General Editor: David Stuart Davies

THE DRUG
and Other Stories

THE DRUG

and Other Stories

Aleister Crowley

Edited with an Introduction by
William Breeze

Foreword by
David Tibet

WORDSWORTH EDITIONS

FOR KENNETH ANGER

Readers interested in other titles from
Wordsworth Editions are invited to visit our
website at www.wordsworth-editions.com

For our latest list and a full mail-order service contact
Bibliophile Books, Unit 5 Datapoint,
South Crescent, London E16 4TL
Tel: +44 (0) 20 74 74 24 74
Fax: +44 (0) 20 74 74 85 89
orders@bibliophilebooks.com
www.bibliophilebooks.com

First published 2010 by
Wordsworth Editions Limited
8B East Street, Ware, Hertfordshire SG12 9HJ

Second edition, revised and expanded, 2015

ISBN 978-1-84022-734-5

Wordsworth Editions is
the company founded in 1987 by
MICHAEL TRAYLER

Typeset in the United States by O.T.O.
Printed in Great Britain by Clays Ltd, St Ives plc

CONTENTS

Foreword

As an author, Aleister Crowley is usually associated with his writings on Magick (to use the technical term he himself preferred and which identifies his own system), and, after those works, with his remarkable and hallucinatory novels *Moonchild* (1929) and *The Diary of a Drug Fiend* (1922). His talents as a playwright, poet and author of short stories are still in the main unappreciated except by aficionados and collectors of his work, and those who follow the new dispensation that he announced and then codified as the religion of *Thelema*.

Perhaps we should not be surprised that his poetry and plays remain generally unknown today. Poetry long ago fell out of favour as a way of expressing truths too subtle, too secret, or too nebulous to be expressed in prose. Plays, once read aloud by intimate groups in family parlours, have given way to isolating vices such as television.

The difficulty of accessing the pieces collected here for the first time – scattered as they were through obscure journals such as *The Equinox* or *The International* or appearing in extremely rare first editions – has prevented their author from being reassessed as a remarkable and idiosyncratic short story writer of the highest order.

Crowley's *œuvre* of short stories is amongst the most interesting – and entertaining – of the many written in the first half of the twentieth century, a period in which the form, as a creative vehicle, was both commercially popular and highly regarded as a demanding medium by some of the most talented writers of the time. Despite his reputation as a rebellious degenerate in both art and morals, his writing is always clear and, though often luxuriant, never descends into the affectation of the more extreme types of purple prose; in this he resembles Count Stenbock (1860–1895), acknowledged in lifestyle and desires as the most decadent of the English *fin de siècle* poets of the nineteenth century who yet wrote short tales of beautiful and haunting simplicity in his exceedingly rare volume from 1894, *Studies of Death*.

If Crowley's wit is not quite as consistently barbed as that of Saki (1870–1916), it certainly covers a wider range of social (and sexual!) situations. And if his alter ego, the psychic detective Simon Iff (who features in an eponymous short stories collection not included here, as well as his novel *Moonchild*) could never be as humble as G.K. Chesterton's Father Brown, Iff's methods of deduction were also informed by a deep spirituality. John Silence, the mystical investigator created by Algernon Blackwood (1869–1951) – himself a member, along with Crowley, of the magical order the Golden Dawn – is a more sympathetic companion to Iff. The exotic psychedelic in 'The Drug,' that unlocks so many secrets, must surely have been one that M.P. Shiel's (1865–1947) decadent detective Prince Zaleski also knew of. Crowley admired the writings of Arthur Machen (1863–1947) – an admiration that was *not* reciprocated – and Machen's works, especially the stories 'The Inmost Light' and 'The Great God Pan,' seem to have been among his influences.

John Symonds, the earliest, best-known and often most inaccurate of the biographers of the Beast, remarked that 'The Stratagem' was one of the poorest stories he had ever read, an unfair slur on a tale that has always reminded me of some of the beautiful and bizarre *non sequitur* works of Ray Bradbury and Borges. By contrast, the editor and author Frank Harris said that 'The Testament of Magdalen Blair' was the most terrifying tale ever written.

Crowley used his short stories as a medium of entertainment, but wrote both himself and his evolving belief system into them on many levels. As with all of his writing, one way of looking at these tales is as manifestations of a continual autobiography. The stories thus resonate on several levels, from that of pure entertainment, to those of self-promotion and occult instruction. The author was no stranger to problems with censorship; one can well imagine that if this collection had been published during his lifetime, it would have been damned by the yellow press. The collapse of the moral and political order of the hypocritical *imperium* of Christendom was one he enthusiastically sought and, in foreseeing this and so much else that is manifest in the world around us and its masks, he was a prophet.

Is this the first instance of a god in the making (for Crowley was finally to say about himself 'as God goes, I go') writing short stories? It is time to reassess these witty, strange and occasionally very dark works as the rare and lovely jewels they are.

DAVID TIBET

INTRODUCTION

This volume brings together the uncollected short fiction of the poet, writer and religious philosopher Aleister Crowley (1875–1947). Much of it has languished for a half century or more in old journals and archives, and is long overdue for a critical appraisal.

Crowley went up to Trinity College, Cambridge in 1895 and obtained leave from his tutor to read modern literature, then not in the curriculum. He embraced the Romantics and emulated them in his early poetry; after a brief flirtation with Æstheticism, he then embraced the Decadents and Symbolists. Along with Balzac and Verlaine, Baudelaire was a major literary influence, almost a lifetime preoccupation; like most Europeans at the time, he was probably introduced to the writings of Poe by Baudelaire. His French was very good – beginning in 1902, he occasionally lived in Paris – and he translated Baudelaire, Verlaine and Balzac's friend, the magician Éliphas Lévi. Through his translations, criticism and occult writings he imported Symbolist sensibilities to England and America in all but name. His rival, the poet and occultist W. B. Yeats, was similarly influenced, but with Crowley it was imbued with an un-Gallic, decidedly English sense of humour, a disarming self-effacement through levity that was nonetheless serious, underpinned as it was by a preternaturally acute occult world view. His stance was predicated on an initiated – i.e., experientially real, and hence true even if opaque to noninitiates – view of life's realities. His early attraction to magick, Buddhism and yoga evolved into a lifelong preoccupation with the true nature of the self and its transcendence.

And what a self to transcend! Crowley was many things and excelled at most: a record-setting mountaineer, a competition-level chess player, the best metrical poet of his generation in the estimation of some, a literary critic of international reputation, an innovative editor and book designer, a pioneer in the use of entheogens, and a lion of sexual liberation – he was above all a lover, of men, women, gods, goddesses and himself. Outsiders to Crowley's milieu often suspect that he exerted some baleful, sinister hold on his enthusiasts and friends. Not at all: the key to his appeal was (and is) that he was as *fun* as he was smart. In truth his only satanic feature was his pride, which was admittedly of Miltonian proportions.

The revelation received in 1904, *The Book of the Law*, led him to found Thelema – a joyous religion, but one that grew out of personal sorrow. He was determined to break the stranglehold of sin-obsessed religious morality and fight an establishment that usurped individuality, sneered at aspirations outside class barriers and crippled its victims with guilt, leaving them spiritually maimed. He called it 'the world's tragedy'; in response he revived the Comedy of Pan.

His inspirations come into focus through a reverse reading of his voluminous essays and criticism. These ran deep, and were as likely to be literary as philosophical. For example, in Balzac's *Louis Lambert* (one of the *Études philosophiques* in *La Comédie humaine*), the title figure is a young prodigy who develops an occult philosophy of will; like Balzac (and the fictional Lambert), Crowley suffered social alienation and abuse at boarding school. Other influences apparent in his stories include his friend and early mentor Marcel Schwob, as well as Poe, de Maupassant, Butler, Stevenson and his late *Vanity Fair* colleague O. Henry.

Crowley was highly mobile in every sense. He lived and moved easily in most of the defining countercultures of his times: decadent Cambridge, Montmartre and the Left Bank of Belle Époque Paris, Cheyne Walk and Fitzrovia of Edwardian London, pre-revolutionary Moscow, wartime Greenwich Village, the Paris and Côte d'Azur of the Lost Generation, and Weimar Berlin – they were all his haunts.

Literary circles have a centre and a periphery, and Crowley swiftly moved to the centre by honing his skills as a critic, reviewer, editor and fiction author. But his career in literary journalism would only last about fifteen years, from 1908 through 1922.

Of his early prose efforts, Crowley wrote in his *Confessions* that

> Most of these were written from a very curious point of view. It was not exactly that I had my tongue in my cheek, but I took a curious pleasure in expressing serious opinions in a fantastic form. I had an instinctive feeling against prose; I had not appreciated its possibilities. Its apparent lack of form seemed to me to stamp it as an essentially inferior means of expression. I wrote it, therefore, in a rather shame-faced spirit. I deliberately introduced bad jokes to show that I did not take myself seriously;

whereas the truth was I was simply nervous about my achievement, just as a man afraid to disgrace himself as a boxer might pretend that the bout was not in earnest. My prose is consequently marred by absolutely stupid blasphemies against itself.

I now began to see that this was schoolboyish bashfulness, and to feel my responsibility as an exponent of the hidden knowledge, to treat my prose as reverently as my verse, and (consequently) to produce masterpieces of learning and wit.

He began to write short stories in 1908:

I had begun, I do not in the least remember how, to try my hand at short stories. Even today having written more than seventy such, I do not quite understand why this form of art should appeal to me. I take fits of it. I go for a month without thinking of the subject at all, and then all of a sudden I find myself with ideas and writing them down. I entirely agree that the short story is one of the most delicate and powerful forms of expression. It forms a link with poetry because one can work up to ecstasy of one kind or another in a more lyric manner than is possible in a novel; the emotion evoked is doubtless more limited, but it can be made for this very reason better defined.

The title story 'The Drug' was Crowley's first sale of a fully developed short story, appearing in London's *The Idler* for January 1909. It shows him consciously crafting the elements of character, setting and atmosphere, while exercising the restraint necessary for effective and memorable short fiction, where less is usually more.

Crowley was an early advocate of the psychedelic mescaline, which he called by a now obsolete taxonomic name for the peyote cactus, *Anhalonium lewinii*. Yeats tried it once a little earlier, but it was Crowley who fostered its use in literary and occult circles in Europe and America. While there was a sizable body of fiction dealing with drugs by 1909, especially in French, most if not all of it dealt with opium and its derivatives, or with hashish. 'The Drug' stands as one of the first – if not *the* first – accounts of a psychedelic experience.

Beginning in March of 1909 Crowley had a ready outlet for new fiction in his biannual journal *The Equinox*, an imposingly large 'little magazine' with a solid backbone of advanced occultism. It carried fiction by Frank Harris, Katharine Susannah Prichard and Lord Dunsany, as well as by Crowley and his immediate circle. Crowley contributed so much fiction that he ran most stories anonymously or pseudonymously; in the four years from spring 1909 to spring 1913, of his seventeen stories, three appeared anonymously, seven more under four pseudonyms, and seven under his own name.

Crowley came to earn the respect of several editors responsible for the best English language literary journalism on both sides of the Atlantic for several decades. He reviewed Frank Harris' novel *The Bomb* in early 1908, and Harris gave him crucial early encouragement by publishing his poetry and travel writing in the London edition of *Vanity Fair*. Within a few years he was a regular contributor of poetry and criticism to *The English Review*, then the most prestigious literary journal in English; its editor Austin Harrison bought his story 'The Stratagem' in 1914. After moving to New York – he arrived in New York Harbor on Halloween 1914 – he became a regular contributor to the American edition of *Vanity Fair*, edited by Frank Crowninshield, where his criticism and translations from French were published alongside the criticism of A. J. A. Symons. The American editor H. L. Mencken also bought 'The Stratagem,' for *The Smart Set* in 1916. Crowley came to know Harris and Harrison quite well; his relationship with Crowninshield was more professional. Mencken, who described him in his memoirs as 'something of an eccentric,' was more an acquaintance.

British espionage and counterespionage figures would develop close ties to fiction, from Basil Thomson, J. C. Masterman and Alan Hillgarth to Ian Fleming and John le Carré. Once in New York, Crowley did his best to discredit the well-funded German propaganda effort, which sought to keep neutral America out of World War 1. He became a regular contributor to the magazine *The Fatherland*, where he posed as an over-the-top pro-German Irish author who hated England. The Germans also subsidised *The International*, an arts monthly edited by the poet George Sylvester Viereck; it published eighteen of his stories between August 1915 and April 1918. Crowley was possibly the first 'agent of influence' to publish fiction as part of a fictive cover legend. He served as *The International*'s contributing editor for its last year of existence before it folded in summer 1918. He contributed to its demise by padding out its later issues with his pseudonymous esoteric works.

Crowley returned to England in late 1919 under his own name and unmolested by the authorities: clearly not a traitor. But he had conducted his war work in his own name, and by the strange rules of intelligence he could never be given public absolution. In January 1920 he lunched in Paris with the Hon. Everard Fielding (1867–1936), an intelligence officer who was the basis for the fictional Earl of Granchester in the story 'Colonel Pacton's Brother' written later that year.

All we know of their lunch is that there was 'conflict'; official denial would prevail. Crowley's student Norman Mudd later tried to obtain a file of letters from Crowley to Fielding that might have exonerated his master. Fielding politely and regretfully informed Mudd that they had been destroyed.

Crowley's reputation was in tatters and his literary career in ruins. Only Frank Harris – who really *had* been pro-German in the war – would publish work credited to him; his last sale of a short story was 'Face,' in *Pearson's Magazine* in 1920. But Crowley carried on and kept writing, noting on June 20:

> Finished a fairly short story – the first since last September or earlier, I forget exactly whether I worked on Simon Iff after Montauk – called 'Dedit.' It has the merit of being extremely stern in its morality, and is therefore quite unpublishable in England or in America.

His last short story appears to have been 'Colonel Pacton's Brother,' written that August.

Austin Harrison at *The English Review* bought a few pieces of non-fiction and poetry in 1922, but would only issue it anonymously or pseudonymously.

Perversely, Crowley tried to reverse his fortunes by publishing, under his own name, a provocative *roman à clef* depicting his experimental spiritual commune in Sicily – the novel *The Diary of a Drug Fiend* (1922). This backfired badly and reaped a whirlwind of bad press in England, compounded by the death by mischance of a disciple, for which Crowley was unfairly blamed, followed by several former residents selling lurid stories to the press. Attacks in the gutter press would rise to a crescendo in 1922–23.

The Mandrake Press issued the only collection of short stories published in Crowley's lifetime, *The Stratagem and Other Stories* (1929). A spirited attempt was made to rehabilitate Crowley's reputation by its editor, P. R. Stephensen, in his *The Legend of Aleister Crowley* (1930, 2d ed. 2007), but this had little effect on Crowley's popular aura of dangerous diabolism. This persisted in the public mind until his death in 1947 at age 72, and still reverberates today.

Crowley stopped producing fiction around 1922 and assessed his output: more than seventy stories, including two short 'novels' that were extended short stories on the original French model of the novel. Of the fifty-four stories in the present volume, he had published thirty-five. The rest remained unpublished at his death; most appear in this collection for the first time.

This collection is organised into two subseries: stories published in his lifetime, ending with the last tale he published in life, 'Face,' and stories first published posthumously or unpublished, beginning with what is probably his earliest story, 'Which Things are an Allegory.' These groups are arranged chronologically, the first by date of first publication, and the second by the known or likely year of creation. This collection omits stories belonging to his two well-defined collections: the eight stories in his mythological *Golden Twigs* tales, and the seventeen stories in his Simon Iff detective series, *Simple Simon*; these have appeared in another volume published by Wordsworth, *The Scutinies of Simon Iff and Other Works* (2012). Also omitted are two pornographic novelettes ('The Nameless Novel' and 'The Bromo Book,' written to entertain his first wife) from *Snowdrops from a Curate's Garden* (1904). His coded sexual autobiography, which he termed a 'novelissim,' *Not the Life and Adventures of Sir Roger Bloxam*, an unfinished novella, 'The Fish,' and a fragment of a short story, 'The Russian Butler,' are also omitted. A few other works that may have been short stories, known only by their titles in his diaries, are probably now lost.

A few of his stories have autobiographical elements, dealing with Crowley's childhood religious sect the Plymouth Brethren ('A Death Bed Repentance'), his mountaineering ('The Escape'), and his failed first marriage ('The Argument that Took the Wrong Turning'). Others are autobiographical satire or spiritual allegory; he portrays himself as the Maitreya Buddha ('The Three Characteristics'), the Egyptian priest Ankhefenkhons 1 ('Across the Gulf'), and the Chinese Taoist master Kwaw Li Ya ('T'ien Tao').

This revised second edition includes four additional stories. Two were excluded from the first edition for reasons of space and their ambiguous standing as short stories. 'The Murder on X. Street' was a puzzle contest serialised in *What's On* with clever characterisation and plotting. Some solutions to the puzzles propounded would require a Cambridge maths wrangler to solve, and were either never published, or the issue with the answers is no longer extant. 'The Electric Silence' is a fictionalised treatment of Crowley's early spiritual career featuring strong prose writing. Two very short stories, 'The Ideal Idol' and 'The Professor and the Plutocrat,' were overlooked for the first edition. Crowley had failed to notate them as his writing in the text of his set of *The International*, where they appeared pseudonymously; however, he claimed their authorship by ticking their titles in the contents pages.

Sources vary greatly for the stories. Some have only the published version, others just a typescript or manuscript, still others have multiple sources with variants, sometimes with no single source that is wholly satisfactory. The endnotes give the sources for texts, when and where stories were written, details of his inspirations and dedicatees, Crowley's marginalia to some stories, citations for some quotations, details of obscure references and allusions, as well as identifications of some individuals who formed the basis for some characters.

Crowley's later marginal notes to his copies of the various journals are given as footnotes to the texts wherever appropriate, but many notes seemed too much of a distraction from the fictional narrative to include on the page; these are given in the endnotes as unbracketed endnotes. Endnotes by the present editor have been bracketed to keep them distinct from Crowley's notes.

As readers should not need to reach for references to follow fiction, translations are given as footnotes in editorial brackets. Problems with paragraphing, missing dialogue quotation marks, dialogue synchronisation, punctuation modernisation, clear misquotations and missing numbered subtitles have been silently repaired, as have obvious clerical errors; the few glosses are noted in the endnotes. Transliterations have been conformed to Crowley's later standards, and further modernised in keeping with his practice of adopting current accepted standards. Spelling has been standardised to British.

I wish to thank Cody Grundy, who thoughtfully gave the Crowley estate, Ordo Templi Orientis (o.t.o.), a photocopy of Crowley's working typescript of *The Banyan Tree*, an important late fiction collection featuring many unique stories as well as Crowley's final edits to some of his best tales. I also wish to thank Kenneth Anger for his gifts of many typescripts.

For research assistance, I wish to thank Vivian Burgess, Clive Harper, Jean-Matthieu Kleemann and Clint Warren. I also wish to thank the Warburg Institute; the Harry Ransom Center, University of Texas at Austin, especially Elspeth Healy; the Widener Library, Harvard; the New York Public Library; and the British Library, especially Lisa Kenny at the old serials division at Colindale.

Several colleagues should be thanked for their contributions. Bill Heidrick typed the stories from *The Equinox* and most of those from *The International*; Darryl Emplit typed *The Banyan Tree* stories. Michael Estell provided assistance with translations and classical sources and gave helpful editorial advice. Robin Matthews read the proofs of the stories expertly, and offered sound editorial counsel.

For this revised second edition I am again indebted to Robin Matthews and Michael Estell, as well as Bill Heidrick and John Brunie, two highly capable editors whose earlier republication of the *International* stories in the O.T.O. journal *Thelema Lodge Calendar* belatedly made me aware of two stories omitted in the first edition; see www.billheidrick.com. I also wish to thank J. Daniel Gunther for editorial advice, and William and Antje Peters for translation assistance.

This book came about through the divine intervention of David Tibet, who suggested a Crowley fiction collection to a Wordsworth editor, Mark Valentine, who in turn brought the idea to the general editor of their *Tales of Mystery and the Supernatural* series, David Stuart Davies. Wordsworth's finance and marketing director, Derek Wright, worked with O.T.O. to make this edition possible. Wordsworth excels at affordable editions of public domain literature, but, whilst Crowley's works published before 1923 are public domain in America, in Europe the works authorised in his lifetime are in copyright through 2017, and his posthumous works through 2039. As O.T.O. shares Wordsworth's wish to make Crowley's uncollected fiction widely available, we agreed to a nominal royalty. This is in keeping with the philosophy of the original Wordsworth. I like to think that Crowley's maternal great-grandparents, the legendary horologist James Cole (1769–1838) and his wife Catherine, would have approved. Both were great friends of William and Dorothy Wordsworth, as well as Samuel Taylor Coleridge and his wife, their neighbours on Lime Street in Nether Stowey, Somerset. Known as 'Conjuror' or 'Philosopher' Cole for his scientific bent and radical views, he and his wife witnessed the birth of the Romantic movement through the *Lyrical Ballads* (1798).

If strangeness is any test of how well Crowley carried on the great Romantic literary experiment, then a few friendly words of warning from the preface to *Lyrical Ballads* clearly apply to the present volume as well. Wordsworth wrote:

> Readers accustomed to the gaudiness and inane phraseology
> of many modern writers, if they persist in reading this book
> to its conclusion, will perhaps frequently have to struggle with
> feelings of strangeness ...

WILLIAM BREEZE

THE DRUG

and other stories

The Three Characteristics

I

'Listen to the *jataka*!' said the Buddha. And all they gave ear.

'Long ago, when King Brahmadatta reigned in Benares,[1] it came to pass that there lived under his admirable government a weaver named Suraj Ju[2] and his wife Chandi.[3] And in the fulness of her time did she give birth to a man child, and they called him Perdu' R Abu.[4]

'Now the child grew, and the tears of the mother fell, and the wrath of the father waxed: for by no means would the boy strive in his trade of weaving. The loom went merrily, but to the rhythm of a *mantra*; and the silk slipped through his fingers, but as if one told his beads. Wherefore the work was marred, and the hearts of the parents were woe because of him.

'But it is written that misfortune knoweth not the hour to cease, and that the seed of sorrow is as the seed of the Banyan Tree. It groweth and is of stature as a mountain, and, ay me! it shooteth down fresh roots into the aching earth. For the boy grew and became a man; and his eyes kindled with the lust of life and love; and the desire stirred him to see the round world and its many marvels. Wherefore he went forth, taking his father's store of gold, laid up for him against that bitter day, and he took fair maidens, and was their servant. And he builded a fine house and dwelt therein. And he took no thought. But he said: "Here is a change indeed!"

'Now it came to pass that after many years he looked upon his lover, the bride of his heart, the rose of his garden, the jewel of his rosary; and behold, the olive loveliness of smooth skin was darkened, and the

---

[1] The common formula for beginning a *jataka*, or story of a previous incarnation of Buddha. Brahmadatta reigned 120,000 years.

[2] The Sun.

[3] The Moon.

[4] Perdurabo, Crowley's motto.

flesh lay loose, and the firm breasts drooped, and the eyes had lost alike the gleam of joy and the sparkle of laughter and the soft glow of love. And he was mindful of his word, and said in sorrow, "Here is then a change indeed!" And he turned his thought to himself, and saw that in his heart was also a change, so that he cried, "Who then am I?" And he saw that all this was sorrow. And he turned his thought without and saw that all things were alike in this: that nought might escape the threefold misery. "The soul," he said, "the soul, the I, is as all these; it is impermanent as the ephemeral flower of beauty in the water that is born and shines and dies ere sun be risen and set again."

'And he humiliated his heart and sang the following verse:

> Brahmā, and Viṣṇu, and great Śiva! Truly
> I see the Trinity in all things dwell,
> Some rightly tinged of Heaven, others duly
> Pitched down the steep and precipice of Hell.
> Nay, not your glory ye from fable borrow!
> These three I see in spirit and in sense,
> These three, O miserable seer! Sorrow,
> Absence of ego, and impermanence!

'And at the rhythm he swooned, for his old *mantra* surged up in the long-sealed vessels of subconscious memory, and he fell into the calm ocean of a great Meditation.'

2

'Jehjaour[1] was a mighty magician; his soul was dark and evil; and his lust was of life and power and of the wreaking of hatred upon the innocent. And it came to pass that he gazed upon a ball of crystal wherein were shown him all the fears of the time unborn as yet on earth. And by his art he saw Perdu' R Abu, who had been his friend; for do what he would, the crystal showed always that sensual and frivolous youth as a Fear to him – even to him the Mighty One!

But the selfish and evil are cowards; they fear shadows, and Jehjaour scorned not his art.

'"Roll on in time, thou ball!" he cried. "Move down the stream of years, timeless and hideous servant of my will! Taph! Tath! Arath!"[2]

---

[1] Allan MacGregor Bennett (whose motto in the 'Hermetic Order of the Golden Dawn,' was Iehi Aour, i.e., 'Let there be light'), now Ananda Metteyya, to whom the volume in which this story was issued is inscribed.

[2] Taphtatharath, the spirit of Mercury.

'He sounded the triple summons, the mysterious syllables that bound the spirit to the stone.

'Then suddenly the crystal grew a blank; and thereby the foiled wizard knew that which threatened his power, his very life, was so high and holy that the evil spirit could perceive it not.

"Avaunt!" he shrieked, "false soul of darkness!" And the crystal flashed up red, the swarthy red of hate in a man's cheek, and darkened utterly.

'Foaming at the mouth, the wretched Jehjaour clutched at air and fell prone.'

3

'To what God should he appeal? His own, Hanuman, was silent. Sacrifice, prayer, all were in vain. So Jehjaour gnashed his teeth, and his whole force went out in a mighty current of hate towards his former friend.

'Now hate hath power, though not the power of love. So it came about that in his despair he fell into a trance; and in the trance Māra[1] appeared to him. Never before had his spells availed to call so fearful a potency from the abyss of matter.

'"Son," cried the Accursèd One, "seven days of hate unmarred by passion milder, seven days without one thought of pity, these avail to call me forth."

'"Slay me my enemy!" howled the wretch.

'But Māra trembled.

'"Enquire of Gaṇeśa concerning him!" faltered at last the fiend.

'Jehjaour awoke.'

4

'"Yes!" said Gaṇeśa gloomily, "the young man has given me up altogether. He tells me I am as mortal as he is, and he doesn't mean to worry about me any more."

'"Alas!" sighed the deceitful Jehjaour, who cared no more for Gaṇeśa and any indignities that might be offered him than his enemy did.

'"One of my best devotees too!" muttered, or rather trumpeted, the elephantine anachronism.

'"You see," said the wily wizard, "I saw Perdu' R Abu the other day, and he said he had become *sotāpanna*. Now that's pretty serious. In seven births only, if he but pursue the path, will he cease to be reborn. So you have only that time in which to win him back to your worship."

---

[1] The archdevil of the Buddhists.

The cunning sorcerer did not mention that within that time also must his own ruin be accomplished.

"'What do you advise?" asked the irritated and powerful, but unintelligent deity.

"'Time is our friend," said the enchanter. "Let your influence be used in the Halls of Birth that each birth may be as long as possible. Now the elephant is the longest lived of all beasts —"

"'Done with you!" said Gaṇeśa in great glee, for the idea struck him as ingenious. And he lumbered off to clinch the affair at once.

'And Perdu' R Abu died.'

5

'Now the great elephant strode with lordly footsteps in the forest, and Jehjaour shut himself up with his cauldrons and things and felt quite happy, for he knew his danger was not near till the approaching of Perdu' R Abu's *arhant*-ship.

'But in spite of the young gently-ambling cows which Gaṇeśa took care to throw in his way, in spite of the tender shoots of green and the soft coconuts, this elephant was not as other elephants.

'The seasons spoke to him of change – the forest is ever full of sorrow – and nobody need preach to him the absence of an ego, for the brutes have had more sense than ever to imagine there was one. So the tusker was usually to be found, still as a rock, in some secluded place, meditating on the Three Characteristics.

'And when Gaṇeśa appeared in all his glory, he found him to his disgust quite free from elephantomorphism. In fact, he quietly asked the God to leave him alone.

'Now he was still quite a young elephant when there came into the jungle, tripping merrily along, with a light-hearted song in its nucleolus, no less than a Bacillus.

'And the elephant died. He was only seventeen years old.'

6

'A brief consultation; and the *sotāpanna* was reincarnated as a parrot. For the parrot, said the wicked Jehjaour, may live five hundred years and never feel it.

'So a grey wonder of wings flitted into the jungle. So joyous a bird, thought the God, could not but be influenced by the ordinary passions and yield to such majesty as his own.

'But one day there came into the jungle a strange wild figure. He was a man dressed in the weird Tibetan fashion. He had red robes and hat, and thought dark things. He whirled a prayer-wheel in his hands; and ever as he went he muttered the mystic words "*Auṁ Mani Padme Hūṁ.*"[1]

'The parrot, who had never heard human speech, tried to mimic the old *lama*, and was amazed at his success. Pride first seized the bird, but it was not long before the words had their own effect, and it was in meditation upon the conditions of existence that he eternally repeated the formula.

*
**

'At home in distant Inglistan. An old lady, and a grey parrot in a cage. The parrot was still muttering inaudibly the sacred *mantra*.

'Now, now, the moment of Destiny was at hand! The Four Noble Truths shone out in that parrot's mind; the Three Characteristics appeared luminous, like three spectres on a murderer's grave; unable to contain himself, he recited aloud the mysterious sentence.

'The old lady, whatever may have been her faults, could act promptly. She rang the bell.

'"Sarah!" said she, "take away that dreadful creature! Its language is positively awful."

'"What shall I do with it, mum?" asked the "general."

'"*Auṁ Mani Padme Hūṁ,*" said the parrot.

The old lady stopped her ears.

'"Wring its neck!" she said.

'The parrot was only eight years old.'

7

'"You're a muddler and an idiot!" said the infuriated God.

'"Why not make him a spiritual thing?"

'"A *nat*[2] lives 10,000 years."

'"Make him a *nat* then!" said the magician, already beginning to fear that fate would be too strong for him, in spite of all his cunning. "There's someone working against us on the physical plane. We must transcend it."

'No sooner said than done: a family of *nats* in a big tree at Anuradhapura had a little stranger, very welcome to Mamma and Papa *nat*.

---

[1] 'O the jewel in the Lotus! *Auṁ!*' The most famous of the Buddhist formularies.
[2] The Burmese name for an elemental spirit.

'Blessed indeed was the family. Five-and-forty feet[1] away stood a most ancient and holy dagoba; and the children of light would gather round it in the cool of the evening, or in the misty glamour of dawn, and turn forth in love and pity towards all mankind – nay, to the smallest grain of dust tossed on the utmost storms of the Sahara!

'Blessed and more blessed! For one day came a holy *bhikkhu* from the land of the Peacock,[2] and would take up his abode in the hollow of their very tree. And little Perdu' R Abu used to keep the mosquitoes away with the gossamer of his wings, so that the good man might be at peace.

'Now the British Government abode in that land, and when it heard that there was a *bhikkhu* living in a tree, and that the village folk brought him rice and onions and gramophones, it saw that it must not be.

'And little Perdu' R Abu heard them talk; and learnt the great secret of Impermanence, and of Sorrow, and the mystery of Unsubstantiality.

'And the Government evicted the *bhikkhu*; and set guard, quite like the end of Genesis III, and cut down the tree, and all the *nats* perished.

'Jehjaour heard and trembled. Perdu' R Abu was only three years old.'

8

'It really seemed as if fate was against him. Poor Jehjaour!

'In despair he cried to his partner, "O Gaṇeśa, in the world of Gods only shall we be safe. Let him be born as a flute-girl before Indra's throne!"

'"Difficult is the task," replied the alarmed deity, "but I will use all my influence. I know a thing or two about Indra, for example —"

'It was done. Beautiful was the young girl's face as she sprang mature from the womb of Matter, on her life-journey of an hundred thousand years. Of all Indra's flute-girls she played and sang the sweetest. Yet ever some remembrance, dim as a pallid ghost that fleets down the long avenues of deodar and moonlight, stole in her brain; and her song was ever of love and death and music from beyond.

'And one day as she sang thus the deep truth stole into being and she knew the Noble Truths. So she turned her flute to the new song, when – horror! – there was a mosquito in the flute.

---

[1] The Government, in the interests of Buddhists themselves, reserves all ground within fifty feet of a dagoba. The incident described in this section actually occurred in 1901.
[2] Siam.

'"Tootle! Tootle!" she began.

'"Buzz! Buzz!" went the mosquito from the very vitals of her delicate tube.

'Indra was not unprovided with a disc.[1]

'Alas! Jehjaour, art thou already in the toils? She had only lived eight months.'

9

'"How you bungle!" growled Gaṇeśa. "Fortunately we are better off this time. Indra has been guillotined for his dastardly murder; so his place is vacant."

'"Eurekas!" yelled the magus, "his very virtue will save him from his predecessor's fate."

'Behold Perdu' R Abu then as Indra! But oh, dear me! what a memory he was getting!

'"It seems to me," he mused, "that I've been changing about a lot lately. Well, I am virtuous – and I read in Crowley's new translation of the *Dhammapada*[2] that virtue is the thing to keep one steady. So I think I may look forward to a tenure of my *mahākalpa* in almost Arcadian simplicity.

'"Lady Bhavāni, did you say, boy? Yes, I am at home. Bring the betel!"

'"*Jeldi!*" he added, with some dim recollection of the British Government, when he was a baby *nat*.

'The Queen of Heaven and the Lord of the Gods chewed betel for quite a long time; conversed of the weather, the crops, the *affaire Humbert*, and the law in relation to motor-cars, with ease and affability.

'But far was it from Indra's pious mind to flirt with his distinguished guest! Rather, he thought of the hollow nature of the Safe, the change of money and of position; the sorrow of the too confiding bankers, and above all the absence of an Ego in the Brothers Crawford.

'While he was thus musing, Bhavāni got fairly mad at him. The *spretæ injuria formæ*[3] gnawed her vitals with pangs unassuagable; so, shaking him quite roughly by the arm, she Put It To Him Straight.

'"O Madam!" said Indra.

---

[1] A whirling disc is Indra's symbolic weapon.

[2] He abandoned this. A few fragments are reprinted [from *Oracles* (1904); in *The Collected Works of Aleister Crowley*, vol. II (1906), p. 44].

[3] [The insult to her scorned beauty.]

'This part of the story has been told before – about Joseph; but Bhavāni simply lolled her tongue out, opened her mouth, and gulped him down at a swallow.

'Jehjaour simply wallowed. Indra had passed in seven days.'

10

'"There is only one more birth," he groaned. "This time we must win or die."

'"Goetia[1] expects every God to do his duty," he excitedly lunographed to Svarga.[2] But Gaṇeśa was already on his way.

'The elephant-headed God was in great spirits.

'"Never say die!" he cried genially, on beholding the downcast appearance of his fellow-conspirator. "This'll break the slate. There is no change in the *arūpa-brahma-loka*!"[3]

'"Rupe me no rupes!" howled the necromancer.

'"Get up, fool!" roared the God. "I have got Perdu' R Abu elected Mahābrahmā."

'"Oh Lord, have you really?" said the wizard, looking a little less glum.

'"Ay!" cried Gaṇeśa impressively, "let Æon follow Æon down the vaulted and echoing corridors of Eternity; pile *mahākalpa* upon *mahākalpa* until an *asankhayā*[4] of *crores*[5] have passed away; and Mahābrahmā will still sit lone and meditate upon his lotus throne."

'"Good, good!" said the magus, "though there seems a reminiscence of the *Bhagavad-gītā* and *The Light of Asia* somewhere. Surely you don't read Edwin Arnold?"

'"I do," said the God disconsolately, "we Hindu Gods have to. It's the only way we can get any clear idea of who we really are."

'Well, here was Perdu' R Abu, after his latest fiasco, installed as a Worthy, Respectable, Perfect, Ancient and Accepted, Just, Regular Mahābrahmā.

'His only business was to meditate, for as long as he did this, the worlds – the whole systems of 10,000 worlds – would go on peaceably. Nobody had better read the lesson the Bible – the horrible results to mankind of ill-timed, though possibly well-intentioned, interference on the part of a deity.

---

[1] The world of black magic.
[2] Heaven.
[3] The highest heaven of the Hindu. 'Formless place of Brahmā' is its name.
[4] 'Innumerable,' the highest unit of the fantastic Hindu arithmetic.
[5] 10,000.

'Well, he curled himself up, which was rather clever for a formless abstraction, and began.

'There was a grave difficulty in his mind – an obstacle right away from the word "Jump!" Of course there was really a good deal: he didn't know where the four elements ceased, for example;[1] but his own identity was the real worry. The other questions he could have stilled; but this was too near his pet *cakra*.[2]

'"Here I am," he meditated, "above all change; and yet an hour ago I was Indra; and before that his flute-girl; and then a *nat*; and then a parrot; and then a Hathi –

> Oh, the Hathis pilin' teak
> in the sludgy, squdgy creek!"

sang Parameśvara.

'"Why, it goes back and back, like a biograph out of order, and there's no sort of connection between one and the other. Hullo, what's that? Why, there's a holy man near that Bo-Tree. He'll tell me what it all means."

'Poor silly old Lord of the Universe! Had he carried his memory back one more step he'd have known all about Jehjaour and the conspiracy, and that he was a *sotāpanna* and had only one more birth; and might well have put in the 311,040,000,000,000 myriads of æons which would elapse before lunch in rejoicing over his imminent annihilation.

'"Venerable Sir!" said Mahābrahmā, who had assumed the guise of a cowherd, "I kiss your worshipful Trilbies;[3] I prostrate myself before your estimable respectability."

'"Sir," said the holy man, none other than Our Lord Himself! "thou seekest illumination!"

'Mahābrahmā smirked and admitted it.

'"From Negative to Positive," explained the Thrice-Honoured One, "through Potential Existence, eternally vibrates the Divine Absolute of the Hidden Unity of processional form masked in the Eternal Abyss of the Unknowable, the synthetical hieroglyph of an illimitable pastless futureless PRESENT. To the uttermost bounds of space rushes the Voice of Ages, unheard save in the concentrated unity of the thought-formulated Abstract, and eternally that Voice formulates

---

[1] See the witty legend in *The Questions of King Milinda*.
[2] Meditation may be performed on any of seven *cakras* (wheels or centres) in the body.
[3] Feet.

a Word which is glyphed in the vast ocean of limitless life.[1] Do I make myself clear?"

"'Perfectly. Who would have thought it was all so simple?" The God cleared his throat, and rather diffidently, even shamefacedly, went on: "But what I really wished to know was about my incarnation. How is it I have so suddenly risen from change and death to the unchangeable?"

"'Child!" answered Gautama, "your facts are wrong – you can hardly expect to make correct deductions."

"'Yes, you can, if only your logical methods are unsound. That's the Christian way of getting truth."

"'True!" replied the sage, "but precious little they get. Learn, O Mahābrahmā" (for I penetrate this disguise), "that all existing things, even from thee unto this grain of sand, possess Three Characteristics. These are Mutability, Sorrow and Unsubstantiality."

"'All right for the sand, but how about Me? Why, they *define* me as unchangeable."

"'You can define a quirk as being a two-sided triangle," retorted the Saviour, "but that does not prove the actual existence of any such oxymoron.[2] The truth is that you're a very spiritual sort of being and a prey to longevity. Men's lives are so short that yours seems eternal in comparison. But – why, *you're* a nice one to talk! You'll be dead in a week from now."

"'I quite appreciate the force of your remarks!" said the seeming cowherd; "that about the Characteristics is very clever; and curiously enough, my perception of this has always just preceded my death for the last six goes."

"'Well, so long, old chap," said Gautama, "I must really be off. I have an appointment with Brother Māra at the Bo-Tree. He has promised to introduce his charming daughters —"

"'Goodbye, and don't do anything rash!"

Rejoice! our Lord wended unto the Tree![3]

'As blank verse this scans but ill, but it clearly shows what happened.'

---

[1] This astonishing piece of bombastic drivel is verbatim from a note by S.L. Mathers to *The Kabbalah Unveiled*.
[2] A contradiction in terms.
[3] Arnold, *Light of Asia*.

11

'*The Nineteenth Mahākalpa* brought out its April number. There was a paper by Huxlānanda Swāmi.

'Mahābrahmā had never been much more than an idea. He had only lived six days.'

12

'At the hour of the great Initiation,' continued the Buddha, 'in the midst of the Five Hundred Thousand *Arhants*, the wicked Jehjaour had joined himself with Māra to prevent the discovery of the truth. And in Māra's fall he fell.

'At that moment all the currents of his continued and concentrated hate recoiled upon him and he fell into the Abyss of Being. And in the Halls of Birth he was cast out into the Lowest Hell – he became a clergy-man of the Church of England, further than he had ever been before from Truth and Light and Peace and Love; deeper and deeper enmeshed in the net of Circumstance, bogged in the mire of *taṇhā*[1] and *avijjā*[2] and all things base and vile.

'False *vicikicchā*[3] had caught him at last!'

13

'Aye! The hour was at hand. Perdu' R Abu was reincarnated as a child of Western parents, ignorant of all his wonderful past. But a strange fate has brought him to this village.'

The Buddha paused, probably for effect.

A young man there, sole among all them not yet an *arhant*, turned pale. He alone was of Western birth in all that multitude.

'Brother Abhavānanda,[4] little friend,' said the Buddha, 'what can we predicate of all existing things?'

'Lord!' replied the neophyte, 'they are unstable, everything is sorrow, in them is no inward Principle, as some pretend, that can avoid, that can hold itself aloof from, the forces of decay.'

'And how do you know that, little Brother?' smiled the Thrice-Honoured One.

'Lord, I perceive this Truth whenever I consider the Universe. More, its consciousness seems ingrained in my very nature, perhaps through

---

[1] Thirst; i.e., desire in its evil sense.
[2] Ignorance.
[3] Doubt.
[4] 'Bliss-of-non-existence.' One of Crowley's eastern names.

my having known this for many incarnations. I have never thought otherwise.'

'Rise, Sir Abhavānanda, I dub thee *arhant!*' cried the Buddha, striking the neophyte gently on the back with the flat of his ear.[1]

And he perceived.

When the applause of praise and glory had a little faded, the Buddha, in that golden delight of sunset, explained these marvellous events.

'Thou, Abhavānanda,' he said, 'art the Perdu' R Abu of my lengthy tale. The wicked Jehjaour has got something lingering with boiling oil in it, while waiting for his clerical clothes; while, as for me, I myself was the Bacillus in the forest of Lanka; I was the old Lady; I was (he shuddered) the British Government; I was the mosquito that buzzed in the girl's flute; I was Bhavāni; I was Huxlānanda Swāmi; and at the last, at this blessed hour, I am – that I am.'

'But, Lord,' said the Five Hundred Thousand and One *Arhants* in a breath, 'thou art then guilt of six violent deaths! Nay, thou hast hounded one soul from death to death through all these incarnations! What of this First Precept[2] of yours?'

'Children,' answered the Glorious One, 'do not be so foolish as to think that death is necessarily an evil. I have not come to found a Hundred Years Club, and to include mosquitoes in the membership. In this case to have kept Perdu' R Abu alive was to have played into the hands of his enemies.

'My First Precept is merely a general rule.[3] In the bulk of cases one should certainly abstain from destroying life, that is, wantonly and wilfully: but I cannot drink a glass of water without killing countless myriads of living beings. If you knew as I do – the conditions of existence: struggle deadly and inevitable, every form of life the inherent and immitigable foe of every other form, with few, few exceptions – you would not only cease to talk of the wickedness of causing death, but you would perceive the First Noble Truth, that no existence can be free from sorrow; the Second, that the desire for existence only leads to sorrow; that the ceasing from existence is the ceasing of sorrow (the Third); and you would seek in the Fourth the Way, the Noble Eightfold Path.

---

[1] The Buddha had such long ears that he could cover the whole of his face with them. Ears are referred to Spirit in Hindu symbolism, so that the legend means that he could conceal the lower elements and dwell in this alone.

[2] Here is the little rift within the lute which alienated Crowley from active work on Buddhist lines; the orthodox failing to see his attitude.

[3] A more likely idea than the brilliantly logical nonsense of *pansil*.

'I know, O *arhants*, that you do not need this instruction; but my words will not stay here: they will go forth and illuminate the whole system of ten thousand worlds, where *arhants* do not grow on every tree.

'Little brothers, the night is fallen: it were well to sleep.'

Ambrosii Magi Hortus Rosarum[1]

Translated into English by Christeos Luciftias.
Printed by W. Black, at the Wheatsheaf in Newgate,
and sold at the Three Keys in Nags-Head Court, Gracechurch St.

Opus[2] It is fitting that I, Ambrose, called I.A.O., should set
down the life of our great Father (who now is not, yet
whose name must never be spoken among men), in
order that the Brethren may know what journeys he
undertook in pursuit of that Knowledge whose attainment is their constant study.

Prima It was at his 119th year,[4] the Star Suaconch[5] being
Materia[3] in the sign of the Lion, that our Father set out from
A.O. his Castle of Ug[6] to attain the Quintessence or Philo-
sophical Tincture. The way being dark and the Golden

---

[1] [The Rose Garden of Ambrose the Mage.]
   [*Note to 1906 2nd ed.:*] It would require many pages to give
   even a sketch of this remarkable document. The Qabalistic
   knowledge is as authentic as it is profound, but there are also
   allusions to contemporary occult students, and a certain very
   small amount of mere absence of meaning. The main satire
   is of course on *The Chymical Marriage of Christian Rosencreutz.*
   A few only of the serious problems are elucidated in footnotes.
   [*Note to 2015 3rd ed.:* Annotations by Crowley from his copy
   of *The Sword of Song* (1904) appear in braces { }.]
[2] [The work.]
[3] [The first matter.]
[4] I.e., when 118 = change, a ferment, strength. Also = before he
   was 120, the mystic age of a Rosicrucian. {Before 120 = ☉.}
[5] [*Lat., sua concha =*] Her-shell = {H͜H} Herschel, or Uranus, the
   planet which was ascending (in Leo) at Crowley's birth.
[6] *Vau* and *gimel*, 'The Hierophant' and 'High Priestess' in the
   Tarot. Hence 'from his Castle of Ug' means 'from his initiation.'
   We cannot in future do more than indicate the allusions.

Dawn at hand, he did call forth four servants to keep him in the midst of the way, and the Lion roared before him to bid the opposers beware of his coming. On the Bull he rode, and on his left hand and his right marched the Eagle and the Man. But his back was uncovered, seeing that he would not turn.

Custodes[1]

ﬢ   And the Spirit of the Path met him. It was a young girl of two and twenty years, and she warned him fairly that without the Serpent[3] his ways were but as wool cast into the dyer's vat. Two-and-twenty scales had the Serpent, and every scale was a path, and every path was alike an enemy and a friend.

Sapiens Dominabitur Astris[2]

So he set out, and the darkness grew upon him. Yet could he well perceive a young maiden[4] having a necklace of two-and-seventy pearls, big and round like the breasts of a sea-nymph; and they gleamed round her like moons. She held in leash the four Beasts, but he strode boldly to her, and kissed her full on her full lips. Wherefore she sighed and fell back a space, and he pressed on.

S.S.D.D.

Now at the end of the darkness a fire glowed; she would have hindered him; clung she to his neck and wept. But the fire grew and the light dazzled her, so that with a shriek she fell. But the beasts flung themselves ﬣ against the burning gateway of iron, and it gave way. Our Father passed into the fire. Some say that it consumed him utterly and that he died; howbeit, it is certain that he rose from a sarcophagus, and in the skies stood an angel with a trumpet, and on that trumpet he blew so mighty a blast that the dead rose all from their tombs, and our Father among them.

Intellectio[5]

Deus[6]

---

[1] [Guards.]

[2] [Some marginal notes in roman refer to individuals; these are identified in the editorial notes.]

[3] See Table of Correspondences [in *Liber* 777].

[4] The 22nd Key of the Tarot. The other Tarot symbols can be traced by anyone who possesses, and to some degree understands, a pack of the cards. The occult views of the nature of these symbols are in some cases Crowley's own.

[5] [Understanding.]

[6] [God.]

'Now away!' he cried. 'I would look upon the sun!' And with that the fire hissed like a myriad of serpents and went out suddenly.

It was a green sward golden with buttercups; and in his way lay a high wall. Before it were two children, and with obscene gestures they embraced and laughed aloud, with filthy words and acts unspeakable. Over all of which stood the sun, calm and radiant, and was glad to be.

Now, think ye well, was our Father perplexed; and he knew not what he would do. For the children left their foulness and came soliciting with shameless words his acquiescence in their sport; and he, knowing the law of courtesy and of pity, rebuked them not. But master ever of himself he abode alone, about and above. So saw he his virginity deflowered, and his thoughts were otherwhere.

Now loosed they his body; he bade it leap the wall.

The giant flower of ocean bloomed above him! He had fallen headlong into the great deep. As the green and crimson gloom disparted somewhat before his eyes, he was aware of a Beetle that steadily and earnestly moved across the floor of that Sea unutterable. Him he followed; 'for I wit well,' thought the Adept, 'that he goeth not back to the gross sun of earth. And if the sun hath become a beetle, may the beetle transform into a bird.' Wherewith he came to land.

Night shone by lamp of waning moon upon a misty landscape. Two paths led him to two towers, and jackals howled on either. Now the jackal he knew; and the tower he knew not yet. Not two would he conquer – that were easy; to victory over one did he aspire. Made he therefore toward the moon.

Rough was the hillside and the shadows deep and treacherous; as he advanced the towers seemed to approach one another closer and closer yet.

He drew his sword; with a crash they came together, and he fell with wrath upon a single fortress. Three windows had the tower, and against it ten cannons thundered. Eleven bricks had fallen dislodged by lightnings;

Margin notes:
H. *et* S.V.A.

Luna[1]

*Quid
Umbratur
In Mari*[2]

Deo Duce
Comite Ferro

Marginal Hebrew letters: ר פ נ

---

[1] [The moon.]
[2] [What is veiled in the sea.]

it was no house wherein our Father might abide. But there he must abide.

'To destroy it I am come,' he said. And though he passed out therewithal, yet 'twas his home until he had attained.

ל So he came to a river, and sailing to its source he found a fair woman all naked, and she filled the river from two vessels of pure water.

'She-devil,' he cried, 'have I gone back one step?' For the Star Venus burned above.

And with his sword he clave her, from the head to the feet, that she fell clean asunder.

Cried the echo: 'Ah! thou hast slain hope now!'

Our Father gladdened at that word, and wiping his blade he kissed it and went on, knowing that his luck should now be ill.

ע And ill it was, for a temple was set up in his way, and there he saw the grisly Goat enthroned. But he knew better than to judge a goat from a goat's head and hoofs. And he abode in that temple awhile, therefore, and worshipped ten weeks.

And the first week he sacrificed to that goat[2] a crown every day.

The second, a phallus.

The third, a silver vase of blood.

The fourth, a royal sceptre.

The fifth, a sword.

The sixth, a heart.

The seventh, a garland of flowers.

The eighth, a grass-snake.

The ninth, a sickle.

And the tenth week did he daily offer up his own body.

Said the goat: 'Though I be not an ox, yet am I a sword.'

'Masked, O God!' cried the Adept.[3]

'Verily, an thou hadst not sacrificed' –

There was silence.

---

[1] [Love appears by the secret rose.]
[2] The sacrifices are the ten Sephiroth.
[3] {ע = '.}

And under the Goat's throne was a rainbow[1] of seven colours; our Father fitted himself as an arrow to the ס string – and the string was waxed well, dipped in a leaden pot wherein boiled amber and wine – and shot through stormy heavens. And they that saw him saw a woman wondrous fair,[3] robed in flames of hair, moon-sandalled, sun-belted, with torch and vase of fire and water. And he trailed comet-clouds of glory upward.

Hermaphro-ditus[2]

Thus came our Father (Blessed be his name!) to Death,[4] נ who stood, scythe in hand, opposed. And ever and anon he swept round, and men fell before him.

'Look,' said Death, 'my sickle hath a cross-handle. See how they grow like flowers!'

Mors Janua Vitae[5]

'Give me salt!' quoth our Father. And with sulphur (that the Goat had given him) and with salt did he bestrew the ground.

'I see we shall have ado together,' says Death.

'Aye!' and with that he lops off Death's cross-handle.

Now Death was wroth indeed, for he saw that our Father had wit of his designs (and they were right foul!); but he bade him pass forthwith from his dominion. And our Father could not at that time stay him; though for himself had he cut off the grip, yet for others – well, let each man take his sword!

Adeptus[6]

The way went through a forest. Now between two trees hung a man by one heel (Love was that tree).[7] מ Crossed were his legs, and his arms behind his head that hung ever downwards, the fingers locked.[8]

'Who art thou?' quoth our Father.

'He that came before thee.'

'Who am I?'

---

[1] See [*Liber* 777].
[2] [Hermaphrodite.]
[3] Ancient form of the Key of ס.
[4] Considered as the agent of resurrection.
[5] [Death is the gateway of life.]
[6] [Adept.]
[7] In the true key of מ the tree is shaped like the letter ד = Venus or love.
[8] The figure of the man forms a cross above a triangle, with apex upwards, the sign of redemption. {☥}.

'He that cometh after me.'

With that worshipped our Father, and took a present of a great jewel from him, and went his ways. And he was bitterly a-cold, for that was the great Water he had passed. But our Father's paps glittered with cold, black light, and likewise his navel. Wherefore he was comforted.

Terrae Ultor
Anima Terrae[1]

Now came the sudden twittering of heart, lest the firmament beneath him were not stable, and lo! he danceth up and down, as a very cork on waters of wailing.

'Woman,' he bade sternly, 'be still. Cleave that with thy sword; or that must I well work?'

But she cleft the cords, bitter-faced smiling goddess as she was, and he went on.

'Leave thine ox-goad,'[2] quoth he, 'till I come back an ox!'

And she laughed and let him pass.

Now is our Father come to the Unstable Lands, 'Od wot, for the Wheel whereon he poised was ever turning. Sworded was the Sphinx, but he out-dared her in riddling; deeper pierced his sword; he cut her into twain: her place was his. But that would he not, my Brethren; to the centre he clomb ever, and having won thither, he vanished.

Sapientiae Lux
Viris Baculum[3]

As a hermit ever he travelled, and the lamp and wand were his.

In his path a lion roared, but to it ran a maiden, strong as a young elephant, and held its cruel jaws. By force he ran to her; he freed the lion – one buffet of his hand dashed her back six paces! – and with another blow smote its head from its body. And he ran to her and by force embraced her. Struggled she, and fought him; savagely she bit, but it was of no avail: she lay ravished and exhausted on the Lybian plain. Across the mouth he smote her for a kiss, while she cried:

Femina Rapta
Inspirat
Gaudium[4]

---

[1] [The soul of the earth is the avenger of the earth.]

[2] *Lamed* means 'ox-goad'; *aleph*, 'an ox.' *Lamed aleph* means 'No,' the denial of *aleph lamed*, El, 'God.' {ל = ox-goad and balance.}

[3] [The light of wisdom is a walking stick for man.]

[4] [The woman, ravished, inspires joy.]

'O! thou hast begotten on me twins. And mine also is the Serpent, and thou shalt conquer it, and it shall serve thee; and they, they also for a guide!'

She ceased; and he, having come to the world's end, prepared his chariot. Foursquare he builded it, and that double; he harnessed the two sphinxes that he had made from one and sailed, crab-fashion, backwards, through the amber skies of even. Wherefore he attained to see his children.

Lovers they were and lovely, those twins of rape. One was above them, joining their hands.

'That is well,' said our Father, and for seven nights he slept in seven starry palaces, and a sword to guard him. Note well also that these children, and those others, are two, being four.

Pleiades

And on the sixth day (for the seven days were past) he rose and came into his ancient temple, a temple of our Holy Order, O my Brethren, wherein sat that Hierophant who had initiated him of old. Now read he well the riddle of the Goat (Blessed be his name among us for ever! Nay, not for ever!), and therewith the Teacher made him a master of the Sixfold Chamber and an ardent Sufferer toward the Blazing Star. For the Sword, said the Teacher, is but the Star unfurled.[2] And our Father being cunning to place *aleph* over *tau* read this reverse, and so beheld Eden, even now and in the flesh.

Dignitates[1]

Whence he sojourned far, and came to a great Emperor, by whom he was well received and from whom he gat great gifts. And the Emperor[4] (who is Solomon) told him of Sheba's Land and of one fairest of women there enthroned.

Amicitia[3]

So he journeyed thither, and for four years and seven months[6] abode with her as paramour and light-of-love, for she was gracious to him and showed him those things

Amor[5]

---

[1] [Honours.]
[2] Read [in] reverse, the Star {= the Will and the Great Work} is to fold up the Sephiroth; i.e., to attain *nirvāṇa*. {The ☆ is the ⚹ folded, i.e., the Will, and the ☉ is to fold back the Sephiroth.]
[3] [Friendship.]
[4] {⊕.}
[5] [Love.]
[6] {ד = 4. ♀ = 7.}

that the Emperor had hidden: even the cubical stone and the cross beneath the triangle that were his and unrevealed.

And on the third day he left her and came to Her who had initiated him before he was initiated; and with her he abode eight days and twenty days,[2] and she gave him gifts.[3] *Sophia*[1]

The first day, a camel;
The second day, a kiss;
The third day, a star-glass;
The fourth day, a beetle's wing;
The fifth day, a crab;
The sixth day, a bow;
The seventh day, a quiver;
The eighth day, a stag;
The ninth day, an horn;
The tenth day, a sandal of silver;
The eleventh day, a silver box of white sandalwood; *Dona Virginis*[4]
The twelfth day, a whisper;
The thirteenth day, a black cat;
The fourteenth day, a phial of white gold;
The fifteenth day, an eggshell cut in two;
The sixteenth day, a glance;
The seventeenth day, an honeycomb;
The eighteenth day, a dream;
The nineteenth day, a nightmare;
The twentieth day, a wolf, black-muzzled;
The twenty-first day, a sorrow;
The twenty-second day, a bundle of herbs;
The twenty-third day, a piece of camphor;
The twenty-fourth day, a moonstone;
The twenty-fifth day, a sigh;
The twenty-sixth day, a refusal;
The twenty-seventh day, a consent; and the last night she gave him all herself, so that the moon was eclipsed and earth was utterly darkened. *Puella Urget Sophiam Sodalibus*[5]

---

[1] [Wisdom.]
[2] The houses of the Moon. {☽ = 28 days.}
[3] All the gifts are lunar symbols.
[4] [Gifts of the Virgin.]
[5] [The girl urges wisdom upon her companions.]

And the marriage of that virgin was on this wise: She had three arrows, yet but two flanks; and the wise men said that who knew two was three[1] should know three was eight,[2] if the circle were but squared; and this also one day shall ye know, my Brethren!

And she gave him the great and perfect gift of Magic, so that he fared forth right comely and well-provided.[3] ב

The Sophic Suggler

Now at that great wedding was a Suggler,[4] a riddler, for he said, 'Thou hast beasts; I will give thee weapons one for one.'[5]

For the Lion did our Father win a little fiery wand like a flame, and for his Eagle a cup of ever-flowing water; for his Man the Suggler gave him a golden-hilted dagger (yet this was the worst of all his bargains, for it could not strike other, but himself only), while for a curious coin he bartered his good Bull.

Alas for our Father! Now the Suggler mocks him and cries: 'Four fool's bargains hast thou made, and thou art fit to go forth and meet a fool[6] for thy mate.'

But our Father counted thrice seven and cried: 'One for the fool,' seeing the Serpent should be his at last.[7]

'None for the fool,'[8] they laughed back – nay, even his maiden queen. For she would not any should know thereof.

Yet all were right, both he and they. But truth ran quickly about; for that was the House of Truth; and

Hammer of Thor

Mercury stood far from the Sun. Yet the Suggler was ever in the Sign of Sorrow, and the Fig Tree was not far.

So went our Father to the Fool's Paradise of Air. But א it is not lawful that I should write to you, brethren, of

---

[1] 3, the number of ג. 2, the number of the card ב.
[2] The equality of three and eight [8° = 3°] is attributed to Binah, a high grade of Theurgic attainment. {3° = 8°.}
[3] {Grades in order and ☉.}
[4] *Scil.* "Juggler," the 1st Key.
[5] The magical weapons correspond to the Kerubim. {Weapons and Cherubs interchanged.}
[6] The Key marked o and applied to *aleph*, 1.
[7] {21 + 1 = 22.}
[8] {א = o in Tarot.}

what there came to him at that place and time; nor indeed is it true, if it were written. For alway doth this Arcanum differ from itself on this wise, that the Not[1] and the Amen,[3] passing, are void either on the one side or the other, and Who shall tell their ways?

Arcanum[2]

So our Father, having won the Serpent Crown, the Uræus of Antient Khem, did bind it upon his head, and rejoiced in that Kingdom for the space of two hundred and thirty and one days[4] and nights, and turned him toward the Flaming Sword.[5]

Now the Sword governeth ten mighty Kingdoms, and evil, and above them is the ninefold lotus,[6] and a virgin came forth unto him in the hour of his rejoicing and propounded her riddle.

'The first riddle: The maiden is blind.'[7]

Griphus I[8]

Our Father: 'She shall be what she doth not.'

And a second virgin came forth to him and said: 'The second riddle: *Detegitur Yod*.'[9]

Griphus II

Quoth our Father: 'The moon is full.'[10]

So also a third virgin the third riddle: 'Man and woman: O fountain of the balance!'[11]

Griphus III

To whom our Father answered with a swift flash of his sword,[12] so swift she saw it not.

Came out a fourth virgin, having a fourth riddle: 'What egg hath no shell?'

Griphus IV

---

[1] {אין.}

[2] [Secret.]

[3] This is obscure. {אמן.}

[4] $0 + 1 + 2 + \ldots + 21 = 231$.

[5] The Sephiroth. {ﬡ.}

[6] {Ain Soph Aur.}

[7] The maiden (Malkuth) is blind (unredeemed). Answer: She shall be what she doth not, i.e., see. She shall be the sea, i.e., 'exalted to the throne of Binah' (the great sea), the Qabalistic phrase to express her redemption. We leave it to the reader's ingenuity to solve the rest. Each refers to the Sephira indicated by the number, but going upward.

[8] [Riddle 1.]

[9] [The *yod* is uncovered.] {' = Generation.}

[10] {☽ in Yesod = Chastity.}

[11] [☿ as Hermaphrodite in Salmacis.}

[12] [☿ as speed.}

And our Father pondered a while and then said: 'On a wave of the sea, on a shell of the wave; blessed be her name!'

Griphus v

The fifth virgin issued suddenly and said: 'I have four arms and six sides; red am I, and gold.'[1]

To whom our Father: *'Eli, Eli, lama sabachthani!'*[2]

(For wit ye well, there be two Arcana therein.)

Griphus vi

Then said the sixth virgin openly: 'Power lieth in the river of fire.'[3]

And our Father laughed aloud and answered: 'I am come from the waterfall.'

So at that the seventh virgin came forth, and her countenance was troubled. 'The seventh riddle: The oldest

Griphus vii

said to the most beautiful: "What doest thou here?"'[4]

Our Father:

And she answered him: 'I am in the place of the bridge. Go thou up higher: go thou where these are not.'[5]

Thereat was commotion and bitter wailing, and the eighth virgin came forth with rent attire and cried the

Griphus viii

eighth riddle: 'The sea hath conceived.'[6]

Our Father raised his head, and there was a great darkness.[7]

Griphus ix

The ninth virgin, sobbing at his feet, the ninth riddle: 'By wisdom.'[8]

Then our Father touched his crown and they all rejoiced; but laughing he put them aside and he said: 'Nay! By six hundred and twenty[9] do ye exceed!'[10]

Whereat they wept, and the tenth virgin came forth, bearing a royal crown having twelve jewels;[11] and she

---

[1] {Christ crucified.}

[2] Thou hast forsaken/glorified me! [*Lit.* My God, my God, why have you forsaken me?]

[3] {Geburah = Power.}

[4] {♄ to ♀ in Chesed as 4 = ⊓.

[5]
{♄ ○ ♀ ○.}

[6] {Binah as mother.}

[7] {Binah as darkness.}

[8] {By Chokmah only one may grasp Kether.}

[9] Kether adds up to 620.

[10] {He wished 0.}

[11] {12 = HVA.}

had but one eye, and from that the eyelid had been torn.[1] A prodigious beard had she, and all of white; and they wist he would have smitten her with his sword. But he would not, and she propounded unto him the tenth riddle: 'Countenance beheld not countenance.'[2]

Griphus x

So thereto he answered: '– Our Father, blessed be thou! – Countenance?'[3]

Then they brought him the Sword and bade him smite withal; but he said: 'If countenance behold not countenance, then let the ten be five.'

Culpa Urbium Nota Terrae[4]

And they wist that he but mocked them, for he did bend the sword fivefold and fashioned therefrom a Star, and they all vanished in that light;[5] yet the lotus abode nine-petalled and he cried: 'Before the wheel, the axle.'

So[6] he chained the Sun,[7] and slew the Bull,[8] and exhausted the Air,[9] breathing it deep into his lungs. Then he broke down the ancient tower[10] – that which he had made his home, will he nill he, for so long – and he slew the other Bull,[11] and he broke the arrow[12] in twain. After that he was silent, for they grew again in sixfold order, so that this latter work was double; but unto the first three he laid not his hand, neither for the first time, nor for the second time, nor for the third time.

So to them he added[13] that spiritual flame (for they were one, and ten, and fifty, thrice, and again) and that was the Beast, the Living One that is Lifan.

---

[1] {See [*The Zohar*,] I[dra] R[abba] Q[adisha] ['The Greater Holy Assembly,'] for Eye of Macroprosopus.}

[2] {Affirms Unity prior to Sephiroth.}

[3] {Doubts everything.}

[4] [The fault of cities is known to the earth.]

[5] {⚕ to ☆ = ♄.}

[6] These [following] are the letters of Ain Soph Aur, the last two [words] of which [סוף אור, Soph Aur] he destroys so as to leave only Ain, 'Not,' or 'Nothing.'

[7] {ר = ☉.}

[8] {ו = ♉.}

[9] {א = △.}

[10] {פ = ♂ 'Tower.'}

[11] {ו = ♉.}

[12] {ס = ♐.}

[13] To (1 + 10 + 50) 3 × 2 he adds 300, *shin*, the flame of the Spirit = 666. {אי׳ן = 61. [61] × 3 = 183. [183] 'and again' [i.e., × 2 =]

Let us be silent, therefore, my brethren, worshipping the holy sixfold Ox[1] that was our Father in his peace that he had won into, and that so hardly. For of this shall no man speak.

Now therefore let it be spoken of our Father's journeyings in the land of Vo[2] and of his suffering therein, and of the founding of our holy and illustrious Order.

Nechesh

Abiegnus

Our Father, Brethren, having attained the mature age of three hundred and fifty and eight years,[3] set forth upon a journey into the Mystic Mountain of the Caves. He took with him his Son,[4] a Lamb,[5] Life,[6] and Strength, for these four were the Keys of that Mountain.[7] So by ten days and fifty days and two hundred days and yet ten days he went forth.

Mysterium
I.N.R.I.[8]

After ten days fell a thunderbolt, whirling through black clouds of rain; after sixty the road split in two, but he travelled on both at once; after two hundred and sixty, the sun drove away the rain, and the Star shone in the daytime, making it Night.

After the last day came his Mother, his Redeemer, and Himself; and joining together they were even as I am who write unto you. Seventeen they were, the three Fathers; with the three Mothers they were thirty-two, and sixfold therein, being as countenance and countenance. Yet, being seventeen, they were but one, and

---

366. [366] + 300 (ש) = 666.}

[1] 666 = 6 × 111. 111 = *aleph*, the Ox.

[2] His journeys as Initiator.

[3] Nechesh the Serpent and Messiach the Redeemer.

[4] {Abigenos. Son of the Father.} [Born of the father.]

[5] {Abiagnus. Lamb.} [Lamb of the father.]

[6] {Biagenos. Life.} [Born of strength.]

[7] Abigenos, Abiagnus, Biagenos, Abiegnus, metatheses of the name of the Mystic Mountain of Initiation.

[8] {I = 10   '   Isis   ϟ = Bolt
   N = 50   ג   Apophis   Υ = 2 roads
   R = 200   ר = ☉   Osiris   ☆
   I = 10   '

$$IAO = 17 + (3 \times ר =) 15$$
$$= 32$$

Six letters = AHIHVH

17 = squares of ϟ = א

= I = o.}

that one none, as before hath been showed. And this enumeration is a great Mysterium of our art. Whence a light hidden in a Cross.

Mysterium
L.V.X.[1]

Now therefore having brooded upon the ocean, and smitten with the Sword, and the Pyramid being builded in its just proportion, was that Light fixed even in the Vault of the Caverns.[2]

With one stroke he rent asunder the Veil; with one stroke he closed the same. And entering the Sarcophagus of that Royal Tomb he laid him down to sleep.

Pastos

Four guarded him, and One in the four;[3] Seven enwalled him, and One in the seven,[4] yet were the seven ten, and One in the ten.[5]

Now therefore his disciples came unto the Vault of that Mystic Mountain, and with the Keys they opened the Portal and came to him and woke him. But during his long sleep the roses had grown over him, crimson and flaming with interior fire, so that he could not escape. Yet they withered at his glance; withat he knew what fearful task was before him. But slaying his disciples with long Nails,[6] he interred them there, so that they were right sorrowful in their hearts. May all we die so!

And what further befell him ye shall also know, but not at this time.

Going forth of that Mountain he met also the Fool. [Hear] [t]hen the discourse of that Fool, my Brethren; it shall repay your pains.[7]

'They think they are a triangle,'[8] he said; 'they think as the Picture-Folk. Base they are, and little infinitely.

Trinitas[9]

---

[1] {Now 𝕭 = L
    Y = V
    ☆ = X
    = LVX, Light ✕ }.

[2] {Ritual of flaming light.}

[3] {IHVH and Sh. [יהוה and ש = יהשוה].}}

[4] {7 planets and Daäth.}

[5] {10 Sephiroth and Daäth. 7 = 10 by Palaces.}

[6] {ו = 'Hierophant' = nail.}

[7] [The following] has been explained in the essay 'Qabalistic Dogma.'

[8] The belief in a Trinity – ignorance of Daäth. {△ for △.}

[9] [The Trinity.]

'Ain Elohim.[1]

Unitas[2] 'They think, being many, they are one.[3] They think as the Rhine-Folk think. Many and none.

'Ain Elohim.

Serpentes[4] 'They think the erect[5] is the twined,[6] and the twined is the coiled,[7] and the coiled is the twin,[8] and the twins are the stoopers.[9] They think as the Big-Nose-Folk.[10] Save us, O Lord!

'Ain Elohim.

'The Chariot. Four hundred and eighteen. Five are one, and six are diverse, five in the midst and three on

Abracadabra[11] each side. The Word of Power, double in the Voice of the Master.

'Ain Elohim.

Amethsh 'Four sounds of four forces. O the Snake hath a long tail! Amen![12]

'Ain Elohim.

'Sudden death; thick darkness; ho! the ox![13] One, and one, and one: Creater, Preserver, Destroyer, ho!

Ye Fylfat ✝ the Redeemer! Thunder-stone; whirlpool; lotus-flower; ho! for the gold of the sages![14]

'Ain Elohim.'

And he was silent for a great while, and so departed our Father from Him.

Mysterium Matris[15] Forth he went along the dusty desert and met an antient woman bearing a bright crown of gold, studded

[1] [*Lit.*, 'no God' = the Negative Unity.]
[2] [The Unity (Monad).]
[3] Belief in Monism, or rather Advaitism. Crowley was a Monist only in the modern scientific sense of that word. {Advaitism denied.}
[4] [Serpents.]
[5] Confusion of the various mystic serpents. We leave the rest to the insight of the reader.
[6] {Uraeus, Nechesh.}
[7] {Nehushtan.}
[8] {Twins on wand, etc.}
[9] {Stooping dragon.}
[10] The Big-Nose-Folk = the Jews.
[11] {ח = חית = 418 = Abrahadabra *q.v.*}
[12] {אמן = 741 = AMThsh [אמתש] the elements if נ be counted ן.}
[13] {פלא. אפל. אלף = ox.}
[14] {א = 111 = אעם 卐.}
[15] [Mystery of the mother.] This is all obscure.

with gems, one on each knee. Dressed in rags she was, and squatted clumsily on the sand. A horn grew from her forehead; and she spat black foam and froth. Foul was the hag and evil, yet our Father bowed down flat on his face to the earth.

'Holy Virgin of God,' said he, 'what dost thou here? What wilt thou with thy servant?'

At that she stank so that the air gasped about her, like a fish brought out of the sea. So she told him she was gathering simples for her daughter that had died to bury her withal.

Now no simples grew in the desert. Therefore our Father drew with his sword lines of power in the sand, so that a black and terrible demon appeared squeezing up in thin flat plates of flesh along the sword-lines. *Evocatio*[1]

So our Father cried: 'Simples, O Axcaxrabortharax, for my mother!'

Then the demon was wroth and shrieked: 'Thy mother to black hell! She is mine!'

So the old hag confessed straight that she had given her body for love to that fiend of the pit.

But our Father paid no heed thereto and bade the demon to do his will, so that he brought him herbs many, and good, with which our Father planted a great grove that grew about him (for the sun was now waxen *Lucus*[2] bitter hot) wherein he worshipped, offering in vessels of clay these seven offerings:[3]

The first offering, dust;
The second offering, ashes;
The third offering, sand;
The fourth offering, bay-leaves;[4]
The fifth offering, gold;
The sixth offering, dung;
The seventh offering, poison.

With the dust he gave also a sickle to gather the harvest of that dust.

---

[1] [Evocation.]
[2] [Grove.]
[3] Refer to the planets. {♄, ♃, ♂, ☉, ♀, ☿, ☽.}
[4] {Apollo.}

With the ashes he gave a sceptre, that one might rule them aright.

With the sand he gave a sword, to cut that sand withal.

With the bay-leaves he gave a sun, to wither them.

With the gold he gave also a garland of sores, and that was for luck.

With the dung he gave a Rod of Life to quicken it.

With the poison he gave also in offering a stag and a maiden.

But about the noon came one shining unto our Father and gave him to drink from a dull and heavy bowl. And this was a liquor potent and heavy, by'r lady! So that our *Somnium Auri* Father sank into deep sleep and dreamed a dream, and *Potabilis*[1] in that mirific dream it seemed unto him that the walls of all things slid into and across each other, so that he feared greatly, for the stability of the universe is the great enemy; the unstable being the everlasting, saith Adhou Bin Aram, the Arab. O Elmen Zata, our Sophic Pilaster!

Further in the dream there was let down from heaven a mighty tessaract, bounded by eight cubes, whereon sat a mighty dolphin having eight senses.

Further, he beheld a cavern full of most ancient bones of men, and therein a lion with the voice of a dog.

Tredecim Then came a voice: 'Thirteen[3] are they, who are one.
Voces[2] Once is a oneness; twice is the Name; thrice let us say not; by four is the Son; by five is the Sword; by six is the Holy Oil of the most Excellent Beard, and the leaves of the Book are by six; by seven is that great Amen.'

Then our Father saw one hundred and four horses that drove an ivory car over a sea of pearl, and they received him therein and bade him be comforted.

With that he awoke and saw that he would have all his desire. In the morning therefore he arose and went his *Ordinis* way into the desert. There he clomb an high rock and *Inceptio*[4] called forth the eagles, that their shadow floating over the desert should be as a book that men might read it.

---

[1] [The dream of potable gold.]

[2] [Thirteen voices.]

[3] Achad, unity, adds to thirteen. There follow attributions of the 'thirteen times table.' {26 = IHVH. 39 = [...]. 52 = BN. 65 = sq[uare] of ☾. 78 = MZLA – Tarot. 91 = AMN, etc. 104 = 13 × 8 = 8 = Π.}

[4] [The founding of the Order.]

The shadows wrote and the sun recorded; and on this wise cometh it to pass, O my Brethren, that by darkness and by sunlight ye will still learn ever these the Arcana of our Science. Lo! who learneth by moonlight, he is the lucky one!

So our Father, having thus founded the Order, and our sacred Book being opened, rested awhile and beheld many wonders, the like of which were never yet told. But ever chiefly his study was to reduce unto eight things his many.

And thus, O Brethren of our Venerable Order, he at last succeeded. Those who know not will learn little herein; yet that they may be shamed all shall be put forth at this time clearly before them all, with no obscurity nor obfuscation in the exposition thereof.

'Writing this,' saith our Father to me, the humblest and oldest of all his disciples, 'write as the story of my Quintessential Quest, my Spagyric Wandering, my Philosophical Going.

'Write plainly unto the Brethren,' quoth he, 'for many be little and weak; and thy hard words and much learning may confound them.'

Therefore I write thus plainly to you. Mark well that ye read me aright!

Our Father (blessed be his name!) entered the Path on this wise. He cut off three from ten:[1] thus he left seven. He cut and left three; he cut and left one; he cut and became. Thus fourfold. Eightfold.[2] He opened his eyes; he cleansed his heart; he chained his tongue; he fixed his flesh; he turned to his trade; he put forth his strength; he drew all to a point; he delighted. *Viae*[3]

Therefore he is not, having become that which he was not. Mark ye all: it is declared.

Now of the last adventure of our Father and of his going into the land of Apes – that is, England – and of what he did there, it is not fitting that I, the poor old *Vitae Reliquiae*[4]

---

[1] These are the Buddhist 'paths of enlightenment.' {*Sotāpanna*, etc., to *arhant*.}
[2] The eightfold path. The rest is very obscure.
[3] [The paths.]
[4] [The remainder of his life.]

fool who loved him, shall now discourse. But it is most necessary that I should speak of his holy death and of his funeral and of the bruit thereof, for that is gone into diverse lands as a false and lying report, whereby much harm and ill-luck come to the Brethren. In this place, therefore, will I set down the exact truth of all that happened.

Mirabilia[1]

In the year of the Great Passing Over were signs and wonders seen of all men, O my Brethren, as it is written,

1. *Signum*[2] and well known unto this day. And the first sign was of dancing: for every woman that was under the moon began to dance and was mad, so that headlong and hot-mouthed she flung herself down, desirous. Whence the

II. *Signum* second sign, that of musical inventions: for in that year, and of Rose-women, came A and U and M,[3] the mighty

III. *Signum* musicians! And the third sign likewise, namely, of animals: for in that year every sheep had lambs thirteen,

Alii Signa[4] and every cart[5] was delivered of a wheel! And other wonders innumerable; they are well known, insomuch that that year is yet held notable.

Now our Father, being very old, came into the venerable Grove of our August Fraternity and abode there. And so old was he and feeble that he could scarce lift his hands in benediction upon us. And all we waited about him, both by day and night lest one word should fall, and we not hear the same. But he spake never unto us, though his lips moved and his eyes sought ever that which we could not see.

At last, on the day of D., the mother of P.,[6] he straightened himself up and spake. This his final discourse was written down then by the dying lions in their own blood, traced willingly on the desert sands about the Grove of the Illustrious. Also here set down;

---

[1] [Miracles.]

[2] [The first sign.]

[3] *Aum!* The sacred word.

[4] [Other signs.]

[5] *Qy.* Π (the cart) becomes O (a wheel). The commentators who have suspected the horrid blasphemy implied by the explanation 'becomes Ɔ, "The Wheel of Fortune,"' are certainly in error.

[6] Demeter and Persephone

but who will confirm the same, let him seek it on the sands.

'Children of my Will,' said our Father, from whose grey eyes fell gentlest tears, 'it is about the hour. The chariot (Ch.) is not, and the chariot (H.) is at hand.[1] Yet I, who have been car-borne through the blue air by sphinxes, shall never be carried away, not by the whitest horses of the world. To you I have no word to say. All is written in the sacred Book. To that look ye well!

'Ambrose, old friend,' he said, turning to me – and I wept ever sore – 'do thou write for the little ones, the children of my children, for them that understand not easily our high Mysteries; for in thy pen is, as it were, a river of clear water; without vagueness, without ambiguity, without show of learning, without needless darkening of counsel and word, dost thou ever reveal the sacred Heights of our Mystic Mountain. For, as for him that understandeth not thy writing, and that easily and well, be ye well assured all that he is a vile man and a losel of little worth or worship; a dog, an unclean swine, a worm of filth, a festering sore in the vitals of earth; such an one is liar and murderer, debauched, drunken, sexless and spatulate; an ape-dropping, a lousy, flat-backed knave; from such an one keep ye well away! Use hath he little;[3] ornament maketh he nothing; let him be cast out on the dung-hills beyond Jordan;[4] let him pass into the S.P.P., and that utterly!'

With that our Father sighed deep and laid back his reverend head, and was silent. But from his heart came a subtle voice of tenderest farewell, so that we knew him well dead. But for seventy days and seventy nights we touched him not, but abode ever about him; and the smile changed not on his face, and the whole grove was filled with sweet and subtle perfumes.

Pater Jubet Scientiam Scribere[2]

Sedes Profunda Paimonis[5]

Oculi Nox Secreta[6]

---

[1] Ch = Π; H = Hades. See the Tarot cards, and classical mythology, for the symbols. {Π Lord of [the] Triumph of Light. H = Hades.}

[2] [The Father bids me write of this knowledge.]

[3] {N[o] B[loody] U[se]. L.B.O.}

[4] {'To the other side of Jordan.'}

[5] [The deep abode of Paimon.]

[6] [The secret night of the eye.]

Now on the 71st day arose there a great dispute about his body; for the angels and spirits and demons did contend about it, that they might possess it. But our eldest brother V.N.[3] bade all be still; and thus he apportioned the sacred relics of our Father.

Portae Silentium[1]

Partitio[2]

To the Angel Agbagal, the fore part of the skull;

To the demon Ozoz, the back left part of the skull;

To the demon Olcot,[4] the back right part of the skull;

To ten thousand myriads of spirits of fire, each one hair;

To ten thousand myriads of spirits of water, each one hair;

To ten thousand myriads of spirits of earth, each one hair;

To ten thousand myriads of spirits of air, each one hair;

To the archangel Zazelazel, the brain;

To the angel Usbusolat, the medulla;

To the demon Ululomis, the right nostril;

To the angel Opael, the left nostril;

To the spirit Kuiphiah, the membrane of the nose;

To the spirit Pugrah, the bridge of the nose;

To eleven thousand spirits of spirit, the hairs of the nose, one each;

To the archangel Tuphtuphtuphal,[5] the right eye;

To the archdevil Upsusph, the left eye;

The parts thereof in trust to be divided among their servitors; as the right cornea, to Aphlek; the left, to Urnbal; – mighty spirits are they, and bold!

To the archdevil Rama,[6] the right ear and its parts;

To the archangel Umumatis, the left ear and its parts;

The teeth to two-and-thirty letters of the sixfold Name: one to the air, and fifteen to the rain and the ram, and ten to the virgin, and six to the Bull;

The mouth to the archangels Alalal and Bikarak, lip and lip;

The tongue to that devil of all devils Yehowou.[7] Ho, devil! canst thou speak?

---

[1] [The silence of the gate.]

[2] [The distribution.]

[3] {[G. Cecil] Jones.}

[4] Col. Olcott, the theosophist.

[5] ? the spirit of motor-cars.

[6] Viṣṇu, the preserver.

[7] Jehovah.

The pharynx to Mahabonisbash,[1] the great angel;

To seven-and-thirty myriads of legions of planetary spirits the hairs of the moustache, to each one;

To ninety and one myriads of the Elohim, the hairs of the beard; to each thirteen, and the oil to ease the world;

To Shalach, the archdevil, the chin.

So also with the lesser relics; of which are notable only: to the Order, the heart of our Father; to the Book of the Law, his venerable lung-space to serve as a shrine thereunto; to the devil Aot, the liver, to be divided; to the angel Exarp[2] and his followers, the great intestine; to Bitom[2] the devil and his crew, the little intestine; to Aub, Aud and Aur,[3] the venerable Phallus of our Father; to Ash,[4] the little bone of the same; to our children K., C., B., C., G., T., N., H., Y. and M.,[5] his illustrious fingernails, and the toenails to be in trust for their children after them; and so for all the rest: is it not written in our archives?

As to his magical weapons, all vanished utterly at the moment of his Passing Over.

Therefore they carried away our Father's body piece by piece and that with reverence and in order, so that there was not left of all one hair, nor one nerve, nor one little pore of the skin. Thus was there no funeral pomp; they that say other are liars and blasphemers against a fame untarnished. May the red plague rot their vitals!

Thus, O my Brethren, thus and not otherwise was the Passing Over of that Great and Wonderful Magician, our Father and Founder. May the dew of his admirable memory moisten the grass of our minds, that we may bring forth tender shoots of energy in the Great Work of Works. So mote it be!

BENEDICTVS DOMINVS DEVS NOSTER

QVI NOBIS DEDIT SIGNVM

R. C.[6]

---

[1] {Mahabone.}

[2] {Names on tablets.}

[3] {3 names = ˘ = △ = Phallus.}

[4] {Fire.}

[5] {Sephiroth.}

[6] [Blessed be the Lord our God who has given to us the sign R[osae] C[rucis].]

The Wake World

A TALE FOR BABES AND SUCKLINGS

(WITH EXPLANATORY NOTES IN HEBREW AND LATIN
FOR THE USE OF THE WISE AND PRUDENT)

My name is Lola, because I am the Key of Delights,[1] and the other children in my dream call me Lola Daydream. When I am awake, you see, I know that I am dreaming, so that they must be very silly children, don't you think? There are people in the dream, too, who are quite grown up and horrid; but the really important thing is the wake-up person.[2] There is only one, for there never could be anyone like him. I call him my Fairy Prince. He rides a horse with beautiful wings like a swan,[3] or sometimes a strange creature like a lion or a bull, with a woman's face and breasts, and she has unfathomable eyes.[4]

My Fairy Prince is a dark boy, very comely;[5] I think everyone must love him, and yet everyone is afraid. He looks through one just as if one had no clothes on in the Garden of God, and he had made one, and one could do nothing except in the mirror of his mind. He never laughs or frowns or smiles; because, whatever he sees, he sees what is beyond as well, and so nothing ever happens. His mouth is redder than any roses you ever saw. I wake up quite when we kiss each other, and there is no dream any more. But when it is not trembling on mine, I see kisses on his lips, as if he were kissing someone that one could not see.

Now you must know that my Fairy Prince is my lover, and one day he will come for good and ride away with me and marry me. I shan't tell you his name because it is too beautiful. It is a great secret between us. When

---

[1] *Virgo Mundi*. [Virgin of the World.]
[2] Adonai.
[3] Pegasus.
[4] Sphinx.
[5] V.V.V.V.V.

we were engaged he gave me such a beautiful ring. It was like this. First there was his shield, which had a sun on it and some roses,[1] all on a kind of bar; and there was a terrible number written on it.[2] Then there was a bank of soft roses with the sun shining on it,[3] and above there was a red rose on a golden cross,[4] and then there was a three-cornered star,[5] shining so bright that nobody could possibly look at it unless they had love in their eyes; and in the middle was an eye without an eyelid. That could see anything, I should think, but you see it never could go to sleep, because there wasn't any eyelid. On the sides were written I.N.R.I. and T.A.R.O., which mean many strange and beautiful things, and terrible things too. I should think anyone would be afraid to hurt anyone who wore that ring. It is all cut out of an amethyst, and my Fairy Prince said: 'Whenever you want me, look into the ring and call me ever so softly by my name, and kiss the ring, and worship it, and then look ever so deep down into it, and I will come to you.' So I made up a pretty poem to say[6] every time I woke up, for you see I am a very sleepy girl, and dream ever so much about the other children; and that is a pity, because there is only one thing I love, and that is my Fairy Prince. So this is the poem I did to worship the ring, part is words, and part is pictures. You must pick out what the pictures mean, and then it all makes poetry.

The Invocation of the Ring

> ADONAI! Thou inmost $\triangle$,
> Self-glittering image of my soul,
> Strong lover to thy Bride's desire,
> Call me and claim me and control!
> I pray Thee keep the holy tryst
> Within this ring of Amethyst.
>
> For on mine eyes the golden $\odot$
> Hath dawned; my vigil slew the Night.
> I saw the image of the One:
> I came from darkness into L.V.X.
> I pray Thee keep the holy tryst
> Within this ring of Amethyst.

---

[1] *Sigilla annuli.* [The figures of the ring.]
[2] 1. *Cognominis* 666. [Of the name 666.]
[3] 2. *I Ordinis.* [Of the First Order.]
[4] 3. *II Ordinis.* [Of the Second Order.]
[5] 4. *III Ordinis.* [Of the Third Order.]
[6] *Incantatio.* [Spell.]

I.N.R.I. – me crucified,
Me slain, interred, arisen, inspire!
T.A.R.O. – me glorified,
Anointed, fill with frenzied △
I pray Thee keep the holy tryst
Within this ring of Amethyst.

I eat my flesh: I drink my blood
I gird my loins: I journey far:
For thou hast shown ○, +,[1]
ע, 777, καμήλον,[2]
I pray Thee keep the holy tryst
Within this ring of Amethyst.

Prostrate I wait upon Thy will,
Mine Angel, for this grace of union.
O let this Sacrament distil
Thy conversation and communion.
I pray Thee keep the holy tryst
Within this ring of Amethyst.

I have not told you anything about myself, because it doesn't really matter; the only thing I want to tell you about is my Fairy Prince. But as I am telling you all this, I am seventeen years old,[3] and very fair when you shut your eyes to look; but when you open them, I am really dark, with a fair skin. I have ever such heaps of hair, and big, big, round eyes, always wondering at everything. Never mind, it's only a nuisance. I shall tell you what happened one day when I said the poem to the ring. I wasn't really quite awake when I began, but as I said it, it got brighter and brighter, and when I came to 'ring of amethyst' the fifth time (there are five verses, because my lover's name has five V's in it), he galloped[4] across the beautiful green sunset, spurring the winged horse, till the blood made all the sky turn rosy red. So he caught me up and set me on his horse, and I clung to his neck as we galloped into the night. Then he told me he would take me to his Palace and show me everything, and one day when we were married I should be mistress of it all. Then I wanted to be married to him at once, and then I saw it couldn't be, because I was so sleepy and had bad dreams, and one can't be a good wife if one is always doing that sort of thing. But he said I would be older one day, and not sleep so much, and everyone slept a little, but the great thing was not to be lazy and contented with the dreams, so I mean to fight hard.

---

[1] The Rose, the Rood, the Eye, the Sword, the Silver Star.
[2] [Camel.]
[3] יא [IAO]. The Masculine Trinity.
[4] *Advenit Adonai.* [Adonai arrives.]

PART I

By and by we came to a beautiful green place[1] with the strangest house you ever saw.[2] Round the big meadow there lay a wonderful snake,[3] with steel grey plumes, and he had his tail in his mouth, and kept on eating and eating it, because there was nothing else for him to eat, and my Fairy Prince said he would go on like that till there was nothing left at all. Then I said it would get smaller and smaller and crush the meadow and the palace, and I think perhaps I began to cry. But my Fairy Prince said: 'Don't be such a silly!' and I wasn't old enough to understand all that it meant, but one day I should; and all one had to do was to be as glad as glad. So he kissed me, and we got off the horse, and he took me to the door of the house, and we went in.[4] It was frightfully dark in the passage, and I felt tied so that I couldn't move, so I promised to myself to love him always, and he kissed me. It was dreadfully, dreadfully dark though, but he said not to be afraid, silly! And it's getting lighter, now keep straight forward, darling! And then he kissed me again, and said: 'Welcome to my Palace!'

I will tell you all about how it was built, because it is the most beautiful Palace that ever was.[5] On the sunset side were all the baths, and the bedrooms were in front of us as we were. The baths were all of pale olive-coloured marble, and the bedrooms had lemon-coloured everything. Then there were the kitchens on the sunrise side, and they were russet, like dead leaves are in autumn in one's dreams.[6] The place we had come through was perfectly black everything, and only used for offices and such things. There were the most horrid things[7] everywhere about; black beetles and cockroaches, and goodness knows what; but they can't hurt when the Fairy Prince is there. I think a little girl would be eaten though if she went in there alone.

Then he said: 'Come on! This is only the Servants' Hall, nearly everybody stays there all their lives.' And I said: 'Kiss me!' So he said: 'Every step you take is only possible when you say that.' We came into a dreadful dark passage[8] again, so narrow and low, that it was like a dirty old tunnel, and yet so vast and wide that everything in the whole world was contained

---

[1] *Regnum Spatii.* [The Kingdom of Space.]

[2] *Palatium Otz Chiim.* [Of the First Order.]

[3] *Draco* תל. [Dew of the Serpent.]

[4] *Ceremonium* o°= o°. [The o°=o° Ceremony.]

[5] *Domus X vel Porta vel Regnum.* [The Tenth House or the Kingdom or the Gate.]

[6] 4 *loci secundum Elementa.* [Four Places according to the Elements.]

[7] Qliphoth. [Shells.]

[8] *Via* ת *vel Crux.* [The Path of *tau* or the Cross.]

in it. We saw all the strange dreams and awful shapes of fear, and really I don't know how we ever got through, except that the Prince called for some splendid strong creatures to guard us. There was an eagle[1] that flew, and beat his wings, and tore and bit at everything that came near; and there was a lion that roared terribly, and his breath was a flame, and burnt up the things, so that there was a great cloud; and rain fell gently and purely, so that he really did the things good by fighting them. And there was a bull that tossed them on his horns, so that they changed into butterflies; and there was a man who kept on telling everybody to be quiet and not make a noise. So we came at last in the next house of the Palace.[2] It was a great dome of violet, and in the centre the moon shone. She was a full moon, and yet she looked like a woman quite, quite young. Yet her hair was silver, and finer than spiders' webs, and it rayed about her, like one can't say what; it was all too beautiful. In the middle of the hall there was a black stone pillar,[3] from the top of which sprang a fountain of pearls; and as they fell upon the floor, they changed the dark marble to the colour of blood, and it was like a green universe full of flowers, and little children playing among them. So I said: 'Shall we be married in this House?' and he said: 'No, this is only the House where the business is carried on. All the Palace rests upon this House; but you are called Lola because you are the Key of Delights. Many people stay here all their lives though.' I made him kiss me, and we went on to another passage which opened out of the Servants' Hall. This passage[4] was all fire and flame and full of coffins. There was an Angel blowing ever so hard on a trumpet, and people getting up out of the coffins. My Fairy Prince said: 'Most people never wake up for anything less.' So we went (at the same time it was; you see in dreams people can only be in one place at a time; that's the best of being awake) through another passage,[5] which was lighted by the Sun. Yet there were fairies dancing in a great green ring, just as if it was night. And there were two children playing by the wall, and my Fairy Prince and I played as we went; and he said: 'The difference is that we are going through. Most people play without a purpose; if you are travelling it is all right, and play makes the journey seem short.' Then we came out into the Third (or Eighth, it depends which way you count them, because there are ten) House,[6] and that was so splendid you can't imagine. In the first place it was a bright, bright,

---

[1] Cherubim.

[2] *Domus IX vel Fundamentum.* [The Ninth House or the Foundation.]

[3] ' *vel Membrum sancti foederis.* [*Yod* or the Organ of the Sacred Covenant.]

[4] *Via* ש *vel Dens.* [The Path of *shin* or the Tooth.]

[5] *Via* ר *vel Caput.* [The Path of *resh* or the Head.]

[6] *Domus VIII vel Splendour.* [The Eighth House or Splendour.]

bright, orange colour, and then it had flashes of light all over it, going so fast we couldn't see them, and then there was the sound of the sea and one could look through into the deep, and there was the ocean raging beneath one's feet, and strong dolphins riding on it and crying aloud, 'Holy! Holy! Holy!' in such an ecstasy you can't think, and rolling and playing for sheer joy. It was all lighted by a tiny, weeny, shy little planet, sparkling and silvery, and now and then a wave of fiery chariots filled with eager spearmen blazed through the sky, and my Fairy Prince said: 'Isn't it all fine?' But I knew he didn't really mean it, so I said 'Kiss me!' and he kissed me, and we went on. He said: 'Good little girl of mine, there's many a one stays there all his life.' I forgot to say that the whole place was just one mass of books, and people reading them till they were so silly, they didn't know what they were doing. And there were cheats, and doctors, and thieves; I was really very glad to go away.

There were three ways into the Seventh House, and the first[1] was such a funny way. We walked through a pool, each on the arm of a great big Beetle, and then we found ourselves on a narrow winding path. There were nasty Jackals about, they made such a noise, and at the end I could see two towers. Then there was the queerest moon you ever saw, only a quarter full. The shadows fell so strangely, one could see the most mysterious shapes, like great bats with women's faces, and blood dripping from their mouths, and creatures partly wolves and partly men, everything changing one into the other. And we saw shadows like old, old, ugly women, creeping about on sticks, and all of a sudden they would fly up into the air, shrieking the funniest kind of songs, and then suddenly one would come down flop, and you saw she was really quite young and ever so lovely, and she would have nothing on, and as you looked at her she would crumble away like a biscuit. Then there was another passage[2] which was really too secret for anything; all I shall tell you is, there was the most beautiful Goddess that ever was, and she was washing herself in a river of dew. If you ask what she is doing, she says: 'I'm making thunderbolts.' It was only starlight, and yet one could see quite clearly, so don't think I'm making a mistake. The third path[3] is a most terrible passage; it's all a great war, and there's earthquakes and chariots of fire, and all the castles breaking to pieces. I was glad when we came to the Green Palace.[4]

---

[1] *Via ק vel Cranium.* [The Path of *qoph* or the Cranium.]

[2] *Via צ vel Hamus.* [The Path of *tzaddi* or the Fish Hook.]

[3] *Via פ vel Os.* [The Path of *pé* or the Mouth.]

[4] *Domus VII vel Victoria.* [The Seventh House or Victory.]

It was all built of malachite and emerald, and there was the loveliest
gentlest living, and I was married to my Fairy Prince there, and we
had the most delicious honeymoon, and I had a beautiful baby, and
then I remembered myself, but only just in time, and said: 'Kiss me!'
And he kissed me and said: 'My goodness! But that was a near thing
that time: my little girl nearly went to sleep. Most people who reach
the Seventh House stay there all their lives, I can tell you.'

It did seem a shame to go on; there was such a flashing green star to
light it, and all the air was filled with amber-coloured flames like kisses.
And we could see through the floor, and there were terrible lions, like
furnaces for fury, and they all roared out: 'Holy! Holy! Holy!' and leaped
and danced for joy. And when I saw myself in the mirrors, the dome was
one mass of beautiful green mirrors, I saw how serious I looked, and that
I *had* to go on. I hoped the Fairy Prince would look serious too, because
it is a most dreadful business going beyond the Seventh House; but he
only looked the same as ever. But oh! how I kissed him, and how I clung
to him, or I think I should never, never have had the courage to go up
those dreadful passages, especially knowing what was at the end of them.
And now I'm only a little girl, and I'm ever so tired of writing, but I'll tell
you all about the rest another time.

Explicit Capitulum Primum vel De Collegio Externo.[1]

PART II

I was telling you how we started from the Green Palace. There are
three passages that lead to the Treasure House of Gold, and all of them
are very dreadful. One is called the Terror by Night, and another the
Arrow by Day, and the third has a name that people are afraid to hear,
so I won't say.

But in the first[2] we came to a mighty throne of grey granite, shaped
like the sweetest pussy cat you ever saw, and set up on a desolate heath.
It was midnight, and the Devil came down and sat in the midst; but
my Fairy Prince whispered: 'Hush! it is a great secret, but his name
is Yeheswah, and he is the Saviour of the World.' And that was very
funny, because the girl next me thought it was Jesus Christ, till another
Fairy Prince (my Prince's brother) whispered as he kissed her: 'Hush,
tell nobody ever, that is Satan, and he is the Saviour of the World.'

---

[1] [Here ends Section the First, or, Concerning the Outer College.]
[2] *Via ע vel Oculus.* [The Path of *ayin* or the Eye.]

We were a very great company, and I can't tell you of all the strange things we did and said, or of the song we sang as we danced face outwards in a great circle ever closing in on the Devil on the throne. But whenever I saw a toad or a bat, or some horrid insect, my Fairy Prince always whispered: 'It is the Saviour of the world' and I saw that it was so. We did all the most beautiful wicked things you can imagine, and yet all the time we knew they were good and right, and must be done if ever we were to get to the House of Gold. So we enjoyed ourselves very much and ate the most extraordinary supper you can think of. There were babies roasted whole and stuffed with pork sausages and olives; and some of the girls cut off chops and steaks from their own bodies, and gave them to a beautiful white cook at a silver grill, that was lighted with the gas of dead bodies and marshes; and he cooked them splendidly, and we all enjoyed it immensely. Then there was a tame goat with a gold collar, that went about laughing with everyone; and he was all shaved in patches like a poodle. We kissed him and petted him, and it was lovely. You must remember that I never let go of my Fairy Prince for a single instant, or of course I should have been turned into a horrid black toad.

Then there was another passage[1] called the Arrow by Day, and there was a most lovely lady all shining with the sun, and moon, and stars, who was lighting a great bowl of water with one hand, by dropping dew on it out of a cup, and with the other she was putting out a terrible fire with a torch. She had a red lion and a white eagle, that she had always had ever since she was a little girl. She had found them in a nasty pit full of all kinds of filth, and they were very savage; but by always treating them kindly they had grown up faithful and good. This should be a lesson to all of us never to be unkind to our pets.

My Fairy Prince was laughing all the time in the third path.[2] There was nobody there but an old gentleman who had put on his bones outside, and was trying ever so hard to cut down the grass with a scythe. But the faster he cut it the faster it grew. My Fairy Prince said: 'Everybody that ever was has come along this path, and yet only one ever got to the end of it.' But I saw a lot of people walking straight through as if they knew it quite well; he explained, though, that they were really only one; and if you walked through that proved it. I thought that was silly, but he's much older and wiser than I am; so I said nothing. The truth is that it is a very difficult Palace to talk about, and the further you get in, the harder

---

[1] *Via* ☉ *vel Sustentaculum*. [The Path of *samekh* or the Prop.]
[2] *Via* ☽ *vel Piscis*. [The Path of *nun* or the Fish.']

it is to say what you mean because it all has to be put into dream talk, as of course the language of the Wake-World is silence.

So never mind! let me get on. We came by and by to the Sixth House.[1] I forgot to say that all those three paths were really one, because they all meant that things were different inside to outside, and so people couldn't judge. It was fearfully interesting; but mind you don't go in those passages without the Fairy Prince. And of course there's the Veil. I don't think I'd better tell you about the Veil.[2] I'll only put your mouth to my head, and your hand – there, that'll tell anybody who knows that I've really been there, and that it's all true that I'm telling you.

This Sixth House is called the Treasure House of Gold; it's a most mysterious place as ever you were in. First there's a tiny, tiny, tiny doorway,[3] you must crawl through on your hands and knees;[4] and even then I scraped ever such a lot of skin off my back; then you have to be nailed on a red board with four arms,[5] with a great gold circle in the middle, and that hurts you dreadfully. Then they make you swear the most solemn things you ever heard of, how you would be faithful to the Fairy Prince, and live for nothing but to know him better and better. So the nails stopped hurting, because, of course, I saw that I was really being married, and this was part of it, and I was as glad as glad; and at that moment my Fairy Prince put his hand on my head, and I tell you, honour bright, it was more wake up than ever before, even than when he used to kiss me. After that they said I could go into the Bride-chamber,[6] but it was only the most curious room that ever was with seven sides. There was a dreadful red dragon on the floor, and all the sides were painted every colour you can think of, with curious figures and pictures. The light was not like dream light at all; it was wake light, and it came through a beautiful rose in the ceiling. In the middle was a table all covered with beautiful pictures and texts, and there were ever such strange things on it. There was a little crucifix in the middle, all of diamonds and emeralds and rubies, and other precious stones, and there was a dagger with a golden handle, and a cup full of the most delicious wine, and there was a curious coin with the strangest writing on it, and a funny little stick that was covered with flames, like a rose tree is with roses. Beside the strange coin was a heavy iron chain, and I took it and put it round my neck because I was bound

---

[1] *Domus VI vel Pulchritudo.* [The Sixth House or Beauty.]
[2] פרכת. [Paroketh.]
[3] *Ceremonium* $5°=6°$. [The $5°=6°$ Ceremony.]
[4] *Humilitas.* [Humbleness.]
[5] *Supplicium.* [Punishment.]
[6] *Sepulchrum.* [The Tomb.]

to my Fairy Prince, and I would never go about like other people till I found him again. And they took the dagger and dipped it in the cup, and stabbed me all over to show that I was not afraid to be hurt, if only I could find my Fairy Prince. Then I took the crucifix and held it up to make more light in case he was somewhere in the dark corners, but no! Yet I knew he was there somewhere, so I thought he must be in the box, for under the table was a great chest;[1] and I was terribly sad because I felt something dreadful was going to happen. And sure enough, when I had the courage, I asked them to open the box, and the same people that made me crawl through that horrid hole, and lost my Fairy Prince, and nailed me to the red board, took away the table and opened the box, and there was my Fairy Prince, quite, quite dead. If you only knew how sorry I felt! But I had with me a walking-stick with wings,[2] and a shining sun at the top that had been his, and I touched him on the breast to try and wake him; but it was no good. Only I seemed to hear his voice saying wonderful things, and it was quite certain he wasn't really dead. So I put the walking-stick on his breast, and another little thing he had which I had forgotten to tell you about. It was a kind of cross with an oval handle[3] that he had been very fond of. But I couldn't go away without something of his, so I took a shepherd's staff, and a little whip[4] with blood on it, and jewels oozing from the blood, if you know what I mean, that they had put in his hands when they buried him. Then I went away, and cried, and cried, and cried. But before I had got very far they called me back; and the people who had been so stern were smiling, and I saw they had taken the coffin out of the little room with seven sides. And the coffin was quite, quite empty.[5] Then they began to tell us all about it, and I heard my Fairy Prince within the little room saying holy exalted things, such as the stars trace in the sky as they travel in the Car called 'Millions of Years.' Then they took me into the little room, and there was my Fairy Prince standing in the middle. So I knelt down and we all kissed his beautiful feet, and the myriads of eyes like diamonds that were hidden in his feet laughed joy at us. One couldn't lift one's head, for he was too glorious to behold; but he spoke wonderful words like dying nightingales that have sorrowed for the fading of the roses, and pressed themselves to death upon the thorns; and one's whole body became a

---

[1] *Pastos Patris nostri C.R.C.* [The Bridal Chamber of our Father C.R.C.]

[2] *Baculum I. Adepti.* [The Staff of the First Adept.]

[3] *Crux Ansata.* [The Cross with a Handle.]

[4] *Pedum et Flagellum Osiridis.* [The Shepherd's Crook and Whip of Osiris.]

[5] *Curinter mortuos vivum petes? Non est hic ille; resurrexit.* [Why will you seek a living one among the dead? He is not here; he has risen again.]

single eye, so that one saw as if the unborn thought of light brooded over an eternal sea. Then was light as the lightning flaming out of the east,[1] even unto the west, and it was fashioned as the swiftness of a sword.

By and by one rose up, then one seemed to be quite, quite dead, and buried in the centre of a pyramid of the most brilliant light it is possible to think of. And it was wake-light too; and everybody knows that even wake-darkness is really brighter than the dream-light. So you must just guess what it was like. There was more than that too; I can't possibly tell you. I know too what I.N.R.I. on the Ring meant: and I can't tell you that either, because the dream-language has such a lot of important words missing. It's a very silly language, I think.

By and by I came to myself a little, and now I was really and truly married to the Fairy Prince, so I suppose we shall always be near each other now.

There was the way out of the little room with millions of changing colours,[2] ever so beautiful, and it was lined with armed men, waving their swords for joy like flashes of lightning; and all about us glittering serpents danced and sang for joy.[3] There was a winged horse ready for us when we came out on the slopes of the mountain. You see the Sixth House is really in a mountain called Mount Abiegnus,[4] only one doesn't see it because one goes through indoors all the way. There's one House you have to go outdoors to get to, because no passage has ever been made; but I'll tell you about that afterwards; it's the Third House. So we got on the horse and went away for our honeymoon. I shan't tell you a single word about the honeymoon.

Explicit Capitulum Secundum vel
De Collegio ad S. S. Porta Collegii Interni.[5]

PART III

You mustn't suppose the honeymoon is ever really over, because it just isn't. But he said to me: 'Princess, you haven't been all over the Palace yet. Your *special* House is the Third, you know, because it's so convenient for the Second where I usually live. The King[6] my Father lives in the

---

[1] *Advenit* L.V.X. *sub tribus speciebus.* [L.V.X. arrives under three forms.]
[2] *Symbola Hodos Chamelionis.* [The Symbol the Path of the Chameleon.]
[3] *Symbola Gladius et Serpens.* [The Symbol the Sword and the Serpent.]
[4] *Mons Abiegnus vel Cavernarum.* [Mount Abiegnus or the Mountain of Caverns.]
[5] [Here ends Section the Second, or Concerning the College that is the Gate to the S.S. of the Inner College.]
[6] *Caput candidum.* [White Head.]

First; he's never to be seen, you know. He's very, very old nowadays;
I am practically Regent of course. You must never forget that I am really
He; only one generation back is not so far, and I entirely represent
his thought. Soon,' he whispered ever so softly, 'you will be a mother;[1]
there will be a Fairy Prince again to run away with another pretty little
Sleepyhead. Then I saw that when Fairy Princes were really and truly
married they became Fairy Kings;[2] and that I was quite wrong ever to
be ashamed of being only a little girl and afraid of spoiling his prospects,
because really, you see, he could never become King and have a son a
Fairy Prince without me.

But one can only do that by getting to the Third House, and it's a
dreadful journey, I do most honestly assure you.

There are two passages, one from the Eighth House and one from
the Sixth; the first is all water, and the second is almost worse, because
you have to balance yourself so carefully, or you fall and hurt yourself.

To go through the first[3] you must be painted all over with blood
up to your waist, and you cross your legs, and then they put a rope
round one ankle and swing you off. I had such a pretty white petti-
coat on, and my Prince said I looked just like a white pyramid with a
huge red cross on the top of it, which made me ever so glad, because
now I knew I should be the Saviour of the World, which is what one
wants to be, isn't it? Only sometimes the world means all the other
children in the dream, and sometimes the dream itself, and sometimes
the wake-things one sees before one is quite, quite awake. The prince
tells me that really and truly only the First House where his Father
lived was really a wake-House, all the others had a little sleep-House
about them, and the further you got the more awake you were, and
began to know just how much was dream and how much wake.

Then there was the other passage[4] where there was a narrow edge
of green crystal, which was all you had to walk on, and there was a
beautiful blue feather balancing on the edge, and if you disturbed the
feather there was a lady with a sword, and she would cut off your head.
So I didn't dare hardly to breathe, and all round there were thousands
and thousands of beautiful people in green who danced and danced
like anything, and at the end there was the terrible door of the Fifth
House,[5] which is the Royal armoury. And when we came in, the House

---

[1] אמא *erit* אימא. [AMA will be AIMA.]
[2] *Arcanum de Via Occulta.* [Secrets of the Hidden Path.]
[3] *Via* מ *vel Aqua.* [The Path of *mem* or Water.]
[4] *Via* ל *vel Pertica Stimulans.* [The Path of *lamed* or the Goading Rod.]
[5] *Domus V vel Severitas.* [The Fifth House or Severity.]

was full of steel machinery, some red hot and some white hot, and the din was simply fearful. So to get the noise out of my head, I took the little whip and whipped myself till all my blood poured down over everything, and I saw the whole house like a cataract of foaming blood rushing headlong from the flaming and scintillating Star of Fire that blazed and blazed in the candescent dome, and everything went red before my eyes, and a great flame like a strong wind blew through the House with a noise louder than any thunder could possibly be, so that I couldn't hold myself hardly, and I took up the sharp knives of the machines and cut myself all over, and the noise got louder and louder, and the flame burnt through and through me, so that I was very glad when my Prince said: 'You wouldn't think it, would you, sweetheart? But there are lots of people who stay here all their lives.'

There are three ways into the Fourth House from below. The first passage[1] is a very curious place, all full of wheels and ever such strange creatures, like monkeys and sphinxes and jackals climbing about them and trying to get to the top. It was very silly, because there isn't really any top to a wheel at all; the place you want to get to is the centre, if you want to be quiet. Then there was a really lovely passage,[2] like a deep wood in Springtime, the dearest old man came along who had lived there all his life, because he was the guardian of it, and he didn't need to travel because he belonged to the First House really from the very beginning. He wore a vast cloak and he carried a lamp and a long stick; and he said that the cloak meant you were to be silent and not say anything you saw, and the lamp meant you were to tell every-body and make them glad, and the stick was like a guide to tell you which to do. But I didn't quite believe that, because I am getting a grown-up girl now, and I wasn't to be put off like that. I could see that the stick was really the measuring rod with which the whole Palace was built, and the lamp was the only light they had to build it by, and the cloak was the abyss of darkness that covers it all up. That is why dream-people never see beautiful things like I'm telling you about. All their houses are built of common red bricks, and they sit in them all day and play silly games with counters, and oh! dear me, how they do cheat and quarrel. When anyone gets a million counters, he is so glad you can't think, and goes away and tries to change some of the counters for the things he really wants, and he can't, so you nearly die of laughing, though of course it would be dreadfully sad if it were

---

[1] *Via* כ *vel Pugnus.* [The Path of *kaph* or the Hand.]
[2] *Via* י *vel Manus.* [The Path of *yod* or the Fist.]

wake-life. But I was telling you about the ways to the Fourth House, and the third way[1] is all full of lions, and a person might be afraid; only whenever one comes to bite at you, there is a lovely lady who puts her hands in its mouth and shuts it. So we went through quite safely, and I thought of Daniel in the lions' den.

The Fourth House[2] is the most wonderful of all I had ever seen. It is the most heavenly blue mansion; it is built of beryl and amethyst, and lapis lazuli and turquoise and sapphire. The centre of the floor is a pool of purest aquamarine, and in it is water, only you can see every drop as a separate crystal, and the blue tinge filtering through the light. Above there hangs a calm globe of deep sapphirine blue. Round it there were nine mirrors, and there is a noise that means when you understand it, 'Joy! Joy! Joy!' There are violet flames darting through the air, each one a little sob of happy love. One began to see what the dream-world was really for at last;[3] every time anyone kissed anyone for real love, that was a little throb of violet flame in this beautiful House in the Wake-World. And we bathed and swam in the pool, and were so happy you can't think. But they said: 'Little girl, you must pay for the entertainment.' {I forgot to tell you there was music like fountains make as they rise and fall, only of course much more wonderful than that.} So I asked what I must pay, and they said: 'You are now mistress of all these houses from the Fourth to the Ninth.[4] You have managed the Servants' Hall well enough since your marriage; now you must manage the others, because till you do you can never go on to the Third House. So I said: 'It seems to me that they are all in perfectly good order.' But they took me up in the air, and then I saw that the outsides were horribly disfigured with great advertisements, and every single house had written all over it:

FIRST HOUSE

THIS IS HIS MAJESTY'S FAVOURITE RESIDENCE.
NO OTHER GENUINE. BEWARE OF WORTHLESS IMITATIONS.
COME IN HERE AND SPEND LIFE!
COME IN HERE AND SEE THE SERPENT EAT HIS TAIL!

So I was furious, as you may imagine, and had men go and put all the proper numbers on them, and a little sarcastic remark to make them ashamed; so they read:

---

[1] *Via ⊙ vel Serpens.* [The Path of *teth* or the Serpent.]
[2] *Domus IV vel Benignitas.* [The Fourth House or Mercy.]
[3] *Ratio Naturae Naturatae.* [The Scheme of Created Nature.]
[4] *Adeptum Oportet Rationis Facultatem Regnare.* [The Adept should Rule over the Faculty of Reason.]

FIFTH HOUSE,
AND MOSTLY DREAM AT THAT.

SEVENTH HOUSE.
EXTERNAL SPLENDOUR AND INTERNAL CORRUPTION.

and so on. And on each one I put:

NO THOROUGHFARE FROM HERE TO THE FIRST HOUSE.
THE ONLY WAY IS OUT OF DOORS.
BY ORDER.

This was frightfully annoying, because in the old days we could walk about inside everywhere, and not get wet if it rained, but nowadays there isn't any way from the Fourth to the Third House.[1] You could go of course by chariot from the Fifth to the Third, or through the House where the twins live from the Sixth to the Third, but that isn't allowed unless you have been to the Fourth House too, and go from there at the same time.

It was here they told me what T.A.R.O. on the ring meant. First it means gate,[2] and it is the name of my Fairy Prince, when you spell it in full letter by letter.[3]

There are seventy-eight parts to it, which makes a perfect plan of the whole Palace, so you can always find your way, if you remember to say T.A.R.O.[4] Then you remember I.N.R.I. was on the ring too. I.N.R.I. is short for L.V.X.,[5] which means the brilliance of the wide-wide-wake Light, and that too is the name of my Fairy Prince only spelt short.[6]

The Romans said it had sixty-five parts, which is five times thirteen, and seventy-eight is six times thirteen. To get into the Wake World you must know your thirteen times table quite well. So if you take them both together that makes eleven times thirteen, and then you say 'Abrahadabra,' which is a most mysterious word, because it has eleven letters in it. You remember the Houses are numbered both ways, so that the Third House is called the Eighth House too, and the Fifth the Sixth, and so on. But you can't tell what lovely things that means till you've been through them all, and got to the very end. So when you look at the Ring and see

---

[1] *Gladium, quod omnibus viis custodet portas Otz Chiim.* [The sword which on all paths guards the gates of the Tree of Life.]

[2] *Nomen* תרעא. [The Name THROA.]

[3] *Nomen* ADNI אלף דלת נון יוד. [The Name Adonai [Adonai spelt in full].]

[4] *Cartae Tarot vel Aegyptiorum.* [The Cards of the Tarot or of the Egyptians.]

[5] I.N.R.I. = י.נ.ר.י. = ♍.☉.♏.♍ = I.A.O. = L.V.X.

[6] אדני = 65. L.V.X. = LXV.

I.N.R.I. and T.A.R.O. on it that means that it is like a policeman keeping on saying 'Pass along, please!' I would have liked to stay in the Fourth House all my life, but I began to see it was just a little dream House too; and I couldn't rest, because my own House was the very next one. But it's too awful to tell you how to get there. You want the most fearful lot of courage, and there's nobody to help you, nobody at all, and there's no proper passage. But it's frightfully exciting, and you must wait till next time before I tell you how I started on that horrible journey, and if I ever got there or not.

Explicit Capitulum Tertium vel De Collegio Interno.[1]

PART IV

Now I shall tell you about the chariot race in the first passage.[2] The chariot is all carved out of pure, clear amber, so that electric sparks fly about as the furs rub it. The whole cushions and rugs are all beautiful soft ermine fur. There is a canopy of bright blue with stars (like the sky in the dream world), and the chariot is drawn by two sphinxes, one black and one white. The charioteer is a most curious person; he is a great big crab in the most lovely glittering armour, and he can just drive! His name is the mysterious name I told you about with eleven letters in it, but we call him Jehu for short, because he's only nineteen years old.[3] It's important to know though because this journey is the most difficult of all, and without the chariot one couldn't ever ever do it, because it is so far – much farther than the heaven is from the earth in the dream world.

The passage where the twins live[4] is very difficult too. They are two sisters; and one is very pure and good, and the other is a horrid fast woman. But that shows you how silly dream language is – really there is another way to put it: you can say they are two sisters, and one is very silly and ignorant, and the other has learnt to know and enjoy.

Now when one is a Princess it is very important to have good manners, so you have to go into the passage, and take one on each arm, and go through with them singing and dancing; and if you hurt the feelings of either of them the least little bit in the world it would show you were not really a great lady, only a dress lady, and there is a man with a bow and

---

[1] [Here ends Section the Third, or, Concerning the Inner College.]

[2] *Via* ח *vel Vallum.* [The Path of *cheth* or the Fence.]

[3] *Nomen* יהוה = 22. 22 = 19 = 418 = Abrahadabra. [The Name IHVH (etc.)]

[4] *Via* ז *vel Gladium.* [The Path of *zayin* or the Sword.]

arrow in the air, and he would soon finish you, and you would never get to the Third House at all.

But the real serious difficulty is the outdoors. You have to leave the House of Love, as they call the Fourth House.[1] You are quite, quite naked:[2] you must take off your husband-clothes, and your baby-clothes, and all your pleasure clothes, and your skin, and your flesh, and your bones, every one of them must come right off. And then you must take off your feeling clothes; and then your idea clothes; and then what we call your tendency clothes which you have always worn, and which make you what you are. After that you take off your consciousness clothes, which you have always thought were your very own self, and you leap out into the cold abyss, and you can't think how lonely it is. There isn't any light, or any path, or anything to catch hold of to help you, and there is no Fairy Prince any more: you can't even hear his voice calling to you to come on. There's nothing to tell you which way to go, and you feel the most horrible sensation of falling away from everything that ever was. You've got no nothing at all; you don't know how awful it all is. You would turn back if you could only stop falling; but luckily you can't. So you fall and fall faster and faster; and I can't tell you any more.

The Third House is called the House of Sorrow.[3] They gave me new clothes of the queerest kind, because one never thinks of them as one's own clothes, but only as clothes.[4] It is a House of utmost Darkness. There is a pool of black solemn water in the shining obsidian, and one is like a vast veiled figure of wonderful beauty brooding over the sea;[5] and by and by the Pains come upon one.[6] I can't tell you anything about the Pains. Only they are different from any other pains, because they start from inside you, from a deeper, truer kind of you than you ever knew. By and by you see a tremendous blaze of a new sun in the Sixth House,[7] and you are as glad as glad as glad; and there are millions of trumpets blown, and voices crying: 'Hail to the Fairy Prince!' meaning the new one that you have had for your baby; and at that moment you find you are living in the first Three Houses all at once, for you feel the delight of your own dear Prince and his love;

---

[1] *Via quae non est.* [The Path which does not exist.]
[2] *Vaginae Quinque Animae.* [The Five Sheaths of the Soul.]
[3] *Domus III vel Intellectio.* [The Third House or Understanding.]
[4] *Abest Egoitas.* [Selfhood is Absent.]
[5] *Ego est Non-ego.* [Ego is Non-ego.]
[6] *Puerperium.* [Childbirth.]
[7] *Partus.* [Delivery.]

and the old King stirs in his Silence in the First House, and thousands of millions of blessings shoot out like rays of light, and everything is all harmony and beauty below, and crowned above with the crown of twelve stars, which is the only way you can put it into dream talk.

Now you see you don't need to struggle to go on any more, because you know already that all the House is one Palace, and you move about in your own wake world, just as is necessary.[1] All the paths up to the Second House all open – the path of the Hierophant[2] with the flaming star and the incense in the vast cathedral, and the path of the Mighty Ruler,[3] who governs everything with his orb and his crown and his sceptre. There is the path of the Queen of Love[4] which is more beautiful than anything, and along it my own dear lover passes to my bridal chamber. Then there are the three ways to the Holy House of the old King, the way by which he is joined with the new Fairy Prince,[5] where dwells a moonlike virgin with an open book, and always, always reads beautiful words therein, smiling mysteriously through her shining veil, woven of sweet thoughts and pure kisses. And there is the way[6] by which I always go to the King, my Father, and that passage is built of thunder and lightning; but there is a holy Magician called Hermes, who takes me through so quickly that I arrive sometimes even at the very moment that I start. Last of all is the most mysterious passage of them all,[7] and if any of you saw it you would think there was a foolish man in it being bitten by crocodiles and dogs, and carrying a sack with nothing [of] any use at all in it. But really it is the man who meant to wake up, and did wake up. So that is his House, he is the old King himself, and so are you. So he wouldn't care what anyone thought he was.

Really all the passages to the first Three Houses are very useful; all the dream-world and the half-dream world, and the Wake-World are governed from those passages.

I began to see now how very unreal even the Wake-World is, because there is just a little dream in it, and the right world is the Wide-Wide-Wide-Wake-World. My lover calls me little Lola Wide-awake, not Lola Daydream any more. But it is always Lola, because I am the Key of Delights. I never told you about the first two houses, and really

---

[1] *Vita Adepti.* [The Life of the Adept.]
[2] *Via* ו *vel Clavus.* [The Path of *vau* or the Nail.]
[3] *Via* ה *vel Fenestra.* [The Path of *hé* or the Window.]
[4] *Via* ד *vel Porta.* [The Path of *daleth* or the Gate.]
[5] *Via* ג *vel Camelus.* [The Path of *gimel* or the Camel.]
[6] *Via* ב *vel Domus.* [The Path of *beth* or the House.]
[7] *Via* א *vel Bos.* [The Path of *aleph* or the Ox.]

you wouldn't understand. But the Second House[1] is grey, because the light and dark flash by so quick it's all blended into one; and in it lives my lover, and that's all I care about.

The First House[2] is so brilliant that you can't think; and there, too, is my lover and I when we are one. You wouldn't understand that either. And the last thing I shall say is that one begins to see that there isn't really quite a Wide-Wide-Wide-Wake-World till the Serpent outside has finished eating up his tail, and I don't really and truly understand that myself. But it doesn't matter; what you must all do first is to find the Fairy Prince to come and ride away with you, so don't bother about the Serpent yet. That's all.

Explicit Opusculum in Capitulo Quarto vel De Collegio Summo.[3]

---

[1] *Domus II vel Sapientia.* [The Second House or Wisdom.]
[2] *Domus I vel Corona Summa.* [The First House or the Highest Crown.]
[3] [Here ends the Little Work in the Fourth Book, or, Concerning the Highest College.]

T'ien Tao

OR, THE SYNAGOGUE OF SATAN

My object all sublime
I shall achieve in time –
To let the punishment fit the crime –
The punishment fit the crime

— *W. S. Gilbert*

I

The Decay of Manners

Since nobody can have the presumption to doubt the demonstration of St Thomas Aquinas that this world is the best of all possible worlds, it follows that the imperfect condition of things which I am about to describe can only obtain in some other universe; probably the whole affair is but the figment of my diseased imagination. Yet if this be so, how can we reconcile disease with perfection?

Clearly there is something wrong here; the apparent syllogism turns out on examination to be an enthymeme with a suppressed and impossible Major. There is no progression on these lines, and what I foolishly mistook for a nice easy way to glide into my story proves but the blindest of blind alleys.

We must begin therefore by the simple and austere process of beginning.

The condition of Japan was at this time (what time? Here we are in trouble with the historian at once. But let me say that I will have no interference with my story on the part of all these dull sensible people. I am going straight on, and if the reviews are unfavourable, one has always the resource of suicide) dangerously unstable. The warrior aristocracy of the Upper House had been so diluted with successful cheesemongers that adulteration had become a virtue as highly profitable as adultery. In the Lower House brains were still esteemed, but they had been interpreted as the knack of passing examinations.

The recent extension of the franchise to women[1] had rendered the Yoshiwara the most formidable of the political organisations, while the physique of the nation had been seriously impaired by the results of a law[2] which, by assuring them in case of injury or illness of a life-long competence in idleness which they could never have obtained otherwise by the most laborious toil, encouraged all workers to be utterly careless of their health. The training of servants indeed at this time consisted solely of careful practical instruction in the art of falling down stairs; and the richest man in the country was an ex-butler who, by breaking his leg on no less than thirty-eight occasions, had acquired a pension which put that of a field-marshal altogether into the shade.

As yet, however, the country was not irretrievably doomed. A system of intrigue and blackmail, elaborated by the governing classes to the highest degree of efficiency, acted as a powerful counterpoise.[3] In theory all were equal; in practise the permanent officials, the real rulers of the country, were a distinguished and trustworthy body of men. Their interest was to govern well, for any civil or foreign disturbance would undoubtedly have fanned the sparks of discontent into the roaring flame of revolution.

And discontent there was. The unsuccessful cheesemongers were very bitter against the Upper House; and those who had failed in examinations wrote appalling diatribes against the folly of the educational system.

The trouble was that they were right; the government was well enough in fact, but in theory had hardly a leg to stand on. In view of the growing clamour, the official classes were perturbed; for many of their number were intelligent enough to see that a thoroughly irrational system, however well it may work in practise, cannot for ever be maintained against the attacks of those who, though they may be secretly stigmatised as doctrinaires, can bring forward unanswerable arguments. The people had power, but not reason; so were amenable to the fallacies which they mistook for reason and not to the power which they would have imagined to be tyranny. An intelligent *plebs* is docile; an educated *canaille*[4] expects everything to be logical. The shallow sophisms of the socialist were intelligible; they could not be

---

[1] Cf. Mrs Pankhurst and Co.
[2] Workman's Compensation Act 1907.
[3] S[outh] A[frica] Commission, Dublin Castle, etc.
[4] [Scoundrel.]

refuted by the profounder and therefore unintelligible propositions of the Tory.

The mob could understand the superficial resemblance of babies; they could not be got to understand that the circumstances of education and environment made but a small portion of the equipment of a conscious being. The brutal and truthful 'You cannot make a silk purse out of a sow's ear' had been forgotten for the smooth and plausible fallacies of such writers as Ki Ra Di.[1]

So serious had the situation become, indeed, that the governing classes had abandoned all dogmas of Divine Right and the like as untenable. The theory of heredity had broken down, and the ennoblement of the cheesemongers made it not only false, but ridiculous.

We consequently find them engaged in the fatuous task of defending the anomalies which disgusted the nation by a campaign of glaring and venal sophistries. These deceived nobody, and only inspired the contempt, which might have been harmless, with a hate which threatened to engulf the community in an abyss of the most formidable convulsions.

Such was the razor-edge upon which the unsteady feet of the republic strode when, a few years before the date of my visit, the philosopher Kwaw[2] landed at Nagasaki after an exhilarating swim from the mainland.

2

Standing Alone

Kwaw, when he crossed the Yellow Sea, was of the full age of thirty-two years.[3] The twenty previous equinoxes had passed over his head as he wandered, sole human tenant, among the colossal yet ignoble ruins of Wei-hai-wei.[4] His only companions were the lion and the lizard, who frequented the crumbling remains of the officers' quarters; while in the little cemetery the hoofs of the wild ass beat (uselessly, if he wished to wake them) upon the tombs of the sportsmen that once thronged those desolate halls.[5]

---

[1] Keir Hardie.
[2] Kwaw Li Ya, Crowley's Chinese name.
[3] 32 paths of S[epher] Y[etzirah].
[4] Wei-hai-wei, deserted by British in 190[2].
[5] Omar Khayyam, [*Rubáiyát*] v. [18].

During this time Kwaw devoted his entire attention to the pursuit of philosophy; for the vast quantities of excellent stores abandoned by the British left him no anxiety upon the score of hunger.[1]

In the first year he disciplined and conquered his body and its emotions.[2]

In the next six years he disciplined and conquered his mind and its thoughts.[3]

In the next two years he had reduced the Universe to the *yang* and the *yin*[4] and their permutations in the trigrams of Fu-hsi and the hexagrams of King Wên.

In the last year he abolished the *yang* and the *yin*, and became united with the Great Tao.[5]

All this was very satisfactory to Kwaw. But even his iron frame had become somewhat impaired by the unvarying diet of tinned provisions;[6] and it was perhaps only by virtue of this talisman[7]

N	A	H	A	R	I	A	M	A
A			Q					
H							E	
A		Q						
R								
I								
A							Q	
M						Q	A	
A								

that he succeeded in his famous attempt to outdo the feats of Captain Webb. Nor was his reception less than a triumph. So athletic a nation as the Japanese still were could not but honour so superb an achievement, though it cost them dear, inasmuch as the Navy League (by an astute series of political moves) compelled the party in power to treble the Navy, build a continuous line of forts around the sea-coast, and expend many billions of yen upon the scientific breeding of a more voracious species of shark than had hitherto infested their shores.

---

[1] Kitchener.
[2] Nephesch.
[3] Ruach.
[4] Binah. Chokmah.
[5] Kether.
[6] A.C. on Baltoro.
[7] Abramelin talisman 'to swim for twenty-four hours without fatigue.'

So they carried Kwaw shoulder-high to the Yoshiwara, and passed him the glad hand, and called out the Indians, and annexed his personal property for relics, and otherwise followed the customs of the best New York Society,[1] while the German Band accompanied the famous Ka Ru So to the following delightful ballad:[2]

CHORUS

Blow the tom-tom, bang the flute!
Let us all be merry!
I'm a party with acute
Chronic beri-beri.

1

Monday I'm a skinny critter
Quite Felicien-Rops-y.
Blow the cymbal, bang the zither!
Tuesday I have dropsy.

Chorus

2

Wednesday cardiac symptoms come;
Thursday diabetic.
Blow the fiddle, strum the drum!
Friday I'm paretic.

Monday I'm a skinny critter
Quite Felicien-Rops-y.
Blow the cymbal, bang the zither!
Tuesday I have dropsy.

Chorus

3

If on Saturday my foes
Join in legions serried,
Then, on Sunday, I suppose,
I'll be beri-beried!

Monday I'm a skinny critter
Quite Felicien-Rops-y.
Blow the cymbal, bang the zither!
Tuesday I have dropsy.

Chorus

---

[1] Prince Henry's visit to New York.
[2] Cf. Monson, *Tropical Diseases*.

One need not be intimately familiar with the Japanese character to understand that Kwaw and his feat were forgotten in a very few days; but a wealthy Daimio, with a taste for observation, took it into his head to enquire of Kwaw for what purpose he had entered the country in so strange a manner. It will simplify matters if I reproduce *in extenso* the correspondence, which was carried on by telegram.[1]

(1) Who is your honourable self, and why has your excellency paid us cattle the distinguished compliment of a visit?

(2) This disgusting worm is Great Tao. I humbly beg of your sublime radiance to trample his slave.

(3) Regret great toe unintelligible.

(4) Great Tao – t.a.o. – Tao.

(5) What is the Great Tao?

(6) The result of subtracting the universe from itself.

(7) Good, but this decaying dog cannot grant your honourable excellency's sublime desire, but, on the contrary, would earnestly pray your brilliant serenity to spit upon his grovelling *joro*.[2]

(8) Profound thought assures your beetle-headed suppliant that your glorious nobility must meet him before the controversy can be decided.

(9) True. Would your sublimity condescend to defile himself by entering this muck-sweeper's miserable hovel?

(10) Expect leprous dragon with beri beri at your high mightiness' magnificent heavenly palace tomorrow (Thursday) afternoon at three sharp.

Thus met Kwaw, the poet-philosopher of China; and Juju, the godfather of his country.

Sublime moment in eternity! To the names of Joshua and Hezekiah add that of Kwaw![3] For though he was a quarter of an hour late for the appointment, the hands went back on the dial of Juju's chronometer, so that no shadow of distrust or annoyance clouded the rapture of that supreme event.

---

[1] See any book on Far Eastern etiquette.
[2] *Joro* = strumpet.
[3] See Bible.

3

The Manifesting of Simplicity

'What,' said Juju, 'O Great Tao, do you recommend as a remedy for the ills of my unhappy country?'

The sage replied as follows: 'O mighty and magniloquent Daimio, your aristocracy is not an aristocracy because it is not an aristocracy. In vain you seek to alter this circumstance by paying the noxious vermin of the Dai Li Pai Pur to write fatuous falsehoods maintaining that your aristocracy is an aristocracy because it is an aristocracy.

'As Heracleitus overcame the antinomy of Xenophanes and Parmenides, Melissus and the Eleatic Zeno, the *ens* and the Non-*ens* by his Becoming,[1] so let me say to you: the aristocracy will be an aristocracy by becoming an aristocracy.

'Ki Ra Di and his dirty-faced friends wish to level down the good practise to the bad theory; you should oppose them by levelling up the bad theory to the good practice.

'Your enviers boast that you are no better than they; prove to them that they are as good as you. They speak of a nobility of fools and knaves; show to them wise and honest men, and the socialistic ginger is no longer hot in the individualistic mouth.'

Juju grunted assent. He had gone almost to sleep, but Kwaw, absorbed in his subject, never noticed the fact. He went on with the alacrity of a steam-roller, and the direct and purposeful vigour of a hypnotised butterfly.

'Man is perfected by his identity with the Great Tao. Subsidiary to this he must have balanced perfectly the *yang* and the *yin*. Easier still is it to rule the sixfold star of Intellect; while for the base the control of the body and its emotions is the earliest step.

'Equilibrium is the great law, and perfect equilibrium is crowned by identity with the Great Tao.'[2]

He emphasised this sublime assertion by a deliberate blow upon the protruding abdomen of the worthy Juju.

'Pray continue your honourable discourse!' exclaimed the half-awakened Daimio.

Kwaw went on, and I think it only fair to say that he went on for a long time, and that because you have been fool enough to read thus far, you have no excuse for being fool enough to read farther.

---

[1] See Erdmann, *History of Philosophy*, vol. I.
[2] See Fuller, *The Star in the West*, cap. ult.

'Phenacetin is a useful drug in fever, but woe to that patient who shall imbibe it in collapse. Because calomel is a dangerous remedy in appendicitis, we do not condemn its use in simple indigestions.

'"As above so beneath!" said Hermes the thrice greatest. The laws of the physical world are precisely paralleled by those of the moral and intellectual sphere. To the prostitute I prescribe a course of training by which she shall comprehend the holiness of sex. Chastity forms part of that training, and I should hope to see her one day a happy wife and mother. To the prude equally I prescribe a course of training by which she shall comprehend the holiness of sex. Unchastity forms part of that training, and I should hope to see her one day a happy wife and mother.

'To the bigot I commend a course of Thomas Henry Huxley; to the infidel a practical study of ceremonial magic. Then, when the bigot has knowledge and the infidel faith, each may follow without prejudice his natural inclination; for he will no longer plunge into his former excesses.

'So also she who was a prostitute from native passion may indulge with safety in the pleasure of love; she who was by nature cold may enjoy a virginity in no wise marred by her disciplinary course of unchastity. But the one will understand and love the other.

'I have been taxed with assaulting what is commonly known as virtue.[1] True; I hate it, but only in the same degree as I hate what is commonly known as vice.

'So it must be acknowledged that one who is but slightly unbalanced needs a milder correction than whoso is obsessed by prejudice. There are men who make a fetish of cleanliness; they shall work in a fitter's shop, and learn that dirt is the mark of honourable toil. There are those whose lives are rendered wretched by the fear of infection; they see bacteria of the deadliest sort in all things but the actual solutions of carbolic acid and mercuric chloride with which they hysterically combat their invisible foemen; such would I send to live in the bazaar at Delhi, where they shall haply learn that dirt makes little difference after all.

'There are slow men who need a few months' experience of the hustle of the stockyards; there are business men in a hurry, and they shall travel in Central Asia to acquire the art of repose.

'So much for the equilibrium, and for two months in every year each member of your governing classes shall undergo this training under skilled advice.

---

[1] *Cambridge Review.*

'But what of the Great Tao? For one month in every year each of these men shall seek desperately for the Stone of the Philosophers. By solitude and fasting for the social and luxurious, by drunkenness and debauch for the austere, by scourging for those afraid of physical pain, by repose for the restless, and toil for the idle, by bull-fights for the humanitarian, and the care of little children for the callous, by rituals for the rational, and by philosophy for the credulous, shall these men, while yet unbalanced, seek to attain to unity with the Great Tao. But for those whose intellect is purified and coordinated, for those whose bodies are in health, and whose passions are at once eager and controlled, it shall be lawful to choose their own way to the One Goal; *videlicet*, identity with that Great Tao which is above the antithesis of *yang* and *yin*.'

Even Kwaw felt tired, and applied himself to sake-and-soda. Refreshed, he continued:

'The men who are willing by this means to become the saviours of their country shall be called the Synagogue of Satan, so as to keep themselves from the friendship of the fools – who mistake names for things. There shall be masters of the Synagogue, but they shall never seek to dominate. They shall most carefully abstain from inducing any man to seek the Tao by any other way than that of equilibrium. They shall develop individual genius without considering whether in their opinion its fruition will tend to the good or evil of their country or of the world; for who are they to interfere with a soul whose balance has been crowned by the most holy Tao?

'The masters shall be great men among men; but among great men they shall be friends.

'Since equilibrium will have become perfect, a greater than Napoleon shall arise, and the peaceful shall rejoice thereat; a greater than Darwin, and the minister in his pulpit give open thanks to God.

'The instructed infidel shall no longer sneer at the churchgoer, for he will have been compelled to go to church until he saw the good points as well as the bad; and the instructed devotee will no longer detest the blasphemer, because he will have laughed with Ingersoll and Saladin.

'Give the lion the heart of the lamb, and the lamb the force of the lion; and they will lie down in peace together.'

Kwaw ceased, and the heavy and regular breathing of Juju assured him that his words had not been wasted; at last that restless and harried soul had found supreme repose.

Kwaw tapped the gong.

'I have achieved my task,' said he to the obsequious major-domo, 'I pray leave to retire from the Presence.'

'I beg your excellency to follow me,' replied the gorgeous functionary, 'his lordship has commanded me to see that your holiness is supplied with everything that you desire.'

Then the sage laughed aloud.

4

Things to be Believed

Six months passed by, and Juju, stirring in his sleep, remembered the duties of politeness, and asked for Kwaw.

'He is on your lordship's estate at Nikko,' the servants hastened to reply, 'and he has turned the whole place completely upside down. Millions of yen have been expended monthly; he has even mortgaged this very palace in which your lordship has been asleep; a body of madmen has seized the reins of government —'

'The Synagogue of Satan!' gasped the outraged Daimio.

'— And you are everywhere hailed as the Godfather of your country!'

'Do not tell me that the British war has ended disastrously for us!' and he called for the elaborate apparatus of *hara-kiri*.

'On the contrary, my lord, the ridiculous Sa Mon, who would never go to sea because he was afraid of being sick, although his genius for naval strategy had no equal in the Seven Abysses of Water, after a month as stowaway on a fishing boat (by the order of Kwaw) assumed the rank of Admiral of the Fleet, and has inflicted a series of complete and crushing defeats upon the British Admirals, who though they had been on the water all their lives, had incomprehensibly omitted to acquire any truly accurate knowledge of the metaphysical systems of Sho Pi Naour and Ni Tchze.

'Again, Hu Li, the financial genius, who had hitherto been practically useless to his country on account of that ugliness and deformity which led him to shun the society of his fellows, was compelled by Kwaw to exhibit himself as a freak. A fortnight of this cured him of shyness; and within three months he has nearly doubled the revenue and halved the taxes. Your lordship has spent millions of yen; but is today a richer man than when your excellency went to sleep.'

'I will go and see this Kwaw,' said the Daimio. The servants then admitted that the Mikado in person had been waiting at the palace door for over three months, for the very purpose of begging permission to conduct him thither, but that he had been unwilling to disturb the sleep of the Godfather of his country.

Impossible to describe the affecting scene when these two magnanimous beings melted away (as it were) in each other's arms.

Arrived at the estate of Juju at Nikko, what wonder did these worthies express to see the simple means by which Kwaw had worked his miracles! In a glade of brilliant cherry and hibiscus (and any other beautiful trees you can think of) stood a plain building of stone, which after all had not cost millions of yen, but a very few thousands only. Its height was equal to its breadth, and its length was equal to the sum of these, while the sum of these three measurements was precisely equal to ten times the age of Kwaw in units of the span of his hand. The walls were tremendously thick, and there was only one door and two windows, all in the eye of the sunset. One cannot describe the inside of the building, because to do so would spoil all the fun for other people. It must be seen to be understood, in any case; and there it stands to this day, open to anybody who is strong enough to force in the door.

But when they asked for Kwaw, he was not to be found. He had left trained men to carry out the discipline and the initiations, these last being the chief purpose of the building, saying that he was homesick for the lions and lizards of Wei-hai-wei, and that anyway he hadn't enjoyed a decent swim for far too long.

There is unfortunately little room for doubt that the new and voracious species of sharks (which Japanese patriotism had spent such enormous sums in breeding) is responsible for the fact that he has never again been heard of.

The Mikado wept; but, brightening up, exclaimed: 'Kwaw found us a confused and angry mob; he left us a diverse, yet harmonious, republic; while let us never forget that not only have we developed men of genius in every branch of practical life, but many among us have had our equilibrium crowned by that supreme glory of humanity, realisation of our identity with the great and holy Tao.'

Wherewith he set aside no less than three hundred and sixty-five days in every year, and one extra day every fourth year, as days of special rejoicing.

The Stone of the Philosophers

WHICH IS HIDDEN IN ABIEGNUS,
THE ROSICRUCIAN MOUNTAIN OF INITIATION

> And a certain woman cast a piece of a mill stone
> upon Abimelech, and all to brake his skull.
>
> — *Anon.*

> Whomsoever shall fall upon this stone shall be
> broken; but upon whomsoever it shall fall, it will
> grind him to powder.
>
> — *Anon.*

> Qu'est-ce donc, en vérité, que cette pierre? C'est
> le fondement de la philosophie absolue, c'est le
> suprême et inébranlable raison.[1]
>
> — *Lévi*

> One day when I was all alone
> I found a wondrous little stone.
> It lay forgotten on the road
> Far from the ways of man's abode.
> When on this stone mine eyes I cast
> I saw my Treasure found at last.
>
> . . . .
>
> O stone, so red and rare and wise
> O fragment of far Paradise!
>
> — *Machen*

---

[1] [So what, in truth, is this stone? It is the basis of the absolute philosophy, it is the
supreme and unshakeable reason.]

Holbein House suggests rather Hogarth. It is one of those sordid barracks where the Martinet of Realism, Society, pens his privates. Whoso sees an inhabitant thereof thenceforward for ever must believe in the predestination of the damned. Are we so far progressed as to interpret the saying 'The Englishman's house is his castle' in the light of the fact that once a man lay dead in his room for seven weeks, all undisturbed?

Thus far the Socialist. To him enter a Man. Sayeth, the fate of men is naught; we measure mountain ranges by their peaks, not by their plains. And forthwith the Man must seek in Holbein House for some crown of the age, some Venus floating new-born in that Dead Sea, some God new-lit upon that Limbo. As also it is written.

We follow him to its smallest garret, deserted by the rats, since they found nor room nor victual, but tenanted by men. Arthur Gray was a poet who had abandoned alike his father's favour and his jam factory. Caring for nothing but his books, he lived in Holbein House, year in, year out. Looking at the blank wall opposite, he had seen God face to face, and died. When he spoke he was not understood, for his words were the words of a dead God.

Basil Gray, his brother, had come hot-foot from West Africa to see him. Basil had just made the great march from Tetuan to Lagos, and the love of his only brother burnt strong in him, and the hunger for his face.

Basil, looking upon the blind face of the desert, his body withered in the furnace of the sand, had seen God face to face, and died.

Basil spoke, therefore, as a dead God speaks, and only children understood him.

At Gibraltar, on the way home, he had fallen in with Denzil Roberts, that foolish globe-trotter, secularist and philanthropist-at-large. Denzil had just returned from a silly 'sentimental journey' through Spain, and gazing on the sunset from the western tower of the Alhambra he had come nigh to seeing God.

Saddened and sane, he yet could recognise the magnificent insanity of Basil, and had come home with him to learn the way to the gate that men call Madness.

The fourth occupant of the room was Arthur's oldest friend – nay, master.

Desperate research, life risked again and again in strange ways, incomprehensible to the swinish multitude, steady purpose ever equilibrating each thought with its opposite, had brought him at the end to the mastery of things.

So earnestly would he gaze on God, and die, that God had given him of His own life, and sent him among men.

But men knew him not. Only the babes could understand his strange grave smile.

The fifth man was a classical scholar; much learning had made him mad. Yet, well as he knew Greek and Latin, he had not yet read enough to see therein the luminous image of the Creator.

Last was a doctor who, gazing ever on madness, had himself become mad. He, too, saw God, but, being already mad, died not. Men thought they understood him, and for that reviled him. Being mad, he did not care.

All these men smoked heavily, and the silence of the world lay upon them.

It was only when the Man and the Socialist, invisibly seeking some pinnacle in the plains of Holbein House, as Sigiri springs from the flat table of the central province of Ceylon, came upon them, that their influence woke them into life.

'I will cause them to converse,' said the Man (who was the Devil), 'as it were to take you upon an high mountain and show you all the kingdoms of the earth.'

'I have seen them,' said the Socialist.

'But,' said the Man, 'things look very different from that height.'

'Poverty and vice are the same from any point of view,' began the Socialist.

'Listen!' said the other.

Arthur Gray stretched his legs as well as the room would allow. 'Master, your pipe is out. Read us that yarn of your turn-to with Asmodee in Scotland. If ever a place seemed to defy God, "it is this, it is this, it is this." Tune our instruments, master!'

The big man put away his pipe. 'Your brother,' he said, 'will recognise the title.'

And clearing his throat, he began:

هو الله الذى لا اله الا هو

Or the Devil's Conversion

> I see o' nights among the whins
> The Devil walking widdershins.[1]
> As stony silent as the Sphinx
> I sit upon the sandy links,

---

[1] Widdershins ☽.

And listen to the glittering spell
Of Asmodee the Goat of Hell.

He conjures up the nights of grey
And cardinal in Dahomey,
Where before kings and caboceers
The flaming cat of Hell careers;
Where witches whirl their flapping teats
Still shrieking to the drum that beats
Its monstrous call to flesh of man
Hissing and bubbling in the pan –
'Hua is God' it spelt to me;
'There is none other God than He.'

He conjures up the seas[1] that swell
Before the hosts of Gabriel
Between the Lights in Ibis flight
Who whirls the Sword and Scales of Right.[2]
The tall ship strikes: the rending roar
Of death devours the horrid war
Where men dash women to the deck,
Leave children wailing on the wreck....
Behold the lightning's jagged flash
Spell out the signal with its lash –
'Hua is God' (it tore the sea)
'There is none other God than He.'

He conjures up the greasy glare
Of Rupert Street by Leicester Square,
Whose sodden slaves with sweat and paint
Sicken the soul and make it faint.
Build of the slimy scales of vice
One concentrated cockatrice!
'Think!' laughs the devil, 'everywhere
Is Rupert Street by Leicester Square.'
'True!' I replied, 'it spells to me:
There is none other God than He.'

He conjures up the loathly rout
Of Christians crawling in and out,

---

[1] For Gabriel is the archangel of ▽.

[2] ג = ☽
ב = ☿ } See [*Liber*] 777.
ר = ☉

י
א } Sword and Scales. [See] G∴ D∴ lecture on telesmatic images.
ל

A sight as lovely to the wise
As maggots in a maiden's eyes.
From chapel, church, and meeting-room,
From brothel, hospital, and tomb,
From palace, gin-shop, workhouse, prison,
Factory, slum, their slime is risen.
The Devil said 'Bestir thy wits!
Spew out these dysenteric ——' 'It's
A pity' (thus I cut him short)
'Your boyhood was so badly taught.
The riddle's simple – here's the key!
There is none other God than He.'

He conjures up the Universe,
Men bitter bad, and women worse.
The whole disgusting Pan is shown,
Filth from the spirit to the stone.
'Read that!' he yelled. 'Your eyeballs squint,
But That is surely plain as print.'
'It is,' I said, 'for all to see –
There is none other God than He.'

And now the Devil strides and spins
Most furiously widdershins.
He causes two deceitful moons
To dance upon the driving dunes.
'If all's illusion, gentle youth,
All is the enemy of Truth.
Where are you now?' 'My worthy friend!'
(I answered) 'take it to the end.
I do not think you prove it quite
That truth and lies are opposite.
But upon This we can agree:
There is none other God than He.'

He wrote in flame upon the grass
'This person is a perfect ass.'
He vanished in a cloud of musk.
He sent the demons of the dusk
To ramp and rage about the links
To tease me – Me, the stony Sphinx!
I smiled; I bent them to my will;
I set them dancing deosil,[1]

---

[1] Deosil ◌.

And singing with seraphic glee
'There is none other God than He.'

The devil saw that he had failed.
He came back very draggle-tailed;
And, poised above me in the air,
Whined 'Mr. Sphinx, now, is it fair?
My business is to rack the bones
Of saints like you and Mr. Jones!
I'm paid to accuse the brethren, sir!'[1]
'I do not blame you, Lucifer.
I take my pleasure in your frown
Because you "represent the Crown."
And all your prattle means to me:
There is none other God than He.'[2]

The Devil seemed to see the point.
Pleased that I did not say 'Aroint!'
Pleased that in Asmodee I sight
Brave Lucifer, the Lord of Light,
Pleased with my Qabalistic pun
(Really a very clever one!),
Accepted all and none; became
A perfect vessel of the Flame.
He flapped his crook'd and gloomy wing
And swore by God the Holy King

That all his malice should confine
Itself to this one sin of mine
And this alone, when neophytes
(Confused by the excess of lights)
Perceive not what they ought to see:
'There is none other God than He.'

Oh how the good converted Fiend
Worries those Postulants unweaned!
Though now he dances deosil
He pounds them many a purging pill.
He cleans them from their piggish food;
He brings them to beatitude.
'Hua is God!' quoth Asmodee:
'There is none other God than He.'

---

[1] The Devil 'represents the Crown' as Crown Counsel in criminal proceedings.
[2] The Crown is Kether – the Highest – and I like anything that symbolises that Crown.

A silence ensued. At last, from Denzil: 'You mean very much what the Hindus mean by their doctrine of *māyā*?'

'Exactly so; but of course they cannot mean what they say. The thinkable is false. All our attempts to crystallise Truth in words are just as futile as the trickery by which the artist gets his sunlight effects with some dull ochre. The impression's good enough, maybe, at a distance, as an impression. Examine it close; it goes. God sees the clever composition; man sees the untidy brushwork. So logic destroys our religions, despite their truth.'

'But,' said Denzil, 'surely it is better to get nearer truth. I hate all the evil that religion has wrought. As I looked on Granada and its cathedral, this is what I thought. Can you blame me?'

And from a little leathern pocket-book he began to read these lines:

On a Prospect of Granada Cathedral from the Alhambra

> Brown bloated toad that squattest in the sun!
> Loose thankless mouth whose greed is never done
> Old spider waiting with thy web aspin
> Till all Granada thou hast gathered in!
> The blood of bulls and goats would satisfy
> Of old the hellish thirst of the Most High.
> Well – at the worst Jehovah's altars smoke
> And hiss with flesh of his own favoured folk.
> But Thou, O Christ, dost glut thy lust refined
> Upon the ravaged souls of all mankind.

'An excellent photograph,' said the big man. 'My own words just now were as strong, I think. Yet the one answer answers all.'

Arthur Gray broke in. 'You should hear the whole story,' he said. 'Look at the inmost as well as the middle. Under correction, sir' (politely to the doctor), 'I find that human beauty fades if we dissect the body. Yet your microscopist (in the first place) will find the detail of blood beautiful, just as I its banners in my lady's face. And in the second place, does the dissection table reveal all? Is there no spirit, lovely even to me, of which my lady's bones and nerves are but the weak expression?'

'So strongly do I agree with you,' returned the madman, 'that I have written a poem on the unattractive subject of ovariotomy. It must not shock you; I am mad, and claim the immunities of my limitations. I say nothing of your spirit theory; to me, ignorant as we all are, it seems easier to call a nerve God and so explain its functions, than to imagine a God using that nerve as an instrument. We can kill a nerve;

can we then baulk God of His effects? This is no less blasphemous than to say we kill God as we cut the nerve. If a man understand not his brother whom he hath seen, how shall he understand God whom he hath not seen? Materialism is fertile, though it lead to its opposite.[1] Theism is sterile. How would you treat an engine-driver who tried to make his engine go by prayer and philosophy? But I am mad. Here is my poem, then.'

Having the memory of a madman, he recited it by heart.

Ovariotomy

I love you, lass, and you alone.
   What shall I say now death and life
Wrangle before the jasper throne
   And cry to God to end the strife?

Kind words? a little good advice?
   Patience, and fortitude, and prayer?
Tracts are so suitable, and nice?
   "Dear chyild, there'll be no parting there!"?

O bourgeoisie! you read no doubt,
   But still you have a lot to learn.
I am a lover, not a lout.
   My thoughts take quite another turn.

I who have bitten through your skin
   Envy the surgeon who could dip
His deft and conscious fingers in
   Your bowels, and twitch a scornful lip.

I would have paddled in you, played
   Childlike and cloudless of your pain.
I would have kissed the wound, and made
   A pleasant ripple in your brain.

Within the startling lovelier mouth
   New-cut my brother torch should flare
And pour to ease its awful drouth
   The poison of a Baudelaire.

O fool! not thus the Intimate
   Gives up its secret to the soul.
Truth flies beyond, inviolate,
   And slips beside the glancing goal.

---

[1] Atheism = Theism.

Who probes the body gains a fact,
   Yet leaves an equal fact behind;
So gathering for the cataract
   Roll up the rapid waves of mind.

Swift as the light at last they leap
   Into the chasm of despair;
Of all their freshet force they keep
   But froth and smoke and empty air.

O fool! to deem dissection truth
   And paint and patches but a blind!
The enthusiasm of a youth
   Is worth the sage and cynic mind.

O Buddha! couldst thou nowhere rest
   A pivot for the universe?
Must all things be alike confessed
   Mere changes rung upon a curse?

I swear by all the bliss of blue
   My Phryne with her powder on
Is just as false – and just as true –
   As your disgusting skeleton.

Each to his taste: if you prefer
   This loathly brooding on Decay,
I call it Growth, and lovelier
   Than all the glamours of the day.

Which of us likes his house the best?
   You who find filth on every floor?
I, in the privy who attest
   A something worthy to adore?

The end is – you are always sick;
   You always quarrel with your meat.
My raptures follow fast and thick:
   I even tend to overeat.

You would not dally with Doreen
   Because her fairness was to fade,
Because you know the things unclean
   That go to make a mortal maid.

I, if her rotten corpse were mine,
   Would take it as my natural food,

Denying all but the Divine
　　Alike in evil and in good.

Aspasia may skin me close,
　　And Lais load me with disease.
Poor pleasures, bitter bargains, those?
　　I still despise Diogenes.

Why must the prig be still the judge?
　　The Deadly-Livelies audit life?
Ask of the drone about the drudge!
　　Compute the mistress by the wife!

Why? Because Jesus helps them to!
　　Converted William snubs the King.
No doubt the soapy godly crew
　　Can turn their hands to anything!

Alas! the days of Christ are gone:
　　The callous King supports the snub:
Campaspe's lips gush Lethe on
　　The schoolboy-trickster in the Tub.

O restless rats that gnaw the bones
　　Of Aristophanes and Paul!
Come up to me and Mr Jones
　　And see the rapture of it all!

This moral sense is sorry stuff –
　　You take the peas – give me the pod!
Follow your fancy far enough!
　　At last you surely come to God.

'Who is Mr Jones?' asked Denzil. 'We have heard of him from our friend here already.'

'Mr Jones,' said the big man, 'is the Unutterable Tao.'

'Mr Jones,' said the doctor, 'is (on this illusory plane of *māyā*) one of the wonders of the world. He is never seen or heard, felt or smelt. Nor hath he been at any time tasted of any. Yet he is everywhere; in all, and causer of all, and apart from all. By profession he is a curator in the British Museum; but that is going very low indeed upon the plane of *māyā*.'

'I have already told you,' said the big man, 'that Mr Jones is the Unutterable Tao. Why not leave it at that?'

'I will,' said Basil, 'if Arthur will read us something. I know what he was leading up to when our friend – played with his opponent's ball.'

'A brother is a dreadful handicap!' sighed Arthur. 'Still, here you are!'
And he read:

The Wife-Beater

I bruised your body with the whip:
    Its wheals stand out in ridgéd azure.
The savage blood upon your lip
    Images hurt, and hurt's erasure.

The pain transmuted into passion;
    And passion's ruin was not pain;
But my pain wears another fashion;
    My dead men do not rise again.

You hurt me, and the silent skin
    Whispers no word of bleeding bruises;
Your subtle hate, your cunning sin
    Brands and corrodes me where it chooses.

I fear not them that kill the body,
    But rather them that hurt the soul:
My soul with your disdain is bloody:
    Your stripes are none to make me whole.

Could you but see my vitals torn,
    My nerves on rack, my tortured spirit –
Of all the ills to mortals born
    This is the sorest to inherit.

If you could see the branded token
    Of your invisible whip, the scars
Of your intangible knife, the unspoken
    Agonies, silent as the stars!

Then you should count the agéd lines
    That wrinkle up my boy's blithe beauty: –
The Judge of all the Earth divines.
    My wrongs and yours, and does his duty.

For you in heaven shall bloom and burgeon,
    And I in hell shall howl and groan.
Ah! God is an unskilful surgeon;
    We both shall weep to be alone!

For we are one and may not part;
    And though we hurt, we love, believe me!
Nor would I in my inmost heart
    Of one of all your stabs bereave me.

No man can hurt the indifferent stranger,
  No woman wound the casual friend.
There is a glory born of danger;
  What anger gat, desire may end.

Give me the frenzy of your lip!
  My heart accepts your usurpature.
Your body leaps beneath the whip;
  Our pain is in love's very nature.

It is enough. The woe is over,
  The woe begins; the vial brims,
And all the anguish of your lover
  And you is hidden in wrestling limbs.

Drain the black cup of bruiséd blood!
  Its bitter shall beget devotion,
And Bacchus sweep its frenzied flood
  Into the Eleusinian ocean!

'Certainly, the plane is very low indeed. We hardly came here to learn that!' said Basil indignantly. 'We all know that cold-blooded murder (even) may become a duty – witness Hodson and the pistolling of the Delhi Princes!'

His brother laughed: 'I don't know about duty, but to murder you in cold blood would be a pleasure.'

'Dear old chap!' responded Basil, with a warm pressure of the hand. 'Open the whisky, and you'll feel better!'

Which being gone about, the irrepressible doctor broke in with a story of his youth.

'I will never assent to murder,' said he. 'It's inartistic. I dined forty years ago in the Apennines with an Italian Prince, and he entirely converted me. I put down his words in verse. They are being published by the Society for the Abolition of Capital Punishment. If a supreme æsthete like the Prince botches it (this is their idea) how much more must we detest the crude melodramas of the Law! The proceeds are to be devoted to the artistic education of the Common Hangman – as a palliative measure.'

'Wiertz and Beardsley, Sime and O'Sullivan?' suggested the Scholar, separating his fingers widely to illustrate his 'Three fingers only, please!' to their host.

'Now, doctor,' said Basil, 'your Italian Prince!'

The Disappointed Artist

Shall we sit here? A lovely night! —
What you were saying, though, is right:
Man scorns repulsion and attraction;
Woman is wholly reflex action. —
I'll tell you of a splendid joke
I had once. Have another smoke?
No? Well. I wanted to determine
Rightly the nature of the vermin.
(A pity scientific study
Makes the hands poisonous and bloody!)

You see yon finger chaste and cool
That moonlight flings across the pool?
It seems to tempt a man to swim.
I have as sharp and straight and slim
A blade whose glamour makes one reel
And dazzles death upon the steel.
Oh! the stiletto! supple joy –
As if some soft Italian boy
With all his slender strength alive
Laughed in a deep Narcissus dive.

I used to poise its light aloft
Above Carlotta sleepy-soft.
The dusky gold enamoured eyes
And bloom of down would harmonise.
She used to scold it in pretence
Of envy of its excellence.

We laughed – but not at the same joke.
All girls are blind with their own smoke.
A man may come, his lazy day,
Cuddle and coo an hour away,
Yet in his heart is bound to feel:
'No woman's worth an inch of steel.'

Woman has always played the sphinx.
An open secret! How the minx
Covers her single aim, poor saint!
With many a foxy futile feint.
The same thing civilised or wild:
'I want a man: I want a child.'

Man has a real secret – kept
Close as a Rosy Cross adept!

The safer that the sapient sheep
Have never guessed he'd one to keep.
Unveil the Pyramid of Stone!
He simply wants to be alone.

Women suspect it. Tell one that
To change her to a frenzied cat!
'Tis the one cliff where all their waves
Break back to spumed and shattered graves.
A man (at heart they're well aware)
May love, maybe! can never care.

I bore you with an old fool's prosing?
No? I was right, then, in supposing
Modern conditions hamper youths
Who seek to grasp these simple Truths.

But to my yarn. Carlotta lay
So sleepy-soft one summer's day
That really I could not resist it.
I took the dagger out and kissed it.
Like a cat's tongue that daintily laps,
I slipped it in between her paps.
At first, of course, the shrieking swerves
One's thought: it irritates the nerves;
And out of tone the laughter lies
At the poor innocent's surprise.
But soon there triumphs cool and clean
The touching pathos of the scene.
No word of anger, be assured!
A strange soft wonder, long immured
Within her, lit her lovely face
With something of Our Lady's grace.
'What did you kill me for, my Lord?'
As if my answer must accord
With some most lucid miracle
Of love too sweet to think or tell.
'Kiss me again before I die!'
And, as I kissed her, tenderly
Shone like pale flames the sudden spheres
Of dewy light, of eager tears.
She touched my soul's divinest chord:
'I am so happy, dear my Lord.'
And, breaking to the spirit bliss,

'I go, dear. O so keen to kiss
Our baby when I get to God!"

Charming! Why, damn it now! that's odd.
I'm surely in my dotage, Dick!
A sniveller makes me fairly sick.
– Well, here's the Devil in Eden still;
No good we do but turns to ill:
Art's but a crust o'er Nature's chasms.
Death caught her with his comic spasms.
They turned her fairly inside out,
Jerking her legs and arms about
Like a damned dancing marionette.

I could not light my cigarette:
I started laughing. Laugh? I laughed –
I rocked my body fore and aft –
I fairly yelled! To crown the event
Her wonder at my merriment:
That beat the band. I really wonder
However I came to, by thunder! —

Ha! Ha! You hear – it somehow jars.
Bad art, my boy! The Devil mars
Our best. You want a tender grey,
Prepare your palette half the day,
Take brush, and find to your surprise
The snout of scarlet stab your eyes.
Bad art, my boy! I never cared
To try the piece again.

　　　　　　　　　— We've aired
Our dinner. By the way, though, here
You are. That's it! How smooth and clear
The moonlight runs from point to hilt!
Steel in the end beats silver-gilt!
Well, there's an end of my cigar:
The girls will wonder where we are.

'Strange! how this question of motive deceives historians – and others!'
said the scholar. 'Froude was hardly a fool; but his *Henry the Eighth* is
incredible. So is the conventional monster. I for one shall not be surprised
at the Day of Judgement to hear that the Constantine of Protestantism
was actuated by some quite simple motive like suppressed vegetarianism.'

'Very likely it never happened at all,' said Denzil thoughtfully. 'Nothing ever did. Look at the Christ-myth. The Trial and Death and so on – mere stage-directions from a ritual of Mithraism....'

'But who was Mithras?' asked the big man. 'Like any other question, it goes on for ever, till you get to the big question.'

'With your answer to it,' said Basil.

'On the question of motive, though,' said the Doctor, 'I like your theory of Messalina as an ascetic. Since the divine consciousness only appears as the negation of the human, and is only to be attained by wearing out all the sensation-points, till no response occurs to any stimulus —'

'Nonsense!' interjected the big man, 'one can control them, not destroy them. Only morbid "Union with God" is attained by fast, vigil, scourging and the like.'

'Morbid or no,' continued the doctor, 'most saints have used this method. What I was about to say was that since we wish to overcome the body by fatigue, we shall do just as wisely to seek Union with God in excessive debauch. If done with the same purpose, and sleep successfully banished, the same result will occur. If your Messalina failed – well, what does the poet say? Try, try, try again! Read us your verses, Jack!'

And with a disdainful glance at his clothes, as much as to say 'Where's my toga?' the scholar began:

The Return of Messalina

From the marsh of the Maremma the malaria is drawn
By the grey and chilly breezes of the autumn and the dawn.
In the silence as we shiver who is yonder that we see
With the hair fallen loose about her, with the stole about her knee?
All her flesh is loose and fallen, and her eyes are wet and wild,
And she staggers as she wallows like a woman big with child.
How she gasps and stares about her! How she shivers! Are the hosts
Of her lovers there to haunt her, life's lupanar thick with ghosts?
How her teeth are clenched with horror! How her lips are curled and wried
As she staggers to the palace weary and unsatisfied!

Surely I have done the utmost! (all the demon in her wails)
Is it spirit that disdains me? Is it only flesh that fails?
Did Danae win to slumber at the thrust of grievous gold?
Did the Bull bring Pasiphae to the palace of the cold?
Could the sea avail to Sappho drifting dead upon the foam?
What shall save me, Messalina, save the majesty of Rome?

Shall I wreck my life with roses, hurt my flesh with flames and rods?
All is vain! – for I have conquered both the mortals and the Gods.
In the garden of Priapus, in the land of lost desire,
I have made myself a monster and my soul a snake of fire.
Ho! it stings me! Ho! it poisons! all the flesh is branded through,
Branded with the steel of Vulcan, with the lava's deadly dew.
All the kisses of the satyr, all the punishments of Pan,
All Eros hath given of arrows to the eyes of maid and man,
At their lips and lives I suffered – I have borne me as a queen:
Hear the roar of after æons that acclaim me Messaline!
Woe is me! the waves of ages – icier, icier as they roll –
May not cover up my stature, may not quench this devil-soul.

Here's the palace. I must enter sly and secret as a thief.
I would rather blazon, blazon, this my night beyond belief.
I, a worn Suburrian Venus reeking with a fouler foam,
Sucked within me in the darkness the virility of Rome.
Now's the light, the light accurséd: I must get me to the feast,
Stupefy this Panic spirit, throw a posset to the beast.
– Hail, ye Gods! ye Gods infernal! here salutes ye Hercules!
I am come to bring my spirit free of ye and forth of these.
I am Orpheus! I will charm ye, bring Eurydice to light –
Ah, my lords! Alas the omen! who shall turn me all to right?
Who of all our proud Olympus shall avail me or befriend?
Ah, my lords! but I am weary.
                              See ye any one the end?
Nay! we saw her grope and stumble for the secret sidelong door,
Lift the latch with trembling fingers, pass within and be no more.
There we stood and worshipped sadly (for the cry had touched us home),
Worshipped till the grey was azure as the sun rekindled Rome.

'You may be right,' said Basil, 'in thinking as you evidently do that
much of the ceremonial debauchery of the Pagan worships was a true
mystical process. Indeed, at this day there are many cults in India
(also, I believe, in the South Seas) of what is called *vāmacaryā*. Religious frenzy is invoked by the aid of the Erotic and Bacchic frenzies
mingled with that of the Muse of the Tom-Tom. Soma, *bhang*, *arraq*,
and the Uniting of the *liṅga* and the *yoni*! All, mind you, by a most
elaborate ritual.

'But, on the other hand, there is a perfect purity of thought in
much of the avowedly Phallic symbolism of the world. For just as
the sexual pleasure is entirely in a class by itself among (or rather,
above) physical pleasures; so is *samādhi* – union with God – in a class
by itself among (or rather, above) mental pleasures. Who, therefore,

would make an hieroglyph of the latter formless ecstasy can do no better than by drawing a picture of the former, under the image of its physical instruments.

'Hence the Rose and Cross, Sphinx and Pyramid, Sulphur and Salt, Black and White Pillars of the temple – in short, all the "pairs of opposites" in the world.' (Politely, to the big man.) 'As you were saying just now.'

'Their literature?' hinted the scholar.

Basil took up the glove. 'The Eastern is such a paradox that one hates to lay down the law. A Sufi (for example) no doubt writes erotic verse for the divine reason I have stated; but also, I believe him to be very glad of the excuse, because he is just as dirty-minded a beast as you and I.

'I suspect the semi-erotic verse more than that which is untinctured. Why conceal your meaning under a symbol and then go on to explain it all? If language is valid, why use the symbol? If invalid, why use it at all?

'Thus I can believe the Song of Solomon (unadulterated filth, with not a word about Yoga) to be a purely mystic treatise; but if the writer had inserted the inane "explanations" which pollute our Bibles – Christ and the Church, and that stuff – faugh! – I should certainly have thought he was trying to palm off his purulence under the guise of religion.'

'An Oriental Kensit!' cried the scholar.

'Just so, and the pious prurient would buy it and taboo "Dolores,"' added Arthur Gray.

'Well, judge this!' concluded Basil. 'It's a pretty free adaptation from the Arabic – or what passes for Arabic in Morocco!' he contemptuously added.

And diving into his shooting-jacket, he produced and read:

Inspiration

O desert sand! how still and prone the large-eyed boy upon thy breast
Lies in El Maghrab' in the West, and makes his low luxurious moan!
How still the stars that watch above! how still his lover, lapsed for joy
To death upon the dying boy, the boy dissolved and lost in love!
Even as a serpent in the grass their passion stole upon them there.
Within the warm ambrosial air, the intoxicating midnight mass.
The pale boy lifted high the cup; the swarthy priest insanely poured
That utmost unction of the Lord, that only Gods might drink it up.
Wherefore indeed the holy Jinn that have embraced 'addin Islam'
Arose from their colossal calm, and smote the paramours of sin.
Shrieking they fled, and all was still; the perfume of the place was spilt

Even on the domes of ivory gilt that soar on Allah's holy hill.
I saw the threescore iron kings smite thrice upon the Burning Throne
Till Mecca's black enchaunted stone resolved the rapture of their wings.
The proud Emirs bowed low before the awful fervour of the wind
That rose their steely flight behind, and set him lion-like to roar.
And as the Dervish howls and whirls its savour catches him and lifts
His soul (beyond the mind that drifts) into the Treasure House of Pearls.
Even to the icy solitude of death a gust of scent is borne
An herald of the awaking morn to that unhappy brotherhood;
An herald of the healing kiss of maids with eyes of white and black
Whose heavenly lips shall woo them back into a bright eternal bliss.
O laughter of delicious boys that bring the cup and pour the wine
And with their rosy limbs entwine fresh garlands of mirific joys!
The boy is prone upon the sand; he lies as one who nestles in
Some arbour delicate of sin built by the Everlasting Hand.
His lover is the Open Eye, that kindles Light within the Abyss,
And wakes with His immortal kiss enthusiastic energy.
Weep Thou again, O weeping One! Thy tears that gush within the goal
Are songs that shudder in the soul, and springs that gladden at the sun.
They flood me with irradiate tunes of life and ecstasy and light
As though some misty maid of night were girded with a million moons.
They make my pulsing blood to pour in rhythmic throbs of music rare;
My songs shall course the choral air from Mazaghan to Mogador.
And leaping all the lesser bars I shall become the One and All,
And cry the cross-dissolving call, and lose myself among the stars.

'This is indeed paradox,' cried the scholar. 'You embolden me to read my "Mask of Gilt." I defy the subtlest of you to find a moral or a hieroglyph in it; so according to you it must be the only decent poem read as yet.'

'You are itching to read it,' said the big man, 'for you love the bestial. We are fairly trapped. Open the window, someone, and remember that He is God alone, and that there is none other God than He!'

'Right as usual,' said the scholar. 'It's a true story, though, in a way. I've seen the mask myself, and I believe it.'

The Gilt Mask

In Florence in the days of old there dwelt a craftsman pale and grim.
The Devil entered into him, and fanned his soul with plumes of gold.

He offered all he chose to ask. 'O snatch this itching soul away,
So that thou animate my clay and finish me this magic mask!'

The Devil brought him graving tools; the first a ravening disease,
The cold corrupting masterpiece of Christ the god of weeping fools!

The second, bright as burning coal, a white and wanton wolf of sin
Who had an icy flame within the ulcer that she called her soul.

Long years he bent him to the task; he worked his torture and his lust
Out of the horror of the dust into the horror of the mask.

The mewing lecherous devils crept out of the strongholds of the hills,
And filled their blood with noisome thrills before the work of the adept.

The ghuls that gloat on corpses cold would gather, glutted with their meat,
And give it dead man's chops to eat, and dead man's bones to rub the gold;

While stinking goats and cats would come to link in infamies unheard;
While beat the witches oiled and furred their buttocks on the devil's drum.

Yet still the dying craftsman strove to work his lust and pain within
The glittering avatar of sin that seemed to mock him as he wove.

At last his visage pale and grim lights with the laughter of the Pit.
The Devil comes and praises it, and lays a wreath of fire on him.

'Well hast thou wrought, O Florentine! Thy work hath gathered in its spell
The Daughters of the Lords of Hell, the Goddess-goats, the Women-swine!

'These shall adore it age by age; to these shall it give lust and force,
Absolve their spirits of remorse, and make them sage among the sage.

'Its eyes shall gleam when Borgia goes simpering to her stallion,
Her hair bedecked, her jewels on – to please her neighing, champing spouse.

'It shall smile loose on Katherine wallowing in the mire of blood,
Her lover's cold congealing flood paying their silly hour of sin.

'Salammbô mated with an asp shall shudder at its leering face,
And kiss the gilded lips, and lace her serpent in a closer clasp.

'It shall inspire the dews of death that stand on Brinvilliers the smooth
And strangle all her woman's ruth, envenoming the baby breath.

'It shall revolve to hellish bliss the water-torture and the wheel;
In all their pangs she shall not feel aught but my soul-devouring kiss.

'Its satyr lips shall writhe in prayer to nameless Nubian whores that mate
With swinish kisses to abate the black desire of Baudelaire.

'So after many a house of sin it finds at last a pungent home
Sweet as a poisoned honeycomb – a fairer fouler Katherine!

'With cooing laughter she shall press the monster to her golden teats,
Feed its desire on all her sweets with many a masterful caress.

'Its wisdom shall invigorate her soul to heights of hideous joy
To match her with the equal boy that shall be master of her fate.

'She shall attain a man to excel her strong satanic womanhood:
Their love shall break the mask of wood, reveal the authentic face of Hell.'

All this the craftsman heard with pride: he called: his sickness and his whore
Together at his vitals tore, and rent him that he laughed and died.

So, with the last convulsive shred of spending life, his fingers fold
So subtly on that face of gold that all its peace is perfected.

* * *

And there it hangs, a thought obscene, to haunt our love with damnéd ghosts –
Hark to their execrable hosts exulting as I kiss Katrine!

It conquers? We will show it things memorial of its splendours gone,
Things grosser than it looked upon where Neva rolls or Tiber swings.

We shall exceed: its lips unclean shall answer at the Judgement Day:
'The greatest of them all, I say, were this my poet and his queen!'

Ah, God! we look upon the Thames; the Arno's palaces are gone.
Dull glows the misty horizon with London's stinking stratagems.

But lift the lid of earth and see the good flame gush and wrap us round!
For us, the Gods of the Profound, may England equal Italy.

And I who revelled with Faustine in Rome make madder music here
Who poise upon my bleeding spear the severed kisses of Katrine.

I eat her flesh: I drink her blood. God! could I love a woman more
By Arno's flower-enamelled shore, or Father Tiber's tawny flood?

And reeking with her lusty life I hack the gilded mask and burn
With joy and hate. Aha! to turn to my own guts the glutted knife!

O Satan! stand morose and cold above our bodies swimming thus
And plunge thy glory into us, and fan our death with plumes of gold!

Write with our blood before thee spilt on catafalque and catacomb
The dire monition of our doom, the story of the Mask of Gilt!

'The paradox *is* right, by Heaven!' exclaimed the big man. 'That poem
is bad enough, but a long explanation – *qui s'excuse s'accuse*.[1] Better look
for God in the filth itself than in the lame excuse for it!'

'I once knew people as mad as that,' said the Doctor. 'They were all
right; they knew their own business; but they were misunderstood –
and they're in the Asylum at this minute.'

'Misunderstanding!' said the big man; 'why *will* people try to judge
others? I know less of my own brain – and *à fortiori* of my brother's –
than I do of an oyster. Yet I try to instruct my brother, and let the
oyster gang his ain gait.'

'Read that jest of yours about the Qabalistic Rabbi!' said Arthur.

---

[1] [He who apologises accuses himself.]

'I will. He was the dearest old man in the world; absolutely incapable of doing anything to shock the most puritanical. Yet his curious studies in the *Zohar* got him a reputation unfit even to speak of.

'He was too innocent to guess what trouble he was making! Let it be a warning to us!'

So he read:

The Rabbi Misunderstood

'Temurah tells us – praise to Adonai!'
Rabbi Mephibosheth Ben Mordecai
Was wont to say, 'that the Adepti see
Sa-Ma-Dhi equalised with So-Do-My.
That transcends Short o' Face and Longnose both:
This is the deepest den of the Qliphoth.
Match them! the Tree of Life in Eden Bower
Grows balanced perfectly from root to flower.'
— This may be why the Reverend Mrs Grundy
Called him a sodomite the other Sunday.

'Good!' chuckled Basil, when they had done laughing. 'If he'd worked that out as a boy, his alleged character might have forced him to its own path.

'When I was in Marrakesh, they lynched a poor old man because their mosque had been defiled in some real or imaginary way (with which he had in any case nothing to do, having been paralysed for years). The excuse was, on the soles of his feet the creases formed the word Allah, so that he always trod upon the name of God! They killed Burckhardt for that, by the way. A pure invention in both instances. I saw his feet, and they were just like anybody else's, only dirtier.

'Poverty and paralysis were *his* crimes, I warrant ye, my masters! Anyway, it was a great joke, and I made a splendid Arabian Tale of it.'

'Read it!' was the chorus.

Which he did.

The Mosque Bewitched

An aged sorcerer there dwelt within the town of Marrakesh
The fangs of Hell in life who felt twitching his soul out through the flesh.

Though not originally bad his moral ruin was complete:
His pious parents said he had the devil's claw-marks on his feet.

An outward wart upon the nose spells inward malice in the gizzard.
The path is easy, I suppose, for such an one to play the wizard.

In any case he took the risk, and left off things like soap and eating,
Till he could give the world a bisque, ten spells in thirty, and a beating.

Well, at the age of eighty-eight he found himself the One-horse Wire
For the Jehannum Maiden Plate – by Satan, out of Lake o' Fire.

So, calling Iblis of the Jinn (a god among the damnéd Ghebers!)
He offered up a final sin to play a last joke on the neighbours.

The deed was signed in fire and blood; and ere the morn was dewy wet
An hog for the Muezzin upstood, and chanted from the Minaret.

'There is no God! no God' (he sware) 'Mohammed was a charlatan!
'Sleep is more excellent than prayer! and pork is pleasant in the pan!'

The elders knew that only one could crack such execrable quips.
They hurried off to have the fun of slicing him in little strips.

But Iblis met him with a grin worth ninety-nine per cent. per annum.
'You've missed the fun – but pray walk in! – we're off this minute to Jehannum!'

In sooth, the fiend's unseemly mirth mocked all their wagging beards alike,
As from the bowels of the earth quacked an ironical 'Labbaik!'

The moral is – if all your folk are sure you are a black magician,
You may as well enjoy the joke; you cannot damage your position.

The moral is – when mothers crossed perform the usual Christian revel
And tell their children they are 'lost,' they simply drive them to the devil.

   'What's "*Labbaik*"?' asked Denzil.
   'The pious "*Adsum*"[1] of the Pilgrim when he reaches the holy ground
of Mecca. So you may imagine the horror of the Muslim on hearing it
float cheerfully up from Hell!'
   'Talking of Black Magic,' said the big man, 'the belief in it is probably as strong as ever. I myself am inclined to laugh: "Who believes
in Black Magic proves himself to be bewitched!" I had a horrible case
of it once – I shudder yet! I could imagine the time when my poor
friend's disease was epidemic; when the panic madness seized even on
the government —'
   'I hae my doots!' said the scholar. 'Popular beliefs furnish convenient stalking-horses for political subterfuge.'
   'No!' said the Doctor. 'Disease of the mind as well as that of the
body attacks all classes. While man is as subject to suggestion as he is,
the simulation of belief is almost surrender to the belief itself. Constantine probably became a real Christian in the end.'
   'Tell us about your friend, though!' from Basil.

---

[1] [I am present.]

'I hitched it into verse and good,' said the big man. 'But as it's a tale with a moral, please imagine yourselves to be a set of children. I wrote it for them. Here goes!'

The Suspicious Earl

There was a poor bedevilled Earl
Who saw a Witch in every girl,
A Wehr-Wolf every time one smiled,
A budding Vampire in a child,
A Sorcerer in every man,
A deep-laid Necromantic plan
In every casual word; withal
Cloaked in its black horrific pall
A Vehmgericht obscenely grim,
And all designed – to ruin him!

He saw in every passer-by
Black Magic and the Evil Eye,
Interpreting the simplest act
As being a Satanic Pact.
Of course at times there were a few
In some sort victims of the crew;
For when his Countess coughed or sneezed,
'Obsessed!' the poor old fellow wheezed.

He sought the Mighty Powers of Good,
Invoked the Great White Brotherhood.
Like smart and punctual business men,
They sent a man round there and then.
How gladly reverent doth he greet
The sage's venerable feet!

But in a while suspicion grows.
'This fellow, now, by Jove, who knows?
Perhaps he too is in the Plot.
I like Scotch Whisky: he does not.
He prefers Job to Second Kings.
We disagree on many things.'

He sniffed around the Adept (who lay low).
He searched his luggage for his halo.
He asked him frequently to dine
Forgetting purposely the wine
(Though the arcana of *nibbāna*
Ignore the very name of Cana).

He could not pass a herd of swine
Without a hint; in fact, in fine,
He took His Silence as a sign:
'This is an Enemy of mine!'

To cut the story short, we skip
A year or two, and in we chip
(Invigorated by our rest)
Just where the jury at the 'Quest
At the Asylum duly find
'Suicide while of Unsound Mind.'
This time we skip from earth to heaven
God stands among the Spirits Seven.
The Seven Lamps about Him flame.
Myriad archangels cry His name.
Millions of elders, prophets, preachers,
Saints, martyrs, virgins, hermits, teachers,
Angels, evangelists, apostles
All singing like a lot of throstles
All out of tune with one another,
And every one a Plymouth Brother,
With praise set heaven in a whirl.
Up slinks the poor bedevilled Earl,
Saved after all! The grateful tears
Course down his cheeks for several years.
But when he pulls himself together
And gets accustomed to the weather
He wants to poke his fingers in
To see if God is genuine.
Too soon he stripped (this cunning clod!)
Gilt off the gingerbread of God;
And sipping His nepenthe clear,
Sniffed 'Bah! plain gin and gingerbeer'
– That night he happened to be sick:
'Poisoned,' he yelled, 'with Arsenic!'

He left – his boomerang suspicions
Created hosts of Black Magicians.
His leaky lordship they annoyed
All through the immeasurable void
– Until his pallid voice confessed
Himself in league with all the rest.

(The breathless children round me crowd.
I pause. At last one says aloud:

'But tell us how he got to glory!'
– I'm very sorry. That's the story.

But what's the moral? asks a big
Girl with the makings of a prig.
First. Golf is long, and life is fleeting:
Only one Bogey is worth beating.
Moral the Second (Quiet, girls!)
A sane squire is worth ten mad earls.
And, most important, Number Three:
Everyone must trust somebody.)

'You do well to treat it lightly,' said Basil. 'It's the most terrible story I ever heard. A fico for your tragedies of blood and bones!'

'Indeed, 'tis the one hopeless hell,' added the Scholar. 'It is true? You knew the man?'

'I did,' returned the big man. 'As nice a fellow as you could find in three continents. And lost! lost! lost!'

'Oh! when will men be free of all this superstition?' groaned Denzil.

'Never,' said the Scholar.

'Now,' said the big man.

'I can't see it,' cried Denzil, 'but it shall be! it shall be!' And he rolled off this great oath:

I swear by all the stars that stream
Through all the lofty leaves of night:
I swear by the tremendous towers
That crown Granada's vale of flowers:
I swear by their impending gleam,
The Sierra's snowy swords of light!

By all the cruel and cold despair
That Christ hath brought upon the land:
By Mary and the false blind beastly
Lies of the prudish and the priestly:
By God and death and hate I swear
That man shall rise, shall understand.

I swear by this my lucid Eye,
By all the freedom I have won,
That men shall learn to love and doubt,
Put faith and slavery to the rout,
And eagle-pinioned even as I
Soar to the splendour of the sun!

'All right! all right!' said the doctor, rather testily. 'But you want every-body to use your methods. Hurrah for Huxley! Down with Jesus! By heaven, your tyranny will soon be as bad as that of Rome or Geneva. Every man must find his own way to freedom.

'Let me read to you about my mad friends. One of the most interesting cases of symbolic coitus I know of. The man wasn't of the hunting class; he was a head waiter, child of some Russian exiles of the so-called student persuasion, and his only notions of fox-hunting were taken from the Christmas numbers of the illustrated papers of his childhood!

'Strange how things stick!'

The Symbolists

Titan Eve was thewed and sinewed: all the blood of Mother Earth
Sang within her veins and gave her all the might of all her girth.
Vladimir was small and dainty like a fairy knight to brand
Greener circles with his dancing on the green enamoured land.
Strange that in the silent city, Eve should play the horsing mare,
Eve should whinny for a stallion, snuffing up the scented air!
Strange that breeched and scarlet-coated, brave with wealth of boot and spur,
He should hunt the fox Jehovah through the world astride of her.
But his whip! the flame that lashes blood from out her flanks afoam,
Strips the flesh and leaves the spirit bridle-free to gallop home!
But the screams of pain that stab him, drunk with lust of spur and rod,
As the rowels and the whalebone send his spirit back to God!
So in madness is attainment that inspirits and endures.
– Who are you to blame their folly, ask them to assent to yours?
Be ye sure, the Eye Unlidded measures by another rod!
Be ye sure, the human balance looks distorted to a God!
To yourselves be slaves and masters; stand or fall to self alone;
Human ethics will not loosen our Astarte's crimson zone.
You will never fit your forehead with your father's fancy hats:
You know more about salvation than the Reverend Robert Rats.

'Well, you have most certainly met an unpleasant set of people,' ex-claimed the big man. 'Can't we be a bit cheerful for a change? The night wears on; we must part.'

'I think you would like my Gipsy girl,' said Denzil, without scruple or diffidence.

'If she's a sane clean human being, we shall.' So Arthur Gray voiced the general feeling.

Without further debate he set to.

La Gitana

Your hair was full of roses in the dewfall as we danced,
The sorceress enchanting and the paladin entranced,
In the starlight as we wove us in a web of silk and steel
Immemorial as the marble in the halls of Boabdil,
In the pleasaunce of the roses with the fountains and the yews
Where the snowy Sierra soothed us with the breezes and the dews!
In the starlight as we trembled from a laugh to a caress
And the god came warm upon us in our pagan allegresse.
Was the Baile de la Bona[1] too seductive? Did you feel
Through the silence and the softness all the tension of the steel?
For your hair was full of roses, and my flesh was full of thorns,
And the midnight came upon us worth a million crazy morns,
Ah! my Gipsy, my Gitana, my Saliya! were you fain
For the dance to turn to earnest? – O the sunny land of Spain!
My Gitana, my Saliya! more delicious than a dove!
With your hair aflame with roses and your lips alight with love!
Shall I see you, shall I kiss you once again? I wander far
From the sunny land of summer to the icy Polar Star.
I shall find you, I shall have you! I am coming back again
From the filth and fog to seek you in the sunny land of Spain.
I shall find you, my Gitana, my Saliya! as of old
With your hair aflame with roses and your body gay with gold.
I shall find you, I shall have you, in the summer and the south
With our passion in your body and our love upon your mouth –
With our wonder and our worship be the world aflame anew!
My Gitana, my Saliya! I am coming back to you!

The men breathed freer. So powerfully did the song lift them that
through the open window all the fragrance of Spain and its roses seemed
to flow into the room.

Only Arthur Gray never smiled.

The big man looked at him. 'What is it?' he said sharply.

'We are all Gods!' (said Arthur) 'knowing good and evil, and that
which is beyond. But I love Holbein House and London – dear vile
London!

'What can I do?'

And he began mournfully to recite:

---

[1] A gipsy dance; boy and girl play at copulation.

The Poet

> Bury me in a nameless grave!
> I came from God the world to save.
> I brought them wisdom from above:
> Worship, and liberty, and love.
> They slew me for I did disparage
> Therefore Religion, Law, and Marriage.
> So be my grave without a name
> That earth may swallow up my shame!

'Arthur!' said the big man, more tenderly than he had yet spoken, 'there was once a man like you. He wished your wish, not with tears, but with laughter; he had his wish, as you shall have yours. In spite of all, that nameless man is widely known as any in the world; they know not his name: they call him Jesus Christ. Now all the evil wrought by Jesus Christ is as nothing to the wish of that unknown poet. From this pinnacle of Adeptship we weigh the Universe in other scales – but this doctrine is known to you and understood of you, and I need say no more.'

Then said Arthur: 'Verily, all is *māyā*, all! He is God, and there is none other God than He!'

In silence his guests went down the narrow stairs. Arthur Gray turned him to the window and looked out on the blank wall of Holbein House.

'Well?' said the Man.

But the Socialist had hanged himself in his own red necktie. He had seen God, and died.

The Murder in X. Street

Rupert Lascelles had been dining too freely, a fact that accounts for his extraordinary mistake about the time. He had steered a fairly successful course down the Strand, avoiding the few passengers who were still loitering in that never deserted thoroughfare, and now paused at the corner of X. Street. Here, seeking support against a convenient lamppost, he fumbled with his watch chain, and at last succeeded in snapping open the case of his gold hunter repeater.

At this moment a rough, uncouth man, who had been lurking under the shadow of the houses, came across and addressed him:

'Wot's the time, guv?' he asked.

'Pasht two,' replied Lascelles.

'Ho! is it?' said the rough man, making a deft grab at the watch. The next moment Lascelles found himself alone.

Now, it appeared afterwards that Lascelles had made a mistake in his estimate of the time, since he had mistaken the long and short hands of his watch for each other, a mistake which caused him to believe that the time was between 55 and 57 minutes later than it actually was.

(What was the real time?)

For a moment Lascelles was too startled to grasp the fact that he had been robbed; then, pulling himself together with an effort, he started down X. Street in a belated chase after the pickpocket, who had by this time safely made his escape.

At the bottom of the street, however, Lascelles saw two men bending over some object on the ground, and, believing that one of them was his late assailant, he slowed down and approached them cautiously, with the result that he was enabled to overhear the following extraordinary conversation which was being held between them: –

Said the first: 'I will take the red things; you shall have the rest.'

'Agreed,' said the second, 'but I will take from the red things such as are round.'

'Very good,' said the first, 'but, of course, anything that is not round, even in your original portion, comes to me.'

'That is hardly fair,' replied the second. 'If I agree to that you must let me have all the red not round things that are golden.'

'Done,' cried the first, 'on condition that you give up from all you are at present entitled to everything which is neither silver nor gold.'

'An easy condition,' said the second, 'for everything I am entitled to is silver.'

As they laughed and shook hands on the bargain, Lascelles lurched forward: 'Shay, ol' pals,' he observed, *'what was the swag, anyway?'*

'You'd better ask the readers of *What's On*,' replied the thieves, making off hurriedly.

At this dramatic moment a series of heart-rending shrieks broke the silence of the night, and a book was thrown furiously from an upper window.

'Murder! Murder!' came the appalling and inhuman yell.

'Thine hour is come, oh, execrable hag!' replied a firm but courteous voice. 'Thou worthy spouse of Ahab! I am not employed in the royal household – far from it! But permit me to take the liberty!' – and he plunged her after the book. A grey-headed, wizened, monkey-like mass fell upon the pavement with a resounding plunk.

'Life is not extinct,' exclaimed Lascelles, sober in a moment. 'Run, one of you, and get *a word of seven letters which spells the same forward and backwards.*'

But it was useless. The victim of the dastardly outrage was as dead as mutton.

The question then most seriously arose – How dead is mutton? But Lascelles easily showed to the satisfaction of the bystanders and Mr Algernon Ashton, that it was as dead as anything can be.

'Why!' he said, 'I can easily think of six words implying death or burial whose initials form the word "mutton."'

With a muttered curse, Robert Caldwell slunk away!

(What six words can you suggest?)

II

By this time there was quite a crowd. In fact, on looking round him, he saw no less than forty people who stood in a circle; one of them was his old friend Josephus Jones.

'Somebody,' he said, placing himself in the rank, 'had better go for the police. I would suggest that we send every third man – starting from you, sir!' (addressing a stranger distinguished by his height) – 'until all have gone but one, who shall stay and keep watch.'

They agreed.

(Of course his real intention was to secure a private interview with Josephus Jones. *How did he place himself and Jones so as to secure this result?*)

'Jones, old chap,' he said, 'while we are waiting, lend me a hundred pounds!'

'Gladly,' replied his friend, 'if, using nine digits – 1, 2, 3, 4, 5, 6, 7, 8, 9 – each once and only once, you will mention four mathematical expressions whose sum is 100.'

Lascelles complied and pocketed the money, just as the detective-inspector strolled up.

'You're drunk!" said the detective-inspector.

'I am,' admitted Lascelles, 'but you are more so.'

(Explain this allusion after solving 8.)

'You know me, then?' said the surprised official.

'I do,' said Lascelles; 'your name has six letters, but what value have they?'

'The usual values,' returned the inspector. '*A* is *1*, *B* is *2*, and so on, up to *Z* is *26*.'

'Why, then, surely the sum total is equal to twice the square of the first added to twice the difference of the first and the fifth?'

The inspector admitted that it was so, and similarly added that the third and fourth were equal, and equal together alike to the sum of the first and the last, and to the first multiplied by the square root of the difference of the second and the fifth, just as the second less the first was to the fifth as the last to the first.

'For the benefit of this gentleman,' said Lascelles, 'let us add that the sum of the second and the fifth exceeds the square root of the fifth by 1.'

'I don't tumble,' growled the dastard; *'who is he?'*

They ignored him.

'But whom have we here?' asked the inspector. 'I will proceed to seek for traces of the victim's identity.'

In the old woman's card-case he found a visiting card on which were nine letters.

'Who is she?' asked Lascelles.

'I daresay you would like to know, young man. Here is a hint: if I place a suitable letter between the first and the second of the letters on this card, I get a word of three letters meaning to spoil; between the second and third with an 'ound at its 'eels' (for the inspector was a little slack with his aspirates) 'is to make a big noise; between third and the fourth, and I get a word meaning to droop heavily; between the fourth and the fifth, force. I place, as before, a letter between the fifth and sixth, add a barb thereto, and obtain a most valuable drug; a letter between the sixth and seventh, and I get a receptacle for human remains; between the seventh and eighth, to assent; between the eighth and ninth, a period of time.'

'What!' said the thief; 'all words of three letters?'

'Yes.'

'Then I'll run and report the death and earn a "fiver." This murder is going to make a stir, I can tell you.' And off he went.

He was rather hampered at first by his pet flying-pig. This animal – fast enough when he got going – could only move an inch to his first yard, two inches to his second yard, four inches to his third yard, and so on. It was exactly 200 yards to the newspaper office. On arrival he looked round for his pet, but could not see him. 'Where in goodness,' he exclaimed irritably, 'is that pig got to?'

Where, I wonder? *The readers of* What's On *will tell us.*

Another annoyance was the rudeness of the office-boy, who refused to receive him without these silly riddles being answered. What newspaper proprietors remind one of: – blood-money, the heir to a barony, Mary, expensive mud, the adverb fundamentally, reddish cindery-coloured?

Lascelles was, however, easily able to answer these questions. *Can you?*

The Editor was overjoyed to hear of the murder. 'Just what we wanted to brighten us all up!' He smiled with all the innocent happiness of a readily-pleased child. 'I only wish it were two!'

'It is two,' said Lascelles.

'You said "one" just now!'

'Two, I say – and I'll prove it.'

'What? Two is the same as one?'

'Yes. Let $a = 2$, $b = 1$, and $c = 1\frac{1}{2}$

'Then $a + b = 2c$

'$(a + b)(a - b) = 2c(a - b)$

'$\therefore a^2 - b^2 = 2ac - 2bc$

'$\therefore a^2 - 2ac = b^2 - 2bc$

'$\therefore a^2 - 2ac + c^2 = b^2 - 2bc + c^2$

'$\therefore (a - c)^2 = (b - c)^2$

'$\therefore a - c = b - c$

'$\therefore a = b$

'Therefore,' he concluded triumphantly, '2 equals 1. There were *two* murders in X. Street!'

III

The inspector then proceeded to examine the body.

'Lucky!' he murmured, 'the card might have been a "plant," but this tattooing is a sure test.'

For on the old woman's right arm was this curious figure,

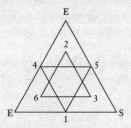

and on the left arm, as if to explain the figure, the following table: –

E21	A measure of work.
56E	A device to conceal age and shabbiness.
s34	The all-beholder.

'It is she! It is she!' groaned the Pride of Scotland Yard. Let me get assistance from these offices!'

(Read her name.)

He went and knocked at a green door, bearing the legend: –

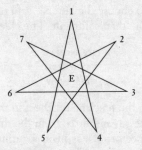

Beneath it the office-boy had scribbled: –

12E34	is often cornered, always beaten.
5E3	is always wet
46E	is 1234 1E usually have 4E7 of
7E54	has a bird in it.
1E54	has a star in it.

Better 4231 your 765E. Rub it with 5761.

'Oh, *those* people!' muttered the inspector. *'I'm sure of intelligent assistance here!'*

(Read the cipher and signify the letters denoted by the figures at the points of the star.)

'Come in!' said a weary voice, and the inspector, entering, saw a young man with his eyes standing out from his head.

'I am a member of a secret society,' he explained, 'and the Chiefs have sent me a secret order to watch over the life of one of its most valued members.'

'Show it to me!' commanded the inspector. And the young man produced the following note:

> THIS HAG
> SHALL RUE
> OUR HANDY CREW.

'I am to take one letter from the first line, two (consecutive in all cases) from the second, three from the third,' he explained, 'and arrange them in a triangle, thus: –

$$\begin{matrix} & 1 & \\ 2 & & 3 \\ 4 & 5 & 6 \end{matrix}$$

and 123456 will spell the name of my protégé.'

'But how are you to choose the letters?' said the inspector.

'Oh,' said the youth, 'that is difficult. The clue is: –

> THE WOMAN
> WAS DREAD
> FULLY UGLY.

I take one letter from the first line for the 4 in the triangle, two from the second line for the 52, and three from the third line for the 631.'

'Bah!' said the inspector; 'it's as plain as print. Your stupidity has cost you dear; you are too late. The woman is already dead.'

'What is her name?' gasped the youth.

'It's up to you,' he said.

'I heard two dreadful bumps,' said the youth.

'A book and a woman,' said the inspector. 'By the Jumping Frog, I forgot all about the book! Let us go and see what it is!'

'What do I care about books?' muttered the young fellow, 'am I not on the Best Weekly in London? As the poet says in his double acrostic: –

> This place is like a wood-yard – packed with poles.
> This exports horses to make sausage-rolls.
> Here a grandee rides gaily on the moors,
> And here a treaty arméd peace assures;
> This is a faery spot, an Alpine dip in,
> And this a lake, that famous waters chip in,
> While this is noted for a simple pippin.'

The inspector was duly impressed.
(Read this acrostic, and give name of paper.)

IV

'What is your name?' the inspector asked the pallid youth.

'Carstairs.'

'What knowledge have you of the crime? What are your hours in office?'

Carstairs smiled. 'My movements are easy to trace. The master is a very methodical man; he leaves nothing to chance. See!' – and he pointed to the wall.

On the wall of the office were the following rules for clerks, of whom there were six: –

1. On Monday and Tuesday no four can go out together.
2. On Thursday, Friday and Saturday no three can stay in together.
3. On Tuesday, Wednesday and Saturday, if Burton and Carstairs are together, then Aliston, Burton, Edwards and Francis must be together.
4. On Monday and Saturday, Burton cannot go out unless either Despard, or Aliston, Carstairs and Edwards stay at home. Aliston and Burton have the right to choose first what they will do, then Carstairs, then the others.

'Now,' said the inspector, 'let us trace your movements, Carstairs. First, *when must you go out; second, when must you stay in; third, when can you do as you choose?'*

These questions having been satisfactorily answered, the detective's manner relaxed a little. 'Got a good berth here, I suppose?'

'Oh, dear, yes! a very soft thing, indeed,' chuckled the clerk. 'Only the other day the boss came in and raised our salaries all round. We had been getting a half-yearly rise of £10, but now we get a rise of £20 yearly. Fancy that!'

'You have indeed a generous employer,' sneered the detective. *'How much (do you think) have you gained by the exchange?'*

It doesn't matter what he thought; the detective soon set him right.

These matters having been satisfactorily settled they proceeded to the street.

The book was quite unrecognisable, being partially burnt, and partially rotted, and partially covered with blood. But the title was readily enough found from the double acrostic which some reader had scribbled in a blank leaf.

1. This word indicible has four good letters.
2. This sort of person forges his own fetters.
3. This is as good as any Guildhall banquet.
4. This person has a mischievous and crank wit.
5. This ends the glacial age of frozen rocks.
6. This heroine pleases some – though some she shocks.
7. This horny brute is dangerous to hit.
8. Whatever those may be, this last is it.

Very little of the book itself was legible. There was, however, one superb passage which the inspector proceeded to spell out with great enthusiasm.

'Thnmstrgrwthsnsfgdwthtndgdwsndnthngmghtxst Sbsstrbtlltsdf-mmslfstncfxstncs.'

'He's forgotten the vowels!' exclaimed Lascelles.

'Here they are, in a note, all in their correct order. Eiieeeeeooiouaoai-aoiieiuioeaaouieoeyeeieeoeiee. He was certainly right: this magnificent passage *is* the very consummation of idealism!'

(Restore the passage.)

'How many pages of this sort of rubbish are there?' dissented the unamiable Lascelles.

'More than 99 and less than 1,000,' replied the detective. 'The square of the first figure added to the square of twice the second figure is equal to the square of the difference of the third and second figures. The product of all the figures less their sum is equal to the product of the first two figures multiplied by their sum. The square of the last figure is equal to the sum of the product of the figures and the last figure; and the square of the first figure to the sum of the other two. How old was the author when he wrote it, should you say? The sum of all the integral subdivisors of his age was equal to that age itself – a man in the prime of youth.'

(What was his age?)

v

When he had perfected this, the inspector reminded him of their search.

'Are you sure about the title of the book?" asked Lascelles.

'Well, we'll go and ask Madame Aganda, the clairvoyant,' and off they went.

The lady promptly fell into a trance.

'Five goddesses appear!' she murmured. 'The first cries "Justice" and shakes her sword and scales. Alas! all is dark: for I know that in her name is concealed the first word of the five words that shall shake the world.

'The second binds me with her fair green girdle and I am blinded with the brilliance of her bloom – alas! for in her name is concealed the second word of the five words that shall shake the world.

'The third gives me to eat of a pomegranate – I am drunk thereon – alas! for wist I but her name, I should perceive therein concealed the third word of the five words that shall shake the world.

'The fourth with spear and shield assails me sore, so that, alas! I cannot learn her name, wherein is concealed the fourth word of the five words that shall shake the world.

'The fifth bears a lamp shining for ever with clear light and lustrous – joy! in her name the last word is concealed of the five words that shall shake the world.'

'I don't think we're much enlightened,' muttered Lascelles.

'I think it is wonderful for six bob, in spite of the confusion of V and W. *But what does she mean?*'

'That's her way of telling us the title of the book, and it certainly confirms my conjecture. By the Jumping Frog, here's the author coming along Cockspur Street now – in the usual trouble with his children, of course.'

'What's that?' asked Lascelles.

'Well, he has sixteen of them. Thomas, Timothy, Titus and Tibullus are quadruplets, Ethel, Emily and Emma are triplets, Henry and Herbert, Sarah and Susan are twins; and Arthur, Robert, Ivan, Nathaniel and Willie were born one at a time. Now he likes them to walk in a solid square, but he won't allow any of them to be next to one of the same age, either before or behind, or sideways, or skew-whiff.'

'Can he manage it?'

'Oh yes! but he wants their initials to spell out the title of his best masterpiece without any jumps, but moving regularly from one square to the next as the King moves at chess. There are two or three ways of doing that, even; look now! he has got them right at last, with the quadruplets one at each corner.'

(How did he do it?)

'He's certainly a family man.'

'I should think he was! He's so fond of his family that he never stirs without his father's brother-in-law, his brother's father-in-law, his father-in-law's brother, his brother-in-law's father, his sister's father-in-law, and his sister-in-law's father.'

'He can't be very fond of solitude!'

'Oh! yes, he is. In fact, he is very often alone.'

'How can that be?'

'Ask *What's On!*'

(Show the necessary relationships.)

But without waiting to hear the answer, which is indeed quite obvious, the inspector and Lascelles strolled back down the Strand to the scene of the murder.

In the west there appeared suddenly a star of dazzling brilliance. It was a star of twelve magnificent rays, each ray a letter.

The First	ray	suggests	Water.
The Second	"	"	Existence.
The Third	"	"	Debt.
The Fourth	"	"	Marriage.
The Fifth	"	"	Punishment.
The Sixth	"	"	Sight.
The Seventh	"	"	Doubt.
The Eighth	"	"	Grass.
The Ninth	"	"	Maternity.
The Tenth	"	"	Personality.
The Eleventh	"	"	A heap of sand.
The Twelfth	"	"	Reason.

All these things, in short, which it has come to take away.

Whereof was gladness in the land.

The Drug

I

I never suspected that my quiet friend was a wizard. Until that fatal Sunday afternoon I had always supposed that the little black door was a cupboard.

This was the way of it.

It had long been my habit to spend Sunday with my quiet friend. I believe in Sunday as the Day of Rest, and the British Sunday is usually the acme of restless misery. But in my friend's house and its quiet park the wheels of the week went round very smoothly. Especially so in the little observatory which he had built over the lake. It had no door upon the landward side, but a quay ran within it and beneath, so that (entering by boat) one found oneself at the foot of a small spiral staircase, narrow and dark, which led one out into a bright room, windowed on every side, at a height of near fifty feet from the water. So large and lofty was the room, so narrow seemed the tower, that I may surely be excused for having thought that the little black door in the East was but a shallow cupboard.

Many a Sunday had passed pleasantly within this room. Now we would read, now play chess or cards; or now he would play upon the violin, when our morning's sport among the trout was over. It was our custom to broil the fish over a clear fire, and to eat it with bread and the fruit of his beautiful orchards, while certain goodly vintages refreshed us with their subtle enthusiasm.

I should like you to picture my friend. He was still young, pale and slim, with a certain remote beauty dwelling lively on his cheeks, deep in his eyes. He was quiet as few men are quiet, yet every gesture glittered with starry joy. His quiet, indeed, was the twinkling quiet of the stars.

Upon this fatal Sunday afternoon, as we played chess together, I noticed thrice that his attention wandered to the clock with grave enquiry.

So preoccupied, indeed, was he that the game languished, and we agreed to a draw. 'Will you forgive me,' he said, 'for a moment if I leave you? As you know, I dabble slightly in chemistry, and an important operation awaits a particular instant of time this afternoon. Stay!' he added, 'why should you not become (as Kelly says) "partaker of the mysteries of the creation"?'

Thus saying, he opened the door – the little black door – with a key (for it had no handle), and I beheld a curious apartment built in the thickness of the wall.

Very long, very narrow, very lofty; its walls of dead black. At one end hung in the midst a tall, slim tube of pale violet – a film of fire in whose light we seemed colourless spectres.

On the walls were shelves full of strange apparatus, mostly of glass or – as it seemed – silver.

My quiet friend executed some intricate movements with deft elegance.

'Enough!' he smiled – ''twas but a moment's work, yet many a month have I had to wait for the right instant.'

'I had no idea,' said I, 'that so strange a laboratory existed.'

'The products,' he answered, 'are in keeping. Look at this flask!'

'Twas a queer twisted shape, greenish with gold flecks – something not inhuman, perhaps; something sinuous and serpentine, beyond a doubt.

'This liquor,' he continued, as we moved back into the other room, 'is made by taking pure mercury and exposing it in a certain manner to the action of the sun and of the air. The fire then passes over it and it is ready to receive the influence of the constellation of Virgo, and of Saturn the planet. Thus it grows exceeding dark – yet at the end? Behold!'

He placed a drop upon the palm of his hand. 'Twas a drop of purest opal, flashing with many tints, self-luminous. A light smoke floated up from it into the still air; a moment, and it was vanished altogether.

''Tis a volatile drug!' explained my friend; 'even now I am at work upon it, that I may fix it. But the task is passing hard.'

'What is its name?' I asked.

'Surely you are not one of those who think that by naming aught they have explained it! Suffice it,' he added, 'that all men drink once of this drug, but no man twice!'

'Then,' I laughed, 'the name of it must be Death.'

'No!' he smiled, 'I think not. Come, drink, my friend! It is the drug that giveth strange vision.'

He poured about a drachm of the fluid into a tall glass. Its appearance was quite altered, being now of a grey pearly sheen.

'Drink!' he cried, 'drink!'

I lifted the glass and drank. Its taste was subtle and sweet as a kiss is; an ecstasy woke in me for an instant. Then I sank down, out of things, into a rich red gloom that grew blacker and blacker. Meseems that much time passed; but who can measure the time of a consciousness that is but the negation of all things?

Yet was I content in annihilation, and – as it seemed – at rest.

2

Quite suddenly consciousness returned. I was muffled in black night, suffocated by darkness, awake to a strange nameless fear.

Hardly was I aware of this when from all sides came upon me an agonising pressure, like the frenzied grip of some giant hand. Even as my bones crushed beneath it, it relaxed. But my peace was gone; I was disturbed, anxious; I waited.

Not in vain. Again and again came the clutch upon me, each time more terrible than the last.

'Twas all so meaningless – I never guessed – how could I guess? –

Also I tried to struggle and to shriek. Useless; my voice seemed gone.

Then – ah God! one spasm of steel ten thousand times fiercer than all the rest – a blaze of light in my eyes – and a wail of helpless agony, as it were, crushed out of me, that turned into a shrill scream of pain – of pain – unspeakable – unthinkable – I cannot bear to write of it.

Then a long lull.

A certain animal content, reaction from the agony.

A certain animal discontent, echo of the agony.

And dawning vistas of strange visions.

Vast was the concave of the orb of light wherein I found myself. The light was of a cool, early green, filtered through dew and reflected by flowers. A soft alluring scent was in the air; and a ripple as of slow, invisible waters.

A tide of happiness and expectation played in my soul like the wind in the branches of an oak, making delicious music. Yet still there came now and again swift, strange pangs memorial of that past agony, and sudden fits of weeping shook me. But, one dream with another, the scene was inexpressibly delightful.

The sole avenue open to the forces of mental discomfort was the budding sense of insecurity. Pleasures and pains alike had no obvious source; their function and purpose were still more obscure. The question even arose: Are all these phenomena *detached*? Or, in a word, Am I insane?

The stress of this particular anxiety was increased by the alluring paths of research that opened to me. As vision after vision passed in fleeting rapture over my gaze, I seemed to grasp a certain shadowy nexus; then would arise another in the light of which the whole grouping broke down.

It seems trifling; you would hardly believe the mental agony that this simple matter caused; and – now – rose ever the mocking query: Insane?

However, as I became more used to the scene, certain facts did become clearer. The faint greenish luminosity was certainly due to the concourse of bright stars that hung in the limpid, colourless ether. One of these stars would now and again come dropping through the sky, and each, as it dropped, would burst into flame, shaped into some strange vision which riveted my attention. It would perhaps pass near me, so that the wind of its presence would tinge my being with some portion of its influence. But none of these actually struck me until one – 'twas a bigger star than most – burst into a glorious face more beautiful than sea-born Aphrodite. As it streamed through the sky, the flame of its pace became an aureole of wondrous hair. Nearer, nearer it came; my soul leapt out to meet it. Innocence, godhead, peace, love, gentleness, all infinite rapture were hers. My soul leapt out to meet her. Now! Now! And waves of purest gold streamed through all my being as our lips met in one long passionate kiss.

But, as this endured, it changed. Her lips grew hot – horrible. Beneath her mouth my lips rotted away; unutterable pangs tore asunder my whole being.

Suddenly, as a shock, all that soul-shaking vision passed; but it left me trembling. Now, too, all the rapture of joyous expectation began to cloud. The vivid stream of blood in me began to slacken. The faint dawn-blush of the universe tinged its green with rose, with gold – and dull grey patches in the gold. And then I became aware of certain faces behind me. Behind me – however swift I turned, I could only catch the vaguest glimpses of them. But the impression was that of forces too unutterably malignant, menacing.

Yet the flood of the exaltation of the vision bore me away, and they were easily forgotten. Until in the full current the star swept upon me from the height, and I recognised the type of face that I had known as Theirs. It passed me, but so close that, fast as it fell, it chilled me horribly. It seemed, too, as if I had moved swiftly to avoid it. And therewith came a sinking fear. Before I had always been stable in a world of change. Now forsooth I too am mobile! the fear shook me horribly.

Then, too, a spasm of remembrance of the evil woman. It was as if her nature had passed into me, become part of me. And I loathed myself. Thus the dreadful war began; that war wherein a man is set against himself – the strife that hath no end.

Yet at this very moment a strange, new phenomenon took away my breath – my whole life lost itself therein.

A star grew, brighter than a million stars, and headlong from the vault it fell, rayed with gossamer gold that streamed and filled the whole bright heaven.

And as it came to me it loved me – I saw a face of sorrow and strange longing, of hunger for the unattainable mingled with ecstasy for what it had attained. This face drew near to me; and the hands pressed mine, and put them to its lips, and my lips trembled.

Then we kissed, and the vision dissolved into an ecstasy too serene and exquisite to have any object.

As did the other visitor, this too suddenly passed – yet still that star hangs in the vault (so I felt), and will hang ever.

This was a mighty consolation. For now the vision swiftly shifted, and took new forms and lives.

As if the subtle poison of the drug had taken on a new phase.

Not only were the objects of the vision altered, but my point of view began to change.

3

It was now no longer expectation of some bliss ineffable that informed the dream. This was remembered, indeed, but with a sneer. Instead of it, dominant, compelling, an apprehension of some horror beyond naming.

So terrible seemed the meaning of the vision – that meaning which I had sought so long – that I strove to shut out all reflection upon it, to busy myself with the phenomena themselves.

Yet as I came to myself out of this resolution, it was to see the vulture eyes of one of the Faces, that regarded me, a triumph unholy in its hate against me.

I swooned.

Coming to myself again, I strove to regain the lost control. I clung to the tangible, the visible. Yet these gradually deteriorated as time passed. The heaven of gold was almost hidden by angry clouds, the sun, dull, rayless red of dying fire, became an hateful thing.

Anon more shakings of the fear unnameable; anon more visions of corruption, more urgent intimations of the close hostility of those fearful Faces.

Only by stern grip of myself could I shut out this terror – and, once it had entered in, I found strange liability to recurrence.

Yet upon the things visible and tangible, I still gained; their mastery became easy to me. Save only that the action of clasping them as I needed them seemed (it may be) to recall the clutch upon me at the beginning of the vision. With this result, that I became instantly conscious of the fatuity of my state, that the thing I grasped eluded me even *because* I had succeeded.

Yet so terrible was any inward reflection that I clung still fiercely and more fiercely to the visible gains. How they had changed! Beauty had almost vanished; harmony was clean gone; the one thing desirable yet was a certain rod of iron that hung above me. This I aspired to; this was alike my fear and my desire.

For I feared that it might come whirling through the air and destroy me – unless I could reach up to it – grasp it – make it mine.

So thereunto I strove.

And behold I found myself sitting in a great concourse of monkeys, whose jabber deafened every other sound. Six hundred and sixty-nine there were, and I among them, I one of them.

Yet even so I strove. I aped their cunning, their avarice, their folly; in the end I became head of them.

And now – yes, now at last! the iron rod was in my hand. I raised it to smite – when, lo!

In my struggles I had almost forgotten the Faces. One of them was gazing at me between the eyes.

Yet this time came no merciful swoon to my relief. Conscious of the horror I stood, gasping; while he, no longer an elusive phantom, but real, positive, awful, shot the dreadful pain, the paralysing fear, through every tiniest path of my whole being.

Then the supreme, the unutterable pang – and blackness – blackness – blackness.

* * *

I came to myself. My quiet friend stood smiling by me.

'Well!' – his soft voice wooed my sense to life – 'how do you like the vision?'

I was still shaking, sweating, shrivelled by the terror of it all.

'You were wise,' I replied, 'did you call the name of it Death!'

'Nay!' he answered, with grave sorrow in his eyes, 'methinks its name is Life.'

Cancer?

A STUDY IN NERVES

I

Bertie Bernard, Sociétaire of the Salon des Beaux Arts, an officer of the Légion d'Honneur, looked at the world from the window of his favourite café. In front, behold the hideous façade of the Gare Montparnasse and the clattering devastation of the Place de Rennes! It was a chill summer morning; a thin rain fell constantly. Great columns of ice came into the restaurant on men's backs; waiters with napkins knotted round their necks sprinkled the sandy boards with water, laid the tables for lunch, bore great basins piled with slabs of sugar here and there; in short, began the day. Behind a small bar, perched, the lady cashier performed mysterious evolutions with a book of green tickets and counterfoils; a small blind puppy nestled into the crook of her elbow.

There was a greyness in everything. Without the good sun's kiss, or the glare of the lights and the kaleidoscope of the demimonde, Paris is a sad city. Nowhere, I think, are the distances so great, the communications so bad. Nowhere do the pavements tempt so, and tire so.

Nor, as it happened, was Bernard full of that internal sunlight which transforms the world. For four months he had worked like a demon. Six pictures – 'twas his right – hung on the walls of the Salon, excellent in a wilderness of mediocrity or worse – nay, nothing is worse! but one cannot live on a reputation alone, and the American Slump had hit the painters hard.

His was a solitary life at the best of times, and, when one works, that life offers indeed the best of times. But when work is over, when one has worked so hard that there is no longer energy to play – a gloomy world for the solitary!

So here he sat in the Café de Versailles and droned through the inanities of *The Overseas* (as distinguished from the Half-Seas-Over) *Daily Wail*. His eye caught a sudden paragraph: 'Death of a Well-Known Baronet.' 'He had been complaining,' said the paper, 'of his throat for some time, but had not thought it worth while to consult a doctor. On Saturday last he saw Sir Herpes Zoster, who took so serious a view of the matter that he advised an immediate operation. Unhappily, pneumonia supervened, and death ensued early on Tuesday morning....'

Cancer! read Bernard between the lines. At the word a whole cohort of ancient thoughts, armed and angry, swept up the glacis that defended his brain, and entering put the defenders to the sword.

Cancer! The one great memory of his boyhood; his mother's illness. They had shown him – idiots! – the dreadful tumour that was – uselessly, of course – to be cut away from the breast that, eight years before, had been his life. The bedside, the cold cleanliness of things, the false-smiling faces that failed to hide their fear, his mother's drawn face and staring eyes, the hideous disease itself – all this stood out in his mind, clear-cut and vivid as it had been yesterday; a violence done to his childhood.

Then, his face already blanched, rose in his memory certain episodes of youth. Once in Switzerland, sleeping out on the mountains, a stone had bruised his side as he lay on it, and two days after, having forgotten the origin of the blue-brown stain, he had thought it cancer, and been laughed at by a medical friend in the hotel. But again the thought, 'Is it hereditary?' leapt at him. Nobody knows – that is the trouble! Nobody knows anything at all about the cause of cancer. There are no precautions, no prognoses, no diathesis except (as some said) the negative one of incompatibility with tubercle.

Bernard would have liked a little tubercle. There's Luxor, Davos, Australia – but for cancer? Cancer is everywhere. Cancer takes no account of conditions.

Now Bernard was a brave man. For sheer devilment he had gone over and taken a hand in the Cuban mix-up. He had shot tigers on foot in Burma, and was indeed so afraid of fear that he had always refused to take the least care of his health. Better die facing death! One must die. It is no good running away. One may as well live a man's life. So he fished for salmon without waders, and found by immunity that the doctors know as little about rheumatism as about anything else.

But on this morning at the Café de Versailles things went ill with his thoughts. All that he had ever read about cancer; all the people he had ever heard of who had died of it; all the false wicked bombast of the newspapers (once a week on an average) that an 'eminent Scientist' – whatever a 'scientist' may be – had discovered a perfect cure – puppy's livers, roseleaves, tomato-juice, strange serums, anything and everything. All Ignorance! Ignorance!! Ignorance!!!

He dropped the paper with listless anger, rapped on the marble, threw down his franc, and rose. And as he caught the sharp air of the street a little cough took his throat. 'God! God!' he cried, 'I have it at last!' And the precise parallelism between his symptoms and those of the dead baronet hit him, as it were a giant with a club.

He, too, had been troubled for a long while. He, too, had not thought it worth while to consult a doctor.

Then the healthy reaction surged up in him. 'You're a hysterical fool, my lad, and I'll teach you a lesson. You shall go and see a doctor, and be laughed at, and pay ten francs for your cowardice!'

Up sprang the assailing thought. 'On Saturday he saw Sir Herpes Zoster, who took so serious a view of the matter that ...'

'I daren't! I daren't!' he cried inwardly, with bitter anguish. Bowed and old, his face wrinkled and blue-grey with fear, he faltered and turned back. He sat down on a little cane chair outside the café, and drove his nails into the palms of his hands.

Abject indecision had him by the throat. He would do this, he would do that. He would go to Italy, to New York, to ride horseback through Spain, to shoot in Morocco, to – half a hundred schemes....

Each impulse was inhibited. He half rose from his chair again and again, and always fell back as the terrible reply beat him down. For New York he must have a new trunk, and the idea of going into a shop and buying one seemed as insanely impossible as if he had needed a live dodo. For Spain, the terrors of the Custom House on the frontier smote him back. Trifle after trifle, fierce and menacing, beat upon him, and the cry of his sane self: 'Don't be a fool, it's only nerves, get away anywhere; eat, sleep, amuse yourself and you'll be all right in a day or so!' grew feebler and feebler as the dominant demon swung his fell spear, 'Go away? you've got cancer – cancer – cancer – you can't go away from cancer!' He knew, too, that did he but once decide to do anything, the cloud would clear. But decide he could not.

If only a good hearty stupid Briton had come along and taken him out of himself for a moment!

But he was a solitary; and the early morning is not the time for meeting such few acquaintances as he possessed. He might have called on one or two friends, but he dared not. Laden with his terrible secret, he could not confront them.

At last he rose, still purposeless, driven by physical disquietude. The muscles, irritated by the anguish of the nerves, became uneasy, sent jerky, meaningless messages to the brain. He walked and walked, feebly and foolishly, everywhere and yet nowhere – the muscles of his back ached.

Cancer of the kidney! he thought, and was swept into a whirlpool of fear. He had once been supposed to have weak kidneys. 'The seat of a previous lesion' was a likely spot. He put his hand to his neck to adjust his collar. There was a small 'blackhead' half formed. Cancer!

He remembered how the previous evening – no! last week, last year – what did it matter? – one of his friends had told of a man in South America who had died of a cancer on the neck, caused, he thought, by the irritation of his collar. Bernard wrenched at his collar to tear it off. 'Useless! too late!' cried one interior voice. 'Nothing is known of the cause,' whispered the consoler, common-sense. Then, louder: 'My dear good ass, every man wears a collar; only one man in twenty-one dies of cancer, and probably not one in twenty-one of those have cancer of the neck.' Louder, for the physical violence of his wrench had sent his blood faster, pulled him together a little.

In the newfound courage he began again to contemplate a change, for it was only too clear that his nerves were wrong. But the enemy had an answer to this: 'One of the most painful features of the disease is the dreadful anxiety —' he remembered from some old medical book.

It had begun to rain more heavily; he was wet. The physical dis-comfort braced him; he looked up.

He was in the Rond-Point des Champs-Elysées, not a hundred yards from his doctor's house.

In a flash his mind was made up. He strode at six miles an hour to the physician, an old friend, one Dr Maigrelette, and was shown into the consulting room. If the doctor had happened to see him as he entered, he would not have had to wait, as was the case.

Waiting, he could not tolerate the alleged amusing journals. He looked for the poison that was eating out his soul. Soon he happened on *The Lancet*, and found to his taste an authoritative article on 'Cancer of the Ileum,' urging speedy operation before – so he gathered – the appear-ance of any symptoms whatever. 'Unfortunately,' wrote the great surgeon, 'cancer is a painless disease for many months.'

God! God! *He, too, had no pain!* He did not know where the ileum might be; he never even knew that he *had* an ileum. And what an awakening! He had got cancer of it. For many, many months he had had no pain!

His perception of the absurd was utterly snowed under.

With clenched teeth, the sweat rolling from his brow, he rushed from the house.

What followed he never really knew. The agony of the mind had gone a step too far, and dropped below the human into a dull animal consciousness of fear. He was being hunted for his life. The instinct of flight became dominant. He found himself feverishly packing his bag; he found himself at the Gare de Lyon, with no very clear conception of how he came there.

Hunger brought him to. Luckily the restaurant of the station – one of the best in Paris – was full of the cheeriest memories. Time and again he had left the station for Italy, Switzerland, Algiers, always with high hope, good courage, pleasurable anticipation.

Almost himself again for the moment, he feasted superbly on a Caneton Rouennais au Sang, with a bottle of the ripe red Burgundy.

A peace stole over him. 'I have had a bad attack of nerves,' he thought; 'I will go away and rest. Worry and overwork, that's what it is. Where's the laziest place on earth? Venice.'

And to Venice he went, almost gaily, in a *wagon-lit*.

Gaily? At the back of his consciousness was a dull sphere of some forgotten pain, some agony in abeyance.

The exhaustion of the day and the last benediction of the good wine together drove him down the slopes of sleep into the Valley of deepest Anæsthesia. Almost trance.

2

The dull viewless journey up the Rhone Valley, with its everlasting hint of great things beyond, did Bernard good. More than a touch of mountain freshness in the air, nay! the very loathsomeness of the Swiss – that nation with the Frenchman's meanness without his insouciance, the German's boorishness without his profundity, the Italian's rascality without his picturesqueness, all these things reminded him of his happy youth spent among the glaciers. At lunch he ordered a bottle of Swiss champagne, drank that infamous concoction with a certain relish piercing through the physical disgust at its nauseousness, as remembering the joy of the opened bottle on some peak yet unclimbed by the particular ridge he had chosen. Life seemed very different nowadays. He would hardly have taken the trouble to climb Mount Everest, had a *djinn* borne him to its foot upon a magic carpet. Fame, love, wealth, friendship – these things seemed valueless. He knew now what he wanted – rest – rest. Death would have pleased him. He thought of the Buddhist *nibbāna*, and almost determined to become an *arhant*, or at least a *bhikkhu*, the stage preliminary.

So the long day went by; at its end, Venice, a vulgar approach, a dead level of shapeless houses with insignificant church spires scarce visible.

Then the sudden wonder of the gondola, gliding between the tall jagged subtly-coloured palaces, the surprise of the moon, glittering down some unexpected alley. And again the sleep of utmost fatigue, only accentuated by the violent stimulus of the wonderful city, its un-deniable romance, its air of dream, of enchantment.

In the morning he rose early. The Grand Canal was stirring, lively, with the pale gold of sunrise kindling it. He hailed a gondola, and until lunch-time drifted about in the narrow waterways, seeking to discover by some subtle mental process the secret which he imagined, as one is compelled to imagine, that each tall house contains.

Yet, lost as he was in the dream, there was ever present in the back-ground of his mental picture, the waking life. What he conceived as the waking life was but that formless mass of horror, the disease whose fear was yet upon him.

In short, he was drugged with Venice, as with an opiate. There would come a reckoning. Life itself was poisoned. The mask matters little; the face behind the mask is all. And for Bernard, behind the mask of Venice, glittered the eyes of Cancer – Cancer – Cancer!

But as health came back, he consciously fought the demon.

One may as well die of cancer as anything else, he would think. He insisted on the word; he said it aloud, watching his voice to detect the tremor of fear. He would contemplate death itself – the worst (after all!) that would come, and discovered death to be but a baseless illusion. He made a dilemma for death. If consciousness ceases, he argued, there is no death, for one is not conscious of it, and nothing exists for the individual of which he is not conscious. If consciousness does not cease – why, that is life!

And so on, making a brave show of the feeble weapon of intellect, as one sees a frightened insect try to appear terrible. Or as a guardsman struts with moustache and busby.

But this same bold analysis was, as he soon saw, but another shape of fear. It was courage, true! but courage implies fear. There was but one cure, absorption in work. So, as he rested the capacity for work returned. He began, first sketches, then fair-sized pictures of the ever-changing, ever-identical beauty of Venice. He spent an altogether joyous morning buying materials for his art.

He met a charming child of Venice in black shawl, with Madonna's face and Venus' body; he painted her into all his foregrounds. In the evening, sitting together in the café of the Rialto Inn, he sketched her. He projected a large and sacred picture, full of the sensual strength of Rubens. His tired soul took her virgin vigour into itself; he became like a boy; he idealised, adored his mistress. He would learn a little Italian, so that they might talk together easily, no longer in broken French-Italian.

So one morning he strolled down to the old Dandolo Palace, glorious with memories of Georges Sand and de Musset, and consulted the jolly bearded blonde beautiful hall-porter about lessons in Italian.

The porter gave him an address. Would he had added, 'Venice is the most relaxing city in the five continents. A week will cure you, a fortnight kill you!'

So our friend was soon knocking at the door of the Signora who taught English.

She was a faded widow, her dyed blonde hair eked out with an improbable fringe, rouged and wrinkled, intensely respectable, Scotch, Presbyterian, sentimental, scented. The room was musty and ill-sized, an imported lodging-house from Ramsgate! The decorations in keeping. Undusted furniture, portraits of 'Victoria the Good,' and of the lady's 'poor dear husband,' a Bible, English and Italian novels and grammars. All frivolities, all dullnesses, all inessentials. The very piano had the air of an accident. Poor tired woman! Long since all hope, all purpose, is lost for you, he thought. And 'Am I otherwise?' Vital scepticism tinged his disgust with the teacher as, mastering his repulsion, he arranged for a series of lessons.

It was on the third day of these lessons that he saw Germanica Visconti. She was a few minutes early at the teacher's, and intruded on his hour. Paler than death, and clad in deepest mourning, she had yet beauty rare and rich, a charm irresistible. The great sense of beauty that had made him the famous painter that he was allured him.

Voilà une belle idée[1] – he scented intrigue. All night he dreamt of her, gliding as a gondola glides into the room. (For so do all Venetian women glide.)

The next day he began – the cunning fellow! – with a little apology. Had he overstayed his hour? She was rather a pretty girl (no Don Juan would openly say that; it was a clever subterfuge).

The old-young widow rose easily to the bait. The Visconti had just lost her father. Poor man, he had suffered terribly for two years. Smokers' cancer, they called it. You can operate twice, but the third time he must die. Oh, yes! it is very, very common in Venice.

The pipe in his pocket burnt him like a red-hot coal. The whole horror came flooding back, tenfold stronger for its week of abeyance. Good God! he had come to the very place of all places where he was sure to get it. Yet he was master of himself enough to sit out the lesson,

---

[1] [There's a lovely idea.]

to bow gracefully to Germanica as she came up the stairs. Thence he went shaking into Florian's, and thought filth of all the world.

The city, ever a positive impression, unlike most other cities, which one can ignore, hurt him. Very common here, he mused – and his throat, really a little irritated by the slackness and the sirocco, became dominant and menacing. He put his hand to his larynx, imagined a tumour. The word 'induration' afflicted him, throbbed in his brain. He could not bear society: he got rid of his model, cruelly and crudely. Nothing but his stubborn courage saved him from throwing his pipe into the canal. By bravado, he smoked double his usual allowance. His throat naturally got worse, and his distress correspondingly increased.

He simply could not stand Venice any longer. Two days of speechless agony, and he went suddenly back to Paris, the dust of the journey aggravating his sore throat, and its misery dragging him ever lower into the abyss of despair. His indecision increased, invaded the smallest details of life. He walked miles, unable to find a restaurant to suit his whim. He would reach the door, perhaps enter, suddenly remember that the coffee was never good there, go out again, walk, walk, walk, repeat the folly again and again, until perhaps he would go to bed foodless. His sore throat (always a depressing influence on all of us) grew worse, and his soul sagged in sympathy.

He could not work, he could not read, he could do nothing. He went out to play Pelota at Neuilly one afternoon, and his very natural failure to play decently increased his misery. I am no more good, he thought, I am getting old. Thirty-six, he mused, and a sob came to his throat – the very age when cancer most begins to claim its prey.

He engaged a model, and discovered that he could no longer draw. He tried everything, and gave up after an ineffectual hour.

His throat grew worse: it pained him really very badly. The follicles of his tongue, too, inflamed sympathetically, and the horrid vision of a bottled cancerous tongue that he had once seen at the College of Surgeons stood luminous in his mind – an arched monstrous tongue of a hideous brown colour, with the ulcer just visible in the dorsum. It looked too big to be a human tongue at all, he had thought. Would his own tongue be bottled in a year from now?

He was afraid to go to a doctor; he could hear the diagnosis; the careful preparation to break it gently to him, the furtive eye that would assure itself of the presence of some necessary stimulant; the ——

His thought shot on prophetic to the operation. Would he sink under it? He hoped so. 'Early and successful operations afford a respite of from three to five years,' he had read. Think of the waiting through those years for its recurrence! Think of Carrière – he, too, dead of throat-cancer – who had said after the operation, 'If it comes back I'll shoot myself' – Carrière – his colleague – his friend.

He had once had an operation, a minor affair. He could picture every-thing – 'extirpate the entire triangle,' the surgeon would say – and do. He did not know what would be left of himself. Would he be able to speak, to swallow, during those horrible three, four, five years while he waited (in Hell!) for 'recurrence'?

Liability to recurrence! he sneered angrily; they know it means al-ways, the dogs!

He thought of the title of a book he had seen advertised, *How Sur-gery Blocks the Way to the Cure of Cancer*, and foamed against the folly of the surgeon, then against the blatant quackery of the alternatives. He hated mankind. He hated God, who had made such a world. Why not have ——? and discovered that it is not as easy as it sounds to devise a genuine undeniable improvement upon the universe.

He fought against the notion that his throat was cancerous, did it good with a simple gargle, made it worse again by smoking; finally the shocking anxiety of the terror that he dared not reveal operated to make him really ill.

Only his magnificent constitution had saved him from being very ill indeed long before this.

As it was, the genuine physical suffering took his mind to some ex-tent off his supposed disease, and in a fit of annoyance he determined to put an end of the matter one way or the other.

He got into a fiacre, and drove off – idiot! – to the great Cancer Specialist, Dr Pommery.

3

It was the very worst thing he – or anyone – could have done. Dr Pommery was famous as having – regardless of expense – grafted the skin of a pig's belly on to the face and hands of a negress, who was thereby enabled to marry a crazy Vicomte, whose parents objected to black blood in the family. True, she had died. He, too, had dis-covered the bacillus of cancer, the only flaw in his experiments being that the said bacillus was to be found in all known organic substances except sterilised agar-agar. He had prepared a curative serum which killed cancer patients before the disease got half a chance, and he had received the record fee of £5,000 sterling for killing the actress wife of an English Duke – or so the Duke's friends laughed over his Grace's cigars and '47 port in his Grace's smoking-room.

He welcomed Bernard with a kindling eye. 'Dear me!' (in his kindest professional manner) 'Don't worry! don't worry, my dear young friend! I think we shall be able to help the little trouble. At the same time, I must ask you to realise that it is somewhat serious, not at all a matter to neglect. In fact, I ought to tell you – you are a man, and should be well able to bear a little shock – that – that ——'

Bernard had heard him with set face, afraid no more but of showing the white feather. Now as he caught the expression of the great specialist's eyes, the long strain broke. He burst into a torrent of glad tears, caught the doctor's hands in his, and wrung them hard. 'I know!' he cried. 'It's cancer – cancer! Thank God! Thank God!'

His fear was over.

He sobered himself, arranged to go the next day to Dr Pommery's private hospital for the treatment, and went off. His throat was better already. Almost joyfully, he went about his affairs. He bade goodbye to his one good friend at lunch, not wishing to sadden her by telling her the truth. He found a sombre pleasure in keeping the secret. 'The next she hears of me, I shall be dead. She will remember this lunch, think kindly of me that I would not spoil her pleasure.' Then – 'Poor girl, how will she live when I am gone?'

Bernard had a small regular income; he had no relations; he would leave it to her. So off he went to the Rive Droite to make his will.

The lawyer was an old friend, was grievously shocked at his story, made the usual attempts to minimise the affair, told a long story of how he too had been condemned to death by a doctor – 'Twenty years ago, Herbert, and – well, I feel sure I shall die, you know, if I have to wait another forty years for it.'

Bernard laughed duly, and was cheered; yet the lawyer's sympathy jarred. He detected a professionalism, an insincerity, in the good cheer. He was quite wrong; his friend did think him scared, and was honestly trying to give him courage. He asked him to come back to tea. Bernard accepted.

Now who should chance to drop in but Maigrelette, that same old medical friend of Bernard's, from whose consulting-room he had fled in terror a month before! They were four at tea, Jobbs the lawyer and his wife, Maigrelette and the dying man.

At the proper moment Bernard began his sad story; it was necessary to say farewell.

Maigrelette heard him with patient impatience. To his look, that asked for sympathy, he said but one explosive word, 'Pommery!' It sounded like an oath!

'Come here!' he said, catching Bernard by the shoulder and dragging him to the window. He thrust a spoon, snatched from the tea-table, into his mouth. 'Say R!'

'R-R-R-R-R,' said Bernard obediently, wondering whether to choke or vomit.

'You d——d ass!' thundered Maigrelette, shaking him to and fro till his teeth chattered, 'I beg your pardon, Mrs Jobbs – what you've got is a very mild go of tonsillitis, and a very bad go of funk. What you're going to do is to go away with my brother Jack tomorrow morning for a month. He'll teach you what speed means. No nonsense, now! Hold up!'

But Bernard went limp, fainted.

While he lay unconscious, 'You can tear up that will, Jobbs,' said Maigrelette, 'but it's a bad nervous case, as bad as I want to see. I don't think we'll trust him to go home alone, do you know?'

Bernard came to. The doctor took him back to his studio, packed his bag for him, carried him off to dinner. 'Jack,' he said to his brother, in a swift aside, 'take the big Panhard, and L for leather all the way to Madrid! Let him out of your sight, day or night, for the next week, and I won't answer for it! After that, if he stops brooding – well, I'll have a look at him myself before you relax.'

Jack nodded comprehension, and after the cigars had been converted into ash and contentment, he went off with Bernard pounding through the night in a great journey to the south.

Bernard, exhausted, dozed uneasily in the tonneau, the wind driving out of his brain the phantoms of its disorder. All day they raced through the haze and heat; fed like giants here and there. The patient grew visibly sleek, his face got blood, his eyes brightness, the furtive inwardness of them sucked out by the good sun, the wild fresh air.

They stopped their headlong course at a small town in the Pyrenees. Bernard was honestly sleepy, as a tired man is, not as an exhausted man. As for Jack, he thought he could never get enough sleep. He had held the wheel nearly all day.

They dined, smoked, took a tentative walk cut short by the eagerness of the air and their own great fatigue. Bernard threw himself upon his bed, and slept instantly. Jack, with a glad sigh, 'Safe till the morning!' imitated him.

So abode the utter stillness of the night upon them; so the dawn arose. A shaft of sunlight came through the mountain cleft, and fell obliquely upon Bernard's face. He half woke, wondered. His memory played him false. Where was he? The strange room baffled him. And suddenly his face whitened.

'I have got cancer,' he thought. And again: 'It is I that have got cancer. It is I.' The emphasis of egoity rose to a perfect shriek of nerve, dominated all other chords in the brain, once and for all.

He rose calm and smiling, like a little child, went on tiptoe to the window, kissed his hand to the sun, whose orb now rose clear of the mountain and looked full upon him. 'What a ripping score off old Jack!' he said in a soft voice, laughing, and after a minute's search in his dressing-case, drew his razor with one firm sweep across his throat.

As he turned and fell, the bright blood sprang, a slim swift jet, and fell bubbling upon the face of the sleeper.

At the Fork of the Roads

Hypatia Gay knocked timidly at the door of Count Swanoff's flat. Hers was a curious mission, to serve the envy of the long lank melancholy unwashed poet whom she loved. Will Bute was not only a poetaster but a dabbler in magic, and black jealousy of a younger man and a far finer poet gnawed at his petty heart. He had gained a subtle hypnotic influence over Hypatia, who helped him in his ceremonies, and he had now commissioned her to seek out his rival and pick up some magical link through which he might be destroyed.

The door opened, and the girl passed from the cold stone dusk of the stairs to a palace of rose and gold. The poet's rooms were austere in their elegance. A plain gold-black paper of Japan covered the walls; in the midst hung an ancient silver lamp within which glowed the deep ruby of an electric lamp. The floor was covered with black and gold of leopards' skins; on the walls hung a great crucifix in ivory and ebony. Before the blazing fire lay the poet (who had concealed his royal Celtic descent beneath the pseudonym of Swanoff) reading in a great volume bound with vellum.

He rose to greet her.

'Many days have I expected you,' he exclaimed, 'many days have I wept over you. I see your destiny – how thin a thread links you to that mighty Brotherhood of the Silver Star whose trembling neophyte I am – how twisted and thick are the tentacles of the Black Octopus whom you now serve. Ah! wrench yourself away while you are yet linked with us: I would not that you sank into the Ineffable Slime. Blind and bestial are the worms of the Slime: come to me, and by the Faith of the Star, I will save you.'

The girl put him by with a light laugh. 'I came,' she said, 'but to chatter about clairvoyance – why do you threaten me with these strange and awful words?'

'Because I see that today may decide all for you. Will you come with me into the White Temple, while I administer the Vows? Or will you enter the Black Temple, and swear away your soul?'

'Oh really,' she said, 'you are too silly – but I'll do what you like next time I come here.'

'Today your choice – tomorrow your fate,' answered the young poet. And the conversation drifted to lighter subjects.

But as she left she managed to scratch his hand with a brooch, and this tiny blood-stain on the pin she bore back in triumph to her master; he would work a strange working therewith!

* * *

Swanoff closed his books and went to bed. The streets were deadly silent; he turned his thoughts to the Infinite Silence of the Divine Presence, and fell into a peaceful sleep. No dreams disturbed him; later than usual he awoke.

How strange! The healthy flush of his cheek had faded: the hands were white and thin and wrinkled: he was so weak that he could hardly stagger to the bath. Breakfast refreshed him somewhat; but more than this the expectation of a visit from his master.

The master came. 'Little brother!' he cried aloud as he entered, 'you have disobeyed me. You have been meddling again with the *Goetia*!'

'I swear to you, master!' He did reverence to the adept.

The new-comer was a dark man with a powerful clean-shaven face almost masked in a mass of jet-black hair.

'Little brother,' he said, 'if that be so, then the *Goetia* has been meddling with you.'

He lifted up his head and sniffed. 'I smell evil,' he said; 'I smell the dark brothers of iniquity. Have you duly performed the Ritual of the Flaming Star?'

'Thrice daily, according to your word.'

'Then evil has entered in a body of flesh. Who has been here?'

The young poet told him. His eyes flashed. 'Aha!' he said, 'now let us Work!'

The neophyte brought writing materials to his master: the quill of a young gander, snow-white; virgin vellum of a young male lamb; ink of the gall of a certain rare fish; and a mysterious Book.

The master drew a number of incomprehensible signs and letters upon the vellum.

'Sleep with this beneath the pillow,' he said; 'you will awake if you are attacked; and whatever it is that attacks you, kill it! Kill it! Kill it! Then instantly go into your temple and assume the shape and dignity of the god Horus; send back the Thing to its sender by the might of the god that is in you! Come! I will discover unto you the words and the signs and the spells for this working of magic art.'

They disappeared into the little white room lined with mirrors which Swanoff used for a temple.

* * *

Hypatia Gay, that same afternoon, took some drawings to a publisher in Bond Street. This man was bloated with disease and drink; his loose lips hung in an eternal leer; his fat eyes shed venom; his cheeks seemed ever on the point of bursting into nameless sores and ulcers.

He bought the young girl's drawings. 'Not so much for their value,' he explained, 'as that I like to help promising young artists – like you, my dear!'

Her steely virginal eyes met his fearlessly and unsuspiciously. The beast cowered, and covered his foulness with a hideous smile of shame.

* * *

The night came, and young Swanoff went to his rest without alarm. Yet with that strange wonder that denotes those who expect the unknown and terrible, but have faith to win through.

This night he dreamt – deliciously.

A thousand years he strayed in gardens of spice, by darling streams, beneath delightful trees, in the blue rapture of the wonderful weather. At the end of a long glade of ilex that reached up to a marble palace stood a woman, fairer than all the women of the earth. Imperceptibly they drew together – she was in his arms. He awoke with a start. A woman indeed lay in his arms and showered a rain of burning kisses on his face. She clothed him about with ecstasy; her touch waked the serpent of essential madness in him.

Then, like a flash of lightning, came his master's word to his memory – Kill it! In the dim twilight he could see the lovely face that kissed him with lips of infinite splendour, hear the cooing words of love.

'Kill it! My God! Adonai! Adonai!' He cried aloud, and took her by the throat. Ah God! Her flesh was not the flesh of woman. It was hard as india-rubber to the touch, and his strong young fingers slipped. Also he loved her – loved, as he had never dreamt that love could be.

But he knew now, he knew! And a great loathing mingled with his lust. Long did they struggle; at last he got the upper, and with all his weight above her drove down his fingers in her neck. She gave one gasping cry – a cry of many devils in hell – and died. He was alone.

He had slain the succubus, and absorbed it. Ah! With what force and fire his veins roared! Ah! How he leapt from the bed, and donned the holy robes. How he invoked the God of Vengeance, Horus the mighty, and turned loose the Avengers upon the black soul that had sought his life!

At the end he was calm and happy as a babe; he returned to bed, slept easy, and woke strong and splendid.

* * *

Night after night for ten nights this scene was acted and re-acted: always identical. On the eleventh day he received a postcard from Hypatia Gay that she was coming to see him that afternoon.

'It means that the material basis of their working is exhausted,' explained his master. 'She wants another drop of blood. But we must put an end to this.'

They went out into the city, and purchased a certain drug of which the master knew. At the very time that she was calling at the flat, they were at the boarding-house where she lodged, and secretly distributing the drug about the house. Its function was a strange one: hardly had they left the house when from a thousand quarters came a lamentable company of cats, and made the winter hideous with their cries.

'That' (chuckled the master) 'will give her mind something to occupy itself with. She will do no black magic for our friend a while!'

Indeed the link was broken; Swanoff had peace. 'If she comes again,' ordered the master, 'I leave it to you to punish her.'

* * *

A month passed by; then, unannounced, once more Hypatia Gay knocked at the flat. Her virginal eyes still smiled; her purpose was yet deadlier than before.

Swanoff fenced with her a while. Then she began to tempt him.

'Stay!' he said, 'first you must keep your promise and enter the temple!'

Strong in the trust of her black master, she agreed. The poet opened the little door, and closed it quickly after her, turning the key.

As she passed into the utter darkness that hid behind curtains of black velvet, she caught one glimpse of the presiding god.

It was a skeleton that sat there, and blood stained all its bones. Below it was the evil altar, a round table supported by an ebony figure of a negro standing upon his hands. Upon the altar smouldered a sickening perfume, and the stench of the slain victims of the god defiled the air. It was a tiny room, and the girl, staggering, came against the skeleton. The bones were not clean; they were hidden by a greasy slime mingling with the blood, as though the hideous worship were about to endow it with a new body of flesh. She wrenched herself back in disgust. Then suddenly she felt it was alive! It was coming towards her! She shrieked once the blasphemy which her vile master had chosen as his mystic name; only a hollow laugh echoed back.

Then she knew all. She knew that to seek the left-hand path may lead one to the power of the blind worms of the Slime – and she resisted. Even then she might have called to the White Brothers; but she did not. A hideous fascination seized her.

And then she felt the horror.

Something – something against which nor clothes nor struggles were any protection – was taking possession of her, eating its way into her …

And its embrace was deadly cold.… Yet the hell-clutch at her heart filled her with a fearful joy. She ran forward; she put her arms round the skeleton; she put her young lips to its bony teeth, and kissed it. Instantly, as at a signal, a drench of the waters of death washed all the human life out of her being, while a rod as of steel smote her even from the base of the spine to the brain. She had passed the gates of the abyss. Shriek after shriek of ineffable agony burst from her tortured mouth; she writhed and howled in that ghastly celebration of the nuptials of the Pit.

Exhaustion took her; she fell with a heavy sob.

* * *

When she came to herself she was at home. Still that lamentable crew of cats miauled about the house. She awoke and shuddered. On the table lay two notes.

The first: 'You fool! They are after me; my life is not safe. You have ruined me – Curse you!' This from the loved master, for whom she had sacrificed her soul.

The second a polite note from the publisher, asking for more drawings. Dazed and desperate, she picked up her portfolio, and went round to his office in Bond Street.

He saw the leprous light of utter degradation in her eyes; a dull flush came to his face; he licked his lips.

The Dream Circean

I

Au 'Lapin Agile'

Perched at the junction of two of the steepest little streets in Montmartre shines the 'Lapin Agile,' a tiny window filled with gleaming bottles, thrilled through by the light behind, a little terrace with tables, chairs, and shrubs, and two dark doors.

Roderic Mason came striding up the steepness of the Rue St Vincent, his pipe gripped hard in his jaw; for the hill is too abrupt for lounging. On the terrace he stretched himself, twirled round half a dozen times like a dervish, pocketed his pipe, and went stooping through the open doorway.

Grand old Frédéric was there, in his vast corduroys and sou'-wester hat, a 'cello in his hand.

His trim grey beard was a shade whiter than when Roderic had last patronised the 'Lapin,' five years before; but the kindly, gay, triumphant eyes were nowise dimmed by time. He knew Roderic at a glance, and gave his left hand carelessly, as if he had been gone but yesterday. Time ambles easily for the owner of such an eyrie, his life content with wine and song and simple happiness.

It is in such as Frédéric that the hope of the world lies. You could not bribe Frédéric with a motor-car to grind in an office and help to starve and enslave his fellows. The bloated, short-of-breath, bedizened magnates of commerce and finance are not life, but a disease. The monster hotel is not hospitality, but imprisonment. Civilisation is a madness; and while there are men like Frédéric there is a hope that it will pass. Woe to the earth when Bumble and Rockefeller and their victims are the sole economic types of man!

Roderic sat down on his favourite bench against the wall, and took stock of things.

How well he remembered the immense Christ at the end of the room, a figure conceived by a giant of old time, one might have thought, and now covered with a dry, green lichenous rot, so that the limbs were swollen and distorted. It gave an incredibly strong impression of loathsome disease, entirely overpowering the intention of picturing inflicted pain.

Roderic, who, far from being a good man, was actually a Freethinker, thought it a grimly apt symbol of the religion of our day.

On His right stood a plaster Muse, with a lyre, the effect being decidedly improved by someone who had affixed a comic mask with a grinning mouth and a long pink nose; on His left a stone plaque of Lakṣmī, the Hindu Venus, a really very fine piece of work, clean and dignified, in a way the one sanity in the room, except an exquisite pencil sketch of a child, done with all the delicacy and strength of Whistler. The rest of the decoration was a delicious mixture of the grotesque and the obscene. Sketches, pastels, cuts, cartoons, oils, all the media of art, had been exhausted in a noble attempt to flagellate impurity – impurity of thought, line, colour, all we symbolise by womanhood.

Hence the grotesque obscenity in nowise suggested Jewry; but gave a wholesome reaction of life and youth against artificiality and money-lust.

As it chanced, there was nobody of importance in the 'Lapin.' Frédéric, with his hearty voice and his virile roll, more of a dance than a walk, easily dominated the company.

Yet there was at least one really remarkable figure in the pleasant gloom of the little cabaret.

A man sat there, timid, pathetic, one would say a man often rebuffed. He was nigh seventy years of age, maybe; he looked older. For him time had not moved at all, apparently; for he wore the dress of a beau of the Second Empire.

Exquisitely, too, he wore it. Sitting back in his dark corner, the figure would have gained had it been suddenly transplanted to the glare of a State ball and the steps of a throne.

Merrily Frédéric trolled out an easy, simple song with perfect art – how different from the labourious inefficiency of the Opera! – and came over to Roderic to see that his coffee was to his liking.

'Changes, Frédéric!' he said, a little sadly. 'Where is Madeleine la Vache?'

'At Lourcine.'

'Mimi l'Engeuleuse?'

'At Clamart.'

'The Scotch Count, who always spoke like a hanging judge?'

'Went to Scotland – he could get no more whisky here on credit.'

'His wife?'

'Poor girl! poor girl!'

'Ah! it was bound to happen. And Bubu Tire-Cravat?'

Frédéric brought the edge of his hand down smartly on the table, with a laugh.

'He had made so many widows, it was only fair he should marry one!' commented the Englishman. 'And Pea-Shooter Charley?'

'Don't know. I think he is in prison in England.'

'Well, well; it saddens. "Where are the snows of yesteryear?" I must have an absinthe; I feel old.'

'You are half my years,' answered Frédéric. 'But come! If yesteryear be past, it is this year now. And all these distinguished persons who are gone, together are not worth one silver shoe-buckle of yonder —'

Frédéric nodded towards the old beau.

'True, I never knew him; yet he looks as if he had sat there since Sedan. Who is he?'

'We do not know his name, monsieur,' said Frédéric softly, a little awed; 'but I think he was a duke, a prince – I cannot say what. He is more than that – he is unique. He is – *le Revenant de la Rue des Quatre Vents!*'

'The Ghost of the Street of the Four Winds?' Roderic was immensely taken by the title; a thousand fantastic bases for the sobriquet jumped into his brain. Was the Rue des Quatre Vents haunted by a ghost in his image? There are no ghosts in practical Paris. But of all the ideas which came to him, not one was half so strange as the simple and natural story which he was later to hear.

'Come,' said Frédéric, 'I will present you to him.'

'Monseigneur,' he said, as Roderic stood before him, ready to make his little bow, 'let me present Monsieur Mason, an Englishman.'

The old fellow took little notice. Said Frédéric in his ear: 'Monsieur lives on the Boulevard St Germain, and loves to paint the streets.'

The old man rose with alacrity, smiled, bowed, was enchanted to meet one of the gallant allies whose courage had – he spoke glibly of the Alma, Inkerman, Sebastopol.

The little comedy had not been lost on Roderic. Wondering, he sat down beside the old nobleman.

What spell had Frédéric wrought of so potent a complexion?

'Sir,' he said, 'the gallantry of the French troops at the Malakoff was beyond all praise; it will live for ever in history.'

To another he might have spoken of the *entente cordiale*; to this man he dared not.

Had not his brain perhaps stopped in the sixties?

Had the catastrophe of '70 broken his heart?

Roderic must walk warily.

But the conversation did not take the expected turn. Elegantly, wittily, almost gaily, the old gentleman chattered of art, of music, of the changed appearance of Paris. Here, at any rate, he was *au courant des affaires*.

Yet as Roderic, puzzled and pleased, finished his absinthe he said more seriously than he had yet spoken: 'I hear that monsieur is a great painter' (Roderic modestly waved aside the adjective), 'has painted many pictures of Paris. Indeed, as I think of it, I seem to remember a large picture of St Sulpice at the Salon of eight years ago – no, seven years ago.'

Roderic stared in surprise. How should anyone – such a man, of all men – remember his daub, a thing he himself had long forgotten? The oldster read his thought. 'There was one corner of that picture which interested me deeply, deeply,' he said. 'I called to see you; you had gone – none knew where. I am indeed glad to have met you at last. Perhaps you would be good enough to show me your pictures – you have other pictures of Paris? I am interested in Paris – in Paris itself – in the stones and bricks of it. Might I – if you have nothing better to do – come to your studio now, and see them?'

'I'm afraid the light—' began Roderic. It was now ten o'clock.

'That is nothing,' returned the other. 'I have my own criteria of excellence. A match-glimmer serves me.'

There was only one explanation of all this. The man must be an architect, perhaps ruined in the mad speculations of the Empire, so well described by Zola in *La Curée*.

'At your service, sir,' he said, and rose. The old fellow was surely eccentric; but equally he was not dangerous. He was rich, or he would not be wearing a diamond worth every penny of two thousand pounds, as Roderic, no bad judge, made out. There might be profit, and there would assuredly be pleasure.

They waved, the one an airy, the other a courteous, good-night to grand old Frédéric, and went out.

The old man was nimble as a kitten; he had all the suppleness of youth; and together they ran rapidly down to the boulevard, where, hailing a fiacre, they jumped in and clattered down towards the Seine.

Roderic sat well back in the carriage, a little lost in thought. But the old man sat upright, and peered eagerly about him. Once he stopped the cab suddenly at a house with a low railing in front of it, well set back from the street, jumped out, examined it minutely, and then, with a sigh and a shake of the head, came back, a little wearier, a little older.

They crossed the Seine, rattled up the Rue Bonaparte, and stopped at the door of Roderic's studio.

2

La Rue des Quatre Vents

'Ah, well,' said the old man, as he concluded his examination of the pictures, 'what I seek is not here. If it will not weary you, I will tell you a story. Perhaps, although you have not painted it, you have seen it. Perhaps – bah! I am seventy years of age, and a fool to the end.

'Listen, my young friend! I was not always seventy years of age, and that of which I have to tell you happened when I was twenty-two.

'In those days I was very rich, and very happy. I had never loved; I cared for nobody. My parents were both dead long since. A year of freedom from the control of my good old guardian, the Duc de Castelnaudary (God rest his soul!), had left me yet taintless as a flower. I had that chivalrous devotion to woman which perhaps never really existed at any time save for rare individuals.

'Such a one is ripe for adventure, and since, as your great poet has said, "Circumstance bows before those who never miss a chance," it was perhaps only a matter of time before I met with one.

'Indeed (I will tell you, for it will help you to understand my story), I once found myself in an extremely absurd position through my fantastic trust in the impeccability of woman.

'It was rather late one night, and I was walking home through a deserted street, when two brutal-looking ruffians came towards me, between them a young and beautiful girl, her face flushed with shame, and screaming with pain; for the savages had each firm hold of one arm, and were forcing her at a rapid pace – to what vile den?

'My fist in the face of one and my foot in the belly of the other! They sprawled in the road, and, disdaining them, I turned my back and offered my arm to the girl. She, in an excess of gratitude, flung her arms round my neck and began to kiss me furiously – the first kiss I had ever had from a woman, mind you! Maybe I would not have been altogether displeased, but that she stank so foully of brandy that – my gorge rises at the memory. The ruffians, more surprised than hurt, began laughing, but kept well away. I tried to induce the girl to come home; in the end she lost her temper, and fell to belabouring me with her fists. I was not strong enough or experienced enough to contend with a madwoman, and I could not allow myself to strike her. She beat me sore....

'I can remember the scene now as if it were yesterday: the bewildered boy, the screaming, swearing, kicking, scratching woman, the two "savages" (honest bourgeois enough!) reeling against the houses, crying with laughter, too weak with laughter to stand straight.

'By-and-by they took pity, came forward, and released me from my unpleasant situation.

'But the shame of me, as I slunk away down the streets! I would not go home that night at all, ashamed to face my own servants.

'I told myself, in the end, that this was a rare accident; but for all that there must have remained a slight stain upon the mirror of perfect chivalry. In the old days when they taught logic in the schools one learnt how delicate a flower was a "universal affirmative."

'It was some uneventful months after this "tragedy of the ideal" that I was again walking home very late. I had been to the Jardin des Plantes in the afternoon, and, dining in that quarter, had stayed lingering on the bridge watching the Seine. The moon dropped down behind the houses – with a start I realised that I must go home. There was some danger, you understand, of footpads. Nothing, however, occurred until – I always preferred to walk through the narrow streets; there is romance in narrow streets! – I found myself in the Rue des Quatre Vents; not a stone's-throw from this house, as you know.

'I had been thinking of my previous misadventure, and, with the folly of youth, had been indulging in a reverie of the kind that begins "If only." If only she had been a princess ravished by a wicked ogre. If only … If only …

'On the south side of the Rue des Quatre Vents is a house standing well back from the street, with a railing in front of it – a common type, is it not? But what riveted my attention upon it was that while the front of the house was otherwise entirely dark, from a window on the first floor streamed a blaze of light. The window was wide open to the street; voices came from it.

'The first an old, harsh, menacing voice, with all the sting of hate in it; nay, the sting of something devilish, worse than hate. A corrupt enjoyment of its malice informed it. And the words it spoke were too infamous for me to repeat. They are scarred upon my brain. Addressed to the vilest harridan that scours the gutter for her carrion prey, they would have yet been inhuman, impossible; to the voice that answered …!

'It was a voice like the tinkling of a fairy bell. Whoever spoke was little more than a child; and her answer had the purity and strength of an angel. That even the foul monster who addressed her could support it, unblasted, was matter for astonishment.

'Now the older voice broke into filthy insult, a very frenzy of malice.

'I heard – O God! – the swish of a whip, and the sound of it falling upon flesh.

'There was silence a while, save for the hideous laughter of the invisible horror inside.

'At last a piteous little moan.

'My blood sang shrill within me. Out of myself, I sprang at the railings, and was over them in a second. Rapidly, and quite unobserved (for the scene was strenuous within), I climbed up the grating of the lower windows, and, reaching up to the edge of the balcony, swung myself up to and over it.

'As I stopped to fetch breath, as yet unperceived, I took in the scene, and was staggered at its strangeness.

'The room, though exquisitely decorated, was entirely bare of furniture, unless one could dignify by that name a heap of dirty straw in one corner, by which stood a flattish wooden bowl, half full of what looked like a crust of bread mashed into pulp with water.

'Half turned away from me stood the owner of the harsh voice and soul abominable. It was a woman of perhaps sixty years of age, the head of an angel – so regular were the features, so silver-white the hair – set upon the deformed body of a dwarf. Hairy hands and twisted arms, a hunched back and bandy legs; in the gnarled right hand a terrible whip, the carved jade handle blossoming into a rose of fine cords, shining with silver – sharp, three-cornered chips of silver! The whole dripped black with blood. Upon the angel face stood a sneer, a snarl, a malediction. The effect upon one's sense of something beyond the ordinary was, too, heightened by her costume; for though the summer was at its height she was clad from head to foot in ermine, starred, more heavily than is usual, with the little black tails in the form of *fleurs-de-lis*.

'In extreme contrast to this monster was a young girl crouching upon the floor. At first sight one would have hardly suspected a human form at all, for from her head flowed down on all sides a torrent of exquisite blonde gold, that completely hid her. Only two little hands looked out, clasped, pleading for mercy, and a fairy child-face, looking up – in vain – to that black heart of hatred. Even as I gazed the woman hissed out so frightful a menace that my blood ran chill. The child shrank back into herself. The other raised her whip. I leapt into the room. The old hag spat one infamous word at me, turned on me with the whip.

'This time I was under no illusions about the sanctity of womanhood. With a single blow I felled her to the ground. My signet ring cut her lip, and the blood trickled over her cheek. I laughed. But the child never moved – it would seem she hardly comprehended.

'I turned, bowed. "I could not bear to hear your cries," I said – rather obviously, one may admit. "I came —," adding under my breath, "I saw, I conquered." "Who is that?" I added sternly, pointing to the prostrate hag.

'"Ah, sir" (she began to cry), "it is my mother." The horror of it was tenfold multiplied. "She – she —" The child blushed, stammered, stopped.

'"I heard, mademoiselle," I cried indignantly.

'"I am here" (she sobbed) "for a month, starved, whipped – oh! By day the window barred with iron; by night, open, the more to mock my helplessness!" Then, with a sudden cry, her little pink hand darting out and showing a faultless arm: "Look! look! she is on you."

'The mother had drawn herself away with infinite stealth, regained her feet, and, a thin stiletto in her hand, was crouched to spring. Indeed, as she leapt I was hard put to it to avoid the lunge; the dagger-edge grazed my arm as I stepped aside.

'I turned. She was on me, flinging me aside with the force of her rush as if I had been a straw. The snarl of her was like a wolf.

'This time she cut me deep. Again a whirl, a rush. I altered my tactics; I ran in to meet her. Hampered as she was by her furs, I was now quicker than she. I struck her dagger arm so strongly that the blade flew into the air, and fell quivering on the floor, the heavy hilt driving the thin blade deep into the polished wood. Even so I had her by the waist, catching her arm, and with one heave of my back I tossed her into the air, careless where she might fall.

'As luck would have it, she struck the balcony rail, broke it, and fell upon the pavement of the court. There was a crash, but no cry, no groan. I went to the balcony. She lay still, as the living do not lie, and her white hair was blackening, lapped by a congealing stream.

'I withdrew into the room. Since I have learnt that any death brings with it a strange sense of relief. There is a certain finality. *La comédie est jouée*[1] – and one turns with new life to the next business.

'The golden child had never stirred. But now she crouched lower, and fell to soft, sweet crying.

'"Your mother is dead," I said abruptly. "May I offer you the guardianship of my godmother, the Duchess of Castelnaudary? Come, mademoiselle, let us go."

'"I thank you, sir," she answered, still sobbing; "but Jean is awake and at the door. Jean is fierce and lean as an old wolf."

---

[1] [The comedy has been performed.]

'I pulled the dagger from the floor. "I am fierce and lithe as a young lion!" I said. "Let the old wolf beware!"

'"But I cannot, sir, I cannot. I ..." Her confusion became acute.

'"I dare not move, sir – I – I – my mother has taken away all my clothes."

'I marvelled. In her palace of gold hair nobody could have guessed it. But now I blushed, and lively. The dilemma was absurd.

'"I have it," said I. "I will climb down and bring up the ermine."

'She shuddered at the idea. Her dead mother's furs!

'"It must be," I said firmly.

'"Go, brave knight!" – a delicate smile lit up her face – "I trust myself to you."

'I bent on my right knee to her. "I take you," I said, "to be my lady, to fight in your cause, to honour and love you for ever."

'She put out her right hand – oh, the delicate beauty of it! I kissed it. "My knight," she said, "Jean is below; he may hear you; you go perhaps to your death – kiss me!"

'With a sob I caught her once full in my arms, and our mouths met. I closed my eyes in trance; my muscles failed; I sank, my forehead to the ground before her.

'When I opened my eyes again she too was praying. Softly, without a word, I stepped to the window, took the dagger in my teeth, dropped from the edge, landed lightly beside the corpse. She was quite dead, the skull broken in, the teeth exposed in a last snarl. She lay on her back; I opened the coat, turned her over. The gruesome task was nearly finished when the door of the house opened, and an old man, his face scarred, one lip cut half away in some old brawl, so that he grinned horribly and askew, rushed out at me, a rapier in his hand. My stiletto, though long beyond the ordinary, was useless against a tool of such superior reach.

'A last wrench gave me the ermine cloak, an invaluable parry. Could I entangle his sword, he was at my mercy. He saw it, and fenced warily. Indeed, I had the upper hand throughout. Threatening to throw the cloak, catch his sword, blind him, rush in with my dagger – he gave back and back in a circle round the courtyard.

'No sound came from the room above. Probably we three were alone. The fight was not to be prolonged for ever; the weight of the fur would tire me soon, counterbalance the advantage of age. Then, almost before I knew what had happened, we were fighting in the street. I would not cry for help; one was more likely to rouse a bandit than a guardian of the peace. And, besides, who could say how the law stood?

'I had certainly killed a lady; I was doing my best, with the aid of her stolen cloak, to kill a servant of the house; I contemplated an abduction. Best kill him silently, and be gone.

'But when and how had Jean pulled open the iron gates and retreated into the street?

'It mattered little, though certainly it left an uneasy sense of bewilderment; what mattered was that here we were fighting in semi-darkness – the dawn was not fairly lifted – for life and death.

'"Ten thousand crowns, Monsieur Jean," I cried, "and my service!" – I gave him my style – "I see you can be a faithful servant."

'"Faithful to death!" he retorted, and I was sorry to have to kill him.

'We fenced grimly on.

'"But," I urged, "your mistress is dead. Your duty is to her child, and I am her child's –"

'He looked up from my eyes. "An omen!" he cried, pointing to the great statue of St Michael trampling Satan, for we had come fighting to the Place St Michel. "Darkness yields to light; I am your servant, sir." He dropped on one knee, and tendered the hilt of his sword.

'But as I put out my hand to take it (guarded against attack, I boast me, but not against the extraordinary trick which followed) he suddenly snatched at the ermine, which lay loosely on my left arm, and, leaving me with sword and dagger, fled with a shriek of laughter across the Place St Michel, and, flinging the furs over the bridge, himself plunged into the Seine and swam strongly for the other bank.

'There was no object in pursuing him; I would recover the furs, and return triumphant. Alas! they had sunk; they were now whirled far away by the swift river. Where should I get a cloak?

'How stupid of me! The old woman had plenty of other clothes beneath her furs; I would take them.

'And I set myself gaily to run back to the house.'

3

'Whether by excitement I took the wrong turning, or whether – but you will hear! – in short, I do not clearly understand even now why I did not at once find the road. But at least I did fail to find it, discovered, as I supposed, my error, corrected it, failed once more…. In the end I got flustered – so much hung on my speedy return! – I fluttered hither and thither like a wild pigeon whose mate has been shot. I stopped short, pulled myself together. Let me think it out! Where am I now? I was under the shadow (the dawn just lit its edge) of the mighty shoulder of St Sulpice. "More haste, less speed!" I said to myself. "I will walk deliberately down to the boulevard, turn east, and so I cannot possibly miss the Carrefour de l'Odéon" – out of which, as I knew of old, the Rue des Quatre Vents leads. Indeed, I remembered the *carrefour* from that night. I had passed through it. I remembered hesitating as to which turning to take. For, as you know, the *carrefour* is a triangle, one road leading from the apex, four (with two minor variations just off the *carrefour*) from the base.

'Following this plan, I came, sure enough, in three minutes or so into the Rue des Quatre Vents. It is not a long street, as you know, and I thought that I remembered perfectly that the house faced the tiny Rue St Grégoire, which leads back to the Boulevard St Germain. Indeed, it was down that obscure alley that Jean and I had gone in our fight. I remembered how I had expected to meet somebody on issuing into the boulevard; and then ... I must have been very busy fighting: I could not remember anything at all of the fight between that issue and the place of Jean's feint and flight.

'Well, here I was: the house should have been in front of me – and it was not. I walked up and down the street; there was no house of the kind, no railings. No residential house. Yet I could not believe myself mistaken. I pinched myself; I was awake. Further, the pinching demonstrated the existence of a sword and dagger in my hands. I was bleeding, too; my left arm twice grazed. I took out my watch; four o'clock. Since I left the bridge – ah! when had I left the bridge? I could not tell – yes, I could. At moon-set. The moon was nine days old.

'No; everything was real. I examined the sword and the stiletto. Silvergilt; blades of exquisite fineness; the cipher of a princely house of France shone in tiny diamonds upon the pommels.

'The thought sent new courage and determination thrilling through me. I had saved a princess from shame and torture; I loved her! She loved me, for I had saved her – ah! but I had not yet saved her. That was to do.

'But how to act? I had plenty of time. Jean would not return to the house, in all probability. But the markets were stirring; the weapons and my blood would arouse curiosity. Well, how to act?

'The positive certitude that I had had about the name of the street was my bane. Had I doubted I could have more easily carried out the systematic search that I proposed. But as it was my organised patrol of the quarter was not scientific; I was biased. I came back again and again to the street and searched it, as if the house might have been hidden in the gutter or vanished and reappeared by magic; as if my previous search might (by some incredible chance) have been imperfect, through relaxed attention. So one may watch a conjuror, observing every movement perfectly, except the one flash which does the trick.

'The search, too, could not be long; so I reflected as disappointment sobered me. One cannot go far from the Carrefour de l'Odéon in any direction without striking some unmistakable object. The two boulevards, the schools, the Odéon itself, St Sulpice – one could not be far off. Yet – could I possibly have mistaken the Odéon for the Luxembourg?

'Could I ...? ...? A host of conjectures chased each other through my brain, bewildering it, leading the will to falter, the steps to halt.

'Beneath, keener anguish than the thrust of a poisoned rapier, stabbed me this poignant pang: my love awaits me, waits for me to save her, to fly with her ...

'Where was she?

'It was broad day; I cleansed myself of the marks of battle, sat down and broke my fast, my sane mind steadily forcing itself to a sober plan of action, beating manfully down the scream of its despair. All day I searched the streets. Passing an antiquary, I showed him my weapons. He readily supplied their history; but – there was none of that family alive, nor had been since the great Revolution. Their goods? The four winds of heaven might know. At those words "the four winds" I rushed out of the shop, as if stung by an adder.

'I drove home, set all my servants hunting for railed houses. They were to report to me in the Rue des Quatre Vents. Any house not accounted for, any that might conceal a mystery, these I would see myself.

'All labour lost! My servants tried. I distrusted their energy: I set myself obstinately to scour Paris.

'There is a rule of mathematics which enables one to traverse completely any labyrinth. I applied this to the city. I walked in every road of it, marking the streets at each corner as I passed with my private seal. Each railed house I investigated separately and thoroughly. By virtue of my position I was welcome everywhere. But every night I paced the Rue des Quatre Vents, waiting ...

'Awaiting what? Well, in the end, perhaps death. The children gibed at me; passers-by shunned me.

'"*Le Revenant*," they whispered, "*de la Rue des Quatre Vents*."

'I had forgot to tell you one thing which most steadfastly confirmed me in the search. Two days after the adventure I passed, hot on the quest, by the Morgue. Two women came out. "Not pretty, the fish!" said one. "He with the scarred lip—"

'I heard no more, ran in. There on the slab, grinning yet in death, was Jean. His swim had ended him. Faithful to death!

'I watched long. I offered a huge sum for his identification. The authorities even became suspicious: why was I so anxious? How could I say? He was the servant of ——

'I did not know my sweet child's name!

* * *

'So, while a living man, I made myself a ghost.'

4

'It may have been one day some ten years later,' continued the old nobleman, 'when as I paced uselessly the Street of the Four Winds I was confronted by a stern, grey figure, short, stout, and bearded, but of an indescribable majesty and force.

'He laid his hand unhesitatingly upon my shoulder. "Unhappy man!" he cried, "thou art sacrificing thy life to a phantom. 'Look not,' quoth Zoroaster, 'upon the Visible Image of the Soul of Nature, for Her name is Fatality.' What thou hast seen – I know not what it is, save that it is as a dog-faced demon that seduceth thy soul from the sacred Mysteries; the Mysteries of Life and Duty."

'"Let me tell my story!" I replied, "and you shall judge – for, whoever you may be, I feel your power and truth."

'"I am Éliphas Lévi Zahed – men call me the Abbé Constant," returned the other.

'"The great magician?"

'"The enemy of the great magician."

'We went together to my house. I had begun to suspect some trick of Hell. The malice of that devilish old woman, it might be, had not slept, even at her death. She had hidden the house beneath a magic veil? Or had her death itself in some strange way operated to – to what? Even conjecture paled.

'But magic somewhere there must be, and Éliphas Lévi was the most famous adept in Paris at the time.

'I told my story, just as I have told it to you, but with strong passion.

'"There is an illusion, master!" I ended. "Put forth the Power and destroy it!"

'"Were I to destroy the illusion," returned the magus, "thinkest thou to see a virgin with gold hair? Nay, but the Eternal Virgin, and a Gold that is not gold."

'"Is nothing to be done?"

'"Nothing!" he replied, with a strange light in his eyes. "Yet, in order to be able to do nothing, thou must first accomplish everything.

'"One day," he smiled, seeing my bewilderment, "thou wilt be angry with the fool who proffers such a platitude."

'I asked him to accept me as a pupil.

'"I require pay," he answered, "and an oath."

'"Speak; I am rich."

'"Every Good Friday," said the adept, "take thirty silver crowns and offer them to the Hospital for the Insane."

'"It shall be done," I said.

'"Swear, then," he went on, "swear, then, here to me" – he rose, terrible and menacing – "by Him that sitteth upon the Holy Throne and liveth and reigneth for ever and ever, that never again, neither to save life, nor to retain honour, wilt thou set foot in the Street of the Four Winds; so long as life shall last."

'Even as he bade me, I rose with lifted hand and swore.

'As I did so there resounded in the room ten sharp knocks, as of ivory on wood, in a certain peculiar cadence.

'This was but the first of a very large number of interviews. I sought, indeed, steadfastly to learn from him the occult wisdom of which he was a master; but, though he supplied me with all conceivable channels of knowledge – books, manuscripts, papyri – yet all these were lifeless; the currents of living water flowed not through them. Should one say that the master withheld initiation, or that the pupil failed to obtain it?

'But at least time abated the monomania – for I know now that my whole adventure was but a very vivid dream, an insanity of adolescence. At this moment I would not like to say at what point exactly in the story fact and dream touch; I have still the sword and dagger. Is it possible that in a trance I actually went through some other series of adventures than that I am conscious of? May not Jean have been a thief, whom I dispossessed of his booty? Had I done this unconsciously it would account for both the weapons and the scene in the Morgue.... But I cannot say.

'So, too, I learnt from the master that all this veil of life is but a shadow of a vast reality beyond, perceptible only to those who have earned eyes to see withal.

'These eyes I could not earn; a faith in the master sustained me. I began to understand, too, a little about the human brain; of what it is capable. Of Heaven – and of Hell!

'Life passed, vigorous and pleasant; the only memory that haunted me was the compulsion of my oath that never would I again set foot in the Rue des Quatre Vents.

'Life passed, and for the master ended. "The Veil of the Temple is but a Spider's web!" he said, three days before he died. I followed Éliphas Lévi Zahed to the grave.

'I could not follow him beyond.

'For the next year I applied myself with renewed vigour to the study of the many manuscripts which he had left me. No result could I obtain; I slackened. Followed the folly of my life: I rationalised.

'Thus: one day, leaning over the Pont St Michel, I let the whole strange story flow back through my brain. I remembered my agony; my present calm astonished me. I thought of Lévi, of my oath. "He did not mean *for all my life*," I thought; "he meant until I could contemplate the affair without passion. Is not fear failure? I will walk through just once, to show my mastery." In five minutes – with just one inward qualm – again I was treading the well-worn flags of that ensorcelled road.

'Instantly – instantly! – the old delusion had me by the throat. I had broken my oath; I was paying the penalty.

'Crazier than ever, I again sought throughout changed Paris for my dream-love; I shall seek her till I die. If I seem calmer, it is but that age has robbed me of the force of passion. In vain you tell me, laughing, that if she ever lived, she is long since dead; or at least is an old woman, the blonde gold faded, the child-face wrinkled, the body bowed and lax. I laugh at you – at you – for a blaspheming ass. Your folly is too wild to anger me!'

'I did not laugh,' said Roderic gravely.

'Well,' said the old man, rising, 'I fear I have wearied you … I thank you for your patience … I know I am a mad old fellow. But, if you should happen – you know. Please communicate. Here is my card. I must go now. I am expected elsewhere. I am expected.'

Illusion d'Amoureux

She lay, the gilded lily with geranium lips, in the midst of the flower of night. Kindlier than the moon, her body glowed with more than harvest gold. Fierier than the portent of a double Venus, her green eyes shot forth utmost flames. From the golden chalice of love arose a perfume terrible and beautiful, a perfume strong and deadly to overcome the subtler fragrance of her whole being with its dominant, unshamed appeal.

She lay with arms outstretched, as if awaiting the visitation of some god.

Some ghastly god, for sure? For where she lay, the gilded lily with geranium lips, was, as it were, a flower of night.

It was a small square room, black from edge to edge. A dull dead black that gave back no light from the two solemn candlesticks of silver, crowned with long guttering tapers, which gave the only relief in all that world of night.

These stood at the head of her strange couch. It was a huge coffin, lidless, with hinged sides, whereon she lay. She had loosened the girths and lowered the sides, to stretch herself at ease. Six black ropes of silk hung from the ceiling with their hooks, which could be attached to rings on the sides of the coffin, so that at will it might be made to swing slowly to and fro.

A heavy rug of black cats' skin was spread under her, as if her body, gleaming now like moonstone, now like amber, would coax electric sparks from the fur.

Wonderful was the body of the woman; she changed ever as she lay. She outran the gamut of all music and flowers and jewels and soft words; there is nothing beautiful upon the earth that she did not resemble. At the sides of the room stood tall pier-glasses in black frames, cunningly disposed so that from the centre one could see endless avenues of her beauty, reaching out into infinity.

Even the roof was mirror-clad, so that as she lay upon the furs she might look upward, and see herself hanging like a star from the black vault of night.

Beside her in the temple was but one strange image. Carved of that polished black granite of Egypt, which seems, as it were, the very bodily form of the Night of Time, there squatted a god upon his pedestal; an inscrutable god, smiling, ever smiling with a smile that spoke unfathomable lust and cruelty resolved – by what theurgic alchemy? – into a pure and passionless bliss. It was a thing eternal as the stars – nay, before it the very stars might bow as in the reverence of Youth to age! Yet in it stood a strength and beauty as of golden youth.

Its skin was polished and shining, not as if reflecting the guarded light of the electric globes, but as if the very soul of light – a light too essential to be recognised as light by men – did inhabit and inform it.

As she lay, the gilded lily, she moved the passionate lips in some mysterious orison that was subtler and stronger than prayer.

'O beautiful, adorable, wonderful! O soul of wickedness! Supreme abomination, I invoke Thee! I worship Thee! I love Thee! Body and soul, I invoke Thee! Awake! Arise! Move! Manifest thy bliss to me, the soul that hungers for thy wisdom, as my body aches for thy kisses!

'Have not I wooed Thee and awaited Thee? But Thou comest not. By what spell may I conjure Thee? Am I the mock of Thy majesty? Ah, my god, my master, my lover – nay, that Thou art not.

'But I love Thee! I worship Thee!'

With supreme force she cried out upon the God; she tore at her beautiful flesh with her fingers; she writhed upon the fur; words of dreadful passion bubbled at her lips; her mouth was like a raging sea of blasphemy; she moaned and struggled, torn by some internal force even as a woman in childbirth; she sank back into black silence, exhausted, numb.

But now the words came back like echoes from the infinite – I love thee! I worship thee!

The lights went out; the black god gathered himself together; his mighty form outran the limits of space. He gathered himself in force and fire; he concentrated himself; as a black cloud he wrapped her round – body and soul. He ate her up with his first kiss; his arms crushed her into his mouth as a boy might crush some golden grape; the majesty of his passion clove her with white-hot steel; her life rushed headlong down the steeps of annihilation.

Yet in her rose the awful dawn of a new life, vast and magnificent. She became the god, absorbed in His being; her dreadful shriek – the cry of a soul at Heaven's gate smitten by the lightning into the abyss – changed to a marvellous laughter of love as she touched the summit of felicity.

* * *

So much I saw; yet the cloud withdrew itself; the lights redeemed their lustre. There in the midst my love awaited me – me – and I stood, as a diver that hesitates, so that he may enjoy to the full the foretaste of the plunge.

I stood there, very God of very God, in the glittering green of her eyes, that darted flames of exquisite ardour upon me – ay, upon me.

Had I been standing there a moment or an æon?

The Soul-Hunter

UNPUBLISHED PAGES FROM THE DIARY OF
DR ARTHUR LEE – 'THE MONTROUGE VAMPIRE'

I bought his body for ten francs. Months before I had bought his
soul, bought it for the first glass of the poison – the first glass of the
new series of horrors since his discharge, cured – cured! – from the
'retreat.' Yes, I tempted him, I, a doctor! Bound by the vows – faugh!
I needed his body! His soul? pah! but an incident in the bargain. For
soul is but a word, a vain word – a battlefield of the philosopher fools,
the theologian fools, since Anaximander and Gregory Nanzianus. A
toy. But the consciousness? That is what we mean by *soul*, we others.
That then must live somewhere. But is it, as Descartes thought,
atomic? or fluid, now here, now there? Or is it but a word for the
totality of bodily sense? As Weir Mitchell supposed. Well, we should
see. I would buy a brain and hunt this elusive consciousness. Just so,
luck follows skill; the brain of Jules Foreau was the very pick of the
world's brains. The most self-conscious man in Europe! Intellectual
to an incredible point, introspective beyond the Hindus, *and* with the
fatal craving which made him mine. Jules Foreau, you might have
been a statesman; you became a sot – but you shall make the name
of doctor Arthur Lee famous for ever, and put an end to the great
problem of the ages. Aha, my friend, how mad of me to fill my diary
with this cheap introspective stuff! I feel somehow that the affair will
end badly. I am writing my *defence*. Certainly that excuses the form. A
jury can never understand plain facts – the cold light of science chills
them; they need eloquence, sentiment.… Well, I must pay a lawyer
for that, if trouble should really arise. How should it? I have made all
safe – trust me!

I gave him the drug yesterday. The atropine was a touch of almost
superhuman cleverness; the fixed, glassy stare deader than death itself.
I complied with the foolish formulæ of the law; in three hours I had

the body in my laboratory. In the present absurd state of the law there is really nobody trustworthy in a business of this sort. *Tant pis!*[1] I must cook my own food for the next month or so. For no doubt there will be a good deal of noise. No doubt a good deal of noise. I must risk that. I dare not touch anything but the brain; it might vitiate the whole experiment. Bad enough this plaster of Paris affair. You see a healthy man of thirteen stone odd in his prime will dislike any deep interference with his brain – resent it. Chains are useless; nothing keeps a man still. Bar anæsthesia. And anæsthesia is the one thing barred. He must feel, he must talk, he must be as normal as possible. So I have simply built his neck, shoulders, and arms into plaster. He can yell and he can kick. If it does him any good he is welcome. So – to business.

10.30 A.M.	He is decidedly under the new drug – ή; yet he does not move. He takes longer to come back to life than I supposed.
10.40.	Warmth to extremities. Inhalations of λ. He cannot speak yet, I think. The glare of eyes is not due to hate, but to the atropine.
10.45.	He has noticed the plaster arrangement and the nature of the room. I think he guesses. A gurgle. I light a cigarette and put it in his mouth. He spits it out. He seems hardly to understand my good-humour.
10.47.	The first word – 'What is it, you devil?' I show him the knife, *et cetera*, and urge him to keep calm and self-collected.
10.50.	A laugh, not too nervous. A good sign. 'By George, you amuse me!' Then with a sort of wistful sigh, 'I thought you just meant to poison me in some new patent kind of way.' Bad; he wants to die. Must cheer him up.
11.0.	I have given my little scientific lecture. The patient unimpressed. The absinthe has damaged his reasoning faculty. He cannot see the *à priori* necessity of the experiment. Strange!
11.10.	Lord, how funny! – he thinks I may be mad, and is trying all the old dodges to 'humour' me! I must sober him.
11.15.	Sobered him. Showed him his own cranium – he had never missed it, of course. Yet the fact seemed to surprise him. Important, though, for my thesis. Here at least is one part of the body whose absence in nowise diminishes the range

---

[1] [Too bad!]

of the sensorium – soul – what shall we call it? '*x*.' Some important glands, of course, rule a man's whole life. Others again – what use is a lymphatic to the soul? To '*x*'? Well, we must deal with the glands in detail, at the fountain-head, in the brain.

11.20. My writing seems to irritate him. Daren't give drugs. He flushes and pales too easily. Absence of skull? Now, a little cut and tie – and we shall see.

N.B. – To keep this record very distinct from the pure surgery of the business.

11.22. A concentrated, sustained yell. It has quite shaken me. I never heard the like. 'All out' too, as we used to say on the Cam; he's physically exhausted – *e.g.*, has stopped kicking. Legs limp as possible. Pure funk; I never hurt him.

11.25. A most curious thing: I feel an intense dislike of the man coming over me; and, with an almost insane fascination, the thought, 'Suppose I were to *kiss* him?' Followed by a shiver of physical loathing and disgust. Such thoughts have no business here at all. To work.

12.0. I want a drink; there are most remarkable gaps in the consciousness – not implying unconsciousness. I am inclined to think that what we call continuous pain is a rhythmic beat, frequency of beat less than one in sixty. The shrieks are simply heartbreaking.

12.5. Silence, more terrible than the yells. Afraid I had had an accident. He smiles, reassures me. Speaks – 'Look here, doctor, enough of this fooling; I'm annoyed with you, I really don't know why – and I yell because I know it worries you. But listen to this: under the drug I really died, though you thought I was simulating death. On the contrary, it is now that I am simulating life.' There seemed to me, and still seems, some essential absurdity in these words; yet I could not refute him. I opened my mouth and closed it. The voice went on: 'It follows that your whole experiment is a childish failure.' I cut him short; this time I found words. 'You forget your position,' I said hotly. 'It is against all precedent for the vivisectee to abuse his master. Ingrate!' So incensed was I that I strode angrily to the operating-chair and paralysed the ganglia governing the muscles of speech. Imagine my surprise when he proceeded, entirely incommoded: 'On

the contrary, it is you who are dead, Arthur Lee.' The
voice came from behind me, from far off. 'Until you die
you never know it, but you have been dead all along.' My
nerve is clearly gone; this must be a case of pure hallucination. I begin to remember that I am alone – alone in
the big house with the ... patient. Suppose I were to fall
ill? ... Was this thought written in my face? He laughed
harsh and loud. Disgusting beast!

12.15.   A pretty fool I am, tying the wrong nerve. No wonder he
could go on talking! A nasty slip in such an experiment
as this. Must check the whole thing through again....

1.0.   O.K. now. Must get some lunch. Oddly enough, I am pretty
sure he was telling the truth. He feels no pain, and only yells
to annoy me.

2.10.   Excellent! I suppress all the senses but smell, and give
him his wife's handkerchief. He bubbles over with amorous drivel; I should love to tell him what she died of, and
who.... A curious trait, that last remark. Why do I *dislike*
the man? I used to get on A1 with him. (N.B. to stitch
eyelids with silk. Damn the glare.)

2.20.   Theism! The convolution with the cause-idea lying too
close to the convolution with the fear-idea. And imagination at work on the nexus! About 24μ between Charles
Bradlaugh and Cardinal Newman!

2.50.   So for faith and doubt? Sceptical criticism of my whole
experiment boils up in me. What is 'normality'? Even
so, what possible relation is there between things and
the evidence of them recorded in the brain? Evidence of
something, maybe. A thermometer chart gives a curve;
yet the mercury has only moved up and down. What
about the time dimension? But it is not a dimension; it is
only a word to explain multiplicity of sensation. Words!
words! words! This is the last straw. There is no conceivable standard whereby we may measure anything
whatever; and it is useless to pretend there is.

3.3.   In short, we are all mad. Yet all this is but the expression
of the doubt-stop in the human organ. Let me pull out
his faith-stop!

4.54.   Done; the devil's own job. He seems to be a Pantheist
Antinomian with leanings towards Ritualism. Not impres-
sive. My observation-stop (= my doubt-stop nearly) is full

out. (Funny that we should fall into the old faculty jargon.) Perhaps if one's own faith-stop were out there would be a fight; if one's reception-of-new-ideas-stop, a conversion.

5.12. I only wish I had two of them to test the 'tuning-up' theory of Collective Hallucination and the like. Out of the question; we must wait for Socialism. But enough for the day is the research thereof. I've matter for a life's work already.

7.50. An excellent scratch dinner – none too soon. Turtle soup, potted char, Yorkshire pie, Stilton, burgundy. Better than nothing. Tomorrow the question of putrefactive changes in the limbs and their relation to the brain.

3.1. Planted bacilli in left foot. Will leave him to sleep. No difficulty there; the brute's as tired as I am. Too tired to curse. I recited *Abide with Me* throughout to soothe him. Some lines distinctly humorous under the circumstances. Will have a smoke in the study and check through the surg. record. Too dazed to realise everything, but I am assuredly an epoch. Whaur's your Robbie Pasteur noo?

12.20 A.M. So I've been on a false trail all day! The course of the research has led right away from the '*x*-hunt.' The byways have obscured the main road. Valuable though; very, very valuable. In the morning success. Bed!

12.30. Yells and struggles again when I went in to say good-night. As I had carefully paralysed *all* the sensory avenues (to ensure perfect rest), how was he aware of my presence? The memory of the scented handkerchief, too, very strong; talked a lot of his wife, thinking her with him. Pah! what beasts some men must be! Disgusting fellow! I'm no prude either! If ever I do a woman I'll stop the Filth-gutter. *Ce serait trop.*[1]

12.40. Maybe he did *not* know of my presence; merely remembered me. He has cause. How much there is in one's mind of the merely personal idea of scoring off the bowlers. And every man is a batsman in a world of bowlers. Like that leg-cricket game, what did we call it? Oh! bed, bed!

5.0. Patient seriously ill; plaster irks breathing; all sorts of troubles expected and unexpected. Putrefaction of left foot well advanced: promises well for the day's work if I can check collapse.

---

[1] [This would be too much.]

5.31.   Patient very much better; paralysed motor ganglia; safe
               to remove plaster. Too much time wasted on these fool-
               ish mechanical details of life when one is looking for the
               Master of the Machine.

6.12.   Patient in excellent fettle; now to find '*x*' – the soul!

11.55.   Worn out; no '*x*' yet. Patient well, normal; have checked
               shrieks, ingenious dodge.

2.15.   No time for food; brandy. Patient fighting fit. No '*x*.'

3.1.   *Dead!!!* No cause in the world – I must have cut right into
               the '*x*,' the soul.

               The meningeal —

* * *

{Dr Lee's diary breaks off abruptly at this point. His researches
were never published. It will be remembered that he was convicted of causing the death of his mistress, Jeannette Pheyron,
under mysterious circumstances, some six months after the
date of the above. The surgical record referred to has not been
found.– *Editor*.}

The Daughter of the Horseleech

A FABLE

Tria sunt insaturabilia, et quartum, quod nunquam
dicit: Sufficit. Infernus, et os vulvæ....[1]

— *Prov.* 30:16

The Great White Spirit stretched Himself and yawned. He had done
an honest six days' work if ever a man did; yet in such physical training
was He from His lengthy 'cure' in that fashionable Spa Pralaya that
he was not in the least fatigued. It was the Loi du Répos Hebdomad-
aire that had made Him throw down His tools.

'Anyway, the job's finished!' He said, looking round Him compla-
cently. Even His critical eye assured Him that it was very good.

And indeed it must be admitted that He had every right to crow.
With no better basis than the Metaphysical Absolute of the Qabalists
he had unthinkably but efficiently formulated Infinite Space, filled the
said Space with Infinite Light, concentrated the Light into a Smooth-
pointed Whitehead (not the torpedo) and emanated Himself as four
hundred successive intelligences all the way from Risha Qadisha in Atzi-
luth down to where intelligence ends, and England begins.

He took a final survey and again faintly murmured: 'Very good!
Beautifully arranged, too!' He added, 'not a hole anywhere!'

It somewhat surprised Him, therefore, when a tiny, tiny silvery little
laugh came bell-like in His ear. It was so tiny that he could hardly
credit the audacity of the idea, but for all its music, the laugh certainly
sounded as if someone were mocking Him.

He turned sharply round (and this was one of His own special attributes, as transcending the plane where activity and rotundity are
incompatibles) but saw nothing; and putting His legs up, lighted His

---

[1] [There are three insatiable things, and a fourth, which never says: 'It is sufficient.'
The underworld, and the mouth of the womb....]

long pipe and settled down to a quiet perusal of a fascinating 'cosmic romance' called *Berashith* by two pseudonymous authors, G.O. Varr and L.O. Heem – of ingenious fancy, exalted imaginative faculty, and a tendency, which would later be deemed undesirable, to slop over into the filthiest details whenever the love-interest became dominant. Oh, but it was a most enthralling narrative! Beginning with a comic account of the creation, possibly intended as a satire on our men of science or our men of religion – 'twould serve equally well in either case – it went on to a thrilling hospital scene. The love-interest comes in chapter 2; chapter 3 has an eviction scene, since when there have been no snakes in Ireland; chapter 4 gives us a first-rate murder, and from that moment the authors never look back.

But the Great White Spirit was destined to have his day of repose disturbed.

He had just got to the real masterpiece of literature 'And Adam knew Hevah his woman,' which contains all that ever has been said or ever can be said upon the sex-problem in its one simple, sane, clean truth, when glancing up, he saw that after all He had overlooked something. In the Infinite Universe which he had constructed there was a tiny crack.

A tiny, tiny crack.

Barely an inch of it.

Well, the matter was easily remedied. As it chanced, there was a dainty little Spirit (with gossamer wings like a web of steel, and scarlet tissue of silk for his robes) flitting about, brandishing his tiny sword and spear in a thoroughly warlike manner.

'Shun!' said the Great White Spirit.

'By the right, dress!

'Sappers, one pace forward, march!

'Prepare to stop leak!

'Stop leak!'

But the matter was not thus easily settled. After five hours' strenuous work, the little spirit was exhausted, and the hole apparently no nearer being filled than before.

He returned to the Great White Spirit.

'Beg pardon, sir!' he said; 'but I can't fill that there 'ole nohow.'

'No matter,' answered the Great White Spirit, with a metaphysical double entendre. 'You may go!'

If anything, the crack was bigger than before, it seemed to Him. 'This,' He said, 'is clearly the job for Bartzabel.' And he despatched a 'speed' message for that worthy spirit.

Bartzabel lost no time in answering the summons. Of flaming, radiant, far-darting gold was his crown; flashing hither and thither more swiftly than the lightning were its rays. His head was like the Sun in its strength, even at high noon. His cloak was of pure amethyst, flowing behind him like a mighty river; his armour was of living gold, burnished with lightning even to the greaves and the armed feet of him; he radiated an intolerable splendour of gold and he bore the Sword and balance of Justice. Mighty and golden were his wide-flashing wings!

Terrible in his might, he bowed low before the Great White Spirit, and proceeded to carry out the order.

For five and twenty years he toiled at the so easy task; then, flinging down his weapons in a rage, he returned before the face of his Master and, trembling with passion, cast himself down in wrath and despair.

'Pah!' said the Great White Spirit with a smile; 'I might have known better than to employ a low material creature like yourself. Send Graphiel to Me!'

The angry Bartzabel, foaming with horrid rage, went off, and Graphiel appeared.

All glorious was the moon-like crown of the great Intelligence Graphiel. His face was like the Sun as it appears beyond the veil of this earthly firmament. His warrior body was like a tower of steel, virginal strong.

Scarlet were his kingly robes, and his limbs were swathed in young leaves of lotus; for those limbs were stronger than any armour ever forged in heaven or hell. Winged was he with the wings of gold that are the Wind itself; his sword of green fire flamed in his right hand, and in his left he held the blue feather of Justice, unstirred by the wind of his flight, or the upheaval of the universe.

But after five and sixty centuries of toil, though illumined with intelligence almost divine, he had to confess himself defeated.

'Sir,' he cried strongly, 'this is a task for Kamael the mighty and all his host of Seraphim!'

'I will employ them on it,' said the Great White Spirit.

Then the skies flamed with wrath; for Kamael the mighty and his legions flew from the South, and saluted their Creator. Behold the mighty one, behold Kamael the strong! His crownless head was like a whirling wheel of amethyst, and all the forces of the earth and heaven revolved therein. His body was the mighty Sea itself, and it bore the scars of crucifixion that had made it two score times stronger than it was before. He too bore the wings and weapons of Space and of Justice; and in himself he was that great Amen that is the beginning and the end of all.

Behind him were the Seraphim, the fiery Serpents. On their heads the triple tongue of fire; their glory like unto the Sun, their scales like burning plates of steel; they danced like virgins before their lord, and upon the storm and roar of the sea did they ride in their glory.

'Sir,' cried the Archangel, 'sir,' cried Kamael the mighty one, and his legions echoed the roar of his voice, 'hast Thou called us forth to perform so trivial a task? Well, let it be so!'

'Your scorn,' the Great White Spirit replied mildly, 'is perhaps not altogether justified. Though the hole be indeed but a bare inch – yet Graphiel owns himself beaten.'

'I never thought much of Graphiel!' sneered the archangel, and his serpents echoed him till the world was filled with mocking laughter.

But when he had left, he charged them straitly that the work must be regarded seriously. It would never do to fail!

So for æons three hundred and twenty and five did they labour with all their might.

But the crack was not diminished by an hair's breadth; nay, it seemed bigger than before – a very gape in the womb of the Universe.

Crestfallen, Kamael the mighty returned before the Great White Spirit, his serpents drooping behind him; and they grovelled before the throne of that All-powerful One.

He dismissed them with a short laugh, and a wave of His right hand. If He was disturbed, He was too proud to show it. 'This,' he said to himself, 'is clearly a matter for Elohim Gibor.'

Therefore He summoned that divine power before Him.

The crown of Elohim Gibor was Space itself; the two halves of his brain were the Yea and Nay of the Universe; his breath was the breath of very Life; his being was the *mahālinga* of the First, beyond Life and Death the generator from Nothingness. His armour was the Primal Water of Chaos. The infinite moon-like curve of his body; the flashing swiftness of his Word, that was the Word that formulated that which was beyond Chaos and Cosmos; the might of him, greater than that of the Elephant and of the Lion and of the Tortoise and of the Bull fabled in Indian legend as the supports of the four letters of the Name; the glory of him, that was even as that of the Sun which is before all and beyond all Suns, of which the stars are little sparks struck off as he battled in the Infinite against the Infinite – all these points the Great White Spirit noted and appreciated. This is certainly the person, thought He, to do my business for me.

But alas! for five, and for twenty-five, and for sixty-five, and for three hundred and twenty-five myriads of myriads of myriads of *kotis* of *crores* of *lakhs* of *asankhayās* of *mahākalpas* did he work with his divine power – and yet that little crack was in nowise filled, but rather widened!

The god returned. 'O Great White Spirit!' he whispered – and the Universe shook with fear at the voice of him – 'Thou, and Thou alone, art worthy to fill this little crack that Thou hast left.'

Then the Great White Spirit arose and formulated Himself as the Pillar of Infinitude, even as the *mahālinga* of Great Śiva the Destroyer, who openeth his eye, and All is Not. And behold! He was balanced in the crack, and the void was filled, and Nature was content. And Elohim Gibor, and Kamael the mighty and his Seraphim, and Graphiel, and Bartzabel, and all the inhabitants of Madim shouted for joy and gave glory and honour and praise to the Great White Spirit; and the sound of their rejoicing filled the Worlds.

Now for one thousand myriad eternities the Great White Spirit maintained Himself as the Pillar of Infinitude in the midst of the little crack that he had overlooked; and lo! He was very weary.

'I cannot stay like this for ever,' He exclaimed; and returned into His human shape, and filled the bowl of His pipe, and lit it, and meditated....

And I awoke, and behold it was a dream.

Then I too lit my pipe, and meditated.

'I cannot see,' thought I, 'that the situation will be in any way amended, even if we agree to give them votes.'

The Violinist

The room was cloudy with a poisonous incense: saffron, opoponax, galbanum, musk and myrrh, the purity of the last ingredient a curse of blasphemy, the final sneer; as a degenerate might insult a Raphael by putting it in a room devoted to debauchery.

The girl was tall and finely built, huntress-lithe. Her dress, close-fitted, was of a gold-brown silk that matched, but could not rival, the coils that bound her brow – glittering and hissing like snakes.

Her face was Greek in delicacy; but what meant such a mouth in it? The mouth of a satyr or a devil. It was full and strong, curved twice, the edges upwards, an angry purple, the lips flat. Her smile was like the snarl of a wild beast.

She stood, violin in hand, before the wall. Against it was a large tablet of mosaic; many squares and many colours. On the squares were letters in an unknown tongue.

She began to play, her grey eyes fixed upon one square on whose centre stood this character, N. It was in black on white; and the four sides of the square were blue, yellow, red and black.

She began to play. The air was low, sweet, soft and slow. It seemed that she was listening, not to her own playing, but for some other sound. Her bow quickened; the air grew harsh and wild, irritated; quickened further to a rush like flames devouring a hayrick; softened again to a dirge.

Each time she changed the soul of the song it seemed as if she was exhausted: as if she was trying to sound a particular phrase, and always fell back baffled at the last moment.

Nor did any light infuse her eyes. There was intentness, there was weariness, there was patience, there was alertness. And the room was strangely silent, unsympathetic to her mood. She was the dimmest thing in that grey light. Still she strove. She grew more tense, her mouth tightened, an ugly compression. Her eyes flashed with – was it hate? The soul of the song was now all anguish, all pleading, all despair – ever reaching to some unattainable thing.

She choked, a spasmodic sob. She stopped playing; she bit her lips, and a drop of blood stood on them scarlet against their angry purple, like sunset and storm. She pressed them to the square, and a smear stained the white. She caught at her heart; for some strange pang tore it.

Up went her violin, and the bow crossed it. It might have been the swords of two skilled fencers, both blind with mortal hate. It might have been the bodies of two skilled lovers, blind with immortal love.

She tore life and death asunder on her strings. Up, up soared the phœnix of her song; step by step on music's golden scaling-ladder she stormed the citadel of her Desire. The blood flushed and swelled her face beneath its sweat. Her eyes were injected with blood.

The song rose, culminated – overleapt the barriers, achieved its phrase.

She stopped; but the music went on. A cloud gathered upon the great square, menacing and hideous. There was a tearing shriek above the melody.

Before her, his hands upon her hips, stood a boy. Golden haired he was, and red were his young lips, and blue his eyes. But his body was ethereal like a film of dew upon a glass, or rust clinging to an airy garment; and all was stained hideously with black.

'My Remenu!' she said. 'After so long!'

He whispered in her ear.

The light behind her flickered and went out.

The spirit laid her violin and bow upon the ground.

The music went on – a panting, hot melody like mad eagles in death struggle with mountain goats, like serpents caught in jungle fires, like scorpions tormented by Arab girls.

And in the dark she sobbed and screamed in unison. She had not expected this: she had dreamt of love more passionate, of lust more fierce-fantastic, than aught mortal.

And this?

This real loss of a real chastity? This degradation not of the body, but of the soul! This white-hot curling flame – ice cold about her heart? This jagged lightning that tore her? This tarantula of slime that crawled up her spine?

She felt the blood running from her breasts, and its foam at her mouth.

Then suddenly the lights flamed up, and she found herself standing – reeling – her head sagging on his arm.

Again he whispered in her ear.

In his left hand was a little ebony box; a dark paste was in it. He rubbed a little on her lips.

And yet a third time he whispered in her ear.

With an angel's smile – save for its subtlety – he was gone into the tablet.

She turned, blew on the fire, that started up friendly, and threw herself in an arm-chair. Idly she strummed old-fashioned simple tunes.

The door opened.

A jolly lad came in and shook the snow from his furs.

'Been too bored, little girl?' he said cheerily, confident.

'No, dear!' she said. 'I've been fiddling a bit.'

'Give me a kiss, Lily!'

He bent down and put his lips to hers; then, as if struck by lightning, sprawled, a corpse.

She looked down lazily through half-shut eyes with that smile of hers that was a snarl.

The Vixen

TO AND FROM N. I. L. B. W.

Patricia Fleming threw the reins to a groom, and ran up the steps into the great house, her thin lips white with rage.

Lord Eyre followed her heavily. 'I'll be down in half an hour,' she laughed merrily, 'tell Dawson to bring you a drink!' Then she went straight through the house, her girlish eyes the incarnation of a curse.

For the third time she had failed to bring Geoffrey Eyre to her feet. She looked into her hat; there in the lining was the talisman that she had tested – and it had tricked her.

'What do I need?' she thought. 'Must it be blood?'

She was a maiden of the pure English strain: brave, gay, honest, shrewd – and there was not one that guessed the inmost fire that burnt her. For she was but a child when the Visitor came.

The first of the Visits was in a dream. She woke choking; the air – clear, sweet and wholesome as it blew through the open window from the Chilterns – was fouled with a musty stench. And she woke her governess with a tale of a tiger.

The second Visit was again at night. She had been hunting, was alone at the death, had beaten off the hounds. That night she heard a fox bark in her room. She spent a sleepless night of terror; in the morning she found the red hairs of a fox upon her pillow.

The third Visit was nor in sleep nor waking.

But she tightened her lips, and would have veiled the hateful gleam in her eyes.

It was that day, though, that she struck a servant with her riding-whip.

She was so sane that she knew exactly wherein her madness lay; and she set all her strength not to conquer but to conceal it.

Two years later, and Patricia Fleming, the orphan heiress of Carthwell Abbey, was the county toast, Diana of the Chilterns.

Yet Geoffrey Eyre evaded her. His dog's fidelity and honesty kept him true to the little north-country girl that three months earlier had seduced his simplicity. He did not even love her; but she had made him think so for an hour; and his pledged word held him.

Patricia's open favour only made him hate her because of its very seduction. It was really his own weakness that he hated.

Patricia ran, tense and angry, through the house. The servants noticed it. The mistress has been crossed, they thought, she will go to the chapel and get ease. Praising her.

True, to the chapel she went; locked the door, dived behind the altar, struck a secret panel, came suddenly into a priest's hiding-hole, a room large enough to hold a score of men if need be.

At the end of the room was a great scarlet cross, and on it, her face to the wood, her wrists and ankles swollen over the whip lashes that bound her, hung a naked girl, big-boned, voluptuous. Red hair streamed over her back.

'What, Margaret! so blue?' laughed Patricia.

'I am cold,' said the girl upon the cross, in an indifferent voice.

'Nonsense, dear!' answered Patricia, rapidly divesting herself of her riding-habit. 'There is no hint of frost; we had a splendid run, and a grand kill. You shall be warm yet, for all that.'

This time the girl writhed and moaned a little.

Patricia took from an old wardrobe a close-fitting suit of fox fur, and slipped it on her slim white body.

'Did I make you wait, dear?' she said, with a curious leer. 'I am the keener for the sport, be sure!'

She took the faithless talisman from her hat. It was a little square of vellum, written upon in black. She took a hairpin from her head, pierced the talisman, and drove the pin into the girl's thigh.

'They must have blood,' said she. 'Now see how I will turn the blue to red! Come! don't wince; you haven't had it for a month.'

Then her ivory arm slid like a serpent from the furs, and with the cutting whip she struck young Margaret between the shoulders.

A shriek rang out: its only echo was Patricia's laugh, childlike, icy, devilish.

She struck again and again. Great weals of purple stood on the girl's back; froth tinged with blood came from her mouth, for she had bitten her lips and tongue in agony.

Patricia grew warm and rosy – exquisitely beautiful. Her babe-breasts heaved; her lips parted; her whole body and soul seemed lapped in ecstasy.

'I wish you were Geoffrey, girlie!' she panted.

Then the skin burst. Raw flesh oozed blood that dribbled down Margaret's back.

Still the fair maid struck and struck in the silence, until the tiny rivulets met and waxed great and touched the talisman. She threw the bloody whalebone into a corner, and went upon her knees. She kissed her friend; she kissed the talisman; and again kissed the girl, the warm blood staining her pure lips.

She took the talisman, and hid it in her bosom. Last of all she loosened the cords, and Margaret sank in a heap to the floor. Patricia threw furs over her and rolled her up in them; brought wine, and poured it down her throat. She smiled, kindly, like a sister.

'Sleep now a while, sweetheart!' she whispered, and kissed her forehead.

It was a very demure and self-possessed little maiden that made dinner lively for poor Geoffrey, who was thinking over his mistake.

Patricia's old aunt, who kept house for her, smiled on the flirtation. It was not by accident that she left them alone sitting over the great fire.

'Poor Margaret has her rheumatism again,' she explained innocently; 'I must go and see how she is. Loyal Margaret!'

So it happened that Geoffrey lost his head. 'The ivy is strong enough' (she had whispered, ere their first kiss had hardly died). 'Before the moon is up, be sure!' and glided off just as the aunt returned.

Eyre excused himself; half a mile from the house he left his horse to his man to lead home, and ten minutes later was groping for Patricia in the dark.

White as a lily in body and soul, she took him in her arms.

Awaking as from death, he suddenly cried out, 'Oh God! What is it? Oh my God! my God! Patricia! Your body! Your body!'

'Yours!' she cooed.

'Why, you're all hairy!' he cried. 'And the scent! the scent!'

From without came sharp and resonant the yap of a hound as the moon rose.

Patricia put her hands to her body. He was telling the truth. 'The Visitor!' she screamed once with fright, and was silent. He switched the light on, and she screamed again.

There was a savage lust upon his face.

'This afternoon,' he cried, 'you called me a dog. I looked like a dog and thought like a dog; and, by God! I am a dog. I'll act like a dog then!'

Obedient to some strange instinct, she dived from the bed for the window.

But he was on her; his teeth met in her throat.

In the morning they found the dead bodies of both hound and fox – but how did that explain the wonderful elopement of Lord Eyre and Miss Fleming? For neither of them were ever seen again.

I think Margaret understands; in the Convent which she rules today there hangs beside a blood-stained cutting-whip the silver model of a fox, with the inscription:

PATRICIA MARGARITÆ VULPIS VULPEM DEDIT.[1]

---

[1] [Patricia gave a fox's fox to Margaret.]

The Electric Silence

{This parable is a synopsis of *The Temple of Solomon the King*, with which it may be collated.—Ed.}

I waited for news that my heart beat. The severing night was between me and my love. There was no god of sleep; sleep were traitor. I sought to praise my love, and to lament the hours that divided us; and I could not. Therefore I wrote down the story of my life.

And it is this:

* * *

Gilded and painted to hide its worm-eaten planks, my pleasure-boat was foundering.[1] I cursed the treachery of the workmen, and resolved to trust myself to my own arms rather than to abide any longer therein.

No sooner had I taken off my clothes and plunged into the river than I perceived that it was now become dark. On the one hand glowed a star,[2] curious indeed, but of no great brightness, and promising but little; while on the other was a sombre and fantastic lamp,[3] whose fascination was its horror.

If I swam lazily towards either of these, it was because their light, confused and difficult on the one part, and tenebrous on the other, was yet light in comparison with that aimless and abiding gloom which had now settled upon the bosom of the river.[4] And these lamps were above the river, children of a nobler element. And in the river is the great Leviathan that devours men.[5]

---

[1] 1897.
[2] Alchemy.
[3] Black Magic.
[4] Life.
[5] Death.

But before I had come within the sphere of attraction of either of these, suddenly mine eyes were gladdened with a marvellous vision. Infinitely far off, as it seemed, a ray of sunlight shot through the Saturnine gloom of the skies, and lit the surface of the water. And then I perceived that upon the river there floated, within that small circle of light, an ark, or as it might be, a coffin. Then looking up into that pierced cloud I saw within the light a certain house surrounded by a grove. Within, all was dark; yet from it proceeded a ray as silvery as the first ray was golden.[1]

And I desired ardently to enter that house. Yet, having no wings, the task appeared beyond my human force. Then the heavens closed as suddenly as they had opened, and I was left darkling. Yet I had this candle of hope, that within the ark, could I reach it, might be some help of knowledge or power whereby that house might be attained.

So I swam steadily toward, though with some fear, for the eddies in that great stream were numerous, and my sole guide was a slender snake of light that moved upon the water.

Or so it appeared; for I have since discovered that I had an interior sense of direction as trusty as the mariner's compass; so that, though I knew it not, it was never possible for me to go astray.

Now as I swam I came upon one[2] floundering and spluttering in the stream, who with mighty puffings urged me to continue.

For but a little way beyond us (quoth he) is a mighty swimmer and a dexterous.

So with a mighty effort my comrade put forth all his strength, and we gained upon this one, and greeted him.

Thereupon he (and he was a goodly man, and fair)[3] did most heartily welcome me as a fellow-traveller to that house, and confirmed me in my belief that the ark did indeed hold the secret of the way thereto. And as for the guide that might convey us through the darkness and the tumult of the stream, he spoke (something darkly) of one appointed,[4] and more clearly that he was aware of divers marks upon the way; for, said he, to them that view it from above this trackless waste of water is mapped out and charted with a perfect science.

'Behold!' quoth he. And at that moment was there a glimmer just before me of a white shining triangle,[5] and what was most strange, rather

---

[1] Sanctuary described by von Eckartshausen.
[2] Julian L. Baker.
[3] George Cecil Jones.
[4] The Holy Guardian Angel.
[5] $\triangle$ symbol of G∴D∴.

an impression than a vision of a man that hung upon a gibbet by one heel. 'This,' said the fair man, 'is a most notable sign that we travel the right road.'

Now by the light of the triangle I perceived another wonder; for my friend was not swimming as I was in the stream, but was borne by a boat, frail indeed, yet sufficient. Within this shallop or cockleshell he pulled me, and set me at the bench. Then (still by the light of the triangle) I saw a dark man[1] at the thwart, rowing a strong stroke.

We pulled on almost in silence; for when I asked of the fair man his name he answered me only 'I wish to know,'[2] and of the dark man 'I wish it were light,'[3] the first clearly a confession of ignorance, the second a patent evasion; which things discomforted me much.

Yet we progressed evenly and rapidly, and were mightily cheered after a while to see just a flash of lightning[4] sundering two dark clouds; next a pale crescent,[5] heavy and slow, yet silvered; next, as if it had dropped from the stars, an unicorn[6] galloped past us and was gone ere we could fix it; next a tall lighthouse[7] upon the water.

'Here,' said the dark man my comrade, 'is a pleasant place for refreshment before we turn to the further journey.'

As he spoke, although no sun was visible, a mighty rainbow[8] appeared, and crowned the tower. I cried out joyfully, 'The bow of promise,' but they answered nothing. And at that I understood that they had travelled further already, and were but returned for an hour to succour me who had no boat.

Seven days[9] then we remained in the tower, eating and drinking. Also in my sleep I had many marvellous dreams,[10] of greater sustenance than sleep itself. And there was given unto me by my fair brother (for so I may now call him) a little book,[11] wherein it was written how a man might build himself a shallop, and have for steersman one appointed thereunto.

---

[1] Allan Bennett.
[2] 'I wish to know.' Volo Noscere—[George Cecil] Jones' motto.
[3] 'I wish it were light.' Iehi Aour—Allan [Bennett]'s motto.
[4] $1° = 10°$.
[5] $2° = 9°$.
[6] $3° = 8°$.
[7] $4° = 7°$.
[8] *Pharos Illuminans*, bow of קוב. [The illuminating lighthouse, bow of the crown.]
[9] Months.
[10] Astral visions.
[11] [*The Book of the Sacred Magic of*] *Abra-Melin* [*the Mage*, tr. S.L. MacGregor Mathers (1898)].

This then I laboured to build, and the toil was great. Moreover, certain vile fish[1] rose from the water, and with their fins beat upon the planks of my boat, that I might not end it.

However, at last I had it perfect, and was about to set sail at dawn. But first the dark man my brother departed from us, and went his way.[2] And then the old man[3] of the tower took me aside and offered me a seat at the funeral feast of his master. And although I verily believe that this old man was a rogue, a very knavish fellow, and a sot, yet in that funeral[4] I took great pleasure. For the gentlest perfume was borne upon the breeze, and the air was lit with faint electric flames that gathered themselves into a hill of light. So I, being lifted up, and my heart overflowing, came into the funeral chamber that was exceeding bright, and there was the table for the feast, and beneath it the coffin wherein lay the body of the master. There too I saw barren wood bear roses, and I heard the voice of the master. After that I was shewn all the kingdoms of the world[5] in a moment of time, and many other things of great use and beauty.

Then I took my leave of the old man of the tower, and boarded the shallop that I had made, when he cried out piteously that he feared earthquake,[6] and asked me for my aid.

So with a heart both heavy and light I abandoned my shallop and the dreadful labour of its fashioning, and came back to him.

Then came earthquake as he had foreseen; and he and the boats also were swallowed up. In the tidal wave of the earthquake I was borne far away,[7] even from the fair man my brother; and in the darkness he was lost to me. I knew not even whether he had perished.

But fashioning a raft from the loose planks of the wreckage, I made shift to paddle.[8] The ark was invisible, and I had no more memory thereof, so turned away was I and absorbed in the bright signs upon the way. And now my raft was like to sink, and my arms were exceeding weary, when a voice sounded but a little above me: 'Enter the ark!'[9]

---

[1] The demons.
[2] To Ceylon.
[3] [S. L. MacGregor] Mathers.
[4] $5° = 6°$.
[5] *Minutum Mundum*, etc.
[6] The row in the Order.
[7] To Mexico.
[8] I practised Magick.
[9] Meditation.

And I looked up and beheld a bearded man,[1] mighty, with the signs of labour and long journeying writ upon him. I knew him; and for this reason was I much amazed, for I had believed him far from that place.[2] But taking my hand he drew me not without pain into the ark. Here (quoth he) forget all that thou hast seen and heard;[3] for in this ark they are not lawful.

So I obeyed him, else I had drawn after me the raft that had brought me thither.

Then he questioned me, saying: 'What lieth above the ark?'

And I answered him: 'The house of the silver ray,[4] that is lighted by the ray of gold.'

He: 'How many roofs hath the ark?'

I: 'One.'

He: 'Thou must pass through this one. Yet thou lookest eagerly upon the four walls of the ark.'

I: 'I seek a door.'

He: 'The door is in the roof.'

I: 'Lead me to it, I pray thee!'

He: 'Fix thine eyes upon it.'

I: 'Sir, I will. Yet I pray thee to tell me thy name.'

He: 'Thou didst know it of old, didst thou not?'

I: 'The son of the mountain?'[5]

He: 'The Stone of the Crossways.'

I: 'It is enough. Let me fix mine eye upon the door.'

He: 'It is well.'

Then I obeyed him, and in that obedience forgot him. For though mine eye wandered often, and although once the planks beneath me threatened to give way and plunge me once more into the stream,[6] yet I strove as a man may.

Then,[7] mine eye being accustomed to the gloom, I beheld by my side, yet a little above me, the dark man my brother. Him I greeted most gladly, and told him of the earthquake. Whereat he sighed heavily.

'Brother,' quoth I, 'canst thou now tell me thy name?'

---

[1] [Oscar] Eckenstein.
[2] I didn't know he was an adept.
[3] I.e., my G∴ D∴ work.
[4] $8° = 3°$.
[5] Oscar Eckenstein.
[6] The *Alice* episode.
[7] In Ceylon.

But he only answered me: 'It is a pity!'[1]

And with that I returned to my task, and he guided me therein with his counsel and example. Yet in the ark the gloom is fierce; the river without is but twilight, wherein shadows are free; within is darkness itself, and the essence and quintessence of darkness.

In this terrific silence I abode for very long; then for an instant that seemed longer than many lives the sun of heaven[2] broke in and smote mine eye, so that I fell backward nigh fainting. But he bade me be of good cheer and return to the task. I obeyed; and behold! again the sun, and behind the sun a glimpse of one appointed equally to be hidden and to be seen, each as may be fitting.

But the brightness of the sun and its heat dazzled me and scorched me. My members refused to obey; and I slid backward into the great stream that was here so icy cold, and it refreshed me and comforted me.[3]

Now then I was minded to enter again the ark when there flew unto me, I wot not whence, a dove,[4] and perched upon my shoulder. And thus I swam for a while, and the waters of the stream were soft and warm, caressing me.

Yet I felt that this aimless drifting was enervating my limbs; so I gathered some stray planks of my raft—for they still floated round the ark—and began half playfully to paddle, with what purpose I cannot tell.[5]

And so it was ordered that the dove flew to me with an oak-leaf in its beak.[6]

Thereat I was silent. But gazing eagerly thereon, I beheld one appointed, and I understood that the oak-leaf was sent from the House.

Then I took counsel of him who is to this end appointed, and with his own hand he brought to me a champak-blossom, a mustard-seed, and again an oak-leaf.[7]

And these I treasured in my bosom, though I hardly knew wherefore. Nor could I understand what purpose they should serve, save darkly. And seeing this, the dove came to me again bearing an olive-branch;[8]

---

[1] Ananda Metteyya.
[2] *Dhyāna* Oct. 1902.
[3] I gave up med[itation] and went to Chogo Ri.
[4] Rose [Crowley].
[5] 1904.
[6] Revelation of Eq[uino]x of the Gods.
[7] *Liber Legis*. Nuit. Hadit. Ra Hoor Khuit.
[8] The baby [Nuit Crowley].

and with this I was so mightily pleased that for a while I forgot all else, and swam lustily in the stream for my pleasure.

But now came a current of ice-cold water and enwrapped me; and when I looked, it bore spots of blood upon it.[1] Then I went hastily into the ark that was ever near by; and, climbing to the roof by the ladder that I had before made, looked through. And all the sky was a hurricane, a madness of storm.[2]

Now in my eagerness I had approached closely to the roof, so that the storm whirled me away into itself. One might say that I was the storm.[3] And when I came to myself[4] I was floating upon the bosom of the river, borne by that very bark that once I had built myself in the lighthouse. And in the storm I had lost my hair and beard; for the wind had torn all out by the root. So that I heard a voice saying, 'It is a babe upon the waters.' And looking at the bark, I found it refashioned by him that is appointed to refashion. For it had planks of my old shallop, and planks also of the ark, and it was shaped like a cradle rather than like a boat. And I heard the voice of one appointed to speak saying: 'Behold thou me!' And I could not. Nevertheless I gazed earnestly, and paddled in the direction of the sound.

While this was a-doing suddenly the river fell in a cataract. And I looked for the olive-branch, and it was withered, and sunk beneath the stream.[5] And I looked for the dove, and it was wrapped round with a most hideous serpent.[6] And I was helpless. In the end he devoured that rose-winged companion of my journey, and went seeking a new prey.

Now in this cataract I had most surely been wrecked but that I clung tightly to the boat. This indeed floated as serenely as if it had been upon the still waters of a lake; and when I had a little plucked up courage,[7] I saw sitting at the helm him that is appointed to steer; I saw him face to face.

This then endured for a space; and with his aid I began ship-building. 'For' (said he) 'there are many that swim, and find no boats. Be it thy task to aid them.'

Of my journey to the House he spake nothing. But in the ship-building came the fair man my brother to my help; and one evening as

---

[1] Kangchenjunga accident.
[2] Babe of the Abyss.
[3] Experience.
[4] Back to Holy Guardian Angel Work.
[5] Death of the baby.
[6] Rose [Crowley] a dipsomaniac.
[7] Oct. 1906.

we sate at meat he said: 'May it please you to enter the House; for there is prepared for you a goodly bedchamber.' But I would not at that time; for I was ashamed, being unclothed,[1] not understanding that in the House robes are provided by him that is appointed to provide them.

Thus we laboured, and built many fair shallops upon the model of that wherein we sailed.[2] In all these there was not one splinter of wood too much, or too little; and there was no ornament; and neither paint nor varnish covered the planks, for they were planks of a tree that cometh neither from the East nor from the West. But the sails were of gold tissue, very brave, with figures inwoven.

Now at last the time being come, did I take my chamber in the House.[3] And upon the secret things that were there shown to me I ponder yet; so that in this place I shall make no mention of them. But this treasure will I give out, that everything noble in that House seemeth vile to them that are swimming in the stream; and everything vile to them appeareth noble. Thus they endure not the delicate stuffs with rough and impure handling; and the rubbish they carry away with them, and devour. Thus wisely hath the master of the House ordained.

Now of the silver radiance that issueth from the darkness of the House I will say nothing; nor of the golden ray that illuminateth the darkness of the House.

But for the sake of one that may come to share my bed-chamber will I speak of the last adventure.

Upon the breast of the river came a wild swan,[4] singing, and for a moment rested upon mine image reflected in the water. And I said: 'Come up hither.'

And the wild swan said: 'How shall I come up thither?'

I: 'I will guide thee.'

The Swan: 'Who art thou?'

I: 'My Father is the keeper of the King's Cup; I have prepared a little ship wherein I may go my journeys upon the great river.

'Who will draw it?'

The Swan: 'I will draw it.'

So we set forth together; and of the horrible tempests that arose it is unworthy discourse.[5] And of what followed after is discourse unprofitable; but the wild swan still guides my ship.

---

[1] $8° = 3°$ grade offered and refused.
[2] The sacred books and rituals.
[3] $8° = 3°$ accepted.
[4] Leila Waddell.
[5] Rites of Eleusis row.

And the end shall be as is appointed by the master of the House; but this I know, that this ship is the King's ship. And in my bosom are the champak-blossom, and the mustard seed, and the oak-leaf, more lovely than before.

And upon us watcheth ever he that is appointed to watch.

And the wild swan sings ever; and my heart sings ever.

* * *

Now then I had laid aside the pen, and a voice cried: Write!

Fear not!

Turn not aside!

Is it not written that Sorrow may endure for a night, but joy cometh in the morning?

Sleep therefore in peace and in faith: shall he not watch whose eye hath no eyelid, who to this end is appointed?

And my heart answered: Amen!

The Ordeal of Ida Pendragon

I

The Red Hour

There was myrrh in the honey of the smile with which Edgar Rolles turned from the façade of the Panthéon. '*Aux grands hommes la patrie reconnaissante*'[1] – he reflected that the grateful fatherland never gives her great men anything but a tomb.

Then the full blast of it struck him. The Gargantuan jest! The solemn ass that had devised the motto; the labourious ass that had put it up there; the admiring asses that had warmed their skinny souls at the false fire of its pompous sentimentality.

Perhaps he was the first to see the joke! He rocked and reeled with laughter – to find himself caught, as he stumbled against a table, in the sturdy arms of a solidly built young woman, who – he had in her a glance – joined in Celtic harmony the robust brutality of the peasant to the decadent refinement of the latter Greek. The face of a Bacchanal, even of a satyr, perhaps; but a satyr of Raphael; the face of a madonna, perhaps; but a madonna of Rodin. Besides this, she was seductive, alluring, a Messalina rather than an Aspasia. *Chienne de race!*[2] She was young, and her lips rather sneered than smiled, rather gloated than sneered. One instinctively muttered the word cannibal. She had a perfect and perverse enjoyment of life, a perfect and perverse contempt of life; the contempt of the philosopher, the enjoyment of the wallowing pig. *Porcus e grege Epicuri.*[3]

---

[1] [To its great men, a grateful fatherland.]
[2] [Bitch of the breed!]
[3] [A pig from the herd of Epicurus.]

This much Edgar Rolles smelt rather than saw; for as he turned to her, he caught her eyes. They were the eyes of an enthusiast, of a saint, of an ascetic – but of a saint who, strong in his agony through faith and hope and love, still endures the Dark Night of the Soul.

'You shall lunch with me, nice boy' (she said), 'and beg my pardon for your stumble, and pay for your lunch by telling me what drives you mad with laughter at the sight of the Panthéon. Is it "*L'homme aux trois sous*"?'[1] For so the irreverent Frenchman, mindful of his daily need, calls Rodin's *Le Penseur*.

'Mademoiselle,' said Rolles, 'I accept your kind invitation; I abandon the Church for the Tavern.' They turned into the Taverne du Panthéon, threading their way through the professors and their mistresses, a clever, incurious, domestic, fascinating crowd.

'I kiss your hands and your feet, and I will tell you the joke before lunch; so that you may repent in time if it is not amusing. In your ear, enchantress! The truth is – I am a great man.'

She saw it in a flash. 'Then, my friend, I must bury you!'

'In your hair!' he cried. She had huge rolling masses of brown-bronze hair, as if a great sculptor had wished to immortalise the sea in storm.

'Anoint me first,' he added, with a low sob, suddenly clairvoyant of some vision of Christ and Magdalene.

'Need you die?' They were seated, and her hand fell on his lap. 'Great men die never.'

'Nor kind words,' he retorted. 'You have flattered me; *tu veux me perdre*.'[2] His English had no equivalent. She gave a little shiver.

'What do you want?' he said, with the man's alarm when he at last meets the woman he may be able to love.

'Your body and soul,' she answered solemnly; her eyes sank into his, like a dagger into the belly of a faithless Kabyle woman. 'But beyond that, your secret! You know life, yet you can laugh from a mad heart!'

'It is easily said. I am going to London tomorrow. There they will make me bankrupt, because I love my neighbour better than myself, and prosecute me for blasphemy and indecency, because I uttered a few simple truths that everybody knows.'

'Why, my friend, you will be famous!' she cried. '*Aux grands hommes la patrie reconnaissante!*'

---

[1] [The man with three cents.]
[2] [You want to ruin me.]

'Probably,' said he. 'Already I run to a full page in the American papers, my name intimately coupled with that of a duke's daughter whom I have never seen.'

'Good, good!' she agreed – 'so much for fame. But are you really great? Your laughter was better than Zarathustra! What is your real secret? Why did you love your neighbour? Why did you speak the truth? How did you come to know anything at all well enough to be able to laugh as you laughed! Such abandonment to mirth implies a standard of seriousness unshakable.'

'You are a witch,' said he. 'It is sorcery to know that I have a secret. But to discover it you must be an adept.'

'I know this,' she answered, making a secret sign.

'This,' he retorted, with the *mano in fica*.[1]

'If you can laugh at me,' she said, 'you must indeed be a great man!'

'Know,' said he pompously, 'that you speak to an Absolute Grand Patriarch of the Rite of Mizraim.'

'A button!' she laughed back. 'I was born to undo them. So I always wear laced boots.'

'True enough,' said Edgar Rolles. 'I will take you seriously then. If you really understand the sign you gave me, you know that the *mano in fica* is but a caricature of the answer to it. Why are you painted and perfumed?'

'Because I am ambitious, may I not be vicious?' she rimed. 'If I see anyone that seems likely to amuse me, I try and amuse him – or her,' she laughed. 'Is not that the Golden Rule?'

'Well,' said Edgar hesitatingly, 'well …'

'I am so abstemious, so self-restrained, that I fear the reproach of the ascetic. Love is my balancing-pole.' She threw her arm round his neck, and her mouth shuddered on his in a long, deliberate, skilful kiss.

'Art?' sighed he, fallen back half fainting in his seat.

'Art concealed'; she glowed, radiant, intoxicated with her own enthusiasm.

'Yes,' he agreed, 'consummate art!'

'And to all arts there is but One summit!' continued the girl.

'You are a *nymphomane*,' he said; 'your aspiration is the lie you tell yourself.'

She struck him across the face. 'Devil!' she cried, so loud that even in the Taverne Panthéon folk looked up and laughed, 'have I not heard that from conscience since I was sixteen? A blow is the one answer possible.'

'A blow is but your male desire,' he said, unmoved.

---

[1] [The hand in the shape of a fig.]

'How shall I prove my truth?' she sobbed, disquieted and angry.

'Live it down, little girl,' he said kindly. 'Trust me; I will prove you and justify you. Afterwards!'

'Do you think? – now—?' she began indignantly.

'I know it,' said he. 'In the grey light, tomorrow, we will talk.'

She suddenly felt chill and afraid. 'I am not ready,' she said; 'I am not worthy …'

'It is to prove you worthy,' said he, 'that I was sent to you.'

'Well, God aid me,' said the girl. She was serious and almost sobbing, her face drawn and white beneath its paint. Her emotion added piquancy to her voluptuousness, pathos to her brute appeal.

'At this moment, of all moments? How should I find you? It was one chance in a million million.'

Edgar lifted the knife that lay by his side. There was a fly on the tablecloth. Adroit and salmon-swift, he cut it fairly in half. 'Bad luck on the fly?' he laughed. 'But I did it. Chance only means ignorance of causes.'

'Then you believe in the Brothers?'

'As I revel in the kisses of your mouth,' said the boy, crushing her face against his.

A rich gladness filled her eyes, moist gladness; one might say the first gush of an artesian well amid the seas of sand.

'Well,' quoth she, cheerful and brisk, to let the mask fall on her blushing soul, 'we have got through six dozen oysters and a devil of a lot of Burgundy.… I wonder if I am hungry!' She looked him between the eyes.

'Hors d'œuvres!' said Edgar. 'I have a box for the Sam Hall fight.'

'Oh do take me,' she panted. 'Will he beat Joe Marie?' she added, with a touch of anxiety. 'He has the weight, and the experience, and the record.'

'Fools are betting he will. My money is on the man with three years younger, six inches taller, and twelve inches longer reach to his credit. And a twenty-four times harder skull.'

'It's his skin I love.'

'The only thing a woman ever can love.'

'And his activity.'

'Exactly. You cannot understand Being, which is Peace.'

'Don't! You are near *my* secret, now.'

'Wait till the grey hours!'

She dropped three napoleons on the plate, and disdaining to wait for the change, took Edgar's arm in hers. They hailed a fiacre.

'By the way, I don't know your name,' he began, as they clattered down the Boul' Mich'.

'Ida Pendragon. But call me Poppy, because my lips are red, because I give sleep, and death!'

A pause. 'And your name, nice boy?'

'Edgar Rolles – you may call me Monkshood.'

'What – *the* Edgar Rolles?'

'As ever is.'

'Oh, they'll hang you! They'll certainly hang you! for that last book of yours…. But you shall hang here first.' Her long white fingers went to her neck, like a cuttle-fish feeling for its prey. Her eyes closed: her throat worked convulsively for a moment. Rolles too leaned back, pale with excitement. He drank the fresh air. Then, like a man shot, he lifted himself and fell forward, his head in the nest of her bosom.

'Please sit up and behave sensibly, Mr Rolles!' was the next word that fell on his ears. 'We are crossing the Seine. Passion may not pass the gloomy river; here stalks Vice, and the Englishman on its heels. The very coffee *sent son Anglais*.'[1]

'*Et les femmes*,'[2] muttered Edgar.

She slapped his hand half fiercely.

'It's Poster Art of immorality.'

'I remember going with an American girl to the Guignol once. They played a comedy one could have acted in a Sunday-school in Glasgow; but Verro-nika, as they called her, who didn't understand a word of French, said the atmosphere was one of the most awful lust. Poor girl! she had paid a lot to see Yurrup and its wickedness. I had not the heart to undeceive her.'

'You sympathised, and offered to take her away?'

'Of course.'

'And she preferred to stay?'

'Of course.'

'Here's the Cirque, anyhow.'

'We'll hope for a clean fight.'

The second round was just over as they took their seats. Sam Hall was solid and furious, looking an ounce or two overtrained; Joe Marie looked hardly human, his black skin gleaming, his arms so long as to seem almost disproportionate. He seemed apathetic; he reminded one of India rubber.

---

[1] [Savours of its Englishness.]
[2] [And the women.]

It was not till the sixth round that any warm exchanges took place. Then Ida sat up. Joe had sent a sharp upper cut to the Englishman's lip. She dug her nails into Rolles' hand, that lay idly on her knee. Sam Hall returned a blow on the heart that sent the negro staggering across the ring. He was after him like a flash, thinking to finish the fight; but the black countered unexpectedly hard, and the round finished in a clinch.

In the seventh round both men seemed cautious and afraid of punishment. Joe Marie, in particular, seemed half asleep. The lazy grace of his feints was admirable; he was tiring the Englishman, and paying nothing for the advantage.

In the ninth round Sam Hall reached his eye; but he only laughed, and leapt at his opponent, rushing him to the ropes despite the extra stone and a half. In the furious exchanges both men gave and took a great deal of punishment. In a sense, it was bad boxing.

The tenth round showed Joe Marie awake at last. He led repeatedly, and thrice got home on the white man's face.

Ida was rubbing her body against Edgar's like a cat. 'He is like a black leopard,' she purred. 'Is anything in the world so beautiful as that lithe black body?'

'I have seen blood in the sunlight on a bull's shoulder,' replied Rolles.

'I love to see the pure animal beat the mere brute. White men ought not to fight: they ought to think, and do lovely physical things, things gracious and of good report.'

'Ida! my Ida! Could you see your nostrils twitching! I can imagine you fighting with all their fierceness, incapable of keeping to the rules of boxing.'

'I hate you,' she said. 'In everything you see—'

'Your lust of blood,' he answered gravely.

'It is true,' said Ida slowly. 'There is no light of battle in your eye. You see it as a picture.'

'It is a hieroglyph.'

'But it is a fight!'

'I do not believe in fights. I only believe in beauty.'

'Oh how true, how right your are! How noble!' She hid her face in her hands and began to cry to herself. 'I see! I see! That is how God must see the Universe, or He could never tolerate such cruelty, such idiotcy, ineptitude.'

'Exactly. Suppose now that the world is only symbol – I had rather say sacrament – suppose for example that all these stars swimming in boundless æther are but corpuscles in the blood of some toy terrier of the Creator.'

'You frighten me. I don't want to suppose.'

'Think of the eternal battles of hæmoglobin, oxyhæmoglobin, carboxyhæmoglobin in our blood. It is the same idea. Do we express sympathy for the fallen? Have we a stop-the-war party? On the contrary, we take good care that these murderous conflicts shall go on. So when you call the God to whom you aspire "The Compassionate," "The Merciful," pray be very careful as to exactly what you mean!'

'I am cold. I am frightened. The world has fallen away from me. Take me away. Put me into the ordeal; I have nothing more to lose.'

'In the grey hours of the morn.'

But the crowd was already on its feet, cheering. Joe Marie had fallen on his opponent, now too weak to counter or to guard, and smashed him here, there, and everywhere. It was as one-sided as a man beating a carpet. Twice he knocked him through the ropes. The first time he rose unsteadily, only to fall instantly. The second time his friends, careless of the rules, helped him to rise. A mistaken kindness; the black rushed him round the ring under a hail of pitiless blows, and with a last smashing drive flung him clean through the ropes out of the ring before the referee had time to stop the fight.

Edgar Rolles drove Ida Pendragon back to his studio in Montparnasse. All the way she clung to him, sobbing like a child. He sat very still, save to caress her hair from which the turban had fallen. 'It is the victory of Essence over Form,' he mused, 'of Matter over Motion. Woman is Form, and thinks Form is Being. Oh my God!' he started up. 'I am a man. Suppose I, who am Being, think Being is Form! ... I cannot even attach a meaning to the phrase! I am blinder than shorn Samson. Both must be equal, equally true, equally false, in His eyes wherein all is false and true, He being beyond them. Only the brains of a child – of The Child – can grasp it. "Except ye become as little children, ye cannot enter the Kingdom of Heaven!" I am blinder than shorn Samson! ... Well, I'm in charge of Delilah at present, and here's the House where we don't admit Philistines! Get up, little girl!'

He lifted her gently from the fiacre and paid the driver. 'Stamp!' said he, 'stamp like Dr Johnson! The ground is firm.'

'*E pur si muove*,'[1] murmured she, and clung (O illogical sex!) still closer to his arm.

---

[1] [And yet it moves.]

2

The Grey Hour

'To resume,' observed Rolles as he removed the tea-tray, 'since you have done no prescribed practises (wicked little sister!) you cannot banish the body by bidding it keep silence. So it must be banished by exhaustion, and the spirit awakened by a sevenfold dose of the Elixir.'

'Have you the Elixir?' she asked, rather awed.

'It is entrusted to me,' he answered simply. 'To this laudable end I have appointed a sufficiency of Bisque Kadosh at the Café Riche, followed by Homard Cardinal and Truffes au champagne. With a savoury of my own invention. The Truffes au champagne of the Café Riche are more to be desired than all the hashish dreams of all the wicked, and than all the divine dreams of all the good. We shall walk there, and drive back. This incense shall be kindled, and this lamp left burning.'

He took a strange object from a locked cabinet. It had flowered chased pipes of gold, copper and platinum, coiling about an egg of crystal. The three snakes met just above the egg, as if to bite or to kiss. Rolles filled the egg with a pale blue liquid from a Venetian flask, then pressed the heads of the serpents just a little closer together. Instantly a coruscating flame leapt between them, minute, dazzling, radiant. It continued to burn with a low hissing noise rarely interrupted by a dry crackle.

'It is well,' said Rolles, 'let us depart.'

Ida Pendragon had not said a word. She put on her hat and followed to the door as fatalistically as the condemned man walks to the gallows. She had passed through anticipation; she was content to await what might be.

At the door she whispered, hushed in awe of the real silence of the room with its monotonous hiss, in his ear. 'You have the Lamp. I almost begin to wonder if you have not the Ring!'

'"This is a secret sign,"' he quoted, '"and thou shalt not disclose it unto the profane." Tonight yours be the ring – the Eternal Ring, the Serpent to twine about my heart.'

'Ah! could I crush it!'

He closed the door. Like a priest celebrating his first high mass he led her through Paris. Neither spoke. Only as they mounted the steps of the Café he took her arm and said, sharply and sternly: 'Attention! From this moment I am Edgar Rolles, and you are Ida Pendragon. No more: not a thought of our real relation. Man and woman, if you will; beasts in the jungle, if you will; flowers by the wayside, if you will; but nothing more. Else you will not only fail in the ordeal, but you will be swept aside out of the Path. You were in greater danger than you knew this afternoon; you will yet pay the price.'

'I understand,' she said. 'You devil! I love you.'

'And I love every inch of your white body!'

They ran laughing arm in arm through the swing doors.

* * *

Edgar Rolles sat curled up Hindu fashion on his bed. The sacred lamp still hissed. At his side lay Ida, her arms stretched out cruciform. She hardly breathed; there was no colour in her face. One would have said the corpse of a martyred virgin. On her white body its own purity hovered like a veil.

Edgar Rolles watched the lamp, erect, attentive. It went out. Hardly a hint of grey filtered through the blackness. In his hands he held two threads. 'One is black, and one is white,' he mused, 'and only God knows which is which. So only God knows what is sin. In our darkness we who presume to declare it are liars – charlatans, groping quacks at the best. Will the sun never dawn? For us on whom the lightning of ecstasy hath flashed for a moment – "much may be seen by its light" – the light of the tempest. But the Light of the Silver Star? Oh, my Brothers' (he began to speak aloud) 'give me wisdom as you have given me understanding! Knowledge and grace and power? These are nothing and less than nothing. Is not this a precious thing that you have given into my charge? Am not I too young among you to bear so wonderful a burden? It is the first time that I have dared so far. The Abyss! The Razor-Edge! Frail bridge and sharp! Yet is it not a ray of the Evening Star, a ray of Venus, of the Love Supernal! ...

'Can I tell black from white? It seems I can – and then the certainty flickers, and I doubt. I doubt. I am always doubting. Perhaps a wise man grows angry, and declares his will. "It shall be what o'clock I say it is," or ... see! I lay the threads on her white breast. No doubt remains.'

Then clear and loud: '*Ave Soror!*'[1]

The girl, as it seemed mechanically, murmured the words '*Rosæ Rubeæ.*'[2]

'*Et Aureæ Crucis,*'[3] he rejoined.

Then together, very slowly and distinctly: '*Benedictus sit Dominus Deus Noster qui nobis dedit signum.*'[4]

---

[1] [Hail, sister!']

[2] [Of the Red Rose.]

[3] [And of the Gold Cross.]

[4] [Blessed be the Lord Our God who gave us the sign.]

It seemed hardly possible that her voice joined his. The lips hardly moved; it was as if an interior voice spoke in her heart. Yet the room was suddenly filled with a pale green light – or was it rosy? – or was it golden? – or was it like the moon? That was the strange thing about it. To every name one put to it an inward voice answered: No, not that; like that, but not quite that. Luminous, spectral, cloudy, shimmering – it was all these, and something more.

He placed his hand upon the girl's forehead.

'Are you perfectly awake?'

'I am awake, *frater*.'[1]

'Can you give me the sign of your grade?'

'I must not move. But I am poised for diving, *frater*.'

'The word?'

Haltingly came the answer: 'Ar – ar – it – a.'

'One is His beginning; one is His individuality; His permutation one. Do not forget it, little sister.'

'Are you ready?'

'I am ready. Farewell – farewell for ever!'

'Farewell.'

He took his signet-ring, and pressed a spring. The bezel opened and disclosed a small jewelled wheel, divided into many compartments. He pressed a second spring. The wheel began to revolve, and in the silence sang a tiny tune. It was a faint tinkle, like a distant cow-bell, or like a chime heard far off, heard from the snow. There was an icy quality in the note.

'Where are you?'

'I – I—' she broke off.

His eyes lit with joy.

'I am in the sand; I am buried to the waist in the sand. I see nothing but sand.'

His face fell again.

'What is sand?' he asked.

'Oh – just sand, you know. Leagues and leagues of sand; like a great bowl of sand.'

'But what is sand?'

'Sand – oh! sand is God, I suppose.' There was a patience and weariness in her voice, as of one who has suffered long and is at rest, or convalescent.

'And who are you?'

---

[1] [Brother.]

She did not answer the question. 'Now I see sky,' she said. 'Sky is God, too, I think.'

'Then do you see God?'

'Oh no! I think I am God, somehow. It is all like it was before, long ago. I was once a spider in the sand. God is a spider; the Universe is flies. I am a fly, too.... And now the desert is full of flies.'

Rolles bit his lip; his face was drawn with pain. At that moment he looked an old man.

'Black flies,' she went on. 'Horrible white maggots. And now there are corpses. The maggots play about their mouths and eyes. There are three corpses that were God when they were alive. I killed Him. That was when I was a camel in the sand. Now there are only my bones.'

'It may be only a veil,' he muttered, not wishing her to hear. But she heard.

'It is a veil,' she said. 'But is there anything behind veils?'

'Look!'

'Only the sand.'

'Tear it down!'

'There might be Nothing behind.'

'There is Nothing behind. It is through that that you must pass.'

'This veil is God. I am a holy nun in the trance called *Rāmapurāṇa*. I am canonised. My name is on every banner. My face is worshipped by every nation. I am a pure virgin; all the others are soiled. Thought is worse than deed. All my thoughts are holy. I think. I think. I think. By the power of my thought I created the Word; and by the Word came the Worlds. I am the creator. I will write my law upon tablets of jade and onyx.'

Rolles bowed his head in silence.

'I am thought itself,' she went on quietly. 'And all thought is I. I am knowledge. All knowledge is in three. Three hundred and thirty-three. I am half the Master. I have cut him in two.'

The adept shuddered.

'That was when I was an axe. I will not be an arrow. I will be an axe....' She gave a giggle.

'I am gleeful by reason of hate.'

There was a pause.

'And I am gleeful because I am reason....'

'All reason ends in two. I have cut the Master in two.'

'Can she pass through?' wondered Edgar. 'Is it a fault to be identified so well with that which she beholds?'

'There are devils,' she cried. 'Black, naked screaming devils. They touch, and at a touch each oozes back to his slime. This slime is Chaos.'

'Ararita!' he breathed the word upon her brow.

'Don't touch me! don't touch me!' she screamed. 'I am holy! I am God! I am I!' Her face was black and distorted with sudden passion.

'It's quite different to my own experience in many ways,' thought the watcher. 'Yet – is it not the essence of all ordeal, all initiation, that it should be unexpected? Otherwise, the candidate would have passed through the gate before he approached it. Which is absurd.'

The last word must have been audible.

'Absurd!' she cried. 'Indeed, it is not absurd. It is all rational. It is you who are absurd.'

'Do you understand what you are saying?'

'No! No! I hate all who understand. I will bite them. I will bite their waists.' Dropping her voice suddenly: 'That was when I was a mouse-trap.'

'Dear God! this is like delirium.'

'Oh! go on about God. I don't mind God. I could tell you wonderful things about what I have done to God. I was a Nonconformist preacher once: I had secret sins. They were mine! Mine! How proud I was of them! Every Sunday I used to preach against the sin that I had done most in the week. There are many butterflies in the desert; ever so many more than one would think. This proves that God is good. And then, you see, there are beetles. Beetles and beetles. And scorpions. Dear little amber beasts. There! one has stung me. It is the sacrament of hate. I will sleep in a bed of scorpions and rose-leaves. Scorpions are better than thorns. Why do I wander about naked? And why do I thirst? And this torment of cold? It ought to be hot in the desert. And it isn't. Now that proves – oh yes, my cat! you shall have milk. I will strike a rock for you. Milk and honey.'

She started up suddenly, and put her hands to her face, then threw them round his neck.

'Edgar, darling!' she cried, 'your pussy has had such a dreadful dream. Come and love his girl!'

He dared not tell her that she had tried and failed, that she had come back as she set out. He flung his will into that act of mercy; his kisses ravished her into delight.

It was late morning when they woke, faint with rapture, fresh kisses blossoming on their young lips, as the sun himself lit their awakening with his love.

Only then came memory, and solemnity, and sorrow.

'I must catch the four o'clock,' he said, as he left her; 'one of these addresses always finds me. Telegraph if you need me. I would come from the ends of the earth, if I must: but you know the Brothers? When you

need me really I shall be at your shoulder. O my darling! my darling!'
he broke out, falling to tenderness, half human and half superhuman;
'how I love you! how I love you! I hate going to England.'

'Oh yes! your martyrdom! I wish I were worthy to share it.'

'God! God! why must we part? It's my fool vanity that makes me
want the martyrdom. And all the time I only want you.'

'But you're not only Edgar Rolles.'

'And when I return, be more than Ida Pendragon. Keep a stout heart,
wench!'

So, with a thousand tears and kisses, they parted. She would not come
to see him off; her self-command was weakened alike by her new love
and by the terrible ordeal that she had undergone. Her mind remembered nothing of it – such is the merciful order of things; but her soul,
beaten with rods, was sore.

So Edgar Rolles went to England to his martyrdom, with a lock of
her hair in his pocket-book; and he turned martyrdom to battle, and
battle to victory. Kingdoms have been won for an eyelash, before now.

3

The Black Hour

'Disgusting!' said Ida Pendragon. She was at the Luxembourg Gallery,
regarding a too faithful portrait of an orator addressing his constituents.
She spoke over her shoulder to the long negro, Joe Marie. His eyes
rolled, and his hands twitched, and his thick mouth grinned. He seemed
to sniff her hair. A pitiable creature – a tamed leopard. All smiles and yes!
yes! to a discourse of whose purport he had no idea.

'Realism!' she went on. 'We want truth, but we want beauty too. We
don't want what our silly eyes call truth. We want the beauty that is
seen by artists' souls. A photograph is a lie because a camera is not a
God. And we would rather the truth coloured by the artist's personality
than the lie that his mere eyes tell him. The women of Bougereau and
Gerôme are more like what the eyes tell one of life than the women of
Degas and Manet. I want the truth of Being, not the truth of Form. Do
you hear?' she cried, 'I want truth, I want Truth.'

'I want you,' said Joe Marie.

'We are both in trouble, then,' she smiled back. 'And perhaps if
we had our wish, we should both be disappointed. Now I am going
home to write letters, and if you are good you shall lunch with me
tomorrow.'

'Then let me pay! I want to pay for your lunch.'

'You shall have a great treat, Joe! I have a friend and his girl coming, too. You shall pay for all of us.'

The negro beamed. 'Ida Pendragon!' he spluttered. 'I love you, Ida Pendragon.'

'And Ida Pendragon loves her leopard. Now leave me.' She glanced round. They were alone in the gallery.

'You may kiss the back of my neck, if you like.'

The negro buried his head between her shoulders.

She shivered; her hair hissed under his kiss. She writhed round, and gave her mouth to his for one clinging moment. Then she pushed herself away, and he, poor troubled animal, went swiftly and sleekly from the room. At the corner he staggered. The girl saw it; her smile was like sheet lightning.

A quarter of a mile away, at that moment, Edgar Rolles was tearing the edges from a '*petit bleu.*'

'I am paying the penalty,' he read. 'Lunch with me at Lavenue's at one tomorrow. Bring a girl.'

'Right,' said he. 'But I wonder what she means.' And he strolled out to the Dôme to find good-hearted Ninon, '*la grande hystérique*'[1] of the Quarter, half-mad and wholly amorous, half gamine and half great lady, satiated and unsatisfied indeed, but innocent withal. *La Dame de Montparno*[2] they called her; she dominated her surroundings without effort. Yet none could analyse or explain the fascination to which all surrendered. She had more friends than lovers, and no one ever told a lie about her, or let her want for anything.

She welcomed the invitation with joy. 'Ida Pendragon!' she said, 'Oh! I know the type. Name of a tigress ...' and she rattled off a story of a stag-hunt at Fontainebleau in which the Cornish girl had played the principal, an incredible part.

The café pricked up its ears, and dissolved in laughter at the culminating impossibility.

But Edgar Rolles only frowned. 'I am sorry for Ida,' he said slowly. 'If your story were true I should be glad; but she is only the painter with his palette mixing paints: she never gives her soul up to the canvas. Tigress? yes: but not the *bodhisattva* who let the tigress eat him. She always wins; she cannot lose. As the proverb says: "Lucky at play, unlucky in love" – and "God is love."'

---

[1] [The great hysteric.]
[2] [The Lady of Montparno, i.e., Montparnasse.]

'Listen! he is saying the Black Mass again,' cried Ninon, and springing on a table began the Dance of the Postman's Knock, just then the rage of Montparnasse before the infection spread to Paris and London. A Polish youth jumped on to the table opposite and joined her; in a minute the whole café was aflame with it.

But Edgar Rolles, his hands thrust deep into his pockets, and the threat of tears in his eyes, was walking back to his studio.

'If only life were folly!' he sighed. 'But the silliest things we do are wisdom – somehow, somewhere—'

And he let himself in.

* * *

The lunch in the private room at Lavenue's was secretly amusing. Joe Marie had only dog's eyes for Ida; Ninon amused herself by trying to distract him. Edgar held forth at length upon Art, passionlessly expository.

'Art,' said he, 'and do not imagine that Art or anything else is other than High Magic! – is a system of holy hieroglyph. The artist, the initiate, thus frames his mysteries. The rest of the world scoff, or seek to understand, or pretend to understand; some few obtain the truth. The technical ability of the artist is the lucidity of his language; it has nothing to do with the degree of his illumination. Bougereau is better technically than Manet; he explains more clearly what he sees. But what does he see? He is the priest of a false God. Form has no importance except in this sense: we must not be revolted by the extravagance of new symbolic systems. Gauguin and Matisse may live to be understood. We acquiesce in the eccentricities of Raphael.'

Ida gave a little laugh of pleased scorn of him.

'My good girl, perspective is an eccentricity, a symbol: no more. How can one ever represent a three-dimensional world in two dimensions? Only by symbolism. We have acquiesced in the method of the primitives – do you think men and women are really like Fra Angelico's pictures look to the eye of the untaught? We may one day acquiesce in all the noughts and crosses of Nadelmann! It's the same everywhere. I draw a curve and a circle and a waggle up and down; and everybody who can read English is perfectly satisfied that I mean that placid ruminant, female, herbivorous, and lactiferous, to which we compare our more domesticated courtesans and our less domesticated policemen. So Being is not in Form; it is however only to be understood through Form. Hence incarnations. The Universe is only a picture in the Mind of the Father, by which He wishes to convey –

what? It is our Magnum Opus to discover what He means! Hence "the eye of faith." Mere eyesight tells us that a plaster mould is truer to nature than the greatest masterpiece of Phidias; so does science, with her gross calipers. Sensible men prefer a good photograph of nature to a bad landscape. The photograph shows them the view of their own normal eye through the medium of an accepted symbolism; the picture shows the view of an indifferent bad soul through a medium of mud. But Corot! But Whistler! But Morrice! Corot sees a wood, and paints Pan; Bougereau sees a pretty model, and paints a pretty model. He doesn't paint Woman. Morrice paints the Venice of Byron, of our historic and voluptuous dreams; not the Venice of the Yankee and the churning steamers. Raphael found Madonna in his mistress; Rembrandt a queen of sombre passion and seduction in his wife. In one way or another we must get to God's meaning through a medium that itself is meaningless.'

'Just as through *déjeuner* we get to the dessert!' laughed Ida, who had something more to say than her face showed. All through lunch she had allured the big black savage, until beneath her glances he was in agony. All the primitive passions fought one another in his heart. He could have killed Rolles for the very nonchalance of his small-talk. It hurt him that anyone should speak to Ida save in words of love. Equally, he could have killed him for a trace of inflection in his voice.

Edgar Rolles understood his torture, understood the suppressed intensity of Ida's purpose, though he could not guess its nature. Somehow he distrusted the event.

'Take literature!' he went on, in that even vigilant voice of his. 'Take Zola with his million marshalled facts. What do they matter? Nothing. We get the truth about the Second Empire – and if Zola's facts were all false, it would not alter the truth he came to tell, poor, provincial, time-serving truth as it is.

'Take Ibsen! It is no accusation to say that Norwegians never act as his characters do; no defence to prove that Norwegians always do act so. It has nothing to do with the question. Romeo and Juliet make love in English – nobody minds! Macbeth is not obliged to say, "Hoots! ma leddy!" every time he addresses his wife. The fool who bothers with local colour misses the sunshine. The man with the burette misses the sea. Some pious Dutchman of yore, who wanted to paint Abraham and Isaac, gave the old man a blunderbuss. Why not? You can shoot your son with a blunderbuss! I tell you it's all symbolism, all hieroglyphics. Take Wagner!'

'Take a cigarette,' said Ida.

He shrugged his shoulders, and surrendered to the event.

'Mr Rolles,' she said, 'it is your advice on life that we are asking. Let us talk seriously. This dear boy (she took the negro's lips in her slim fingers and pinched them) likes me.'

'I love her! I would die for her!' broke in the black, crying with pleasure and pain, utterly unable to hold himself in. He caught the table to draw himself to it, so violently that two glasses fell. 'I love her! I love her! I want her.'

'Hush, Joe! Well, you see, Mr Rolles, I love him too....' Rolles flashed one glance at her. She would not see it. – 'I love him passionately, indeed I do. Oh, I love him, I love him!'

She threw herself on the broad chest of the boxer and hid her face. His long arms wound convulsively round her. His eyes seemed to start from his head; foam gathered on his dry lips; he could not speak. The breath came through his dilated nostrils hot and fierce; one would have said a bull in the arena. She disengaged herself.

'You see, he wants to marry me. I love him! I want to be with him for ever. But – ' the great fighter was limp in his chair. 'It is difficult,' she went on. 'There are complications. My mother ...'

Edgar Rolles detected the false note in her voice. He understood. He was angry, angry at his implication in such an affair. His teeth snapped.

'Yes?' he said, though he wanted to shout, to break the furniture.

'We cannot marry,' she went on, and this time the mordant malice almost tore her silky pathos with a rending shriek. 'So, Joe ...' She turned her great eyes on him, lustrous, pleading.

'I want you!' was all he said. But his voice was like the low and terrible cry of an elephant.

'You would not make me' – she hesitated a moment – 'you would not make me – *impure*?' Her inflection was low and tremulous; but the Caucasians understood. It was like the scream of the typhoon, ripping the sails.

Ninon broke into a high hysterical sob of utmost laughter. She had not seen such a comedy since – she had never seen such a comedy. What a dull brute that black creature was!

Edgar Rolles rose with a jerk. He did not know what was coming.

And then light dawned in the dense brain of the African. The thousand meshes of her spider web were torn. He understood. He understood that she cared nothing, had never cared, would never have given a hair of her head for all his body and soul. Understanding was to his brain a momentary death.

Then with a silent snarl he sprang at her. She and her chair crashed backwards to the floor, and the black leopard was upon her, his teeth sunk in her throat.

Edgar Rolles was only just in time. His boot caught the murderer behind the ear – and Edgar Rolles had played football.

The beast was dead.

Edgar stooped and caught her up, blood leaping from her throat, while Ninon, shriek upon shriek rising in torment, rushed to rouse the people of the restaurant.

'Oh, my brother,' gasped the girl. 'Could you not understand? I wanted to die, so.'

They were her last words for long.

Lavenue's was a storm of chattering and gesticulating fools. The police pushed them aside. The corpse to the mortuary; the girl to the hospital; the man to the Poste. Ninon, wringing her hands and crying and laughing, had run like a Bacchante up the Boulevard to the Dôme.

4

The Hour of Gold

It was easy to satisfy French justice. Ida Pendragon was compared to several early Christian martyrs whose names I have forgotten; Edgar Rolles was asked to sit for a picture of St George by Follat, the success of the year's salon. Humanitarian papers urged the law to suppress boxing and its brutalities. Texans in Paris argued and rejoiced; Parisians in Texas went with a clear conscience to such lynchings as occurred.

Ida was convalescent. She would never lose the awful scars that jagged her throat; but would her face ever lose its mysterious exaltation? When Edgar saw her, he was almost afraid to understand. Leaving her, he went through the heart of Paris to a certain house. He wished to be certain; he wished to consult a Brother of the Silver Star.

Now it is very easy to find a Brother, when you know the password. But it is not always easy to get that Brother to tell you what you want. He is almost certain to be exceedingly rude; he is extremely likely to insist on talking common sense, which is annoying when you go for exalted mysticism; and quite possibly he may just nod, and continue his labours, which is maddening when your business is of the highest importance to you, and to him, and to the Brotherhood itself, not to mention humanity – while he is occupied in playing spillikins, and further insults you by explaining that he is trying to prove that, if you only do it carefully enough, you can detach planets from the solar system without hurting it.

On this occasion, however, Rolles was fortunate enough to find the Brother whom he knew at leisure – even for him. His feet were on the mantlepiece; a long pipe was in his mouth, and he was twiddling his thumbs.

'*Ave, Frater!*'[1] said he, as Rolles entered. 'Also *Vale*.[2] How you young brothers manage to find trouble!'

'Miss Pendragon will be out of the hospital in four days,' began Edgar in explanation.

'Lucky dog!' said the great man. 'But the funny thing is that I am in trouble too.'

'Oh! I am sorry.'

'I wonder if you could help. It's this way. Sometimes I twiddle my thumbs so – we call that the plus direction: and sometimes *so* – the minus direction. Now I lost count years and years ago; and so whichever way I twiddle, I may be getting further and further from equality. Then how – I ask you! – may man attain to the Universal Equilibrium?'

'Wouldn't it be safer not to twiddle at all?' suggested Rolles meekly.

'Inglorious youth!' retorted the Brother. 'Base Buddhist! So you could never equalise the count! No! My plan is – always to twiddle one way. It is an even chance that my way is right.'

'But if you should be wrong?'

'I shall be damned, I suppose.'

'And if you should succeed, and equalise the count?'

'I have no idea.'

'But—'

'Ungenerous, unsympathetic youth! I wager you have not divined my difficulty?'

'It *all* seems very difficult.'

'But my supreme, my crushing doubt?'

'I cannot guess, sir.'

'This! In your ear, my young friend. This! I cannot remember which way always to twiddle.'

Rolles drew back dazed.

'Read Nietzsche!' snapped the Brother.

---

[1] [Hail, brother!]
[2] [Farewell.]

'But – but –' he stammered. 'Oh! this is it. Miss Pendragon comes out in four days' time ...'

'I wish you'd learnt twiddling,' said the Brother sadly.

'But what am I to do, sir?'

'Twiddle, you damned fool!'

'I know you always mean something ...'

'Never. There is Nothing to mean!'

'Oh!'

'Be off, I can't be bothered with you – be off! I send you packing. Is *that* clear?'

'You have nothing to say to me?'

'What have I been saying this priceless past fourteen minutes twenty-seven seconds? Ape! Goat! Imbecile! Dullard! Poopstick! Do you think one can recover lost time? One must talk English to you – English, you hotel blotting-paper, you unabsorbent wad of pulp! English, you Englishman!'

Rolles nearly lost his temper at the final insult.

'Well, then, I send you packing. Go and pack, dolt! Pack! Trunks, portmanteaux, bags, boxes, and for the Lord's sake pack some brains! Take the girl to Jericho or Johannesburg, and get some sense, and triplets, if you can!

'Twiddle so – Being! Twiddle *so* – Form! Balance them, cheating grocer! Nation of shopkeepers! Twiddle! Twiddle! Twiddle! Isn't the Balance in the Babe? Teach her to understand children!' The Brother paused to re-light his pipe, thrusting the bowl into the glowing carbon of the grate.

'To understand children? It is hard. But we love children, sir.'

'And what the devil is the difference between love and understanding? If you have one, you have the other. Oh, twiddle, twiddle! – You can send me one of those rotten paper knives from Jericho,' added the adept more peaceably. 'With the rotten Sephardi pointing – blasphemers! And here! don't *you* blaspheme, young feller my lad. You've got a good woman: make the most of her.'

'A great woman, perhaps.'

'A good woman. In the next siege of Paris I hope I shall not have to boil your head; I prefer thick soup. A good woman. A sister of the Silver Star, my good goat!'

'I do not understand, master!'

'You never will, I think. O generation of vipers! O prosy princox! O coxcomb of Kafoozelum!'

'I beg your pardon, sir! You know she failed in the abyss?'

'I? You? This is intolerable. Give me more Hafiz! Here, thickhead!'

'She was your mistress, I suppose? Most women in Paris seem to be. Sir! Yes or no? Well, silence gives consent—'

'No! she wasn't!'

'You lie!

'She never gave herself but once – go and look at the mark on her throat!'

Rolles reeled back, stunned by the bludgeon truth.

'I am a Fool!'

'Not by a long chalk! Keep your end up, and you'll be a Magus in this life yet, though. In the meantime – oh, be a Devil!'

The younger man divined the infinite love and wisdom beneath the brusquerie of the Brother.

His eyes filled with tears.

'I'll win her, sir, by God!' he said enthusiastically.

'Lose yourself to her. Only so. Off now, boy! I am busy. I must twiddle – twiddle – twiddle.'

Edgar bowed and went. He could not trust himself to speak: the Love that was the whole being of the Brother melted the snow of his soul. He loved. Not Ida, not the world, not anything. It was pure love: love without object, love as love is in itself. He did not love; he was Love.

But he strode straight back to Ida Pendragon. Before she left her bed, they were married. A week later they drove through the cool swift air to the South; and there, among the vines, they learnt how – once in a century – the phœnix Passion may rise from the fire of Vice, and how in the beak of the phœnix proved by the fire is the ring of Love.

* * *

A year later. They were in a villa at Mustapha. The sea and sky strove enviously which should best answer the sun's question with the word blue.

But Ida Pendragon, pale and fragile as rare porcelain, twisted herself and found no peace. Edgar bent over her, as vigilant as on the night of her first ordeal. In the shadow stood a physician; at the bedside sat a nurse, and in her arms a child.

'Brother!' she said faintly, 'the number of the grade is Three, and I have given myself three times. Once to the brute, once to the man – my man!' (her hand pressed his, oh! too feebly!) 'and now – to God!'

The tears sprang to his eyes.

'It is for you,' she whispered, 'to understand the child.'

She fell back. The physician ran forward. He knew that he had no useful purpose there; but he motioned Edgar away. Too late. Edgar had understood the Event.

He fell upon the dead girl's breast, crash!

The nurse shook herself, half angrily, as a retriever shakes off water. Then she put the child into his arms.

Apollo Bestows the Violin

I

The pastureland reached from the border of the olives and figs that garlanded the village to the upper slopes of the mountain, whose tumbled rocks, fire-scarred, frowned the menace of eternal sterility, the Universe against struggling man.

It was not often that Daphnis led his goats too far toward the crags, for the plain was green and gracious. Only in one spot was the sward broken. There did mosses and flowers, yellow, blue, and white, cover a mound as soft and firm as a maiden's breast.

Daphnis, true child, loved to make believe that this mound was sacred to some nymph. He would never invade the circle, or allow his goats to wander on it. But he would take his flute and invoke the nymph, or express the faint stirrings of manhood in his boyish breast by some such simple song as this: –

> Goats of mine, give ear, give ear!
> Shun this mound for food or frolic!
> Heaven is open; gods are near
> To my musings melancholic.
> Spring upon the earth begets
> Daffodils and violets.
>
> Here it was maybe that Zeus
> With his favourite took his pleasure;
> Here maybe the Satyrs use
> With the nymphs to tread a measure.
> Let no wanton foot distress
> This encircled loveliness!
>
> Oh, some destined nymph may deign
> Through the lilies to come gliding,
> Snatch from earth the choral swain,
> Hold him in her breast in hiding!

> See, they stir. It is the wind:
> Of my case they have no mind.

Thus lamenting and complaining the days found him, a monotony pastoral whose cycle was but peace.

But on the day of the summer solstice, as he plainted with the old refrain, the lilies stirred more violently; and the day was windless. Also it seemed to him as if a faint mist inhabited their midst. And he sang: –

> Mist, is this the fairy veil
> Of the bright one that's for me?
> Too fantastic, false and frail,
> See, it melts to vanity!

Yet was he eagerly afoot with curiosity, for now the mist rose in fiercer puffs, and little jets of flame spurted and sparkled amid the lilies: –

> Is it earth herself (he sang) that breathes
> In the bosom of the flowers?
> Is it fatal fire that seethes
> From the heart of hateful powers?

And the tumult of the mound increasing ever, he went forward a step toward the circle; yet again his self-set fear caught him, and he drew back – yet again his eagerness lured him. In the end, reality conquered imagination; he advanced delicately up the knoll.

Like the nipple of a breast, earth protruded, red, puckered, fissured. This Daphnis saw as he broke through the tall lilies. From its centre jetted the dusky, rose-red mist. As he thrust forward his arms to divide the flowers, the breeze caught a curl of smoke and mixed it with his breath.

His head went back: he half choked. Then a strangled cry broke from him, turning to wild laughter. His limbs caught the craze. He leapt and twirled and pirouetted like one stung by a tarantula: and all the while meaningless cries issued from his throat.

The nearer he approached the nipple the more fantastic were his antics, the more strident his laughter.

Now at the foot of the mound appeared a company of merchants and slaves journeying in caravan. All these, attracted from their path by the unwonted sounds, beheld him thus dancing. The whisper went round: 'He is possessed of the spirit of some God,' and they all fell upon their faces and worshipped.

Then followed the wonder of all; for at high noon was the sun wrapped in blackness of eclipse. In the gathering darkness and the strange shadows Daphnis still leapt and laughed; but as the sun was wholly swallowed by the dragon, he gave one supreme shriek, and fell exhausted.

2

That which had been a mound of flowers was hidden deep beneath a floor of marble, translucent as mother-of-pearl. Along each side four elephants of obsidian, crouching, did homage to the central object of the hall, a slim tripod of silver, and on their backs eight pillars of porphyry were swathed with pythons of gold and black. These supported the dome, which glittered with lapis-lazuli. The shape of the temple was that of a fish or vesica, and nowhere was there any cross or tau to be seen.

Beneath the tripod a circular hole in the marble admitted the dusky vapours which two centuries before had filled Daphnis with enthusiasm.

Beyond and between each elephant stood five priestesses in white robes, their faces wrapped closely even to the eyes, lest the fumes should cause them to fall into trance. Each of these held in her hand a torch filled with oil pressed from the sacred olives that grew in the groves of the temple, and each was blind and deaf from too long continuance in the shrine whose glory was so dazzling and whose music so intense. Each might have been a statue of snow at some antique revelry of a Tsar.

Beyond the last of these, where the temple narrowed, was a shrine hidden, for from the roof hung a veil of purple, on which were written in golden letters the names and titles of Apollo.

It was the hour of worship; with uplifted hands a bearded priest in a voluminous robe of azure and gold cried aloud the invocations. He stood beyond the tripod, his face toward the shrine.

> Hail to the Lord of the Sun!
> Mystic, magnificent one!
> Who shall contend with him? None.
> Hail to the Lord of the Sun!
>
> Hail to the Lord of the Bow!
> He hath chosen an arrow, and lo!
> Shall any avail with him? No!
> Hail to the Lord of the Bow!

And then turning towards the tripod: –

> Hail to the Lord of the Lyre!
> Diviner of death and desire,
> Prophetic of favour and fire,
> Hail to the Lord of the Lyre!

With this he turned again and went up to the veil, prostrating himself seven times. Then again he turned and came to the tripod and sang: –

> Prophetess, pythoness, hear!
> Child of Apollo, descend!
> Smooth from the soul of the sphere
> Of the sun, be upon us, befriend!
> In the soothsaying smoke of the hollow
> Do thou and thine oracle follow
> The word and the will of Apollo!

So saying, he cast incense upon the opening beneath the tripod, and retired into the shrine. As the smoke cleared, there was found seated upon the tripod a maiden in a close-fitting dress of crimson silk broidered with gold. Her masses of black hair, caught at the crown with a fillet of crimson and gold, fell heavily around her. She bore a lyre in her hands. Her eyes were wild and fierce, and she sniffed up the vapours of the cavern with awesome ardour. Feebly at first, afterwards frenetically, she plucked at the strings.

Hardly a minute – a string snapped; the whole music jarred; and the priest ran from the shrine, shrieking 'Apollo! Apollo! Veil your faces! Apollo hath descended.' Himself he flung upon the marble before the tripod. There was a noise as of thunder; the veil was swept open as by a whirlwind, and Apollo, one flame of gold, entered the temple. As he passed, the priestesses fell dead and their torches were extinct. But a ray of glory from above, a monstrance to the God, followed him. Slowly and majestically he moved to the tripod. In his hands he bore an instrument of wood, of unfamiliar shape. Music of triumph and of glory answered his paces.

To the pythoness he advanced, thus dancing. He took the lyre from her hands and broke it. She stared, entranced. He put the strange instrument into her hands and, drawing down her head, pressed his lips to her forehead. Then he breathed lightly on her hands. Darkness fell, and lightnings rent it; thunders answered them. Apollo was gone. After the thunder the temple was filled with rosy radiance. The old priest, still prone, raised and let fall his hands, in mechanical imitation of the signs of invocation. Obedient, the pythoness began to play upon the instrument given of the God, and the temple shuddered at sounds so ethereal, so soul shaking, so divine. A greater music had been given to the world.

She ended. The old priest rose unsteadily to his feet, crying: 'Apollo! Apollo!' staggered, and fell dead before the tripod.

The light went out.

Across the Gulf

I

At last the matter comes back into my mind.

It is now five years since I discovered my stèla at Bulaq, but not until I obtained certain initiations in the city of Benares last year did the memory of my life in the Twenty-Sixth Dynasty when I was prince and priest in Thebai begin to return. Even now much is obscure; but I am commanded to write, so that in writing the full memory may be recovered. For without the perfect knowledge and understanding of that strange life by Nilus I cannot fully know and understand this later life, or find that Tomb which I am appointed to find, and do that therein which must be done.

Therefore with faith and confidence do I who was – in a certain mystical sense – the Priest of the Princes, Ankh-f-na-khonsu, child of Ta-nech, the holy and mighty one, and of Bes-na-Maut, priestess of the Starry One, set myself to tell myself the strange things that befell me in that life.

Thus.

At my birth Aphruimis in the sign of the Lion was ascending, and in it that strange hidden planet that presides over darkness and magic and forbidden love. The sun was united with the planet of Amoun, but in the Abyss, as showing that my power and glory should be secret, and in Aterechinis the second decanate of the House of Maat, so that my passion and pleasure should likewise be unprofane. In the House of Travel in the Sign of the Ram was the Moon my sweet lady. And the wise men interpreted this as a token that I should travel afar; it might be to the great temple at the source of mother Nile; it might be …

Foolishness! I have scarce stirred from Thebai.

Yet have I explored strange countries that they knew not of: and of this also will I tell in due course.

I remember – as I never could while I lived in Khemi-land – all the minute care of my birth. For my mother was of the oldest house in Thebes, her blood not only royal, but mixed with the divine. Fifty virgins in their silver tissue stood about her shaking their sistrums, as if the laughter of the Gods echoed the cries of the woman. By the bed stood the Priest of Horus with his heavy staff, the Phœnix for its head, the prong for its foot. Watchful he stood lest Sebek should rise from the abyss.

On the roof of the palace watched the three chief astrologers of Pharaoh with their instruments, and four armed men from the corners of the tower announced each god as it rose. So these three men ached and sweated at their task; for they had become most anxious. All day my birth had been expected; but as Tum drew to His setting their faces grew paler than the sky; for there was one dread moment in the night which all their art had failed to judge. The gods that watched over it were veiled.

But it seemed unlikely that Fate would so decide; yet so they feared that they sent down to the priest of Thoth to say that he must at all costs avoid the threatening moment, even if the lives of mother and child should pay for it; and still the watchmen cried the hour. Now, now! cried the oldest of the astrologers as the moment grew near – now! Below in answer the priest of Thoth summoned all his skill.

When lo! a rumbling of the abyss. The palace reeled and fell; Typhon rose mighty in destruction, striding across the skies. The world rocked with earthquake; every star broke from its fastening and trembled.

And in the midst lo! Bes-na-Maut my mother; and in her arms myself, laughing in the midst of all that ruin. Yet not one living creature took the slightest hurt! But the astrologers rent their robes and beat their faces on the ground; for the dread moment, the Unknown Terror, had gone by; and with it I had come to light.

In their terror, indeed, as I learnt long after, they sent messengers to the oldest and wisest of the priests; the High-priest of Nuit, who lived at the bottom of a very deep well, so that his eyes, even by day, should remain fixed upon the stars.

But he answered them that since they had done all that they could, and Fate had reversed their design, it was evident that the matter was in the hands of Fate, and that the less they meddled the better it would be for them. For he was a brusque old man – how afterwards I met him shall be written in its place.

So then I was to be brought up as befitted one in my station, half-prince, half-priest. I was to follow my father, hold his wand and ankh, assume his throne.

And now I begin to recall some details of my preparation for that high and holy task.

Memory is strangely fragmentary and strangely vivid. I remember how, when I had completed my fourth month, the priests took me and wrapped me in a panther's skin, whose flaming gold and jet-black spots were like the sun. They carried me to the river bank where the holy crocodiles were basking; and there they laid me. But when they left me they refrained from the usual enchauntment against the evil spirit of the crocodile; and so for three days I lay without protection. Only at certain hours did my mother descend to feed me; and she too was silent, being dressed as a princess only, without the sacred badges of her office.

Also in the sixth month they exposed me to the Sun in the desert where was no shade or clothing; and in the seventh month they laid me in a bed with a sorceress, that fed on the blood of young children, and, having been in prison for a long time, was bitterly an-hungered; and in the eighth month they gave me the aspic of Nile, and the Royal Uræus serpent, and the deadly snake of the south country, for playmates; but I passed scatheless through all these trials.

And in the ninth month I was weaned, and my mother bade me farewell, for never again might she look upon my face, save in the secret rites of the Gods, when we should meet otherwise than as babe and mother, in the garment of that Second Birth which we of Khemi knew.

The next six years of my life have utterly faded. All that I can recall is the vision of the greatness of our city of Thebai, and the severity of my life. For I lived on the back of a horse, even eating and drinking as I rode; for so it becometh a prince. Also I was trained to lay about me with a sword, and in the use of the bow and the spear. For it was said that Horus – or Mentu, as we called Him in Thebai – was my Father and my God. I shall speak later of that strange story of my begetting.

At the end of seven years, however, so great and strong had I waxen that my father took me to the old astrologer that dwelt in the well to consult him. This I remember as if it were but yesterday. The journey down the great river with its slow days! The creaking benches and the sweat of the slaves are still in my ears and my nostrils. Then swift moments of flying foam in some rapid or cataract. The great temples that we passed; the solitary Ibis of Thoth that meditated on the shore; the crimson flights of birds; – but nothing that we saw upon the journey was like unto the end thereof. For in a desolate place was the Well, with but a small temple beside it, where the servants – they too most holy! of that holy ancient man might dwell.

And my father brought me to the mouth of the well and called thrice upon the name of Nuit. Then came a voice climbing and coiling up the walls like a serpent, 'Let this child become priestess of the Veiled One!'

Now my father was wise enough to know that the old man never made a mistake; it was only a question of a right interpretation of the oracle. Yet he was sorely puzzled and distressed, for that I was a boy child. So at the risk of his life – for the old man was brusque! – he called again and said 'Behold my son!'

But as he spoke a shaft of sunlight smote him on the nape of the neck as he bent over the well; and his face blackened, and his blood gushed forth from his mouth. And the old man lapped up the blood of my father with his tongue, and cried gleefully to his servants to carry me to a house of the Veiled One, there to be trained in my new life.

So there came forth from the little house an eunuch and a young woman exceeding fair; and the eunuch saddled two horses, and we rode into the desert alone.

Now though I could ride like a man, they suffered me not; but the young priestess bore me in her arms. And though I ate meat like a warrior, they suffered me not, but the young priestess fed me at her breast.

And they took from me the armour of gilded bronze that my father had made for me, scales like a crocodile's sewn upon crocodile skin that cunning men had cured with salt and spices; but they wrapped me in soft green silk.

So strangely we came to a little house in the desert, and that which befell me there is not given me of the gods at this time to tell; but I will sleep; and in the morning by their favour the memory thereof shall arise in me, even in me across these thousands of years of the whirling of the earth in her course.

2

So for many years I grew sleek and subtle in my woman's attire. And the old eunuch (who was very wise) instructed me in the Art of Magic and in the worship of the Veiled One, whose priestess was I destined.

I remember now many things concerning those strange rituals, things too sacred to write. But I will tell of an adventure that I had when I was nine years of age.

In one of the sacred books it is written that the secret of that subtle draught which giveth vision of the star-abodes of Duaut, whose sight is life eternal in freedom and pleasure among the living, lieth in the use of a certain little secret bone that is in the Bear of Syria. Yet how should I a child slay such an one? For they had taken all weapons from me.

But in a garden of the city (for we had now returned unto a house in the suburbs of Thebaï) was a colony of bears kept by a great lord for his pleasure. And I by my cunning enticed a young bear-cub from its dam, and slew it with a great stone. Then I tore off its skin and hid myself therein, taking also its jaw and sharpening the same upon my stone. Then at last the old she-bear came searching me, and as she put down her nose to smell at me, taking me for her cub, I drove my sharpened bone into her throat.

I struck with great fortune; for she coughed once, and died.

Then I took her skin with great labour; and (for it was now night) began to return to my house. But I was utterly weary and I could no longer climb the wall. Yet I stayed awake all that night, sharpening again upon my stone the jaw-bone of that bear-cub; and this time I bound it to a bough that I tore off from a certain tree that grew in the garden.

Now towards the morning I fell asleep, wrapped in the skin of the old she-bear. And the great bear himself, the lord of the garden, saw me, and took me for his mate, and came to take his pleasure of me. Then I being roused out of sleep struck at his heart with all my strength as he rose over me, and quitting my shelter ran among the trees. For I struck not home, or struck aslant. And the old bear, sore wounded, tore up the skin of his mate; and then, discovering the cheat, came after me.

But by good fortune I found and wedged myself into a narrow pylon, too deep for him to reach me, though I could not go through, for the door was closed upon me. And in the angle of the door was an old sword disused. This was too heavy for me to wield with ease; yet I lifted it, and struck feebly at the claws of the bear. So much I wounded him that in his pain he dropped and withdrew and began to lick his paws. Thus he forgot about me; and I, growing bolder, ran out upon him. He opened his mouth; but before he could rise, I thrust the sword down it. He tossed his head; and I, clinging to the sword-hilt, was thrown into the air, and fell heavily upon my shoulder. My head too struck the ground; and I lay stunned.

When I came to myself it was that a party of men and women had thrown water in my face and uttered the spells that revive from swoon. Beside me, close beside me, lay mine enemy dead; and I, not forgetful of my quest, took the blade of the sword (for it was snapt) and cut off the secret parts of the bear and took the little bone thereof, and would have gone forth with my prize. But the great lord of the house spake with me; and all his friends made as if to mock at me. But the women would not have it; they came round me and petted and caressed me; so that angry words were spoken.

But even as they quarrelled among themselves, my guardian, the old eunuch, appeared among them; for he had traced me to the garden.

And when they beheld the ring of the holy ancient man the astrologer they trembled; and the lord of the house threw a chain of gold around my neck, while his lady gave me her own silken scarf, broidered with the loves of Isis and Nephthys, and of Apis and Hathor. Nor did any dare to take from me the little bone that I had won so dearly; and with it I made the spell of the Elixir, and beheld the starry abodes of Duaut, even as it was written in the old wise book.

But my guardians were ashamed and perplexed; for though I was so sleek and subtle, yet my manhood already glowed in such deeds as this – how should I truly become the priestess of the Veiled One?

Therefore they kept me closer and nursed me with luxury and flattery. I had two negro slave-boys that fanned me and that fed me; I had an harp-player from the great city of Memphis, that played languorous tunes. But in my mischief I would constantly excite him to thoughts of war and of love; and his music would grow violent and loud, so that the old eunuch, rushing in, would belabour him with his staff.

How well I recall that room! Large was it and lofty; and there were sculptured pillars of malachite and lapis-lazuli and of porphyry and yellow marble. The floor was of black granite; the roof of white marble. On the Southern side was my couch, a softness of exotic furs. To roll in them was to gasp for pleasure. In the centre was a tiny fountain of pure gold. The sunlight came through the space between the walls and the roof, while on the other sides I could look through and up into the infinite blue.

There was a great python that inhabited the hall; but he was very old, and too wise to stir. But – so I then believed – he watched me and conveyed intelligence to the old magus of the well.

Now then the folly of my guardians appeared in this; that while all day I slept and languished and played idly, at night while they supposed I slept, I slept not. But I rose and gave myself to the most violent exercises. First, I would go into my bathing-pool and hold my breath beneath the water while I invoked the goddess Auramoth one hundred times. Next, I would walk on my hands around the room; I even succeeded in hopping on one hand. Next, I would climb each of the twenty-four smooth pillars. Next, I would practise the seventy-two athletic postures. Also in many other ways I would strive to make my strength exceeding great; and all this I kept most secret from my guardians.

At last on one night I resolved to try my strength; so, pushing aside the curtain, I passed into the corridor. Springing upon the soldier that guarded me, I brought him to the ground; and with my right hand under his chin, my left on his right shoulder, and my knee at the nape of his neck, I tore his head from his body before he could utter a cry.

I was now in my fifteenth year; but the deed was marvellous. None suspected me; it was thought a miracle.

The old eunuch, distressed, went to consult the magus of the well; whose answer was; 'Let the vows of the priestess be taken!'

Now I thought this old man most foolish-obstinate; for I myself was obstinate and foolish. Not yet did I at all understand his wisdom or his purpose.

It often happens thus. Of old, men sent their priests to rebuke Nile for rising – until it was known that his rising was the cause of the fertility of their fields.

Now of the vows which I took upon me and of my service as priestess of the Veiled One it shall next be related.

3

It was the Equinox of Spring, and all my life stirred in me. They led me down cool colonnades of mighty stone clad in robes of white broidered with silver, and veiled with a veil of fine gold web fastened with rubies. They gave me not the Uræus crown, nor any nemyss, nor the *Ateph* crown, but bound my forehead with a simple fillet of green leaves – vervain and mandrake and certain deadly herbs of which it is not fitting to speak.

Now the priests of the Veiled One were sore perplexed, for that never before had any boy been chosen priestess. For before the vows may be administered, the proofs of virginity are sought; and, as it seemed, this part of the ritual must be suppressed or glossed over. Then said the High Priest: 'Let it be that we examine the first woman that he shall touch with his hand, and she shall suffice.' Now when I heard this, I thought to test the God; and, spying in the crowd, I beheld in loose robes with flushed face and wanton eyes, a certain courtesan well-known in the city, and I touched her. Then those of the priests that hated me were glad, for they wished to reject me; and taking aside into the hall of trial that woman, made the enquiry.

Then with robes rent they came running forth, crying out against the Veiled One; for they found her perfect in virginity, and so was she even unto her death, as later appeared.

But the Veiled One was wroth with them because of this, and appeared in her glittering veil upon the steps of her temple. There she stood, and called them one by one; and she lifted but the eye-piece of her veil and looked into their eyes; and dead they fell before her as if smitten of the lightning.

But those priests who were friendly to me and loyal to the goddess took that virgin courtesan, and led her in triumph through the city, veiled and crowned as is befitting. Now after some days he that guarded the sacred goat of Khem died, and they appointed her in his place. And she was the first woman that was thus honoured since the days of the Evil Queen in the Eighteenth Dynasty, of her that wearied of men at an age when other women have not known them, that gave herself to gods and beasts.

But now they took me to the pool of liquid silver – or so they called it; I suppose it was quicksilver; for I remember that it was very difficult to immerse me – which is beneath the feet of the Veiled One. For this is the secret of the Oracle. Standing afar off the priest beholds the reflection of her in the mirror, seeing her lips that move under the veil; and this he interprets to the seeker after truth.

Thus the priest reads wrongly the silence of the Goddess, and the seeker understands ill the speech of the priest. Then come forth fools, saying 'The Goddess hath lied' – and in their folly they die.

While, therefore, they held me beneath the surface of the pool, the High Priestess took the vows on my behalf saying:

> I swear by the orb of the Moon;
> I swear by the circuit of the Stars;
> I swear by the Veil, and by the Face behind the Veil;
> I swear by the Light Invisible, and by the Visible Darkness;
> On behalf of this Virgin that is buried in thy water;
> To live in purity and service;
> To love in beauty and truth;
> To guard the Veil from the profane;
> To die before the Veil; ...

– and then came the awful penalty of failure.

I dare not recall half of it; yet in it were these words: Let her be torn by the Phallus of Set, and let her bowels be devoured by Apep; let her be prostituted to the lust of Besz, and let her face be eaten by the god ———.

It is not good to write His name.

Then they loosed me, and I lay smiling in the pool. They lifted me up and brought me to the feet of the goddess, so that I might kiss them. And as I kissed them such a thrill ran through me that I thought myself rapt away into the heaven of Amoun, or even as Asi when Hoor and Hoor-pa-kraat, cleaving her womb, sprang armed to life. Then they stripped me of my robes, and lashed me with fine twigs of virgin hazel, until my blood ran from me into the pool. But the surface of the silver swallowed up the blood by some mysterious energy; and they took this to be a sign of acceptance. So then they clothed me in the right robes of a priestess of the Veiled One; and they put a silver sistrum in my hand, and bade me perform the ceremony of adoration. This I did, and the veil of the goddess glittered in the darkness – for night had fallen by this – with a strange starry light.

Thereby it was known that I was indeed chosen aright.

So last of all they took me to the banqueting-house and set me on the high throne. One by one the priests came by and kissed my lips: one by one the priestesses came by, and gave me the secret clasp of hands that hath hidden virtue. And the banquet waxed merry; for all the food was magically prepared. Every beast that they slew was virgin; every plant that they plucked had been grown and tended by virgins in the gardens of the temple. Also the wine was spring water only, but so consecrated by the holy priestesses that one glass was more intoxicating than a whole skin of common wine. Yet this intoxication was a pure delight, an enthusiasm wholly divine; and it gave strength, and did away with sleep, and left no sorrow.

Last, as the first grey glow of Hormakhu paled the deep indigo of the night, they crowned and clothed me with white lotus flowers, and took me joyously back into the temple, there to celebrate the *matin* ritual of awakening the Veiled One.

Thus, and not otherwise, I became priestess of that holy goddess, and for a little while my life passed calm as the unruffled mirror itself.

It was from the Veiled One herself that came the Breath of Change. On this wise.

In the Seventh Equinox after my initiation into her mystery the High Priestess was found to fail; at her invocation the Veil no longer glittered as was its wont. For this they deemed her impure, and resorted to many ceremonies, but without avail. At last in despair she went to the temple of Set, and gave herself as a victim to that dreadful god. Now all men were much disturbed at this, and it was not known at all of them what they should do.

Now it must be remembered that the ceremonies are always performed by a single priestess alone before the goddess, save only at the Initiations.

The others also had found themselves rejected of her; and when they learnt of the terrible end of the High Priestess, they became fearful. Some few, indeed, concealed their failure from the priests; but always within a day and a night they were found torn asunder in the outer courts; so that it seemed the lesser evil to speak truth.

Moreover, the affair had become a public scandal; for the goddess plagued the people with famine and with a terrible and foul disease.

But as for me, I wot not what to do; for to me always the Veil glittered, and that brighter than the ordinary. Yet I said nothing, but went about drooping and sorrowful, as if I were as unfortunate as they. For I would not seem to boast of the favour of the goddess.

Then they sent to the old Magus in the well; and he laughed outright at their beards, and would say no word. Also they sent to the sacred goat of Khem, and his priestess would but answer, 'I, and such as I, may be favoured of Her,' which they took for ribaldry and mocking. A third time they sent to the temple of Thoth the Ibis god of wisdom. And Thoth answered them by this riddle: 'On how many legs doth mine Ibis stand?'

And they understood him not.

But the old High Priest determined to solve the mystery, though he paid forfeit with his life. So concealing himself in the temple, he watched in the pool for the reflection of the glittering of the Veil, while one by one we performed the adorations. And behind him and without stood the priests, watching for him to make a sign. This we knew not; but when it fell to me (the last) to adore that Veiled One, behold! the Veil glittered, and the old Priest threw up his arms to signal that which had occurred. And the flash of the Eye pierced the Veil, and he fell from his place dead upon the priests without.

They buried him with much honour, for that he had given his life for the people and for the temple, to bring back the favour of the Veiled One.

Then came they all very humbly unto me the child, and besought me to interpret the will of the Goddess. And her will was that I alone should serve her day and night.

Then they gave me to drink of the Cup of the Torment; and this is its virtue, that if one should speak falsely, invoking the name of the Goddess, he shall burn in hell visibly before all men for a thousand years; and that flame shall never be put out. There is such an one in her temple in Memphis, for I saw it with these eyes. There he burns and writhes and shrieks on the cold marble floor; and there he shall burn till his time expire, and he sink to that more dreadful hell below the West. But I drank thereof, and the celestial dew stood shining on my skin, and a coolness ineffable thrilled through me; whereat they all rejoiced, and obeyed the voice of the Goddess that I had declared unto them.

Now then was I always alone with that Veiled One, and I must enter most fully into that secret period of my life. For, despite its ending, which hath put many wise men to shame, it was to me even as an eternity of rapture, of striving and of attainment beyond that which most mortals – and they initiates even! – call divine.

Now first let it be understood what is the ritual of adoration of our Lady the Veiled One.

First, the priestess performs a mystical dance, by which all beings whatsoever, be they dogs or demons, are banished, so that the place may be pure. Next, in another dance, even more secret and sublime, the presence of the Goddess is invoked into her Image. Next, the priestess goes a certain journey, passing the shrines of many great and terrible of the Lords of Khem, and saluting them. Last, she assumes the very self of the Goddess; and if this be duly done, the Veil glittereth responsive.

Therefore, if the Veil glittereth not, one may know that in some way the priestess hath failed to identify herself with Her. Thus an impurity in the thought of the priestess must cause her to fail; for the goddess is utterly pure.

Yet the task is always difficult; for with the other gods one knoweth the appearance of their images; and steadily contemplating these one can easily attain to their imitation, and so to their comprehension, and to unity of consciousness with them. But with Our Veiled One, none who hath seen her face hath lived long enough to say one word, or call one cry.

So then it was of vital urgency to me to keep in perfect sympathy with that pure soul, so calm, so strong. With what terror then did I regard myself when, looking into my own soul, I saw no longer that perfect stillness. Strange was it, even as if one should see a lake stirred by a wind that one did not feel upon the cheeks and brow!

Trembling and ashamed, I went to the vesper adoration. I knew myself troubled, irritated, by I knew not what. And in spite of all my efforts, this persisted even to the supreme moment of my assumption of her godhead.

And then? Oh but the Veil glittered as never yet; yea more! it shot out sparks of scintillant fire, silvery rose, a shower of flame and of perfume.

Then was I exceedingly amazed because of this, and made a Vigil before her all the night, seeking a Word. And that word came not.

Now of what further befell I will write anon.

4

So it came to pass that I no longer went out at all from the presence of the goddess, save only to eat and to sleep. And the favour of her was restored to the people, so that all men were glad thereof.

For if any man murmured, he was slain incontinent, the people being mindful of the famine and the disease, and being minded to have no more of such, if it could by any means be avoided. They were therefore exceeding punctual with their gifts.

But I was daily more afraid, being in a great sweat of passion, of which I dared to speak to no man. Nor did I dare to speak even privily in mine own heart thereof, lest I should discover its nature. But I sent my favourite, the virgin Istarah (slim, pallid, and trembling as a young lotus in the West Wind), with my ring of office, to enquire of the old Magus of the well.

And he answered her by pointing upward to the sky and then downward to the earth. And I read this Oracle as if it were spoken 'As above, so beneath.' This came to me as I had flung myself in despair at the feet of my Lady, covering them with my tears; for by a certain manifest token I now knew that I had done a thing that was so dreadful that even now – these many thousand years hence – I dare hardly write it.

I loved the Veiled One.

Yea, with the fierce passion of a beast, of a man, of a god, with my whole soul I loved her.

Even as I knew this by the manifest token the Veil burst into a devouring flame; it ate up the robes of my office, lapping them with its tongues of fire like a tigress lapping blood; yet withal it burnt me not, nor singed one hair.

Thus naked I fled away in fear, and in my madness slipped and fell into the pool of liquid silver, splashing it all over the hall; and even as I fled that rosy cataract of flame that wrapt me (from the Veil as it jetted) went out – went out –

The Veil was a dull web of gold, no more.

Then I crept fearfully to the feet of the goddess, and with my tears and kisses sought to wake her into life once more. But the Veil flamed not again; only a mist gathered about it and filled the temple, and hid all things from my eyes.

Now then came Istarah my favourite back with the ring and the message; and thinking that she brought bad news, I slit her lamb's-throat with the magic sickle, and her asp's-tongue I tore out with my hands, and threw it to the dogs and jackals.

Herein I erred sorely, for her news was good. Having reflected there-on, I perceived its import.

For since the Veil flamed always at my assumption, it was sure that I was in sympathy with that holy Veiled One.

If I were troubled, and knew not why; if my long peace were stirred – why then, so She!

'As above, so beneath!' For even as I, being man, sought to grasp godhead and crush it in my arms, so She, the pure essence, sought to manifest in form by love.

Yet I dared not repeat the ceremony at midnight.

Instead I lay prone, my arms outstretched in shame and pain, on the steps at her feet.

And lo! the Veil flamed. Then I knew that She too blamed Herself alike for her ardour and for her abstinence. Thus seven days I lay, never stirring; and all that time the Veil flamed subtly and softly, a steady bluish glow changing to green as my thought changed from melancholy to desire.

Then on the eighth day I rose and left the shrine and clad myself in new robes, in robes of scarlet and gold, with a crown of vine and bay and laurel and cypress. Also I purified myself and proclaimed a banquet. And I made the priests and the citizens, exceeding drunken. Then I called the guard, and purged thoroughly the whole temple of all of them, charging the captain on his life to let no man pass within. So that I should be ab-solutely alone in the whole precincts of the temple.

Then like an old grey wolf I wandered round the outer court, lifting up my voice in a mournful howl. And an ululation as of one hundred thousand wolves answered me, yet deep and muffled, as though it came from the very bowels of the earth.

Then at the hour of midnight I entered again the shrine and per-formed the ritual.

As I went on I became inflamed with an infinite lust for the Infinite; and now I let it leap unchecked, a very lion. Even so the Veil glowed red as with some infernal fire. Now then I am come to the moment of the Assumption; but instead of sitting calm and cold, remote, aloof, I gather myself together, and spring madly at the Veil, catching it in my two hands. Now the Veil was of woven gold, three thousand twisted wires; a span thick! Yet I put out my whole force to tear it across; and (for she also put out her force) it rent with a roar as of earthquake. Blinded I was with the glory of her face; I should have fallen; but she caught me to her, and fixed her divine mouth on mine, eating me up with the light of her eyes. Her mouth moaned, her throat sobbed with love; her tongue thrust itself into me as a shaft of sunlight smites into the palm-groves; my robes fell shrivelled, and flesh to flesh we clung. Then in some strange way she gripped me body and soul, twining herself about me and within me even as Death that devoureth mortal man.

Still, still my being increased; my consciousness expanded until I was all Nature seen as one, felt as one, apprehended as one, formed by me, part of me, apart from me – all these things at one moment – and at the same time the ecstasy of love grew colossal, a tower to scale the stars, a sea to drown the sun ...

I cannot write of this ... but in the streets people gathered apples of gold that dropped from invisible boughs, and invisible porters poured out wine for all, strange wine that healed disease and old age, wine that, poured between the teeth of the dead (so long as the embalmer had not begun his work), brought them back from the dark kingdom to perfect health and youth.

As for me, I lay as one dead in the arms of the holy Veiled One – Veiled no more! – while she took her pleasure of me ten times, a thousand times. In that whirlwind of passion all my strength was as a straw in the *simoom*.

Yet I grew not weaker but stronger. Though my ribs cracked, I held firm. Presently indeed I stirred; it seemed as if her strength had come to me. Thus I forced back her head and thrust myself upon and into her even as a comet that impales the sun upon its horn! And my breath came fast between my lips and hers; her moan now faint, like a dying child, no more like a wild beast in torment.

Even so, wild with the lust of conquest, I urged myself upon her and fought against her. I stretched out her arms and forced them to the ground; then I crossed them on her breast, so that she was powerless. And I became like a mighty serpent of flame, and wrapt her, crushed her in my coils.

I was the master! ...

Then grew a vast sound about me as of shouting: I grew conscious of the petty universe, the thing that seems apart from oneself, so long as one is oneself apart from it.

Men cried 'The temple is on fire! The temple of Asi the Veiled One is burning! The mighty temple that gave its glory to Thebai is aflame!

Then I loosed my coils and gathered myself together into the form of a mighty hawk of gold and spake one last word to her, a word to raise her from the dead!

But lo! not Asi, but Asar!

White was his garment, starred with red and blue and yellow. Green was his Countenance, and in his hands he bore the crook and scourge. Thus he rose, even as the temple fell about us in ruins, and we were left standing there.

And I wist not what to say.

Now then the people of the city crowded in upon us, and for the most part would have slain me.

But Thoth the mighty God, the wise one, with his Ibis-head, and his nemyss of indigo, with his *Ateph* crown and his Phœnix wand and with his ankh of emerald, with his magic apron in the Three colours; yea, Thoth, the God of Wisdom, whose skin is of tawny orange as though it burned in a furnace, appeared visibly to all of us. And the old Magus of the Well, whom no man had seen outside his well for nigh threescore years, was found in the midst: and he cried with a loud voice, saying:

'The Equinox of the Gods!'

And he went on to explain how it was that Nature should no longer be the centre of man's worship, but Man himself, man in his suffering and death, man in his purification and perfection. And he recited the Formula of the Osiris as follows, even as it hath been transmitted unto us by the Brethren of the Cross and Rose unto this day:

> For Asar Un-nefer hath said:
> He that is found perfect before the Gods hath said:
> These are the elements of my body, perfected through
>   suffering, glorified through trial.
> For the Scent of the dying Rose is the repressed sigh of my
>   suffering;
> The Flame-Red fire is the energy of my undaunted Will;
> The Cup of Wine is the outpouring of the blood of my
>   heart, sacrificed to regeneration;
> And the Bread and Salt are the Foundations of my Body

Which I destroy in order that they may be renewed.

For I am Asar triumphant, even Asar Un-nefer the Justified
One!

I am He who is clothed with the body of flesh,

Yet in Whom is the Spirit of the mighty Gods.

I am the Lord of Life, triumphant over death; he who
partaketh with me shall arise with me.

I am the manifestor in Matter of those whose abode is in the
Invisible.

I am purified: I stand upon the Universe: I am its Reconciler
with the eternal Gods: I am the Perfector of Matter; and
without me the Universe is not!

All this he said, and displayed the sacraments of Osiris before them
all; and in a certain mystical manner did we all symbolically partake of
them. But for me! in the Scent of the dying Rose I beheld rather the
perfection of the love of my lady the Veiled One, whom I had won,
and slain in the winning!

Now, however, the old Magus clad me (for I was yet naked) in the
dress of a Priest of Osiris. He gave me the robes of white Linen, and
the leopard's skin, and the wand and ankh. Also he gave me the crook
and scourge, and girt me with the royal girdle. On my head he set
the holy Uræus serpent for a crown; and then, turning to the people,
cried aloud:

'Behold the Priest of Asar in Thebai!

'He shall proclaim unto ye the worship of Asar; see that ye follow
him!'

Then, ere one could cry 'Hold!' he had vanished from our sight.

I dismissed the people; I was alone with the dead God; with Osiris,
the Lord of Amennti, the slain of Typhon, the devoured of Apophis ...

Yea, verily, I was alone!

5

Now then the great exhaustion took hold upon me, and I fell at the
feet of the Osiris as one dead. All knowledge of terrestrial things was
gone from me; I entered the kingdom of the dead by the gate of the
West. For the worship of Osiris is to join the earth to the West; it is
the cultus of the Setting Sun. Through Isis man obtains strength of
nature; through Osiris he obtains the strength of suffering and ordeal,
and as the trained athlete is superior to the savage, so is the magic of
Osiris stronger than the magic of Isis. So by my secret practices at
night, while my guardians strove to smooth my spirit to a girl's, had

I found the power to bring about that tremendous event, an Equinox of the Gods.

Just as thousands of years later was my secret revolt against Osiris – for the world had suffered long enough! – destined to bring about another Equinox in which Horus was to replace the Slain One with his youth and vigour and victory.

I passed therefore into these glowing abodes of Amennti, clad in thick darkness, while my body lay entranced at the feet of the Osiris in the ruined temple.

Now the god Osiris sent forth his strange gloom to cover us, lest the people should perceive or disturb; therefore I lay peacefully entranced, and abode in Amennti. There I confronted the devouring god, and there was my heart weighed and found perfect; there the two-and-forty Judges bade me pass through the pylons they guarded; there I spoke with the Seven, and with the Nine, and with the Thirty-Three; and at the end I came out into the abode of the Holy Hathor, unto her mystical mountain, and being there crowned and garlanded I rejoiced exceedingly, coming out through the gate of the East, the Beautiful gate, unto the Land of Khemi, and the city of Thebai, and the temple that had been the temple of the Veiled One. There I rejoined my body, making the magical links in the prescribed manner, and rose up and did adoration to the Osiris by the fourfold sign. Therefore the Light of Osiris began to dawn; it went about the city whirling forth, abounding, crying aloud; whereat the people worshipped, being abased with exceeding fear. Moreover, they hearkened unto their wise men and brought gifts of gold, so that the temple floor was heaped high; and gifts of oxen, so that the courts of the temple could not contain them: and gifts of slaves, as it were a mighty army.

Then I withdrew myself; and taking counsel with the wisest of the priests and of the architects and of the sculptors, I gave out my orders so that the temple might duly be builded. By the favour of the god all things went smoothly enough; yet was I conscious of some error in the working; or if you will, some weakness in myself and my desire. Look you, I could not forget the Veiled One, my days of silence and solitude with Her, the slow dawn of our splendid passion, the climax of all that wonder in her ruin!

So as the day approached for the consecration of the temple I began to dread some great catastrophe. Yet all went well – perhaps too well.

The priests and the people knew nothing of this, however. For the god manifested exceptional favour; as a new god must do, or how shall he establish his position? The harvest were fourfold, the cattle eightfold; the women were all fertile – yea! barren women of sixty years bore twins! – there was no disease or sorrow in the city.

Mighty was the concourse of the citizens on the great day of the consecration.

Splendid rose the temple, a fortress of black granite. The columns were carved with wonderful images of all the gods adoring Osiris; marvels of painting glittered on the walls; they told the story of Osiris, of his birth, his life, his death at the hands of Typhon, the search after his scattered members, the birth of Horus and Harpocrates, the vengeance upon Typhon Seth, the resurrection of Osiris.

The god himself was seated in a throne set back unto the wall. It was of lapis-lazuli and amber, it was inlaid with emerald and ruby. Mirrors of polished gold, of gold burnished with dried poison of asps, so that the slaves who worked upon it might die. For, it being unlawful for those mirrors to have ever reflected any mortal countenance, the slaves were both blinded and veiled; yet even so, it were best that they should die.

At last the ceremony began. With splendid words, with words that shone like flames, did I consecrate all that were there present, even the whole city of Thebai.

And I made the salutation unto the attendant gods, very forcibly, so that they responded with echoes of my adoration. And Osiris accepted mine adoration with gladness as I journeyed about at the four quarters of the temple.

Now cometh the mysterious ceremony of Assumption. I took upon myself the form of the god: I strove to put my heart in harmony with his.

Alas! alas! I was in tune with the dead soul of Isis; my heart was as a flame of elemental lust and beauty; I could not – I could not. Then the heavens lowered and black clouds gathered upon the Firmament of Nu. Dark flames of lightning rent the clouds, giving no light. The thunder roared; the people were afraid. In his dark shrine the Osiris gloomed, displeasure on his forehead, insulted majesty in his eyes. Then a pillar of dust whirled down from the vault of heaven, even unto me as I stood alone, half-defiant, in the midst of the temple while the priests and the people cowered and wailed afar off. It rent the massy roof as it had been a thatch of straw, whirling the blocks of granite far away into the Nile. It descended, roaring and twisting, like a wounded serpent demon-king in his death-agony; it struck me and lifted me from the temple; it bore me through leagues of air into the desert; then it dissolved and flung me contemptuously on a hill of sand. Breathless and dazed I lay, anger and anguish tearing at my heart.

I rose to swear a mighty curse; exhaustion took me, and I fell in a swoon to the earth.

When I came to myself it was nigh dawn. I went to the top of the hillock and looked about me. Nothing but sand, sand all ways. Just so was it within my heart!

The only guide for my steps (as the sun rose) was a greener glimpse in the East, which I thought might be the valley of the Nile reflected. Thither I bent my steps: all day I struggled with the scorching heat, the shifting sand. At night I tried to sleep, for sheer fatigue impelled me. But as often as I lay down, so often restlessness impelled me forward. I would stagger on a while, then stumble and fall. Only at dawn I slept perhaps for an hour, and woke chilled to death by my own sweat. I was so weak that I could hardly raise a hand; my tongue was swollen, so that I could not greet the sun-disk with the accustomed adoration. My brain had slipped control; I could no longer even think of the proper spells that might have brought me aid. Instead, dreadful shapes drew near; one, a hideous camel-demon, an obscene brute of filth; another, a black ape with a blue muzzle and crimson buttocks, all his skin hairless and scabby, with his mass of mane oiled and trimmed like a beautiful courtesan's. This fellow mocked me with the alluring gestures of such an one, and anon voided his excrement upon me. Moreover there were others, menacing and terrible, vast cloudy demon-shapes....

I could not think of the words of power that control them.

Now the sun that warmed my chill bones yet scorched me further. My tongue so swelled that I could hardly breathe; my face blackened; my eyes bulged out. The fiends came closer; drew strength from my weakness, made themselves material bodies, twitched me and spiked me and bit me. I turned on them and struck feebly again and again; but they evaded me easily and their yelling laughter rang like hell's in my ears. Howbeit I saw that they attacked me only on one side, as if to force me to one path. But I was wise enough to keep my shadow steadily behind me: and they, seeing this, were all the more enraged: I therefore the more obstinate in my course. Then they changed their tactics; and made as if to keep me in the course I had chosen; and seeing this, I was confirmed therein.

Truly with the gods I went! for in a little while I came to a pool of water and a tall palm standing by.

I plunged in that cool wave; my strength came back, albeit slowly; yet with one wave of my hand in the due gesture the fiends all vanished; and in an hour I was sufficiently restored to call forth my friends from the pool – the little fishes my playmates – and the nymph of the pool came forth and bowed herself before me and cooked me the fishes with that fire that renders water luminous and sparkling. Also she plucked me dates from the tree, and I ate thereof. Thus was I much comforted; and when I had eaten, she took my head upon her lap, and sang me to sleep; for her voice was like the ripple of the lakes under the wind of spring and like the bubbling of a well and like the tinkling of a fountain through a bed of moss. Also she had deep notes like the sea that booms upon a rocky shore.

So long, long, long I slept.

Now when I awoke the nymph had gone; but I took from my bosom a little casket of certain sacred herbs; and casting a few grains into the pool, repaid her for her courtesy. And I blessed her in the name of our dead lady Isis, and went on in the strength of that delicious meal for a great way. Yet I wist not what to do; for I was as it were a dead man, although my age was barely two and twenty years.

What indeed should befall me?

Yet I went on; and, climbing a ridge, beheld at last the broad Nile, and a shining city that I knew not.

There on the ridge I stood and gave thanks to the great gods of Heaven, the Aeons of infinite years, that I had come thus far. For at the sight of Nilus new life began to dawn in me.

6

Without any long delay I descended the slopes and entered the city. Not knowing what might have taken place in Thebai and what news might have come thither, I did not dare declare myself; but seeking out the High Priest of Horus I showed him a certain sign, telling him that I was come from Memphis on a journey, and intended to visit Thebai to pay homage at the shrine of Isis. But he, full of the news, told me that the ancient priestess of Isis, who had become priest of Osiris, had been taken up to heaven as a sign of the signal favour of the God. Whereat I could hardly hold myself from laughter; yet I controlled myself and answered that I was not prepared to return to Memphis, for that I was vowed to Isis, and Osiris could not serve my turn.

At this he begged me to stay as his guest, and to go worship at the temple of Isis in this city. I agreed thereto, and the good man gave me new robes and jewels from the treasury of his own temple. There too I rested sweetly on soft cushions fanned by young boys with broad leaves of palm. Also he sent me the dancing girl of Sleep. It was the art of this girl to weave such subtle movements that the sense, watching her, swooned; and as she swayed she sang, ever lower and lower as she moved slower and slower, until the looker-listener was dissolved in bliss of sleep and delicate dream.

Then as he slept she would bend over him even as Nuit the Lady of the Stars that bendeth over the black earth, and in his ears she would whisper strange rhythms, secret utterances, whereby his spirit would be rapt into the realms of Hathor or some other golden goddess, there in one night to reap an harvest of refreshment such as the fields of mortal sleep yield never.

So then I woke at dawn, to find her still watching, still looking into my eyes with a tender smile on her mouth that cooed whispers infinitely soothing. Indeed with a soft kiss she waked me, for in this Art there is a right moment to sleep, and another to waken: which she was well skilled to divine.

I rose then – she flitted away like a bird – and robed myself; and, seeking my host, went forth with him to the Temple of Isis.

Now their ritual (it appeared) differed in one point from that to which I was accustomed. Thus, it was not death to intrude upon the ceremony save only for the profane. Priests of a certain rank of initiation might if they pleased behold it. I, therefore, wishing to see again that marvellous glowing of the Veil, disclosed a sufficient sign to the High Priest. Thereat was he mightily amazed; and, from the foot judging Hercules, began to think that I might be some sacred envoy or inspector from the Gods themselves. This I allowed him to think; meanwhile we went forward into the shrines and stood behind the pillars, unseen, in the prescribed position.

Now it chanced that the High Priestess herself had this day chosen to perform the rite.

This was a woman tall and black, most majestic, with limbs strong as a man's. Her gaze was hawk-keen, and her brow commanding. But at the Assumption of the God-form she went close and whispered into the Veil, so low that we could not hear it; but as it seemed with fierce intensity, with some passion that knotted up her muscles, so that her arms writhed like wounded snakes. Also the veins of her forehead swelled, and foam came to her lips. We thought that she had died; her body swelled and shuddered; last of all a terrible cry burst from her throat, inarticulate, awful.

Yet all this while the Veil glittered, though something sombrely. Also the air was filled with a wild sweeping music, which rent our very ears with its uncouth magic. For it was like no music that I had ever heard before. At last the Priestess tore herself away from the Veil and reeled – as one drunken – down the temple. Sighs and sobs tore her breast; and her nails made bloody grooves in her wet flanks.

On a sudden she espied me and my companion; with one buffet she smote him to earth – it is unlawful to resist the Priestess when she is in the Ecstasy of Union – and falling upon me, like a wild beast she buried her teeth in my neck, bearing me to the ground. Then, loosing me, while the blood streamed from me, she fixed her glittering eyes upon it with strange joy, and with her hands she shook me as a lion shakes a buck. Sinewy were her hands, with big knuckles, and the strength of her was as cords of iron. Yet her might was but a mortal's; in a little she gave one gasp like a drowning man's; her body slackened, and fell with its dead weight on mine, her mouth glued to mine in one dreadful kiss. Dreadful; for as my mouth returned it, almost mechanically, the blood gushed from her nostrils and blinded me. I too, then, more dead than alive, swooned into bliss, into trance. I was awakened by the High Priest of Horus. 'Come,' he said; 'she is dead.' I disengaged myself from all that weight of madness – and the body writhed convulsively as I turned it over – I kissed those frothy lips, for in death she was beautiful beyond belief, joyous beyond description – thence I staggered to the Veil, and saluted with all my strength, so that it glittered under the force of my sheer will. Then I turned me again, and with the High Priest sought his house.

Strange indeed was I as I went through the city, my new robes dark with blood of that most holy sorceress.

But no one of the people dared so much as lift his eyes; nor spoke we together at all. But when we were come into the house of the High Priest, sternly did he confront me.

'What is this, my son?'

And I weary of the folly of the world and of the uselessness of things answered him:

'Father, I go back to Memphis. I am the Magus of the Well.'

Now he knew the Magus, and answered me:

'Why liest thou?'

And I said 'I am come into the world where all speech is false, and all speech is true.'

Then he did me reverence, abasing himself unto the ground even unto nine-and-ninety times.

And I spurned him and said, 'Bring forth the dancing girl of Sleep; for in the morning I will away to Memphis.'

And she came forth, and I cursed her and cried: 'Be thou the dancing girl of Love!'

And it was so. And I went in unto her, and knew her; and in the morning I girded myself, and boarded the state barge of the High Priest, and pillowed myself upon gold and purple, and disported myself with lutes and with lyres and with parrots, and with black slaves, and with wine and with delicious fruits, until I came even unto the holy city of Memphis.

And there I called soldiers of Pharaoh, and put cruelly to death all them that had accompanied me; and I burnt the barge, adrift upon the Nile at sunset, so that the flames alarmed the foolish citizens. All this I did, and danced naked in my madness through the city, until I came to the Old Magus of the Well.

And laughing, I threw a stone upon him, crying: 'Ree me the riddle of my life!'

And he answered naught.

Then I threw a great rock upon him, and I heard his bones crunch, and I cried in mockery: 'Ree me the riddle of *thy* life!'

But he answered naught.

Then I threw down the wall of the well; and I burned the house with fire that stood thereby, with the men-servants and the maid-servants.

And none dared stay me; for I laughed and exulted in my madness. Yea, verily, I laughed, and laughed – and laughed –

7

Then being healed of my madness I took all the treasure of that old Magus which he had laid up for many years – and none gainsaid me. Great and splendid was it of gold more than twelve bullocks could draw, of balassius rubies, and sardonyx, and beryl, and chrysoprase; of diamond and starry sapphire, of emerald much, very much, of topaz and of amethyst great and wonderful gems. Also he had a figure of Nuit greater than a woman, which was made of lapis lazuli specked with gold, carved with marvellous excellence. And he had the secret gem of Hadit that is not found on earth, for that it is invisible save when all else is no more seen.

Then went I into the market and bought slaves. I bought me in particular a giant, a Nubian blacker than polished granite seen by starlight, tall as a young palm and straight, yet more hideous than the Ape of Thoth. Also I bought a young pale stripling from the North, a silly boy with idle languishing ways. But his mouth burned like sunset when the dust-storms blow. So pale and weak was he that all despised him and mocked him for a girl. Then he took a white-hot iron from the fire and wrote with it my name in hieroglyphics on his breast; nor did his smile once alter while the flesh hissed and smoked.

Thus we went out a great caravan to a rocky islet in the Nile, difficult of access for that the waters foamed and swirled dangerously about it. There we builded a little temple shaped like a beehive; but there was no altar and no shrine therein; for in that temple should the god be sacrificed unto himself.

Myself I made the god thereof; I powdered my hair with gold, and inwound it with flowers. I gilded my eyelids, and I stained my lips with vermilion. I gilded my breasts and my nails, and as God and Victim in one was I daily sacrificed unto that strange thing that was none other than myself. I made my giant Nubian high priest; and I endowed his wand with magic power, so that he might properly perform my rites. This he did to such purpose that many men from Memphis and even from more distant towns, leaving their gods, came thither, and did sacrifice. Then I appointed also the pale boy warder of the Sanctuary: and he swore unto me to be faithful unto death.

Now there arose a great strife in Memphis, and many foolish and lewd women cried out against us. So fierce was the uproar that a great company of women issued forth from the city and came into the island. They slew my pale boy at the gate, though sword in hand he fought against them. Then they frothed on, and I confronted them in my glory. They hesitated, and in that moment I smote them with a deadly itching, so that running forth they tore off their clothes and set themselves to scratching, while my people laughed until they ached.

At the term, indeed, with exhaustion and with loss of blood they died all; four hundred and two women perished in that great day's slaughter. So that the people of Memphis had peace for a while.

But as for me, I mourned the loss of that young slave. I had his body embalmed as is not fitting for other than a king. And at the door of the temple I placed his sarcophagus beneath a hedge of knives and spears, so that there was no other access to my glory.

Like honour hath no slave had ever.

Thus then I abode three cycles of the season; and at the end of that time the High Priest died.

For mine was a strange and dreadful rite to do; none other, and none unfortified by magic power, could have done this thing.

Yet I too sickened of that everlasting sacrifice. I was become worn and wan; there was no blood but ice in my veins. I had indeed become all but a god ...

Therefore I took the body of my Nubian, and slew four young girls, and filled all the hollow spaces of his body with their blood. Then too I sealed up his body with eight seals; and the ninth seal was mine own, the centre of my godhead.

Then he rose slowly and staggeringly as I uttered the dreadful words:

> *A ka dua*
> *Tuf ur biu*
> *Bi aa chefu*
> *Dudu ner af an nuteru!*[1]

Then I touched him with my wand and he rose into full power of his being; and we entered in, and for the last time did he perform (though silent) the ceremony. At whose end he lay shrivelled and collapsed, shrunken like an old wineskin; yet his blood availed me nothing. I was icier than before. Yet now indeed was I Osiris, for I sent out flames of cold grey glory from my skin, and mine eyes were rigid with ecstasy.

Yea, by Osiris himself, I swear it! Even as the eyes of all living men revolve ceaselessly, so were mine fixed!

Then I shook myself and went forth into the city of Memphis, my face being veiled and my steps led by slaves.

And there I went into the temples one by one; and I twitched aside my veil, whereat all men fell dead on the instant, and the gods tumbled from their places, and broke in pieces upon the floor.

And I veiled myself, and went into the market-place and lifted up my voice in a chant and cried:

> Death, and desolation, and despair!
> I lift up my voice, and all the gods are dumb.
> I unveil my face, and all that liveth is no more,
> I sniff up life, and breathe forth destruction.
> I hear the music of the world, and its echo is Silence.
>
> Death, and desolation, and despair!
> The parting of the ways is come: the Equinox of the Gods is past.
> Another day: another way.
> Let them that hear me be abased before me!
> Death, and desolation, and despair!

Then I pulled away my veil, and the cold lightnings of death shot forth, and the people of the city fell dead where they stood.

---

[1] [Oh high one, may he be praised, the one great of power, the spirit great of dignity, who places fear of himself amongst the gods.]

Save only one, a young boy, a flute-player, that was blind, and, seeing not those eyes of mine, died not.

Then to him I spake, saying:

'Arise, summon the priests and the people, all that remain. And let them build a temple unto Osiris the God of the dead, and let the dead be worshipped for ever and ever.'

This I said, and went out from the city with the two slaves that I had left in the gate, and we went unto Nile, unto a cave by the bank of the river; and there I abode for many months, weeping for Isis my Lady. For though I had avenged her in many dreadful deeds, yet I brought her not back unto life. Moreover the love of her was as it were dead in me, so that my heart stirred not at the thought of her. Say that my love wandered like a ghost unburied, frozen, adrift upon the winds!

Now of my deeds at this period it is almost too horrible to tell. For I performed great penance, in the hope of vitalising that dead principle in me which men call the soul.

I starved myself shamefully, in this manner. First surrounding myself with all possible luxuries of food, brought in steaming and savoury from hour to hour, I yet condemned myself to subsist upon a little garlic and a little salt, with a little water in which oats had been bruised.

Then if any wish arose in me to eat of the dainties around me I gashed myself with a sharp stone.

Moreover I kindled a great fire in the cave so that the slaves stumbled and fainted as they approached. And the smoke choked me so that I constantly vomited a black and ill-smelling mucus from my lungs, stained here and there with frothing blood.

Again, I suffered my hair to grow exceeding long, and therein I harboured vermin. Also, when I lay down to sleep, though this I did not till with swollen tongue and blackened throat I could no longer howl the name of my dead Lady, then (I say) did I smear my limbs with honey, that the rats of the cave might gnaw them as I slept. Moreover, I pillowed mine head upon a corpse dead of leprosy, and whenever that dead soul of mine stirred at all with love toward my Lady, then I caressed and kissed that corpse, and sang soft songs to it, playing with gracious words and gestures. All this spoke loudly to my soul, rebuking it for its weakness and corruption. So too the bitterness and foulness of my life would often overleap the limit of sensibility; and then for hours together would I be lost in a raging whirlwind of laughter. At this time my slaves would be afraid to come anigh me, and then darting out of the cave I would catch one by the hair and dragging him within put him to exquisite torture. This indeed was of great use to me; for I would devise atrocious things, and if they served to excite his utmost anguish I would then try them on myself. Thus I would run needles steeped in Nile mud beneath my finger-nails, so that the sores festering might produce a sickening agony. Or again I would cut strips of skin and tear them off; but this failed, though it acted well enough upon the slave, for my own skin had become too brittle. Then I would take a piece of hard wood, and hammer it with a stone against the bones, hurting the membrane that covers them, and causing it to swell. This too I had to abandon, for the limb of the slave died, and he swelled up and rotted and turned green, and in shocking agony he died.

So then I was compelled to cure myself magically, and this was a great loss of force.

Yet was I 'Far from the Happy Ones,' although my lips hung on my fleshless face like bean-pods withered and blackened, and although there was not one inch of skin upon all my body that was not scarred.

Yet my trial was nigh its end. For the people of Memphis, wondering at the frequent purchases of dead lepers made always by the same slave, began, as is the wont of the ignorant, to spread foolish rumours. At last they said openly 'There is an holy hermit in the old cave by Nile.' Then the barren women of the city came out stealthily to me in the hope that by my sanctity their dry sticks might blossom.

But I showed them my dead leper, and said 'Let me first beget children upon this, and after I will do your business.' This liked them not; yet they left me not alone, for they went home and cried out that I was an horror, a ghoul, a vampire.... And at that all the young and beautiful women of the city, leaving their lovers and their husbands, flocked to me, bringing gifts. But I took them to the dead leper and said, 'When you are beautiful as that is beautiful, and when I am weary of its beauty and its delight, then will I do your pleasure.'

Then they all raged vehemently against me, and stirred up the men of the city to destroy me. And I, not being minded to display my magic force, went by night (so soon as I heard of this) and took sanctuary in the shrine of Osiris that I had caused them to build. And there I attained felicity; for uniting my consciousness with the god's, I obtained the expansion of that consciousness. Is not the kingdom of the dead a mighty kingdom?

So I perceived the universe as it were a single point of infinite nothingness yet of infinite extension; and becoming this universe, I became dissolved utterly therein. Moreover, my body lifted itself up and rose in the air to a great height beyond the shadow of the earth, and the earth rolled beneath me; yet of all this I knew nothing, for that I was all these things and none of them. Moreover I was united with Isis the Mother of Osiris, being yet her brother and her lord.

Woe, woe to me! for all this was but partial and imperfect; nor did I truly understand that which occurred.

Only this I knew, that I should return to my city of Thebai, and rule therein as High Priest of Osiris, no longer striving to some end unheard-of or impossible, but quietly and patiently living in the enjoyment of my dignities and wealth, even as a man.

Yet one thing I saw also, that as Isis is the Lady of all Nature, the living; and as Osiris is the Lord of the Dead, so should Horus come, the Hawk-headed Lord, as a young child, the image of all Nature and all Man raised above Life and Death, under the supreme rule of Hadit that is Force and of Nuit that is Matter – though they are a Matter and a Force that transcend all our human conceptions of these things.

But of this more anon, in its due place.

8

Behold me then returned to Thebai! So scarred and altered was I, though not yet thirty years of age, that they knew me not. So I offered myself as a serving-man in the temple of Osiris, and I pleased the priests mightily, for by my magic power – though they thought it to be natural – I sang songs unto the god, and made hymns. Therefore in less than a year they began to speak of initiating me into the priest-hood. Now the High Priest at this time was a young and vigorous man, black-bearded in the fashion of Osiris, with a single square tuft beneath the chin. Him had they chosen after my departure in the whirl-wind. And the High Priestess was a woman of forty and two years old, both dark and beautiful, with flashing eyes and stern lips. Yet her body was slim and lithe like that of a young girl. Now, as it chanced, it was my turn to serve her with the funeral offerings; flesh of oxen and of geese, bread, and wine. And as she ate she spake with me; for she could see by her art that I was not a common serving-man. Then I took out the consecrated Wand of Khem that I had from my father; and I placed it in her hand. At that she wondered, for that Wand is the sign of a great and holy initiation: so rare that (as they say) no woman but one has ever attained unto it. Then she blessed herself that she had been permitted to look upon it, and prayed me to keep silence for a little while, for she had somewhat in her mind to do. And I lifted up the wand upon her in the nine-and-forty-fold benediction, and she received illumination thereof, and rejoiced. Then I fell at her feet – for she was the High Priestess – and kissed them reverently, and withdrew.

Then three days afterwards, as I learnt, she sent for a priestess who was skilled in certain deadly crafts and asked of her a poison. And she gave it, saying: 'Let the High Priest of the God of the dead go down to the dead!' Then that wicked High Priestess conveyed unto him subtly the poison in the sacraments themselves, and he died thereof. Then by her subtlety she caused a certain youth to be made high priest who was slovenly and stupid, thinking in herself 'Surely the god will reject him.' But at his word the Image of the god glowed as was its wont. And at that she knew – and we all knew – that the glory was departed; for that the priests had supplanted the right ceremony by some trick of deceit and craft.

Thereat was she mightily cast down, for though wicked and ambitious, she had yet much power and knowledge.

But instead of using that power and that knowledge she sought to oppose craft with craft. And suspecting (aright) whose cunning had done this thing she bribed him to reverse the machinery, so that the High Priest might be shamed. But shamed he was not; for he lied, saying that the God glowed brighter than the Sun; and he lied securely, for Maat the Lady of Truth had no place in that temple. To such foulness was all fallen by my first failure to assume the god-form, and their priestly falsehood that my sanctity had rapt me into heaven. Nor had the wealth they lied to obtain availed them aught; for Pharaoh had descended upon Thebai, and laid heavy hand upon the coffers of the temple, so that they were poor. Even, they sold good auguries for gold; and these were a very destruction to them that bought. Then they sold curses, and sowed discord in the city. Wherefore the people grew poorer still, and their gifts to the temple waxed even less.

For there is no foolishness like the hunger after gain.

Of old the gods had given blessing, and the people offered freely of their plenty.

Now the priests sowed chaff, and reaped but barrenness.

So I waited patiently in silence to see what might befall. And this foolish priestess could think of no better expedient than formerly. But this young stupid man had guessed how his predecessor was dead, and he touched not the sacraments; but feigned.

Then she called for me – and I was now ordained priest – to take counsel of me; for she was minded to put me in his place.

Thus she made a great banquet for me; and when we were well drunken she laid her head upon my breast and said marvellous things to me of love, to me, who had loved the Veiled One! But I feigned all the madness of passion and made her drunk thereon, so that she talked great words, frothing forth like dead fishes swollen in the sun, of how we should rule Thebai and (it might be) displace Pharaoh and take his throne and sceptre. Yet, foolish woman! she could not think how she might remove this stupid high priest, her own nominee! So I answered her 'Assume the Form of Osiris, and all will be well in the Temple of Osiris.' Mocking her, for I knew that she could not. Yet so drunken was she upon love and wine that there and then she performed the ritual of Adoration and Assumption.

Then I in merry mood put out my power, and caused her in truth to become Osiris, so that she went icy stark, and her eyes fixed....

Then she tried to shriek with fear, and could not; for I had put upon her the silence of the tomb.

But all the while I feigned wonder and applause, so that she was utterly deceived. And being tired of mocking her, I bade her return. This she did, and knew not what to say. At first she pretended to have received a great secret; then, knowing how much higher was my grade initiation, dared not. Then, at last, being frightened, she flung herself at my feet and confessed all, pleading that at least her love for me was true. This may well have been; in any case I would have had compassion upon her, for in sooth her body was like a flower, white and pure, though her mouth was heavy and strong, her eyes wrinkled with lust, and her cheeks flaccid with deceit.

So I comforted her, pressing her soft body in mine arms, drinking the wine of her eyes, feeding upon the honey of her mouth.

Then at last I counselled her that she should bid him to a secret banquet, and that I should serve them, disguised in my old dress as a serving-man.

On the next night after this he came, and I served them, and she made open love (though feigned) to him. Yet subtly, so that he thought her the deer and himself the lion. Then at last he went clean mad, and said: 'I will give thee what thou wilt for one kiss of that thy marvellous mouth.' Then she made him swear the oath by Pharaoh – the which if he broke Pharaoh would have his head – and she kissed him once, as if her passion were like the passion of Nile in flood for the sandy bars that it devoureth, and then leaping up, answered him, 'Give me thine office of High Priest for this my lover!' With that she took and fondled me. He gaped, aghast; then he took off the ring of office and flung it at her feet; he spat one word in her face; he slunk away.

But I, picking up the ring of office, cried after him: 'What shall be done to who insulteth the High Priestess?'

And he turned and answered sullenly: 'I was the High Priest.' 'Thou hadst no longer the ring!' she raged at him, her face white with fury, her mouth dripping the foam of her anger – for the word was a vile word! ...

Then she smote upon the bell, and the guard appeared. At her order they brought the instruments of death, and summoned the executioner, and left us there. Then the executioner bound him to the wheel of iron by his ankles and his waist and his throat; and he cut off his eyelids, that he might look upon his death. Then with his shears he cut off the lips from him, saying, 'With these lips didst thou blaspheme the Holy One, the Bride of Osiris.' Then one by one he wrenched out the teeth of him, saying every time: 'With this tooth didst thou frame a blasphemy against the Holy One, the Bride of Osiris.' Then he pulled out the tongue with his pincers, saying: 'With this tongue didst thou speak blasphemy against the Holy One, the Bride of Osiris.' Then took he a strong corrosive acid and blistered his throat therewith, saying: 'From this throat didst thou blaspheme the Holy One, the Bride of Osiris.' Then he took a rod of steel, white-hot, and burnt away his secret parts, saying: 'Be thou put to shame, who hast blasphemed the Holy One, the Bride of Osiris.' After that, he took a young jackal and gave it to eat at his liver, saying: 'Let the beasts that devour carrion devour the liver that lifted itself up to blaspheme the Holy One, the Bride of Osiris!' With that the wretch died, and they exposed his body in the ditch of the city, and the dogs devoured it.

Now all this while had my lady dallied amorously with me, making such sweet moan of love as never was, yet her face fixed upon his eyes who loved her, and there glared in hell's torment, the body ever striving against the soul which should exceed.

And, as I judge, but the favour of Set the Soul gat mastery therein.

Also, though I write it now, coldly, these many thousand years afterward, never had I such joy of love of any woman as with her, and at that hour, so that as I write it I remember well across the mist of time every honey word she spoke, every witching kiss (our mouths strained sideways) that she sucked from my fainting lips, every shudder of her soft strong body. I remember the jewelled coils of hair, how they stung like adders as they touched me; the sharp rapture of her pointed nails pressing me, now velvet-soft, now capricious-cruel, now (love-maddened) thrust deep to draw blood, as they played up and down my spine. But I saw nothing; by Osiris I swear it! I saw nothing, save only the glare in the eyes of that lost soul that writhed upon the wheel.

Indeed, as the hangman took out the corpse, we fell back and lay there among the waste of the banquet, the flagons overturned, the napery awry, the lamps extinct or spilt, the golden cups, chased with obscene images, thrown here and there, the meats hanging over the edge of their bejewelled dishes, their juice staining the white luxury of the linen; and in the midst ourselves, our limbs as careless as the wind, motionless.

One would have said: the end of the world is come. But through all that fiery abyss of sleep wherein I was plunged so deep, still stirred the cool delight of the knowledge that I had won the hand for which I played, that I was High Priest of Osiris in Thebai.

But in the morning we rose and loathed each other, our mouths awry, our tongues hanging loose from their corners like thirsty dogs, our eyes blinking in agony from the torture of daylight, our limbs sticky with stale sweat.

Therefore we rose and saluted each other in the dignity of our high offices; and we departed one from the other, and purified ourselves.

Then I went unto the Ceremony of Osiris, and for the last time the shameful farce was played.

But in my heart I vowed secretly to cleanse the temple of its chicanery and folly. Therefore at the end of the ceremony did I perform a mighty banishing, a banishing of all things mortal and immortal, even from Nuit that circleth infinite Space unto Hadit the Core of Things; from Amoun that ruleth before all the Gods unto Typhon the terrible Serpent that abideth at the end of things, from Ptah the god of the pure soul of æthyr unto Besz the brute force of that which is grosser than earth, which hath no name, which is denser than lead and more rigid than steel; which is blacker than the thick darkness of the abyss, yet is within all and about all.

Amen!

Then during the day I took counsel with myself, and devised a cunning to match the cunning of them that had blasphemed Osiris, who had at last become my God.

Yea! bitterly would I avenge him on the morrow.

9

Now this was the manner of my working, that I inspired the High Priestess to an Oracle, so that she prophesied, saying that Osiris should never be content with his servants unless they had passed the four ordeals of the elements. Now of old these rituals had been reserved for a special grade of initiation. The chapter was therefore not a little alarmed, until they remembered how shamefully all the true magic was imitated, so that the rumour went that this was but a device of the High Priestess to increase the reputation of the temple for sanctity. And, their folly confirming them in this, they agreed cheerfully and boasted themselves. Now then did I swathe them one by one in the grave-clothes of Osiris, binding upon the breast and image, truly consecrated, of the god, with a talisman against the four elements.

Then I set them one by one upon a narrow and lofty tower, balanced, so that the least breath of wind would blow them off into destruction.

Those whom the air spared I next threw into Nile where most it foams and races. Only a few the water gave back again. These, however, did I bury for three days in the earth without sepulchre or coffin, so that the element of earth might combat them. And the rare ones whom earth spared I cast upon a fire of charcoal.

Now who is prepared for these ordeals (being firstly attuned to the elements) findeth them easy. He remains still, though the tempest rage upon the tower; in the water he floats easily and lightly; buried, he but throws himself into trance; and, lastly, his wrappings protect him against the fire, though all Thebai went to feed the blaze.

But it was not so with this bastard priesthood of Osiris. For of the three hundred only nine were found worthy. The High Priestess, however, I brought through by my magic, for she had amused me mightily, and I took great pleasure in her love, that was wilder than the rage of all the elements in one.

So I called together the nine who had survived, all being men, and gave them instruction and counsel, that they should form a secret brotherhood to learn and to teach the formula of the Osiris in its supreme function of initiating the human soul. That they should keep discipline in the temple only for the sake of the people, permitting every corruption yet withdrawing themselves from it. Is not the body perishable, and the skin most pure? So also the ancient practice of embalming should fall into desuetude, and that soon; for the world was past under the rule of Osiris, who loveth the charnel and the tomb.

All being sworn duly into this secret brotherhood I appointed them, one to preside over each grade, and him of the lowest grade to select the candidates and to govern the temple.

Then did I perform the invoking Ceremony of Osiris, having destroyed the blasphemous machinery; and now at last did the God answer me, glittering with infinite brilliance. Then I disclosed myself to the Priests, and they rejoiced exceedingly that after all those years the old lie was abolished, and the master come back to his own.

But the god uttered an Oracle, saying: 'This last time shall I glitter with brilliance in My temple; for I am the god of Life in Death, concealed. Therefore shall your magic henceforth be a magic most secret in the heart; and whoso shall perform openly any miracle, him shall ye know for a liar and a pretender to the sacred Wisdom.

'For this cause am I wrapped ever in a shroud of white starred with the three active colours; these things conceal Me, so that he who knoweth Me hath passed beyond them.'

Then did the god call us each separately to him, and in each ear did he whisper a secret formula and a word of power, pertaining to the grade to which I had appointed him.

But to me he gave the supreme formula and the supreme word, the word that hath eight-and-seventy letters, the formula that hath five-and-sixty limbs.

So then I devoted myself there and then to a completer understanding of Osiris my God, so that I might discover his function in the whole course of the Cosmos.

For he that is born in the years of the power of a God thinketh that God to be eternal, one, alone. But he that is born in the hour of the weakness of the God, at the death of one and the birth of the other, seeth something (though it be little) of the course of things. And for him it is necessary to understand fully that change of office (for the gods neither die nor are reborn, but now one initiates and the other guards, and now one heralds and the other sanctifies) its purpose and meaning in the whole scheme of things.

So I, in this year v of the Equinox of the Gods (1908) wherein Horus took the place of Osiris, will by the light of this my magical memory seek to understand fully the formula of Horus – Ra Hoor Khuit – my god, that ruleth the world under Nuit and Hadit. Then as Ankh-f-na-khonsu left unto me the stèla 666 with the keys to that knowledge, so also may I write down in hieroglyph the formula of the Lady of the Forked Wand and of the Feather, that shall assume his throne and place when the strength of Horus is exhausted.

So now the service of the Gods was to be secret and their magic concealed from men. They were to fall before the eyes of men from their place, and little sewer-rats were to come and mock at them, no man avenging them, and they utterly careless, not striking for themselves. Yet was there knowledge of them which an initiate might gain, though so much more difficult, immeasurably higher and more intimate.

My life from this moment became highly concentrated upon itself. I had no time either for ascetic practices or for any pleasures; nor would I take any active part in the service of the temple which, purified and regenerated, had become both subtly perfect and perfectly subtle.

It was not all of the people who did at all comprehend the change that had occurred; but the others obeyed and made believe to understand, lest their fellows should despise them. So it happened that the more ignorant and stupid any person was the more he feigned understanding; so that the least devout appeared the most devout – as it is unto this day.

But for me all these things were as nothing; for I studied ever the nature of Osiris, concentrating myself into mysterious pure symbols. I understood why it was said that Isis had failed to discover the Phallus of Osiris, and thus perceived the necessity of Horus to follow him in the great succession of the Equinoxes. Moreover I fashioned talismans of pure light concerning Osiris, and I performed in light all the ceremonies of initiation into his mysteries.

These were interpreted by wise men and translated into the language of the twilight and graven on stone and in the memories of men.

Yet was I even more intrigued in that great struggle to apprehend the course of things, as it is seen from the standpoint of Destiny. So that I might leave true and intelligible images to enlighten the mind of him (whether myself or another) that should come after me to celebrate the Equinox of the Gods at the end of the period of Osiris.

As now hath come to pass.

Thus then three-and-thirty years I lived in the temple of Osiris as High Priest; and I subdued all men under me. Also I abolished the office of priestess, for had not Isis failed to find that venerable Phallus without which Osiris must be so melancholy a god? Therefore was Khemi to fall, and the world to be dark and sorrowful for many years.

Therefore I made mine High Priestess into a serving-maid, and with veiled face she served me all those many years, never speaking.

Yet they being accomplished, I thought fit to reward her. So magically I renewed about her the body of a young girl, and for a year she served me, unveiled and speaking at her pleasure.

And her time being come, she died.

Then I looked again into my destiny, and perceived that all my work was duly accomplished. Nor could any use or worth be found in my body.

So therefore I determined to accept my great reward, that was granted unto me as the faithful minister of the god F.I.A.T. that is behind all manifestation of Will and of Intelligence, of whom Isis and Osiris and Horus are but the ministers.

Of this, and of my death, I will speak on another occasion.

But first I will discourse of the inhabitants of the kingdom that encircleth the world, so that they who *fear* may be comforted.

10

But of these matters I am warned that I shall not now become aware, for that there be great mysteries therein contained, pertaining to a degree of initiation of which I am as yet unworthy.

(Thus the record comes abruptly to an end.)

His Secret Sin

INSCRIBED ADMIRINGLY TO ALEXANDER COOTE

I

Theodore Bugg had made England what she is. The last forty-two years had elevated him from errand-boy to biggest retail grocer in the Midlands. Twenty-eight years of wedded happiness had left him with a clear conscience, a five-year old grave to keep in order 'To the memory of my beloved relict,' as he had written until the clerk suggested a trifling alteration, and a strapping daughter just turned twenty.

I wish I could stop here. But there is a rough side to every canvas, and Theodore Bugg had forgotten all about England, and what she is, and how he had made her. Or if the good work was going on, it was subconscious. He was standing by the gilded statue of Jeanne d'Arc, his mouth wide open, his Baedeker limp in his perspiring hand. 'She's riding astride!' The molten madness throbbed in his brain. 'She's got man's clothes on!'

The shocking truth must out: Theodore Bugg had come to Paris for Pleasure!

He had only been able to spare two days, the Sunday and Monday of Whitsuntide. He had travelled by the night boat on Saturday, arriving in Paris on Sunday morning – the first step downward! The air of Paris intoxicated him; the Grands Boulevards ate into his moral fibre like a dragon chewing butter; and though he had not actually 'been in' anywhere, he felt the atmosphere of the music-halls as Ulysses heard the Sirens. He was fortunately tied to the mast of his ignorance of French and his fear of asking anybody such a very peculiar question, or he would certainly have discovered and visited the Moulin Rouge.

As it was, Joan of Arc was very much more than was good for him. He stared, fascinated as by a basilisk, his eyes starting further and further from his head as his moral sense dragged his body backwards along the Rue de Rivoli. By this means he cannoned into a worthy Frenchman (who refused to take him seriously) and so was shocked into himself.

He pulled out his watch. Only an hour and a half to catch his train. Just as he was beginning to enjoy himself, too. What a shame! He couldn't even send a telegram without letting somebody know where he was – and at home they supposed him to be visiting a business acquaintance in Shropshire.

I'll have a memento, thought he, if I die for it. I'll – I don't care. I may as well be hung for a sheep as a lamb – I'll go the whole hog. I know there's shops about here.

So, turning, in his excitement and determination, he saw – when you invoke the devil he is usually halfway to you – a shop window full of photographs of the pictures and sculptures of the Louvre. He looked up and down the street – the sight of a top hat might have saved him even at the eleventh hour. But no! nothing that looked in the least like an Englishman, even to his overheated fear of discovery. He peered and dodged about for a little like a man stalking dangerous game, and then, with sudden stealth, his back to the door, pushed down the lever and slid into the shop.

'*Avvy-voo photographiay?*' he said hurriedly, with averted face.

'Certainly, sir,' replied the shopkeeper in perfect English. 'What does Monsieur require? Photographs of Paris, of Fontainebleau, of the Louvre, of Versailles?'

But English would not serve the turn of Theodore Bugg. He nearly bolted from the shop. An English voice – it was almost Discovery!

'*Kelker shows,*' he muttered doggedly enough, though his head hung lower than ever. '*Kelker shows tray sho. Voo savvy? – tray tray sho – par propre!*'

The shopman, not yet old enough to master his disgust at the familiar incident, brought forward several books of photographs.

'Perhaps Monsieur will find there what he requires,' he said coldly.

Furtively and hurriedly, his glance divided between the forbidden book and the shop-door, his only safeguard from intrusion the thought that nobody who entered would be in a position to throw stones at a fellow-culprit, Theodore Bugg turned over the pages.

The book began mildly enough with the winged Victory and only entered the rapids with *La Gioconda*. Thence, Niagara-like, one plunge to the abyss – the Venus de Milo.

The blood flamed to his face; his breath came hot and quick.

With fumbling fingers that trembled with excitement he withdrew the photograph from its leaf and half showed it to the proprietor with a whispered '*Comby-ang*?'

'*Trente sous*,' said the shopman in his most rapid French. And in English, 'We take English money here, sir; ten shillings, if you please. May I wrap it up for you?' But Bugg had thrust it into his inner pocket, and, pressing a sovereign into the man's hand, dashed without looking behind him from the shop, eager to put time and space between himself and his compromising position.

He hurried to his hotel, not without many a suspicious glance over his shoulder, and packed his bag. He had ten minutes to spare. He locked the door carefully, sat down with his back to the light, and pulling the photograph from his pocket, indulged in a long voluptuous gloat.

Then the boots knocked with the news of his cab, and Bugg, nobler than Lord Howard of Effingham, thrust his treasure into his pocket, unlocked the door and cried '*Venny!*'

2

Theodore Bugg, a year later, was paying the price of his fall. He had allowed Gertrude to attend Art Classes, although he knew it to be wrong. But he had grown to fear his daughter, and – on such a point especially – he was incapable of fighting her.

For there were times when he tried to persuade himself that there was 'nothing wrong in it.' A brother churchwarden had looked a little askance when the news of Gertrude's 'advanced ideas' had come; but Theodore had stoutly and even a little sternly rebuked him with the original remark: 'To the pure all things are pure.' It was knowing when to be bold that had made Theodore the fine businessman he was.

And very bold it was, for conscience makes cowards of us all. The secret shame of his orgies! Every weeknight – once even on a Sunday! – after everyone had gone to bed, he opened the little safe in the wall at the head of his bed, and drew forth the obscene picture from its envelope marked 'In case of my death or disability THIS PACKET is to be DESTROYED UNOPENED. T. Bugg.' Then he would sit, and hold it in his hot hands, and gloat upon the evil thing, lifting it now and again to his mouth to cover it with greedy, slobbering kisses. And afterwards, when it was safely locked up again, he would undress with a certain unction. Once even he attempted – with the aid of a bath towel – to take the pose before the mirror. And he saw nothing ridiculous in that, just as he saw nothing beautiful in the photograph. Nakedness is lust: so ran his simple gospel of æsthetics.

Shame quickened him, too, to measures of expiation or precaution. He read family prayers twice a day instead of once, and he took the chair at the Annual Meeting of a Society for Sending Out Trousers to Converted Hindoos.

As everybody in the Midlands knows, 'Hindoos' are Naked Savages. And he discharged a groom for whistling on Sunday.

But if these expedients salved his conscience, they did nothing to quell Gertrude's incipient tendency to independence of thought and action. There had been a very unpleasant scene when he threw into the fire a book from Mudie's (I thought one could have trusted Mudie's!) called *The Stolen Bacillus*, which he understood to be of a grossly immoral tendency. (Nasty filth about free love or something, isn't it?)

Theodore Bugg was not a sensitive man; excess of intuitive sympathy had not made his life a hell; but he felt that his domestic relations were strained. Especially since 'that Mrs Grahame' had evinced a liking for Gertrude. Her husband's colonelcy was the gilding of the pill; but the pill was a bitter one, for Mrs Grahame went motoring and even golfing on Sunday instead of going to Church, and once or twice had taken Gertrude with her, to the scandal of the neighbourhood. Colonel Grahame, too, rather got on Bugg's nerves, in spite of the 'honour of his acquaintance.'

Such thoughts went dully through his mind as he waited in the garden for his daughter to come in to tea from the 'Art Class.' But when she arrived, portfolio in hand, her beauty and the splendour of her long easy swing determined him to be gracious.

Under such circumstances conversation is apt to be artificial; but Gertrude was gay and garrulous, and the tea went very pleasantly until her father's eye unluckily fell on the portfolio. 'And what has my little fairy been doing lately?' he asked with elephantine lightness.

'Oh, sketches mostly, father. This week we're copying from old Greek masterpieces, though. Let me show you, father, dear.' She opened the portfolio and turned over the leaves. 'I'm getting on splendidly. Mr Davis thinks I ought to go to Paris and study properly. Do let me.'

'How can you think of such a thing, Gertrude? A daughter of mine! Study properly!!! No indeed! A little sketching is a nice accomplishment for a young lady, but —'

His jaw dropped. A thin, graceful pencil sketch it was that he clutched in frenzied fingers; but he could not mistake the subject.

'Wretched girl,' he shouted, 'where did you get the – the – the – Damn it all, what d'ye call it? – the – ay! that's it! – the model for this vile, filthy, lewd, obscene, lustful thing? Damn it! you're as bad as Cousin Jenny! (Cousin Jenny was a blot on the 'scutcheon of the Buggs.) You're a harlot, miss!' And then, with an awful change as the truth came home to him: 'O my God! O my God! Damn it!' he screamed, 'how did you get the keys of my little safe?'

The girl had frozen colder than the stone, but there was a new light in her eye, and if the curl of a lip could tread a worm into the dust, that lip was hers and that worm the author of her being. She had withdrawn as one who comes suddenly upon a toad, and the first flaming of her face had died instantly to deadlier ice.

Bugg saw his mistake, his masses of mistakes. There being but one more to make, he made it; and, finding himself in the frying-pan of discovery, leapt into the fire of things irrevocable and not to be forgotten. His fat, heavy-jowled, coarse face all twitching, he fell on his knees and clasped his hands together. 'So you found me out? Don't, don't give away your poor old father, Gertie! My little Gertie!'

There was a silence. 'Excuse me, father,' said the girl at last, 'but I've just had a glimpse of you for the first time in my life, and it's a bit of a shock. I must think.'

And she stood motionless until her hapless father attracted her attention by backing into his wicker chair. 'Don't touch holy things,' she snapped suddenly, taking the sketch from his nerveless hand, and replacing it reverently in the portfolio.

The action seemed to decide her.

'I'll give you an address to send my things to,' she said, and walked out of the garden.

Theodore Bugg sat stunned. 'Holy things,' she had said. She called that lustful French photograph holy! Was this Original Sin; or was it that strange new thing people were talking about – what was it? Ah! heredity. Heredity? His secret sin become her open infamy? Truly the sins of the fathers were visited on the children!

By this time he was upstairs and in his bedroom. He must destroy the accursed thing; he must destroy – Ah! yes. He had contaminated Gertrude by having such a thing in his house. He must be the Roman father, and – what would a Roman father do?

He had the match alight, but he could not put it to the edge of the packet. Then the silence of the house hit him; he knew that his daughter would never return, and in a fit of rage he trampled on the envelope like a wild beast mauling a corpse.

He thrust it into the empty grate, lit the paper frills, watched all blaze up. Then, gulping down a sob, he went to the drawer of a cabinet and pulled out the revolver which he had bought (and loaded, under the shopman's guidance) against burglars.

Yes, he must kill himself. He drew back the hammer. Cold sweat beaded his flabby face. He could not; and anyhow, how did one? He thought of many stories of people who had shot themselves ineffectively. He felt for his heart and failed to find it, wondered if it had stopped and he were dying, had a fit of fear paralysing all his will. He thought of himself lying dead.

'No, by God! I can't do it!' he cried, and flung the pistol back into the drawer. As luck would have it, the weapon exploded. The bullet broke his jaw, tore away four molars, smashed the cheekbone, pulped the right eye, and, glancing from the frontal bone, found its billet in the ceiling. He lost consciousness and fell. His head struck the grate where yet smouldered the ashes of the photograph.

It was three months before he recovered, and then with only half a face to face the world with. He still thinks that Gertrude gave him away, for the street-boys have taken to calling him 'old Venus.' But he is wrong; the boys have their æsthetic reasons for the name.

Gertrude in any case is much too busy to bother her head about him; for, after a year in the Latin Quarter, if she has failed to surpass Degas and Manet and O'Conor, she has at least conquered the great pianist Wlodywewsky, and it takes her all her time to manage him and keep the baby out of mischief.

Theodore Bugg needs no help of hers in his moral sculpture of the destinies of England.

The Woodcutter

Placide Gervez was a woodcutter, like his father and grandfather before him. It is to be supposed that Nature was weary of the procession, for Placide had never married, but lived alone in his hut in the forest of Fontainebleau, just too far from the borders for it ever to be worth his while to go into a village for a drink except on very special occasions. He had even been overlooked for military service; and the Prussians had come and gone without interfering with his chopping. He could not read or write, and his language had many less than half a thousand words.

In such conditions he deserved his Christian name. In the forest even an hour calms the most turbulent spirit; a day will cure most worries; and a week with an axe may be recommended to neurasthenics as more than the equivalent of the most expensive Weir-Mitchell treatment and rest-cures. If fashionable doctors could afford to be honest, they would order work-cures for nine-tenths of their patients.

Forty-eight years with an axe in the forest had turned Placide Gervez into a mixture of Stoic, Cynic and Epicurean; he boasted the simplicity and fortitude of each in respect of pain, propriety and pleasure.

The droning hum of the forest, broken rarely by the birds – magpie, crow, cuckoo, and nightingale – meant nothing to him in the summer; nor did the monotonous drip depress him in the winter. The ringing thud of his axe and the crash of the murdered tree were neither history nor tragedy to him; the comic and the pastoral were equally sealed books, for the forest has neither satyrs nor shepherds. He had no sport, since in his boyhood his father had thrashed him for throwing his axe at a stag; and no society, for the nearest forester thought him a boor. He chopped to live, and lived to chop.

It was the philosopher of the Rue de Chevreuse who cast the grain of sand into the wheels of this approximation to the solution of the problem of perpetual motion. The philosopher was really a painter, but so bad a painter that he was only known as a theorist in the café which supplied his crème de menthe. There he would hold forth interminably on God and man.

Blessed with such means as a mediocre father's devotion to cutlery and an only son had supplied, it was his habit on occasion to descend into the country. Picture him, if you please, as very short and moderately fat, middle-aged at thirty-two, clad in a bourgeois suit and an artist's tie, a red handkerchief under a black felt hat upon a bushy head garnished with a little beard and moustache, perspiring in a sandy and interminable bridle-path leading from the Long Rocher to nowhere in particular.

These walks he would undertake (*a*) for his health, (*b*) to absorb the beauties of nature – as he would often demonstrate. Yet the greatest of philosophers are not always logical, and he would have been compelled to discover other reasons for his choice of company. This consisted of a lady whose age was rendered only more uncertain by her efforts to nail conjecture to the number 25. Her hair paled visibly from the scalp, and her neck darkened visibly from the chin. She had made the fortune of India in rice powder, and of China in vermilion. The extravagance of her person and attire, exaggerated even for the Café d'Harcourt, the fortress whence her sallies, was in Fontainebleau a thing to make earth's guardian angels throw up the sponge.

This was a summer's afternoon; and the strange pair, encountering Placide Gervez as he chopped, accosted him. The philosopher, whose irrelevant name was Théophraste Goulet, drew out a cigarette and offered it to his intended victim. It is impossible in a polite nation to leave a man until you have finished the cigarette he gives you – a man, if he was a man, once gave me an Irish cigarette, but that story is a separate cheque – and Placide could not have cut that knot save with his axe. However, in the first pause of the voluble ass for breath, he pointed to his work, uttered the adjective 'Hard,' and continued to chop.

However, the purport of the discourse – in a highly condensed form – was as follows.

God is good, was the First Postulate of Theophrastus. Hence, all God does is good. Hence, since God made man, He meant man to do good. Hence, man should do good. Agreed. Then, what is good? The necessities of life are good, for otherwise no other good were possible without them. Food is good, shelter is good, all that tends to the health of the individual and the reproduction of the species is good. For if not, let food be bad, let art be good. Then, since artists need food, good is based on bad, which is absurd. Agreed, then, that necessary things are good. Yes; but are these the only good? No; for these benefits absorb only part of the time and energy of man. Is it good to chop wood? Yes, undoubtedly; but it is also good to render woodcutting in art. Then why should not the woodcutter be an artist? Why should he not chop miracles of carving? The Michael Angelo of Fontainebleau? Why not? What does Browning say? 'I want to know the butcher paints, the baker rhymes for his pursuit,' and so on. Very well; then what do you do that is truly good? That is, unnecessarily, supererogatively, and therefore superlatively good? You, my friend! You chop wood. Good. You cherish a fair wife; you have strong children to defend the father-land. Good again. You eat, you drink, you make merry: all good. But do you achieve fame? No. Glory? No. Are you a great saint? No. A great artist? No. A great sinner? No. Nothing great? No. Very well, then: not good. Rise up, man! (the peroration) Be not slothful, be am-bitious! Be statesman, artist, divine, strategist, inventor; nay, thief or murderer, if you will! But do not be content to chop wood!

During this quarter of an hour of eloquence his was not the only discourse. The fair friend of the philosopher, eager to impress men in her way as he in his, and equally omnivorous, was busy with Placide Gervez. First a sidelong glance struck armour quite impenetrable to such assault, quickly followed by smiles first secret and then open, gestures at first subtle and at last unmistakable, finally by the unspeak-able grimace of the tongue which she had learnt in her time at the red-shuttered convent in the Rue des Quatre Vents. Her triumph was that once the woodcutter struck aslant, and swore.

Théophraste ended his discourse, and, pleasantly parting, sauntered off with his mistress, arm-in-arm. Neither of them gave their victim another thought. Out of the wood they went, and (thank God!) out of the story.

But Placide leant upon his axe and stared after them. In his brain one thought only remained, which Théophraste might have formulated logically as 'Some men do not chop wood.' And in his heart and eye was a dull animal lust. Two strangers had come to his soul's Inn. There being only one room, he put them to bed together, in this form or something like it: 'Chop – chop – chop – chop; I'm sick of it. Even if I had a fine girl from Paris like that, what could I do but chop – chop – chop – chop?'

For the first time in his life he went home half an hour earlier than his custom, to the accompaniment of a terrific thunderstorm that rolled up from the valley of the Loing and fell like night upon the forest, like a dark winter's night that afternoon of May.

He was wet to the skin before he reached his hut. Opening the door, he glowered with dull surprise. Equally wet, standing in one corner and wringing out a blouse, was a girl of about twenty years old, an Amazon maid. He could see that she was a lady – that is, that she was not a villager; but he had no means of knowing that she was the Honourable Diana Villiers-Jernyngham-Ketteringham.

Placide spoke a patois that a Parisian might have surmised to be Cherokee, and Diana's boarding-school French would have been given up by that Parisian as no earthly language at all.

She told him that she was staying at the Savoy Hotel at Fontainebleau, and had gone for a walk and lost her way in the forest; and she asked him how far was it to the nearest village, and would he please take her there, and she would give him money.

All this while Placide lit his fire, and proceeded to cook beans. He did not understand her, or try to understand her. There was a strange animal in his hut, possibly a human animal; it might like beans; he would offer it beans. It was not his affair; his affair was to chop – chop – chop – chop.

Diana was a little afraid of this silent beast at first. But the offer of food seemed kindly, and she ate some beans lest he should take offence, found them surprisingly good, nodded satisfaction, and even asked for more.

This part concluded, she went to the door. The rain poured unceasingly; the forest stood in pools; and it was too dark to tell one tree from another. The woodcutter joined her, shook his head, said 'far' and 'tomorrow,' and pointed to a heap of straw.

This strong-minded young lady knew when to bow to the inevitable; she took an armful of the straw, and retiring with it to the other end of the hut, made the sleep sign which every savage understands, and lay down.

Placide Gervez grunted assent, and lying down with a surly '*Bon soir*' dropped instantly to sleep. How was he to know what dreams would echo his quarter of an hour with the two philosophers of Paris?

About eleven o'clock the next morning some of the well-horsed search-party from Fontainebleau reached the hut.

At the door, as carefully stacked as the rest, they found the severed limbs of the Honourable Diana. And in the forest the cheery, ringing thud of his axe led them to Placide Gervez, quietly, manfully chopping.

They told him of a Widow Lady in Paris who could beat him at his own game.

Professor Zircon

Muriel Maddox was a blonde frail piquant thing, a fluffy baby of nineteen easy summers. But she was a hard-working orphan, too, with no relations but a semi-mythical brother on the Yukon who had not found enough gold to send her any; and she earned her living – two pounds a week – as violinist to the splendid tea-parties of the Hotel Escoffier.

Her liking for Professor Zircon was little more than a child's, though the shaggy-headed old analyst told another story to his brother experts at the War Office. And indeed, though her nature was incapable of great passion, what she had she gave, and to the innocence of a child added a dog's fidelity and trust.

Professor Zircon was a happy old man; he called her his Chloride of Gold. 'Muriel means salt, you know,' he would explain to the fellows at the Club, 'and salt is a compound of hydrochloric or muriatic acid – I wonder if we shall produce a little Zirconium Chloride!' At this jest thus elaborated he was wont to laugh seven time a week; and trot happily back to his house in Kensington for dinner. Seven times a week he would let himself in through the laboratory and pretend surprise when he found Muriel reading a novelette in his own arm-chair.

'What, what! and how the deuce did you get in?' or 'Tut! tut! my dear madam, to what am I indebted for the honour of this visit?' or 'I beg a thousand pardons, madam, I really thought this was my house,' and Muriel, genuinely pleased and amused, would enter into the little comedy, always ending up with kisses in the old arm-chair, and a dainty dinner.

This had continued for nearly three years with no interruption but once, when the Professor's wife, from whom he had long been separated, succeeded in getting into the house on some pretence, and creating a very considerable uproar before the Professor and his butler could master her rage. She was a big muscular woman from Australia with the body of a tiger and the temper of a snake. She would have made a winning fight of it but for Zircon's adroit sortie to the laboratory and timely return with a bottle of chloroform.

The Professor dined alone that night; at the very outset of the battle Muriel had fled in tears to the little room in Walham Green where she lived under the alleged guardianship of a most paunchy ex-dresser.

No other incident disturbed the ripples of their harmless, petty liaison. Even the earlier rumours of the brother in Alaska had died down to folklore.

The Professor had never got away from his work in time to hear her play the fiddle; anyhow, he hated music. Nor had Muriel ever stayed too late to alarm her landlady, who thought she played at supper as well as at tea.

The illness of the Secretary of War alarmed only the German Ambassador, who could not be positive that in case of his death an accident might not happen and a capable person be appointed to the post. The annoyance of his death – telephoned to the Office at three o'clock one afternoon – was concentrated on Professor Zircon, torn away from a compound with half the Greek Alphabet dotted about its name by a white-haired little Colonel who assured him that it really wasn't decent.

'We won't go to the Club, dear man. We'll just drop in at the Escoffier for tea.'

The Professor grunted an assent; but he was more than half pleased. He wondered what his fairy looked like in her butterfly wings.

The lounge of the Escoffier was full of people; but right across the room Professor Zircon could see Muriel with cornflowers in her yellow-ashen hair and her simple muslin dress. But she wore the diamonds he had given her, a string of starlight at her neck. How well he remembered that evening! He had taken her into the laboratory and heated up some sugar with sulphuric acid, loving her amazement as it swelled and blackened. 'That is carbon now,' he had said, 'if we could only crystallise it, what splendid diamonds we could have! But we can't – not to any effect. Diamonds are always found in a kind of blue mud – I suppose there can't be any here?' leading her to a box full of modelling clay which he used in some of his experiments. And he made her dive and dirty her dear little fingers ever so, before she ran against the necklace. And when they retrieved it quite, and washed it, and he put it round her neck for her very own!

She played in her demure, modest way; not very good, but pleasing enough to people who only wanted an excuse for not having to think sufficiently to talk while they wolfed *foie gras* and watercress, muffins and éclairs, cheesecakes and hot buttered toast. And she seemed to care as little for them as they for her.

The Professor and the Colonel had risen to go.

'That's my little Muriel – I call her the Spirit of Salt – ha! ha! ho!'

'A damn nice little bit of fluff – damn lucky boy!' growled the Colonel, winking at a chorus girl (in two thousand pounds' worth of furs) whose salary was thirty shillings a week.

Suddenly the Professor paled. A last glance over his shoulder showed him that a bearded man had risen and was handing a flower to Muriel. And Muriel was blushing and trembling with some emotion too profound to estimate, but clear enough to the analyst.

When a man has detected a thousandth of a grain of atropine in the carcass of a barmaid, he does not hesitate to read the heart of a girl. And as a Government expert he was clothed with official infallibility – a triple buckler.

He went on casually talking to the Colonel for a few minutes before politeness allowed him to throw himself into a moving taxi-cab and roar his address at the astonished driver. It was the first time he had come home to an empty house since he had picked up Muriel on an omnibus and carried her off to a discreet Italian restaurant near Sloane Square, where a flask of Chianti emptied to the bottom had left not a dreg of discretion.

The arm-chair shocked him. This was the last time that she would sit in it, the false little harlot! The eternal emptiness of things, the unbreakable solitude of life, struck a chill to his marrow. How was he to know that only by uttermost surrender of the self to the Beloved can that curse be broken?

Then a gleam of sanity crossed the bigoted scientific mind of the man. She might be able to explain. But he brushed away the idea. How can a fact ever be upset?

Credulity itself is reason compared to the mind of the logician who has once allowed emotion to infect his brain, who has missed the factor of the personal equation.

The idea returned. So long she had sat there in her childish purity that the conservatism of his hard old brain reacted. It could not be. Things could not change. Yet? In the upshot he was English enough to try her before condemning her, German enough to lay a trap for her in the very nature of that trial.

His consideration passed from judgement to execution, and his face set like a mask. Ultimately he went to a small safe in the wall, took out a half-hoop diamond ring, and dropped it into the coal-scuttle.

Reward or punishment! Either the old trick – or a new one! He turned on his heel and went softly into the laboratory.

Meanwhile Muriel Maddox tripped along from the Escoffier in the bright February air. Her heart was very light and very anxious. The incident of the afternoon – should she tell the Professor? Concealment was foreign to her nature; for the first time in her life she hesitated. How would it affect their relations?

It would be better to think it over, to sleep on it. It never occurred to her for a moment that the Professor might already know. In the end she decided to say nothing; but so absorbed had been her tiny brain in its little problem that she forgot the obvious corollary of removing the flower from her dress.

She was nestled in the arm-chair when the old analyst tiptoed into the room and clapped his hands over her eyes.

'Who is it?' said he gaily.

'Why, you're Jack from Alaska, of course,' she answered, laughing.

'Guess again?'

And the child guessed the German Emperor, and Lewis Waller, and everyone else she could think of.

'Wrong.

'Wrong.

'Wrong.'

'Why,' she cried, jumping up and facing him, 'it's Professor Zircon! The last person in the world I should have expected to find here!'

She threw her arms round his neck and called him a 'dear silly.'

'Well, what's the news, child?'

'No news. I'm so sorry the chief's dead.'

'Doesn't matter to me. What a pretty flower in your dress!'

She had an instinct of sudden and terrible danger; and lied instantly. 'I bought it for your buttonhole.' And she fastened it there.

Professor Zircon called her a sweet, thoughtful fairy, and gave her a kiss. Such a shudder ran through him as rarely stirred his veins. He had some flash of memory, of Judas, perhaps, signalled across the forty years since he had heard the legend of the Gospels at his mother's knee.

'But there is news!' he added gaily. 'I'm going to show you my great discovery. I've found out how to make diamonds. Just crystallising coal, you see; so simple when you know how to do it. Wait a minute!' And he fetched a small electric machine from the laboratory and solemnly made it spark in the coal-scuttle.

'There! he announced triumphantly. Now we'll see if we've managed to crystallise any coal!'

So the child began to hunt in the scuttle, and in a few minutes found the ring glittering in its dusty setting, like the eyes of a snake in the jungle.

'Oh, you darling!' she cried. 'Oh, you old fraud! You said nothing about making gold!'

'Ah! that's a little accident,' replied the Professor. 'Discoveries never come singly.'

'And is it really for me? All my very own?'

'Who else should it be for, darling?'

'You're a darling sweet boy.'

'Run away and wash your hands! I've warmed up your own element for you, you dear little Spirit of Salt!'

She ran gleefully into the laboratory. On the bench stood the basin she had used so often, with the soap and towels neatly at its side. She seized the soap, and plunged both hands into the nearly boiling hydrochloric acid. Then she turned her head to him, her mouth a tragic square, incapable even of uttering even a shriek.

'How will you play the fiddle,' screamed Zircon, 'with no fingers? How will you play the harlot? I saw you and your lover. There's his flower!' He flung it at her. 'But I'm even with you – Oh! I'm even with you!' And he foamed into a spate of the filthiest abuse.

It broke the spell. Scream after scream broke from her mouth until, choking with their very volume, her voice broke to a strangled yell, and the agony of the acid bit into her soul. She fell on the floor fainting.

'Vile thing!' screamed Zircon, spurning her with his foot. He choked; his brain fell suddenly clear with the lucidity of intellect. He walked into the dining-room, and whistled as he walked. There he sat down.

The next move in his infernal revenge was the waking of Muriel, and that might be soon or late. He had not calculated the effect of waiting; his nerves cried out. For the first time he had a glimpse of the doctrine of eternal punishment – perceived that the resurrection of the body was no necessary condition. Tortured, he gazed upon the second hand of his watch. He could have sworn it stopped, when it shook and staggered on with the importance of Big Ben, and he realised that his own time-sense was radically upset. He wondered if it was the same with her – the devil in him gloated.

'A gentleman to see you, sir!' said he butler, opening the door. 'He wouldn't give his name!'

'I'll see him,' said Zircon, as blithe as a lark. 'Show him in!'

In strode the bearded stranger of the afternoon.

'You damned scoundrel!' he addressed the smiling Professor. 'So this is where my sister spends her evenings! Be good enough to explain —'

He broke off, for the Professor had thrust both hands deep into his trouser pockets and leant back against the bookcase, laughing, laughing, laughing.

The Vitriol-Thrower

TO KATHLEEN SCOTT

I

The Boulevard Edgar Quinet is convenient for life and death. There is a squalid toil and squalid pleasure, represented by the Gare Montparnasse and the Rue de la Gaieté; at the other end is the exotic struggle of the quaint little colony of English artists. The boulevard itself hangs between these extremes; but, sinister and terrible omen! the whole of one side is occupied by that vast cemetery of Montparnasse which Charles Baudelaire has honoured by his bones.

I like to think that Baudelaire, brooding like an unquiet fiend above his carrion, may laugh, though it be but the laugh of hell, at this my tale.

A man who has deliberately taken human life on no responsibility but his own enjoys some of the immunities of a God. The habit of acting first and thinking afterwards is surely divine, or how can we explain the universe? Among civilised people few such men are to be found; they may be known by the grave courage of their steadfast eyes. Would you like to meet one? The first place to search is most certainly the Boulevard Edgar Quinet.

At least this is certain, that if you had been strolling down by the cemetery on Monday night before Mardi-Gras, twelve years ago, you would have had your opportunity.

Clement Seton was a tiny little man with a pale face. One would have said that he suffered from a wasting illness. On his finger flashed a single ruby. Very unwise of you, young man! for the boulevard, deserted and leading no whither in particular, is the haunt of the greatest ruffians in Paris.

The two Apaches in the shadow laughed. Silent and swift, they leapt. But the Scot was swifter yet. Ten feet away he stood with a Colt levelled in the gloom, demanding 'Your pleasure, gentlemen?'

They began some stammering excuse; the boy's light laugh trilled out, and he lightly replaced his weapon, turned on his heel, and left them to follow if they dared.

There is almost opposite the end of the boulevard an *impasse* miscalled the Rue Boissonade. A road it would have been, save for the obstinate leases in the midst thereof. A road it one day surely will be, but at present it is certainly trying that from No. n to No. $n+1$ is a circuitous journey of near upon half a mile. On the right as you enter is a small low house, roofed for a studio, old-fashioned, with its ugly modern neighbours sneering over it. It had a bad name, too, even among the easy-going folk of Bohemian Paris.

Is your face the face of a cat or of a pig, strange dweller in that desolate house? Where did you get that shaggy mane of fire? Your face is covered with fine down, every tip whereof stings like a nettle. You have eyes that must devour the soul of a man ere they can sleep. You have long and heavy lips ever twitching; one thinks of an octopus waiting for its prey. Is that your blood that makes them scarlet, or the blood of all those who would not be warned in time?

How is it, too, that all men own you beautiful? How, surer test! that all women deny you beauty?

For beautiful you are. Your face is the face of some divine beast, adored of the Egyptians or the Mexicans.

What of your soul? Is that, too, the soul of a God and a beast? Does your face that warns us, and in vain, tell truth? People are afraid of you, Mirabelle! they cross the road to avoid passing over the pavements you have trod.

Who was that poor Hungarian boy that men cut down one morning from your gate? and the pianist who poisoned himself in Vienna?

What did the painter see in your eyes that he slashed your finished face from his canvas, and drew the second stroke across his throat?

Is there any gate of death, Mirabelle, that some man has not passed – for you?

Why, too, do you tire your hair so carefully tonight? You only lift your finger, and they die for you. Why, then, do you struggle? There is anxiety, not only pride, in the thrice-gazed-on mirror. You have swathed yourself close like a corpse; the amber silk clings to your beautiful body. After all, you have taken down your hair; it flows over your breasts like a river of hell.

How is it that you are waiting? Others should wait, surely; it is not for you to wait. You are in danger, Mirabelle; there is a God in heaven after all.

Yes, and you will have him in your arms.

2

Clement Seton shrugged his shoulders and threw his cigar away with a gesture of weariness. Life in Paris seemed tame after his exploits in Somaliland, where he had won the Victoria Cross standing over a wounded comrade half the day, while the survivors of what had been a very smart little outpost scrimmage tried in vain to come to terms with that waterless warrior.

'Most cowardly thing I ever did,' he would explain. 'The poor beggars couldn't get at us for the rocks. When a head appeared one put a bullet through it. Like bally clay pigeons, by Jove!' and then he would go on, in his talkative nonsensical way, with some absurd paradox in ethics or metaphysics.

Yet what good was to come of Paris? Bitter scorn of the sneaking Apaches ate up his soul. To come to grips with a devil were worth the pains. Murderers, he mused, are the salt of the earth. And lo! the salt hath lost its savour. And he laughed sourly.

At the gate of the lonely house he flung away his cigar, and his hand was on the latch.

Suddenly, a noiseless touch upon the arm, and a low, hurried, pleading voice.

'Clement, my old friend, listen a moment.'

He turned, and saw dear, fat, good-natured old Miss Aitken. What was there in this woman to make her (as she had been) the friend of Swinburne, Carrière and Verlaine?

Artists hate artists, not for envy, but because there can be no companionships among the Gods. Eternally silent in himself, a God sees all, knows all; yet nothing touches him. He can learn nothing from another such, while his study is mankind. So true friendship is their prize; Miss Aitken could not guess their detachment; she thought them human. Maybe this flattered the poor Gods. In their weak hours they accept devotion gladly.

Miss Aitken stood, white to the lips; her terror shining about her visibly.

'That house is fatal, Clement,' she moaned. 'Go anywhere but there!' Patient and smiling, Clement heard her out. Half was he fain to put her off with a lie – some folly about God in heaven.

Then truth urged him to sing the song he had made of Mirabelle –

> The world for a whore!
>   The sky for a harlot!
> All life – at your door –
>   For a Woman of Scarlet!
> A bitter exchange?
>   A bad bargain to strike? It
> May seem to you strange –
>   The fact is – I like it!
>
> You offer me gold,
>   Place, power, and pleasure
> To have and to hold –
>   Inexhaustible treasure!
> I'll give it and more
>   In this planet of boredom
> For a girl that's a whore
>   And is proud of her whoredom.

He reflected that such truth might seem to her but a sneer. So in the end he pressed her hand, thanked her, bade her be of good cheer, passed in.

3

Like a frail ghost, poor worn-out Sylvie glided from the graveyard, and confronted Clement Seton.

Three months had passed since his first visit to Mirabelle the wonderful and beautiful, and still daily he strolled down the boulevard to his destiny. Thin and pale are you growing, my fine fool? Is it the air of Paris that robs you of your blood? We know better. Are you quite besotted? Or would you rather die thus than live otherwise?

This we cannot think; he cannot be absorbed body and soul in the contemplation of Mirabelle's perfections; for when poor worn-out Sylvie, with her harsh cough and hectic cheek, addresses him, he hears.

She took him to a corner of the graveyard, eagerly, with her worn face all fire, ever looking back. For he followed sedately. Clement would run nor to nor fro.

She paused by a low grave. 'Here,' she said, 'lies Sergius, whom I loved – ah God! She took him from me; she threw him away, and laughed when he pistolled himself at her doorstep. You are her lover, monsieur. She will serve you so. I swear it. She lives for nothing else. God! God! to have these fingers but one moment at her throat.'

She burst into a passion of weeping anger.

Seton lit a pipe. 'This Mirabelle!' he mused. 'She leads me to Pisgah,' he thought, 'she feeds me with milk and honey from the Promised Land. But to enter in and to possess it? No. She knows possession is but the prelude to the Captivity, the Exile to great Babylon. But who am I, to waste the months? I have said: Easy to write the curtain-raiser, but few who can pen five pungent acts. Yet, why should I wait? Why not make drama myself? Tragedy, no! for I am God, and must laugh at everything. Well! Well!'

'I will kill her, kill her,' sobbed the girl, kissing the cross upon the tomb.

Seton smiled, bent down caressingly, and whispered in her ear. Then swiftly turning he bent no undecided step towards the Gardens of his Armida.

* * *

Trembling in each other's arms with the violence of their repressed passion, Clement and Mirabelle still lay. Now he put forth all his force; always she easily eluded it.

'For your sake, O goddess!' he exclaimed. 'You are not utterly high, because you have not touched humanity. I sacrifice the splendour of our passion to initiate you.'

'Not you then, but another!' she laughed wildly. 'You are the only one that can play the Game; I will not use you up.'

He looked at her doubtfully; then he knew she lied. Hers was a real prudery.

'Galilean!' he cried, 'thou hast conquered!'

But so shocking was the irony of his voice that for a moment she feared him.

Then, rising up, they talked of many indifferent things; yet, being gods, all language was hieroglyphic to their intimacy; so that she marked a change.

'Am I adream?' she said; 'did not I win the bout?'

'At the odds,' he said.

And again a chill passed over her.

Some premonition of things utterly forlorn?

Some intimate fear of the soul, struck bare and cold in the presence of its God?

'Tire yourself carefully tonight,' wooed Clement in his velvet voice.

She thought of Jezebel, and a third time she shuddered.

Nevertheless, right comely was she, and golden in sheen of gossamer silk.

In the Boulevard Edgar Quinet the wear is not silk, O Mirabelle the beautiful! Rather a shroud. The desolate trees of the boulevard do not rustle like silk; rather do they whisper like murderers in league. The stones of the boulevard do not rustle like silk; they clatter foolishly. Is it not as the tears of your false passion on the adamantine hearts of men?

Mystic and doubtful, from behind a tree leaps out a ghost. With one hoarse word, poor worn-out Sylvie flings her vitriol, and speeds laughing down the boulevard.

Full in the face it splashed her; the great curse rose to a shriek and sank to a moan.

Clement Seton carried her back to the studio.

4

Jolly fat old Miss Aitken! What a treasure you are in a world of sorrow!

Mirabelle's sins, which were many, were forgiven; especially as she could sin no more, thought she.

So she and Clement nursed her back to life; the face no more a face. One blind scar, more fearful to look upon than death. Her hands had escaped; one could judge by her hands what her beauty must have been.

But we are interested in her soul. In her weakness she grew human; and Clement, loving her through the flesh, loved her yet more. Why did he make her his mistress? You shall judge. But why did she comply? Who shall judge that? Judge not too easily; I myself, who am the great God who made these, dare not say.

So in the closest intimacy for more than a year they lived; and good-natured Miss Aitken like a mother to them.

Now was a new life stirred in Mirabelle; when Seton heard it, he called Miss Aitken aside privily, and said to her: 'Dear friend, you may guess what she and I have always known: Love at its climax must decay thence. Such is the common lot; nothing escapes. I have given Mirabelle a child; let her seek there for new worlds to conquer. For me, I have studied her enough. Sylvie is dying; her consumption draws her to a close. I shall go live with her, and feast upon her end.

'She loves me, since I helped her vengeance; and hates me, since I have lifted her victim to such heights of joy. You never guessed? Yes, Sylvie loved Sergius, whom Mirabelle stole from her. 'Twas I that bade her throw the acid. Anon.'

And he went whistling off. But to Miss Aitken, whose excellent memory broke this atrocious speech to Mirabelle, replied that expressionless mask of horror: 'I knew it. I went to the death of myself that night; I went willingly, wittingly. It was Ananke and the Moirai. Moreover, I have had much joy of Clement; I leap with joy, breeding this child to him.

'Let him go to Sylvie: it is a woman's part to see her husband go away on strange errands. Was not Juno foolish, with her gadfly?'

In fact, when Sylvie died, Clement came back to her, brotherly. He had chosen the right moment to break off the tie; Socrates suicide is finer than Socrates turned dotard. So they remained fast friends.

The child was twelve years old last week. In him we see the seeds of miraculous thoughts, things to transcend all limitations mortal and immortal, common to man.

The Overman is surely come; in the second generation is he established.

The Testament of Magdalen Blair

PART I

I

In my third term at Newnham I was already Professor Blair's favourite pupil. Later, he wasted a great deal of time praising my slight figure and my piquant face, with its big round grey eyes and their long black lashes; but the first attraction was my singular gift. Few men, and, I believe, no other women, could approach me in one of the most priceless qualifications for scientific study, the faculty of apprehending minute differences. My memory was poor, extraordinarily so; I had the utmost trouble to enter Cambridge at all. But I could adjust a micrometer better than either students or professor, and read a vernier with an accuracy to which none of them could even aspire. To this I added a faculty of subconscious calculation which was really uncanny. If I were engaged in keeping a solution between (say) 70° and 80° I had no need to watch the thermometer. Automatically I became aware that the mercury was close to the limit, and would go over from my other work and adjust the Bunsen without a thought.

More remarkable still, if any object were placed on my bench without my knowledge and then removed, I could, if asked within a few minutes, describe the object roughly, especially distinguishing the shape of its base and the degree of its opacity to heat and light. From these data I could make a pretty good guess at what the object was.

This faculty of mine was repeatedly tested, and always with success. Extreme sensitiveness to minute degrees of heat was its obvious cause.

I was also a singularly good thought-reader, even at this time. The other girls feared me absolutely. They need not have done so; I had neither ambition nor energy to make use of any of my powers. Even now, when I bring to mankind this message of a doom so appalling that at the age of twenty-four I am a shrivelled, blasted, withered wreck, I am supremely weary, supremely indifferent.

I have the heart of a child and the consciousness of Satan, the lethargy of I know not what disease; and yet, thank – oh! there can be no God! – the resolution to warn mankind to follow my example, and then to explode a dynamite cartridge in my mouth.

2

In my third year at Newnham I spent four hours of every day at Professor Blair's house. All other work was neglected, gone through mechanically, if at all. This came about gradually, as the result of an accident.

The chemical laboratory has two rooms, one small and capable of being darkened. On this occasion (the May term of my second year) this room was in use. It was the first week of June, and extremely fine. The door was shut. Within was a girl, alone, experimenting with the galvanometer.

I was absorbed in my own work. Quite without warning I looked up. 'Quick!' said I, 'Gladys is going to faint.' Everyone in the room stared at me. I took a dozen steps towards the door, when the fall of a heavy body sent the laboratory into hysterics.

It was only the heat and confined atmosphere, and Gladys should not have come to work that day at all, but she was easily revived, and then the demonstrator acquiesced in the anarchy that followed. 'How did she know?' was the universal query; for that I knew was evident. Ada Brown (*Athanasia contra mundum*)[1] pooh-poohed the whole affair; Margaret Letchmere thought I must have heard something, perhaps a cry inaudible to the others, owing to their occupied attention; Doris Leslie spoke of second sight, and Amy Gore of 'sympathy.' All the theories, taken together, went round the clock of conjecture.

Professor Blair came in at the most excited part of the discussion, calmed the room in two minutes, elicited the facts in five, and took me off to dine with him.

'I believe it's this human thermopile affair of yours,' he said. 'Do you mind if we try a few parlour tricks after dinner?'

His aunt, who kept house for him, protested in vain, and was appointed Grand Superintendent in Ordinary of my five senses.

---

[1] [Athanasia against the world.]

My hearing was first tested, and found normal, or thereabouts. I was then blindfolded, and the aunt (by excess of precaution) stationed between me and the Professor. I found that I could describe even small movements that he made, so long as he was between me and the western window, not at all when he moved round to the other quarters. This is in conformity with the 'Thermopile' theory; it was contradicted completely on other occasions. The results (in short) were very remarkable and very puzzling; we wasted two precious hours in futile theorising. In the event, the aunt (cowed by a formidable frown) invited me to spend the Long Vacation in Cornwall.

During these months the Professor and I assiduously worked to discover exactly the nature and limit of my powers. The result, in a sense, was nil.

For one thing, these powers kept on 'breaking out in a new place.' I seemed to do all I did by perception of minute differences; but then it seemed as if I had all sorts of different apparatus. 'One down, t'other come on,' said Professor Blair.

Those who have never made scientific experiments cannot conceive how numerous and subtle are the sources of error, even in the simplest matters. In so obscure and novel a field of research no result is trustworthy until it has been verified a thousand times. In our field we discovered no constants, all variables.

Although we had hundreds of facts, any one of which seemed capable of overthrowing all accepted theories of the means of communication between mind and mind, we had nothing, absolutely nothing, which we could use as the basis of a new theory.

It is naturally impossible to give even an outline of the course of our research. Twenty-eight closely written note-books referring to this first period are at the disposal of my executors.

3

In the middle of the day, in my third year, my father was dangerously ill. I bicycled over to Peterborough at once, never thinking of my work. (My father is a canon of Peterborough Cathedral.) On the third day I received a telegram from Professor Blair, 'Will you be my wife?' I had never realised myself as a woman, or him as a man, till that moment, and in that moment I knew that I loved him and had always loved him. It was a case of what one might call 'Love at first absence.' My father recovered rapidly; I returned to Cambridge; we were married during the May week, and went immediately to Switzerland. I beg to be spared any recital of so sacred a period of my life: but I must record one fact.

We were sitting in a garden by Lago Maggiore after a delightful tramp from Chamounix over the Col du Géant to Courmayeur, and thence to Aosta, and so by degrees to Pallanza. Arthur rose, apparently struck by some idea, and began to walk up and down the terrace. *I was quite suddenly impelled to turn my head to assure myself of his presence.*

This may seem nothing to you who read, unless you have true imagination. But think of yourself talking to a friend in full light, and suddenly leaning forward to touch him.

'Arthur!' I cried, 'Arthur!'

The distress in my tone brought him running to my side. 'What is it, Magdalen?' he cried, anxiety in every word.

I closed my eyes. 'Make gestures!' said I. (He was directly between me and the sun.)

He obeyed, wondering.

'You are – you are' – I stammered – 'no! I don't know what you are doing. I am blind!'

He sawed his arm up and down. Useless; I had become absolutely insensitive. We repeated a dozen experiments that night. All failed.

We concealed our disappointment, and it did not cloud our love. The sympathy between us grew even subtler and stronger, but only as it grows between all men and women who love with their whole hearts, and love unselfishly.

4

We returned to Cambridge in October, and Arthur threw himself vigorously into the new year's work. Then I fell ill, and the hope we had indulged was disappointed. Worse, the course of the illness revealed a condition which demanded the most complete series of operations which a woman can endure. Not only the past hope, but all future hope, was annihilated.

It was during my convalescence that the most remarkable incident of my life took place.

I was in great pain one afternoon, and wished to see the doctor. The nurse went to the study to telephone for him.

'Nurse!' I said, as she returned, 'don't lie to me. He's not gone to Royston; he's got cancer, and is too upset to come.'

'Whatever next?' said the nurse. 'It's right he can't come, and I was going to tell you he had gone to Royston; but I never heard nothing about no cancer.'

This was true; she had not been told. But the next morning we heard that my 'intuition' was correct.

As soon as I was well enough, we began our experiments again. My powers had returned, and in triple force.

Arthur explained my 'intuition' as follows: 'The doctor (when you last saw him) did not know consciously that he had cancer; but subconsciously Nature gave warning. You read this subconsciously, and it sprang into your consciousness when you read on the nurse's face that he was ill.'

This, farfetched as it may seem, at least avoids the shallow theories about 'telepathy.'

From this time my powers constantly increased. I could read my husband's thoughts from imperceptible movements of his face as easily as a trained deaf-mute can sometimes read the speech of a distant man from the movements of his lips.

Gradually as we worked, day by day, I found my grasp of detail ever fuller. It is not only that I could read emotions; I could tell whether he was thinking 3465822 or 3456822. In the year following my illness we made 436 experiments of this kind, each extending over several hours; in all 9363, with only 122 failures, and these all, without exception, partial.

The year following, our experiments were extended to a reading of his dreams. In this I proved equally successful. My practise was to leave the room before he woke, write down the dream that he had dreamt, and await him at the breakfast table, where he would compare his record with mine.

Invariably they were identical, with this exception, that my record was always much fuller than his. He would nearly always, however, purport to remember the details supplied by me; but this detail has (I think) no real scientific value.

But what does it all matter, when I think of the horror impending?

5

That my only means of discovering Arthur's thought was by muscle-reading became more than doubtful during the third year of our marriage. We practised 'telepathy' unashamed. We excluded the 'muscle-reader' and the 'super-auditor' and the 'human thermopile' by elaborate precautions; yet still I was able to read every thought of his mind. On our holiday in North Wales at Easter one year we separated for a week, at the end of that week he to be on the leeward, I on the windward side of Tryfan, at the appointed hour, he there to open and read to himself a sealed packet given him by 'some stranger met at Pen-y-Pass during the week.' The experiment was entirely success-ful; I reproduced every word of the document. If the 'telepathy' is to be vitiated, it is on the theory that I had previously met the 'stranger' and read from him what he would write in such circumstances! Surely direct communication of mind with mind is an easier theory!

Had I known in what all this was to culminate, I suppose I should have gone mad. Thrice fortunate that I can warn humanity of what awaits each one. The greatest benefactor of his race will be he who discovers an explosive indefinitely swifter and more devastating than dynamite. If I could only trust myself to prepare Chloride of Nitrogen in sufficient quantity....

6

Arthur became listless and indifferent. The perfection of love that had been our marriage failed without warning, and yet by imperceptible gradations.

My awakening to the fact was, however, altogether sudden. It was one summer evening; we were paddling on the Cam. One of Arthur's pupils, also in a Canadian canoe, challenged us to a race. At Mag-dalen Bridge we were a length ahead – suddenly I heard my husband's thought. It was the most hideous and horrible laugh that it is pos-sible to conceive. No devil could laugh so. I screamed, and dropped my paddle. Both the men thought me ill. I assured myself that it was not the laugh of some townee on the bridge, distorted by my over-sensitive organisation. I said no more; Arthur looked grave.

At night he asked abruptly after a long period of brooding, 'Was that my thought?'

I could only stammer that I did not know.

Incidentally he complained of fatigue, and the listlessness, which before had seemed nothing to me, assumed a ghastly shape. There was something in him that was not he! The indifference had appeared transitory; I now became aware of it as constant and increasing. I was at this time twenty-three years old. You wonder that I write with such serious attitude of mind. I sometimes think that I have never had any thoughts of my own; that I have always been reading the thoughts of another, or perhaps of Nature. I seem only to have been a woman in those first few months of marriage.

7

The six months following held for me nothing out of the ordinary, save that six or seven times I had dreams, vivid and terrible. Arthur had no share in these. Yet I knew, I cannot say how, that they were his dreams and not mine; or rather that they were in his subconscious waking self, for one occurred in the afternoon, when he was out shooting, and not in the least asleep.

The last of them occurred towards the end of the October term. He was lecturing as usual, I was at home, lethargic after a too heavy breakfast following a wakeful night. I saw suddenly a picture of the lecture-room, enormously greater than in reality, so that it filled all space; and in the rostrum, bulging over it in all directions, was a vast, deadly pale devil with a face which was a blasphemy on Arthur's. The evil joy of it was indescribable. So wan and bloated, its lips so loose and bloodless; fold after fold of its belly flopping over the rostrum and pushing the students out of the hall, it leered unspeakably. Then dribbled from its mouth these words: 'Ladies and gentlemen, the course is finished. You may go home.' I cannot hope even to suggest the wickedness and filth of these simple expressions. Then, raising its voice to a grating scream, it yelled: 'White of egg! White of egg! White of egg!' again and again for twenty minutes.

The effect on me was shocking. It was as if I had a vision of Hell.

Arthur found me in a very hysterical condition, but soon soothed me. 'Do you know,' he said at dinner, 'I believe I have got a devilish bad chill?'

It was the first time I had known him to complain of his health. In six years he had not had as much as a headache.

I told him my 'dream' when we were in bed, and he seemed unusually grave, as if he understood where I had failed in its interpretation. In the morning he was feverish; I made him stay in bed and sent for the doctor. The same afternoon I learnt that Arthur was seriously ill, had been ill, indeed, for months. The doctor called it Bright's disease.

8

I said 'the last of the dreams.' For the next year we travelled, and tried various treatments. My powers remained excellent, but I received none of the subconscious horrors. With few fluctuations, he grew steadily worse; daily he became more listless, more indifferent, more depressed. Our experiments were necessarily curtailed. Only one problem exercised him, the problem of his personality. He began to wonder *who he was*.

I do not mean that he suffered from delusions. I mean that the problem of the true Ego took hold of his imagination. One perfect summer night at Contrexéville he was feeling much better; the symptoms had (temporarily) disappeared almost entirely under the treatment of a very skilful doctor at that Spa, a Dr Barbézieux, a most kind and thoughtful man.

'I am going to try,' said Arthur, 'to penetrate myself. Am I an animal, and is the world without a purpose? Or am I a soul in a body? Or am I, one and indivisible in some incredible sense, a spark of the infinite light of God? I am going to think inwards; I shall possibly go into some form of trance, unintelligible to myself. You may be able to interpret it.'

The experiment had lasted about half an hour when he sat up gasping with effort.

'I have seen nothing, heard nothing,' I said. 'Not one thought has passed from you to me.'

But at that very moment what had been in his mind flashed into mine.

'It is a blind abyss,' I told him, 'and there hangs in it a vulture vaster than the whole starry system.'

'Yes,' he said, 'that was it. But that was not all. I could not get beyond it. I shall try again.'

He tried. Again I was cut off from his thought, although his face was twitching so that one might have said that anyone might read his mind.

'I have been looking in the wrong place,' said he suddenly, but very quietly and without moving. 'The thing I want lies at the base of the spine.'

This time I saw. In a blue heaven was coiled an infinite snake of gold and green, with four eyes of fire, black fire and red, that darted rays in every direction; held within its coils was a great multitude of laughing children. And even as I looked, all this was blotted out. Crawling rivers of blood spread over the heaven, of blood purulent with nameless forms – mangy dogs with their bowels dragging behind them; creatures half elephant, half beetle; things that were but a ghastly blood-shot eye, set about with leathery tentacles; women whose skins heaved and bubbled like boiling sulphur, giving off clouds that condensed into a thousand other shapes, more hideous than their mother; these were the least of the denizens of these hateful rivers. The most were things impossible to name or to describe.

I was brought back from the vision by the stertorous and strangling breath of Arthur, who had been seized with a convulsion.

From this he never really rallied. The dim sight grew dimmer, the speech slower and thicker, the headaches more persistent and acute.

Torpor succeeded to his old splendid energy and activity; his days became continual lethargy ever deepening towards coma. Convulsions now and then alarmed me for his immediate danger.

Sometimes his breath came hard and hissing like a snake in anger; towards the end it assumed the Cheyne-Stokes type in bursts of ever-increasing duration and severity.

In all this, however, he was still himself; the horror that was and yet was not himself did not peer from behind the veil.

'So long as I am consciously myself,' he said in one of his rare fits of brightness, 'I can communicate to you what I am consciously thinking; as soon as this conscious ego is absorbed, you get the subconscious thought which I fear – oh how I fear! – is the greater and truer part of me. You have brought unguessed explanations from the world of sleep; you are the one woman in the world – perhaps there may never be another – who has such an opportunity to study the phenomena of death.'

He charged me earnestly to suppress my grief, to concentrate wholly on the thoughts that passed through his mind when he could no longer express them, and also on those of his subconsciousness when coma inhibited consciousness.

It is this experiment that I now force myself to narrate. The prologue has been long; it has been necessary to put the facts before mankind in a simple way so that they may seize the opportunity of the proper kind of suicide. I beg my readers most earnestly not to doubt my statements; the notes of our experiments, left in my will to the greatest thinker now living, Professor von Bühle, will make clear the truth of my relation, and the great and terrible necessity of immediate, drastic action.

PART II

I

The stunning physical fact of my husband's illness was the immense prostration. So strong a body, as too often the convulsions gave proof; such inertia with it! He would lie all day like a log; then without warning or apparent cause the convulsions would begin. Arthur's steady scientific brain stood it well; it was only two days before his death that delirium began. I was not with him; worn out as I was, and yet utterly unable to sleep, the doctor had insisted on my taking a long motor drive. In the fresh air I slumbered. I awoke to hear an unfamiliar voice saying in my ear, 'Now for the fun of the fair!' There was no one there.

Quick on its heels followed my husband's voice as I had long since known and loved it, clear, strong, resonant, measured: 'Get this down right; it is very important. I am passing into the power of the subconsciousness. I may not be able to speak to you again. But I am here; I am not to be touched by all that I may suffer; I can always think; you can always read my —' The voice broke off sharply to enquire, 'But will it ever end?' as if someone had spoken to it. And then I heard the laugh. The laugh that I had heard by Magdalen Bridge was heavenly music beside that! The face of Calvin (even) as he gloated over the burning of Servetus would have turned pitiful had he heard it, so perfectly did it express the quintessence of damnation.

Now then my husband's thought seemed to have changed places with the other. It was below, within, withdrawn. I said to myself, 'He is dead!'

Then came Arthur's thought, 'I had better pretend to be mad. It will save her, perhaps; and it will be a change. I shall pretend I have killed her with an axe. Damn it! I hope she is not listening.' I was now thoroughly awake, and told the driver to get home quickly. 'I hope she is killed in the motor; I hope she is smashed into a million pieces. O God! hear my one prayer! let an Anarchist throw a bomb and smash Magdalen into a million pieces! especially the brain! and the brain first. O God! my first and last prayer: smash Magdalen into a million pieces!'

The horror of this thought was my conviction – then and now – that it represented perfect sanity and coherence of thought. For I dreaded utterly to think what such words might imply.

At the door of the sick-room I was met by the male nurse, who asked me not to enter. Uncontrollably, I asked, 'Is he dead?' and though Arthur lay absolutely senseless on the bed I read the answering thought 'Dead!' silently pronounced in such tones of mockery, horror, cynicism and despair as I never thought to hear. There was a something or somebody who suffered infinitely, and yet who gloated infinitely upon that very suffering. And that something was a veil between me and Arthur.

The hissing breath recommenced; Arthur seemed to be trying to express himself – the self I knew. He managed to articulate feebly, 'Is that the police? Let me get out of the house! The police are coming for me. I killed Magdalen with an axe.' The symptoms of delirium began to appear. 'I killed Magdalen' he muttered a dozen times, then changing to 'Magdalen with' again and again; the voice low, slow, thick, yet reiterated. Then suddenly, quite clear and loud, attempting to rise in the bed: 'I smashed Magdalen into a million pieces with an axe.' After a moment's pause: 'a million is not very many nowadays.' From this – which I now see to have been the speech of a sane Arthur – he dropped again into delirium. 'A million pieces,' 'a cool million,' 'a million million million million million million' and so on; then abruptly: 'Fanny's dog's dead.'

I cannot explain the last sentence to my readers; I may, however, remark that it meant everything to me. I burst into tears. At that moment I caught Arthur's thought, 'You ought to be busy with the note-book, not crying.' I resolutely dried my eyes, took courage, and began to write.

2

The doctor came in at this moment and begged me to go and rest. 'You are only distressing yourself, Mrs Blair,' he said, 'and needlessly, for he is absolutely unconscious and suffers nothing.' A pause. 'My God! why do you look at me like that?' he exclaimed, frightened out of his wits. I think my face had caught something of that devil's, something of that sneer, that loathing, that mire of contempt and stark despair.

I sank back into myself, ashamed already that mere knowledge – and such mean vile knowledge – should so puff one up with hideous pride. No wonder Satan fell! I began to understand all the old legends, and far more —

I told Doctor Kershaw that I was carrying out Arthur's last wishes. He raised no further opposition; but I saw him sign to the male nurse to keep an eye on me.

The sick man's finger beckoned us. He could not speak; he traced circles on the counterpane. The doctor (with characteristic intelligence) having counted the circles, nodded, and said: 'Yes, it is nearly seven o'clock. Time for your medicine, eh?'

'No,' I explained, 'he means that he is in the seventh circle of Dante's Hell.'

At that instant he entered on a period of noisy delirium. Wild and prolonged howls burst from his throat; he was being chewed unceasingly by 'Dis'; each howl signalled the meeting of the monster's teeth. I explained this to the doctor. 'No,' said he, 'he is perfectly unconscious.'

'Well,' said I, 'he will howl about eighty times more.'

Doctor Kershaw looked at me curiously, but began to count.

My calculation was correct.

He turned to me, 'Are you a woman?'

'No,' said I, 'I am my husband's colleague.'

'I think it is suggestion. You have hypnotised him?'

'Never; but I can read his thoughts.'

'Yes, I remember now; I read a very remarkable paper in *Mind* two years ago.'

'That was child's play. But let me go on with my work.'

He gave some final instructions to the nurse, and went out.

The suffering of Arthur was at this time unspeakable. Chewed as he was into mere pulp that passed over the tongue of 'Dis,' each bleeding fragment kept its own identity and his.

The papillæ of the tongue were serpents, and each one gnashed its poisoned teeth upon that fodder.

And yet, though the sensorium of Arthur was absolutely unimpaired, indeed hyperæsthetic, his consciousness of pain seemed to depend upon the opening of the mouth. As it closed in mastication, oblivion fell upon him like a thunderbolt. A merciful oblivion? Oh! what a master stroke of cruelty! Again and again he woke from nothing to a hell of agony, of pure ecstasy of agony, until he understood that this would continue for all his life; the alternation was but systole and diastole, the throb of his envenomed pulse, the reflection in consciousness of his blood-beat. I became conscious of his intense longing for death to end the torture.

The blood circulated ever slower and more painfully; I could feel him hoping for the end.

This dreadful rose-dawn suddenly greyed and sickened with doubt. Hope sank to its nadir; fear rose like a dragon, with leaden wings. Suppose, thought he, that after all death does not end me!

I cannot express this conception. It is not that the heart sank, it had nowhither to sink; it knew itself immortal, and immortal in a realm of unimagined pain and terror, unlighted by one glimpse of any other light than that pale glare of hate and of pestilence. This thought took shape in these words:

I AM THAT I AM.

One cannot say that the blasphemy added to the horror; rather it was the essence of the horror. It was the gnashing of the teeth of a damned soul.

3

The demon-shape, which I now clearly recognise as that which had figured in my last 'dream' at Cambridge, seemed to gulp. At that instant a convulsion shook the dying man and a coughing eructation took the 'demon.' Instantly the whole theory dawned on me, that this 'demon' was an imaginary personification of the disease. Now at once I understood demonology, from Bodin and Weirus to the moderns, without a flaw. But was it imaginary or was it real? Real enough to swallow up the 'sane' thought!

At that instant the old Arthur reappeared. 'I am not the monster! I am Arthur Blair, of Fettes and Trinity. I have passed through a paroxysm.'

The sick man stirred feebly. A portion of his brain had shaken off the poison for the moment, and was working furiously against time.

'I am going to die.

'The consolation of death is Religion.

'There is no use for Religion in life.

'How many atheists have I not known sign the articles for the sake of fellowships and livings! Religion in life is either an amusement and a soporific or a sham and a swindle.

'I was brought up a Presbyterian.

'How easily I drifted into the English Church!

'And now where is God?

'Where is the Lamb of God?

'Where is the Saviour?

'Where is the Comforter?

'Why was I not saved from that devil?

'Is he going to eat me again? To absorb me into him? O fate inconceivably hideous! It is quite clear to me – I hope you've got it down, Magdalen! – that the demon is made of all those that have died of Bright's disease. There must be different ones for each disease. I thought I once caught sight of a coughing bog of bloody slime.

'Let me pray.'

A frenzied appeal to the Creator followed. Sincere as it was, it would read like irreverence in print.

And then there came the cold-drawn horror of stark blasphemy against this God – who would not answer.

Followed the bleak black agony of the conviction – the absolute certitude – 'There is no God!' combined with a wave of frenzied wrath against the people who had so glibly assured him that there was, an almost maniac hope that they would suffer more than he, if it were possible.

(Poor Arthur! He had not yet brushed the bloom off Suffering's grape; he was to drink its fiercest distillation to the dregs.)

'No!' thought he, 'perhaps I lack their "faith."

'Perhaps if I could really persuade myself of God and Christ – Perhaps if I could deceive myself, could make believe —'

Such a thought is to surrender one's honesty, to abdicate one's reason. It marked the final futile struggle of his will.

The demon caught and crunched him, and the noisy delirium began anew.

My flesh and blood rebelled. Taken with a deathly vomit, I rushed from the room, and resolutely, for a whole hour, diverted my sensorium from thought. I had always found that the slightest trace of tobacco smoke in a room greatly disturbed my power. On this occasion I puffed cigarette after cigarette with excellent effect. I knew nothing of what had been going on.

4

Arthur, stung by the venomous chyle, was tossing in that vast arched belly, which resembled the dome of hell, churned in its bubbling slime. I felt that he was not only disintegrated mechanically, but chemically, that his being was loosened more and more into its parts, that these were being absorbed into new and hateful things, but that (worst of all) Arthur stood immune from all, behind it, unimpaired, memory and reason ever more acute as ever new and ghastlier experience informed them. It seemed to me as if some mystic state were superadded to the torment; for while he was not, emphatically not, this tortured mass of consciousness, yet that was he. There are always at least two of us! The one who feels and the one who knows are not radically one person. This double personality is enormously accentuated at death.

Another point was that the time-sense, which with men is usually so reliable – especially in my own case – was decidedly deranged, if not abrogated altogether.

We all judge of the lapse of time in relation to our daily habits or some similar standard. The conviction of immortality must naturally destroy all values for this sense. If I am immortal, what is the difference between a long time and a short time? A thousand years and a day are obviously the same thing from the point of view of 'for ever.'

There is a subconscious clock in us, a clock wound up by the experience of the race to go for seventy years or so. Five minutes is a very long time to us if we are waiting for an omnibus, an age if we are waiting for a lover, nothing at all if we are pleasantly engaged or sleeping.[1]

We think of seven years as a long time in connection with penal servitude; as a negligibly small period in dealing with geology.

But, given immortality, the age of the stellar system itself is nothing.

This conviction had not fully impregnated the consciousness of Arthur; it hung over him like a threat, while the intensification of that consciousness, its liberation from the sense of time natural to life, caused each act of the demon to appear of vast duration, although the intervals between the howls of the body on the bed were very short. Each pang of torture or suspense was born, rose to its crest, and died to be reborn again through what seemed countless aeons.

Still more was this the case in the process of his assimilation by the 'demon.' The coma of the dying man was a phenomenon altogether out of Time. The conditions of 'digestion' were new to Arthur, he had no reason to suppose, no data from which to calculate the distance of, an end.

It is impossible to do more than sketch this process; as he was absorbed, so did his consciousness expand into that of the 'demon'; he became one with all its hunger and corruption. Yet always did he suffer as himself in his own person the tearing asunder of his finest molecules; and this was confirmed by a most filthy humiliation of that part of him that was rejected.

I shall not attempt to describe the final process; suffice it that the demoniac consciousness drew away; he was but the excrement of the demon, and as that excrement he was flung filthily further into the abyss of blackness and of night whose name is death.

I rose with ashen cheeks. I stammered: 'He is dead.' The male nurse bent over the body. 'Yes!' he echoed, 'he is dead.' And it seemed as if

---

[1] It is one of the greatest cruelties of nature that all painful or depressing emotions seem to lengthen time; pleasant thoughts and exalted moods make time fly. Thus, in summing up a life from an outside standpoint, it would seem that, supposing pleasure and pain to have occupied equal periods, the impression would be that pain was enormously greater than pleasure. This may be controverted. Virgil writes: *'Forsitan haec olim meminisse juvabit'* ['Maybe one day it will be pleasing to remember these things'], and there is at least one modern writer thoroughly conversant with pessimism who is very optimistic. But the new facts which I here submit overthrow the whole argument; they cast a sword of infinite weight on that petty trembling scale.

the whole Universe gathered itself into one ghastly laugh of hate and horror, 'Dead!'

5

I resumed my seat. I felt that I must know that all was well, that death had ended all. Woe to humanity! The consciousness of Arthur was more alive than ever. It was the black fear of falling, a dumb ecstasy of changeless fear. There were no waves upon that sea of shame, no troubling of those accursed waters by any thought. There was no hope of any ground to that abyss, no thought that it might stop. So tireless was that fall that even acceleration was absent; it was constant and level as the fall of a star. There was not even a feeling of pace; infinitely fast as it must be, judging from the peculiar dread which it inspired, it was yet infinitely slow, having regard to the infinitude of the abyss.

I took measures not to be disturbed by the duties that men – oh how foolishly! – pay to the dead; and I took refuge in a cigarette.

It was now for the first time, strangely enough, that I began to consider the possibility of helping him.

I analysed the position. It must be his thought, or I could not read it. I had no reason to conjecture that any other thoughts could reach me. He must be alive in the true sense of the word; it was he and not another that was the prey of this fear ineffable. Of this fear it was evident that there must be a physical basis in the constitution of his brain and body. All the other phenomena had been shown to correspond exactly with a physical condition; it was the reflection in a consciousness from which human limitation had fallen away, of things actually taking place in the body.

It was a false interpretation perhaps; but it was his interpretation; and it was that which caused suffering so beyond all that poets have ever dreamt of the infernal.

I am ashamed to say that my first thought was of the Catholic Church and its masses for the repose of the dead. I went to the Cathedral, revolving as I went all that had ever been said – the superstitions of a hundred savage tribes. At bottom I could find no difference between their barbarous rites and those of Christianity.

However that might be, I was baffled. The priests refused to pray for the soul of a heretic.

I hurried back to the house, resumed my vigil. There was no change, except a deepening of the fear, an intensification of the loneliness, a more utter absorption in the shame. I could but hope that in the ultimate stagnation of all vital forces, death would become final, hell merged into annihilation.

This started a train of thought which ended in a determination to hasten the process. I thought of blowing out the brains, remembered that I had no means of doing so. I thought of freezing the body, imagined a story for the nurse, reflected that no cold could excite in his soul aught icier than that illimitable void of black.

I thought of telling the doctor that he had wished to bequeath his body to the surgeons, that he had been afraid of being buried alive, anything that might induce him to remove the brain. At that moment I looked into the mirror, I saw that I must not speak. My hair was white, my face drawn, my eyes wild and bloodshot.

In utter helplessness and misery I flung myself on the couch in the study, and puffed greedily at cigarettes. The relief was so immense that my sense of loyalty and duty had a hard fight to get me to resume the task. The mingling of horror, curiosity, and excitement must have aided.

I threw away my fifth cigarette, and returned to the death chamber.

6

Before I had sat at the table ten minutes a change burst out with startling suddenness. At one point in the void the blackness gathered, concentrated, sprang into an evil flame that gushed aimlessly forth from nowhere into nowhere.

This was accompanied by the most noxious stench.

It was gone before I could realise it. As lightning precedes thunder, it was followed by a hideous clamour that I can only describe as the cry of a machine in pain.

This recurred constantly for an hour and five minutes, then ceased as suddenly as it began. Arthur still fell.

It was succeeded after the lapse of five hours by another paroxysm of the same kind, but fiercer and more continuous. Another silence followed, age upon age of fear and loneliness and shame.

About midnight there appeared a grey ocean of bowels below the falling soul. This ocean seemed to be limitless. It fell headlong into it, and the splash awakened it to a new consciousness of things.

This sea, though infinitely cold, was boiling like tubercles. Itself a more or less homogeneous slime, the stench of which is beyond all human conception (human language is singularly deficient in words that describe smell and taste; we always refer our sensations to things generally known),[1] it constantly budded into greenish boils with angry red craters, whose jagged edges were of a livid white; and from these issued pus formed of all things known of man – each one distorted, degraded, blasphemed.

Things innocent, things happy, things holy! every one unspeakably defiled, loathsome, sickening! During the vigil of the day following I recognised one group. I saw Italy. First the Italy of the map, a booted leg. But this leg changed rapidly through myriad phases. It was in turn the leg of every beast and bird, and in every case each leg was suffering with all diseases from leprosy and elephantiasis to scrofula and syphilis. There was also the consciousness that this was inalienably and for ever part of Arthur.

Then Italy itself, in every detail foul. Then I myself, seen as every woman that has ever been, each one with every disease and torture that Nature and man have plotted in their hellish brains, each ended with a death, a death like Arthur's, whose infinite pangs were added to his own, recognised and accepted as his own.

The same with our child that never was. All children of all nations, incredibly aborted, deformed, tortured, torn in pieces, abused by every foulness that the imagination of an arch-devil could devise.

And so for every thought. I realised that the putrefactive changes in the dead man's brain were setting in motion every memory of his, and smearing them with hell's own paint.

I timed one thought: despite its myriad million details, each one clear, vivid and prolonged, it occupied but three seconds of earthly time. I considered the incalculable array of the thoughts in his well-furnished mind; I saw that thousands of years would not exhaust them.

But, perhaps, when the brain was destroyed beyond recognition of its component parts —

---

[1] This is my general complaint, and that of all research students on the one hand and imaginative writers on the other. We can only express a new idea by combining two or more old ideas, or by the use of metaphor; just so any number can be formed from two others. James Hinton had undoubtedly a perfectly crisp, simple and concise idea of the 'fourth dimension of space'; he found the utmost difficulty in conveying it to others, even when they were advanced mathematicians. It is (I believe) the greatest factor that militates against human progress that great men assume that they will be understood by others.

Even such a master of lucid English as the late Professor Huxley has been so vitally misunderstood that he has been attacked repeatedly for affirming propositions which he specifically denied in the clearest language.

We have always casually assumed that consciousness depends upon a proper flow of blood in the vessels of the brain; we have never stopped to think whether the records might not be excited in some other manner. And yet we know how tumour of the brain begets hallucinations. Consciousness works strangely; the least disturbance of the blood supply, and it goes out like a candle, or else takes monstrous forms.

Here was the overwhelming truth: *in death man lives again, and lives for ever.* Yet we might have thought of it; the phantasmagoria of life which throng the mind of a drowning man might have suggested something of the sort to any man with a sympathetic and active imagination.

Worse even than the thoughts themselves was the apprehension of the thoughts ere they arose. Carbuncles, boils, ulcers, cancers, there is no equivalent for these pustules of the bowels of hell, into whose seething convulsions Arthur sank deeper, ever deeper.

The magnitude of this experience is not to be apprehended by the human mind as we know it. I was convinced that an end must come, for me, with the cremation of the body. I was infinitely glad that he had directed this to be done. But for him, end and beginning seemed to have no meaning. Through it all I seemed to hear the real Arthur's thought. 'Though all this is I, yet it is only an accident of me; I stand behind it all, immune, eternal.'

It must not be supposed that this in any way detracted from the intensity of the suffering. Rather it added to it. To be loathsome is less than to be linked to loathsomeness. To plunge into impurity is to become deadened to disgust. But to do so and yet remain pure – every vileness adds a pang. Think of Madonna imprisoned in the body of a prostitute, and compelled to acknowledge 'This is I,' while never losing her abhorrence. Not only immured in hell, but compelled to partake of its sacraments; not only high priest at its agapae, but begetter and manifestor of its cult; a Christ nauseated at the kiss of Judas, and yet aware that the treachery was his own.

7

As the putrefaction of the brain advanced, the bursting of the pustules occasionally overlapped, with the result that the confusion and exaggeration of madness with all its poignancy was superadded to the simpler hell. One might have thought that any confusion would have been a welcome relief to a lucidity so appalling; but this was not so. The torture was infused with a shattering sense of alarm.

The images rose up threatening, disappeared only by blasting themselves into the pultaceous coprolite which was, as it were, the main body of the army which composed Arthur. Deeper and deeper as he dropped the phenomena grew constantly in every sense. Now they were a jungle in which the obscurity and terror of the whole gradually overshadowed even the abhorrence due to every part.

The madness of the living is a thing so abominable and fearful as to chill every human heart with horror; it is less than nothing in comparison with the madness of the dead!

A further complication now arose in the destruction irrevocable and complete of that compensating mechanism of the brain, which is the basis of the sense of time. Hideously distorted and deformed as it had been in the derangement of the brain, like a shapeless jelly shooting out, of a sudden, vast, unsuspected tentacles, the destruction of it cut a thousandfold deeper. The sense of consecution itself was destroyed; things sequent appeared as things superposed or concurrent spatially; a new dimension unfolded; a new destruction of all limitation exposed a new and unfathomable abyss.

To all the rest was added the bewilderment and fear which earthly agaraphobia faintly shadows forth; and at the same time the close immurement weighed upon him, since from infinitude there can be no escape.

Add to this the hopelessness of the monotony of the situation. Infinitely as the phenomena were varied, they were yet recognised as essentially the same. All human tasks are lightened by the certainty that they must end. Even our joys would be intolerable were we convinced that they must endure, through irksomeness and disgust, through weariness and satiety, even for ever and for evermore. In this inhuman, this præterdiabolic inferno was a wearisome repetition, a harping on the same hateful discord, a continuous nagging whose intervals afforded no relief, only a suspense brimming with the anticipation of some fresh terror.

For hours which were to him eternities this stage continued as each cell that held the record of a memory underwent the degenerative changes which awoke it into hyperbromic purulence.

8

The minute bacterial corruption now assumed a gross chemistry. The gases of putrefaction forming in the brain and interpenetrating it were represented in his consciousness by the denizens of the pustules becoming formless and impersonal – Arthur had not yet fathomèd the abyss.

Creeping, winding, embracing, the Universe enfolded him, violated him with a nameless and intimate contamination, involved his being in a more suffocating terror.

Now and again it drowned that consciousness in a gulf which his thought could not express to me; and indeed the first and least of his torments is utterly beyond human expression.

It was a woe ever expanded, ever intensified, by each vial of wrath. Memory increased, and understanding grew; the imagination had equally got rid of limit.

What this means who can tell? The human mind cannot really appreciate numbers beyond a score or so; it can deal with numbers by ratiocination, it cannot apprehend them by direct impression. It requires a highly trained intelligence to distinguish between fifteen and sixteen matches on a plate without counting them. In death this limitation is entirely removed. Of the infinite content of the Universe every item was separately realised. The brain of Arthur had become equal in power to that attributed by theologians to the Creator; yet of executive power there was no seed. The impotence of man before circumstance was in him magnified indefinitely, yet without loss of detail or of mass. He understood that The Many was The One without losing or fusing the conception of either. He was God, but a God irretrievably damned: a being infinite, yet limited by the nature of things, and that nature solely compact of loathliness.

9

I have little doubt that the cremation of my husband's body cut short a process which in the normally buried man continues until no trace of organic substance remains.

The first kiss of the furnace awoke an activity so violent and so vivid that all the past paled in its lurid light.

The quenchless agony of the pang is not to be described; if alleviation there were, it was but the exultation of feeling that this was final.

Not only time, but all expansions of time, all monsters of time's womb were to be annihilated; even the ego might hope some end.

The ego is the 'worm that dieth not,' and existence the 'fire that is not quenched.' Yet in this universal pyre, in this barathrum of liquid lava, jetted from the volcanoes of the infinite, this 'lake of fire that is reserved for the devil and his angels,' might not one at last touch bottom? Ah! but time was no more, neither any eidolon thereof!

The shell was consumed; the gases of the body, combined and re-combined, flamed off, free from organic form.

Where was Arthur?

His brain, his individuality, his life, were utterly destroyed. As separate things, yes: Arthur had entered the universal consciousness.

And I heard this utterance: or rather this is my translation into English of a single thought whose synthesis is 'Woe.'

Substance is called spirit or matter.

Spirit and matter are one, indivisible, eternal, indestructible.

Infinite and eternal change!

Infinite and eternal pain!

No absolute: no truth, no beauty, no idea, nothing but the whirl-winds of form, unresting, unappeasable.

Eternal hunger! Eternal war! Change and pain infinite and unceasing.

There is no individuality but in illusion. And the illusion is change and pain, and its destruction is change and pain, and its new segregation from the infinite and eternal is change and pain; and substance infinite and eternal is change and pain unspeakable.

Beyond thought, which is change and pain, lies being, which is change and pain.

These were the last words intelligible; they lapsed into the eternal moan, Woe! Woe! Woe! Woe! Woe! Woe! Woe! in unceasing monotony that rings always in my ears if I let my thought fall from the height of activity, listen to the voice of my sensorium.

In my sleep I am partially protected, and I keep a lamp constantly alight to burn tobacco in the room: but yet too often my dreams throb with that reiterated Woe! Woe! Woe! Woe! Woe! Woe! Woe!

10

The final stage is clearly enough inevitable, unless we believe the Buddhist theories, which I am somewhat inclined to do, as their theory of the Universe is precisely confirmed in every detail by the facts here set down. But it is one thing to recognise a disease, another to discover a remedy. Frankly, my whole being revolts from their methods, and I had rather acquiesce in the ultimate destiny and achieve it as quickly as may be. My earnest preoccupation is to avoid the preliminary tortures, and I am convinced that the explosion of a dynamite cartridge in the mouth is the most practicable method of effecting this. There is just the possibility that if all thinking minds, all 'spiritual beings,' were thus destroyed, and especially if all organic life could be annihilated, that the Universe might cease to be, since (as Bishop Berkeley has shown) it can only exist in some thinking mind. And there is really no evidence (in spite of Berkeley) for the existence of any extra-human consciousness. Matter in itself may think, in a sense, but its monotony of woe is less awful than its abomination, the building up of high and holy things only to drag them through infamy and terror to the old abyss.

I shall consequently cause this record to be widely distributed. The notebooks of my work with Arthur (Vols. I–CCXIV) will be edited by Professor von Bühle, whose marvellous mind may perhaps discover some escape from the destiny which menaces mankind. Everything is in order in these notebooks; and I am free to die, for I can endure no more, and above all things I dread the onset of illness, and the possibility of natural or accidental death.

NOTE

I am glad to have the opportunity of publishing, in a journal so widely read by the profession, the MS. of the widow of the late Professor Blair.

Her mind undoubtedly became unhinged through grief at her husband's death; the medical man who attended him in his last illness grew alarmed at her condition, and had her watched. She tried (fruitlessly) to purchase dynamite at several shops, but on her going to the laboratory of her late husband, and attempting to manufacture Chloride of Nitrogen, obviously for the purpose of suicide, she was seized, certified insane, and placed in my care.

The case is most unusual in several respects.

(1) I have never known her inaccurate in any statement of verifiable fact.

(2) She can undoubtedly read thoughts in an astonishing manner. In particular, she is actually useful to me by her ability to foretell attacks of acute insanity in my patients. Some hours before they occur she can predict them to a minute. On an early occasion my disbelief in her power led to the dangerous wounding of one of my attendants.

(3) She combines a fixed determination of suicide (in the extraordinary manner described by her) with an intense fear of death. She smokes uninterruptedly, and I am obliged to allow her to fumigate her room at night with the same drug.

(4) She is certainly only twenty-four years old, and any competent judge would with equal certainty declare her sixty.

(5) Professor von Bühle, to whom the notebooks were sent, addressed to me a long and urgent telegram, begging her release on condition that she would promise not to commit suicide, but go to work with him in Bonn. I have yet to learn, however, that German professors, however eminent, have any voice in the management of a private asylum in England, and I am certain that the Lunacy Commissioners will uphold me in my refusal to consider the question.

It will then be clearly understood that this document is published with all reserve as the lucubration of a very peculiar, perhaps unique, type of insanity.

V. ENGLISH, M.D.

Ercildoune

A NOVEL

I

The Glacier Camp

Midnight on the Chogo Lungma La. Moonlight. The steady sweep of
the icy blizzards of the north cuts through canvas and eiderdown and
fur. Roland Rex, peering out for a moment from his tiny tent upon
the stupendous beauty of the snows, almost wonders that the stars can
stand before the blast. Yet, dimly and afar, a speck of life stirs on those
illimitable wastes. How minute is a man in such solitudes! Yet how
much man means to man! No avalanche, not the very upheaval of the
deep-rooted mountains, could have held his attention so close as did
that dot upon the wilderness of snow.

So far it was, so heavy the weight of the wind, so steep and slippery
the slopes, that dawn had broken ere the speck resolved itself into a
man. Tall and rugged, his black hair woven into a web over his eyes
to protect them from the Pain of the Snows, as the natives call the
fearful fulminating snow blindness of the giant peaks, his feet wrapped
round and round with strips of leather and cloth, he approached the
little camp.

Patient and imperturbable are these men who face the majesty of
the great mountains: experience has taught them that it is useless to
be angry with a snowstorm. A blizzard may persist for a week; to conquer it one must be ready to persist for many weeks. So, quiet and
at ease, just as if he had not made his two-and-twenty marches in six
days, the messenger fumbled in his clothes and produced the mail.

Two years and more since Roland had been lost in the waste; within
a month of Skardu he had arrived, and sent forward a swift runner with
a letter to the *tehsildar*, the local official, and a budget for his friends at
home. The wind had failed just after dawn, and the sun shone strongly
on the glacier. Every particle of bedding was hung out to dry; the coolies were right merry; it would be easy to cook food today.

Roland had thawed his penultimate tin of sausages, and boiled up his chocolate. Seated on one of the leather-bound baskets which contained his few effects he was now enjoying the warmth, and his pipe, and the rapture of news from home. For though he could expect no letters, the thoughtful Tehsildar had sent him up a newspaper. Mr Justice Billington had hay fever; Lord Wittle had obtained his *decree nisi*; Consols had fallen a point; Sir Julius Boot had left town for his country seat; three pigs had been killed in Staffordshire, and a land agent in Galway; coal would probably soon be dearer; Tariff Reform meant lower income tax and work for all; Peter Briggs, alias 'Peter the Pounder,' had got three years; Buncombe's Bottlettes Cured Constipation; Should Women Wear Braces? and all the weariness of the daily drivel.

But the haunting unreality of the rubbish for a Londoner gives place to a vivid brilliance and charm for one who is far off. Clearly the stuff that dreams are made of; therefore – strange paradox! – convincing. Lord Wittle became for the moment as real as Mr Pickwick. Roland Rex was happy.

Nor was his satisfaction confined to the news of the world. After the starved brain has got every stupid phrase by heart, it turns, still eager, to the report of the Monthly Medal Competition at Little Piddlingborough, and the P. and O. sailings for next month. Even the dull personal column with its hairpin imbecilities and its bogus assignations gives a certain thrill. All is so deliciously fantastic; in the dreary maze of glaciers, in the grim silence of the rocks, in the splendour of the vast, sheathing as they did the iron of reality in the soul of the explorer, the fatuous piffle of the penny-a-liner is like a fairy story told for the first time to a child. Rather a shock to the child when it learns that its Cinderella is not true, but merely a lesson in humility and punctuality; so to the man should he find in his fairy newspaper a paragraph which directly concerns him. Roland Rex found two.

The first, in the memoriam column, read as follows:

> In memory of Lord Marcus Masters, who died —— {a date two years earlier} – never forgotten by his affectionate wife. 'Blessed are the dead that die in the Lord.'

He drew in his breath.

'Poor Marcus!' he exclaimed. And then – Roland Rex looked himself over. His hair and beard had been innocent alike of brush and scissors for three years; his skin was darker than that of his coolies; he would have been taken for a savage in any country of the world.

And he laughed. 'If the Marquis dies tomorrow, I suppose I could hardly take my seat like this!'

Next his eye fell on the personal column. This time he started in genuine surprise.

The paragraph read:

ss. 887. Austria to John. Come home. F.

Roland translated thoughtfully. 'Austria to John'? Now what the devil can he mean by that? I ought to know. But I suppose three years of wilderness dulls the intelligence. 'Come home!' And the old boy has put that message in the paper 887 times!

Go home I will.

He called his head-man, Salama. Laconic as ever. '*Bas! Safar ho-gaya. Panch roz-ka dhal-bat bana'o; Askole-men jeldi jaebne.*' (Enough! The journey is over. Take five days' provisions. We will go quickly to Askole.)

Right enough, in an hour's time, the whole caravan was hurrying down the slopes, tentless and on most meagre rations, if haply they might do fifteen days' march in four. At Askole he paid off the men; and with his gaunt old headman for sole companion, made headlong down the Braldu Valley to Skardu.

2

The River of Mud

Roland Rex had chosen the certain passage down the valley in preference to the dubious shortcut over the Skoro La. Moreover, he wanted news pretty badly, and local rumour had it that a *sahib* was now ascending the Braldu on a sporting trip. So down they slogged over the rough track.

About noon on the second day they met the servants of the sportsman in question preparing his lunch; learning from these that he was probably an hour behind, they pushed on, and found him sitting on the banks of that strange river of mud which flows into the Braldu. Sluggish and even is its course; in normal weather of the consistency of very thick tar, it moves down inch by inch, until at last it oozes over into the pale amber froth of the grey Braldu, and is lost.

Roland Rex had worn his English clothes threadbare long since; he wore the inevitable turban, that best of headgear against both heat and cold, and the rest of his costume was the handiwork of a Yarkand tailor. Small wonder if the natives failed to mark him as a *sahib*, and salute; smaller that the *sahib* sitting by the river equally mistook him. He called authoritatively to the travellers as they approached. Amused at the jest, Roland made his best *salaam*.

'Are there any *sahibs* shooting or travelling in this *nālā*?' he asked.

Roland said that he had heard of one or two.

'Is Rex *sahib* in this district?'

Roland was startled, and showed it; but the spirit of mischief moved him to deny it. What should this stranger want with him?

'You are lying, son of a pig!' said the Englishman coolly, noticing the momentary confusion. It is easy to frighten the truth from an Asiatic by this simple plan. But Roland was really confused, and the stranger accordingly emboldened.

'You are his *dak*-runners!' he exclaimed. 'Where have you left the *sahib*?'

Roland's headman, Salama Tantra, took up the tale. An expert liar for over forty years, he was equal to the situation. Seeing that his master for some reason desired to deny his identity, the grey old hunter began a long tale of woe, beginning nowhere in particular, and ending up, after a series of magnificent falsehoods, with the statement that the *sahib* had sent them on with letters, he himself having turned back up over the Hispar Pass with the intention of visiting Hunza and returning by Gilgit. The stranger was apparently convinced.

'I am going to join him,' he said. 'My own *dak*-runners shall take the mail, and you shall return with me and take me to him. I am glad I have met you.' And with truly royal generosity, he fished out some rupees of his shooting-coat, and bestowed them on the willing *shikari*.

Roland jumped to his meaning in a flash; it was the letters he wanted.

'It is not the order, *sahib*,' he explained, with an artistic cringe. 'It is the order to take these letters to the *tehsildar* of Skardu, and receive a paper from him.'

'Nonsense!' said the stranger. 'My own men can get this paper; I would not lose you for anything. See, I will give you each one hundred rupees.'

'We cannot break an order, *sahib*!' He assumed a gorgeous despair. 'The master would punish us.'

The stranger began to storm, but in vain. The travellers murmured the polite request for permission to leave the presence of the highness, and began to move toward the river, crossable in fairly dry weather by dint of many stones thrown in by gangs of villagers.

Suddenly out lashed the Englishman's revolver and a shot rang through the air. But he only pierced Roland in the thigh.

Long before his finger could press the trigger again, the huntsman had him by the waist; flung him far into the river of mud. Roland ran to save him, but in a trice he was tripped, and down, and the grey old ruffian kneeling on his chest.

'Useless, *sahib*!' he hissed, 'we have no ropes. He tried to kill you, *sahib*, O my father and my mother.'

The poor old fellow was in tears. Shriek after shriek came from the struggling murderer. 'Allah has written it,' the old man went on, 'I saw the mark of death upon his brow.'

In vain did Roland threaten, command, entreat. To all Salama answered, 'The writing!' and kept his hold. The pain of his wound came home to Rex, and he half fainted.

Horrible were the curses of the wretch in the river. The whole valley shuddered. Yet he, too, ceased to struggle, slowly sucked in and down by the insidious mire. The lucid prologue of death's tragedy came upon him, of a sudden, at Roland's cry as he sat up, weak and bleeding, held now in his faithful servant's arms.

'Who are you, in God's name?' he shouted in English, 'and what do you want with Roland Rex?'

'I am mad – I am dying – help! help!' cried the unhappy man. 'How is it you seem to talk my tongue?'

'Why, I am Roland Rex; what do you want with me?'

'A curse on my wry shot,' he shrieked, and fell back to his old raving madness. The calm again. 'I wanted the great reward – the great reward! For news of your death, you fool. So near! So near success!' and again his fury foamed; blood broke black at his lips. But now the midstream strength took him; looking over as he lay half-strangled in the slime, he could see the horror of the Braldu fifty feet below. The roar of it drowned his choking yells. Then, with a last heave and gurgle through its oily mire, the river fell with him and mighty silence swallowed up the scene. Even as he fell, the storm rolled up the valley, and the blaze broke upon the wounded man and his companion.

By now the wound was staunched, for it was but a slight flesh-wound. Limping from the bullet, shaking from the dread mystery of the scene, Roland Rex crossed the treacherous stream, and came to the apricot orchards of Gomboro.

* * *

Stretched upon the green turf in the moonlight, Roland nursed his wound, whose ache, with the fiery events of the day, kept him from sleep.

He mused upon the cipher. The darkness of the letter and the darkness of the deed conspired; and there was light. 'Austria to John!' Aha! *Ivanhoe!* – his thought burnt up – 'The devil is unloosed. Look to yourself!' Then he must mean – oh! but that is too impossible. Let me consider.

And his mind ran back to the strange history of his family.

3

The Doom of Ercildoune

Ewan, fourth Marquis of Ercildoune, was riding alone through the park one drear November day, some eighty years before the beginning of this story. A proud man was he, tracing his descent from True Thomas, the holiest of the ancient Scottish Bards. Of his own house he had predicted glory and earthly power, yet closed it with the weird:

> A red star and a waning moon
> Rede me this true rune.
> A Grey Sun and a bastard loon
> Ding doun Ercildoune.

High in favour with King George and his ministers, his name renowned in Wellington's campaigns, his power absolute as God's for many a mile beyond the eagle-sight from his castle, his wealth well-nigh boundless, four stalwart sons to bear up his age, and lift his honoured coffin to its grave, no man was more enviable in all the realm that the brave sun controls.

Yet his face was dark, and his hand closed convulsively upon the dagger that lurked at his hip. Also his mouth worked strongly.

Presently he dismounted, and, tying his horse to an oak, plunged deep into the glade. Familiar was the way, though obscure; yet even a stranger would have taken the self-same track, for the steady music of a cascade allured the step. High from its narrow channel it tumbled far out into a rock-bound pool, which overflowing rolled forth into a less dominant music among lesser obstacles. Here the Marquis paused a moment, then blew shrill upon a whistle. Instantly, as by enchantment, the volume of the falling water whitened and glowed, shot through by some interior light; then all was dark again. But the Marquis, seeming satisfied, probed his wary way around the base of the pool; the slippery rocks, the mossy knobs and treacherous fern-roots lent an ambiguous aid. He passed behind the water, and the path grew easy. Up into the cave he pressed, and after many twists came to the central hollow. Fashioned more by man than Nature, the room was large and nearly square. A curious table of brass stood in the centre, and a blue flame burnt variably thereon. Behind it stood a man of great stature, his face hidden by a monkish hood.

This man addressed the noble.

'Who art thou?'

'Ewan Dhu, Marquis of Ercildoune.'

'Where is then thy brother the Marquis?'

'Under the heather.' A second pause. 'Shame!' the Marquis added, 'have I come here that you should twit me with this paltry scandal? I never slew him.'

'Not with the sword, but with the pen. Where is the Marquis, his son?'

'Who are you, to press the claim of that bastard brat?'

'I wished to see if the coward who did it was coward enough to lie to me about it.'

The Marquis controlled himself with courage.

'You come to me,' continued the other, 'because your foolish dabbling in the false science of the stars has given you fear. You see a baleful planet threatening your house; you invoke the aid and counsel of the Brethren of the Rosy Cross. With unclean hands you come, Ewan Dhu,' cried the adept, raising his voice, 'and the mire that you have played with shall engulf your proud head. For once your ignorance has taught you all that knowledge could. This is the doom of Ercildoune; your sons shall die before your eyes; your house shall fail utterly, and all your rank and wealth pass to the King. Solitary and silent I see you dying, dying through long months, and no man to take pity.'

'I came to you,' replied Ercildoune, 'that you might aid me, not that you might curse me. I withdraw.'

'Stay!' cried the adept, 'what do you offer me for freedom?'

'Penitence, sincere penitence.'

'You will make amends?'

'Never!' flamed he out, 'for the boy is the vilest of mankind. Before God I say it, I will not believe him of my brother's blood.'

'Then you must suffer the doom.'

'Then be it so! Farewell.'

And he turned to go.

The adept strode swiftly forward. 'Now are you a man, Ewan Dhu!' he cried aloud, and grasped his hand. 'The doom you must dree, for doom is doom; nor you nor I avail; but in – the right – you shall not suffer, and the End is with Him. *Vale! Frater Rosæ —*'[1]

'*Et Crucis!*'[2] answered the nobleman.

Silently and gladly they parted.

The fulfilment of the curse is matter of history.

Taking shelter in a storm during a hunt, Malcolm, the eldest son, died by the lightning flash before his father's eyes. Duncan, the second, plunged into the sea, while they all strove to save a shipwrecked crew, and was drowned. Ivan, the third, racing his horse against his father, was thrown and died. Angus, the fourth, surprised some knowledge of the doom. Maddened by the fear of it, he hanged himself from his own window, even as the Marquis returned from London town, and cried his name to greet him. Then the old man turned melancholy, and shut himself into a Trappist monastery, where in silence and solitude he died.

Title and estates passed to a cousin, one Lord Barfield, not yet to the King. This doom remained undone.

* * *

This Lord Barfield, who had succeeded to the title and estates of Ewan Dhu, was an elderly man of recluse and studious habit. Many years in India had given him the secretiveness and cunning of that strange congeries of nations. He was a widower; his wife had borne him three sons and a daughter; the last had married a Mr Rex, and Roland was the only issue of the marriage.

The Marquis had brought up his sons to follow the colours. Nothing had stirred his placid life until the Mutiny in India, where his eldest son, the Earl of Bannockburn by courtesy, was killed before the walls of Delhi.

Hard upon the news followed a curious box of ebony and silver from the East. Within he read the carved inscription,

LORD BARFIELD, WITH THE COMPLIMENTS OF
THE MARQUIS OF ERCILDOUNE

---

[1] [Farewell! Brother of the Rose.]
[2] [And of the Cross!]

and, lifting the tray, discovered, wrapped and embalmed in costly spices, the head of his best-loved son. This was all mystery, and he sought the clue in vain.

Three years later Lord Arthur, the second son, who was studying Russian in St Petersburg, wrote wildly home that he was stricken by a terrible disease, and the old man, eagerly seeking aid from the Government, learnt that 'studies in Russian' meant little more to Arthur than the acquisition of the gilded vices of that barbaric society. Hastily he dispatched his doctor, a wise old friend of the family, if haply skill and counsel might avail; but in vain. The next month's mail brought irretrievable disaster; Arthur was dead by his own hand.

But oh! strange horror! Clad in fantastic jewel-work, there came a little casket. Within was an empty poison-bottle and the diamond device,

LORD BARFIELD, WITH THE COMPLIMENTS OF
THE MARQUIS OF ERCILDOUNE.

The old man, mastering his grief, was roused.

He devoted his whole time and intelligence, his wealth, and influence, to the discovery of who had woven this chaplet of hell's vine for his grey head.

Who was this devil dressed in the grand name? Why did he pursue and faint not? If human power, and power of prayer, might serve, he would know.

But these availed him not. In the end, an accident lifted the veil. As duly shall follow.

4

Continues the Doom

'Twas a pleasant morning in early October, and the birds were plentiful and strong. The old Marquis, in the joy of his skill, was half forgetting the misfortunes of his family; dwelling rather on the splendid appetite that his morning's pleasure had given him, and the glorious lunch that awaited the party at the corner of the next spinney.

The guests were few. Lord Adolphus Dollymount was an ass, but his friend, Guy Pendragon, was as fine a young man as England can show. Breeding without snobbery, intelligence without pedantry, marked him for a great place in public life. He had been brought up on the Continent, where (it appeared) his family, notorious Jacobites, had long lived in exile, and had, as it were, taken root in the strange soil.

But, he explained, we had had enough of that. England for him, and to serve her was the only life worth living. Besides these were Lord Marcus Masters, the last of the sons of the house, two peers, a cabinet minister, and a famous surgeon, Sir John Bastow.

Guy Pendragon was in the line next to the Marquis, and as they walked, from the fault of one or the other, drew a shade too close together. On a sudden, birds rose, and one fine low-flying cock-pheasant whirred between them. Both swung round, but Pendragon, unable to get a fair shot without danger to his neighbour, withheld his fire and lowered his gun. The Marquis killed his bird.

Then the young man tripped and fell. His gun exploded, and the charge struck the old nobleman in the body. Instantly arose a mighty hubbub. All sprang to his aid; the despair of Pendragon was dreadful to witness. Yet he had sprained his ankle in the fall.

Sir John hurriedly examined the wounded man, pronounced the injuries grave, but not hopeless, rendered first aid, bound up the luckless sportsman's ankle, and saw to the improvising of an ambulance.

The two invalids were carried into the house. The Marquis, in pain as he was, could hardly refrain a smile, as one of the old keepers, boiling over with rage, shook his fist in Guy's face, while he hissed, 'Ye damned fool!'

The fidelity of the servants of a great house like Ercildoune is a thing to restore confidence in human nature.

Soon, too, the old man declared that the accident had shaken him sadly; he would like to spend his last years with his brother's son in far Virginia. The Marquis gave him leave, and in due time he departed.

Pendragon, too, recovered, and went off to Monte Carlo.

* * *

So much for Man; but Fate stepped in, and the carefully skinned poker hand was flung wide on the table by a sudden gust of the Everlasting Wings.

It was left to a nameless Anarchist to save the house of Ercildoune. His brain, tortured and diseased by famine of food and surfeit of cheap philosophy, conceived that the death of a few harmless folk would ease the evil of the Universe.

So he dragged a log of wood across the path of the Marseilles Rapide, and screwed it to the sleepers.

The train staggered, left the line, tore up its universe, crashed into a chaos of blind, foolish agony.

From among the wounded and slain young Guy Pendragon extricated himself.

'Here!' he called to another man, uninjured like himself, 'help me to save my father – my father!'

Stolid and self-possessed, the stranger set himself steadily – for all his rabbit's face and meek shabby-gentility – to the task, and in an hour's hard work that part of the wreckage was cleared. Nigh unto death, they dragged out an old grey man, and bore him to the relief train.

Then the stranger returned to the work of rescue, musing.

What was this man to Guy Pendragon? Father. How father? For this man was the old keeper from Ercildoune!

He knew it all; since long he had been chief of the detectives employed by Lord Ercildoune to track the murderer of his sons. Yet now? Inscrutable. Not altogether, perhaps: a seed-thought had sprouted in his mind; he smiled grimly, seeking amid the tangle of the train for further clues.

He found at last a small pocketbook in the wreck of Guy's portmanteau. The little therein was enough for his trained intelligence; the whole infamy lay bare.

He set wires to work; the authorities came in; and, torn howling from the yet warm corpse of his father, Guy Pendragon faced the rigours of an English court of justice.

Grayson, alias Lord Guy Masters, alias Pendragon, alias Schmidt, alias Laroche, etc., was informed by the Judge that the claim of his father to the Marquisate of Ercildoune was of no importance in the eyes of justice. It had been clearly proved that he did feloniously of his malice aforethought attempt to kill and murder one of his Majesty's subjects, a gentleman of high rank and dignity, who stood to him moreover in the position of host; further that he did conspire with his said father to commit the said murder; further, that all the sentimental considerations which his counsel had so eloquently urged were balanced by the fact that the accused had for years lived by fraud and robbery; and though he (the Judge) regretted that counsel for the Crown had seen fit to try and connect accused with the deaths of Lord Ercildoune's two sons, yet the main charge was abundantly clear, and he had no hesitation in sentencing him to Penal Servitude for Life.

The prisoner had but time to say: 'I am Lord Ercildoune, my Lord, and you shall live to repent it,' before he was removed.

* * *

Nine days, and London had forgotten.

5

Derelict Correspondence

London had forgotten! Yes, even Roland Rex had forgotten in the intensity of his three years' wandering in Central Asia. Now, as he lay in the moonlight in the apricot orchards of Gomboro, the whole history rolled its sinister waves upon him.

That devil unchained? Marcus dead? Was there a link between these evil-omened happenings? What of this strange *sahib* who travelled nine thousand miles, and risked, lost indeed, his life in the hope of meeting Rex or stealing his letters? As the Bralduh roared below, bearing high the funeral dirge of that murderous man of mystery, Roland echoed its eternal restlessness, its unmeaning wail. He could have plunged into the river, and wrested out the heart of that dead mystery....

So came the dawn at last; so, sleepless and stiff, weak from the loss of blood, he and his faithful *shikari* bent themselves to the endless track that leads through that desperate valley at the end of the world to the green glories of Shigar and the whirlwind-haunted circuit of Skardu.

Two days of hellish agony; the torture of the wound, the torment of the sun, the atrocious thirst upon the bare rock walls through which the path winds up and down, and above all the agony of doubt. What should he do? Two years had passed and more. He knew nothing of affairs. To go home as Roland Rex might be the blindest walking into the trap. What might not have happened since? 'Look to yourself' had said the message.

Just then a native passed, giving no salute. Roland started. There was the missing word of wisdom. A native he seemed, a native he would remain. Nothing would be easier; he need not even lack money. He could draw small cheques to his new self as Habib Ju, the first name that came to his mind; he need lack nothing. And it should go hard but he discovered much ere he reached England, and came secretly to his grandfather's house of Ercildoune.

Now they got a raft of swollen goat-skins, and sped down the rushing stream to Skardu. There he wrote a letter to the *tehsildar*, stating his intention to remain in the Braldu Nālā for some weeks, and that the native stories of his disappearance were to cause no anxiety; their origin was quite inexplicable.

Thus he calmed official curiosity, and killing one horse on the Deosai Plains and two more between Burzil and Bandipur, came to Baramula before alarm, either on his account or that of the other man, had yet disturbed the nights of the *tehsildar*, a man naturally lazy, incredulous, and slow to action.

When alarm arose, indeed, it diminished almost as quickly. It was only necessary to construct a plausible, probable story of the death of the two *sahibs*. So the *tehsildar* manufactured an avalanche, and was so thoughtful as to include among the victims not only the two white men, but also those of their servants who might possibly be implicated in any inquiry, and therefore thought that it would be best to lie low for a while.

Thus, six months after, news came to England of the death of Roland Rex.

Meanwhile that worthy was ostensibly engaged in the pilgrimage to Mecca. But he slipped off at Jeddah and took passage in a coaster up the Red Sea. At Cairo he disclosed himself with all due caution to an old schoolfellow at Headquarters, and was able to continue the journey with a bronzed face, a trim foreign beard, and a suit of Greek-cut serge. Here, too, he was able to telegraph to his grandfather that all was yet well. He had only dared to send one other, from Bombay, and that expressed so cautiously that even the recipient might have been pardoned for failing to guess at its meaning.

Roland had not called for his letters at the agent's there, else he would not have missed the following epistle, which had lain awaiting him for more than two years.

'My Dear Roland,' wrote his grandfather,

> Heavy news, heavy news! I fear grievous trouble. Young Grayson has escaped. It seems that while a working party were out in the fog he made a sudden dash for liberty. The whole affair must have been devilish well arranged, for no trace of the fugitives has ever been obtained – save one, of course. A month after the escape I received a parcel from Leipzig which, on being opened, revealed a convict costume with the inscription, beautifully embroidered in silk:
>
> LORD BARFIELD, WITH THE COMPLIMENTS OF THE MARQUIS OF ERCILDOUNE. MERELY A MEMENTO.
>
> As usual! Leipzig is of course worse than no clue at all but one thing we know at least: there is a woman in it. I hope to send

more and better news very shortly. I have wired Arkwright, the
man who caught him before; he must do it again.

Your affectionate grandfather,

ERCILDOUNE

P.S. I am advertising you daily in many papers as your movements are so uncertain; it is but a chance if this letter reaches
you. – E.

P.P.S. For God's sake, dear lad, take care of yourself. Three years
since Marcus married, and no child.

Receiving no answer to this, the Marquis did not write again. Shut
up in Ercildoune, he read deep into the night, and always on the one
subject. As a criminologist he had no rival; from his castle he directed
a vast army of detectives.

Yet with no result. Grayson was lost again.

6

Father Ambrose

Not only did Ercildoune seek Grayson to avenge his dead sons, but to
save his heir. Lord Marcus Masters was a soft youth of a religious turn
of mind. Only at his father's urgent command had he married. Even
so, he married out of his class; it was the niece of the parish priest
of Ercildoune that led him at last as a sheep to the slaughter. Meek
and pious, like the hybrid of a praying mantis and a mouse, she had
but little thought for worldliness. And that caused no grief to the old
Marquis, who thought Marcus safer in the chapel than in the ballroom.

So sped their placid sheepish life; no bucolics were theirs to be disturbed by some such fiery line as 'Formosum pastor Corydon ardebat
Alexin.' The idea of passion was foreign to them. Their idea of love
was verbal; Caroline Masters would have resented the pressure of her
husband's hand.

This indeed would have maddened the old noble, had he guessed
it. But Arthur's debauches in Petersburg had determined him to keep
Marcus innocent, and the frigidity of Caroline was a rare accident such
as the wisest might fail to foresee.

As maturity grew, so religious ardour took the place of virile fervour.
Day by day Marcus and his wife grew closer to Christ, so that in the
end no hour of the day but was given to some devotion or another.

Their guests were itinerant evangelists; their friends converted Atheist cobblers; their enemies imaginary Jesuits.

It so happened one fine summer that the fame of a certain Father Ambrose went abroad. He gave himself out to be a renegade monk from the Benedictine Monastery at Fort Augustus. Convinced of Protestant Truth, he had (it seemed) suffered a martyrdom comparable only to that of Polycarp, and had eventually made his escape in circumstances only paralleled by those of Paul at Damascus.

The statement of the Lord Abbot that the said person had never been a monk at all carried little weight with those who, like Lord Marcus Masters, were acquainted with the depths of the Duplicity of the Devil in particular and the Roman Communion in general.

From town to town the fame of the young convert, who lent piquancy to his personality by retaining semi-monastic garb and traces of the tonsure, leapt like a beacon. He who at Glasgow was starving with a dozen draggle-tailed hearers, was dining well at Manchester, and, under the wing of a leading Elder, addressing some thousand enthusiasts in the local Bethel. At Birmingham the largest hall in the city overflowed. At London all the cranks of all the sects combined to welcome him; the new revival was in every mouth. Even the street-boys whistled the refrain of his famous Redemption Song, which ran: –

> There's salvation in Jesus!
> in Jesus!
> There's salvation in Jesus for you!
> for Me!
> There's salvation in Jesus for all of us!
> There's salvation in Jesus, salvation in Jesus,
> Salvation in Jesus for you –
> and for Me!

The very numerous other verses differed by substituting for the word 'salvation' such words as 'redemption,' 'grace,' 'resurrection,' 'immortality,' 'glory' and the like, I rejoice to say with little consideration for so purely pagan a matter as metre.

No society is so easily carried away by its cranks as London Society. 'Father Ambrose' might have stayed with almost any Duchess in the Kingdom; but when at the end of a long and glorious season, with a ragged throat and a record bag of sinners, his medical adviser insisted on rest, it was the invitation of Lord and Lady Marcus Masters that he accepted.

Absolutely perfect rest! was the doctor's last word; positively *no* society!

So we lose this interesting trinity for a moment and return to the Albert Hall at the close of the last of his meetings.

'Had the man a brother?' asked a rabbit-faced little nondescript of a man with a meek voice.

'I assure you he had not,' replied his interlocutor – who might have been a dog-stealer out of work.

'But it is he himself then!' insisted the first. 'I cannot mistake the voice and the gesture. The face is all wrong, I know, but....'

'Of course; what's in a face? But I went close, I tell you. I went to the "glory form," as they call it, and he prayed with me for twenty minutes.'

'In full light?' asked the first.

'Quite full; yet I can't swear to it that the face is made up.'

'Come, come!' interjected the first speaker, reproachfully.

'I can't, sir!' he insisted. 'But what I can swear to is the eyes; a man can't fake his eyes.'

'Well?'

'Our man's were grey, pale grey. This man's are a strange dark iridescent purple – very catlike.'

'That settles it, of course. But yet – I wish I could feel satisfied.'

A third man touched him on the arm. 'News, sir!' he said: 'strange, grave news!'

'Yes?' turned the other, swift as a snake.

'Father Ambrose is leaving London tomorrow.'

'I knew that, Smithers,' he snapped.

'– with Lord and Lady Marcus Masters.'

'Damn your eyes!' he yelled in excitement – 'sorry, Jackson! I mean the evidence of *his* eyes; there's something up, depend on it. Follow to the office; I must work out a new plan tonight.'

They moved off separately, the man Jackson cursing his superior for a dreaming fool who preferred intuition to plain fact.

7

Literalism in Practise

Despite the merry detective and his gallant men, or possibly because of their unceasing vigilance, nothing whatever happened. Yet Lord Marcus grew ever more pious, and gloomier; he had strange fits of weeping which alarmed his gentle wife; curious blushes would come over him without apparent cause. He grew morose, unkind to village children, who lacked the accustomed smile. He began to neglect his appearance. 'If thy right hand' (he cried one day, reproached for cruelly beating a dog – how unlike our gentle Marcus!) 'offend thee, cut it off! For it is better for thee to enter into Life maimed, than having two hands to be cast into the lake of fire. How much more then, if my dog offend me?'

Father Ambrose was genuinely distressed by these scenes. His influence, and his alone, seemed to calm the unhappy pietist – yet these interviews, beneficial as they seemed at the time, left a deeper irritation behind. Lord Marcus began to treat his wife with contempt and aversion; his temper grew daily more uncertain.

One day his wife took Father Ambrose aside, and suggested that medical treatment would relieve the strain. But the good man forbade all profane interference with 'the wonderful workings of the Lord with the soul.'

'Believe me, dear lady,' he would say, 'in His own good time the dear Lord knows how to bring our dear Marcus into His marvellous light.'

And she was fain to be satisfied.

So far no open scandal.

What brought matters to a climax was this.

One fine holiday, Lord Marcus, in his aimless way, was wandering in the village. Children were sporting in one corner with their big sisters and brothers; some game of forfeits was being played. Lord Marcus looked on moodily, hardly seeing, save to regret that these children were not all groaning over Sin in some damp Bethel.

A great clapping of hands. A buxom wench had broken some rule, or failed in some test; and must pay forfeit. The judge solemnly condemned her: –

> By Peter and Andrew and Mary and Anne
> You must go and kiss the prettiest man!

They all laughed shrill. But the wench, with a snigger, slyly approached the unconscious Marcus, threw her arms round him, and kissed him loud upon the lips.

Marcus started from his reverie, struck her fiercely in the face, and, crying 'Accurséd! accurséd! accurséd!' fled up the street.

The shrieking girl, with her lip bleeding from his signet ring, stared after him – as one who has seen Satan. Sobered, the children ceased their game, and fell to weeping. Some of the lads threw stones at the maniac; some started to follow, with coarse oaths. But he ran like a hare, and shut himself into his house. For three days he would see nobody; at last Father Ambrose, who was going to America to start a great revival there, insisted on bidding him farewell.

The good man found his noble patron in bed, looking like death, yet with a strange light in his eyes.

What passed none knew; but the ex-monk, pale as ashes, came to bid adieu to Lady Marcus. He was deeply moved. 'Do not intrude upon him!' he said, 'the crisis is over. Your husband is a great saint!'

But the American crusade never caught fire. Or the preacher lacked the flint, or his audience the steel, and after a futile fortnight the revival fizzled out. Ambrose gave notice that he must seek counsel of the Lord; something (he thought) was the matter with his personal holiness that the dear Lord no longer saw fit to use him. He disappeared, and none knew whither.

But the Marquis?

One day by post from Lagos came to him a shameful, an atrocious, an abominable packet – a nameless horror. And on the wrapping there was written:

LORD BARFIELD, WITH THE COMPLIMENTS OF
THE MARQUIS OF ERCILDOUNE.

8

The Chapel Of Revenge

Marcus Masters never rallied from the shock.

Tubercle caught his enfeebled frame in its grip; in less than a year he shrivelled to a corpse.

With the aged Marquis of Ercildoune the enemy had become a nightmare, an incubus, an obsession. The poor old man trembled at every whisper. Why did they whisper? What did they wish to hide from him? Some new misfortune? What did this stranger want at the house? Who was he? Lord Barfield feared even his own detectives.

Surely the shadow of the curse lay heavy on the House of Ercildoune.

A certain trusted valet, an old man whom he had known and loved from boyhood, long ere he took on him the fatal marquisate, was his daily companion. Deeply did he scrutinise each visitor to the once great house, now fallen and neglected. What did the Marquis care? Even his giant fortune-tree was somewhat lopped by the maintenance of what had grown to practically a standing army. In every country of the globe his men sought ceaselessly for traces of the escaped convict. Grayson had ten thousand pounds upon his head; yet he seemed safe as Prince Charlie was among his Highland hearts.

Some men doubted nine-tenths of the history. At the worst Grayson must have died somewhere. A desperate life and a desperate death. Why not ere now? He had not been heard of assuredly for years. Wise men remarked that Father Ambrose was certainly not young Grayson. The Marquis was a madman who saw family feuds in stones, and Grayson in everything.

The detectives would joke about it. When one took cold, he would laugh, 'Grayson getting at me again.' A funeral in the force was called a 'Grayson.'

Grim laughter must have filled the soul of that strange man, wherever it was that he lurked.

Ay! the great house of Ercildoune was hushed. Men did not care to pass those portals. Even as the ivy gripped the walls of the castle, so the curse clung upon all the hearts of the great house.

Long and earnestly, therefore, did the old watchdog of the Marquis gaze into the eyes of the strange bearded turbaned man that stole to the side gate one night and asked for admission.

Even so, he refused him. Then the Indian drew off his sandal, and from between the leathers took a scrap of paper. In the well-known cheirograph of Roland Rex, of late so longed-for, were the words, 'Good news of me by mouth.'

The suspicious old man was not yet convinced. This devil Grayson of all devils was most clever to disguise himself as an angel of light.

But the Marquis thought otherwise. 'Bring him in!' he cried. Some intuition told him that the words rang true.

Yet the obstinate old servant took his precautions like a wise general. He led the messenger through a dark passage, and, stumbling, took care to feel him for a hidden weapon. Nor, leading him into the very sight of Ercildoune, did he fail to cover him with his own pistol.

The old man lifted up his head. 'You bring news of my grandson?' he asked in Hindustani.

'The best of news,' was the answer in English, and Roland Rex, shaking off his turban, stepped forward and kissed his grandsire's trembling hand.

Like a stone god, steeled against all emotion, the ancient noble told in chill bleak words the hideous story of Marcus. Then he rose.

'Come!' he said.

At one end of the apartment was a tall door concealed by curtains of black velvet. Beyond lay a strange chapel. Here hung upon the walls the portraits of those dead Ercildounes. Above the altar with its lighted candles flaming was the terrible face of God, a God of Wrath and

Vengeance, the awful God of Judgement, who visiteth the sins of the fathers upon the children.

Upon the altar, draped all in black, stood the ghastly trophies of the curse, each in its casket, each with its sardonic inscription.

And on the empty monstrance was the scroll, 'How long, O Lord, how long?'

Roland started. The terror of the place ate like a cancer into his soul. The curse came home to him. Unreal, in a sense, these old catastrophes had been. These monuments of infernal hate meant little. Now he saw himself as the very target of those frightful arrows, and utmost fear smote him. He feared even lest his old grandfather were an enemy, some appalling avatar of his unresting foe.

Roland sank down before the altar and abased himself, reaching his hands up to Heaven.

A while he prayed; then he arose and swore that by God's help he would root out this monster from the fair earth polluted by his infamy.

The old man followed him in silence, approving. Together they left the chapel, with the echo still afloat in their ears.

The pair spent hours of dreary, profitless talk, wasting days in interviewing detectives, and drafting new plans of campaign. The only profitable work done was the reading of all the reports by Roland, afraid lest he should miss one clue.

At the end he shrugged his shoulders. 'Accident helped us before,' he said, 'and may help us again. But before all let no man know that I am still alive, and I will enter that dark hall of namelessness where Grayson lives. There is, I fancy, one man that may help us, the man that sentenced him – Mr Justice Laycock.'

9

Mr Justice Laycock

Mr Justice Laycock was a capital whip, and his four-in-hand was one of the sights of the Park in the season. If, during the off-season, he chose to keep his hand in by practise in St John's Wood, at midnight, and indoors, well – it was his business, and not ours.

And a very merry old gentleman he was.

Roland Rex just missed him at the club. There was nothing for him to do. He was big and strong, and very tired of tragedy; he had not tasted the over-ripe fruits of London for four years; nor indeed had he the disposition to set his teeth in a hard sharp apple.

He lounged off, with a tired man's eagerness for pleasure, rolled in and out of the Pavilion, stood speechless on the brink of Scott's for minutes that passed like hours, too stupid to go anywhere.

To one who has fallen so far there is but one refuge: – the Continental.

Put your foot on the rung of *that* ladder, and you are safe to reach the bottom!

In sooth, a little past midnight he got away from the drunken turmoil – himself a little enlivened by the light and the laughter and the wine – at the cost of having pledged himself to protect from molestation a beautiful maiden with cheeks far too natural, teeth far too regular, hair far too well-groomed, shoulders far too white, breasts far too well-shaped, dress far too well-cut, to be anything but a hideous monstrosity in the eyes of the healthy man.

The chivalry of his conduct melted the frosty hesitation of the fair one; on arrival at her house she asked him in to rest for a few moments.

The sound of childish laughter from within assured him that he need not fear to disturb the household; so he followed the lady, who took her latchkey and slipped in.

Like an adder he darted back. 'For God's sake, Kissums,' he whispered, catching her by the priceless Mechlin sleeve of her, 'there's the very man I want to see – and if he sees me now there's an end of it!'

For within the door stood Mr Justice Laycock. He had harnessed four pretty girls in reins of blue ribbon, and was driving them gaily up and down the stairs with a whip, while he occasionally blew on the horn that hung from his neck.

It is said that Archimedes, having discovered the principle of the lever, leapt from his bath, shouting 'Eureka' as his sole contribution to the usual toilet of a philosopher; and an equally brilliant idea must, one may believe, have seized the learned judge with equal intensity and suddenness. But if in this respect his costume as coachman seemed incongruous, the same complaint could not have been laid against his steeds, who reproduced the normal costume of a horse with the most scrupulous fidelity.

In the event, Roland suitably bestowed his fair charge at a great West End hotel, and repaired early in the morning to try and interview the judge in chambers.

But he had not appeared; and after an hour of useless waiting Roland strolled back to lunch at the Savoy, and a little later to his rooms.

About four o'clock the posters caught his eye –

MYSTERIOUS
DISAPPEARANCE
OF A
JUDGE

and a brief notice – vilely padded out to trick the public into the idea that the paper possessed some information – told him that it was Mr Justice Laycock that was missing.

'Asses!' chuckled Roland from the height of his superior knowledge. 'Somebody has run off with the old boy's clothes for a lark! Oh! won't I roast him over this!'

By ten o'clock the affair had grown fearful and wonderful. One paper had it that he had been seen at Folkestone: another said that he had received an urgent call to his sick son in Paris; and so on. All to be squelched by the official statement that he was not missing at all, but confined to his room by the very slightest of all possible indispositions, and would almost certainly be at work as usual on the morrow. So simple was this admirable lie that even Roland believed it. Two days elapsed, and he learnt only that 'the indisposition of Mr Justice Laycock had proved more severe than was at first supposed, and his medical advisers had recommended perfect rest for a week. There was no cause whatever for any anxiety.'

But a few noticed that all this did not explain why he was at first reported missing; it did not explain why numberless strangers called at the judge's house: it did not explain the extraordinary activity of Scotland Yard in certain parts of the metropolis.

On the following Sunday *Reynolds's* asked broadly in fat type 'WHERE IS LAYCOCK?' and Roland was still far from an answer when his bell rang, and an inspector from Scotland Yard, accompanied by a little rabbit-faced man, asked for a private interview.

'It's about this business of Mr Justice Laycock,' began the inspector. 'I must ask you to keep it absolutely private, sir, but he is not ill at all. He is really missing; he left his club at nine o'clock last Friday and has not been seen since.'

'Oh, yes, he has!' Roland cheerfully retorted. 'I saw him myself at one o'clock the following morning – I must ask you to keep it absolutely private – driving a very pretty four-in-hand up and down the stairs at 40, Roumania Road, St John's Wood.

The inspector whistled. 'That's the biggest lift yet,' he said.

'Well, this gentleman' – indicating the rabbit-faced man – 'will have it that there's some connection between this case and —'

'This,' said the rabbit-faced man, coming forward.

'What makes you think so?'

'This parcel is addressed to Lord Ercildoune, sir, and I think I know the writing.' He really trembled as he said it. 'You are fully responsible to his Lordship,' he went on, 'I take it; and between you and me, sir, I fear this parcel may be something of a shock, so we took the extreme liberty of delaying it.'

'You did right,' said Rex kindly.

'With your permission, sir, we will open it here and at once.'

The inspector cut the string and tore off the wrapping. A beautiful box of tortoise-shell inlaid with finest filigree of gold lay exposed.

The rabbit-faced man searched for the spring.

'Pull yourself together, sir!' he said sharply.

Lifting the lid, he disclosed a human tongue. To their horrified imagination it seemed still warm and quivering.

'Look! Look!' – the inspector recovered himself quickly enough. Indeed, the inner lid of the box bore this inscription, beautifully chased in gold –

THE TONGUE THAT SENTENCED ME.
LORD BARFIELD, WITH THE COMPLIMENTS OF
THE MARQUIS OF ERCILDOUNE.

They stood, rooted to the ground. Upon that stupendous moment the hateful clamour of the telephone broke in. Rex rushed to it, more to silence than to answer it. But the voice came stern and loud –

'Is that Mr Coffyn?'

'No – yes, of course! What is it?'

It was Rex's assumed name. In that supreme moment he forgot all accidents, stifled with the very breath of hell.

'Is Inspector Maggs with you, sir? May I speak to him?'

Roland handed across the receiver.

'Yes, I'm Maggs. Who are you?'

'Innes. Old Madame Zynscky has owned up: she's here now. Can you come?'

'Right. Ring off, please.'

'Will you come round with us, sir? Your evidence may be useful, if only to get the truth from Mother Zynscky.'

Roland took his hat. The scent was getting warm.

10

Madame Zynscky

Madame Zynscky was the Faubourg St Germain of the underworld. She had been magnificent, and retained alike the appearance and the pride. She was only too ready, once having taken the step, to throw herself into the arms of Justice, and grease the wheels of the chariot of the Law.

Yet it was a black enough business. There was not only the corpse of one of his Majesty's Judges to explain away, but the corpse of a child to whom the most liberal cynic could not give fifteen summers.

The police had started sniffing around on the very morning of the murder, which she had not discovered till eleven o'clock, when, having no sign of her distinguished guest, she had applied her eye to the peephole of the room, and seen the two dead bodies, and a sickening stream of blood, already chill and clotted on the floor.

So much was easy to tell, even if she risked a dose of penal servitude – one could never tell what these police would do! Somehow, she fancied, the matter would not come into court.

But what the inspector did want to know was this: Who had been there that night?

This she rolled off glibly, though she risked her livelihood. But the police were a good sort; they would not hurt an honest woman's trade; she was useful enough to them in a hundred ways, God knew!

They would not let her clients know that she betrayed them. Well, thank God, there was one question that he did not ask; what women were there? That is, other than the ordinary.

Did the inspector know who had done it? She thought perhaps he did. This was no ordinary crime.

Yes! it would be all right for her. They could never bring up the little girl against her; she had her answer for that! She was a cowardly fool not to have come straight to the police on that dreadful first morning, when a thousand expedients worse than foolish jostled each other in her shrewd old skull. No! perhaps it was better to give the man a chance to clear out. The police would prefer that too.

'Mr Fitzgerald would like a word, sir!' came an interruption at the door.

Mr Fitzgerald was Laycock's best friend.

'Any news, inspector?' he whispered.

'The worst, sir, I'm sorry to say.'

'Dead?'

'Ay, sir, and worse!'

'Worse? You are mad!'

'Murdered, so that if I had Grayson here in this office, I wouldn't dare to lay a finger on him. I can't bear it, sir; it's a shame to the force. Go, sir, you must break it to his wife – bear up, sir. We must face it all like men. But – look what I've seen tonight, sir!'

And he silently handed over the tortoise-shell box.

'Look here, gentlemen,' said the rabbit-faced man, who with Roland had joined them at the door. 'That man Grayson has never made but one mistake. He loved his father, and it cost him nigh two years in gaol. He won't do a silly thing like that again! He has committed every crime from petty larceny to murder, these thirty years – and tripped but once. Catch him!' and the little man laughed screechily.

It jarred them, one and all. Indeed there seemed a fate about it.

'I shall go to Lady Laycock,' said Fitzgerald shortly. 'To you, inspector, I only say one word: there is a God above.'

The inspector shrugged his shoulders.

They went back to the adorable Zynscky, who was now quite at her ease. Indeed, had she been Queen of England for a decade she could hardly have borne herself more majestically.

The physical appearance of all her guests supplied her with an inexhaustible fund of talk. Suddenly the inspector stopped her.

'By the way,' he said, 'who was the little girl?'

Madame Zynscky was equal to the occasion.

'Inspector Maggs,' she said solemnly, 'I pledge you my word that it has nothing to do with the case, and I strongly advise you not to ask.'

'H'm' – the inspector was but half convinced.

'The whole affair will be hushed up – you know it as well as I do! Well!' the placid old voice rippled on, 'I will tell you a little story.'

'Nonsense!' said the inspector sternly.

'I knew a very clever policeman in Vienna – never mind how many years ago! – who was engaged in a very similar case. That young man had his fingers on a very great criminal – one of the lowest blackguards in Vienna – but the night before he arrested him he had a very curious dream.'

'Yes?' said the inspector, amused. 'We don't dream much in London, Madame!'

'You'd better learn,' retorted the old woman grimly. 'This young man dreamt that he was hunting for a superintendent's badge in the mud; his fingers closed on it, and – it was a Royal Crown. A red-hot Royal Crown, and it burnt him! 'Twas only the girl with his shaving water that touched his hand with the hot jug to wake him; but while he shaved he thought, and, while he thought, the criminal slipped out of Austria; and the very same post that brought that disappointing news consoled him with the news of his appointment to that very 'surintendance' he had dreamed of.

'Now wasn't that funny?' she concluded, with a chuckle.

'The inspector is a witty man,' interposed Roland, 'but you go and try the joke on the Most Noble the Marquis of Ercildoune. You'll find, inspector,' he added, 'that this affair won't hush up quite as smoothly as all that. I shall see you later. Goodbye!' and he strolled off.

'You may go, Madame,' said the inspector; 'we shall always know where to lay our hands on you – and I'll think it over.'

'Good afternoon, gentlemen!' and the disgusting creature swept out of the office with the airs of a duchess.

Left to themselves, the two men silently produced their pipes. They were nearly through the first before the rabbit-faced man opened his mouth.

'Tell you what, Maggs,' he said, 'if I had Grayson here, I'd choke him right away, and chance what happened after.'

The inspector reached out his hand.

'And not think twice about it,' was his only comment.

11

The Crown Princess

The more Maggs thought about it, the less Maggs liked it. But the certainty of Ercildoune's resentment was bound to outweigh the dubious threats of the old harridan of Roumania Road. After all, she might be bluffing. He determined to go into the case with even more than his accustomed zeal.

But this peculiar case seemed to object to the process.

All his clues were woolly – everybody had a quite straightforward story to tell, and not a soul had heard or seen anything. Of the five or six dapper young men that frequented the house there was not one in the least like the missing Grayson. Every one of them was a fine strapping upstanding healthy clean-living youth, such as England is proud of. Every one of them lived in an honourable way and could be traced back to the cradle.

But they were frankly indifferent to the detective, and had all made a point of seeing and hearing a little less than nothing. Only one, a Mr

Segrave, the private secretary of the Crown Princess (as she was called by everyone), offered to assist him.

'Look here, inspector,' he said, 'for private reasons of my own I should like to see this matter cleared up. Now you're on the wrong tack altogether. Everybody knows all about old Zynscky's men. You have a look round at the women.'

'Well,' said Maggs, 'I have quite certain information that it was done by a man.'

'Or by a woman at his command. You're a smart man, Inspector Maggs; but if you leave out the women, they'll call you Maggots. You have a look round at the women.'

'What do you know, sir?'

'I can tell you of two or three who were there that night – but I shan't. You can find out easily enough from other sources, and —'

'Thank you!' said Maggs, 'you needn't change my name yet; you've told me.'

And off he went.

'There was a Segrave in this case before, too,' mused Maggs. 'Of course. Captain Segrave, killed with Roland Rex in that avalanche. But, Great Scott! Mr Rex was not killed. Where is Captain Segrave, then?'

These lying official reports! Perhaps even Mr Rex himself would hardly know the truth of that story.

Nor did Roland, on being questioned, think the facts of the case good to report, and fubbed off the inspector with the usual commonplaces of official stupidity.

Rex could hardly have explained this reticence, even to himself. Perhaps the shock of the affair had a good deal to do with it. In any case he held his tongue, and a really priceless clue was lost. The inspector left young Segrave to himself, and busied himself with other threads. Yet, had he but known it, young Segrave was like a silken skein of Ariadne, to lead him to the hell-heart of the labyrinth.

* * *

The young man went over to his mistress, to perform his daily secretarial duties. The Crown Princess was known and beloved all over England. The infamous conduct of her vile husband was perhaps but guessed; yet the one shameful bargain, the refusal to accede to which had cost her a throne, was well enough understood to make her the idol of that mean and obscene class of English people that love to think themselves generous and pure.

Divorced though she was, she commanded the esteem and affection of the Court as of the crowd; and if, as a few blackguard busybodies hinted, she sought elsewhere that solace which our beautiful social system had denied her, it was surely her own affair. Not that any decent person listened for an instant to the breath of scandal; in fact, one or two men had been soundly horsewhipped for something less than a whisper to her discredit.

The secretary found his mistress awaiting him. She lay on a magnificent divan of tigers' skins, seriously smoking a cigarette with long deep inhalations. There was more Eastern blood than Austrian in her veins; nay! but the naked Tatar showed clear as noonday in her supple gestures and savage face.

She rose as he entered. She was a woman of full six feet, her body strong and lithe as a leopard's; too slight almost to support the weight of her marvellous head. Of the semi-Mongolian type, with long sleepy eyes, and eyebrows bushy and black as a raven, the nose more snub than straight with the nostrils jutting like an animal's, the mouth a scarlet slit with thinnest lips crowned with a black down, the teeth strong and projecting, the jaw square and portentous. The cheeks were hollow, and they and the whole face glistened with that coarse dead blue (only enlivened by the purple of two moles upon the chin) that one only sees in Eastern Europe. All this was on a mighty model; its poise on the slight shoulders served to accentuate its great size; so did her lustrous hair. Of gleaming dead blue-black, it rolled and twisted tightly about her in innumerable coils. One would have said Medusa with her snakes!

Yet all the wonder and horror of the head was instantly blotted out when she spoke. 'Twas like some gentle far-off silver bell borne down on the Zephyr to one's listening ear. 'Twas of no great volume, but most utter sweet.

So also the sleepy nectar of her long oblique eyes set deep in the rocky fastness of cheekbone and eyebrows stole out to give you of the nectar of her soul.

Verily a marvel! That all the tenderness and truth of a Madonna should force itself to expression through so dark a veil! Yet it did so. Little children ran to kiss the ugly face. When she smiled, it was a world of beauty – and she always smiled.

A marvellous artifice of beauty thus to hide itself in repulsion! She stood upright on the tiger-skins, her body draped in a clinging cas-

cade of scarlet and silver sequins in the half-light against the deep
azure tapestry of the wall, and waited.

12

Miss Arundell

'Mr Segrave,' she said at last, 'I have no letters this morning; but I
have a task of some difficulty for you: well, of absurdity rather, but I
assure you that it is of the last importance to my interests. You will
please go out and buy at the first ironmonger's a hammer and three
long French nails; with these proceed to Guildford Street near Russell Square. You will perceive upon a hoarding a poster bearing the
words "APPLE SOAP." Kindly drive a nail into the centre of each letter
P. You had better leave the motor at the corner of the street. Return,
instantly and without looking round, to the car, drive to Brighton,
and drop the hammer from the pier-head into the sea. Then leave
this cipher message on the ground, and return. You may wait on me
tomorrow morning at the same hour.'

The secretary bowed and withdrew. 'Send Miss Arundell to me as
you go out,' she added: 'I wish to be read to.'

In a few moments the door opened quietly, and Eileen Arundell
appeared.

What a difference to her mistress was this true-hearted English
maiden! Neither tall nor short, but of a graceful habit, the supple
beautiful body was crowned with the daintiest face in the world. A
shade piquant in expression, yet the glorious sincerity of her fearless
eyes stamped her as no coquette. The lips were not too full, not too
red; curved, yet not curved too much; and deliciously tiny was the
whole mouth, set in the delicately chiselled face with its blush ever
flaming over the creamy languor of her cheeks. The eyes were grey
shaded with blue; the hair was of that fine gossamer gold of which the
angels make their harp-strings.

She and her mistress loved each other like twin sisters; the gentle
innocence of the one matched well with the sagacious kindliness of the
other, and the subtle fascination of the ugly Princess was a splendid foil
to the frank appeal of her lovely companion.

Princess Stephanie greeted her with an affectionate caress; then sank
back upon her rugs. '*Je suis énervée!*[1] read me of Flaubert – no, of

---

[1] [I'm upset.]

Balzac. Ah! but not that horrible *Peau de chagrin*, my beautiful. Read me *La Fille aux yeux d'or*.'

Eileen knew the mood. Silently she found the book, and seating herself at the edge of the divan, close to the exquisite feet of the Princess, interpreted in her low melodious voice the inspired words of the great magician of Touraine.

'Eileen,' said Stephanie, after an hour had passed, 'old Mr Jukes will be here this morning. I expect very important news of this projected loan, and I shall require to be quite undisturbed. You must lock the double doors, and see that nobody approaches. You understand quite clearly that a single whisper in the City at this juncture would ruin the whole scheme – and then where would your little fortune be?' she added playfully.

'Do you really mean it, Stephanie darling?' murmured the timid child. 'You will really give me a thousand pounds of stock? I hardly believe there is so much money in the whole world.'

'You have earned it well, kitten!' laughed the Princess. 'You have been very useful to us, I assure you. Who would suspect my beautiful kitten of negotiating a scheme that will startle four capitals when it is made public? Go now, darling one, and see that Mr Jukes enters unobserved.'

The fair girl kissed her mistress, and glided out of the room.

Left to herself, Stephanie gave rein to a tempest of warring passions. She rolled to and fro on the divan like one in grievous pain of body; she lighted a cigarette, and threw it away again; she tried to read, and was revolted by the stupidity of the author in not casting a dazzling light upon her immediate perplexity. She even tried to pray before the dim-lit icon in the little eastern niche; but the Madonna had no message for her.

The paroxysm was luckily soon cut short; the door moved slowly inwards, and the old financier stood before her. The door closed behind him, and Stephanie heard the swish of Eileen's dress, and the turning of the key in the outer lock. She herself made fast the inner door, and turned to greet her visitor.

Mr Jukes was a bent old man of a pronounced Jewish cast of countenance, with bright eyes gleaming from under his shaggy eyebrows. He walked somewhat lamely, and leant upon his serviceable oaken staff.

Stephanie drew the curtains over the window.

The consultation was prolonged and intense. It seemed that the Princess was torn by the claws of many conflicting emotions, those vultures that scent the carcass of the dead soul from afar.

What awful grief had stunned her? What dreadful passion moved her?

How should the cold concentration of high finance admit elements so incongruous?

Nor was the old Jew unmoved by the strange episodes of which she had to inform him. Anger and fear held the situation in a fiery grip. Only the most dazzling brilliance of imagination could inspire dull ingenuity.

Long they talked loud; their voices slowly lessened in volume as the minutes passed; but it was an hour before the conversation sank to confidential whispers. The fusion of these two great intellects, triumphing over personal interest, had produced a gigantic master-piece of intrigue.

Silently and secretly as he had come, the old Hebrew departed; and Eileen returned to her mistress and friend to find fresh vigour and delight replace the apathy and ennui of the morning.

'You have read me Balzac, dear,' she said; 'I in my turn will tell you a stranger story than he ever imagined. First, I have good news for you. A certain young gentleman we know of is not dead at all, but in London.'

Eileen flamed all over with joyful blushes.

'Ah, but there is ill news, too. There are enemies of him and his family; desperate, powerful enemies – and they may seek his life.'

The fair girl paled, but kept her courage.

'I am your friend,' the Princess said, 'and we will try and find a way to defeat them.'

Warmly the two women embraced; the child nestled into the strong white arms.

The tale of family distress that she unfolded has already been in part disclosed.

Some of the earlier, some of the most recent events were yet dark.

Indeed, the long tale which the Princess told to her dependant was but a partial and distorted view of the events.

We shall understand it better if we look on the affair from the im-personal standpoint, if we go back in time a hundred years, to the generation before Ewan Dhu.

13

The Root of the Matter

Long years before, John, third Marquis of Ercildoune, had begotten two strong sons upon Margaret his wife. The elder, Dugal, had proved but a wild lad, and cared more to wander with the gipsy folk and run for lace and French brandy with the smugglers than to acquire the artificial polish of a noble, and to bow and scrape in the gilt flunkeydom of Court society. The old Marquis cared little; 'twas the wild old blood. If he risked life, what care?

But the wildness grew; the heir went wandering for a year and more at once; still the old Marquis went his way, and took but little heed.

Yet suddenly his folly's crown came on him.

Dugal, after an absence of some months, returned one Lammas Eve with a black-browed wench from Brittany for his wife.

Here was a tangle not to be cut; the devout Catholic was bound to respect the blessing of the Church. He could but pray for death to take her. A week they stayed in the castle; the woman sickened of the fine food and fair clothes; she bore herself like an harlot – as indeed she was – bold and impudent and free with the very lacqueys. Nor did her husband care; all day he drank in the great hall, and shamed his father's roof-tree, while his lady, almost as drunk as he, romped with the scullions.

Then the old man, hard stricken, drove them forth to their mates, the outlaws, and set a curse upon his house that he should never enter it.

A year passed. Ewan, a sober goodly lad, did what he could to assuage his father's shame. But that was little. Still, he rode among the people, and sought to fit himself for the duties of a good magistrate.

One winter's night, as he rode homeward, he saw the red flame glitter over the fisher-village by the sea. He set spurs to his horse, and rode in. A band of smugglers, it seemed, had landed their cargo that night, and were carousing in honour of success. Merriness turned to madness, and in their frenzy they set light, for laughter, to some fisher's cot. The flames spread; the fishermen took alarm, and when the smugglers fought against their attempts to extinguish the fire, attacked them. When Ewan arrived, he saw the riot in the darkness lit by the fitful glare of the blazing huts. He joined the fight, and his long sword turned swiftly the issue. The smugglers fled, save one who wheeled a burning brand caught from the fire, and smote therewith lustily about him. The two champions faced each other, knew each other. Ewan let fall his sword.

'Dugal!' he cried.

'Jacob!' answered the other; then laughed. 'But your hour is come, man Ewan!' and lifted his club to strike. But a fisher lad darted in, and with his clasp-knife struck him in the throat. The wild Lord Dugal fell without a sigh.

Death sobered all the storm: the winds and clouds joined in to aid the peace; a clamour of great rain rushed down and quenched the last of the fire. Ewan knelt by his dead brother in the darkness.

Death atoned for all; he bore him to the castle, and they buried him lordly; his life was forgotten, only his birth remembered. Four years passed by, and the old Marquis slept with his fathers; Ewan Dhu inherited the fiefs of Ercildoune. Again twelve years; Ewan was married, and bright sons were born to him.

All was at peace; the land prospered exceedingly. Yet trouble was in store. A hundred miles away in the hills lived an old witch, a miser. News came that she had been robbed and murdered. The runners were hard on the track of the murderer, and but a day after this news arrived Ewan, riding lonely through the park as was his wont, was held by an old woman and a youth. 'Save me, mine uncle!' was his cry.

Then Ewan knew his brother's wife. 'This is Lord Dugal's boy,' she wept, 'Lord Dugal's, foully slain when facing you in fight!' She wove a web of falsehood as to the cause for their plight; and he, always accusing himself of his brother's misfortunes, must haste to hide them in that cavern under the waterfall where, later, he was to meet the Rosicrucian, his master. But he had cherished snakes. The hue-and-cry after the murderer died away; Ewan conveyed the fugitives safely to America. Then they turned and struck. By force of law they sought to oust their benefactor from the Marquisate. But Ercildoune had learnt that it was the murderer of an old woman (though a witch) that he had hidden from the gallows; he determined to hold what he had. 'Wild and foolish was Dugal,' he exclaimed, 'but never sire to this hell-brat, born in wedlock though he may have been.' He sent a trusty servant to the priest who had married his brother, and by money and finesse obtained the mutilation of the register. With his wealth and influence he fought them to the death; it was held not proven that the boy was Dugal's son. It was held proven that two years before his death she had left him for a master-thief named Grayson, whom she had married. This marriage was held good, the former null.

Ewan had triumphed; but his sensitive nature left him never at ease. He sought consolation in the study of the stars, in the companionship of wise and holy men; he was admitted postulant to the mysterious brotherhood of the Rosy Cross. This availed him, maybe, to his own soul; but how could it avoid the Doom of Ercildoune?

As we have seen he surrendered to the curse, and put his trust in God.

Now even as the third distillation of a spirit is purer than the first, so in evil the thief Grayson was but a watery mixture, and the harlot but a child in iniquity. Their son was murderer and traitor from the breast; but genius leapt in him. Conquering his early errors, his futile pettiness of murdering an old woman for her hoarded sixpences, he rose to eminence in infamy. While yet young, he amassed a fortune in the New England states by a supreme exercise of the pharisaical hypocrisy and smug dishonesty for which the people of that part of the world have been and still are justly celebrated.

At thirty-five he had shuffled his now useless old mother into the workhouse, had married the only daughter of the richest man in Boston, had gotten a healthy son, and was ready to devote his life to restoring the rights of primogeniture.

A year in London, and the aid of the cleverest counsel, convinced him that he had no shadow of hope in law. Might should make right, he said, and let loose the leashed passions of his boyhood. A hideous plan leapt full-armed from his mighty yet devilish brain.

His achievements and failures have already been recounted, even unto that colossal stroke of irony that Fate so glibly played on the railway just north of Marseille, where this master-Anarch fell by the hand of the meanest of his tribe.

14

The Flower of the Mischief

That which was the dream of the father became the hope of the son. Rich enough to maintain an obsequious band of clever blackguards, it was easy to arrange his escape from prison, and assure himself a hundred safe retreats. Handsome and fascinating, with a subtle brain, he could bend to his will many of those beyond the lure of gold. He was sharp enough to see from the first that his only chance of regaining the lost glory was not only to carry out his father's ghastly revenge and so stamp out the house of Ercildoune, but to gain such domination in the houses of power that it should become the necessary interest of England herself to gloss over his offences, and establish him in the enviable seat.

To this end, therefore, he worked steadily. Many a lady of high rank was ready to throw herself into his arms, under one of his numberless disguises, which, deep as they might be, could never conceal the essential force and genius of the man. But he threw them aside as quickly as he picked them up. A month to subdue them, a month to test their influence and find it wanting, and a day to rid himself of them.

At last he met and conquered one who could answer fully his ambition. What mysterious levers she controlled he knew not; enough that she controlled him. It was through her that he found a man like Captain Segrave to sink himself in the nullity of a number – 163 – in his accurst band of cut-throats. It was through her that Ercildoune had fallen from favour in the Court; and was openly flouted as a madman.

A prevailing inner sense that Grayson was indeed the rightful Marquis, and likely innocent of all the crimes imputed to him, ruled in the inner circles round the throne. Nor had he failed to bind this woman to him by the deadliest bonds. Little by little he had led her from fair ways to foul; at last he had wrought upon her even to this crowning horror – he had made her commit a crime to serve him. So thought the impostor; but even the most desperate criminal is not always right. Was it possible that for the love of him she had done a deed at whose very contemplation many a hardened ruffian would have blanched? Was it she who had lured Laycock to his doom by the innocent bait, and the knowledge of his hideous greed for maidenhood? Would she not have quailed as she took the knife and did a deed which – had any dared to publish it – would have set the world aghast?

But, whoever had done the deed, none dared to make it public. The newspapers reported all in good faith that Mr Justice Laycock's indisposition had taken an unexpectedly serious turn; that pneumonia had supervened, and a weak heart had proved his bane. Barely a dozen people knew the dread secret; barely a score of others suspected some guile, they knew not what. And every mouth was sealed by interest or fear.

What was the use of Maggs and his determination to see the matter aired? What could he do to upset the bulletins and the death certificate? He threatened this and that; the holders of the secret smiled. He even forced himself upon Lady Laycock, and begged her to avenge her husband – glossing his crime. She half relented; bade him come again. But before the appointment the too zealous detective received a quiet snub from his official chief, and the same evening found in his mail an offer to go to Milan at a very large salary to organise the police force in that city.

What could he do but throw up the sponge? In vain Roland Rex, with whom he had a last stolen interview, urged him to continue his endeavours. Bribes and entreaties were alike of no avail; Maggs had had enough of the task, and rolled off to Italy easier in his mind.

There was but one hope in the fast failing house of Ercildoune. Roland yet lived, and might avenge. The toils closed fast; only this lion might haply break them. Yet hope might well have staggered, had but Ercildoune once guessed that Roland's escape was known to his pitiless and powerful foes.

Nor had they grasped, even with all the evidence before them, the all-reaching mastery of that awful brain. All they had drunk was but the froth upon the hell-brew; they were yet to come down to the dregs.

For while the bastard Marquis yet lay hidden in London, gloating over his last hideous stroke of vengeance, his wily soul grasped out at an idea yet greater than aught he had yet planned.

One master-stroke, one quintessential draught of utmost villany, and the whole problem should be solved, alike on one side and the other, to complete the doom of Ercildoune not only with death but with disgrace.

How? On what obscure and desperate fulcrum would he lean his lever? What lure or menace could bring him to the grievous end? Hath Euclid proved in vain that two circles which cut one another cannot have the same centre? Ah, but geometry is not life.

Even as Roland in despair reached to his youth's dream as his one last hope, so did the deadly malice of the false Ercildoune spit out the name 'Eileen Arundell.'

15

Love Among the Hooligans

So far the adventure of Roland had led him no great distance. He haunted all the dens of vice in London; he consorted with the vilest criminals, and flattered with attention all the old ghouls that batten on the grave of England's youth. He even gave himself out in various quarters as one of Grayson's gang; but to no purpose. Soon, too, he saw that so far from tracking his quarry, he was on the contrary being most adroitly stalked. An unpleasant sensation, as any who have followed a wounded tiger into thick jungle may admit.

Thus, one day a load of bricks fell over him from a ladder, but luckily scattered, so that he escaped with a graze; a second day, his hansom took the wrong turning, and whirled him down strange streets before he was aware. In the upshot, he was free at the cost of a scuffle with a bully.

Several more incidents of this sort occurred. It never stuck him that these were the clumsiest stratagems, that Grayson, if he were so minded, could probably have put him out of the way with ease. That did not occur to him: he attributed his escape to Providence and redoubled his precautions.

But the long search sickened him. Were it not for the terrific evidence of the arch-fiend's presence, he too could have believed him dead.

'I will take the risk,' he said to himself, 'and declare myself to the Beloved One.'

For, ere the shadow of the Curse of Ercildoune fell on him, Roland's youth had been idyllic. Boy and girl together, he had worshipped Eileen Arundell.

What came between them but this doom? His grandfather had taken him aside, and told him all the woe; after that day he had withdrawn himself, and gone to the unknown, if haply he might find forgetfulness. And she? She never guessed – how could she guess? For he had not trusted himself to say 'Farewell!' to her – and so she kept the sorrow at her heart. Old Colonel Arundell died not long after, and left her wellnigh penniless. Fortunate that she had so good a friend as the Princess, who let her lack nothing.

She turned the cold scorn of her eyes on Segrave's measured passion; wherein her faithfulness, though 'twere but a memory – as it chanced – availed to save her lover's life. How, shall be told in its due place.

But how to disclose his identity to his beautiful without letting the world into the secret was harder even than his resolution to trust her had been to take. It might well chance that her great and holy happiness in seeing him alive again would be swallowed up in some dire and irremediable catastrophe. Yet he saw no other road. Her influence with the Crown Princess might restore Ercildoune to favour, and set once more the engines of administration at work upon his side; true! Yet even more important to himself that her simple faith and purity might in some inscrutable manner pierce the awful mask that had so long baffled wealth, intelligence and power.

Of her truth he never doubted; but his late experiences had made him distrust even the Post Office, that sheet-anchor of a Briton's faith.

Even as he sat in his little room in Stepney, where he was hiding since the numerous attempts upon his life had assured him that his enemies had discovered the fraud of the avalanche and were hot on his scent, the problem was solved, and that most strangely.

From the street came a sudden tumult of coarse laughter and jeers, then a cry of anger and alarm above them, then a growing clamour and clatter. He looked out, and saw – Great God! – the very woman of his fantasy – his own Eileen! – running hard with flushed face towards him, pursued by a yelling crowd of young hooligans, the flower of our wonderful social system, and our masters tomorrow when the ideals of Keir Hardie have triumphed over manhood.

In a second he had reached the street door and flung it wide, at the same moment blowing a police whistle with all his force. 'In here, Miss Arundell!' he cried.

She knew him instantly, and obeyed. In another minute some half-dozen of the hooligans lay sprawling on the pavement; the rest sheered off. Roland wasted no more time on them; the police, strolling up sulkily, would attend to them. He found Eileen on the stairs in a dead faint.

Lightly he bore her to his room, and revived her. For a while nothing was said; the tension of the silence grew and grew. Without a word or a look he compelled her by sheer will. For her, fear held her back, but as she gazed she lost the nauseous disease of personality; rapture suddenly overcame her, and with one intense exclaim: 'Roland, ah Roland!' she found herself sobbing in his arms. Closer and yet closer he caught her; his head bowed down – was it in prayer? I believe it – then willed her face to his....

That sun of glory looked up through the showers; the sweet chaste lips kindled, despite themselves; the world was blotted out; they kissed.

An hour later Eileen Arundell, with his mother's ring upon her finger, a new woman by the might of love, was telling her adventure.

The Princess had sent her with a message to one of the many Christian missions, offering her great house for a lecture on the East-End; she would gather many an exalted, many a wealthy listener. Eileen had barely completed her errand and turned homeward when far along the street a dozen boys had begun to follow her with insult. She took no notice; they increased, drew closer, threatened her. At last one bolder and coarser than the rest tore at her hat; she turned, menacing; and at that moment received a cruel blow. She cried for help, and seeing none, began to run.

Roland began to see. The clumsy failures to strike him down were to be followed up more subtly. First, they would perhaps kill her before his eyes. And a blind anguish filled him; a sense of helplessness, like that which grips men in some great earthquake, swallowed up his soul.

If they had hope at all, it was surely in the power and intellect of the Princess. They would go to her and tell the whole strange story; she could not but be moved; she would help, she would save. Yet Eileen hesitated. Might it not be to bring her into the danger? Was anyone so strong, so high, as to escape? Would the hand that had pulled down a Marquis and a Judge be stayed for a Princess?

On the other hand, was not the doubt an insult? Would not the great lady burn red with shame if she could hear? Surely it was a crime to doubt her all-but divinity. Would she ever forgive Eileen if one sorrow of that child-heart were kept back from her? In Roland's absence, her father's death, what sympathy but hers? At the false news of Roland's death, had she not held her up with hope, fed her with sister tears, been as it were mother and sister and husband in one? Had she not already some knowledge of the great conspiracy, and offered her protection?

Then they would go to her. Together, an hour later, they mingled their tears and kisses at her feet, while the royal woman, in a very tiger rage, had sworn by her own soul to save them, to bring them back to happiness, and peace to Ercildoune.

16

The Mental Condition of Mr Segrave

Under the ægis of this Kalmyk Minerva, Roland Rex enjoyed a measure of safety. The attempts on his life ceased; it seemed that the bloodhounds had lost the trail. The Princess hid him in a small house she had in Chelsea; he was wonderfully disguised by an old Hebrew named Jukes, a very master of the art of altering the human face. Luck was with him from the start; he fell in with one of Grayson's gang, and by nearly throttling the fellow in a certain low opium den to which they had retired with the purpose of discussing in private various blackguard schemes, had obtained all sorts of valuable knowledge. Grayson had gone away; the Laycock scent was still warm; he would be back (and God knew Grayson would kill him if he discovered who had betrayed him) in some three months' time. Then let old Ercildoune beware of him! With much more of the same sort.

Roland could enjoy, too, now and again – but not too often! – a stolen interview with exquisite Eileen. Hope and faith and love flowed back into the young man's soul: he felt no doubt as to the issue. When Grayson returned – by God, let him beware of Ercildoune!

It may or may not be true that every pleasure of ours is balanced by some other's pain, but in this instance it was surely so.

The mind of Mr Segrave needed all his ultra-British hatred of visible emotion to hide its anguish from the world. He knew nothing of Roland's return; but he marked the love-light in the wondrous eyes of his adored Eileen, and knew that the flame was none of his kindling. While she was yet a virgin heart (or so he deemed, for the mask of sorrow hid her love) he could afford to wait, to work quietly, to win at his ease. As a jockey in the straight who should have eased his horse to a canter, and finds suddenly some despised outsider furious at his heels, he lost his head a little and lashed in a frenzy at his horse. One evening he caught Eileen alone, and poured out his whole passion.

Gently she put him by.

He could better have borne contempt. He caught her roughly, bruising her almond arms; he called her by the foulest names. Then, suddenly penitent, he flung himself upon the floor in a passion of hysterical weeping. She pitied him, caring little for her own pain and shame; she left him softly and said nothing. Segrave soon conquered himself, and shut himself up in his old suave mask of gentle courtesy and silent devotion, as from afar.

The Princess never guessed what beast might lurk beneath the cultured gentleman, dull in spite of all his intellect, that she had known so long.

Yet the beast grew in cunning and insight; the more Segrave disciplined and controlled it, the mightier it grew. Just as the discipline of physical exercise makes the man stronger at the end, so the first foolish brute impulse, working in ordered channels, became a force to be reckoned with.

Nor was there anyone to reckon with it; Eileen herself never guessed that it was there. She thought his angry fit a passing flash; and her innocence slept sound.

Segrave's awakened judgement soon warned him of what was going on. The absences of Eileen became suspicious; his own foolish missions took on a sinister aspect; it was certain that the Princess was tricking him.

Even his brother's story (which had before seemed commonplace enough) loomed up as a mystery to his newfound subtlety. He reflected upon the sudden mad infatuation that had seized that straight-living soldier; the change in his way of life; the reticence that sat so ill on the frank face; the sudden senseless journey for a sport he had never affected; and the tragic end of him.

Young Segrave brooded overmuch upon these matters. He began to lose sight of the endless kindness of the Princess Stephanie; the fascination of her faded; he began to picture a monster, a vampire that fed upon the lives of men.

Ah! but he would be her master yet. And he began to look about him for a weapon. Always he had felt that he had little share in her true thought, that invisible bars fenced him from her soul. Well, he must penetrate. Perhaps Maggs could have helped him; Maggs knew a deal about most people and their ways. But Maggs was gone abroad. By chance he met the rabbit-faced man one day in Leicester Square. He knew him for an old intimate of Maggs, and the impulse came to him to talk to him. That evening he dined him at his club.

It was a royal pumping-match. During dinner, by common consent, the talk was sterile; yet each casual futility that passed on politics was meant and interpreted alike as a feeler and a thrust. Over their cigars they turned from the skirmish to the battle, and far into the night they plied feint and attack, till the night itself seemed to weary rather than they.

Yet neither obtained much but the increased resolve of silence, and on Segrave's part, an icier gleam in his hatred of the Crown Princess.

As he walked back through the clear morning he swore again to penetrate her fastness, by whatever loophole offered, and to defeat some plan of hers, however trivial, so that he might not feel his manhood shamed.

If he could utterly rout her, and avenge his brother, whom he no longer doubted to have been a victim, in some ambiguous way, to her designs, so much the better.

Thinking over it, he decided to track down first his rival. He paid a man to follow Eileen to what were doubtless assignations. But the girl was clever at throwing off pursuers, and it was not for some weeks that the truth came out. What, then, was Segrave's wrath to find his rival in the person of Roland Rex.

Like all suspicious and jealous persons, he could put two and two together very quickly. But the sum was never less than five, and often reached three figures. So it took him but a moment to convince himself that Rex had killed his brother. Not so bad either! That is the worst of lunatic's arithmetic, the law of chance ordains that now and then the answer shall come right.

All threads, then, were but one. He had but to slay Roland, and the Princess was beaten, his loved Eileen set free (maybe his victory would bring her to his feet – and, by God! how he would trample her!), his brother avenged.

Mr Segrave began to wish that he knew Grayson. That man should have at least one staunch ally. In the meanwhile, he would shadow his victim, even as the silent and terrible man-hunting snake of Yucatan.

17

The Holy Dirk

Lord Ercildoune kept lonely vigil in his ancient castle, brooding over the past terrors that had whitened his still luxurious locks, the future fears that threatened to overwhelm his house thus utterly. Yet tonight he was more cheerful than his wont. Roland's letters had been uniformly hopeful; he seemed to have felt at last upon his own true steel the hitherto invisible foil of his fiendish antagonist; surely, moreover, there was an end to all. 'How long, O Lord, how long?' he murmured with more reverence and confidence than he had felt for many years. Before, the prayer was like a wild outcry for some doubtful justice; now, it seemed that the answer 'Soon! soon!' came like a benediction on his brows. Also, the familiar words wooed him to the familiar way, and he moved solemnly into his little chapel, and bent him in prayer at the altar.

Then he was aware – as we all are at times by some strange sensorium whose paths are yet unknown – that some other person had been before him. A thing surely incredible? His first emotion was of fear. Had the murderer found him? Had the last hour of Ercildoune struck upon the clock of Destiny? Yet a glance reassured him. There was no place of concealment in the chapel.

He betook him again to his prayers.

Again the strange sensation caught him, and more strongly. Yes, there was something new. And on the altar – how did this come to pass? Strange, strange.

There lay upon the black cloth a silver-hilted dirk, sheathless. To his amazement he beheld upon the hilt the well-known cipher of the Rosicrucians. They who had befriended his cousin the late Marquis – had they come at last to his aid? The mystery was explained, for the old man credited the Brotherhood with powers beyond the common. He reverently lifted the dirk. On the sharp shining steel he read in tiny letters of gold the legend –

MASTER, YE SHALL SHEATHE ME SOON
AND BREAK THE CURSE OF ERCILDOUNE.

With a sudden impulse he glanced once fearfully around, and hid the blade in his vest. Then, lingered long, mingling the accustomed prayer with new heart and hope into strains of praise, such as that gloomy chapel, the monument of so many iniquities and woes, had never yet echoed.

The day broke, and Ercildoune still grasped the dagger, and still prayed.

The days passed, and news increased both in volume and excellence. The rabbit-faced man had missed Grayson in Vienna by an hour; Grayson was in hiding, in flight; his band seemed broken up; he struck back no more; the little army of Ercildoune was closing on him. Any moment news might come that he was taken.

One day, too, when he chanced to be confined to the castle by a cold, there came a kindly message of enquiry from the King. It seemed he was restored to favour.

He had not lived as he lived now since he inherited the fatal Marquisate.

Surely Fate had tired of her enmity; he should yet go down to the grave in peace. Then a telegram reached him from London. 'Grayson trapped. Your presence necessary.' It was signed by Eileen Arundell.

All the hope of the last month had strengthened the old man; his virile force came back in floods of anger. 'Now is the time to strike!' he thought; 'now shall I sheathe the holy dirk in the heart of that devil of the pit!'

And, feeling younger and lighter than he had done for many a day, he hurried off to London.

Imagine his joy on reading the morning poster: 'The Scottish Vendetta; Lord Ercildoune's enemy reported under arrest,' as he passed Warrington; his positive rapture at Euston when *The Owl* flamed at him –

GRAYSON SEEN
IN LONDON –
EXCITING CHASE –

at his hotel when the newsboy followed him with –

GRAYSON CAUGHT.

He bought a paper and read the following –

> The mysterious enemy of the Marquis of Ercildoune has, it is alleged, been at last identified. He was seen by one of Lord Ercildoune's private detectives in the act of leaving a famous house in the West-End. As he jumped into a private motor and drove off with all possible speed, it was impossible to arrest him at the moment; but the detective, who was fortunately the chief of Lord Ercildoune's numerous staff, and a man highly esteemed by the police – we break no confidence in mentioning his name, Arkwright, who aided the police so greatly in the

recent Elmstead Tunnel Mystery – was able to set innumerable activities to work.

The motor-car was seen last speeding through Ware, and
hopes of an arrest at any moment are largely entertained. It will
be remembered that Grayson broke prison some years ago —

the paragraph trailed off into a washy résumé of the whole affair.
In the stop press column –

Grayson has been caught at Royston.

But as the old man went gleefully down to dinner the tape-machine
caught his eye. It clicked out –

The reported arrest of Grayson is denied. Turning the sharp
corner at Royston the suspected motor ran into a hedge and
overturned. The chauffeur, arrested, proves not to be the convict
at all. He declares that his master, an undergraduate at Cambridge University, can entirely clear him, and is indignant at his
arrest. On the urgent demand of London, the man is, however,
being detained for enquiries.

So the Marquis enjoyed his dinner but little after all. Much less,
though, the rabbit-faced man Arkwright. His story as he told it to his
most trusted colleague was as follows –

'I was strolling down Hill Street, thinking of nothing in particular,
when I saw the door of a great house open – and out walked my man.

'Grayson in the flesh, I tell you. Grayson as I saw him at Marseille;
Grayson as he was in the dock and the prison. There wasn't a doubt
of it. Well, my gentleman flipped into a motor and is off. You know
the rest.'

'No, I don't!' returned the other. 'You're keeping back the best.'

'For God's sake let us be careful,' said Arkwright, 'this is the biggest
thing for years. I know now what old Zynscky meant.'

'What! Whose house was it?'

He whispered – 'The Duchess of Eltham! There's his influence and
this fool talk of his having been innocent all along! There's his base,
and his cash, and his every mortal thing he wants!'

'Oh rot!' said his Thomasian colleague.

'Well, hear what I did! I enquired. Her Grace was ill, had been ill for
three weeks. The very time, mark you, when Grayson's plans began to
go a bit groggy! Where could I find the gentleman who had just left
the house? My boy, they denied the whole affair!'

'Arkwright,' said the other, solemnly, 'did not one thing strike you as very peculiar about that house?'

'No, by Jove! what?' He was rather annoyed if his usually stolid subordinate had an idea that he was missed. 'What was peculiar?'

'Why, my boy, the blue rats on the ceiling and the pink leopards strolling up the stairs.'

Arkwright was too worried to be angry. He just gave him up.

'My dear man, you're absurd,' continued the critic, 'Here's one of the first ladies in the land, a lady of stainless reputation —'

'Umph!' grunted the rabbit-faced man.

'A lady with the devotion of the handsomest husband, and the three prettiest children in London – I am to believe, am I, that she moves heaven and earth to harbour this convict, on your theory a triple murderer and mutilator and Lord knows what beside? – I'm sick of you! You've talked Ercildoune until you've caught the craze. Why! you ought to be in Parliament! That's the place for *you*.'

'Yes,' retorted the other, 'and I'd make a law to drill your head full of holes and pump a little sense into it. All your argument is *à priori* drivel. Who stole Lady Oldbury's pearls? A prince of the blood royal!'

'Well, but he was mad,' said the sceptic, though a little shaken.

'Of course he was mad. So may Lady Eltham be mad! We're all mad – read your Lombroso, you nincompoop!' After which the conversation became profoundly theoretical, its obscurity hardly illuminated by the fact that neither party to the discussion understood the subject in the least.

We gladly draw a veil over so painful a scene.

18

The Cup Flows Over

Roland Rex was down in the mouth. For one thing, he had been – so Jukes said – spotted during his morning walk by one of Grayson's creatures, and the whole afternoon had been spent in disguising him as a semi-clerical character. Old Jukes had been particularly careful with the make-up, altering it a dozen times till it exactly fitted his ideal. Which had been tedious. On another side, too, he had expected Eileen on the previous evening, and she had not appeared. The failure to capture Grayson had exasperated him, the more so as he knew his foe could not be far away, and might strike home at any moment. He seemed safe enough, yet – what if his previous surmise were correct, and the villain struck at him through his love? Eileen Arundell could not lurk in an obscure nook as he could do, she must be seen and known; she must wait on the Princess. Ah! there was hope. Would she who had helped him so splendidly fail with her own twin soul? Not much!

And even as he thought it, and laughed, came a peculiar knock, the familiar signal of old Jukes. He rose and admitted him; but the old man, usually so calm and steady, seemed perplexed, distressed. His trembling hand thrust a letter into that of Roland.

The latter tore it open.

> Where is Eileen?

it ran.

> She left the house to see you last night at eight, and has not returned. I only got back from Brighton this morning, and of course the servants knew nothing. For God's sake, do something, Mr Rex, I shall go mad.

> Your distracted STEPHANIE

'I will go to her,' he decided without the waste of a moment. 'There must be some more facts to learn than these.' And snatching up his broad-brimmed hat he ran madly to the great house.

He found the Princess in violent fits of rage and tears. She had telephoned to nearly everybody in London, useful or no. For once the giant intellect seemed to have broken down. Roland strove to make light of the affair, though the blackest certainty blotted out the light of all his hope.

Ten minutes, and the great lady was herself again, though now and then she broke into a moan, calling on her loved companion's name, and upon God. Yet she controlled herself, and sternly set herself with Roland to face the situation. Before she had finished imparting the full details of what had passed, the door opened, and a footman entered, with a small package on a silver tray. The Princess took it and opened it mechanically. A card dropped out. She read – 'The Marquis of Ercildoune presents his compliments to ex-Princess Stephanie' (she stamped her pretty foot with anger at the outrage) 'and begs her to hand the enclosed small parcel to Mr Roland Rex, whose present address he despairs of discovering.'

The parcel bore the words: 'For Mr Roland Rex.'

He took it in his hand. 'I no longer fear,' he said, 'I know. There is no God. Leave me alone.'

'No!' she answered, 'you must bear yourself as a man should. I will stay with you, and show you what even a woman may endure.'

In the certitude of calamity they had both grown preternaturally calm.

'So be it!' said Rex, and tore off the wrapper.

A gleam of ivory set with rubies met their eyes. Roland steeled his nerves and pressed the spring: the lid flew open and revealed a little tray beautifully engraved with the fantastic irony as of old –

MR ROLAND REX, WITH THE COMPLIMENTS OF THE
MARQUIS OF ERCILDOUNE.

He lifted out the tray. There lay, fresh-lopped, the flaming lips of his beloved, in their nest of gossamer gold – the hair, the lips he had kissed a thousand times.

'I think, Princess,' he said, 'our jester goes too far. I think the occasion an excellent one for putting to the test our little theories about the existence of a God. You shall soon hear —' There was a sinister significance about his words. He kissed the little box and put it tenderly away.

But the Princess never answered. She sat like Memnon in the uttermost desert, and her eyes were hard and tearless.

Roland went softly from the room. 'There *is* a God! There *is* a God!' he kept on muttering as he walked idly down the street. But for the ashen pallor of his face, men might have thought him a mere curate walking early to his work. A pity that old Jukes had not imagined a more rubicund parson!

His eyes sought out some clue – Nature seemed intelligible to him. He felt that every flag of the pavement was a clue, leading him straight to his enemy.

Or – was he mad? Was the dear God a heartless mocker as well as a cruel tyrant? What was this strange hallucination, then?

Across the road, cheerily striding, was the bronzed and bearded figure of – himself! Himself as he came back to England, hardly a year ago.

Then the truth flamed out in him – this was the very man! Grayson's last surprising masterpiece of insolence was to pass as Roland Rex.

'O Lord!' he cried, 'forgive me for my blasphemy – for Thou hast delivered mine enemy into mine hand!'

Just then the man jumped into a hansom: Roland into another, ordering the cabman to follow.

Up the Edgeware road they turned, and Roland began to wonder whether the pleasure of an interview with Madame Zynscky was to be included in his little outing. Strangely enough, he never gave a thought to his dead love. The horror of his heart had transcended itself, become a compelling purpose, far from the sphere of emotion. He had no doubt of the issue; God, who had shown the quarry, would speed the bolt. So he laughed gaily. The cabman may have wondered at this clerical gentleman apparently engaged in some joyous practical joke.

They went on into St John's Wood; the first cab suddenly stopped at a large house with a garden. The false Roland paid his cab, and swung the gate open. Roland flung half-a-sovereign to his man, stepped up to him, and said gravely, 'Mr Rex, I believe?'

'Yes,' said Grayson, smilingly, 'what can I have the pleasure of doing for you?'

'A few words in private, if it is not troubling you too much.'

'Not at all. Forgive me if I precede you.' And he led the way round the house to a conservatory, and opened the door. Just then a motor-car came noisily up, and stopped.

'It is nothing,' airily explained Grayson, 'only my grandfather, Lord Barfield!' Roland's politeness took a little jar.

Yet one more act of self-control, and the wrath of years should leap out and wither this cynical devil. He merely bowed his head at the taunt.

19
The Trap Closes

Grayson noticed that the gate did not swing open behind them. It was not the old Marquis. Who was it then? Grayson dismissed so idle a query with a slight shrug.

'A seat, Mr ———? I have not the honour of your acquaintance,' he said smiling, and pointing to a chair.

'Thank you, I will stand.' He cast his eye around. Heaven was still on his side; there was some loose rope in the corner. 'My name is a small matter; I think I have had the honour of hearing from you – from your lordship, perhaps I should say – already this morning.'

Grayson laughed out loud. 'Yes! I could not deprive you of such treasures.'

'Come, sir,' said Roland, moved out of all patience: 'this is my errand, to hang you with these hands.'

'Stir!' he said, as Grayson looked about him for a weapon, 'and I will shoot you like a dog.'

The murderer held up his hands.

'The best way, Grayson, perhaps; for as the Lord liveth and as my soul liveth, I will surely hang you with these hands!'

'Ah!' smiled his enemy, 'I am unarmed.'

'I take you at your word,' said Roland; 'do you think there is no God?' And he laid aside his pistol.

'Really, I cannot discuss theology, even with so learned a divine,' he sneered, 'at this early hour of the morning. A divine?' he seemed to muse.

Roland stood ready. 'Ah! I have it,' suddenly yelled Grayson in a voice that shook the house. 'You are Father Ambrose! Father Ambrose! Father Ambrose!' – then he closed with Roland in a death grip. They rolled over, fighting like cats.

But an answering cry woke in the house. From an inner door appeared two figures.

Ah, Roland, had you seen her! had you seen her!

There stood Eileen in life, scatheless and radiant, yet wild with a strange joy, and by her side the old Lord Ercildoune.

'There!' she cried, pointing to Roland, 'is the false priest that murdered poor Lord Marcus.'

Ercildoune with a boy's joy ran down, waving the holy dirk. 'I sheathe thee,' he cried, 'and break the curse of Ercildoune!' But as he lifted up his arm the outer door was burst, and Segrave, ever hot on Roland's track, rushed in and struck away the blade.

Roland had Grayson by the throat. He looked up.

'Grandfather!' he cried.

The old man started back in fear and wonder. How did this Ambrose speak in Roland's voice?

Eileen dashed in. 'Don't you see,' she cried, 'they are all wrong? That gasping cur is Grayson.'

Segrave cried out in terror. 'I have saved the very man I meant to slay,' he roared, entirely losing his self-control.

Ercildoune's shrewd old mind grasped the situation.

'Mr Segrave,' he said, 'if you would save your skin, be a true witness of these proceedings. But if you move or cry, I fear there is but one retort.' He calmly possessed himself of Roland's abandoned revolver. 'A chair, Mr Segrave,' he added, courteous and calm even in that headlong hour.

Segrave subsided, scowling. 'Eileen!' went on the old Marquis, 'you will perhaps be good enough to report to the Princess. She may be anxious about you. I regret to have interrupted you, Roland my lad,' he went on, when she had left the room, 'you had some business with this gentleman.'

'Sit up!' commanded Roland, whom the appearance of Eileen had transfigured with rapture. 'You have been condemned to be hanged; we shall execute the sentence in a quarter of an hour; spend the short minutes in a confession of your sins to God and man.'

'Ah! you want a few things explained!' he jeered. 'Well, then, what is it?'

'No parley,' answered the old Marquis. 'Commit yourself to God!'

'You may as well know all,' he said wearily. 'The whole thing's been a plant right along. The game was to get you – Lord Barfield! to kill your own grandson. Then we should have got you hanged out of the way, had myself declared innocent and my branch legitimate, and – there was I with my rights.' He flamed up; it was plain that the man had been utterly sincere. His fancied wrongs had preyed upon his mind, and turned its mere original evil to a masterpiece of criminal genius.

'But how could you build up such a scheme?' asked Rex. 'It was Miss Arundell herself who called on my grandfather to kill me.'

'Why, you fool, it was our plot from the beginning. We paid the hooligans who threw Eileen into your arms; old Jukes – I have been practically living with you for weeks as old Jukes!' The voice had an ineffable scorn. 'I sent that dodderer his ridiculous dirk.'

'Those eyes of Father Ambrose?'

'Fluorescein,' he retorted; 'why don't you teach your detectives just the rudiments of some one thing?'

'How did you get Lady Eltham to lie for you?'

'Not at all; I had a footman in my pay. I waited till I saw that rabbit-faced idiot nosing about and then gave him the trail – and the slip.'

'But why bring Miss Arundell into it at all?'

'How else could I get him to the intimacy of the Princess? Through that ass Segrave?' he snarled at the embarrassed secretary. 'If I had you to myself for a minute, my boy, I'd teach you something about murder. How did you get here anyway?'

The poor coward winced. 'I saw you hanging about,' he said; 'I thought you were Mr Rex. I wanted Eileen.'

'Pah!' said Grayson.

'But what has the Princess got to do with it?' asked Roland.

There was a rustle behind them, and two women swept into the doorway. 'Everything,' cried the Princess.

20

The Curse Breaks

'You must hang me too,' said Stephanie, seeing Roland busy at his rope. 'Why, I did everything. It was I that lured up the Marquis, and I that arranged for you to think Eileen was killed. Ah! sweet,' she purred, 'you know I would never have let you come to harm. How it hurt me to sacrifice that lock of your gold hair you gave me!' But the girl turned away in horror. 'You plot to kill my lover,' she said, 'and say you would do nothing against me!' and she laughed harshly and hatefully.

'God! I have lost you too,' wailed the wretched woman. 'Ah! let me die! ...'

'Ah! you do not know! Yes, it was I that tore the lying tongue from Laycock, and killed the poor innocent that his ...' she choked with rage and tears. 'Ah! you shall never know what happened in that house! It is between me and God, and I shall not fear to meet Him.'

They all shrank back from her. She towered tremendous above them in the throes of her passion.

'My child,' she sobbed, 'my child!'

Even Grayson gasped. Their loathing turned to mere terror; they were in presence of an elemental force. This was not a woman, but a tempest; they shrank from the right of judging her. The voice of the storm of heaven is louder than man's petty cry.

Only Segrave was so little of a man that his querulous question broke –

'But why did you do it at all? What is this Mr Grayson?'

She turned on him. Like a tree smitten by the lightning he shrank into himself, withered and dumb.

Swifter than an arrow she launched herself at the doomed Grayson. 'Ercildoune!' and her voice was again the gentle far-off bell, 'Ercildoune, my darling, what I have done is for you!'

Again they were still. A sort of mist blinded their apprehension. All this was all so new, so impossible. For a moment Roland dreamt that she was acting a part.

So indeed; yet like all great actresses, the part rang true because she felt its truth.

She kissed him. For an instant the whole world was blank.

Lord Ercildoune rose to end the scene. But she was swifter.

With one deft motion she drew a bottle from her bosom and dashed it on the ground. Dense choking fumes arose, and before anybody could recover from the confusion she had disappeared into the house with her lover.

Eileen had been nearest to the bottle when it broke, and priceless moments were spent in restoring her in the fresh air of the garden. When aid came, no trace could be discovered. Before half the rooms had been searched, the house was found to be on fire. When the engines appeared, it was already but a spout of flame.

Nobody had been seen to leave the garden; it was most sure that they had perished.

* * *

'Roland!' chuckled the old grandfather in the smiling halls of Ercildoune. 'The curse is lifted from us all at last. Eh, my dear? You are all the curse we have at present,' he laughed across at Eileen, now his grandson's six months' bride.

'Well,' answered Roland, with a half-serious shrug, 'the Doom says that the lands shall go back to the King.'

'How stupid you men are!' said Eileen. 'Where were you at school, Roland, not to have learnt that Rex means King?'

'By heaven, she's hit it!' and they all shook hands.

A stalwart ghillie brought in the mail.

Eileen, taking her letter, gave a little wondering cry. The Marquis had a small flat package; his eye fell upon it, and he groaned and fell forward. Roland raised him. 'Wait till you know!' he said. The packet was addressed –

The most noble the Marquis of Ercildoune.

Within was an old miniature on ivory.

With this portrait of the fierce old father of all our mischief, the enclosing letter ran,

I resign the last of the links with Ercildoune. A great sinner asks your pardon for a great wrong.

'Children!' said the Marquis, 'come with me.' Again he led them to the Chapel of Vengeance.

But within there was a change. For the fierce God of Genesis had gone, and in its place was the loving and compassionate figure of the Christ. The monstrance with its angry reproach against the Master had been removed. Instead was a memorial tablet to the Claimant wreathed in flowers, with these words –

God willeth not the death of a sinner, but rather that he should turn from his wickedness and live.

'Children,' said the old man, with tears running down all over his cheeks, 'you see there is a God that answers prayer.'

Eileen looked at her letter, short and pointed:

> Forgive and forget my jealousy, dear one, and all the disastrous passions of an unhappy woman. The madness and misery are over for both of us; we too are married, and all the storm-beacon is burnt out to bliss.
>
> My love, ever my love!
>
> STEPHANIE

Eileen kissed the letter; and, fondly glancing at her husband, slipped it into her bosom.

* * *

Arkwright sat still with his dull colleague, and pulled more gloomily than ever at his pipe.

'So the Ercildoune case is over,' grumbled the dull one, 'and a blessed lot of credit it brought you!'

'Umph!' grunted Arkwright, ''slong it *is* over, I won't complain. I call it a fair sickener.'

'Come, come!' returned the other, ''tain't as bad as all that. Come to think of it, you must 'a' made a tidy bit o' money out o' mad Lord Ercildoune, fust to last.'

'Well,' said the rabbit-faced man, 'I suppose I did. Fust to last, a tidy bit o' money. 'Ave another beer?'

The Stratagem

The fellow-travellers climbed down on to the fiery sand of the platform. It was a junction, a junction of that kind where there is no town for miles, and where the resources of the railway and its neighbourhood compare unfavourably with those of the average quarantine station.

The first to descend was a man unmistakably English. He was complaining of the management even while he extracted his hand-baggage from the carriage with the assistance of his companion. 'It is positively a disgrace to civilisation,' he was saying, 'that there should be no connection at such a station as this, an important station, sir, let me tell you, the pivot – if I may use the metaphor – of the branch which serves practically the whole of Muckshire south of the Tream. And we have certainly one hour to wait, and Heaven knows it's more likely to be two, and perhaps three. And, of course, there's not as much as a bar nearer than Fatloam; and if we got there we should find no drinkable whiskey. I say, sir, the matter is a positive and actual disgrace to the railway that allows it, to the country that tolerates it, to the civilisation that permits that such things should be. The same thing happened to me here last year, sir, though luckily on that occasion I had but half an hour to wait. But I wrote to *The Times* a strong half-column letter on the subject, and I'm damned if they didn't refuse to print it. Of course, our independent press, etc.; I might have known. I tell you, sir, this country is run by a ring, a dirty ring, a gang of Jews, Scotsmen, Irish, Welsh – where's the good old jolly True Blue Englishman? In the cart, sir, in the cart!'

The train gave a convulsive backward jerk, and lumbered off in imitation of the solitary porter who, stationed opposite the guard's van, had witnessed without emotion the hurling forth of two trunks like rocks from a volcano, and after a moment's contemplation had, with screwed mouth, mooched along the platform to his grub, which he would find in an isolated cottage some three hundred yards away.

In strong contrast to the Englishman, with his mustache afforesting a whitish face, marked with deep red rings on neck and forehead, his impending paunchiness and his full suit of armour, was the small active man with the pointed beard whom fate had thrown first into the same compartment, and then into the same hour of exile from all their fellows.

His eyes were astonishingly black and fierce; his beard was grizzled and his face heavily lined and obviously burnt by tropical suns; but that face also expressed intelligence, strength, and resourcefulness in a degree which would have made him an ideal comrade in a forlorn hope, or the defence of a desperate village. Across the back of his left hand was a thick and heavy scar. In spite of all this, he was dressed with singular neatness and correctness; which circumstance, although his English was purer than that of his companion in distress, made the latter secretly incline to suspect him of being a Frenchman. In spite of the quietness of his dress and the self-possession of his demeanour, the sombre glitter of those black eyes, pin-points below shaggy eyebrows, inspired the large man with a certain uneasiness. Not at all a chap to quarrel with, was his thought. However, being himself a widely-travelled man – Boulogne, Dieppe, Paris, Switzerland and even Venice – he had none of that insularity of which foreigners accuse some Englishmen, and he had endeavoured to make conversation during the journey. The small man had proved a poor companion, taciturn to a fault, sparing of words where a nod would satisfy the obligations of courtesy, and seemingly fonder of his pipe than of his fellow-man. A man with a secret, thought the Englishman.

The train had jolted out of the station and the porter had faded from the landscape. 'A deserted spot,' remarked the Englishman, whose name was Bevan, 'especially in such fearful heat. Really, in the summer of 1911, it was hardly as bad. Do you know, I remember once at Boulogne —' He broke off sharply, for the brown man, sticking the ferrule of his stick repeatedly in the sand, and knotting his brows, came suddenly to a decision. 'What do you know of heat?' he cried, fixing Bevan with the intensity of a demon. 'What do you know of desolation?' Taken aback, as well he might be, Bevan was at a loss to reply. 'Stay,' cried the other. 'What if I told you my story? There is no one here but ourselves.' He glared menacingly at Bevan, seemed to seek to read his soul. 'Are you a man to be trusted?' he barked, and broke off short.

At another time Bevan would most certainly have declined to become the confidant of a stranger; but here the solitude, the heat, not a little boredom induced by the previous manner of his companion, and even a certain mistrust of how he might take a refusal, combined to elicit a favourable reply.

Stately as an oak, Bevan answered, 'I was born an English gentleman, and I trust that I have never done anything to derogate from that estate.

'I am a Justice of the Peace,' he added after a momentary pause.

'I knew it!' cried the other excitedly. 'The trained legal mind is that of all others which will appreciate my story. Swear, then,' he went on with sudden gravity, 'swear that you will never whisper to any living soul the smallest word of what I am about to tell you! Swear by the soul of your dead mother.'

'My mother is alive,' returned Bevan.

'I knew it,' exclaimed his companion, a great and strange look of god-like pity illuminating his sunburnt face. It was such a look as one sees upon many statues of Buddha, a look of divine, of impersonal compassion.

'Then swear by the Lord Chancellor!'

Bevan was even more than ever persuaded that the stranger was a Frenchman. However, he readily gave the required promise.

'My name,' said the other, 'is Duguesclin. Does that tell you my story?' he asked impressively. 'Does that convey anything to your mind?'

'Nothing at all.'

'I knew it!' said the Frenchman. 'Then I must tell you all. In my veins boils the fiery blood of the greatest of the French warriors, and my mother was the lineal descendant of the Maid of Saragossa.'

Bevan was startled, and showed it.

'After the siege, sir, she was honourably married to a nobleman,' snapped Duguesclin. 'Do you think a man of my ancestry will permit a stranger to lift the shadow of an eyebrow against the memory of my great-grandmother?'

The Englishman protested that nothing had been further from his thoughts.

'I suppose so,' proceeded the other more quietly, 'and the more, perhaps, that I am a convicted murderer.'

Bevan was now fairly alarmed.

'I am proud of it,' continued Duguesclin. 'At the age of twenty-five my blood was more fiery than it is today. I married. Four years later I found my wife in the embraces of a neighbour. I slew him. I slew her. I slew our three children, for vipers breed only vipers. I slew the servants; they were accomplices of the adultery, or if not, they should at any rate not witness their master's shame. I slew the gendarmes who came to take me – servile hirelings of a corrupt republic. I set my castle on fire, determined to perish in the ruins. Unfortunately, a piece of masonry, falling, struck me on the arm. My rifle dropped. The accident was seen, and I was rescued by the firemen. I determined to live; it was my duty to my ancestors to continue the family of which I was the sole direct scion. It is in search of a wife that I am travelling in England.'

He paused, and gazed proudly on the scenery, with the air of a Selkirk. Bevan suppressed the obvious comment on the surprising termination of the Frenchman's narrative. He only remarked, 'Then you were not guillotined?'

'I was not, sir!' retorted the other passionately. 'At that time capital punishment was never inflicted in France, though not officially abrogated. I may say,' he added, with the pride of a legislator, 'that my action lent considerable strength to the agitation which led to its reintroduction.

'No, sir, I was not guillotined. I was sentenced to perpetual imprisonment on Devil's Island.' He shuddered. 'Can you imagine that accursed Isle? Can your fancy paint one tithe of its horror? Can nightmare itself shadow that inferno, that limbo of the damned? My language is strong, sir; but no language can depict that hell. I will spare you the description. Sand, vermin, crocodiles, venomous snakes, miasma, mosquitoes, fever, filth, toil, jaundice, malaria, starvation, foul undergrowth, weedy swamps breathing out death, hideous and bloated trees of poison, themselves already poisoned by the earth, heat unendurable, insufferable, intolerable, unbearable (as *The Daily Telegraph* said at the time of the Dreyfus case), heat continuous and stifling, no breeze but the pestilential stench of the lagoon, heat that turned the skin into a raging sea of irritation to which the very stings of the mosquitoes and centipedes came as a relief, the interminable task of the day beneath the broiling sun, the lash on every slightest infraction of the harsh prison rules, or even of the laws of politeness toward our warders, men only one degree less damned than we ourselves – all this was nothing. The only amusement of the governors of such a place is cruelty; and their own discomfort makes them more ingenious than all the inquisitors of Spain, than Arabs in their religious frenzy, than Burmans and Kachens and Shans in their Buddhist hatred of all living men, than even the Chinese in their cold lust of cruelty. The Governor was a profound psychologist; no corner of the mind that he did not fathom, so as to devise a means of twisting it to torture.

'I remember one of us who took pleasure in keeping his spade bright – it was the regulation that spades must be kept bright, a torture in itself in such a place, where mildew grows on everything as fast almost as snow falls in happier climates. Well, sir, the Governor found out that this man took pleasure in the glint of the sun on the steel, and he forbade that man to clean his spade. A trifle, indeed! What do you know of what prisoners think trifles? The man went raving mad, and for no other reason. It seemed to him that such detailed refinement of cruelty was a final proof of the innate and inherent devilishness of the universe. Insanity is the logical consequence of such a faith. No, sir, I will spare you the description.'

Bevan thought that there had already been too much description, and in his complacent English way surmised that Duguesclin was exaggerating, as he was aware that Frenchmen did. But he only remarked that it must have been terrible. He would have given a good deal, now, to have avoided the conversation. It was not altogether nice to be on a lonely platform with a self-confessed multiple murderer, who had presumably escaped only by a further and extended series of crimes.

'But you ask,' pursued Duguesclin, 'you ask how I escaped? That, sir, is the story I propose to tell you. My previous remarks have been but preliminary: they have no pertinence or interest, I am aware; but they were necessary, since you so kindly expressed interest in my personality, my family history – heroic (I may claim it) as is the one, and tragic (no one will deny it) as is the other.'

Bevan again reflected that his interlocutor must be as bad a psychologist as the governor of Devil's Island was a good one; for he had neither expressed nor felt the slightest concern with either of these matters.

'Well, sir, to my story! Among the convicts there was one universal pleasure, a pleasure that could cease only with life or with the empire of the reason, a pleasure that the governor might (and did) indeed restrict, but could not take away. I refer to hope – the hope of escape. Yes, sir, that spark (alone of all its ancient fires) burned in this breast – and in that of my fellow-convicts. And in this I did not look so much to myself as to another. I am not endowed with any great intellect,' he modestly pursued, 'my grandmother was pure English, a Higginbotham, one of the Warwickshire Higginbothams ('what has that to do with his stupidity?' thought Bevan), and the majority of my companions were men not only devoid of intelligence, but of education. The one pinnacled exception was the great Dodu – ha! you start?'

Bevan had not done anything of the sort; he had continued to exhibit the most stolid indifference to the story.

'Yes, you are not mistaken; it was indeed the world-famous philosopher, the discoverer of Dodium, rarest of known elements, supposed only to exist in the universe to the extent of the thirty-thousand and fifth part of a milligramme, and that in the star called γ Pegasi; it was Dodu who had shattered the logical process of obversion, and reduced the quadrangle of oppositions to the condition of the British square at Abu-Klea. So much you know; but this perhaps you did not know, that, although a civilian, he was the greatest strategist of France. It was he who in his cabinet made the dispositions of the armies of the Ardennes; and the 1890 scheme of the fortifications of Lunéville was due to his genius alone. For this reason the Government were loth to condemn him, though public opinion revolted bitterly against his crime. You remember that, having proved that women after the age of fifty were a useless burden to the State, he had demonstrated his belief by decapitating and devouring his widowed mother. It was consequently the intention of the Government to connive at his escape on the voyage, and to continue to employ him under an assumed name in a flat in an entirely different quarter of Paris. However, the Government fell suddenly; a rival ousted him, and his sentence was carried out with as much severity as if he had been a common criminal.

'It was to such a man, naturally, that I looked to devise a plan for our escape. But rack my brains as I would – my grandmother was a Warwickshire Higginbotham – I could devise no means of getting into touch with him. He must, however, have divined my wishes; for, one day after he had been about a month upon the island (I had been there seven months myself), he stumbled and fell as if struck by the sun at a moment when I was close to him. And as he lay upon the ground he managed to pinch my ankle three times. I caught his glance – he hinted rather than gave me the sign of recognition of the fraternity of Freemasons. Are you a Mason?'

'I am Past Provincial Deputy Grand Sword-Bearer of this province,' returned Bevan. 'I founded Lodge 14,883, 'Boetic' and Lodge 17,212, 'Colenso,' and I am Past Grand Haggai in my Provincial Grand Chapter.'

'I knew it!' exclaimed Duguesclin enthusiastically.

Bevan began to dislike this conversation exceedingly. Did this man – this criminal – know who he was? He knew he was a J.P., that his mother was alive, and now his Masonic dignities. He distrusted this Frenchman more and more. Was the story but a pretext for the demand of a loan? The stranger looked prosperous, and had a first-class ticket. More likely a blackmailer: perhaps he knew of other things – say that affair at Oxford – or the incident of the Edgware Road – or the matter of Esmé Holland. He determined to be more than ever on his guard.

'You will understand with what joy,' continued Duguesclin, innocent or careless of the sinister thoughts which occupied his companion, 'I received and answered this unmistakable token of friendship. That day no further opportunity of intercourse occurred, but I narrowly watched him on the morrow, and saw that he was dragging his feet in an irregular way. Ha! thought I, a drag for long, an ordinary pace for short. I imitated him eagerly, giving the Morse letter A. His alert mind grasped instantly my meaning; he altered his code (which had been of a different order) and replied with a Morse B on my own system. I answered C; he returned D. From that moment we could talk fluently and freely as if we were on the terrace of the Café de la Paix in our beloved Paris. However, conversation in such circumstances is a lengthy affair. During the whole march to our work he only managed to say, 'Escape soon – please God.' Before his crime he had been an atheist. I was indeed glad to find that punishment had brought repentance.'

Bevan himself was relieved. He had carefully refrained from admitting the existence of a French Freemason; that one should have repented filled him with a sense of almost personal triumph. He began to like Duguesclin, and to believe in him. His wrong had been hideous; if his vengeance seemed excessive, and even indiscriminate, was he not a Frenchman? Frenchmen do these things! And after all Frenchmen were men. Bevan felt a great glow of benevolence; he remembered that he was not only a man, but a Christian. He determined to set the stranger at his ease.

'Your story interests me intensely,' said he. 'I sympathise deeply with you in your wrongs and in your sufferings. I am heartily thankful that you have escaped, and I beg you to proceed with the narration of your adventures.'

Duguesclin needed no such encouragement. His attitude, from that of the listless weariness with which he had descended from the train, had become animated, sparkling, fiery; he was carried away by the excitement of his passionate memories.

'On the second day Dodu was able to explain his mind. "If we escape, it must be by a stratagem," he signalled. It was an obvious remark: but Dodu had no reason to think highly of my intelligence. "By a *stratagem*," he repeated with emphasis.

'"I have a plan," he continued. "It will take twenty-three days to communicate, if we are not interrupted; between three and four months to prepare; two hours and eight minutes to execute. It is theoretically possible to escape by air, by water, or by earth. But as we are watched day and night, it would be useless to try to drive a tunnel to the mainland; we have no æroplanes or balloons, or means of making them. But if we could once reach the water's edge, which we must do in whatever direction we set out if we only keep in a straight line, and if we can find a boat unguarded, and if we can avoid arousing the alarm, then we have merely to cross the sea, and either find a land where we are unknown, or disguise ourselves and our boat and return to Devil's Island as shipwrecked mariners. The latter idea would be foolish. You will say that the Governor would know that Dodu would not be such a fool; but more, he would know also that Dodu would not be such a fool as to try to take advantage of that circumstance; and he would be right, curse him!"

'It implies the intensest depth of feeling to curse in the Morse code with one's feet – ah! how we hated him.

'Dodu explained to me that he was telling me these obvious things for several reasons: (1) to gauge my intelligence by my reception of them; (2) to make sure that if we failed it should be by my stupidity and not by his neglect to inform me of every detail; (3) because he had acquired the professorial habit as another man may have the gout.

'Briefly, however, this was his plan: to elude the guards, make for the coast, capture a boat, and put to sea. Do you understand? Do you get the idea?'

Bevan replied that it seemed to him the only possible plan.

'A man like Dodu,' pursued Duguesclin, 'takes nothing for granted. He leaves no precaution untaken; in his plans, if chance be an element, it is an element whose value is calculated to twenty-eight places of decimals.

'But hardly had he laid down these bold outlines of his scheme when interruption came. On the fourth day of our intercourse he signalled only "Wait. Watch me!" again and again.

'In the evening he manœuvred to get to the rear of the line of convicts, and only then dragged out "There is a traitor, a spy. Henceforth I must find a new means of communicating the details of my plan. I have thought it all out. I shall speak in a sort of rebus, which not even you will be able to understand unless you have all the pieces, and the key. Mind you engrave upon your memory every word I say."

'The following day: "Do you remember the taking of the old mill by the Prussians in '70? My difficulty is that I must give you the skeleton of the puzzle, which I can't do in words. But watch the line of my spade and my heelmarks, and make a copy."

'I did this with the utmost minuteness of accuracy and obtained this figure. At my autopsy,' said Duguesclin, dramatically, 'this should be found engraved upon my heart.'

He drew a note-book from his pocket, and rapidly sketched the subjoined figure for the now interested Bevan.

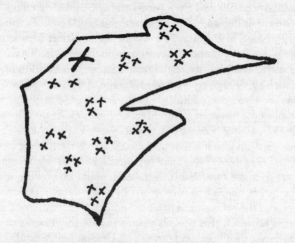

'You will note that the figure has eight sides, and that twenty-seven crosses are disposed in groups of three, while in one corner is a much larger and thicker cross and two smaller crosses not so symmetrical. This group represents the element of chance; and you will at least gain a hint of the truth if you reflect that eight is the cube of two, and twenty-seven of three.'

Bevan looked intelligent.

'On the return march,' continued Duguesclin, 'Dodu said, "The spy is on the watch. But count the letters in the name of Aristotle's favourite disciple." I guessed (as he intended me to do) that he did not mean Aristotle. He wished to suggest Plato, and so Socrates; hence I counted A–L–C–I–B–I–A–D–E–S = 10, and thus completely baffled the spy for that day. The following day he rapped out "Rahu" very emphatically, meaning that the next lunar eclipse would be the proper moment for our evasion, and spent the rest of the day in small talk, so as to lull the suspicions of the spy. For three days he had no opportunity of saying anything, being in the hospital with fever. On the fourth day: "I have discovered that spy is a damned swine of an opium-smoking lieutenant from Toulon. We have him: he doesn't know Paris. Now then: draw a line from the Gare de l'Est to the Étoile; erect an equilateral triangle on that line. Think of the name of the world-famous man who lives at the apex." (This was a touch of super-genius, as it forced me to use the English alphabet for the basis of the cipher, and the spy spoke no language but his own, except a little Swiss.) "From this time I shall communicate in a cipher of the direct additive numerical order, and the key shall be his name."

'It was only my incomparably strong constitution which enabled me to add the task of deciphering his conversation to that imposed by Government. To memorise perfectly a cipher communication of half-an-hour is no mean feat of mnemonics, especially when the deciphered message is itself couched in the obscurest symbolism. The spy must have thought his reason in danger if he succeeded in reading the hieroglyphs which were the mere pieces of the puzzle of the master-thinker. For instance, I would get this message; OWHMOMDVV TXSKZVGKQXZLLHTREIRGSCPXJRMSGAUSRGWHBDXZLDABE, which, when deciphered (and the spy would gnash his teeth every time Dodu signalled a w!), only meant: "The peaches of 1761 are luminous in the gardens of Versailles."

'Or again: "Hunt; the imprisoned Pope; the Pompadour; the Stag and Cross." "The men of the fourth of September; their leader divided by the letters of the Victim of the Eighth of Thermidor." "Crillon was unfortunate that day, though braver than ever."

'Such were the indications from which I sought to piece together our plan of escape!

'Perhaps rather by intuition than by reason, I gathered from some two hundred of such clues that the guards Bertrand, Rolland and Monet had been bribed, and also promised advancement, and (above all) removal from the hated Island, should they connive at our escape. It seemed that the Government still had use for its first strategist. The eclipse was due some ten weeks ahead, and needed neither bribe nor promise. The difficulty was to ensure the presence of Bertrand as sentinel in our corridor, Rolland at the ring-fence, and Monet at the outposts. The chances against such a combination at the eclipse were infinitesimal, 99,487,306,294,236,873,489 to 1.

'It would have been madness to trust to luck in so essential a matter. Dodu set to work to bribe the Governor himself. This was unfortunately impossible; for (*a*) no one could approach the Governor even by means of the intermediary of the bribed guards; (*b*) the offence for which he had been promoted to the governorship was of a nature unpardonable by any Government – he was in reality more a prisoner than ourselves; (*c*) he was a man of immense wealth, assured career and known probity.

'I cannot now enter into his history, which you no doubt know in any case. I will only say that it was of such a character that these facts (of so curiously contradictory appearance – on the face of it) apply absolutely. However, the tone of confidence which thrilled in Dodu's messages, "Pluck grapes in Burgundy; press vats in Cognac: ha!" "The soufflé with the nuts in it is ready for us by the Seine," and the like, showed me that his giant brain had not only grappled with the problem, but solved it to his satisfaction. The plan was perfect: on the night of the eclipse those three guards would be on duty at such and such gates; Dodu would tear his clothes into strips, bind and gag Bertrand, come and release me. Together we should spring on Rolland, take his uniform and rifle, and leave him bound and gagged. We should then dash for the shore, do the same with Monet, and then, dressed in their uniforms, take the boat of an octopus-fisher, row to the harbour, and ask in the name of the Governor for the use of his steam yacht to chase an escaped fugitive. We should then steam into the track of ships and set fire to the yacht, so as to be "rescued" and conveyed to England, whence we could arrange with the French Government for rehabilitation.

'Such was the simple yet subtle plan of Dodu. Down to the last detail was it perfected – until one fatal day.

'The spy, stricken by yellow fever, dropped suddenly dead in the fields before the noon "Cease work" had sounded. Instantly, without a moment's hesitation, Dodu strode across to me and said, at the risk of the lash: "The whole plan which I have explained to you in cipher these last four months is a blind. That spy knew all. His lips are sealed in death. I have another plan, the real plan, simpler and surer. I will tell it to you tomorrow."'

The whistle of an approaching engine interrupted this tragic episode of the adventures of Duguesclin.

'"Yes," said Dodu' (continued the narrator), '"I have a better plan. I have a STRATAGEM. I will tell it you tomorrow."'

The train which was to carry the narrator and his hearer to Mudchester came round the corner.

'That morrow,' glowered Duguesclin, 'that morrow never came. The same sun that slew the spy broke the great brain of Dodu; that very afternoon, a gibbering maniac, they thrust him in the padded room, never again to emerge!'

The train drew up at the platform of the little junction. He almost hissed in Bevan's face.

'It was not Dodu at all,' he screamed, 'it was a common criminal, an epileptic; he should never have been sent to Devil's Island at all. He had been mad for months. His messages had no sense at all; it was a cruel practical joke!'

'But how,' said Bevan, getting into his carriage and looking back, 'how did you escape in the end?'

'By a STRATAGEM,' replied the Irishman ... and jumped into another compartment.

Lieutenant Finn's Promotion

I

Voyage Pénible[1]

Though he had not bought blood-stained laurels on the stricken field, Colonel Koupets was deservedly the pride of the Gallician army.

He had begun as a lion-hunter in Somaliland, and had a wound a foot long in his thigh which had at least the advantage of acting as a barometer. But on his return, grave old Galpoltz had hinted that such talent as he had shown for dealing with strange countries and peoples might be turned to better use than sport.

Accordingly, Koupets had spent his next leave among the lakes that feed the Red Elin River, and a third expedition brought him to Lake Dahet and Northern Melania, and so to the mouth of the Ognoc.[2]

His services to the Gallician government, though secret, were recognisable, and Koupets had a free hand, and aid and glory from the national geographical societies. His adventures had been written up by industrious journalists who spared no yellow. He was beginning to be an eponymous hero in the boulevards of his native Tetulia, when he suddenly became the man of mystery – greater, and yet forgotten.

For Koupets disappeared.

He had been last heard of at Lake Dahet. Thence he had plunged into the jungles of Central Kainogenogy, and the silence swallowed him up.

People began to wonder where he was. Newspapers invented reports, one at least with such claim to authenticity as to be based on the gossip of a sailor's bar. One paper saw an opportunity and published 'The Terrible Tale of Koupets' Last Stand,' with faked diaries, faked last messages and faked photographs complete. Nobody cared much;

---

[1] [Labourious journey.]
[2] Eriaz on the French map.

the editor cut short his feuilleton and began a gorier, while the gloom of the tropical jungle settled over the fate of Koupets. Five years after his disappearance, only one girl in all Gallicia, weeping at the grave of her dead mother, still hoped for his return; hardly a hundred ever gave a thought to him.

But the gathered blackness was not night, but storm; it was to break with a flash and a roar to appall the planet.

2

Colonel Koupets and his eight Gallician brother officers and fourteen soldiers had no intention whatever of going to Adoshaf.

Adoshaf has few charms for anybody, and even if we allow a great deal for eccentricity of taste in a man of Koupets' type, we cannot suppose that he would deliberately go two thousand miles out of his way to get there.

But the traveller in Central Kainogenogy has to reckon with three main matters: savages, jungles and rivers. He consequently provides himself amply with guns, axes and some form of boat. Even so he may get mislaid.

Koupets had been about three years on his trail, heading ever south-west, when he struck an uncharted river where he least expected it. A lieutenant and four men set out in a boat to cross it, and were swept far downstream. Night fell, and they did not return. In the morning Koupets turned northward to try to pick them up. Towards evening a native saw the wreck of the boat on a jutting rock in midstream.

Koupets continued his northern detour on a report of a big village with canoes three days' march downstream.

Rumour told truth, but had omitted to mention that the villagers were warlike and bloodthirsty cannibals.

The peaceable overtures of the traveller, who had exhausted his supply of scarlet umbrellas six months earlier, were scornfully rejected.

Koupets mowed down about three hundred of the deputation of protest with a Maxim, and stormed the village at dawn. Unfortunately, the party which he had detached to capture the canoes found itself cut off by a creek full of soft mud. The natives consequently were able to retreat when they saw their huts on fire, and Koupets was no better off for canoes than before.

Prisoners told him of a village of wizards to the north which no man could reach, since (*a*) the jungle was haunted, (*b*) there was an impassable river, (*c*) the road was very bad, (*d*) the inhabitants, far from being the simple and peaceable folk that informants' martyred tribe was composed of, were incarnate devils. From this Koupets deduced that he would reach it without difficulty in a few days, and meet with a very similar reception.

However, he was wrong. The natives, knowingly or not, failed to find the jungle paths. Koupets was forced more and more to the north and even to the west. He then struck a friendly village, where every white man went down like a log with fever.

Two months later he made a fresh attempt to reach the river. Succeeding in the end, he found wood suitable for rafts, built them, and cast off. One was overturned, and the doctor and all his medicines and all the scientific instruments of the expedition were lost, as well as a great deal of ammunition. Landing on the opposite bank the explorer struck a village too big to attack except as a forlorn hope, and little inclined to amity.

The chief, however, proposed an alliance, as he was about to avenge a raid on his northern territory. A year's campaign followed; the enemy, beaten, pleaded that they had been urged to the raid by a fanatical race of strange complexion who had invaded them from the north. Koupets, who knew that he was a thousand miles or so off his trail, but, since the loss of his instruments, had no real idea where he was on the map, was almost ready to abandon his main object, and get out anywhere he could. The river, always with them, flowed northward as persistently as the Elin itself might have done. He accepted the new alliance, and marched against the 'fanatics of strange complexion,' which he found due to paint and an aged madwoman.

After the pacification of this tribe, he again fell dangerously ill. More of his men died; his resources of every kind were nearly exhausted; it seemed to him a duty to make for the sea as best he could.

He thereupon chose the best canoes of his allies and plenty of provisions, which the grateful chief bestowed on him in abundance. A touching farewell was only marred by a gratuitous and perfectly treacherous attack on the part of the aforesaid grateful chief, who had suddenly wakened to the fact that the strangers were going off with valuable property, and that as soon as the farewell was said, the laws of hospitality no longer applied. Koupets had been expecting this, and a shot from his revolver, striking the chief in the diaphragm, threw the natives into confusion, as the majority of the persons present were booked to be buried alive with the fallen chief. A disordered rush was checked by a single volley, and Koupets and his party reached midstream without a scratch.

The journey downstream was as long as it was uneventful, and the party regained a good deal of its lost strength. It was interrupted by a cataract hedged in by so thick a jungle that it was impossible to cut a way for the canoes. The little army, taking to its legs, came out at last upon an open plain, and sighted a distant village that turned out (in the end) to be Adoshaf.

A few miles from Adoshaf, Koupets found a number of mutilated corpses and a dying maniac, from whom he gleaned no information. A mile further a starving woman told him that the folk of Adoshaf had been exterminated by devils. Two miles from the village the aforesaid devils, perceiving Koupets and his merry men, came out on horseback, with long spears and shrill cries, at the charge.

The wary and resourceful Koupets, who had extended his men in a long line, caused the wings to fall back, and having thus bunched the line of horsemen, unmasked the Maxim and swept them away. The battle was over in three minutes, and an hour later the conquerors were in the marketplace receiving the submission of the 'devils,' who had been utterly demoralised by the annihilation of their fiercest fighting men by what appeared to them to be magic.

Koupets was highly elated at his victory, and dreamt of empire. 'Glory and Gallicia,' said he, 'have always been synonymous.' And forthwith he set up the Gallician flag in the marketplace, unfurled it ceremonially, and took possession of Adoshaf in the name of his country and its government, though, having been seven years lost to civilisation, he had no idea what the form of that government might be, and even less of what is ever the last thing a brave man thinks of – the political situation.

3

Croisière Joyeuse [1]

First Lieutenant Finn was certainly the only man on his ship to be trusted with the navigation. Balustan does not produce born sailors. Finn was of a conquered race of seafaring folk, and hated Balustan as Moses hated the Egyptians. The Khan of Balustan never suspected that the declaration of war would see half his ships sunk by their own officers.

However, the world was at peace, and First Lieutenant Finn saw a brave show of bunting from the bridge of the battleship *Luschbuze*

---

[1] [Merry cruise.]

as she steamed grandly out of the harbour of Sebastian, beneath the muzzles of the biggest fortress guns in the world.

It was a commonplace that Sebastian was impregnable. Though indeed it had once fallen within the memory of living men, conditions of war had changed. It was nowadays not even approachable. It was said that its arsenal held munitions of war sufficient for a three years' siege.

The *Luschbuze* was a battleship-cruiser of the latest pattern, and her armament was superior to that of any other ship in the world. She had been in commission for not quite a year, and hoisted the pennant of Rear Admiral Tsoke. In her bunkers were 3,000 tonnes of the best English steam coal, and her orders were to cruise in the Axine until it was exhausted.

Landsmen have the fixed idea that cruising has something of *dolce far niente*[1] in its constitution. They think of the Norfolk Broads, or Dr Lunn's pleasure parties. But the cruise of a battleship is hard work, the next best thing to action – and hard work formed no portion of the programme of Rear Admiral Tsoke. That gallant seaman – the 'Nelson of the North' of English newspapers – accordingly steamed out of sight of land, and out of the touch of ships, and there by night incontinently emptied two of his three thousand tonnes of coal into the stormy Axine.[2]

This tedious but necessary labour ended, the ward-room returned to its untiring round of baccarat and strong drink, while the Cinderella of the ship, First Lieutenant Finn, went ahead – dead slow – to the convenient harbour of an island most highly favoured by nature, where the hardships of naval discipline might be deservedly mitigated by the amenities of social intercourse with a race whose ladies were renowned throughout three continents for their virtues rather than for their virtue.

It was here that the first ray of the star of First Lieutenant Finn's destiny lit his horizon. 'I shall have to go and blow those poor devils out of the water, I see,' said Rear-Admiral Tsoke, in an expansive moment, to his lieutenant.

'Yes, sir?' interrogatively.

'The brave Koupets has come out at Adoshaf, and raised the banner of Gallicia. See there!' and he handed across a copy of the Balustan *New Times*.

---

[1] [Sweet nothing-doing.]

[2] Improbable statements occurring in this story are facts, for which I can give chapter and verse.

They drank to Koupets the brave, and to Gallicia the glorious, their ally, and heartily wished to God they were in Tetulia, where the girls are gladdest. They also drank the deepest of damnations to treacherous Noibla, the country that had made forcible diplomatic protest against the seizure of Adoshaf, and with a jabber – unintelligible, thank God, to bluff, hardy, honest seamen! – about 'spheres of influence' and the like, raised a little hell in the chancelleries.

There was, however, no anxiety in the simple mind of First Lieutenant Finn. He never expected promotion, having no noble relatives, or even a wealthy lady to interest herself in his career. He knew that war would not come, on the general principle that 'nothing ever happens.' If it did, he conceived it his first duty to God and man to run the *Luschbuze* upon such a rock and in such weather that so much as a splinter of her would never be seen again.

It was the last day of their stay in the island. Tsoke, thinking that the fleet might be mobilised and sent somewhere in such a way that he would have to do something, resolved to lose himself in the Axine until the crisis was over. He hastily got to sea, and cruised about for a fortnight in a choppy temper, which increased upon him daily, the weather becoming and remaining exceedingly bad, and his luck at baccarat worse.

At the end of that period he spoke a British ship, two days out from Sebastian, learnt that the crisis was ended peacefully, and, longing for the flesh-pots of the arsenal, got rid of another 500 tonnes of coal in the night, and ordered Finn to lay a straight course for Sebastian, where he arrived without further adventure.

With a sense of duty done, the Nelson of the North lay to, and went off in a boat with his captain to dinner. No sooner were they landed, however, than the naval police quietly arrested them, and lodged them in separate cells furnished with ample stationery and such other adjuncts to the art of writing as a paternal government deemed fitting for their rank.

4

Alarums and Excursions

It was a serious annoyance to the government of Gallicia that the contents of Colonel Koupets' despatches – forwarded from Adoshaf by special runners – could not have been suppressed. A fortnight before their receipt, the facts, reiterated with constantly accelerated wealth of detail, were in every newspaper, and the official *démentis*[1] grew weaker and weaker. The embassies alone remained officially ignorant of the most startling development of the century. Koupets had blundered into a peaceful powder factory with a Roman candle in full blast.

When he last left Gallicia, the republican government had been extremely popular, and Adoshaf had barely been discovered. During his enforced retirement from clubs and tape telegraphs, the said government had been found out. Singly and collectively, nearly every member of the parliament had robbed the nation wholesale in a way quite apart from the ordinary methods of political graft. It was plain swindling, and its apologists themselves could find no other word for it, but contented themselves with trying to find scapegoats. Several governments fell in quick succession, each being as tainted as its predecessors, the fact becoming more and more conspicuous as its members entered the limelight of office. A great genius – the prince of the thieves – had latterly managed to turn the tables for a moment by unearthing at prodigious cost a most unsavoury scandal against the enemies of the republican form of government, who became daily more numerous and powerful. Most fortunately some six dynasties claimed the crown of Gallicia, and their internecine struggles kept the republic erect though staggering.

A further complication had arisen with regard to Adoshaf. A great diplomatic victory had been won, and a great war averted; and one of the conditions of peace was the recognition of the Elin valley – Adoshaf is on the Elin, though Koupets had no idea of the fact for months afterwards! – as within the 'sphere of influence' of Noibla, the treacherous and hereditary enemy of Gallicia.

And here was the government looking out of its governmental windows and seeing the streets ablaze with enthusiasm and ringing with the cry of *'Krets Koupets!'* (Long live Koupets!), while it had not even received the explorer's despatches and could only wish that he had perished long ago in Central Kainogenogy. It could not even disown Koupets to the Ambassador of Noibla. It could only deny that anything had occurred. And at any moment one of the six pretenders might take it into his head to telegraph *'Krets Koupets!'* to a royalist newspaper, sneak in disguise into Tetulia, and upset the republican apple-cart for a generation.

---

[1] [Denials.]

When the despatches at last arrived, the situation touched boiling-point. Royalist deputies insisted on their being read in parliament, and with a mob of about a million people thronging the parliament square, chanting '*Krets Koupets!*' hour by hour in formidable unison, the government could not refuse.

The house went mad with excitement. Koupets in his elation had been singularly positive and eloquent. 'Light of civilisation in darkest Kainogenogy,' 'Slavery abolished,' 'Fanaticism disarmed,' and above all, 'The flag of Gallicia and glory set up in the metropolis of barbarism.'

The government tried to proceed to the order of the day. It was in vain. '*Krets Koupets!*' resounded inside the house as well as outside. The premier of the government that had fallen only a month earlier mounted the tribunal, his vengeance irresistibly in his hand. He compelled the house to silence. He was very sorry, he said, he was above all a man of moderation. He would be the last to injure a friendly nation such as Noibla. But the flag of Gallicia had been set up in the marketplace of Adoshaf, and where that flag had once floated, who dared pull it down? Not while he lived, or any Gallician worthy of the fatherland.

The government were thunderstruck at this diabolical moderation. Chauvinism they could sneer at; this was unanswerable. They resorted to obstruction. Speaker after speaker mounted the tribunal; each exhausted himself in the effort to glorify Koupets and say nothing compromising. These tactics triumphed; the debate stood adjourned. The Premier returned to the Foreign Office with the Minister of External Affairs – to find what was, in fact, though not in name, an ultimatum from Noibla.

They stood on a crazy pinnacle. Disown Koupets, and they would be lucky if the people did not tear them limb from limb; acknowledge him, and war would follow within forty-eight hours. Dared they fight? They drove to the house of the Minister for the Navy, and pulled him out of bed. The first point of attack would be their great arsenal at Nolout, and the fleet of Noibla lay stripped at Atlam, not a day and a half away.

Was everything ready down to the last gaiter button?

The Minister dared not give an official reply. Instead, he had the line cleared, and went to Nolout on a light engine.

An hour's inspection told him everything. There was no shortage of gaiter buttons, but of the more serious munitions of war there was a most surprising dearth. There was no ammunition for the heavy guns.

There were no mines. There was not ten per cent of the shells that should have been. There were insufficient torpedoes to put half the craft in the harbour on a war footing. Miracles apart, Nolout must fall within three days of a declaration of war. The Minister's telegram to his colleague was terse Gallician for 'peace at any price.'

He remained in Nolout to organise courts-martial on an unprecedented scale, and to escape the fury of the Tetulian mob.

With the fate of the Government we have no concern; with the attitude of Balustan we have. The ambassador of that country represented to the Foreign Minister that a climb-down so ignominious on the part of an ally was a blow to the prestige of his own country.

'My dear Ambassador,' said the Minister in a temper unrestrained by any fear of consequences, since in any case he must fall that day, and for ever, 'we can't fight Noibla without ships. And from all I learn the only wonder is that our chaps didn't try to sell the Navy as a going concern.'

The ambassador, expressing a few apt words of polite sympathy, retired, and sent his most confidential attaché with despatches to the Khan. It might be as well, he opined with deference, to take stock at the arsenal of Sebastian.

The Khan acted on his advice, and found the words of one of the minor prophets about the locust and the grasshopper and the palmer-worm and the canker-worm to be strictly applicable to the situation at Sebastian. The place was a husk; there were not a week's munitions in it.

The Khan ordered the arrest of every officer above the rank of commander. They were put in cells under sentries, furnished with writing materials, and informed that doubtless they would furnish a perfectly satisfactory explanation of the disappearance of some millions of pounds' worth of war stores; but if not (by any chance) they would find loaded revolvers in the room opposite.

At this moment the *Luschbuze* entered the harbour, and two more were added to the bag.

That night every one of the culprits shot himself; during the next six months they were officially killed off – 'Admiral A, promoted, died of heart disease while travelling to take over his new command,' 'Captain B, absent on leave, was thrown from his automobile and killed,' 'Rear Admiral C died of an operation following appendicitis,' 'Captain D drowned at sea while attempting to save the life of a sailor who had fallen overboard' and so on – and First Lieutenant Finn commanded the *Luschbuze*.

Key

Koupets is the Russian word for merchant. Marchand (Major). Elin, Nile. Dahet, Chad. Eriaz, Zaire. Melania, Nigeria. Gallicia, France. Adoshaf, Rashoda. Kainogenogy, Africa (*ex Africa semper aliquid novi*).[1] Tetulla, Lutetia, Paris. Balustan, Bear country, Russia. *Luschbuze*, 'Demon Rum.' Tsoke, Soaker. Sebastian, Sebastopol. Axine, Euxine, Black Sea. *New Times*, *Novoe Vremya*. Noibla, Albion, England. Nolout, Toulon. Atlam, Malta.

---

[1] [From Africa, always something new.]

The Chute

I

Idleness

Mark Lessing was one of nature's monsters. A shy, almost effeminate boy, he had failed to please the proctustes of public school life, and had to be passed to Oxford without that coarseness, cynicism, callousness, hidden brutality and displayed perversion which is the foundation of the Oxford manner. Six years later he was still a ne'er-do-well, wasting his time and money in the Latin Quarter, and acquiring an unsavoury reputation as a painter of what his fellow-artists recognised as master-pieces. At that time his father, a distinguished civil servant, whose last years had been saddened by his only son's failure to live a decent life, took his grey hairs down in sorrow to the grave. Mark's income suddenly stopped, and he had perforce to abandon Paris for London. In Paris, he said, they knew all about pictures and bought none; in London nothing, and bought some. Unfortunately, Lessing was not at all the man to paint the picture of the year at the academy. He could only paint one thing – the nude; and of this he had so extraordinary a perception, and expressed the same with such absolute simplicity, that his work was entirely beneath the notice of those who wished to be excited by the question of whether that sweet child would live or die, whether it was the sinning wife or the faithless husband that went with the title of the picture, who was accusing who of cheating, and why, whether the girl would say yes or no, which horse would win after all, and if the lion would eat the martyr or not.

He did not understand, either, how to sell his work in private. His education had not fitted him to lackey the Johannesburg millionaire, or smirk in the drawing rooms of the 'art patron.' Nor had all Park Lane, with bulging manner and pocketbook, been clamouring at his door, would he have sold a picture. He objected on principle to part-ing with a picture at all, and as for letting it go to other than a 'good home,' it was unthinkable. He would almost rather have burned a work of art than see it go to America. His complete lack of all the finer feelings soured him against humanity. He hated society; preferred to smoke his pipe in a public house. His equals bored him when they did not talk art, and sickened him when they did. He could not tolerate shams of any kind. Age made him more morose than ever. He shunned all folk above the age of ten or thereabouts, with the exception of the honest old fellow with whom he worked in the evenings when it was too dark to paint, two hours of daily toil sufficing to earn enough to supply his simplicity. For the delicacy of touch which served him as a painter was also found useful by polishers of lenses. Mark Lessing could detect and correct errors of a thousandth of an inch with his eyes shut.

When he was forty, a great calamity befell him. The old man died. It had not been his own seeking, this paying work. Now it had ended, he would, of course, live on his savings, and by the sale of his pictures. Of these he had a great collection, having painted about sixty a year for twenty years, and having sold or given away not more than half. However, this was fated not to worry him, for about three months later he was knocked down by a cab and taken to the hospital, where he lay unconscious for over a week, and between life and death for six weeks more.

Before anyone could discover his identity, his landlord sold his few sticks and many canvases to pay himself the rent; and as the aforesaid canvases were distributed among poverty-stricken students to be painted over, they were not recoverable, even had Mark been able to redeem them. Being a man of spirit he would not make his case known to his friends, but bought chalks, and proceeded to decorate a pavement. The police put sudden death to that, and only his university accent saved him from a prosecution, the constable persuading himself that some nob was drawing them ('haw! haw! haw!' behind a glove) for a lark or a bet. So that he escaped with a few remarks, half leering and half jeering, on morality – which jeopardised that constable's life, had he known it, more than many burglars. Thus baffled, the painter took to selling matches, rose by degrees to the power of purchasing paints and brushes, painted a picture and managed to sell it for a ten-pound note to the one dealer in London who would even look at his work. Restored to affluence by this stroke of luck, he was still further favoured by fate, and found a job again at the lenses. He soon had a studio and began his old game of turning out three-score unsaleable pictures per annum. He became casual in the matter of lenses, was paid less, lived on mere scraps of food and kept every available shilling to pay models, and purchase materials.

'Idleness is a bitter curse' (my father used to say), 'it's the mother of all ills, and there's nothing worse.' At this critical point in his downward career he came face to face with vice.

2

Vice

It was the same year in which he entered a public school that Ailsa Roberts joined her eleven brothers and sisters at the little lost vicarage in Gloucestershire. Her father, successful enough in that capacity, had failed in every other, only stumbling into a benefice as a sort of last lurch before the grave. However, her early years were peaceful enough, save that her frivolity, expressed mainly by what can be called vicissitudes of the limbs, caused frowns. When she was twelve years old her father died; the family was scattered; a wealthy aunt sent her to a convent (no place for a Christian child!) and forgot about her the next day. In the convent she still tried to dance until the nuns could think of nothing but the convulsionaries of St Medard. Exorcism proving fruitless, and punishment serving only to confirm the criminal in her crime, she was boarded out. A Russian girl from the opera passing the garden in which she disported, recognising genius, arranged for the girl to go to Moscow to learn the ballet. Here she met Boris Mikhailovich, who was not content to teach her only dancing. At eighteen, under the name of La Koslowskaja, she was dancing in principal parts with him; at twenty she set out to conquer Paris and London, and at twenty-four succeeded. Of strong animal spirits, and weakened moral principles – a convent and a dancing school can undermine even a clergyman's daughter – she allowed herself to amass that collection of sapphires which will be remembered by connoisseurs as the marvel of the decade. She was, however, not without her troubles. For instance, she lost her complexion and several teeth. Then came a year duiring which she could not dance at all, and on her return to the stage the final touch which had made her had departed. She got the usual applause, and looked apparently as well as ever, but the judicious grieved.

Two years later she had already begun to sell her sapphires; and a year after that she – saw a ghost!

There is a point in the downward career of vice when it comes face to face with the idleness whose hours initiated it!

3

Crime

La Koslowskaja was thirty-two, and Mark Lessing forty-seven, when they met on the night boat from Calais. He had been over to Paris for a few weeks of happiness among his old friends, she to fulfil a not too-well-paid engagement at the Alhambra.

'My poor Boris!' cried she, as he walked across the gangway. Boris Mikhailovich had been her first man, the man she really loved, deep down where love lies, God knows where! but most surely immune from all the accidents of life. Now she saw him, as she thought, old and broken down. She became on the instant eternal youth itself, in that aspect of it which we call motherhood.

The mistake was easily explained, but the conversation continued. Ailsa was lost in memories of first love; Mark in contemplation of the body of a perfect dancer. She gladly agreed to sit for him, his simplicity charmed her; his evident poverty moved her to a great resolution. For Boris' memory she resolved to be a mother-daughter to him. With great difficulty she got him to her flat to dine; with greater persuaded him to sell her a picture for ten pounds. He spent over an hour in persuading her to accept one as a gift.

This price of ten pounds deserves comment. Ailsa was singularly ignorant in patches, and had no idea that anything but dress, jewellery, champagne, and women could cost money. She imagined ten pounds to be a sort of fancy price for a picture. She had vaguely heard of Rembrandts bringing £20,000 in the auction room, but never connected it with any fact of life. She had once been offered a particularly fine Conder for fifty pounds, and stamped out of the shop in a rage that anyone should dare to presume so on her inexperience.

The ice once broken, it was the dancer's practise to spend fifteen to twenty pounds a week on Lessing's pictures; and for a year or two he prospered. Greater ease and comfort, combined with complete leisure, overcame advancing age, and he painted harder and better than ever before. Unfortunately his patroness found the contrary. She made less and less, both on the stage and off; her dress cost her more every month, and her hair-dresser and beauty expert ate up all her earnings. There were soon no more supplies; the rent of her flat became a burden. She moved from Mount Street to Victoria Street, from Victoria Street to Russell Square, from Russell Square to Denbigh Street. She bored lesser managers than those who had fought in law courts to secure her services; she who had frowned on dukes now smiled at stockbroker's clerks.

Of all this Mark Lessing was totally unaware. Absorbed completely in his painting, he hardly ever stirred from his studio unless to take the air on the embankment and watch the Titan that is the heart of London's energy tower above the tide. To visit him she always made her finest toilet; she took to feeding in obscure cafés to save the money to buy his pictures. But her visits became less frequent in spite of all that she could do; and a day came when she could no longer hide her poverty, even from his unobservant eye. He flatly refused to sell her another picture, and only woman's wit won out. She burst into tears, and made a great confession. 'All this time,' she said, 'I have been selling your pictures at a profit. It is all I have to live by.'

In plain English, she lied to him. There is a period when the conjunction of vice and idleness gives birth to crime.

4

Virtue

Lady Adelaide Victorine Knowsbagge had never lacked anything, but admirers, and her just indignation against those who had any grew, equal-striding, with what cynics vilely called her age and her despair. She envied even the street walker, and devoted her life to dragging such from their already miserable existence to a world of wash tubs and sewing machines, variegated with sermons. She had lent all her wealth and influence to an agitation against a 'white slave traffic' which existed only in the columns of pornographic newspapers of the basest type, weeklies whose editors had come from every gaol in England to guard the morals of its people. It was principally through her eloquence and intriguing that an act was hurried through Parliament to take away the last happiness of these wretched women by imprisoning and flogging their lovers.

That she did this without self-interest of any kind goes without saying; with her the command of God and the approval of her own conscience were everything. In the career of virtue there are no crises; self-sustained by the consciousness of its own excellence it moves gloriously onwards. Virtue is its own reward.

5

Punishment

It was one of Lady Adelaide's 'censors' – the word 'spy' is highly improper in this connection – who, failing to obtain money and favour from Ailsa Roberts in return for abstinence from offensive measures, resorted to these, and got her fined four pounds for accosting him. This she paid; enraged at his partial failure to revenge alike his pride and cupidity, he resolved upon a subtler plan of persecution, and followed her about for several days. He tracked her to Lessing's studio and made enquiries about the latter, resulting in a visit. When a seedy stranger of villainous appearance offered him a five-pound note for a picture, the painter was not a little taken aback; but being shy and unwilling to wound, accompanied his refusal with the remark that he did not sell his pictures, as he had private means.

'Mark the word, your worship, private means!' was the next act in the comedy, and Lessing found himself in the dock, charged with living on the immoral earnings of Ailsa.

At the trial Mr Justice Sillimore found the opportunity of his life. Counsel for the Crown had told the whole black story by the hour. Although prisoner's father had been a servant of the English Crown, Lessing was a German name – the name, he understood, of a notorious criminal. A voice in court, 'A poet!' and laughter in certain quarters, though the jury became visibly graver.

But the judge out-prosecuted the prosecutor as the sun outshines the moon.

'Prisoner at the bar,' said he, when the jury, without leaving the box, returned a verdict of 'guilty,' 'this has been a very plain and a very shocking case. So far from finding any extenuating circumstance, I can see only aggravations of the most disgusting offence – except one – known to the law. You had a worthy father, and the best of educations. You had, perhaps, at one time, talent. All this you have abused. There is a period when idleness becomes vice; you have long passed that stage. My experience finds no parallel for the brazen effrontery with which you have attempted to defend yourself. Refusing the legal assistance generously offered you by the king you have so grievously offended, you have insulted this court by bringing into it the obscene daubs, fit only for the walls of Parisian brothels, which you call your work. If, indeed, you sell them – which I, thank God, cannot believe – I can only cry shame on the buyer, and it is moreover no principle of English law that a lesser crime can be brought forward as the excuse for a greater. There is a period in the career of idleness when its association with vice engenders crime; and there is a period in the career of crime when it is cut short by punishment.

'I feel it my duty to impose a penalty which, I hope, will deter other lazy rogues from following an example so loathsome and abominable to all decent men; and I therefore sentence you to eighteen months' hard labour and forty-five strokes of the "Cat."'

Amid general applause, the prisoner, who remained silent, was removed to the cells.

6

Hell's Counterstroke

Mark Lessing died under the infliction of the 'Cat.'

Most unfortunately, the story does not end there. It is one of the permitted malices of Satan – in the inscrutable wisdom of God – that even condign punishment, poetic justice, is frustrated; the house is swept and garnished, and seven other devils enter in.

It so happened that a Jewish picture dealer was a witness in the case following *Rex vs. Lessing*, and was in court during the trial. His attention being thus attracted to the 'obscene daubs,' he thought that a success of scandal might possibly attach to the public sale of one or two of them. He therefore approached La Koslowskaja, who sold him three for fifty pounds. She was thunderstruck at the idea of anyone wanting to pay real money for them; had not the dealer been so obviously clean and keen and Hebraic and prosperous, he could have had them for almost nothing.

The sale was widely advertised; decent people turned away disgusted. The day before the sale the dealer returned, with an offer to buy her whole collection – some three hundred pictures, mostly under the bed – but found her reading a telegram from Paris, from a man whose name she knew as one of Lessing's oldest friends, containing these words: 'For God's sake, don't sell any more pictures till after auction. Will call ten o'clock.' Ailsa showed this to the discomfited Hebrew, who retired, objurgating electricity.

The sale was a surprise, even to him, who had wind of what would happen. Painters from Paris who had known Lessing, some of them already successful men, came over in force. Every dealer had been warned, and was there to fight for the fame of his house; everyone bid with no thought but to purchase, careless whether he ever sold again or not; and the Jew went away with what he called a consolation prize of £17,850.

Every year on the anniversary of her meeting with Mark Lessing, and every year on the anniversary of his death, Ailsa Roberts sells a picture, at prices constantly increasing.

For she had built a memorial gallery to the great painter, whom she loved for his likeness to the man who had betrayed her, and after her death there will be no millionaire to filch even one more picture from the nation.

A Death Bed Repentance

I

According to the local G.P., there was no hope for Timothy Bird. There was nothing the matter with him beyond the fact that he was eighty-six and that his weakness was alarming. People snuff out at all ages; accidents apart, our vital clocks vary immensely in the matter of mainspring.

The mind of Timothy Bird was extraordinarily clear and logical; in fact, so logical that he was unreasonable. He was unwilling to die until he had made one further effort to transform that which had most embittered his life into its crowning joy. At the last moment, said he, God will surely touch the heart of my dear lad.

He therefore telegraphed, with a faith which thirty years of disappointment had done nothing to shatter.

The telegram was worded thus:

> John Nelson Darby Bird,
> 99 New Square,
> Lincoln's Inn.

> Jesus calls me at last unless He comes first come to your father and your God. Luke 15.

> FATHER

The curious wording of this message mirrored infallibly the mind of Timothy Bird.

Why (do you interrupt) assert religious beliefs in a telegram? Because the Holy Ghost may 'use' the telegram to 'reach' the clerks in the Post Office. Enough of such querulous query: to the facts!

John Nelson Darby was the founder of the 'Brethren gathered together to the name of the Lord Jesus' and called 'Plymouth

Brethren' owing to their early great successes having been won in Plymouth. This excellent man was a very fine Hebrew scholar, to say nothing of Greek. His eminence had entitled him to the offer of a seat on the Committee of the Revision of the Bible, but he had refused to meet other scholars of heterodox theological views, quoting:

> Matthew 18:17,
> II Thessalonians 3:6 and 14,
> Romans 16:17,

and particularly

> II John 9, 10, 11.

His undoubtedly great all-round mind led him to see that One Infallible Authority is necessary to any religion. Rome had this in the Pope; he followed the apostasy of Luther, and proposed to replace this by the Bible. Now, since the Bible is the actual word of God, dictated by the Holy Ghost – else where is its authority? – this word must be taken literally in every part as well as in the whole. Now you may formulate a sorites from any one text and another sorites from any other. But a contradiction in your conclusions will not invalidate either of your first premises!

This involves a somewhat complex metaphysic, in spite of the fact that metaphysic, being the work of heathen philosophers, is of its father the devil.

It is, however, impossible in practise to corner a Plymouth Brother in these or any other ways, because he scents danger from afar and replies with an *argumentum ad hominem* on these simple lines:

> I am saved.
> You are not I.
> Therefore, you are damned.
>
> (1 John, v. 19.)

In these degenerate days fact is supposed by the ignorant to be truer than fancy, and one must therefore plead for belief by referring the sceptic to Mr Edmund Gosse's *Father and Son*. Reviewers of that book cast doubt on the possibility of such narrow-mindedness as is shown by Philip Gosse. But in the boyhood of another writer sprung of the loins of the Brethren, the poet of *The World's Tragedy*, the name of Philip Gosse was a by-word, a scorn and a reproach; he was an awful warning of the evils of latitudinarianism!

And Timothy Bird was of the anti-Ravenite section of the Exclusive Plymouth Brethren. His had been the dominant voice of that Assembly Judgement which 'delivered' Philip Gosse and his kind 'to Satan for a season'; and he had been the mainstay of the movement which expelled a majority of the remainder when Mr F. E. Raven had 'blasphemed' in a manner so obscure and complex that not one in twenty of the most learned of the seceders ever gained even a Pisgah glimpse of the nature of the controversy.

For Timothy Bird was indeed a Gulliver in Lilliput. He had known John Nelson Darby intimately; he had been the close friend of Wigram and Crowley, even of Kelly before his heresy; he was a scholar of merit if not of eminence; he was a baronet of the United Kingdom and a man of much property. Baronets not being mentioned in the New Testament, he had refused to use his title; but the other brethren, at least those in the lower middle classes, never forgot it.

He lived simply, using his large income principally for the distribution of tracts; he evangelised greatly while he had the strength, going from town to town to establish or confirm the brethren, and it was generally known that he had left the whole of his great fortune in trust to Arthur Horne and Henry Burton for the use of the brethren to the entire exclusion of the aforesaid John Nelson Darby Bird, who had not only backslidden but gone over wholly to Satan, being in fact a barrister of repute, the most distinguished member of the Rationalist Press Association, and, worse than all, a zealous and irrefutable advocate of easy divorce.

This disinheritance weighed little with the younger Bird, who at forty-four was earning some £5,000 a year, and who had such painful memories of eighteen years of the most cruel (because perfectly well-meaning) form of slavery that the word 'home' was habitually used by him in moments of excitement instead of the familiar 'hell' of the pious Englishman.

Now, as Herbert Spencer (a little late in the day) maintained, 'Action and reaction are equal and opposite'; and experience teaches that fanaticism does not escape this law. There are no anti-Christians like the children of Plymouth Brethren. They have the Bible at their fingers' ends; they quite agree that Brethrenism is the only logical form of Bible Christianity; they associate it with every grand tyranny or petty spite of the hated home; and so they are frankly of Satan's party. Terrible opponents they make. The Plymouth Brother can find a text of Scripture to buttress his slightest act, and his son has consequently an equal armory of blasphemy, which, with a little knowledge of Greek and Hebrew and of various infidel writers, makes him unchallengeable in debate.

Timothy Bird had learnt to fear his son. From the age of puberty he had been in fierce revolt; it was the subtleties of that five years' intense struggle that had made him intellectually supreme both in strategy and tactics, the most dangerous advocate at the Bar. He had become a fine psychologist as well; he had penetrated every blind alley of his father's mind, and to that mind he was merciless. He, too, was a fanatic. He really wished (in a way) to avenge the tortures of his boyhood; and perhaps he felt that his emancipation was not complete until he had converted his torturer. However this may be, year after year with ever-gathering strength, he hurled battalion on battalion at the squat blind citadel – to foreseen repulse. It was probably the parable of the importunate widow, or the endurance which his horrible boyhood had taught him, that made him continue. It is impossible to argue with a Plymouth Brother, for his religion is really axiomatic to him, so that everything he says begs the question, and you cannot get him to see that it does so. This is not so unusual as it appears; it requires a very good mind to acquiesce, even for purposes of argument, in non-Euclidean geometry, so fixed is the mind in its certainty that the whole is greater than its part, and the like.

It is good to hear them discuss anything.

Propose the question of the Origin of Evil; your Plymouth Brother will remark sooner or later, but always irrelevantly, 'God is a just God.' You argue that his God is certainly not just, or he would not have commanded the rape of virgins by the thousand, or sent bears to devour forty and two little children whose sole fault was to call attention to the baldness of a prophet.

This is unanswerable; give up the story, as the better mind does, and you are launched for atheism or mysticism; hold to it – the Christian's only hope – and the sole possible reply is 'Shall not the judge of the whole earth do right?' 'Yes,' you retort, 'He shall; that is just my proof that your God is a tribal fetish, and not at all the judge of the whole earth.' The conversation, after a sulphurous interlude, again rises to the dignity of argument, and on some infinitely subtle and obscure minor point which he had never thought of before – I speak of a rare incident much prized by connoisseurs – you do really and truly prove to him from Scripture that he is wrong.

Is he downhearted? No!

The momentary cloud upon his brow passes; the glorious sun shines out amid the wrack:

'The devil can quote Scripture.'

In vain you reply that this consuming doubt invalidates the whole of his arguments, which are all drawn from Scripture; and this again admitting of no reply, the worthy man will continue to breathe out lightnings and slaughter until physical weariness bids him desist.

Yet it was the cherished belief of John Nelson Darby Bird that the last straw will break the camel's back; or, more practically, that if you sandpaper bricks at the base of a building long enough the building will suddenly and without warning reel and fall. You remember that Noah spent 120 years building the ark – with hardly a shower. When the flood came, it came suddenly. J. N. D. Bird, K.C., was quite ready to 'go to the ant, thou sluggard,' or to Noah, as circumstances might indicate.

Before he answered his father's telegram he borrowed the billiard chalk from the waistcoat pocket of his clerk, whose sporting instincts had got the best briefs for his employers in horsey and divorcey circles.

(Lord John Darcy v. the Stewards of the Jockey Club, Riddell v. Riddell, Clay, Arthur, Thompson, Battersby, Jacobs, Bernheim, de la Rue, Griggles, Waite, Shirley, Williamson, Klein, Banks, Kennedy, Gregg, Greg, and others. These were the remarkable cases that established the reputation of Mr Bird. His successful defence of Mrs Riddell had won him, in addition, a vice-presidency of the Anthropological Society.)

To those who are not Plymouth Brethren it will not be obvious why John Bird pocketed the billiard chalk, and a new digression becomes Cocker.

Chalk is the commonest form in which carbonate of calcium is found in Nature. Under the microscope it is seen to be composed of the dust of the shells of minute marine animals. Geologists consider it impossible that a layer of chalk 10,000 feet thick should have been deposited in the course of a week, or even in the course of, say, 4,004 years.

The year after John Bird was called to the Bar he had fleshed his maiden steel upon his father by taking a piece of chalk, a microscope, and twenty-seven volumes of geology to Carnswith Towers for the long vacation. Father and son talked chalk day and night for nine weeks. It was a drawn battle. The father had to admit the facts of geology. 'Then,' said the son, 'I cannot believe that God wrote a lie upon the rocks.' Timothy replied, 'Let God be true, and every man a liar!' He also very ably urged that it was not a lie. If men of science were not blinded by the devil (owing to their seared consciences and their quite gratuitous hatred of God) they would see, as he, Timothy

Bird, saw, that it was obvious from the chalk itself that it had been created in a moment. Alternatively, God *had* written a lie upon the rocks in order to blind them. 'God shall send them strong delusion, that they may believe a lie.'

The immorality of this latter proceeding, of course, led to the old 'God is a just God' line of argument with its inevitable conclusion in Sheol for the younger Bird.

Phœnix-like, however, he caused lumps of chalk to be conveyed to his father at irregular intervals; for he saw, with the astuteness that had discomfited Lord John Darcy, that his father's belief had really been shaken by the argument. The outworks held; the citadel crumbled. In the deepest shrine of subconsciousness Timothy Bird, or, rather, Something that was in very truth *not* Timothy Bird, knew that the world was not made in six days, that the Book of Genesis was a Jewish fable, that the whole structure of 'revelation' was a lie, that the Incarnation and the Atonement were but dreams.

Armed, therefore, with the integrity described by Horace, and the billiard chalk, John Nelson Darby Bird went to Carnswith Towers by the 3.45 for a final wrestle with the Angel.

2

The old man was sitting up when his son arrived. Arthur Horne and Henry Burton, the one pale, the other sallow, the one stumpy and fat, the other dried up, had come to pray with him. The doctor, who was not of the fold, appeared nauseated at the unction of the vultures, and (before he left) communicated a portion of this feeling to the nurse who, although a 'Plymouth Sister,' had experience in her profession of the realities of life, and consequently to some extent saw things, though dimly, as they really were.

Burton was praying audibly as John Bird entered. Without moving a muscle, he directed the current of his supplications into a new channel.

'And, dear Jesus, we beseech Thee, on behalf of one among us, or perhaps now among us, or soon to be present among us (it would not do to admit that he knew of anything that was occurring in the room), one we truly fear dead in trespasses and sins and so it seems far indeed from the precious blood. May it please Thee that this thine aged servant may at last be gladdened, ere he pass into his exceeding great reward, by Thy wonderful mercy working in this hard heart and unregenerate Adam —'

With utter weariness of tautologies and repetitions, the prayer meandered on for another ten minutes. At last came the Amen.

Not until then did Timothy Bird open his eyes and greet his son. Feeble as he was, he began to 'plead with him' to 'come to Jesus.' The son had a terrible temptation to acquiesce, to spare the oldster 'useless' pain. In the stern school of the Brethren, truth, or what passes for truth, must outweigh all human feelings, as if a sword were thrown into a scale wherein two oat-husks were contending. The obstinacy of those five terrible conscious years of revolt assisted his decision to sway to that austerity which here he thought was cruelty.

'Father,' said he, 'don't poison your last hours by these delusions! If there be a God, it is certain that He never trapped man as you say He did.'

Arthur Horne interrupted: 'God is a *just* God.'

'Then why did he make vermin?' retorted the barrister.

A long and laboured explanation followed from the excellent Horne, who never suspected that the repartee was not part of the argument.

It all wound its weary way back to the old subject of the sure and certain damnation of John Bird.

The latter paid no heed. His human feelings swamped all else. He knew instinctively at that moment the supreme human truth that the son *is* the father, literally identical, of one substance. Also, in the great presence of death there is no place for religion of any kind. The sham of it becomes patent – a hideous masque and revelry of mocking thoughts. Even where it is the strongest of all drugs, it lowers; hypnotic cloud or levin of storm, shines never as a sun of life. The Pagans knew; try to write a letter of condolence to a friend bereaved, and you will know it too. Glib consolations are the work of shallow hypocrites, or of cowards too scared to face their fear; they break into a sweat of piety; their eyes glaze with a film – the easy falsehood of immortality. The iridescent bubble of faith is easily burst – woe to the man who dares touch it by so much as one word of truth on any serious subject!

'My son,' began Timothy Bird, to whom the approach of death now lent a majesty indescribable – the feeble baronet might have been a patriarch of the patriarchs – 'my life has failed. Its one desire has been that God would bring my only son to His grace. It was not His will. To that I bow; my times are in His hand. His will, not mine, be done. It may be that my death may be the means —' and on he rambled the well-worn paths of 'pleading with a soul,' things so hackneyed that John Bird, facing his own problem as he was, hardly heard them trickle through his ears. He only marked a stumbling, a growing hesitation, and a look of trouble and of awe. It was a machine interrupted; yet, strangely, not so much as if it were breaking down, but as if a new hand were on the levers. Surely the end was near. The old man himself seemed to think so. He detected his own weakness; he flushed with a sort of shame; he seemed to gather himself for an effort.

'John,' said he firmly, 'shall not the Judge of the whole earth do right? You are a lawyer; you understand the value of testimony. Here are we four, three living and one almost gone to be with Christ, all ready to lift up our voices and testify to the saving grace of God. Is it not so?'

Solemnly enough, Horne, Burton, and the nurse gave their assent.

'Will you not accept their witness?'

'I, too, have witnesses,' replied John Bird; and he drew the billiard chalk from his pocket and laid it on the mantlepiece. 'Let God be true,' said he, 'and every man a liar!'

The light of fanaticism that blazed from the eyes of the moribund man flashed once, and went suddenly out. An uncomprehending stare replaced it. He seemed to search the Infinite. All thought he was at the extreme, and Horne and Butler, intent as they were on their own plans, were frightened into silence. John Bird returned to his problem: it was himself that was dying. And yet no, for the true self was living in himself. And he understood that marriage is a sacrament, and must not be blasphemed by hedging it about with laws of property, and canon prohibitions, and inspection and superintendence sacerdotal. Every man is a king and priest to God; every man is the shrine of a God, the guardian of an eternal flame, the never-extinguished lamp of the Rosicrucian allegory.

The eyes of the old man were still fixed on the chalk in an unwinking stare. His colour heightened and his breath came faster. Yet his muscles grew ever more rigid; he seemed to grip the arms of the chair in which he was propped by pillows.

It was he at last who broke the silence. 'Nurse,' he said, very slowly but firmly and distinctly, 'take my keys and open the buhl cabinet.' The woman obeyed. 'Bring me the paper in the lower middle drawer.' She did so.

With perfect calm and deliberation, but with more vital energy than he had yet shown, and with his eyes shining now with a warm, kindly lustre, he tore the paper across and across.

'Burn it!' said he. The nurse took it to the flame of her spirit lamp and consumed the pieces.

The son understood what had been done.

'Father,' said he, 'I don't want the money. I didn't come down here for that.'

Placidly came the amazing retort: 'Then give it to the Rationalist Press Association!'

Horne and Burton broke into a shrill twittering and rumbling of protest. His mind is gone, was the burden of their swan-song. The old man smiled, like a God smiling at his puppets. Their plaint turned to denunciation.

John Bird aroused himself. 'You must leave the house,' said he. With barely a push they complied; they were too astounded to do themselves justice.

The dying man beckoned his son. 'Your life must have been a hell,' said he, 'and I made it so. But it was blindness and not unkindness, Jack.' His son had not heard 'Jack' for thirty years. He fell on his knees beside his father, and burst into strong sobs. Those thirty years of strife and wrong and misunderstanding came back, single, and in battalions, too!

The old man's head had fallen back; a smile had softened the old stern expression; the eyes closed as if in ecstasy.

Even the nurse was mistaken; she touched the shoulder of the barrister. But John would not move; and suddenly she recognised that the old man was breathing; from swift and shallow it deepened to strong and slow; a great sleep was upon him.

For three hours his son knelt by him, his lips fastened on one hand; and of the experience of those three hours who shall speak?

Then came the doctor – to pronounce the patient 'wonderfully better.'

And indeed he lived three years, sane, healthy, and strong.

I saw him the year after at the annual dinner of the Rationalist Press Association – the weight of his theories rolled off the grand old shoulders. And far down the table I saw Messrs Horne and Burton; but not being encouraged.

There is a cenotaph in the family vault. Following the usual recital of the virtues of the deceased, written in smiling irony by his own hand, comes this text:

THE FATHERS HAVE EATEN SOUR GRAPES,
AND THE CHILDREN'S TEETH ARE SET ON EDGE.

Felo de Se

It lacked a little of midnight. In the east the moon, rising high above the trees that fringed the river, made a lane of light. Her beams fell full upon the face, delicately pensive, with the lips thinly tightened from their drooping corners, of a young exquisite, in whose slender and nervous fingers trembled a gold-headed cane. He was standing at the very edge of the calm water, upon the narrow grass that lay between it and the towing-path. On his right, across the river, rose a hill, cloaked in giant woods, a menace and a mystery. On his left, a clump of beeches sheltered a knoll of velvet grass, one would have said a lover's bower. Behind him lay many miles of pleasant fields and villas. There was no sound in the night but the rare hooting of an owl in the great wood, and the secret undercurrent of sound caused by the commotion of a distant weir.

'Do what thou wilt shall be the whole of the Law. A fine night!' said a strange voice in the young man's ear.

He failed to catch the first part of the greeting, so absorbed was he in his thoughts; to the second he answered mechanically 'a fine night, sir!' As he did so he turned to look at the stranger.

He saw a man between thirty and forty years of age, both full and broad, yet slender, and giving the impression of great strength and activity. It was, however, the face, barbered in Vandyke fashion, which startled him. No one could ever forget it. Deep melancholy lay upon it, yet only as a veil to roguishness. The mouth was small, scarlet and voluptuous, although firm. But in the eyes lay something beyond any of this. The pupils were extremely small, even in that dim light, and the expression was of such intensity that the young man, startled, no doubt, by the suddenness of the apparition, thrilled with fear. By instinct he moved backwards to the towing-path, for in that place the river runs exceeding deep – and who could decipher the portent of such eyes?

'I am afraid that I have broken in upon your meditations,' continued the newcomer. 'Pray excuse me. I will resume my walk.'

But the young man gave a little laugh, harsh and bitter. 'Not at all,' he said with a little sneer. 'I am only going to kill myself.'

'Good,' returned the other, whom we may identify as a Master of the Law of Thelema – and this story will explain what that is – 'I applaud your decision.'

The youth, although not a disciple, failed entirely to understand that the Master meant what he said. He sought instantly to excuse himself.

'If you only knew all my reasons,' he began gloomily.

'I do not ask them,' replied the elder man. 'You have announced your intention. I do you the common courtesy to assume that your intention is in accordance with your Will. That is reason enough and to spare. "There is no law beyond Do what thou wilt." Besides, you'll make a bonny corpse.'

The young man stared rather wildly.

'No, I'm not a lunatic,' smiled the Master; 'would it perhaps bore you if I explained my reasons for not excluding *felo de se* from that infinite list of acts which are now lawful? It may relieve you of some silly scruple, and enable you to take the plunge with that calm ecstasy which should accompany our every act.'

'You interest me greatly,' acquiesced the youth. The other nodded.

'Let us then sit here, where we can enjoy the beauty of the moonlight. Perhaps you will join me in a cigar?'

'I only smoke cigarettes.'

'Every man to his taste. Well,' and he lit up, 'in order to set ourselves right with the Academies we had better begin with Plato. What say you?'

The youth removed his cigarette and bowed with deference.

'The *Phædo*,' continued the adept, 'is certainly the feeblest of all the Dialogues. It is a mass of very silly sophistry, and the classic of *petitio principii*. But the argument against suicide is put with all the cogency of a nursemaid. "The Gods will punish it, probably," is the Alpha and Omega of that monolith of stupidity. Socrates himself saw it, no doubt, for he changed the subject abruptly. His only attempt to save his face is to shelter himself behind Pythagoras. Now he saw, just as you do, that death was desirable to the philosopher – and young though you are, my friend, if I may dare call you so, that brow bespeaks the love of wisdom – yet he would not

> take death the nearest way.
> Gathering it up beneath the feet of love,
> Or off the knees of murder reaching it

because of the gods. He has given the most excellent reasons for wishing to die, but he will not admit their validity. Yet he had himself, as he admits later, committed suicide by not escaping "to Megara or Bœotia." True, he gives an excellent reason for so acting, but to admit one reason is to admit the edge of the wedge. If an act is permissible for love of law and order, even unjust law – and this is, as you know, the reason advanced by Socrates – then why not for – let us say – the safety of the republic? What of the messenger, fallen into the hands of the enemy, who kills himself lest torture wring the army's secret from him; the man who throws himself from the raft, that his comrade may be saved – or his enemy –

> I alit
> On a great ship lightning-split,
> And speeded hither on the sigh
> Of one who gave an enemy
> His plank, then plunged aside to die.

'One can think of a thousand cases from Curtius to Jesus Christ, this last surely the most deliberate suicide possible, since he had planned it from all eternity, even taking the trouble to create a universe of infinite agony in order to redeem it by this suicide. You are, I hope, a Christian?'

The young man declared that he was an humble and erring, but sincere, follower of the Man of Sorrows.

'Then observe how suicide is the hallmark of your religion. "If thine hand offend thee, cut it off." Scourge thy body, starve it, lick the sores of lepers, risk everything, but save the soul. This is all suicide, some partial, some complete. It does not even demand a reason; sheer hatred of the body is sufficient. Again "The carnal mind is enmity against God"; suppress it; faith and obedience are enough; reason will surely destroy them and the soul as well.

'Now, even those unfortunate persons, who, like myself, not being Christians, cannot assent to so much, can at least admit that some one man, in some one strange circumstance, may rightly lay violent hands upon himself. Then who is to judge of such a circumstance? Is the man to consult his lawyer, or to ask for a referendum? Absurd, you will agree. Then what is left but a private judgement? And if it seem good and sufficient cause for self-murder that "I am idle: also, it is true, I have no more money," as in the case of Prince Florizel at the Suicide Club, who shall judge me? You may disagree; you may call me mad and wicked and all manner of names; I can do the same to you with equal right, if I wish to be discourteous. But I can imagine many a situation, incomprehensible to any but its central figure, which would justify such an act in all men's eyes if they understood the case.

'Every man is commander-in-chief of his own life; and his decisions must always be taken in the sanctuary of his own soul. The man who goes to others for advice abdicates his godhead, except so far as he does it merely because he wishes to hear the case argued by another. The final decision is his own responsibility; he cannot really evade it, even if he would, except by a subservience and slavishness which is more horrible than any suicide of the body could be to those who most object to it—'

'Of course, the law forbids suicide,' urged the young man, puffing violently at his seventh cigarette, 'on the ground that a man owes service to the King.'

'It is a convenient weapon, like religion itself, and all its other precepts, of the tyrant against the slave. To admit this argument is to confess yourself a slave. It is a wise weapon to have forged, moreover. If one hundred workmen were to commit suicide simultaneously, instead of starting silly strikes, the social revolution would arrive that day. I did not ask the King for permission to be born; I came here without my own volition; at least allow me the privilege to depart when I please! In the Middle Ages the necessity of preventing suicide was so well understood that they devised horrible and ridiculous maltreatments of the body – as if any sensible suicide would care. Nowadays populations are larger, and it does not matter so much. The tyrants rely on silly superstitious terrors.

'I am supposed, by the way, to have a great deal of what is called occult knowledge, and when I make a magical disappearance, as I do now and then, without warning, my most devoted disciples always console my anxious paramours with the remark that I can't have killed myself because I "know only too well what the penalties are." It would be more sensible to retort, "Anyhow I bet he hasn't killed himself for your sake, you cuckoo!" But my disciples have no sense; they prefer to utter pompous and blasphemous nonsense, and to defame my character.

'James Thomson makes Bradlaugh say, in that stupefying sermon:

> This little life is all we must endure,
> The grave's most holy peace is ever sure,
>   We fall asleep and never wake again;
> Nothing is of us but the mouldering flesh,
> Whose elements dissolve and merge afresh
>   In earth, air, water, plants, and other men.

'— that sermon which concludes on the grand diapason:

> … if you would not this poor life fulfil,
> Lo, you are free to end it when you will,
> Without the fear of waking after death.

'I know of nothing to reply to that. I tell you on my magical honour that it is so. I will admit that I know of states of Being other than that familiar to you as a man. But does the ego persist after death? My friend, you know very well that it does not persist after one breath of the nostrils! The most elementary fact in Buddhist psychology is that! Then (to pursue Gautama into his jungle) "What can be gained, and what lost? Who can commit suicide, and how?"

'But all this metaphysics is more unsatisfying than chopped hay to an alderman. I counsel you, my young friend, to avoid it in your next incarnation, if you have one. (It doesn't matter to you whether you have or not, since you won't know it. What has posterity done for you, anyway?) At least let us avoid it for the few brief moments that remain to us.

'To revert to the question of the right to make away with yourself – if it be denied that you have the right to end your own life, then, *à fortiori*, I think you must admit, you have no right to end another's. Then you should be in revolt against a government whose authority rests in the last resort on the right of capital punishment. You are *particeps criminis*[1] every time a murderer is hanged; you deny the right of peoples to make war, and possibly that of doctors to practise medicine. You have excellent reasons for hanging and shooting others, and do so, by your own hand or another's, without a qualm. Surely then you are on unassailable ground when you sacrifice a victim to Thanatos not against his will but at his express desire. The only objection I know to allowing doctors to offer a fuller euthanasia to hopeless sufferers than is now permitted is that it might facilitate murder. Well, do any further objections to your very sensible decision occur to you?'

---

[1] [A partner in crime.]

'People say it's cowardly,' ventured the young man, who was now enjoying a cigar, slipped to him by the adept, and lit with the acquiescence of one half-hypnotised.

'Shame, foul shame!' returned the Master with indignation, as he started to his feet and began to pace the path to and fro in his honest wrath. 'Shame on the slanderers who try to mask their own cowardice by branding with that stigma of indelible infamy the bravest act that any man can do. Is not Death the Arch-Fear of Man? Do we not load with titles and honours and crosses and pensions the man who dares death even by taking the small chance of it offered in battle? Are we not all dragged piteously howling to the charnel? Is not the fear of death the foundation of religion, and medicine, and much of law, and many another form of fraud and knavery? But you, in perfectly cold blood, face this fiend calmly and manfully – you with no chance of temporary escape like the soldier or the man in the consulting-room – you who face a certainty when the rest of the world trembles at a chance – they call you coward! Why, death is such a fear that the very word is taboo in polite society. Is it not because religion has failed to fortify the soul against this apprehension that religion is no longer the vogue? Instead we indulge in dances and music and wine and everything that may help to banish the thought. We permit no skeleton at modern feasts. Philosophy dwells much upon death; perish philosophy! Mankind today dreads every discussion of realities, because to modern man death is the supreme reality, and they wish to forget it. It is the fear of death that has fooled men into belief in such absurdities and abominations as Spiritualism and Christian Science.

'I would be honoured, sir,' he stopped in front of the youth, 'if you would allow me to grasp the hand of the bravest man that I have ever met, in the very moment of his culmination!'

The youth arose, automatically almost, and gave his hand to the adept.

'I thank you, sir,' continued the latter, 'you have given me an example, as you have taught me a lesson, of sublime courage. You are a thousand times right. When the evils of life become intolerable, they should be ended. I have half a mind to join you,' he added, musing. 'I have many disciples.'

He sighed deeply, and threw away the butt of his cigar, first lighting another from the glow.

'It seems to me that far too much fuss is being made about death nowadays, as it is about death's deadlier twin-sister, Love. The ancients were our masters in these matters, and so are the Japanese and Chinese of today. The fear of these two things – who are but the man and wife at the lodge gates of Life Park – was probably imported from the effeminate, cowardly and degenerate races of the Indian peninsula. Early Christians, with their *agapæ* and their martyrdoms, feared neither. The Crusaders feared neither. But those nations that have become effetes, that preach peace and morality, and women's rights, these have the cur's spirit, the eunuch's soul, and in these nations death is dreadful and love dangerous. The virile temper of the Romans grasped love and death like nettles that excite even as they sting. That temper has decayed – the war should revive it – and men flee from death and love. Love stands apart and weeps; but Death cries Tally-Ho, and hunts them down to hell.

> For dried is the blood of thy lover,
> Ipsithilla, contracted the vein;

'*Novem continuas fututiones!*'[1] ended the adept, raising his voice even more than possibly the best taste would have sanctioned, though after all a river's marge at night is not an alcove. However, he recollected himself, and continued more gently.

'Pardon me, young sir, I beg,' he said, 'my feelings overcame me for the moment. Baulk at love, you baulk at death; baulk at death, you baulk at life. It's hard to score,' he added laughingly, 'with both balls in baulk.'[2]

The young man laughed, not wholly from courtesy, but because he was really amused, despite his tragic situation.

'If we all took things more easily,' the Master added, 'they would go more easily. Confidence is two battalions in every regiment that we have. Fear, and you fumble. Go ahead, a song on your lips and a sword in your hand: and meet what comes with gaiety. Damn consequences! If you see a girl you like, prove it to her by Barbara and Celarent all the way to Fresison or whatever the logician's *omega* is – I forget.'

The boy was unable to remind him. He had taken Paley for the Little-Go.

'If you see a danger, embrace it,' went on the elder man. Nothing seemed to exhaust the energy of his harangue. 'If you escape, you have lived more beautifully and more intensely. If you die, you die, and one

---

[1] [Nine continuous fuckings!]

[2] The allusion is to the English game of billiards.

more bother is done with. Best of all, then, when one is tired of life, to face the Great Adventure gay and gallant – as you do tonight!'

'Then do you see no objection, of any kind,' answered the youth, a trifle more earnestly than his habitual manner (Harrow and Trinity Hall) would have permitted in more usual circumstances, 'to the fatal act which, as soon as you deprive me of your company, I shall have yet one more excellent reason for putting into execution?'

'None,' smiled the Master, bowing rather pontifically at a politeness to which years of the servility of disciples had inured him. 'Unless, perhaps, we look at the matter in this way. Assume one moment that you are what we empirically call an immortal soul incarnating from time to time in various bodies as occasion offers. Very good; then you willed to live in this body. You knew the conditions – assume that! Good; then you formulate the accurséd dyad, you deny your own will, by cutting short this life. Or, say this; assume that your body is an instrument by which you perceive material things, for a whim, or from some inexplicable desire, I know not what. Then, why destroy your instrument? True, it is hopelessly damaged, let us suppose, so that it perceives badly. If it were possible to mend it, you would cheerfully endure the necessary pangs; but all being decayed, scrap it, and get a new instrument. The only argument is that you may have willed to observe the great cruelty of Nature, not only by seeing, but by feeling it, so that you may thereby become fortified in your resolve to "redeem it from all pain." But this is all a mass of assumptions, little better than the twaddle of the Buddhists and the Christians and the Theosophists and all the other guessers. Ignore it – "thou hast no right but to do thy will. Do that, and no other shall say nay." Then since it is your Will to kill yourself, do not be turned from your purpose. That indeed would be a crime.

'The best argument I ever heard against suicide, if you will pardon my introducing a new witness, was an English journalist whose face resembled a cancer of the stomach in a rather advanced stage of the disease. "Excuse a personal remark," said I, "but consider our feelings. Why not blow it all away with a pistol?" He replied with ready wit: "I use it to pour drink into." Clever Cecil!'[1]

The adept rose once more.

'But I detain you,' he murmured apologetically. 'Religion, philosophy, ethics, and common sense concur in approval of your purpose. I am infinitely obliged to you for the pleasure you have given me by your

---

[1] Cecil Chesterton.

elegant and informed conversation. I dare not even voice a regret that I shall have no opportunity of cultivating your acquaintance. Farewell! Love is the law, love under will.'

The Master bowed and moved slowly towards the towering beeches. But the boy – he was barely eighteen years of age – sprang to his feet and followed him. 'You say,' he babbled eagerly, in his enthusiasm a little forgetful of propriety, 'you say you are a Master, that you have disciples. Won't you take me?'

The adept showed no embarrassment. He would not even seem to rebuke the outburst, unconventional as it was.

'Certainly,' he returned. 'Since I have persuaded you with all my power to do a thing and you now desire to do the opposite, you are preeminently fitted for a disciple. You will get on splendidly with the others, I am sure.'

Such ready acquiescence, couched as it was in the delicately-phrased English of which the adept was an acknowledged master, and made tart by that silky subacidity which had made him famous and infamous, delighted the boy beyond all bounds. He sank to his knees, and caught the Master's hand and kissed it, his face wet with tears, and his throat choking.

The Master's own eyes dimmed for a moment; something rose in him that he did not even try to suppress. He stooped and put a friendly arm about the lad and raised him.

'Come,' he said, 'it is no such great matter. Let us talk of other things. Or, if you will, enjoy the silence of this moonlit loveliness.'

Presently the sun rose, and woke the world to a new day's life worth living.

The Argument that Took the Wrong Turning

There was a sombre and a smouldering fire in the eyes of the quiet man in the corner of the ingle. The remarks of the prohibitionist who was holding forth from the big armchair seemed to excite him, but one could hardly have said why. But when that respectable gentleman paused for breath, the fire leapt up.

'May I add my humble testimony?' he said politely. 'I feel more strongly than most men, I think, upon the subject. Were I to tell you my story, perhaps you would admit that I had a right to do so.'

The man from the Anti-Saloon League got out his notebook with undisguised enthusiasm.

'Can't we induce you to tell it?' he asked, scenting something sensational. 'Nothing so aids the cause as the recital of facts.'

'Well,' said the quiet man, 'I don't mind if I do. I was married to a young and beautiful woman. We passed six years of which one could not pick out a single month and say that it was not a honeymoon. She drank herself into a lunatic asylum.'

He stopped there, very suddenly; his words cut bitterly into the heart of every man in the room. They were too shocked for even the conventional murmur of sympathy. But the prohibitionist, with a smirk, asked for further details.

'I shall be happy to gratify you, sir,' replied the other, and there was a subcurrent of severity in his tone which made one or two of the more sophisticated men present prick up their ears. The quiet man lighted his cigar.

'My wife's father,' he said, 'was vicar of one of the most important parishes in London. His wife liked a glass of champagne with her dinner. However, in her position, it would not do. She had to set a good example to the parish. At the same time she was not going to give up her champagne, so she sent for a doctor who prescribed her champagne, and in order more effectually to silence the voice of scandal, it was necessary to prescribe for the children as well. The eldest daughter, at the age of sixteen, was drinking about a quart a day, by the doctor's orders. She married. Two years later, her husband died. Six years after that I married her myself. Presently I discovered that whenever anything happened to depress her she sought consolation in alcohol. The Puritan idea, the necessity of pretending to be what you are not, had destroyed her sense of freedom. She did the drinking secretly. Ultimately the smash came. I had to be away for some months on business. In my absence the baby died. I came back to find her a hopeless dipsomaniac. I tried everything. Naturally it was useless. She lost all moral sense. I was compelled to divorce her because she refused to follow the doctor's last orders, to spend two years in a "home." I would not stand by and let her kill herself so long as I was morally responsible for her moral welfare. Three months after the divorce, she had to be put into a lunatic asylum.'

'A most striking story,' said the prohibitionist. 'A most admirable story, a most useful story for our purpose.'

But the quiet man rose to his feet.

'No,' he said, 'my tragedy is not a tragedy of alcohol, it is a tragedy of humbug. It is the rotten popular Anglo-Saxon cowardice about the use of alcohol which leads inevitably to its abuse. It is people like yourself that are responsible for all the drunkenness, for all the insanity, for all the crime that people resort to. In countries where there is no feeling against alcohol, where, in honesty and decent freedom a man can sit with his family and drink in the open, we find none of these troubles.'

The prohibition orator became exceedingly annoyed.

'I did not expect this treatment,' he said, 'it is most unwarrantable. I have no doubt at all, sir, that the poor woman was driven to drink by your own brutal treatment.'

'Yes,' said the other man, 'I can be both brutal and violent on occasion.' And he was.

The Professor and the Plutocrat

Professor Bugsby was an old man at fifty! Externally nothing much was the matter with him; his cheeks were rosy, and his dreamy blue eye was soft and kindly as ever; but his nervous system, and especially his will, had broken down under the strain of his long fight with Plunks the banker. Bugsby had started out with all the gaiety of youth; he had thought it simple enough to win the fight; he had merely to prove the wickedness of Plunks, and the folly of mankind in allowing him to rob them, and they would rise and end not only Plunks himself, but the system that made Plunks possible. Alas! he only found himself in a welter of intrigue. He was forced to fight fire with fire, to scheme, to agitate, to cabal—and all was in vain. Time and again he had been on the brink of success at least partial. It was all arranged for him to become President of his University; from this vantage he could bombard Plunks more easily; but at the last moment the long arm of the billionaire had moved a pawn, and blocked the check.

So we find poor Bugsby in Chicago in January, 1917. He had attempted to form a triple entente of Chinese laundry men, drugstore clerks and sundial adjusters, which would frustrate the enormous shipping combine which Plunks was supposed by the Sunday newspapers to be meditating.

But the Milkless Milk Company (a mere alias for Plunks, as Bugsby knew only too well!) had stepped in, and by a series of adroit manœuvres had alienated the laundry men from the movement.

Bugsby, his life's work ruined, turned into the Blackstone. Wrong was triumphant—so be it, then! He would have a last dinner, write a last paper of protest, and seal his witness with his blood.

But, as he reached the lobby, who should he see but Plunks himself! By his side was his confidential secretary, Grahame, a villian only slightly less abandoned than his master. A sinister grin of open triumph was on the face of the billionaire. The monster had thrown off the mask! Bugsby had never before seen him in the flesh. He jumped at his opportunity. Walking straight up to the plutocrat, he began, without a word of preface, his harangue.

'Vampire!' he cried, 'at last I confront you! Liar, thief, murderer, for twenty years we have wrestled in a death-grip. Today it seems as if you had won! Railroad wrecker, Wall Street gambler, cornerer of wheat and oil and copper, steamship pirate, land grabber, lobbyist and grafter, in all you have succeeded—so it seems! Seems! Seems! To the philosopher you are but a doomed man. Had you my *Weltanschauung*,[1] you would know it too. The economic forces which I lead, invisible though they may be, are rising to unseat you. The exchange system is tottering; the financial oligarchy crumbles; my *Distanzliebe* is as *lebendig* as your *Pattvereiningdungingen* is *starr*!!!'[2]

The professor paused for breath.

'Forgive me,' said the anarch. 'You have the advantage of me. I know your name perfectly well, of course, but I can't remember your face.'

'Tremble not!' replied the professor, 'tremble not, although my words sear your corrupt brain as with a white-hot shaft of steel. Tremble not! You triumph over me, for I am beaten. Behold in me your sworn, your lifelong enemy! I am the man whom you have fought these twenty years, whom you have kept from the presidency of my university; it is my works that your subsidised publishers have turned down; I am the man whose courage and address have time and again come nigh to hauling you from your bloodstained throne—I am Professor Bugsby of the University of Muttville!'

Plunks interrogated his secretary with a glance. A slight shake of the head was the reply.

'Bugsby!' said the billionaire, kindly; 'of course, of course! Upon my word, my dear fellow, this is very distressing. I hadn't the least idea of all this. Why on earth didn't you come to me direct? Well, well; never too late, you know; I'll found a university for you, and make you president, and we'll get out all your books for you, and you shall knock me as hard as you can for the rest of your natural life. (Just put that through tomorrow morning, will you, Grahame?) Then you'll come and lunch with me here, won't you, my dear Bugsby, at one sharp, and we'll sign the papers. Where are you staying? I'll send a car for you.'

'I'm staying right here,' said the professor.

---

[1] [World-view.]

[2] [My love-at-a-distance is as vital as your stalemated organisation is fossilised!!!]

And when he had brought his grip over, and dined luxuriously, and retired for the night, his dreamy blue eye sought inspiration from the mirror as he adjusted his nightcap.

'I wonder what frightened him,' said the professor, meditatively.

Robbing Miss Horniman

1

I am getting very tired of sitting in the Café Royal without Fée. However, she may be back any day now; and thank God! her health is all right. But people are pointing me out as the lonely poet, which I bar. It must be nearly six months. We had certainly been setting the pace even to Hilda Howard and Campbell and Izeh and John and Euphemia and Shelley and Little Billee and that crowd; and one day Fée just dropped. I took her round to old Jensen. Milk all day, said he, by the gallon; lie about on the grass; general massage an hour every day; no love-affairs; no books. When you can't stick it a day longer you'll know you're better. I gave her a monkey – just half my last thou. – and started to earn some more. I'm still starting. What the devil can I write about?

2

Talk of the devil, *dere diry*! Just as I wrote those words in came Harry Austin, and said he owed me a lunch. I let him pay.

Over the coffee he said: 'Do write me something, *cher maître*!'

'What?' said I.

'Oh, there's a story in that Spalding business, only the journalists have hacked it about. Do it like a tale, only stick to the facts.'

'How many words, and how many quid?' I asked him, as a business poet should.

'Fifty pounds,' said he; 'I'll trust you to do me your best; your wit must tell you how long to make it.' He left me a tenner on account, and went off. Jolly decent.

Well, here goes for the first draft: I'll call it

ROBBING MISS HORNIMAN.

3

The life of the little market town of Spalding in Lincolnshire is as flat as its situation among the fens. In consequence of this circumstance, death and its approaches do not seem to the inhabitants of any importance, since the states of life and death have no such sharp dividing line as in less favoured spots. Miss Anne Horniman, although quite an important inmate, if one may use the word, of Spalding, by reason of her considerable wealth, excellent family and personal refinement, aroused little attention by falling into a decline and going 'abroad' for her health. The town was, however, slightly shocked at hearing of her return, especially as the announcement came in the shape of the arrival of a brisk young architect from London, with orders to make the house up to date for her reception.

'Up to date,' thought Spalding dully, 'What's wrong with 1066?'

However, the activities of the newcomer were not unduly revolutionary. He merely knocked the two main rooms of the ground floor into one, installed an acetylene gas system, and turned the steps that led into the garden and orchard into an inclined plane by the application of a little cement.

He explained his object to the local builder. 'Miss Horniman is a permanent invalid,' he had said; 'she lives between her bed and her bath chair. So it must be easy to wheel her to and from the garden. There is just one other feature of the improvements; she is nervous of robbers, having lived for some years in South Africa; and she has asked me to establish a very complete and elaborate system of burglar alarms.' Ten days later the house was ready, and Miss Horniman arrived with her nurse.

She was a little old lady laid up in lavender from the early days of Queen Victoria, timid and yet positive in her manner, a gentlewoman from her neat bonnet and grey ringlets to the mittens on her wrists and ankles. She covered her poor thin body with a charming grey silk dress, and over her shoulders she wore a shawl of such lace as Venice used to make a century or so ago. The nurse was a stalwart woman, big yet gentle, as is needed where the patient has constantly to be lifted. Miss Horniman had written to the vicar of the parish, a chubby cheery old fellow, asking his assistance in finding servants. He had found her a capable cook, an industrious housemaid; also an honest yokel for the garden, and to wheel her chair should she deem it fit to venture far beyond the grounds of the house, which extended for about an acre, and were devoted to vegetables for use, and tulips for ornament, while some old apple trees served to combine profit with pleasure.

Miss Horniman welcomed the vicar to tea on the day after her arrival. 'I went to South Africa to seek health,' she said in her soft faint voice, 'but I was unsuccessful. So I thought that I would rather lay my bones beside those of my own people.'

'I trust indeed, under Providence,' replied the vicar, 'that the day may be far off for that; but we are all in His hands, dear lady. And we know that all things work together for good.'

But the old lady turned the subject to less distressing themes; she spoke almost brightly of her experiences in South Africa, where she had taken up the hobby of buying diamonds, and had indeed invested a great part of her fortune in them. She drew the attention of the vicar to a varnished chest that stood beside a walnut chiffonier. It was about eighteen inches square, and three feet high.

'Here is where I keep my toys,' she said to the clergyman; 'perhaps you would like to look at them?' She wheeled her chair slowly across, with the aid of her visitor. 'This case is of a special steel,' she explained; 'though thin, it would take a good deal of time and trouble to force it. But I am not afraid of thieves; surely there are none in dear old Spalding, of all places. And I have an efficient system of burglar alarms. Besides this,' she added with a tightening of her thin lips, which showed the vicar that the spirit of Lincolnshire, the last stronghold of resistance to the Normans, was far from being extinct even in this charming old maid, 'in South Africa one learns to protect oneself. Day and night for five years I have had this under my hand.' And she produced from her chair an exceedingly deadly cavalry revolver of old pattern. 'My hand and eye are still true,' she said softly, 'and I think I could hit an apple every time at thirty paces.' She proceeded to open her little safe. The vicar fairly gasped. Tray after tray of perfect shining stones! Each bore a ticket, with the name of the mine where it was found, the date of the finding, the date of the purchase, the price paid, and the name of the seller. The simplicity and beauty of the display reduced the vicar to admiring silence.

'In my will,' she said, as she shut up the trays again and closed the safe, 'I have provided that you shall have the contents of whichever tray you choose, towards the rebuilding of the church. You see, I have made you my partner,' she smiled gently, 'and I will ask you not to mention the existence of these stones to anybody.'

The vicar was overwhelmed; he gladly promised, and presently he took his leave.

The ladies of Spalding made haste – for Spalding! – to welcome the strayed wanderer home; but Miss Horniman was too feeble to exchange more than the few polite words necessary; she seemed to sink more rapidly than ever in the chill and damp of the fens. Certainly the visitors were disappointed; for she never referred in any way to her treasures, of which the jade Rumour had whispered a good deal more than was prudent. For though the vicar had loyally and sensibly held his tongue, he could hardly conceal his exultation, and in that suspicious population any manifestation of life appears eccentric, and due to some great matter.

Now as in Lincolnshire there is nothing to do, the minds of the people ponder incessantly and unfathomably, though with sobriety and even bradytudinity, so that before Miss Horniman had been home more than two months a connection had been established in the public mind between three things: her residence in South Africa, the diamond industry of that country, and her precautions against burglars. A genius for generalisations, named Abraham Perry, at last crystallised the sentiment of the public in one sparkling phrase: 'The old girl's house is chock-a-block o' di'man's,' he stated solemnly before closing time, one Saturday night, at the old 'Bull and Bush.'

As a matter of fact, the syllogism in question had been concluded several days before by cowans and eavesdroppers from London; for on that very night certain knights of the Jimmy, moving in the very best burglarious circles in London, made the first recorded attempt to rob Miss Horniman.

Only one of them was caught, for the Spalding police have to use motor-cycles to pursue a snail; but that one, having a .45 soft-nosed bullet in his hip-joint, was not able even to emulate the humblest creatures of Miss Horniman's garden.

It was expected that further attempts would be few, but this was not the case, though none were attended with quite such disaster as the first. However, Miss Horniman victoriously expelled all assaults without loss. But there are two ways of reducing a fortress. One is to batter down its defences; the other is to induce the garrison to surrender by fair words.

Now the attention of a certain Mr Gordon Leigh of Spalding was attracted by the fame of the adventure. He would have paid little heed to the gossip of the Lincolnshire peasants; but when the stocks of the railways serving Spalding bounded almost daily, owing to the popularity of the excursion in the Underworld of London, he concluded that so much smoke indicated the presence of fire; and he began to angle for an introduction to Miss Horniman.

Mr Gordon Leigh was a person of portly presence. He had amassed a considerable fortune in thirty years of pawn-broking in Conduit Street, London; and a great deal more in his secret trade as usurer. Once, however, he had lost a great deal of money; and that was by the failure of a bank. He had further observed, in common with many others, that those who had disregarded the plain warning of Holy Scripture, and put their faith in princes by investing in British Consols, had lost half their capital in about ten years, for no visible reason. But he had never heard of anybody losing money by keeping it, except the trifle of interest, two or three per cent, which seemed little enough to him who had made his fortune by lending at as many hundreds. So he took the good old way; he built a strong room in his house at Spalding, on his retirement from business, and kept all his money there in gold.

It may well be asked: why Spalding? The worthy man had a second passion in his life, almost rivalling his love of money; and the name of that passion was tulips. Now, outside Holland, there is but one soil in the world which will grow tulips to perfection; and Spalding is the centre of that well-dowered district.

Gordon Leigh had not spared money in the building of his strong room; there was none safer, no, not in London or New York; and he did not spare money on his hobby. Also, there is money in tulips.

But when it came to diamonds! He could smell a diamond across three counties when the wind was in the right direction. But he always took his profit at once when a diamond came into his hands; for he never knew whether de Beers might not suddenly unload and put a hole in the bottom of the market.

Such was the amiable and far-seeing individual who was warily and adroitly approaching Miss Horniman.

When the introduction was at last effected, through the good offices of the vicar, Miss Horniman proved unexpectedly cordial. Leigh had never been to South Africa, but many of his friends had been in the I. D. B. business, and he had a wealth of stories to exchange with the old lady. Their passion for tulips, too, was a bond. In short, the heir of all the Leighs (poll deed, ten pounds, and well worth it) got on much better with her than he had any just reason to expect. For in temperament they were decidedly opposite. Mr Gordon Leigh was a gross and florid person, thick-set and heavy-jowled, with a nose as fleshy and protuberant as Miss Horniman's was delicate, aristocratic and tip-tilted. However, as the novelists assure us, it is between two just such opposites that the spark of love frequently springs up. But let us not insist too closely upon electrical or chemical analogies.

Mr Gordon Leigh pursued his suit with extreme tact. He brought rare tulip bulbs; he read aloud to the old lady by the hour; he often made her simple meals brighter by his presence; and he never referred by so much as a wink to the rumours about treasure, save in the jocular way which had made the affair the staple jest of the district. It had become proverbial to announce the non-success of an enterprise by saying 'I've been robbing Miss Horniman!' It even became a catch-word in London itself. But one dark afternoon in December, after a peculiarly determined attempt on the previous night, the lady broached the subject herself.

'I don't see why I shouldn't treat you as a friend, Mr Leigh. You must be curious to see what it is that they are after.' And she wheeled over to the little safe and opened it. Nonchalantly she drew out tray after tray, and closed them again. 'This,' she said suddenly, picking out the central stone from the lowest drawer, 'is the best in the little collection.' She put it in his hands.

'Wonderful!' he exclaimed, and asked permission, readily accorded, to take it to the light. It was indeed a diamond! Mr Leigh looked at it with keen professional eyes; he even whipped out a glass which he had brought with him every day on the chance of this occasion. It was of the first water; cut in an unusual and most effective shape, it was the finest stone of its size he had ever seen. He would have been glad to lend a thousand pounds on it in his pawn-broking days. And it was only one of many! With many murmurs of congratulation, he returned the stone, and delicately transferred the conversation to tulips.

It was on the following afternoon that Miss Horniman fainted in her chair from weakness. Leigh saw his opportunity, and took it. When she recovered, she could doubt neither the refinement and respect of his conduct, nor the generous warmth of his affection. He did not press the advantage, and her maidenly spirit thanked him also for that courtesy. But on the Sunday following, after church, whither Mr Leigh had accompanied her, she asked him to stay for lunch, and after lunch, the day being bright and sunny, she ventured to wheel her chair into the garden.

'Alas!' she said, with ineffable sadness, looking upon the westering sun, 'it is the sunset of life for me.'

'Say not so, dear lady,' cried the now impetuous lover, 'please God, there are many years of life and happiness before you.'

'It cannot be, sir,' she answered simply, lowering her head. 'I am a doomed woman.'

'If you had someone to love you and care for you,' cried Leigh, ''twould be a new lease of life.'

'I pray you,' she answered, 'not to speak in this way to me; I will not pretend to be ignorant of your chivalrous attention; but I cannot accept it.'

However, Leigh pressed on, and won at last a promise to think of the matter at leisure. He explained that he was no fortune-hunter, that he had eighty thousand pounds in his strong room at Spalding.

'That is a great sum,' answered the invalid, 'it is more than all my pretty toys are worth. But I know your spirit,' she went on, 'it is a noble and chastened one. I could never suspect an unworthy motive in you, Mr Leigh.'

The lover went home in high spirits; he felt sure that she would yield. Ultimately she did so.

'I cannot be a true wife to you, Gordon,' she said, 'we must be resigned to the will of Heaven that we did not meet thirty years ago. But I offer you what I can, and it may be that Heaven will in some way ratify these true vows exchanged on earth.'

And thus the woman who had baffled the greatest crooks in South Africa and London stepped blindly into the net of the wilier scoundrel.

She was to live in Leigh's house, of course; it was far finer than her own, and he had made the necessary alterations for her convenience.

She sent over to his house only two trunks, for she needed few clothes, poor lady; but the little safe went with her on her chair to the church. She would not let it out of her sight, even with Leigh to take the responsibility for its safety. And indeed, the attendants at the wedding included a couple of private detectives paid by him to look out for the London contingent.

After the wedding they went to the house of the bridegroom. Leigh heaved a sigh of relief as he pushed to the door of the strong room the precious little safe.

'Now everything is in good keeping, little wife!' he cried cheerfully, 'I won't reveal the combination, even to you.'

It has previously been remarked that Mr Gordon Leigh had not neglected the study of Holy Scripture in the matter of putting trust in princes; but he should have gone further, and read more attentively that passage which advises the wayfaring man not to lay up treasure upon the earth, where rust and moth do corrupt, and where thieves break through and steal.

For the night had not passed without event. In the morning Mrs Leigh expressed a desire to see her diamonds; she wished to choose a brilliant for her husband's hand. But on arriving at the strong room, the door was found wide open; the little safe had disappeared bodily; and so had Mr Gordon Leigh's eighty thousand pounds.

The police were, of course, notified; London was telegraphed; everything possible was done; but to the hour of this writing no clue has been found.

I wish I could end my story here. But I must add that Leigh's behaviour was insufferably brutal. Marital recriminations became acute, though the bride's health hardly permitted her to raise her voice above a whisper. But she told the Scotland Yard people flatly that she had no evidence of the existence of the gold beyond her husband's word, that she believed the whole affair to be a plot between Leigh and one of his Illicit Diamond Buying Friends to rob her of her property. I doubt whether the Yard dissented very strongly from this view. But when the inspector had gone, Leigh said roughly: 'get out of here, you ——.' I shall not soil my pen with his epithet.

The poor lady burst into tears. Half fainting, she was wheeled back to her own house by the indignant nurse.

The next day the vicar called to condole with her – and incidentally, with himself.

'You shall not lose,' she said, 'by this affair. I shall see to it that on my death an equivalent sum reaches your fund. I have still some private fortune. As for me, after this loss, and what is more to me, this humiliation, I cannot remain in Spalding. I will rest my bones elsewhere. This blow has broken me.'

The good vicar did his best to cheer her.

'No,' she sighed, with yet a sweet and subtle smile that bore witness to her resignation to the will of heaven, 'no. I feel myself fading imperceptibly away.'

Here, in tragedy and pathos, ends the record of a true Englishwoman.

4

Virtue rewarded! I had just finished my diligent account when Fée came into the café. With her was our friend Sid Sloper, known to the world of racing as the Mite, in allusion to his stature, on the one hand, and his fondness for cheese, on the other. He shook hands with me; Fée embraced me before all the multitude.

'Journeys end in lovers' meetings,' she cried. 'Now, Sid, you be off; don't dare miss the boat!

'He's riding at Monte Carlo,' she explained, when he had gone. 'But you, sir? Did I kiss you too soon? Have you been faithful to me?'

'I have, Cynara, in my fashion,' I evaded.

'Well, I've been faithful in the old fashion, by the simple process of fidelity,' she laughed. 'And, I say, let's get married this very afternoon as ever is, and go off round the world!'

'We will not,' I said. 'I don't know what you've been doing, but I've been "robbing Miss Horniman." Ten is all I have in the world!'

'You shouldn't have robbed the poor old lady,' she pouted. 'Now, I did better. I *was* Miss Horniman!'

'Your rest-cure seems to have done you no good!'

'I'm serious, boykins dear. You know what the doctor said – milk – complete rest – massage – no love – no books. You see, Miss Horniman really happened to be my aunt, and she left me the house when she died, two years ago. So I made up like her, and had duplicate safes, one with a nice nest for the Mite, the other with trays and paste diamonds, and the one real one that Euphemia lent me to fool Mr Gordon Leigh, of whose little idiosyncrasies I had wind. So all I had to do was to get Sid into the strong room; at night he just walked out, and let in two pals, and they took all the gold to a car, and O! to see London once again! They took a quarter; I've got ten thousand in notes sewn in my frock; and the rest is in your name in about twenty different banks. So come along right down to the Strand and marry me, dear! It's not tainted money!'

'The money's all right,' I said, 'though I must say it's playing it rather low down to spring all this Wooden-Horse–Ali Baba stuff on us in the twentieth century.'

'You told me to read the classics!' she chirped. 'Now for the *Wedding March*.'

'But I can't marry you – you're the wife of that ass Leigh!'

'Wife – I don't think!' she laughed, dragging me from my settee. 'I kept my fingers crossed!'

I felt that the Café Royal was no place for a difficult legal argument with one's intended wife. Time enough for that on the way to Biskra!

The Ideal Idol

TWO STORIES IN ONE, BUT WITH ONLY ONE MORAL

Reggie Van Rensesslaer was forty-two and a bachelor. For just half his life he had been looking for a wife, and he had turned down a thousand promising opportunities, just because he was particular. He was handsome and distinguished above all men; he had a nice little fortune in copper and the control of one of the biggest banks in New York. His manners were superfine triple X, formed in the best universities, and later in those foreign courts whither he had gone as a diplomatist. He was crazy to marry, but he had his pick of Europe and America. But he had not found his ideal. He wished a woman of birth, breeding, and fortune comparable to own; she must be beautiful and brilliant, yet modest and domesticated; and there were various other points, hardly worth discussion on this page, yet vitally important to the happiness of our gay and gallant hero. There had been several near-engagements; but sooner or later something had always turned up to prevent the wedding bells from ringing. It was by pure accident that Reggie discovered that the Marquise de Vaudeville had a bunion on the third toe of her left foot; the Gräfin von Solingen was barred by an unfortunate habit of lisping; the Princess Politzsky had once smoked a cigarette; Lady Viola Vere de Vere failed to laugh at one of Reggie's puns; Señorita de Sota had a question mark on part of her escutcheon in the earlier half of the twelfth century – there was always something.

But in the winter of 1916 the ideal idol came to Washington. This time there could be no doubt. Flossie Russell was of the most aristocratic of all the families that came over in the *Mayflower*; through her mother she was allied with the royal families of half the countries of Europe; her father controlled most of the railroads and shipping and mines in the United States, owned two of the largest packing houses in Chicago, and was one of the biggest men in the Corn Trust.

Incidentally, he had used his leisure hours in making an immense fortune in munitions. It would endanger the reason of the printer were I to describe her beauty; and as for her manners, it would endanger my own reason to attempt the task in detail. I will only say, in a word, they were American manners.

It was at White Sulphur that she and Reggie met. Swift but thorough investigation on his part assured him that at last he had found his destined bride. To avoid precipitation, he determined to take a long motor ride by moonlight – alone. Absorbed in his own thoughts, he failed to notice an old woman who was crossing the road with a bundle of sticks in her arm. He knocked her down and broke her leg. The automobile swerved violently, and he was obliged to pull up in order to avoid running into a tree. It stuck him that his number might have been seen, and with admirable prudence got out of the car and returned to where the old woman was lying, intending to compensate her with some small change which he was wont to carry on his person precisely in view of such emergencies as this.

'I see,' said she, 'that you are one of Nature's noblemen! Chivalrous as you are handsome, you should also be fortunate. Take this black stone – for I am a witch! And if ever you should be in despair, dash it upon the ground; then you shall have your heart's desire.'

Reggie, charmed with her courtesy, was seized with an impulse of mad generosity, added a dollar bill to his already noble largesse, and even promised to stop at the next village, and tell someone of the accident.

The next morning dawned sunny and glorious; all nature seemed to conspire to aid our hero in his suit. After lunch he sought the fair Flossie; together in the exhilarating air they rode for many miles. They stopped on a great height to admire the romance; he seized the moment. 'Will you be mine?' he murmured.

'Well,' answered Flossie, brightly, 'I guess not. You're about twenty years too old.'

Words cannot depict the rage and horror of our hero. Like a madman he thrust in the clutch; the auto leapt forward; he never stopped until – the following morning – he found himself held up in 42nd Street by the wreck of a Fifth Avenue stage and a lorry. At that moment he realised what the despair was. As in a dream, he pulled out the black stone and dashed it on the ground.

When he raised his eyes, wonder of wonders! They fell upon the ideal idol of his dreams. It was another Flossie, but a Flossie raised in every point to the twenty-seventh power. Her name – as the event showed – was Nina Yolande de Montmorency de Carbajal y Calvados.

This time there was no hitch. The most rigid investigation proved her as pure as she was fair, as rich as she was well born; in short, she was it. Even her modesty could not withstand even for an hour the impetuous advances of our hero; and when he said, only a fortnight after their first meeting, 'Let us be married next week in the Cathedral,' she replied, blushing divinely and with downcast eyes, 'Why not this afternoon, at the City Hall?'

No sooner said than done. A sumptuous banquet succeeded the ceremony; intoxicated with champagne and with delight, the happy couple retired to their luxurious suite in the Hotel Evangeline. Reggie Van Rensesslaer locked the door.

As it happened, however, the Hotel Evangeline was an unusually family hotel, and on the dressing table was a copy of the Holy Scriptures, placed there by the Gideons, whoever they may be.

Instantly that her eyes fell upon the book, the bride uttered a piercing scream. A moment later, and she had disappeared. In her place, smiling and bowing, stood Mephistopheles himself!

'Young man!' he said to the astounded Reggie, 'learn that humanity implies imperfection; those who, not content with the ordinary limitations of life, demand perfection, are liable to find the ideal idol an illusion created by the Devil. However, you have willed it; so if you would be so kind as to throw that book out of the window, I will turn back into Nina Yolande (and all the rest of it) and we can get to bed. It has been a tiring day.'

Reggie's answer has not been recorded; but six months later we hear of him on his honeymoon. The happy lady was a mulatto widow of forty-eight with three children, a slight spinal curvature, a cast in her remaining eye, six gold teeth and the manners of a dock labourer. And a jolly good wife she makes him!

Face

I

'There is the symbol of your race,' said Huang Ming to his friend Andrew Ker, pointing to Edinburgh Castle, that rose like an angry lion above Princes Street. 'You have taken the thistle for your emblem, and the motto *Nemo me impune lacessit*.[1] That is the secret of Scottish success: endure no insult, but avenge it at whatever price. In China we have a similar pride; we must "save face," even if we die for it; but we do not dominate the world as you do, because we refuse to injure others.'

Andrew Ker received the compliment to his nation with unaffected pleasure. He was very devoted to his distinguished friend. Huang Ming was a pure Chinese of the most illustrious descent. His father was Viceroy of Szechuan Province. But he was also of individual distinction, having taken the highest medical honours in Berlin; subsequently, he had specialised in psychotherapeutics both at Nancy and the Salpêtrière. He had come to Edinburgh to complete his knowledge by an advanced course in surgery, and incidentally to learn the language. He was boarding with the widowed mother of Andrew, who was still a student of medicine, in his fifth year. Proud as the Scot was of his long line of ancestors, with their high tradition of aristocracy, he could not but envy the superior manners of the Chinese doctor.

The idea of any other relation than that of friendship had never even entered the mind of Andrew Ker. Nor had his sister Madeline any suspicion of what transformation had been wrought by her beauty in the mind of Huang. He gave no hint of serious attention to any subject outside his profession, and contented himself with a sort of unassuming demonstration of his superior excellence in every act which he condescended to perform. He was peculiarly assiduous in his treatment of Mrs

---

[1] [No one provokes me with impunity.]

Ker, who suffered greatly from nervous headaches. By skilful treatment he had reduced their frequency very greatly, as well as their urgency. He was able to cut short even the severest attack by a few soothing words, accompanied by gentle gestures which seemed to combine the beneficent effects of mesmeric passes with those of massage.

To one of his progressive intelligence it was naturally clear that medical science could develop only through great advances in physiology, and the complete unification of that science with psychology. His constant effort was to discover means by which various organs of the body could be studied separately; he was already noted for his experiments with curare. His improvements had made it possible to carry out the now classical researches of Menzies and Moulton. It had always been simple, by the administration of curare, to paralyse the muscular system completely, while leaving all other functions normal; but unfortunately the cardiac and respiratory muscles were paralysed with the rest, and the animal had to be kept alive by artificial breathing during the whole duration of the experiment. Huang had found that by the injection of a mixture of strychnine, cocaine and digitalin into certain of these muscles, they were enabled to combat the action of the curare in an entirely local and very feeble manner.

Just a flutter of life was maintained, but strong enough and long enough to enable the patient to survive. He had himself been the first human subject of his experiment, which had been successful beyond expectation. Others had been somewhat reluctant to lend themselves to Science, but Andrew Ker had been enthusiastic. About once a month, for it was not prudent to repeat the operation too frequently, he gave up an afternoon to the work.

Huang's room was fitted up as a laboratory; a narrow plank in a recess, supported on trestles, was the only bed he would use. 'Ignorance,' said he to Mrs Ker, who protested in her kindly Scottish way, 'is the hardest of all beds!'

His ardour and devotion were indeed in all ways incomparable. He had taken down the old Moorish lamp that hung from a stout hook screwed into the central rafter of the room, and installed a weighing-machine. To his precise mind a quarter of a pound too much meant idleness and fat, a quarter of a pound too little meant overwork and exhaustion; and he regulated his diet, his labour, and his exercise entirely by the daily report of the machine.

It is probable that he planned his campaign against the fortress of Madeline's heart with very much the same well-calculated ardour. At one time he would astonish the girl with stories of the viceregal court in Szechuan; at another he would overwhelm her with his lofty aspirations towards the release of humanity from the fetters of ignorance and ill-ordered desire; at another time he would kindle the longing for travel within her by showing her photographs and pictures of the Yangtze basin, and of Szechuan itself, perhaps the loveliest of all the provinces of China. In short, while guarding assiduously against any suspicion of ulterior purpose on his part, he imbued her mind with ideals of rank, wealth, beauty, power and knowledge, identifying himself subtly with those glowing abstractions. He was at no pains to show himself the courteous and honourable cavalier, for perfect breeding was implicit in his ancestry for generations; and he was equally distinguished in athletics, whose appeal to woman is so irresistible, playing cricket, golf and football with equal skill and vigour. He thus succeeded in establishing in the mind of Madeline Ker a sort of affectionate reverence, which evidently needed but the spark struck from opportunity to blaze into a soul-fulfilling love.

2

Doctor Huang Ming had been with the Kers for nearly two years before he reaped his reward. It was spring; Madeline had suffered from nervous perturbations of an obscure sort for a month or more; the Chinese had treated her by suggestion, and restored her to the perfection of health and good spirits. It was then that the girl began to wonder whether her feeling for him was limited to gratitude and admiration.

An accident determined her to consult the experience of her mother. It fell thus. During the experiments on curare of which her brother was the subject, he was unable to speak or move, although in full possession of all his other faculties, for about an hour after the experiment proper was concluded. This being a period of great tedium, it had been determined to enliven it by the introduction of Madeline, and occasionally of Mrs Ker. Sometimes they would engage in lively conversation; sometimes Madeline would read aloud. On the occasion of which we are about to speak she had been reading, came to the end of the story, jumped up, crying 'Now let's talk!' and as was her frequent custom, threw herself into the seat of the doctor's weighing machine.

As chance would have it, the spring broke, and she was thrown to the ground. Huang picked her up immediately with the polite regret and the swift-skilled scrutiny which his qualities as a man and a physician enabled him so admirably to command. But Madeline, finding herself lifted in his arms, suddenly fainted. When she came to herself, she understood that a crisis had occurred in her emotional nature, and, excusing herself, ran to seek her mother, that she might gain counsel from experience, and formulate as a conscious thought that which was but a disturbance nameless and inchoate in the subliminal sphere of her intelligence. Mrs Ker was not unskilled in the emotions of the heart; she divined instantly the nature of the psychosis which troubled her daughter. 'Child!' she exclaimed, 'I have long feared this moment. You are in love with Dr Huang.'

The words came to Madeline as a surprise and a shock, but only served to reinforce her. The identification of the obscure catastrophe in her being with all she had read of love and of romance came as a revelation. In a moment, so to speak, she had become one with all the heroines of history and of song.

'You understand, of course,' continued Mrs Ker, 'that it is your duty to combat the feeling which instinct has aroused within you. In the Pentateuch we are repeatedly warned against mixed marriages; the later history of Israel, and the experience of our own times, bears out to the full the righteousness and wisdom of God in establishing this commandment. In the circumstances, I will not speak at once to Dr Huang, who, I doubt not, is insensible to the foolish passion which he has inspired. I will allow you a period of three weeks in which to make yourself mistress of those inclinations which, unless conquered (by the Grace, and with the aid, of God), are capable of destroying the soul, and, by consequence, the body.'

To so just, reasonable and moderate an adjuration Madeline could only reply by golden looks and respectful assent.

But the conquest of herself proved a more difficult matter than she had supposed. The crystallisation in words of her long latent emotions seemed to intensify them to the utmost. Night after night she lay awake, clutching the sheets and gnawing the pillow, saying over and over to herself, 'I am in love with Dr Huang.'

The physician gave no sign of any perception of the cause of the trouble; his demeanour was as studiously correct as ever; but as the girl was patently in a highly nervous condition, he exerted all his hypnotic skill to restore her equilibrium. Mrs Ker herself suffered acutely to watch her daughter's struggles; and the ministrations of the doctor were frequently required for her also.

When the appointed period had elapsed, Madeline, although decid-edly relieved by the care and skill of Huang, was yet obliged to confess to her mother that she was still in love. Mrs Ker resolved to acquaint the doctor with the situation, and suggest to him the propriety of a change of residence. In the absence of the beloved object, she argued, time may be trusted to expunge its traces.

She approached the doctor that same afternoon. 'I fear,' she began, 'that your kindness to my daughter, much as we all appreciate it, is equally the cause as the cure of her affection. Dr Huang, we all like you, and we all respect you; but my unfortunate Madeline, imprudent as are too often the young, has permitted that liking and that respect to deepen into a feeling at once more tender and more fatal.'

The Chinese interupted. 'Before you speak further, madam, let me ask whether you blame me for the circumstance.'

'If I blame you, I blame only your excellences and your virtues.'

'I may then say what I have hitherto concealed, from motives of delicacy as from those of a sense of what I already owe to your hospitality. I have never loved hitherto; my work has absorbed me heart and soul; but I love your daughter. My father is one of the greatest men in China, and I can make Miss Ker one of the highest ladies in the Kingdom of Flowers. Her influence as my wife must be as a very beacon to my countrymen. Not only personal but political and even loftier considerations urge your consent to that proposal which I now formally proffer. Madam, I solicit the honour of your daughter's hand in marriage.'

'Dr Huang,' replied the widow, 'no one can be more sensible than myself of the honour which you do us by your offer; no one will more willingly testify to the propriety of your conduct and to the nobility of your disposition. But the primary fact of race remains as as inexorable bar. It is with the sincerest regret, believe me, that I feel obliged to return an unfavorable answer.'

'Madam,' replied the Chinese, impassive as ever, 'I had anticipated no less from the fine qualities of your heart and mind. Wounded as I must be by your refusal, allow me to say that its manner stirs in me a reverence for your very inflexibility itself. I bow to your decision. I have left my ancestors too long unhonoured. In four days I make the last of our series of experiments with my good friend your son, for whose preferment in his profession I shall labour while I live. I will then make immediate arrangements to remove to the palace of my father. And I ask your pardon that, although inadvertently, I have brought misfortune on your house. In the meanwhile, let us not speak again of this.'

'You are a thousand times right,' answered Mrs Ker. 'I shall rejoice to say that, although barred by the hand of Nature, or rather, by the command of God, from the formation of those ties of family affection which seal respect and friendship, I shall rejoice (let me repeat) to say that the truest gentleman I ever knew was a Chinese physician.'

Huang could not answer but by placing the hand of the widow respectfully, almost reverently, to his lips.

3

The room of Dr Huang Ming was tidier even than its wont. Only on the bureau remained a few papers which he could throw into a bag at the last moment. He was sitting at the bureau, making notes of the final experiment.

'Well,' said he, brightly, to Andrew, who lay upon the operating table with a faint fixed smile upon his lips, and his eyes alight with intelligence, 'that concludes everything. So we have made one more step toward the eternal city of wisdom, piety and peace.'

The young Scot, unable to move or to speak, showed, in the purely physical aspect of him, that these words failed to engage his full interest. Huang watched him closely. Andrew's eyes were fixed upon the door; for, as it seemed to him, it opened. Mrs Ker advanced into the room, followed closely by Madeline. Both were poised on tiptoe, as if they feared to be discovered. Neither spoke, yet each moved with the utmost rapidity and precision, as if they were going through a well-rehearsed performance on the stage. Yet the procedure was extraordinary beyond dream. Andrew, watching every movement, concluded that a new action of curare had been developed; he was acutely conscious of hallucination, and burningly eager for the passing away of the action of the poison, so that he might report it to his friend.

He saw Mrs Ker go to a drawer, and take out a coil of rope used by him and the doctor on some of their climbing expeditions with the Scottish Mountaineering Club. Madeline, drawing a chair and table to the centre of the room, took part of this rope, and, climbing upon the table and then upon the chair which she had placed upon it, passed it over the hook from which the weighing machine had been removed by Dr Huang in the course of his packing. Meanwhile Mrs Ker made a running noose in the rope. Madeline then removed the chair and table to their original positions in the room. Of all this the Chinese doctor took not the smallest notice. It confirmed Andrew in his belief that he was hallucinated. He watched the scene with scepticism.

The girl then approached Dr Huang Ming, and drew him to the middle of the room. Mrs Ker slipped the noose over his head, and pulled on the rope; while her daughter supported his weight by clutching his legs. When his feet were a yard from the ground, Mrs Ker fastened the rope to the head of the bedstead, and Madeline released him. Huang made not the smallest resistance; and the women, having thus deliberately hanged him, went quietly from the room.

An hour later Andrew Ker found that he could move his fingers. Power over the wrists and elbows followed; then the facial muscles were released from their paralysis, and he began at once to speak. 'Huang, dear man,' he cried, 'I've had a most extraordinary hallucination; I saw mother and Madeline come in and hang you – and I still see your body hanging – and I can't see you!'

There was no answer. Ker turned his head; the room was certainly vacant. A few moments later he regained control of his legs. He got off the couch, and went to the body. It answered his touch; it was a real body – and it was already cold.

The student now understood that the curare had definitely paralysed his brain. He was not merely insane visually, but totally. His one thought was to seek Huang; the man who had brought about this state was surely the one to relieve it. He went downstairs. In the parlour Mrs Ker was sitting at tea with Madeline.

'You're late, Andrew!' cried his mother, 'and where's the doctor?'

'He must have gone back to the hospital,' said the lad, mastering himself with a tremendous effort. 'I'll go and look for him. No; I don't want tea, thanks, mother dear!'

At the hospital there was no news of Huang; Andrew determined to consult an alienist at once. He caught Dr Simmons, the Visiting Medical Officer, just as he was leaving.

'You are an excellently sane young man' pronounced the specialist after an examination, 'except on the one point of this hallucination. That was evidently the result of your experiment with curare; don't do it again! Meanwhile, take me home with you; we will put an end to the bogle. When you find Dr Huang alive and well, you will soon forget that you thought you saw him hanged!'

A quarter of an hour's brisk walk brought them to the house. On the steps stood a wizened little old man, a shrewd rat of a lawyer named Watt who, as luck would have it, was well known to both of them.

'Hullo!' cried the alienist, 'what brings you to this gate, man?'

The lawyer stayed his hand upon the knocker. 'I represent the executors of the late Dr Huang Ming,' he said solemnly as the others joined him, 'who, as I understand, is lying dead in this house.'

Simmons and Ker gazed at each other in the extreme of consternation. 'For God's sake, the key!' cried Simmons, recovering himself. Ker opened the door with trembling hand; the three men ran up the stairs. There, sure enough, was the corpse of the Chinese as Ker had left it.

'But it's impossible in nature,' stammered Ker. 'My mother! my sister! the gentlest creatures on God's earth, to have deliberately hanged our dearest friend!'

'Tut, lad, you're dreaming still,' said Simmons, sharply. 'It's a clear case of suicide. He had only to stand on a chair and kick it over. There must be an inquest, of course; but I'll certify the cause of death.'

'But where's the chair?' broke out the little lawyer.

'Here!' replied the alienist, sternly, picking one from the wall side and throwing it over, about a yard from the feet of the corpse.

'Man!' said Watt, 'this is a suspeecious business.'

'It is that,' replied Simmons, 'and I don't know all of it. But, in God's name, the less said the better!'

'The deed maun ha' been planned.'

'Surely so,' answered the physician, 'and if you wish to make a full enquiry, let us begin. How was it that you were at the door to take possession of the body within two hours of the death?'

'O that's a' richt; I had wurrd fower days bye!'

Simmons looked at his old friend, as much as to say: 'Does that really make it all so simple and straightforward?'

Watt rubbed his jaw. 'I doot ye're i' the richt, Jock; the least said the soonest mended.'

During this dialogue Andrew stood dazed. The alienist, however, was not idle. He examined the corpse with the most minute scrutiny; and, to his unutterable horror, Andrew saw him detach a number of long hairs from the trousers of the Chinese. His mind was so utterly paralysed by the impossibilities of the case, where the evidence of sense, reinforced at every step, was at grips with the psychological experience of a life-time, that he literally ceased to think. As the conversation terminated, he heard himself, as one far-off, echoing in a hollow voice: 'The least said the soonest mended.'

So nothing transpired at the inquest. 'Suicide while of unsound mind' was quite long enough epitaph for any Chinaman in the minds of a Scottish jury; and the body of Huang, who had honoured his ancestors, went to join them in the sacred soil of China.

4

Andrew Ker made the discovery that hell is in the heart. The life of the family was broken up entirely; he, who (as he thought) knew all, said nothing to his mother and sister of the frightful scene that he had witnessed.

Out of sheer need of distraction, he forced himself to redouble his studies; and he passed his final examinations with distinction. The effort ended, he sank into apathy. Mrs Ker did not seem to have suffered beyond the natural shock incidental to a suicide in the house; but Madeline was utterly broken. She became pale and listless, sat hour after hour at the piano, beginning one piece after another, and dropping her hands each time after the first few bars.

The moment came when Andrew could not bear the situation. He resolved to have the matter out with Madeline. He could only suspect one thing; imagine some hideous wrong that might demand (in the sight of the stern Scottish puritan) such vengeance as he had seen. But in that case, why had not Huang resisted? Or was his vision, as Simmons pretended to believe, partial hallucination? That hypothesis did not touch the question: what was killing Madeline before his very eyes?

'Girl!' he said, one day after breakfast, 'come up to Arthur's Seat; it's a glorious day.' She pleaded weariness; Andrew insisted.

On the summit they sat down to take breath. The lad put his arm about his sister. 'You're ailing,' he said, softly; 'and it's the mind, not the body. You'd better tell me the whole story. I know what happened; tell me why it happened.'

Madeline broke down in a flood of tears. Presently: 'I loved him. Mother refused our marriage because of the difference of race. He killed himself for love of me.'

'I was awake,' replied her brother, 'I watched every movement in the room. Is that your last word?'

The girl still sobbed: 'He killed himself for love of me. I loved him.'

Was she lying? Could she have assisted unconsciously in that ghastly ritual? Could Huang have hypnotised the women? Absurd. Had he such power, what easier than to force a consent to the marriage? The darkness was deeper than before.

Acting under the impulse of an uncontrollable emotion, Ker sprang to his feet, and walked he knew not whither. When his mind cleared, he found himself in Leith, among the ships.

'Ahoy there! What's the game?' was the word that wakened him. He looked up to see a bearded skipper scowling over the bulwark of a big steamer.

'Take me somewhere!' said Andrew, 'I'll work my passage!'

'Not much!' said the sailor, 'got no use for anybody but a doctor. Ours fell overboard, drunk, in last night's fog. Dirty swab!'

'That's funny,' said Andrew, 'you're my man. It's just Providence! I've got one of the best and freshest diplomas in this University. If you'll only ship me somewhere where the wind will blow my mind clear of memories!'

'Come aboard and sign on! The North Sea's the place you need!'

The next morning found Andrew still pacing the ship's deck. But stormy weather, and the cares of his work, which chanced to be onerous, including a broken leg, a couple of smashed ribs, and a severe case of scalding, took his mind to more wholesome channels.

At Petrograd they picked up a British Consul who was returning from Odessa to take up a new post. With this man Ker struck up a warm friendship. In the course of talk, it appeared that the Consul had spent ten years in China. The old agony seized Andrew; he seized the opportunity to pour out the vials of his woe.

'I don't see much mystery,' said the Consul. 'The man had got hypnotic control over the women; they obeyed; and they have no memory of what they did.'

'But why in Heaven's name not use the power to gain his end? My mother could have been brought to consent just as easily as to hang him!'

'You don't understand the Chinese mind. An insult had been put upon him. He would no more have married your sister after that than I would marry my dog! He had to avenge himself. He had only to kill himself in your house to cause his spirit to haunt you.'

'But he was a man of science.'

'He was a Chinaman. My ten years taught me to think that their wisdom may not be altogether the folly our cocksureness calls it. Look how effectively he has done his work! His bringing them in as agents, and you as witness, was a master-stroke. What hell you have all suffered! Indeed he has avenged himself – and his spirit has haunted you – in a sense quite real enough for his purpose. Also – as we say in China – he has "saved his face."'

'Thank God!' burst out the young surgeon, 'I shall clear up the whole thing the minute I get home. Thank God! The fiend shall yet be conquered.'

But when Andrew Ker reached home, he found that – two days earlier – his sister had thrown herself from Salisbury Crags.

Which Things are an Allegory

The little black demon sat in his corner and grinned. Outside the toads held ghastly revel over that thing, that thing unholy, that lay in the shadow of the old cathedral, that thing so lately a living, loving creature and now a blackened, swollen and already rotting corpse. And it lay in the shadow of the old cathedral, and the little black demon sat in his corner, in the red light of a dying fire, and smacked its fleshless lips and grimaced and aped and gibbered and grinned. And then it laughed out loud and shrunk back frightened at its own hellish mirth. And the thick black London fog shut all the mystery in with a horrid pall.

There came the morning, if we call it morning when the black only fades to an orange hue, a sickly yellow hue, the hue of the dead, and even under the shadow of the cathedral there came a man in blue. And the thing was found.

And men came stealing through the midday murk and bore it through the crowded streets, the streets where men smile with black hate beneath the mask, the streets where no honest man can live, no pure woman eke out her daily bread, where the Devil is crowned king under his best-loved name – the name of Gold. And the liars that minister to their thirst for news broke through all rule, and told the truth about this thing. And they called it Murder. As if Murder were new in London, where every young life's Hope is stamped out under the golden hoof of Mammon – not once a day, nor twice.

And lo! the orange is become black again, and the streets of the City are deserted. And the little black demon gibbered in his corner and laughed and now arose and went out. And he grinned hideously on his dear sisters as he twisted through the Haymarket and marked the putrefaction beneath their paint and the Death beneath their dye. And he chuckled as he passed his dear brothers and saw them stagger through the by-ways. Ha! how he gloated.

And now he is in an alley bleak and lone and the fog is thicker and darker than before. And silently he dances – yes! he dances now – he is so glad! – down the streets and calls a woman to him that stands there in the shadow. And she comes and he leaps on her and licks her with that black tongue that foams with a foul sweat. And she falls still in the shadow. And he licks and still licks with that black tongue and the clothes rot from her as it touches them. And he licks and still licks while the corpse swells to a black putrid mass three times the size God made it, sprinkled with leprous patches of a dead white. And he has finished, and the toads crawl out and sit upon her and hold a ghastly revel. And the black fog is over all. And the little black devil is in his corner and still sat and gibbered.

And this happened day by day, and the people were afraid. And the liars wrote many lies and gave much advice so quaintly worded by their art that nothing or anything might be understood by it. And the little black devil sat in his corner still and grinned.

And then after seven days nothing more happened. And the liars forgot and wrote new lies about other things. And so the world went on.

Now there was a man in this city who was much honoured. For his name was noble and his money measureless. But he had no character and less virtue. So for these qualities he was much esteemed. And he knew also a woman whose name was not noble, who had no money, but whose character and virtue were even as his. And the generous world thought that the last good thing might outweigh the other two for she, with it, could borrow a noble name and gain much money also. And this indeed she did, and was much esteemed of all men. But the women hated her.

Now for a long time had she held this nobleman in her thrall, but he (having no virtue of any sort) grew tired of her. And his friends said 'Get rid of this woman, but shabbily, so that you may be the more esteemed by all men and all shall be well.' For the men of London think that, by reason of the fog, the Eye of God seeth not the deeds that are done in London.

And so he went and took another woman to him. But she, the first, went to her Father, and did consult. And he, from the flames everlasting, bid her be of good cheer. And the room was dark and the woman grew cold and shrank now into a corpse, nor was any breath left in her. And her heart sprang out and arose and went into the outer room. And that black corpse that lay in the shadow of St Paul's had been the rival of her, and was now – and again some other child of hate, and again even for seven days. And after seven days the heart came back and entered again into her and the life came into her again and she arose and went out and so lived on.

Now it came to pass that the year passed by until the day before the anniversary of the first day of this. And she was merry at supper and grew drunken. And being maddened, she passed out into the street and began to rave in the market-place and tore her clothes. And the man in blue came to her and took her. For the men of London do all drink, and the women also. But they say outwardly that it is a horrid thing and so appoint a punishment for the poor who are drunken in the street. But for the rich the man in blue procureth a cab that he may be driven home. And this man in blue that met the woman knew not that she was rich and so forced her to come with him.

And the morning came and she was brought before him who was to judge her. But he was late, having been himself drunken the night before, and having had a headache in consequence. But at last he came and spake loud and virtuously, even giving a long moral lecture on the vice of drink. But while he yet spake, the woman grew cold and shrank up and now there was no life left in her, even as before. And the liars wrote much of this. But her heart had sprung out as before and went about with its black tongue, licking and slaying. And the liars wrote much of this also.

And so seven days passed and the woman was buried. And over her they signed the Cross. And the nobleman knew that it was she and over her grave he raised a cross of marble.

And at the end of the seven days the little black devil ceased his gibbering and came and sought her. But he found her not, for when he came to the grave he might not pass the cross. So he wandered up and down in unclean places and sought rest and found it not. And he went to the Patriarch of the fallen of London. And he was sad for, he said, 'this child of mine has grown to my will and there is nothing left for me to do. I am not needed here.'

'Let us flee,' said the little black demon gibbering and grimacing again, 'let us flee away even to the nearest place we may.'

'Yes,' howled that old Patriarch, lashing a forked tail with a horrid thud, 'let us out of this fog.' For the thick black fog still hung down over all the city. 'Let us to the nearest place where we may find some good we may corrupt.'

And they arose and went through the black streets and away, away. And they fled very far.

The Crime of the Impasse de l'Enfant Jésus

I

Huysbroeck the painter sat in his studio. It was a disgusting world: Red Thérèse had demanded her week's money, the little savage! Ah, but her curling ashen blonde hair; her dead white face, and its thin splash of red; her animal lips, and the strong white teeth of her! Her supple muscular body, that he so loved to paint! Yet because she demanded her week's money, he had turned her out of the studio.

He had – yes, he had struck her. Only with a paintbrush (for look you! reader, this Huysbroeck was a weak man), but yet a blow. The paint – *terre verte* – had stained her bare shoulder; she would not let him cleanse it. 'I know something to wipe that well away,' she had snarled, caught up her shawl, and run down the stairs. Bah! She would come back.

But – would he be there? The outlook was not promising for the painter.

To look at the studio one would not have guessed his embarrassment. True, the quarter is not fashionable; the *impasse* is the haunt of characters dubious and worse; but the house stood alone, lofty and commodious, well-appointed in every respect. The studio was a model of luxury; money could do no more. That money, having supplied the studio, could not supply the painter, was not the fault of money's quantity, but of its quality. Money cannot buy genius or intelligence.

Arsène Huysbroeck was a really bad painter. Years of copying the most horrible chromolithographs could not have taught any ordinary painter the fatuous smoothness of his canvases. It was a very genius of badness that informed his work. So too the shoddy sentimentality of his subjects, his habit of making his pictures speak – either to tell a complete *Bow Bells* novelette to preach a prig's sermon or to ask an absurd question as to its own meaning – all these things endeared him to the highest authorities on art. Almost alone among French painters, his works were extremely popular in England. The bob-a-nob exhibition in Bond Street was a permanent feature of the landscape. Mr M.H. Spielmann had put the seal on his fame by some discreet epigram about combining the noble enthusiasms of Sir Noel Paton and the artistic restraint of the Honourable John Collier.

'How true!' thought the suburbs. 'How choicely expressed!' said Bayswater. Park Lane had him in to paint the already too much painted.

He was known, too, as the perpetrator of the portrait of ex-President Sisse, whose term at the Elysée had so tragically and mysteriously closed. Huysbroeck had been a genuine mourner at the great funeral; for in Sisse he had lost an intimate friend and generous patron. In certain obscure ways he had repaid his benefactor; the President had found him a useful tool in various affairs – hostile rumour said, affairs so shady that the great man himself could not appear in them.

After the President's death commissions had not been quite so frequent. Expenses had increased. Madame Huysbroeck had presented him with two more children; and the painter cursed the name of Zola. A book like *Fécondité* ought to be suppressed. Pornography! Filth! and they would take this dog's bones to the Panthéon! Freemason! Jew! *Canaille!*[1]

An Italian gentleman living in Rome drew a regular income from our painter, thanks to the very vagueness of the threat, for Huysbroeck maintained in his own soul a skilful torturer. Zélie's milliner was really too outrageous, and Madame Huysbroeck's name was Aline.

I must think, he said aloud, throwing down the papers he had been morosely studying, I must think of a jolly good lie!

(I believe I mentioned that Huysbroeck was a weak man.)

2

As he sat moodily revolving the possibilities of the situation the door opened and his family appeared. Madame Dupont, his mother-in-law, was a cunning old peasant woman from Rouen, her blank eyes beady and bright, her face a mass of wrinkles; all the art of the beauty doctor and the milliner – who had worked with set teeth at it! – had failed to persuade those features to resemble the ideal combination of a young coquette at the Bal Tabarin with a duchess of the *ancienne régime*.

Madame Huysbroeck followed her into the studio. In great contrast to her mother, she was a plump, fluffy blonde, considerably above the average height. She was dressed gorgeously in a broidered walk-

---

[1] [Scoundrel!]

ing costume of dove-coloured cloth with a hem of black and scarlet braid, echoed by similar devices at her wrists and breast. She wore an immense hat of white straw with a scarlet chiffon trimming and an ample tuft of black eagle's feathers.

Her daughter Félise followed her, a clear throwback to old Madame Dupont. Her small black eyes, her petite figure, her straight black hair, all echoed the old harridan. She was sixteen years old, but as undeveloped as a child of twelve, which was just as well for her. She would not be allowed to look sixteen for another ten years yet.

'I thought I would come and show you my new hat, Arsène; we are going to the races.'

Madame curtseyed.

'Very nice, Hélène, but not very patriotic!'

'Eh, why?'

'The colours, my dearest!'

'Ah, maman,' broke in the child, clapping her hands, 'maman is a German!'

'What nonsense!' said Madame Huysbroeck angrily. 'And you, child, be quiet!'

She was furious: she wanted compliments, for she was herself a little doubtful about the perfect taste of her costume; and she was getting raillery.

Arsène, a man of peace, hastened to soothe her.

'The hat is beautiful, astonishing, soul-shaking,' said he. Her mother joined him. 'And for the colours, that is an omen. Back all the German horses, my daughter.'

Arsène jumped up, slapping his fat thigh. 'Good little maman,' said he, running to the old woman and kissing her. 'It is an omen! Eureka!' and he went dancing about the studio; a great idea had struck him.

Hélène was annoyed again; she was 'not there.' 'Come,' she said, 'we are late, let us be off.' Out she swept, and the two little women after her.

'Goodbye, black eagle!' laughed Arsène, 'if you cost a hundred francs you shall earn a hundred thousand.'

'Come, let us investigate the affair in detail!' He took down from a shelf a portfolio, and studied it intently for a few minutes. Satisfied, he went off to the post office and sent a telegram to a certain Socialist newspaper in Berlin: 'Can you tell me anything about von Hühne?' and got the extremely mysterious reply: 'The same. Proof enough to sink a warship.'

But Arsène was very satisfied. The same evening he wrote a charming little note to an aristocratic friend, by name Comte de la Souricière, inviting him next day to a little al fresco lunch at the Cascade in the Bois de Boulogne.

Arsène was early at the restaurant, and as he sat sipping an apéritif he patted cheerfully the pocketbook which held the telegrams. 'My friend,' he said, referring to the pocketbook, 'you are going to put on flesh: you will be very, very fat!'

3

The Comte de la Souricière had fallen into a copper and got starched. The imperial, black as night; the black silk hat, the black frock-coat, unrelieved by the expectable red *botton*, the black cravat, fastened by a black pearl – there was not one touch of colour in the whole figure. Even his cheeks were of that colourless white which somehow suggests black, as it were an underlying force.

One would have said that the Count was in mourning. Indeed, it was so; but it was an Empire that he mourned.

Beneath his passionless exterior was a flame of devotion to the house of Napoleon – a monomania, one almost might say.

He was perhaps the only man in Paris who did not spit when the news came that the prince for whom all was prepared – a new *coup d'état* which had every chance of success – did not propose to risk his worthless neck in what he called his capital.

No! The Comte de la Souricière had not spat; a rare devotion, that!

He greeted Huysbroeck with a certain formal frigidity. He was a gentleman, with all a gentleman's fastidiousness; and he could not conceal from himself that he was lunching with a reptile. Clearly he had some very important object in view; when one sees a man of this sort out of his element, in a crank food-dive, or at tea with an Anarchist Communist, it is safe to assume that he is not doing it for fun, or even out of curiosity.

During lunch they discussed the politics of France; Huysbroeck with a cunning, and knowledge of rascality, that served him better than intelligence; the Count with a cold contempt only tempered by an indifference which seemed to imply that the matter concerned him just as much and as little as the affairs of sewer-rats.

When, however, the coffee and cognac were going and the cigars lighted, the Count shifted abruptly to the business of the assignation.

'You wrote me,' he said shortly, 'that you had your hand on D. at last.'

He watched the painter carefully; he had his suspicions that he was being played with beyond the conventional limits of political intrigue.

'Indirectly, yes. We can disgrace L. – von Hühne, you remember?' answered the painter. 'Do me the favour to cast your eye over these telegrams.'

The Count disdainfully complied. His scorn turned to active disgust: the black shape of him seemed to quiver from its eternal rigidity. A second, no longer.

'What do you advise?' he asked.

'Offer L. the old terms; this time he will comply, if we threaten him with this exposure. A telegram to good Editor Soften in Berlin, the storm roars in the distance just as he gets our offer – what choice has he?'

'And you need?'

'Only your letter and eight hundred thousand francs.'

'Sir,' replied the other, with great dignity, his black eyes seeking to read the soul of the wretched spy, 'let me speak to you quite frankly. In the course of the last six years, since the death of President Sisse, His Imperial Majesty's humble servants have been paying you very large sums for certain correspondence to which your intimacy with the President entitled you. We do not think – I tell you simply and clearly – that that correspondence has been worth what we have paid for it. Besides this, you have negotiated with the German Secret Service agent L. who you say – I admit a good deal of corroboration – possesses all the documents necessary to prove the treachery of D. and thereby destroy the Republic —'

He raised his hat for a moment; his lips moved in prayer. For twenty years he had not heard the name of the Republic without an earnest appeal to the Powers celestial to bring back the Empire.

'L.,' he continued, 'has always refused our really magnificent offers on the ground that his career in Germany would be broken. The treachery of D. was of no common sort; the Kaiser would appear in a very undignified aspect. The whole policy of the Empire is compromised.

'Now, as I understand, you propose that we should break his career by the help of this reptile Socialist fellow, so that our offer is his one opportunity. Have I understood?'

'Perfectly, Monsieur le Comte!' replied the painter. 'But I cannot conceive why you should have thought it necessary to recapitulate.'

'Simply that you may understand our present position. You have been bound to our party by ties of extraordinary strength; for this reason you have been trusted with the disposal of immense sums of money; trusted – I say it without offence – more than, in my opinion, any man ought to be trusted. We continue to trust you; but it is only fair to yourself that you should be warned that certain gentlemen of our party dislike you and distrust you. They are incredulous about the possibilities of L.; one or two doubt – I am sorry to say – whether D. was a traitor after all.'

Huysbroeck displayed weak irritation, which, so far as it was intentional, was meant to represent the indignation of a patriot who had suffered all things for his country and was now wounded by the mouth that his hand had fed.

'I still do not see,' he said rudely, 'why the devil this long rigmarole. I have served His Majesty well these long years, without reward – well, quite inadequate when you think of all I have suffered – and – and —.' He did not know what to say, stammered, and broke down, confused.

'I merely wish you to understand that this transaction must be entirely satisfactory. Innuendo and the opinions of third parties, however eminent, are useless to us. We are paying this large sum for official correspondence, and for nothing else. And I am rather afraid that if —'

'You need not go on,' said Huysbroeck, a red flush in his face. Was it anger or fear? 'If I play you false, you will have me murdered. *Air connu!*'[1]

'Let us sing it no more, then!' smiled the Count. 'You have been unfortunate, hitherto; you are going to retrieve all that by a brilliant success on the present occasion.'

'Sir, I will do my best,' answered the painter, affecting a dogged honesty combined with a pathetic assumption of the young-man-placed-for-the-first-time-in-a-position-of-danger-and-responsibility-saying-goodbye-perhaps-for-ever-to-his-chief manner.

'Well,' replied the count, 'we trust you. I need say no more.' He excused himself politely, and drove off.

The painter sat down again and ordered an absinthe. 'I wonder,' he mused, 'how little I can call half when I see L.?'

4

But for the astuteness of old Madame Dupont, Arsène would have made shipwreck many a time ere now. In the present instance he was wise enough to consult her.

'Fine affair,' she cried, as he entered the 'drawing room. 'That little slut of a model was here asking for money. I slapped her face fiercely for her, I can tell you. I really wish, Arsène,' she said more soberly, 'that you would employ a little more discretion in the conduct of affairs!'

---

[1] [Familiar tune!]

'Dear mother,' he began.

'I know, I know,' she snapped. 'But the girl shouted out the story down the *impasse*. Fine, if we had neighbours!'

'Little mother,' he said, 'we will leave that for the moment. I am in terrible trouble.'

'What is it?'

'I have,' he said sombrely, 'in this coat pocket, the sum of eight hundred thousand francs.'

'Poor boy!' chirped the little old woman, 'there is a trouble indeed. Let me share it with you!'

'They will cost me honour, perhaps life,' he replied. 'You know my old dealings with the agent whom we call L.'

'The Prussian spy-king?'

'Right, maman! Well, that hat of Aline's suggested a new scheme to me' – and he went on to unfold the story which our readers know.

'Well,' said the old woman, 'go and buy them! You will always have a large profit on the business!'

'The trouble is, little mother, that for all I know – Listen: L. has not got any papers. Perhaps there are no such papers. Perhaps D. is really a much-abused man. I have got the money, but I can't keep it. I must return it. Or could we fly to —'

'Don't talk like a fool!' snapped the old woman. 'Return money you have your fist on! Fly? To some savage country with no boulevards, no Bois, no Longchamps, no Faubourg? Say nothing; let me think!'

The old woman shrank into herself for full five minutes. Then she straightened herself out again.

'You will go to Berlin,' she said. 'You will change the money into gold there. You will go to this Herr Soften, and give him a thousand francs. You will promise him nine thousand more on the day that L. leaves Germany. Of course you must hide your visit from L. What name does he know you by? A false one? Good; use your own.

'You will telegraph from Berlin to this foolish Count that the papers are entirely satisfactory, that he is to call here for them on Sunday morning. You are then to telegraph that you fear you are watched by Republican spies, and will be a day late. In the train, when everyone is asleep, you will go into the corridor, fire a revolver through the window at your bed, throw away the revolver through the outer window, rush into your compartment, and pretend that the ball whistled past your head, and woke you. Telegraph to the Count that you have been shot at, but escaped, and that the papers are safe.

'In the meanwhile, I will do what is necessary in Paris; for, understand, my son, that the papers will be stolen from this house.'

'But, little mother, it would be easier to pretend to lose them on the journey.'

'Exactly; you are not very bright today, Arsène! It is necessary that people should say: Had he been a rogue, how much more easily —'

'But this is dangerous, very dangerous. The police of Paris are not foolish!'

Mme Dupont gave a sniff; she did not believe in official acumen. 'Leave it to me!' she said; 'I will throw dust in the eyes of a dozen as smart as M. Homard.'

Arsène Huysbroeck knew his mother-in-law from of old; he could trust her.

Abandoning all objections, they threw themselves heart and soul into the details of the pretended burglary.

Madame Huysbroeck must be told of the scheme; the girl Félise must be sent into the country where her two little brothers already were. With her could go the watch-dog Jack, of whom she was extremely fond.

Raymond, the valet, must be told to sleep soundly. He was a fool; almost a 'natural.' Madame Dupont would get Antorino, Arsène's favourite model, to come with a friend and do the 'burglary.' There must be evidence that the safe yielded to no bungler. Antorino would be sure to know somebody expert.

Nothing of great value must be in the house; it would never do for the sham burglary to become a real one.

Very good then; all Arsène need do was pack a toothbrush.

5

If all that Huysbroeck desired was the vindication of his honour, he had it. No breath of suspicion touched him. The Imperialists mourned, but blamed him not.

For when the frightened valet brought in the police, and the police telephoned for the great M. Homard himself, that gentleman was confronted by an impenetrable mystery of quite another sort than that proposed by the ingenuity of Madame Dupont.

In his bed lay the painter, bound, gagged, strangled and mutilated.

Upon the floor not far off see Madame Dupont in a similar condition.

In her child's room lay the painter's wife, bound and gagged. The house had been ransacked for papers, which lay in confusion on the floor.

Atlantis

Last year I was chosen to succeed the venerable K… Z…, who had it in his mind to die, that is, to join Them in Venus, as one of the Seven Heirs of Atlantis, and I have been appointed to declare, so far as may be found possible, the truth about that mysterious lost land. Of course, no more than one seventh of the wisdom is ever confided to any one of the Seven, and the Seven meet in council but once in every thirty-three years. But its preservation is guaranteed by the interlocked systems of 'dreaming true' and of 'preparation by antinomy.' The former almost explains itself; the latter is almost inconceivable to normal man. Its essence is to train a man to be anything by training him to be its opposite. At the end of anything, think they, it turns out to be its opposite, and that opposite is thus mastered without having been soiled by the labours of the student, and without the false impressions of early learning being left upon his mind.

I myself, for example, had unknowingly been trained to record these observations by the life of a butterfly. All my impressions came clear on the soft wax of my brain; I had never worried because the scratch on the wax in no way resembled the sound it represented. In other words, I observed perfectly because I never knew that I was observing. So, if you pay sufficient attention to your heart, you will make it palpitate.

I accordingly proceed to a description of the country.

I

Of the Plains beneath Atlas, and its Servile Race [1]

Atlas is the true name of this archipelago – continent is an altogether false term, for every 'house' or mountain peak was cut off from its fellows by natural, though often very narrow waterways. The African

---

[1] There were four (some say five) distinct races, each having several sub-races. But the main characteristics were the same. Some allege the Portuguese and the English to be survivals of this or kindred stock.

Atlas is a mere offshoot of the range. It was the true Atlas that supported the ancient world by its moral and magical strength, and hence the name of the fabled globe-bearer. The root is the Lemurian *tla* or *tlas*, 'black,' for reasons which will appear in due course. *A–* is the feminine prefix, derived from the shape of the mouth when uttering the sound. 'Black woman' is therefore as near a translation as one can give in English; the Latin has a closer equivalent.

The mountains are cut off, not only from each other by the channels of the sea, but from the plains at their feet by cliffs, naturally or artificially smoothed and undercut for at least thirty feet on every side, in order to make access impossible.

These plains had been made flat by generations of labour. Vines and fruit-trees growing only on the upper slopes, they were devoted principally to corn, and to grass pastures for the amphibian herds of Atlas. This corn was of a kind now unknown, flourishing in sea-water, and the periodical flood-tides served the same purpose as the Nile in Egypt. Enormous floating stages of spongy rock – no trees of any kind grew anywhere on the plains, so wood was unknown – supported the villages. These were inhabited by a type of man similar to the modern Caucasian race. They were not permitted to use any of the food of their masters, neither the corn, nor the amphibians, nor the vast supplies of shell-fish, but were fed by what they called 'bread from heaven,' which indeed came down from the mountains, being the whole of their refuse of every kind. The whole population was put to perpetual hard labour. The young and active tended the amphibians, grew the corn, collected the shell-fish, gathered the 'bread from heaven' for their elders, and were compelled to reproduce their kind. At twenty they were considered strong enough for the factory, where they worked in gangs on a machine combining the features of our pump and treadmill for sixteen hours of the twenty-four. This machine supplied Atlas with its *zro*[1] or 'power,' of which I shall speak presently. Any worker showing even temporary weakness was transferred to the phosphorus works, where he was sure to die within a few months. Phosphorus was a prime necessity of Atlas; however, it was not used in its red or yellow forms, but in a third allotrope, a blue-black or rather violet-black substance, only known in powder finer than precipitated gold, harder than diamond, eleven times heavier than yellow phosphorus, quite incombus-

---

[1] Or *zra'e*. The *zr* is drawled slowly; the lips are suddenly curled back in a sneering snarl, and the vowel sharply and forcibly uttered. It is disputed whether this word is connected with the Sanskrit *srī*, holy.

tible, and so shockingly poisonous that, in spite of every precaution, an ounce of it cost the lives (on an average) of some two hundred and fifty men. Of its properties I shall speak later.

The people were left in utmost slavery and ignorance by the wise counsel of the first of the philosophers of Atlas, who had written: 'An empty brain is a threat to Society.' He had consequently instituted a system of mental culture, comprising two parts:

1. As a basis, a mass of useless disconnected facts.
2. A superstructure of lies.

Part 1 was compulsory; the people then took Part 2 without protest.[1]

The language of the plains was simple but profuse. They had few nouns and fewer verbs. 'To work again' (there was no word for 'to work' simply), 'to sleep again,' 'to eat again,' 'to break the law' (no word for 'to break the law again'), 'to come from without,' 'to find light' (i.e., to go to the phosphorus factory), were almost the only verbs used by adults. The young men and women had a verb-language yet simpler, and of degraded coarseness. All had, however, an extraordinary wealth of adjectives, most of them meaningless, as attached to no noun ideas, and a great quantity of abstract nouns such as 'Liberty,' 'Progress,' without which no refined inhabitant could consider a sentence complete. He would introduce them into a discussion on the most material subjects. 'The immoral snub-nose,' 'the unprogressive teeth,' 'lascivious music,' 'reactionary eyebrows' – such were phrases familiar to all. 'To eat again, to sleep again, to work again, to find the light – that is Liberty, that is Progress' was a proverb common in every mouth.

The religion of the people was Protestant Christianity in all essentials, but with an even closer dependence upon God. They asserted its formulæ, without attaching any meaning to the words, in a manner both reverent and passionate. Sexual life was entirely forbidden to the workers, a single breach implying relegation to the phosphorus works.

In every field was, however, an enormous tablet of rock, carved on one side with a representation of the three stages of life: the fields, the labour mill, the phosphorus factory; and on the other side with these words: 'To enter Atlas, fly.' Beneath this an elaborate series of graphic pictures showed how to acquire the art of flying. During all the generations of Atlas, not one man had been known to take advantage of these instructions.

---

[1] The same danger to society in our own time has been foreseen, and an identical remedy discovered and applied in compulsory education and cheap newspapers.

The principal fear of the populace was a variation of any kind from routine. For any such the people had one word only, though this word changed its annotation in different centuries. 'Witchcraft,' 'Heresy,' 'Madness,' 'Bad Form,' 'Sex-Perversion,' 'Black Magic' were its principal shapes in the last four thousand years of the dominion of Atlas.

Sneezing, idleness, smiling, were regarded as premonitory. Any cessation from speech, even for a moment to take breath, was considered highly dangerous. The wish to be alone was worse than all; the delinquent would be seized by his fellows, and either killed outright or thrust into the compound of the phosphorus factory, from which there was no egress.

The habits of the people were incredibly disgusting. Their principal relaxations were art, music and the drama, in which they could show achievement hardly inferior to that of Henry Arthur Jones, Piñero, Lehar, George Dance, Luke Fildes and Thomas Sidney Cooper.

Of medicine they were happily ignorant. The outdoor life in that equable climate bred strong youths and maidens, and the first symptom of illness in a worker was held to impair his efficiency and qualify him for the phosphorous factory. Wages were permanently high, and as there were no merchants even of alcohol, whose use was forbidden, every man saved all his earnings, and died rich. At his death his savings went back to the community. Taxation was consequently unnecessary. Clothes were unnecessary and unknown, and the 'bread from heaven' was the 'free gift of God.' The dead were thrown to the amphibians. Each man built his own shelter of the rough stone sponge which abounded. The word 'house' was used only in Atlas; the servile race called its huts *bloklost* (equivalent to the English word 'home'). Discontent was absolutely unknown. It had not been considered necessary to prohibit traffic with foreign countries, as the inhabitants of such were esteemed barbarians. Had a ship landed men, they would have been murdered to a man, supposing that Atlas had permitted any approach to its shores. That it hindered such, and by infallible means, was due to other considerations, whose nature will form the subject of a subsequent chapter.

This then is the nature of the plains beneath Atlas, and the character of the servile race.

2

Of the Race of Atlas

In the city or 'house' which was formed from the crest of every mountain, dwelt a race not greatly superior in height to our own, but of vaster frame. The bulk and strength of the bear is not inappropriate as a simile for the lower classes; the higher had the enormous chest and shoulders and the lean haunches of the lion. This strength gave an infallible beauty, made monstrous by their most inexorable law, that every child who developed no special feature in the first seven years should be sacrificed to the Gods. This special feature might be a nose of prodigious size, hands and wrists of gigantic strength, a gorilla jaw, an elephant ear – any of these might entitle its owner to life;[1] for in all such variations from the normal they perceived the possibility of a development of the race. Men and women were hairy as the orangutang, and all were closely shaven from head to foot. It had been found that this practice developed tactile sensibility. It was also done in reverence to the 'Living Atla,' of whom more in its place.

The lower class was few in number. Its function was to superintend the servile race, to bring the food of the children to the banqueting hall, to remove the same, to attend to the disposition of the 'light screens,' to ensure the continuance of the race by the begetting, bearing and nourishing of the children.

The priestly class was concerned with the further preparation of the Zro supplied by the labour mills, and its impregnation with phosphorus. This class had much leisure for 'work,' a subject to be explained later.

The High Priests and High Priestesses were restricted in number to eleven times thirty-three in any one 'house.' To them were entrusted the final secrets of Atlas, and to them was confided the conduct of the experiments in which every will was bound up.[2]

The colour of the Atlanteans was very various, though the hair was invariably of a fiery chestnut with bluish reflections. One might see women whiter than Aphrodite, others tawny as Cleopatra, others yellow as Ta-chi, others of a strange, subtle blue like the tattooed faces of Chin women, others again red as copper. Green was however a prohibited hue for women, and red was not liked in men. Violet was rare, but highly prized, and children born of that colour were specially reared by the High Priestesses.

However, in one part of the body all the women were perfectly black with a blackness no negro can equal; from this circumstance comes the

---

[1] Gautama Buddha was the reincarnation or legend of a previous Buddha who was a missionary from Atlas, hence the account of his immovable neck, the ears that he could fold over his face, and other monstrous details.

[2] There was a Governor of these, of whose name, nature and function I am not permitted to speak.

name Atlas. It is absurdly attributed by some authors to the deposit of excess of phosphorus in the Zro. I need only point out that the mark existed long before the discovery of black phosphorus. It is evidently a racial stigma. It was the birth of a girl child without this mark which raised her mother to the rank of goddess, and ended the terrestrial adventure of the Atlanteans, as will presently appear.

Of the ethics of this people little need be said. Their word for 'right' is *phph*, made by blowing with the jaw drawn sharply across from left to right, thus meaning 'a spiral life contrary to the course of the Sun.' We may sum it as 'contrary.' 'Whatever is, is wrong' seems to have been their first principle. Legs are 'wrong' because they only carry you five miles in the hour; let us refuse to walk; let us ride horseback. So the horse is 'wrong' compared to the train and the motor-car; and these are 'wrong' to the æroplane. If speed had been the Atlantean's object, he would have thought æroplanes 'wrong' and all else too, so long as the speed of light was not surpassed by him.

Curious survivals of these laws are found in the Jewish transcript of the Egyptian code, which they, being a slave race, interpreted in the reverse manner.

'Thou shalt not make any graven image.' Every male child, on attaining manhood, had a graven image given him to worship, a miracle-working image, whose principal exploits he would tattoo upon it.

'Remember the Sabbath Day to keep it holy.' The Atlantean kept one day in seven for all purposes unconnected with his principal task.

'Thou shalt not commit adultery.' Though the Atlanteans married, intercourse with the wife was the only act forbidden.

'Honour thy father and thy mother.' On the contrary, they worshipped their children, as if to say: 'This is the God whom I have made in my own likeness.'

Similarly, there is one exception and one only to the rule of silence. It is the utterance of the 'Name' which it is death to pronounce. This word was constantly in their mouths; it is *Zcrra*, a sort of venomous throat-gargling. Hence, possibly, the Gælic *scurr* 'speak,' English *scaur* or *scar* in Yorkshire and the Pennines. *Zcrra* is also the name of the 'High House,' and of the graven image referred to above.

Others traces may be found in folklore, some mere superstitions. Thus the correct number for a banquet was thirteen, because if there were only one more sign in the Zodiac, the year would be a month longer, and one would have more time for 'work.' This is probably a debased Egyptian notion. Atlanteans knew better than anyone that the Zodiac is only an arbitrary division. Still it may be laid down that the impossible never daunted Atlas. If one said 'Two and two make Four,' his thought would be 'Yes, damn it!'[1]

I now explain the language of Atlas. The third and greatest of their philosophers saw that speech had wrought more harm than good, and he consequently instituted a peculiar rite. Two men were chosen by lot to preserve the language, which, by the way, consisted of monosyllables only, two hundred and fourteen in number, to each of which was attached a diacritical gesture, usually ideographic.

Thus 'wrong' is given as *phph*, moving the jaw from right to left. Wiping the brow with *phph* means 'hot,' hollowing the hands over the mouth 'fire,' striking the throat 'to die'; so that each 'radical' may have hundreds of gesture-derivatives. Grammar, by the way, hardly existed, the quick apprehension of the Atlanteans rendering it unnecessary.

These two men then departed to a cavern on the side of the mountain just above the cliff, and there for a year they remained, speaking the language, and carving it symbolically upon the rock. At the end of the year they returned; the elder is sacrificed, and the younger returns with a volunteer, usually one who wishes to expiate a fault, and teaches him the language. During his visit he observes whether any new thing needs a new name, and if so he invents it, and adds it to the language. This process continued to the end. The rest of the people abandoned altogether the use of speech, only a few years' practise enabling them to dispense with the radical. They then sought to do without gesture, and in eight generations the difficulty was conquered, and telepathy established.[2] Research then devoted itself to the task of doing without thought; this will be discussed in detail in the proper place. There was also a 'listener,' three men who took turns to sit upon the highest peak, above the 'light screens,' and whose duty it was to give the alarm if any noise disturbed Atlas. On their report that High Priest charged with active governorship would take steps to ascertain and destroy the cause.

The 'light screens' spoken of were a contrivance of laminæ of a certain spar such that the light and heat of the sun were completely cut off, not by opacity, but by what we call 'interference.' In this way other subtler rays of the sun entered the 'house,' these rays being supposed to be necessary to life. These matters were the subjects of the deepest controversy. Some

---

[1] One of the most brilliant children committed suicide on learning that he could not move his upper jaw. This boy is one of the eleven heroes who had statues in the High House. And the Atlantean for 'sorrow' in its ultimate sense (*dukkha* or '*Weltschmerz*') is to wrench at the upper jaw.

[2] This system of communication has great advantages over any other. It is independent of distance, and dependent on the will of the transmitter. Telepathic messages could not be 'tapped' or miscarry in any way.

held that these rays themselves were injurious, and should be excluded. Others considered that the light screens should be put in position during moonlight, instead of being opened at sunset, as was the custom. This, however, was never attempted, the great mass of the people being devoted to the moon. Others wished full sunlight, the aim of Atlas being (they thought) to reach the sun. But this theory contradicted the prime axiom of attaining things through their opposites, and was only held by the lower classes, who were not initiated into this doctrine.

The 'houses' of Atlas were carved from the living rock by the action of Zro in its seventh precipitation. Enormously solid, the walls were lofty and smoother than glass, though the pavements were rough and broken almost everywhere for a reason which I am not permitted to disclose. The passages were invariably narrow, so that two persons could never pass each other. When two met, it was the law to greet by joining in 'work' and then going away together on their separate errands, or passing one above the other. This was done purposely, so as to remind every man of his duty to Atlas on every occasion on which he might meet a fellow citizen.

The Banqueting Hall of the children was usually very large. The furniture, which had been brought by the first colonists, and gradually disused by adults, never needed repair. A vast open doorway facing North opened on the mountainside on to the vineyards and orchards, the meadows and gardens, in which the children passed their time. Suckled by the mother for three months only, the child was then already able to nourish itself on the bread and wine, and on the flesh of the amphibian herds, of which there were several kinds; one a piglike animal with flesh resembling wild duck, another a sort of manatee tasting like salmon, its fat being somewhat like caviar in everything but texture, and a sure specific for any of childhood's troubles. A third, the ancestor of our hippopotamus, was really tamed, and was employed by the serviles for preparing the ground for the corn, trampling through the fields while they were covered with sea-water, and thus leaving deep holes in which the seeds were cast. Its flesh was not unlike bear, but more delicate. Notable, too, was the great quantity of turtle; also the giant oysters, the huge deep sea crabs, a kind of octopus whose flesh made a nutritious and elegant soup, and innumerable shell-fish, added to the table. The waterways were haunted by shoals of a small and poisonous fish,[1] whose bite was immediate death to man, a fact which altogether cut off communication between one island and an-

---

[1] Called by them *Zhee-Zhou*, in imitation of the swish of its tail and the cry of its victim.

other except by air, as the hippopotamus-animal, although immune to its bite, was unable to swim.

Of the sleeping chambers I shall tell more particularly in the course of my remarks on Zro.

3

Of the Aim of the Magicians of Atlas;
of Zro, and its Properties and Uses;
of That which is Combined with It; and of Black Phosphorus

It was the most ancient tradition of the Atlantean magicians that they were the survivors of a race inhabiting a country called Lemuria, of which the South Pacific archipelago may be the remains. These Lemurians had, they held, built up a civilisation equal, if not superior to their own; but through a misunderstanding of a magical law – some said the 2nd, some the 8th, some the 23rd – had involved themselves and their land in ruin. Others thought that the Lemurians had succeeded in their magical task, and broken their temple. In any case, it was the secret Lemurian tradition that they themselves represented the survivals of a yet earlier race who lived in ice, and they of yet another who lived in fire, and they again of the earliest colonists from Mars. The theory, in fine, was that the aim of man is to attain the Sun, whence, according to one school of cosmology, he was exiled in the cosmic catastrophe which resulted in the formation of Neptune. His task on any given planet was therefore to overturn the laws of Nature on that planet, thus mastering it sufficiently to enable him to make the leap to the next planet inward. Exactly how and in what sense the leap was made remains obscure, even to heirs of Atlantis.[1]

The men of Atlas could fly, it is true, and that by a method so simple that men will laugh outright when it is rediscovered; but they needed air to support them; they could not confront the cold and emptiness of space. Was it in some subtler body that they conveyed their Palladium? Or, content to die, could they project that supreme vehicle across so great a distance? The answer to such questions probably lies in the recovery by mankind of the knowledge of Zro and its properties.

Beneath the labour mills run[2] troughs[3] in which the sweat of the workers collects and drains off into an open basin without the mill.

---

[1] The point was discussed fully, and finally relegated, in the Council of Stockholm, 1913.

[2] The scene is so real to me that I find it impossible to avoid using the historic present here and elsewhere, inadvertently.

[3] There are six other pieces of apparatus to insulate and carry to the basin the six subtler principles of sweat.

In this basin churns with immense rapidity – through multiple bevel gearing – a sort of paddle with knife edges. The sweat is thus churned into froth, and gradually disappears, and is as constantly replaced. The workers toil in shifts – eight hours work, four hours repose, eight hours work, four hours rest and recreation. The mills never cease day or night.

The basin is of polished silver and agate, and is set at an angle, facing two enormous spheres of crystal, encased in a sort of trellis made of a certain greenish metal, its optical focus at a point midway between the two.

The only sign of activity is that out of this focus a spark crackles unless the air be dry, a condition difficult to secure in this part of the world, although fans blow air, dried over chloride of calcium and sulphuric acid, over the globes and their focus. These fans are worked by tidal power, human labour being appropriated absolutely to the one use.

In the temple of the 'house' are two globes similar to those upon the plains, and the mysterious force generated below is transferred to those above, collecting within them. Now the name of this substance is always Zro, but in its first state the gesture is a twiddling of the thumbs. In its second, it is a rapid twittering of the fingers, and in its third state of distillation it is a screwing of the hands together. Within the spheres it sublimes suddenly in the air as a snaky powder (4) of silver, which immediately turns to an iridescent fluid (5) that is forced up, by its own need of expansion, through a fountain into the temple, on whose floor it lies (6) in a semi-solid condition. Expert priests then gather this in their hands, and rapidly shape it into its seventh state, when it is like a knife of diamond, but alive. An instrument like a Mexican machete is used to carve rocks. The edge shears them, the back smoothes them. The rock behaves exactly like wax, responsive to the lightest touch. What is not used for weapons is then gathered up swiftly and kneaded by women of the rank of high priestess. It is not known even to the high priests with what they knead it, but in its eighth stage it is a substance solid enough to support great weight, but eternally heaving of its own force. Of this they make beds, so that the sleeping Atlantean is (as it were) continually massaged. To this they attribute the fact that Atlanteans sleep never more than half an hour, though they do so four times daily. These beds remain active only for a few days, and they are then thrown into the ninth stage by being taken into a room where is a cauldron of great size. They are thrown into this and sprinkled with black phosphorus.[1] The

---

[1] Only the smallest quantity is required, and it is unchanged, its function being purely catalytic. This form of phosphorus is one of the most stable of elements. It combines (so far as is known) only with Zro. But if thrown out of such a combination, it becomes ordinary yellow phosphorus.

Zro then divides into two parts, one liquid, one solid. Neither of these has any ascertainable properties, for it is absolutely passive to the will of the user, who may taste therein his utmost desire, whether for food or drink. Among adults there is no other food or drink than this. The children are not allowed to taste it.

The black phosphorus is always added by a high priestess, and it is not known to me in what manner she does this. The Zro that may remain is the subject of eternal experiments by the Magicians. It is generally thought by the greatest of them that an error was committed in bringing it to a ninth stage of division into two, and many openly deplored the discovery of black phosphorus. All however strive in harmony to produce a tenth stage that shall surpass the virtues of the ninth. Theoretically it is possible to reach an eleventh stage wherein the Zro takes human form, and lives! Opinion is divided as to whether this was not actually done by a certain magician at the time of the passing of Atlas. In any case, I beg the reader to remember that I have only described one seventh of the virtues of Zro, and I have even omitted this, that in its ninth stage it is not only food and drink, but universal medicine, if properly understood. For Zro is also a vision and a voice!

Now the muscles of the people of Atlas are the muscles of giants, and yet they do one thing only. And this thing is combined by the wisdom of the Magicians, so that it is at the same time work, exercise, sport, game, pleasure, and all else that may fulfill life.

This work never ceases. It has these parts:

1. Working *at* Zro, i.e., bringing it from the first stage to the ninth.
2. Working *with* Zro, i.e., for one's own particular purpose.
3. Working *for* Zro. This is the common and most honourable task, the Zro eaten and drunken being worked by the working into a quintessence of higher power, though identical in property with the common Zro.

This new Zro (Atlas Zro) goes through the same stages as the common Zro of the serviles. But it is the result of free and joyful labour, and so serves the Magicians in their experiments, and the Governor of all for his sustenance. None by the way is ever wasted. For example, a tunnel was drilled completely through the Earth and filled with Zro, and it is said that by this tunnel the Atlanteans escaped.

This working, whether *with* or *for* Zro, requires two persons at least at any one time and place. Great heat is generated in the working, and the bodies of the workers are therefore sprinkled heavily with the black phosphorus, which is incombustible. This black phosphorus, poisonous to the servile race, becomes innocuous to anyone who has been in any way impregnated with Zro. This itself, in its first state, is as dangerous as electricity of high voltage.

The reverence attached to Zro is unbounded. At one time it was hymned as the father of the gods, and till the end all children were thought to be 'begotten of Zro,' though everyone might know who was the father.[1] All such conception was however held indignity. Its official name was 'the old experiment.' It was carried on simply because the new methods of continuing the race were not perfected. Childbirth was therefore in one way an accident; although a duty, everyone shrank from it. For though no pain or discomfort attached to the process, it was a sort of second-best achievement from which proud women turned contemptuously. This was in part the reason why the father's name was never mentioned.

On several occasions in the history of Atlas the Zro 'failed.' Although not changed in appearance, its properties were lost or diminished. In such a case young men and maidens in great numbers were captured on the plains, brought into Atlas, and offered in sacrifice to the Gods. Their blood[2] was mingled with Zro in its third stage, and the latter regained its potency. Their flesh was eaten by the high priests and priestesses in penance for the unknown wrong. It was subject to other and terrible scourges, being the most sensitive as well as the strongest thing on earth. On one occasion it had to be treated with a fox-like perfume prepared by the chief magician; on another it was subjected to streams of moonlight from parabolic mirrors.

The most serious crisis was some two thousand years before the destruction of Atlas. One of the serviles, riding his 'hippopotamus' to the ploughing, fell off and was instantly bitten by the poisonous fish previously described. Through an accident of boyhood he had, however, for a reason too obscure to describe here, no such vulnerable spot as suited the Zhee-Zhou. He survived, and went to work, as it chanced, the next day. The Zro was poisoned; a third of Atlas died within the hour; the plant on the affected island had to be destroyed, and all its people. It was only repopulated some three hundred and eighty years later, and then for particular reasons of magical economy impossible to dwell upon in this account.

---

[1] In spite of the absolute promiscuity of the Atlanteans, this was never in doubt, owing to the special mark of each man, whose stigma or variation was infallibly transmitted.

[2] This item is loosely used, as equivalent of 'life.' The sacrifice is described later, and the point made clear.

Marriage was compulsory on all those whose passion had been so exclusive and enduring as to produce two children. Further intercourse between the pair was thus barred. The Magicians thought that it was inimical to variation for a woman to have more than one child (*à fortiori* two) by the same father; and the custom further prevented those stupid sporadic outbursts of burnt-out lust which make so many modern marriages intolerable.

Closely connected with marriage, the close of the reproductive life, is that of death, the close of the little that remains. Death hardly threatened the Atlantean; he would decide to 'go and see,' as the old phrase ran, and take an overdose of a particular preparation of black phosphorus mixed with a very little Zro in the ninth stage, which ensured a painless death. That none ever returned was taken as proof of the supreme attractiveness of death.

The ghoulish and necromantic practices with which Atlanteans have been unjustly reproached never occurred. A little vampirism, perhaps, in the early days before the perfecting of Zro; but no Atlantean was ever so stupid or so ignorant as to confuse death with life.

Beside this voluntary death only one danger existed. As the use of Zro guaranteed life and health and youth – a centenarian high priest was no better than a kitten! – so did its abuse spell instant corruption of those qualities. As mentioned above, now and then the Zro itself was at fault, and caused epidemics; but from time to time there were deaths in a particularly loathsome form caused by what they called 'misunderstanding' the Zro.[1] Such mistakes were particularly common in the early days of its discovery, and before its use had become well nigh a worship. The first symptom was a crack in the skin of the temple, or sometimes of the bridge of the nose, more rarely of the eyelid or cheek. Within a few minutes this crack became an open sore, of horrid fœtor, and within twenty-four hours, the patient was completely rotted away, bone and marrow. A circumstance of singular atrocity was that death never occurred until the spinal column collapsed. No treatment could be found even to prolong the agony by an hour. This being recognised, sufferers were thrown from the cliffs at the first sign of the malady. In this way too were all other corpses disposed. It was the most honourable death possible, for becoming 'bread from heaven' for the serviles, they were again worked up into Zro itself, a transmutation which in their view would be well worth all

---

[1] No other disease was known after the bringing of the Zro to its ninth stage, all indisposition being instantly cured by a single dose.

the 'resurrections of the body' and 'immortalities of the soul' of the theoretical, dogmatic, hearsay religions.

So much then concerning Zro, and the matters immediately connected with it.

4

Of the So-called Magic of the Atlanteans

Magic in Atlas was a 'Science of Sciences.' It was the final integration of all knowledge. In method its theory was differentiation, and in theory its method was integration. For example, the fifth of the great philosophers indicated 'Everything is Zro' to the Keeper of the Speech at the annual sacrifice. This in spite of the fact that in that very year two new forms of Zro had been discovered by that same philosopher. It was the third of the galaxy who announced 'the ultimate analysis of sensation is pain; that of thought, madness; that of super-consciousness (a state of trance induced by Zro and valued above all things) annihilation.'

His successor had retorted that in this was implicit a postulate that pain, madness and annihilation were undesirable. The third admitted that he had so meant his phrase, but destroying the postulate, still stuck to it. All this was the foundation of much magical theory, and on these purely psychological researches was based the whole magical practice. 'There is no God' was a commonplace. It only implied that the mind was wrong to try to conceive within it what was by definition without it. To set limits to anything whatever seemed to them the greatest of crimes, the exact opposite of the true path to the Sun.

The practical side of magic was for the most part a mere utilisation of known forces, such as are employed by modern science. But the resources of Atlas were as great, and the advantages incomparably greater. The whole archipelago was a laboratory. There was no question of the 'cost of research'; every man was devoted to it. Every man thought only of the main problem 'How to reach Venus' and its sub-issues. Further, the main laws of magic had always been found to govern and include chemical and physical laws.

In the early days of colonisation Zro was only known in its crude state; it was the genius of a single man that obtained the third state in purity. From this state to the seventh it moved almost of itself, very much as radium does. The genius, having sufficient in this pure seventh state, made a sword, and completed in three days the subjugation of the servile races. It was a stroke of fortune, this quickness, for on the fourth day the

Zro began to disintegrate. The magicians then began to seek a means of making this state permanent. But in this they failed,[1] so that knives had always to be replaced twice weekly; but in the course of their failures they discovered the infinitely more valuable eighth and ninth states of Zro. Tradition has preserved a hint of their efforts in Alchemy with its problems of the fixation of the Universal Mercury, the secret of perpetual motion, and 'potable gold – the Universal Medicine.' It had been theoretically determined towards the end of the tenth state, that Zro should be a solid, but whether this was confirmed is beyond my knowledge.

To return to the main magical theory, the Quintessence, said they, or Universal Substance (which some strove to identify with Hyle, others with the Luminiferous Æther) is the two-in-one, liquid and solid, the former part being also twofold, fluid and gaseous, and the latter earthy and fiery. The combination of these four phases of Zro accounted for the universe. This quintessence is Zro in some state unknown and incalculable. Some expected to find it in its twelfth state, some in a seventeenth, others in a thirty-seventh: all this was pure guess-work. Some tradition to this effect appears to have reached Plato; and the neo-Platonists combined with those Jews who had preserved fragments of the Egyptian tradition to form a new initiated hierarchy, the echo of whose teaching is found in Paracelsus. At one period, too, missionaries (not colonists, as has been ignorantly asserted; there was no trouble of over-population in Atlas) were sent to the four quarters, and parties landed in Mexico, Ireland and Egypt. The adventures of the party who travelled South form an astounding chapter in the history of Atlas. It was they who discovered the Magnetic South, and whose observations rendered possible the theory which resulted in the piercing of the Earth by Zro.[2]

Besides all I have recounted, Zro had many extraordinary powers. These were however called 'lesser,' and discarded and forgotten in the absorption in the principal work. Nearly all of these are found in the combinations of Zro in its sixth state with black phosphorus in varying proportions. Thus one product is called 'fiery flying serpent.' A pellet pinched off and thrown into the air elongates itself and flies in the direction desired, killing the person whom it strikes. Another was called 'Eye of the Gods.' It was a metal resembling platinum, and

---

[1] No known state of pure Zro is stable. From this it will be seen how entirely Atlas was in the hands of the servile races. Fortunately no trouble ever arose; the supply of labour was always ample.

[2] There was also a settlement in Finland. Its only remains in historic periods is 'Lapland Witches.'

made into tiny mirrors worn in rings, or even attached by a special process to the thumbnail. The seer could then behold any place or person he chose to name. A similar product, nearly all phosphorus, was like vulcanite, and was worn inside the ear by anyone who wished to hear anything that was being said anywhere. There was also a red transparent lip-salve, which compelled love in any who saw it. Its use had been abandoned early in the history of Atlas, through the witty satires of a poet, and the more serious strictures off a philosopher who perceived its liability to abuse. Again a thin paste of almost pure Zro made the wearer invisible. The poet was again successful in bringing this into contempt by suggesting that people resorted to it to hide their ugliness. This poet was one of the few Atlanteans who suffered violent death, except in voluntary sacrifice.

There were also preparations of Zro which increased the size of the user, and others which diminished it. In general use among the lower classes, until the very end, was that composition which made the body light. Careful adjustment would equalise its weight with that of the displaced air, and movements of the limbs would then permit flying. In this way the overseers visited the plains and returned. The other and earlier art of flying needed no apparatus, but I am forbidden to disclose the method, except to hint that it is connected closely with the art of 'dreaming true.'

These are but a few of the magic powers so-called of the compounds of Zro; but they will indicate the power of Atlas by showing what it could afford to neglect. Yet all these powers were implicit in the process of 'working.'

The art of prediction was in the same unsatisfactory state as it is in England today. Nor was its practise encouraged. A magician makes the future, and does not seek to divine it. All true prediction was therefore necessarily catastrophe. The greatest good fortune seemed worthless to an Atlantean, since it was accident, and if accidents are to happen, one of them may be fatal. They believed themselves to be equal to the whole tendency of things, and proudly gazed on Nature as a man might upon a virgin captive to his spear. Everything that was Being was Zro; everything that was Energy was 'working for Zro.' Outside this was but by-product and waste-heap.

The arrangement of the houses was in accordance with the magical theory. There was first the High House, then four (later six, last ten) 'Houses of Houses'; and to each of these was attached a varying number of ordinary houses. The High House was the central shrine of the whole archipelago, and must be separately described.

5

Of the High House of Atlas, of its Inhabitants,
and of their Manners and Customs, and of the Living Atla

The High House was separated from its nearest neighbour by over twenty miles of sea. Its diameter was about an half-mile and its height some four miles. It had no plains at the base, and its cliffs went absolutely sheer and smooth into the water. It was in shape a flattish cylinder, but the top broadened into a pointed knob, somewhat in the style of St Basil's at Moscow. There was not a trace of vegetation, which, by the way, was despised by the Atlanteans. A child would kick a flower contemptuously, thinking 'Thou cannot even move about,' or pet it as an English degenerate woman does a dog. The only entrance was by an orifice at the top. But the base was tunnelled so that from every house was a channel for the Zro which having been brought to the highest perfection was thus transferred to headquarters. The receptacle at the base being far below the earth, and the Zro further heated by friction, it seethed constantly into a bluish or purplish smoke. This was the sole sustenance of the inhabitants of the High House. In early days the old High House, in an island since destroyed by order of the Atla, had been called the House of Blood, the inhabitants subsisting only on blood sucked from the living. The improvements in Zro had changed all that; but the idea was the same, to live only on the Quintessence of Life. Hence while the 'houses' ate and drank Zro, the High House drank its vapour. No children were born in it, and none below the rank of High Priest dwelt there.

Except for one matter which was never thought of, though constantly spoken, the inmost mystery of the High House was the 'Living Atla.' This had many names, 'Wordeater,' 'Unshaven' (because the razors of Zro were turned on its hair), 'Fireheart,' 'Beginning and End' and so on; but especially a word I can only translate as 'To Her,' a defective pronoun existing only in the Dative. What the Living Atla really was, is a secret of secrets.[1] We know it only from its epithets, its veils. Thus it was 'That Black which makes black white.' It was 'twenty-six feet high and fifteen feet across – Oh my Lords, it is the essence of the Incommensurable!' It was 'the wife of Zro,' 'the heart of Zro,' 'the desire of Zro,' 'the Atla that eats Atlas,' 'the swallower-up

---

[1] There are various theories: one a sort of avatar affair, another that the Atla is a quintessence of some kind; another calls 'To Her' the 'Angel of Venus, the force of our aspiration.'

of her own house,' 'the pelican,' 'the fire-nest of the Phœnix,' according to the greatest of the poets. And the burden of his hymns of worship was that it must be destroyed.

It was impossible to approach the Atla without being instantly sucked up and devoured by it. This was the greatest death, and ardently desired by all. The favour was accorded only to those who discovered improvements in Zro, or otherwise merited signal and supreme recognition from the state. Hidden men listened to the cries of the victim, and thus learned the nature of the death. It appears that the black suddenly broke into a fiery rose, 'the only[1] luminous thing in Atlas,' and shooting forward enclosed him. For some reason which was never even guessed the Atla refused women. Those who had seen Atla were however useless to instruct. They came forth from the Presence smiling, and even under the most fearful tortures that the magicians could devise, continued to smile. This smile never left them during life, and the conscious superiority of it was so irritating, and so contrary to the harmony of life in Atlas that the women were killed, and their companions for the future forbidden to approach the Atla.

Whatever theories as to its nature may have been formed by the magicians were upset by a famous experiment. A most holy high priest, a man who at puberty had insisted on immediate marriage with all the women of his house, a magician who had formed four new compounds of Zro, and discovered how to pass matter through matter, was honoured by the great death. On reaching the last corridor, where the concentrated spirals of Zro vapour whirled up into the Presence of Atla, he bade farewell to the appointed listeners in the manner suitable to his dignity, and then, taking a last deep draught of Zro into his lungs, rushed into the antrum. They heard him cry aloud 'O!' with surprise, and then with inexpressible rapture the words 'Behind Atla, Otla!' which were, and still are, completely unintelligible. Their surprise was greater when, seven days later, he came striding past them without greeting. He went to his 'house' and shut himself up, was never seen or heard again, but was assuredly living at the time of the 'catastrophe.' This man founded a school of philosophy, or rather, it founded itself on what it supposed him to have discovered; and this school disputes with the orthodox the credit of the final success.

The lesser mysteries of the High House were concerned almost entirely with the creation of life, and the bridging of the gulf between Earth and Venus. These were connected intimately; the theory was that

---

[1] A mere compliment.

if Atlantean brains could exist in bodies sufficiently subtle to traverse æther, the task was done. Some of the experiments were crude enough, and, to our minds, horrible. They attempted to breed a new race by crossing with snakes, swans, horses and other animals.[1] The Greek legends of such monsters as Chimæra, Medusa, Lamia, Minotaur, the Centaurs, the Satyrs and the like are mere filtrations of the Atlantean tradition. The only theory behind such experiments was that they were contrary to the natural order, and so worth trying. Men of more scientific mind more plausibly passed Zro vapour through sea-water; but they only created serpents of vast size, which they cast into the sea about the High House as guardians. The sea-serpent, whether legend or fact, is derived from this experiment. It is quite possible that some such survive. Another school, objecting strongly to the sex-process, 'which must be transcended as the Lemurians overcame gemmation,' vivisected men and women, taking various parts of the brain, especially the cerebellum, the pineal gland, and the pituitary body, and cultivated them in solutions of Zro under the invisible rays of black phosphorus. The best result of this work was a race of translucent jelly-folk of great intellectual development; but so far from being able to travel through space, they could hardly move in their own element. Another school argued that as Zro in vapour combined the virtues of the liquid and the solid Zro, so a fiery state might be produced which would so impregnate their bodies as to make them 'mates of the æther.' This school held that fiery Zro already existed in Nature, 'in the heart of the Living Atla,' and asserted that those who died by absorption into Atla passed straight to Venus. Many of them therefore tried hard to obtain messages from that planet. Familiar with Newton's first law of motion, they further held it possible to prepare Zro in such a state that a current of it could never be deflected or dissipated, and so, if it could be made in sufficient quantity, a bridge to Venus might be built by which they might travel. They therefore tunneled through the planet, as previously explained, to have a sort of cannon for the Zro. But as their supply was pitifully insufficient, they endeavoured also to prepare a Zro which would have the power of multiplying itself. Alchemical tradition has some record of this problem.

Yet another group of magicians argued that as Nature had cast off the planets from the Sun – a disputed point, some thinking this due to magic, which if so completely destroys the argument – it would be

---

[1] Especially monkeys. The results of this experiment were sent to colonise an island, but escaped, and after many journeys, reached Japan, where their descendants flourish still.

contrary to Nature to cause the planets to fall back into it. They busied themselves with attempts to increase the Earth's gravitational pull, and (alternatively) to check her course. Their schemes were generally regarded as Utopian – yet they could boast of the discovery of the Zro that lightened bodies, and of a kind of æther-screen which generated mechanical power in inexhaustible quantities by making matter slightly opaque to æther. This engine only worked on a very small scale. A screen two inches long would tear itself from fastenings what would have held an earthquake, while the rocks in its neighbourhood would melt in a few minutes, and the sea boil instantly where its rays struck. The most brilliant of this school asserted 'Matter is a disease of Zro,' which may be translated nearly enough 'Matter is a strain in the æther.' He explained gravitation in this way. Place two ivory spheres in a rubber tube; the strain on the tube is least when the balls touch. The tendency is therefore for them to come together. Friction alone checks them. Now æther is infinitely elastic and without friction. From these data he calculated the Law of Inverse Squares.

A more mystic school saw life everywhere. It knew all that we know, and more, about ions and electrons; it saw every phenomenon as a manifestation of will. The crowning glory of this school was the discovery that Zro in its ninth stage, eaten and drunk with concentrated intention, produced the desired result, whatever (within wide limits) that result might be. This went far to supersede the use of all specialised forms of Zro, and so to unify the magical practice.

It seems curious with all this magic, magic itself should be the thing most deplored. But it was the means, and, as such, 'that which is in particular not the end.' The word for Magic, *Ijynx*, was the only dissyllable in the language, for Magic was the essentially twofold thing, more twofold (in a way) than the number two itself. It is interesting here to sketch briefly the mathematics of Atlas. The task is not easy, as their minds worked very differently from ours.

The number 1 was a fairly simple idea; but two was not only two, but also 'the result of adding 1 to 1' and 'the root of 4.' The numbers grew in complexity out of all reason. Seven was 6 plus 1, and 5 plus 2, and 4 plus 3, and so on; as well as 'the root of 49,' 'half 14,' and the like. They even distinguished 4 plus 3 from 3 plus 4. Each number also represented an idea or group of ideas on all sorts of planes. It would have been quite possible to discuss dressmaking in terms of pure number. To give an example of the way in which their minds thought, consider the number three. Three, in so far as it gives the first plane figure, suggests superficies; with regard to the dimensions of space, solidity. Three itself is therefore 'that ineffably holy thing in which the superficies is the solid.' Of course hundreds of other ideas must be added to this; and to grasp and harmonise them all in one colossal supra-rational idea was the constant task of every mathematician. The upshot of this was that all numbers above 33 were regarded as spurious, illusionary; they had no real existence of their own;[1] they were temporary compounds, unreal in very much the same sense as our $\sqrt{-1}$. They were always expressed by graphic formulæ, like our own organic compounds. To take an example, the number 156 was regarded as a sort of efflorescence of the number 7; it was never written but as $77 + \frac{7+7}{7} + 77$. Again, 11 was usually written 3 + 5 + 3. It was always the aim to find symmetry in these expressions, and also 'to find an easy way to 1.' This last is difficult to explain.

Eleven was their great 'Key of Magic.' It is a twofold number in 'the act of becoming 1.' Thirty-seven was 'the essence of 1' inasmuch as multiplying it by 3 gives 111, three ones, which divided again by 3 in another manner, yield 1. 'One would rather think of 48 as 37 plus 11 than as 4 times 12' is the statement of an elementary textbook dating from the earliest days of Atlas. It was a sort of moral duty to teach the mind to think in this manner.

The number 7 was the 'perfect number' with them as with us, but for very different reasons. It was the link between Earth and Venus, for one thing; I cannot explain why. It was 'the number of the Atla,' and the 'house of success' (two being the 'house of battle'). It was also grace, softness, ease, healing, and 'joy of Zro' as well as 'play of phosphorus.' Many mathematicians, however, attacked it with vigour; there was at one time an almost general consent to replace it by 8, and its 'rapture-combination' 31, by 33. Despite the intense preoccupation with such ideas, mathematics as we know them had reached a perfection which, if it does not surpass that of our own civilisation, fails principally because its theorems, handed down to Euclid and Pythagoras, although imperfectly, formed a springboard whence we might leap.

The initiation of children was also a matter reserved for the High House. Weaned at three months, the children were tended by the lower classes until the age of puberty, an occurrence which fitted them at once for initiation. A legate from the High House was sent for, and in his presence the child was brought, acquainted with Zro by both its father and its mother, and full instruction in 'working' was further

---

[1] A partial exception existed for prime numbers, as being 'self-generated,' and each of these which had been investigated had its special (and comparatively simple) signification.

conferred by any member of the 'house' who chose to do so, this in practise meaning by everybody. The ceremonies were frequently long and exhausting; children often enough died in the course of them. This was not regarded as a serious calamity; some schools of magicians even pretended to rejoice. The representative of the High House had a prior right to the parents of the child; at times he conducted the initiation in person, a high honour, but invariably fatal. On rare occasions male children were sent over to the Atla to be devoured. The parents of so fortunate a child were advanced in rank on the spot, and had special privileges conferred on them, sometimes even being transferred to a 'House of Houses.' All those who dwelt in the High House were veiled whenever they appeared, in order to prevent it being known that they were of the same appearance in all respects as their inferiors. This ordinance had been made after the Great Conspiracy, with which I shall deal in the chapter on History.

6

Of the Underground Gardens of Atlas,
and of the Alleged Commerce of the Atlanteans
with Incubi, Succubi, and the Demons of Darkness

I have referred to the contempt with which the Atlanteans were prone to regard the vegetable kingdom. Animals, including men, shared their scorn. The idea may have been that with their advantages they ought to have done much better for themselves. Minerals, however, were regarded as helpless; and hence the extraordinary attention paid to them. Beneath the 'houses' the rock had been tunnelled out into grottos, some in odd fantastic forms, but most in immense polyhedra or combinations of curves. Each 'house' had some twenty of such gardens. Three reagents were used in the cultivation: the 'seed of metals,' the 'seed of Light,' and the 'seed of　,' an untranslatable idea approximating to our mystic's interpretation of 'Alpha and Omega.' The two former produced simple effects: the first formed jewels, self-luminous, which yet grew like flowers, the second similar effects with metals; while the third brought any mineral to flower in the most extravagant combinations of colour and form. All such conditions as texture, hardness, elasticity, and physical attributes in general, were considered worthy of the profoundest attention.

As an instance of these, I may describe particular gardens. One would have a roof of softly-glowing sapphires, foxglove, bluebell, or gentian, and between these champak stars of ruby. The walls would be covered with tendrils of vine within whose depths lurked tiny blossoms of amethyst. The floor would be of malachite, but alive, growing as coral does, softer than any earthly moss and more elastic to the tread. On every darker leaf might glow dew-drops of self-strung diamond formed from the carbon dioxide of the air by the action of the 'seed of light.' Another grotto would be a monochrome of blue, various copper salts being 'planted' everywhere, and growing in incrustations and festoons of every shade of blue from the faintest tinge of cœrulean azure to the depth of ultra marine and indigo. The floor would be mingled, translucent blue and green and grey, in whose abyss would be seen shapes of anemones, perhaps of such hues as iron oxide, silver chromate, and cuprammonium cyanurate. All this floor would in all respects resemble water but for its greater solidity, and floating on it would be giant lilies, great green leaves of emerald with cups of pearl not less than twelve feet in diameter, with corollæ of pure gold, so fine that they glimmered green, with pistils of platinum on whose tops trembled great pigeon-blooded rubies. Another might be wholly of metal, a mere bower of jasmine, with its floor of violets. The law of growth of these creatures of wisdom was not that of plants or animals, or even of crystals; it was that of the earth. Constantly growing as the planet approached the sun, they as steadily shrank as she departed to aphelion. This was not growth and decay, but the rise and fall of an eternal bosom. It is probable, too, that this is one of the reasons why Atlas neglected the higher kingdoms; they had learned to grow, but on wrong lines, and it was too late to endeavour to correct the error.

These gardens were the principal places of working. It was hardly possible to pass from one place to another without coming upon one of them, so cunningly were they distributed; and in every garden would be found, joyful and noble, parties of workers intent upon their beloved task. The passer-by would gladly join one of such parties, engage in the work for so long as he wished, and then proceed upon his private business. In these same gardens, too, were salvers and goblets always filled with Zro, and after toil, refreshment fitted the workers to return to labour.

Now of these workings in the gardens strange tales are told. It is said that the inhabitants falling to repose were visited in sleep by incubi and succubi (whatever the nature of these may be, and I by no means concur in the opinion of Sinistrari),[1] and that they welcomed such with eagerness. Nay, darker legends tell of infamous commerce and inter-

---

[1] He wrote the classic on Incubi and Succubi.

course with demons foul and malicious, and pretend that the power of Atlas was devilish, and that the catastrophe was the judgement of God. These mediæval fables of the debased and perverted phallicism miscalled Christianity are unworthy even to be refuted, founded as they are on hypotheses contrary to common sense. Nor would they who knew themselves masters of the earth have deigned to degrade themselves, and moreover to vitiate their whole work, by commerce with inferiors. If there be any truth whatever in these stories, it will then be more easily supposable that the Atlanteans, aspiring to journey sunwards to Venus, might invoke the beings of that planet, should it be possible for them to travel to us. And that this is impossible who can assert? On the theory of the Magicians, power increases as the Sun is approached, the inhabitants of earth being more highly infused with the magical force of Our Star than those of Mars, and they again more than those of great Jupiter, gloomy and disastrous Saturn and Uranus, or Neptune lost in star-dreams. Again, the powers of each particular planet may, nay must, be wholly diverse. So fundamental a condition of existence as the value of *g* being vastly various, must not the inhabitants differ equally in body and in mind? What lives on the minute and airless moon can be no inhabitant of what may hide beneath the flaming envelope of the sun, with its fountains of hydrogen flaming an hundred thousand miles into the æther. And surely so wild an ambition as that of Atlas would not have been held by beings so wise and powerful for so many centuries had they not either a sure memory of their coming from Mars, or some earnest of their eventual departure to Venus. Man does not persist in the chimerical for more than a few generations. Alchemy achieved results so startling and so beneficial to humanity at large – one need only mention the discovery of zinc, antimony, hydrogen, opium, gas itself – that the original ideals were changed for others more limited and more practical – or at least more immediately realisable.

Nor is this view unsupported by testimony of a sort.

> Great and glorious, rays of our father the Sun,

says one of the poets of Atlas,

> are they within us. Let us call them forth by utterance that is not uttered, by the gesture that is not made, by the working that is above all working, for they are great and glorious, rays of our father the Sun. Then from our bride that waits for us in the nuptial chamber, green in the green West, blue in the blue East, exalted above our father in the even and in the morn,

spring forth our heirs and our hosts, to greet us in the darkness. Dim-glimmering are our gardens in the light of the seed of light; they are peopled with shadows; they take form; they are as serpents, they are as trees, they are as the holy *Zcrra*, they are as all things straight or curved, they are winged, they are wonderful. With us do they work, and that which was but one is seven, and that which was two is become eleven! With us do they work, and give us of the draught miraculous; us do they instruct in Magic, and feed us the delicate food. Let us call forth them that are within us, that they that are without may enter in, as it was made manifest by Him that maketh secret.

This passage, not devoid of a rude eloquence, makes clear what was held in exoteric circles. For in Atlas the poet was not as in England a holy and exalted being, one set apart for his high calling, throned in the hearts of the people, cherished by kings and nobles, one on whom no wealth and honour are too great to shower, but one of the people themselves, of no greater consequence than any other. Every man was an artist in so far as he was a man; and every man being equally so in nature, whether so in achievement or not mattered nothing, as appreciation was of no moment. Accomplishing Art for the sake of Art, the interest of the creator in his work died with its creation. It may therefore be possible that these words are those of poetic exaggeration, or that there is a concealed meaning in them, or that they are intended to mask and mislead, or that the poet was not himself fully instructed. Indeed it is certain that only the High House had the secrets of Atlas, and that the Magicians of that House held the undeniable if sometimes dangerous doctrine that the truth and falsehood of any statement alternated as do day and night according to the status of the hearer of the statement. However, so strong is the tradition concerning the 'Angel of Venus' that it must at least be considered carefully. The theory appears to have been that if the magicians of Venus invited the Atlanteans, means would assuredly follow, just as if a King summons a paralysed man to his presence, he will also send officers to convey him. Now whether the 'Angel of Venus' is really an angel in anything like the modern sense of the word, or merely a title of one of the principal magicians of that planet, it is evident that the High House ardently desired his presence. That this might be manifested by the birth of a child 'without the stain of Atla' was clearly an ultimate desideratum, an outward and visible sign of redemption, an obvious guarantee of the reality of the occurrence. It was then a Virgin high priestess who achieved so notable a renown; whether or not this is a mere poetic parable of the abiogenesis – if it is indeed fair so to describe it – of the eleventh stage of Zro is another and an open question. In any case, such is the tradition, and numerous parodies of it are still extant in the stories of the births of Romulus and Remus, Bacchus, Buddha and many other legendary heroes of modern times; we even catch an echo in the myths of such barbarian lands as Syria.

So much and no more concerning the Underground Gardens of Atlas, and of their commerce with the inhabitants of Venus.

7

Of Marriage and other Curious Customs of the Atlanteans;
and of Sacrifices to the Gods

I have already adverted to that most singular conception of the duty of the married which opposes the customs of Atlas to those of any other race on Earth. But the considerations which established it have yet to be discussed. I will not insist on that gross and cynical point of view which might perceive in English marriage today a practical vindication of the Atlantean position. On the contrary, in Atlas marriage formed the loftiest of ideals. It resembled the 'Hermetic marriage' of certain alchemists. The bond between the parties was only stronger for the absence of the lower link. The idea underlying this was in the main a particular case of the general proposition that whatever was natural should be transcended. As will be seen in the final chapter, the very stigma of success in their Great Work was the transcending of the sexual process. The bond of marriage was not, however, entirely of this negative character. It had its positive side, and here closely resembled the so-called Christian doctrine of Christ and the church. Husband and wife were to be father and daughter, mother and son, brother and sister, teacher and pupil, and above all, friends. And this relation was to subsist on all planes. The hieroglyph of love was a cross; that of marriage, parallel straight lines; and as the cross was to be transcended in the circle, so were these lines to converge not on earth, but in Venus. In the meanwhile each partner led his own free life; and it often occurred that a woman, having borne two children to a man and married him, would bear two children to another man, and so on for perhaps for two centuries, thus acquiring a cohort of husbands. Such an arrangement must clearly have led to grave confusion had any question of property and inheritance been involved, but notions so unfortunate were unknown. Where all had every heart's desire, of what value were they? It is true that some division of labour (though little) was involved in the social scheme, but it occurred to no one to regard the supervision of the serviles as less honourable than the offering of the great sacrifices. In a perfect organism one part is as necessary and decent as any other part, and no sane observer can reason otherwise. For a perfect organism has a single definite aim, and the only dishonourable feather on an arrow would be one that was out of place. Human nature being what it is, one may nevertheless agree that this measureless content with the existing order, except in so far as the purpose of the establishment of that order was unfulfilled, was rendered possible by the extreme lightness of the toil demanded of any individual. But it is impossible for slaves to understand free men. It is always a wonder to Englishmen that a man should devote himself to unremitting toil for an idea. He is called a crank, basely slandered, the lowest motives being without any reason assigned to his actions, mocked, persecuted, perhaps crucified. This is partly forgivable, as in England philanthropy is almost invariably the mask of vice and fraud.

The ceremony of marriage[1] was simple, dignified, yet poignant. The lovers, in the presence of their whole house, publicly embraced for the last time. Their two children pressed them apart. Elevating their hands in a crossed clasp they gave way, and the children passed through, preceding a most holy image which was borne by a priest and priestess between them. They then parted, and each was severally congratulated and embraced by any of the others who chose, and the priest and priestess then, exalting the image and setting it in a suitable shrine, closed the ceremony by the command 'To work' and adding force to the same by their example.

The education of the children was another important matter in which their ideas were wholly opposed to our own. It ceased altogether at the age of puberty, which was sometimes as early as six, never later than fourteen. Were it so delayed, the delinquent was crowned in mockery with a square black cap, sometimes tasselated, and sent among the serviles to instruct them in religion and similar branches of learning, and never permitted to return to Atlas. The ignorance and superstition of the plains was thus kept at a proper height.

The method of education was indeed singular. Certain Atlanteans who made it their study would place various articles in the hands of infants, and observe what use they made of them. In the course of a few months the experts had accurately mapped the psychology of the child, and it was led in accordance therewith. The marriage customs

---

[1] There was also the marriage of those of the Magicians who refused all intercourse with the opposite sex, and were therefore married to the whole sex as such. Here was no ceremony used; but each had a special mark signifying that he or she was thus consecrated.

of Atlas allowed no too rapid growth in numbers, and it was there-fore easy to give each child attention. The method of opposition was again employed in education, the child's natural wish being constantly stimulated by a parallel training in the contrary subject. Children were also shown a series of ordered facts, and an explanation given. But not the least pains was taken to ascertain whether the child had retained those instructions; they were left as impressions on the mind. The brain was not injured by the strain of being constantly forced to bring up its stores from subconsciousness. It was found in practise that every child learnt everything that it was shown, and that this learning was always ready for use, while the consciousness was never wearied or overcrowded. It was also found that those whose memories were what we call good were precisely those who failed to develop in other ways more useful to society.

The most peculiar of all their methods was the search for genius. It was the business of the experts to pay the most serious and reverent attention to all that a child did, and whenever they failed to under-stand the workings of its mind, to place it under the charge of a special guardian, who did his utmost to comprehend sufficiently to be able to encourage it to become yet more unintelligible.

> Apud eos membrum virile membrano lucido erat; ob quod qualis circumcisio die nativitatis facta erat. Vix credere dignum est, tanquam verum, feminarum montes venereales similitudine facies fuere, facies demoniacæ, sardonicæ, Satyricæ, cujus os erat os vulvæ, res horribilis atque ridiculosa. Ferunt similia de virorum membris, quæ fingunt sicut imagines homunculorum fuere. Lege – Judica – Tace.[1]

Many of the men had ossified extensions of the frontal process which amounted to horns, and the formation was occasionally found in the higher types of women. Curiously carven headdresses of gold were worn by both sexes, and those of priestly rank adorned these with living serpents, and the high priests yet further with feathers or with wings, such being not the spoils of dead birds, but the blossoms of the live gold of the crowns. Some tradition of this custom is found in the pictures of the 'Gods' of Egypt, these gods being merely the Atlanteans whose

---

[1] [Among them, the male member had a clear skin; because of what sort of circum-cision had been done on the day of birth. It is hardly worth believing, yet it is true, the womens' pubic mounds were, in likeness, faces – faces demonic, scornful, satyr-like, whose mouth was the vulva, a thing horrible and laughable. They pro-duce similar things from the mens' members, which they shape as if they were images of little men. Read – judge – be silent.]

mission civilised the country. The names of some of the earlier gods confirm this. Nu (*Heb.* Noah) is Atlantean for 'arch'; Zu (*Egypt.* Shu) for many ideas connecting with wind; Asi means '*cunnus quasi serpens*,'[1] obviously the name of an actual High Priestess. Ra is pure Atlantean for sun, and 'Mse (*Egyptian* Chomse) for moon. The idea in 'Mse is that of a strong woman ('M) closing the mouth of a serpent (S) or dragon, and from this we have the xɪth card of the Bohemian Tarot, and the legend in the Apocalypse. In the mystic Greek used by the Gnostics we find similar traces, Σοφια being from S Ph, giving the idea of 'serpent breath,' i.e., wisdom. IAO is φαλλος, κτεις, προκτος. The word ΛΟΓΟΣ means the Boy (γ) naturally engendered of the Virgin (λ) and the Serpent (σ). ΘΕΟΣ (root ο) means the sun in his strength and also *linga-yoni* conjoined. ΧΡΙΣΤΟΣ is 'The love of passion of the Rising Sun (P) and the Serpent (Σ).' The I and T indicate certain details which are foreign to the present discussion. NEYMA (*Atlantean* ΝΜ) is the 'Arch of the Woman'; ΜΑΡΙΑ, the 'Woman of the Sun.'[2] The words ΜΕΙΘΡΑΣ and ΑΒΡΑΧΑΣ are again derived from Atlas. 'The woman entered, *linga* being conjoined with the *yoni*, bears the Sun from her serpent womb,' and 'From the womb's mouth the Sun (coming seeketh) a womb for his desire, even the womb of a serpent,' the course of the year being signified in this manner, as usual with the ancients. This plan of an idea corresponding to each letter was carried out very strictly: thus ΤΛΑ, 'black,' means the stigma or mark of the virgin's womb, ɪΑ (Hail! Greeting!) 'face to Face,' from the other peculiarity described above. These few examples will suffice to indicate the singular character of the language,[3] and the way in which its essential dogmatic symbols have been incorporated by the heirs of Atlas in the inmost sanctuaries of races which they deemed worthy of such assistance.

I must not pass over in silence the question of the sacrifice to the gods, to which a passing reference has already been made. Such sacrifices were not very frequent; the victims were the 'failures,' those who were useless to the social economy.[4] As they represented capital expenditure, the object was to recover this, at least, since no interest

---

[1] [*Lat.*, 'vulva like a serpent.']

[2] ΜΑR is Atlantean (also Sanskrit!) for 'die.' This word throws light on their conception of death.

[3] Note that no tautologies defile its linguistic wells. 'As I have written' is never changed to 'as I have observed, noted, described, said, indicated, remarked, pointed out' and so on.

[4] I must revert for a moment to the language. ΟΙΚ, Greek Ὀικες, meant the 'House of the penetrating men.' ΝΟΜ, Greek Νομος, the 'arch of the House of the Women,' i.e., that which roofed them in or protected them. Hence 'the law.'

could be expected. The victim was therefore handed over to a High Priest or Priestess, who extracted the life by an instrument devised for and excellently adapted to the purpose, so that it died by exhaustion. The life thus regained was given to 'the gods' in a manner too complex to be described in this brief account.

The early age at which puberty occurred was due to design. The normal period of gestation had also been shortened to four months. This was all part of the scheme to economise time. Old age had been almost done away with by the great readiness of the Atlanteans to 'go and see' at the first sign of failing power. No doubt, further improvements would have been made but for the loss of interest in the matter, all generation being regarded as 'the old experiment,' not likely to repay the trouble of further research. In the two or three hundred years of a man's full vigour, only eight years on an average was the wastage of childhood, and even this was not all waste, since some time at least must be necessary for the experts to discover and direct the tendencies of the mind. The body ought therefore to be regarded as an engine, the theoretical limit of whose efficiency had been reached.

So much I mention of the customs of the Atlanteans with regard to marriage, education and religious sacrifices.

8

Of the History of Atlas, from its Earliest Origins
to the Period Immediately Preceding the Catastrophe

The origin of Atlas is lost in the obscurity of antiquity. The official religious explanation is this: 'We came across (under) the waters on the living Atla,' which is pious but improbable. A mystic meaning is to be suspected. The lay historian says 'We came, escaping from destruction, eight persons in a ship, bearing the living Zro.' This reminds one of later legends of presumably equal value. Poets frankly claim 'We descended from heaven,' and it has been seriously urged that seafarers would have preferred the plains to the rocks. The law of contrariety to Nature explains this away. Others maintain that the earliest settlers came 'by air,' or, 'through air.' This must mean balloons or æroplanes, as flying was not known till centuries after. What is definitely known is that the earliest settlers were of a purely fighting race. An Atlantean Homer, Ylo, has described the first battle in such detail as to leave no doubt that he is retailing facts – a marked contradiction to his earlier books. There appear to have been but few Atlanteans, unless the names given are those of chiefs, which internal evidence controverts. Their valour seems to have been prodigious. The natives were armed with every possible instrument of precision, having cavalry and artillery in abundance, as well as weapons that must have been as superior to the modern rifle (unless Ylo exaggerates) as that is to the arquebus. In spite of this the men of Atlas 'smote them with rods' or 'fell upon them with their cones,' and routed them utterly. This mention of rods and cones has absurdly suggested to commentators that the Atlanteans used their eyes, and hypnotised the enemy. To state such an opinion is sufficient to expose its author to the contempt of the thoughtful. Altogether eighty-six battles were fought, extending over five years, before the natives were reduced to sue for peace. This was granted on generous terms, which the colonists broke, as soon as they dared to do so, in accordance with the invariable practise of colonists, then as much as today. However, it was nigh on an hundred years before the first college of magic was established. Previously the Atla had been carried about as occasion demanded. It was now enshrined with some decency of ceremonial upon a mountain. About three hundred years later we find ourselves face to face with the first great Mystery of Atlas. This is a translation of the record of that most strange event:

> Now it came to pass that all men turned black and died, and that the living Atla abode alone, bearing Mercury, whereof the Sun knoweth. Thus came again the true men of Atlas, and their women, bearing gods and goddesses. And the void suffered nothing, and the earth was at peace. Now then indeed arose Art, and men builded, being blind. And there was light, and the sons of light wrought mischief. Wherefore the wise men destroyed them with their magic, and there is no record because it is written in that which now is.

A sort of '*Si monumentum quæris, circumspice*'[1] seems here implied. In any case there were clearly two gaps unbridgeable between the early struggles of the settlers, the period of great buildings, and the modern period, which proved stable, of 'houses.' The 'houses' were only made possible by the perfecting of Zro, and this helps considerably to fix the date. The next 2,500 years were years of peaceable progress; the labourmills were run without a hitch, and the next event was the discovery of black phosphorus. It had been the custom to worship the Atla with lights, and these lights had been candles of yellow phosphorus in golden sheathes. At that time the Atla was veiled. At one festival of Spring the

---

[1] [If you seek a monument, look around.]

veils were burnt up, the lights extinguished, and the yellow phosphorus was found to have been turned into the black powder. The magicians examined this, and brought Zro to its ninth stage. This revolutionised the condition of things: old age and disease were no more, and death voluntary. Strangely enough this led directly to the Great Conspiracy.

At the end of this period of 2,500 years the system of 'houses' was well established. There were over four hundred such 'houses,' each of perhaps a thousand souls on an average. These were governed by four 'houses of houses' whose rulers took orders from the High House, at the head of which was the living Atla. The plain principle of Atla was revolution; and like all revolutionary bodies, it was obliged to adopt the strictest form of autocracy. A democracy is always soddenly conservative. The only hope is to catch it in one of its moments of crazy enthusiasm, and crush it before it has time to recover. Cæsar and Napoleon both did this so far as they could; Cromwell and Porfirio Díaz did the same within narrower limits.

Now a certain sophist – for philosopher one cannot call him – tried to enunciate a magical law to the effect that the present standard of life was all that could be desired; that further progress would be harmful, that Venus was not worth attaining, and that the sole endeavour of the Magicians should be to preserve things as they were. That such a proposition could be supposed a 'law' reflects no credit on its author or its supporters. Yet of these it found many. The ninth stage of Zro was a leap calculated to unsettle the calmest mind. Its reality had beggared the optimist's daydream. Poets had thrown down their stilettos.[1] High Priests who had spent decades in hopeful experiment saw their results attained by an entirely different method. In short, two thirds of the people were infected with the heresy, and hoped to hear it promulgated as a Law of Magic.

It should here be explained that every Law of Magic had its turn as the principal law of practical working, and the school supporting any law, or insisting on it, became prominent with it. Every dominant law in all history had always been made insignificant by a new discovery about Zro, or other matter of practical importance, just as the 'Peace with Honour' battle-cry of Disraeli was drowned by the calculation of the cost of warships, soldiers and patriotism. Each step in Zro had consequently implied the rise to power of a new school;

---

[1] Needle-sharp daggers of Zro in its seventh stage were used to write on the rock walls of Atlas.

and the sophist was ambitious, and yet the law he wished to establish was the ruling law of the servile races!

The 'law' was accordingly sent to the High House for approval. Some opposition may have been foreseen, but no one was prepared for the blackness of disapproval which actually radiated, striking hearts cold. A course without precedent, no answer was vouchsafed. On the contrary, even normal communication was suspended. The houses which favoured the innovation – 333 in number – took counsel, came to the decision that it was useless to oppose the High House, and were about to acquiesce when a woman who had once been in the Presence of 'To Her' rose and thought vehemently 'The Living Atla is the head of our conspiracy.' In other words, they were the loyalists, the Magicians of the High House the rebels. This was why they had cut themselves off, because their own head was against them. It was instantly resolved to go to the High House, and demand the custody of 'To Her.' Nearing the goal, however, a remnant of the ancient reverence half cowed even the ringleaders – I may mention that five of every six of the heretics were women – when they saw a stern phalanx of magicians, its point threatening their centre. As they wavered, a woman cried 'They are only men such as we are.' The ranks stiffened; on all sides the army closed upon the tiny phalanx, which only numbered sixty-six all told. It was then that the truth was known. Ere a blow could be struck, the attacking party vanished; it was instantaneous and complete annihilation. From that moment it was certain that the ruling power in Atlas was Something[1] infinitely more awful than even the Living Atla. In order to avoid any possible repetition of such a disaster – for the Magicians of the High House knew that any manifestation of the Supreme must undo the work of centuries – they gave out that they had become too terrible to look upon, and for the future they always appeared with heavy veils, or rather masks, since for the most part they were carven fantastically by the wearers in their leisure hours. A further alteration was made in the system of government. The head of one of the 'houses of houses' was made supreme: the High House took no part in affairs of state. Thus the Atla was to all intents and purposes deposed, although the same reverence and sacrifice were paid to it as formerly. It became a 'constitutional monarch,' in our modern jargon.

The next thousand years were years of serious trial in other ways. The toil of repopulation was excessive, and there was a revolt or rather strike of the servile races, which was ended by the substitution of 'bread from

---

[1] This matter is not open for discussion. Even at this distant date it would be dangerous to do so much even as indulge in speculation.

heaven' for those products of the earth on which they had formerly been fed, a diet which proved so adapted to their natures that no labour troubles ever recurred.

The Greek legends of the wars between Gods, giants, Titans are traditional of a real war or series of wars which continued with intervals for over two hundred years. The enemy had developed naval armament to an extreme. Their tactics were these:

1. To wipe out the servile races and so interfere with the production of Zro.
2. To rush and destroy the High House.

The first of these met with a great deal of success, the floating rock being struck with projectiles and sunk. This occurred chiefly on the outlaying islands, where they were not too much afraid to make raids in force. They also sent epidemic disease of many kinds. Atlas was reduced to such extremity in these ways that at one time the waterways were forced and the assault on the High House was actually carried out, bombardment continuing day and night for months together. Through a misunderstanding of a well known magical law, Atlanteans at that time considered themselves prohibited from employing any other defence than the rods and the cones of their forefathers; and these, it appears, were useless against machinery, or against men protected by fortification in such a way that they could not be got at from any quarter. Thus the sharklike submarines of the enemy were unassailable. The war was therefore at first entirely one-sided. A certain youthful magician, however, resolving to die for his country if need were, decided to retaliate. He had found that Zro in its nascent state (i.e., between the globes) had the power of bringing about endothermic reaction, seawater, for example, becoming caustic soda and hydrochloric acid; and further that this acid thus produced was many thousand times more active than in its normal state. For example, the rock basins in which he conducted his first experiment dissolved as rapidly as butter under boiling oil. He then prepared a number of pairs of receiver-globes, and dropped them in the vicinity of the enemy's submarines by night. In this manner he destroyed the hulls of almost the whole fleet in a single night; and the remainder fled in panic at dawn. They returned the following year, carrying out daylight raids only and devoting themselves chiefly to destroying the labour-mills. The young magician had been rewarded for his services by being presented to the Atla, and this example encouraged others to find means of attacking the invaders. Artificial darkness was therefore invented, and combined with the former method; but this was only partially successful, the tremendous pace of the 'sharks' enabling them to evade any threatening clouds. They did enormous damage, and the supplies of Zro were seriously curtailed. Things now went from bad to worse, and culminated in the attack on the High House, the besiegers keeping their battleships surrounded by rafts of fire, so that attack was impossible even by night. It was then that the High House called on the heroism of its sons. Armed with long swords of Zro, they plunged into the sea, to perish under the tooth of the Zhee-Zhou, but not before they had time to hack the invading battleships to shreds. Their floating torch-rafts only assisted the attack by directing the swimmers to their quarry. The attack on the High House had aroused Atlas at last. A counter-invasion was plotted and carried out with immediate and complete success, the enemy being exterminated, and their country not merely ravaged but destroyed by arousing the forces of earthquake. All activity of this kind being however deprecable, a recurrence was guarded against by removing the High House to the lofty mountain previously described, and a 'house' was chosen to cultivate the art of war, and entrusted with the duty of destroying any living thing that might approach within a hundred miles of Atlas.

Only one other adventure of historical importance remains to be recorded. It is the attempt of some foolish Atlanteans to found an 'Empire,' and so to be entirely distinguished from the missionary effort referred to previously. The original settlement of Atlas, as has been the case with all flourishing colonies, was made by a few hardy pioneers, who strengthened themselves gradually by growth. But Atlas in her momentary madness poured out blood and treasure in the fatuous attempt to impose alien domination on lands utterly unsuited to the genius of the people. The idea, of course, was to increase the supply of labour and consequently the output of crude Zro. In the first place the adventure was expensive. It was uneconomical (in the scientific sense) to send ships with less than a thousand fighting men. The Zro required for these meant the employment of at least seven thousand serviles, and naval construction was therefore of a colossal order. But although little difficulty was found in conquering the country in the military sense, the natives had to be almost exterminated, and the labour of the survivors proved difficult to enforce. It was even then not a tenth as efficient as that of the serviles at home. The imported serviles moreover caught native diseases, and died in hundreds; and though by prodigious sacrifices the West African Empire was kept going for nearly two hundred years, it had to end at last no less ingloriously than the French adventure in Mexico, or the English in India, Egypt and South Africa.[1]

The main causes were the impossibility of breeding children in a climate so unsuitable, even of maintaining their own women, and above all the fact that the crude Zro was not of quality equal to that obtained in Atlas, and that the Zro generated by the Atlanteans themselves was not to be made at all outside their own country. The lesson was learnt. Until the end no further attempt was made to advance in any but the true direction. The great majority of the colonists returned to Atlas; but many, degenerating as is the fashion with colonists of this conquering kind, abandoned Zro for gross food, intermarried with the natives, and have generally degenerated yet further to races inferior even to the present descendants of those who were in those days the equivalents of the serviles of Atlas.

9

Of the Catastrophe, its Antecedents and Presumed Causes

In my remarks on Zro I gave a necessarily somewhat diffuse account of the properties of this remarkable substance. It must now be made clearer that the crude Zro in its nine stages produced by the serviles, and consumed in the 'houses,' was in each stage of inferior quality to that of the same degree produced by the Atlanteans, and consumed by the High House. For example, the crude Zro was made in a labour-mill with all sorts of insulations. The first stage of the priest's Zro could be made anywhere and at any time, and naturally directed itself to the receptacle for it without any precautions. It must, I think, be presumed that the Zro generated in the High House was again of far greater purity and potency. Very little of it can have been used in the experiments of the magicians, and it is therefore necessary to account for enormous quantities, produced during many centuries of uninterrupted labour. I have, however, no data of any kind for this investigation; the mysteries of the High House have ever been inscrutable, and were not wholly delivered to the Heirs of Atlas. They must be rediscovered by the magicians of the new race. It may be that in some form or other the Zro had been made stable, and used to impregnate the column which is alleged to have been driven

---

[1] I write a little, but not much, in advance of the events. To illustrate the theory here advanced I will ask the reader to compare the results of the attempts to colonise America by (*a*) the whole military power of Spain at her zenith, (*b*) the handful of exiles in the *Mayflower*.

'through the earth'; perhaps, and less improbably, only to the depth of a few hundred miles. This column, however long it may have been, had certainly its top immediately beneath the reservoir of the High House. It had been completed about seventy years before the 'catastrophe,' but apparently no effort was made to utilise it in any way. To me it appears probable that in some one mind the whole 'catastrophe' was brooding, that the column was part of the device, and that the event which I shall now describe was the other part.

This event was the birth of a child in the High House, a child without the distinguishing mark of the daughters of Atlas. That any child at all should have been born there is so incredible that I am inclined to suspect an improper use of the word 'born.' I think rather that a magician brought Zro to its eleventh stage, when it takes human form, and lives! The alternative theory is that of the 'Angel of Venus,' described in the chapter on the underground Gardens of Atlas. The supporters of this theory hold that the child was not born of a priestess, but of the Living Atla.

In any case, the whole country gave itself to unbridled rejoicing. Work was carried on at a greater speed than ever before: one might say a delirium of labour. For eleven years this continued without cessation, and then without warning came the order to repair to the High House – every man, woman and child of Atlas. What was then done I know not, and dare not guess; that same day seven volunteers, heroic exiles from the reward of so many centuries of toil, voluntary maroons on the discarded planet, the Heirs of Atlas, turned their faces from the High House, and severally sought distant mountains, there each to guard his share of the Secrets of the Holy Race, and in due time to discover and train up fit children of other races of the earth so that one day another people might be founded to undertake another such task as that now ended.

Hardly had the pinnacle of Atlas melted into the sea behind them, than the 'catastrophe' occurred. The High House and the column beneath it, with all the inhabitants of Atlas, shot from the Earth with the vehemence of a million lightnings, bound for that green blaze of glory that scintillated in the West above the sunset.

Instantly the earth, its god departed, gave itself up to anguish. The sea rushed unto the void of the column and in a thousand earthquakes Atlas, 'houses' and plains together were overwhelmed for ever in the ocean. Tidal waves rolled round the world; everywhere great floods carried away villages and towns; earthquakes rocked and tempest roared; tumult was triumphant. For years after the catastrophe the dying tremors of the Event still shook mankind with fear.[1] And the eternal waves of the great mother rolled over Atlas, save where earth in her agony thrust up gaunt pinnacles, bare masts of wreckage to mark the vanished continent. Save for its heirs, of whose successors it is my highest honour to be the youngest and least worthy, oblivion fell, like one last night in which the sun should be for ever extinct, upon the land of Atlas and its people.

Shall such high purpose fail of emulation, such achievement not example and excite us to like striving? Then let earth fall indeed from her high place in heaven, and mankind be outcast for ever from the sun! Men of earth! seek out the heirs of Atlas; let them order you into a phalanx, let them build you into a pyramid, that may pierce that appointed which awaits you, to establish a new dynasty of Atlanteans to be the mainstay and mainspring of the earth, the pioneers of their own path to heaven, and to our lord and father, the sun! And he put his hand upon his thigh, and swore it.

By the ineffable .... TLA, and by the holy Zro, did he swear it, and entered into the body of the new Atla that is alive upon the earth.

---

[1] The Legend of the Deluge is derived from this event.

The Mysterious Malady

The case is certainly a puzzle ....

I wonder if my old diaries would throw any light upon it. Often I have thought that if only our intelligence were super-subtle as it should be, we could detect – and check – every disease at the outset. I have always advocated trimensual examinations, even for the healthiest persons. The dentist admits already that it is only common sense to do as much for the teeth. Why then not for those far more delicate organs, the heart, the kidneys, and the brain?

I met Anna in 1904. I'll start there and make extracts for my casebook.

EXTRACTS, 1904

JAN. 13. Two years since I qualified, and the horizon absolutely black. The rent of this house in Devonshire Street eats up my capital; but I have aspired to be a consulting physician, and I'll go through with it. If it weren't for my U.C.H. job, though, a month would see me starving.

It is too one-sided, life. All day I sit idle in my office, and the rich, who need me much, do not come to me. In the evenings I go out to help the poor, who need me less, in many ways, and often hardly thank me. The rich seem to think it divine right that they should live in luxury on what the poor should share; and the poor seem to grasp angrily and blindly. Was not I the son of poor peasants in Ayr? Have not I toiled night after night to earn knowledge? And what can I do but give what blessings I can to my ain fowk? But they resent my rise; had I been born rich, they would bow and lick my boots. It is because I am one of themselves, that I am not popular with them. O strange, blind race! How pitiful you are! Well, let me spend and be spent for you, as all the helpers of man must be!

JAN. 24. A real patient. A Brightic, too; I can keep him going for three years, with luck. Like finding money!

P.S. One swallow doesn't make a summer.

It is surely monstrous that we doctors should thrive on human misery. The Son of Æsculapius should have a heart tenderer than all other men. Yet all his training goes to make him callous. He sees – he must see – suffering; it is presented to him at such a pace that he has no time to feel sorrow. He is taught to handle the body without emotion; and he is economically tied to the chariot-wheels of Death.

Oh God, if thou be Love, keep me loving! If thou be Mercy, keep me merciful! Do not let the hardness of life contaminate my spirit!

FEB. 3. No luck with appointments. Jealousy, of course. Amazing that medicine, which of all studies should make men benevolent and broadminded, should breed practitioners full of hatred, envy, malice, and all uncharitableness. Petty! Petty! Petty!

FEB. 8. My Brightic has committed suicide. Was ever such rotten luck? Lord knows when I shall ever see another! What mockery! There are thousands of them, that don't know it even; and if they came to me I could prevent the disease from ever taking hold.

Once again the rotten economics of the day piles wretchedness on wretchedness. If medical men of distinction were paid salaries by the state, they would have time to work, and their hearts would be in their work. As it is, they are all driven to do as little as they can for the money they earn, and they are bound to seek palliatives rather than cures. The conquest of tuberculosis, gout and rheumatism would bankrupt every mother's son of us. Can this be why medicine has hardly advanced since Galen?

FEB. 9. I wish I had specialised in Lunacy. The subject attracts me hugely, and with the present appalling increase of insanity, there's plenty of room!

The main cause of insanity is metaphysical, of that I am convinced. It is a disease of the ego, fundamentally; and drink, worry, and all the other so-called causes are but secondary, just as chill is only a secondary cause of phthisis. Those men whose heart is in their work, who are devoted to ideals, to humanity, those in short who love, in the best and biggest sense of the word, never become insane. Objectivity of thought, and hard work, are prophylactics absolute.

The spring is bitter indeed, this year. All last night I worked in Hoxton with the Mission. Heart-breaking, the poverty of the place. And I myself too poor to pay my 'bus fare home! So I walked back, and saw the grey dawn break in the mist – a very Scottish morning – and my heart filled with wonder and hope. I do not know why. Some angel came upon me as I walked – more sensibly: the fresh air and brisk exercise chased away the cobwebs of a sordid night!

Why 'more sensibly'? I believe there is some truth in the poets' visions – else, how could they dominate the centuries? There is a truth of the heart as well as of the brain; 'I love' is explained by the Song of Solomon quite as well as by medical treatises on the physiology of it. (I wonder why I thought of love? I have never so much as noticed a woman. I have had no thought but to help humanity. God help me to do it.)

MARCH 12. It's a regular conspiracy at the hospital: Hemming, and Flint, it appears, have sworn revenge upon me for some imaginary insult – more likely envy, plain black envy. How can men (!) of science (!) be so *small*?

MARCH 20. The Hospital Ball. The best luck in the world – I wonder – or the worst! It's certainly too good to be true ...... and yet it can't be false, or there's no worth in my judgement of human nature. Lady Anna Cleveland! Oh no! I'm dreaming!

I must set my thoughts in order. I went to the ball more lest my absence be remarked than for any other reason. Social functions have always seemed to me so useless that they have bored me. I was introduced to this woman and that woman, and was, I hope, as polite as a Scots peasant lad with nothing in his head but pathology can hope to be. (I know I am awkward.) But I took no notice. Then, all of a sudden, I found myself looking into wonderful deep eyes. It seems we had been talking for some time, and I had not realised the fact. I blushed all over. I had never looked into a woman's eyes before. She did not appear to notice my confusion; she only went on (as I thought) with more comprehending kindliness. She made me talk of my work; I did so like a man hypnotised. Then, I do not quite know how, I found myself asking her to dance. And, wonder of wonders, I found that I *could* dance! I have always been as clumsy with my feet as I am deft with my fingers. By-and-by we sat down and talked again. Her voice is very soft and gentle and far-away. She has brown hair curling over the temples, and her eyes always smile. Otherwise her face is very grave and motherly, although she is quite young.

She is nearly as tall as I am, lissom and slender. At least, so says my memory. All I really remember is the glow of great kindliness that radiated from her.

We parted: I was still adream. She put both her hands in mine, and she said 'Come to see me!' That was all; but there is more in manner than in matter. If she had said 'I love you. I adore you. I am yours in body and soul' it could have meant no more.

MARCH 21. I'm not dreaming – but I think I'm raving mad. I called this afternoon; and not only was she gracious as during that wonderful waltz, but I felt the same subcurrent in her voice. We laugh at the quacks with their 'Magnetism' – but what is it? It is *something*. And I've never been 'in love' – am I 'in love' now? I'd better see a doctor!!!

During the whole interview I was terribly shy. It is new to me to have to keep back what I want to say. I am sure that she would not have been offended; but some silly idea of etiquette prevented me. Besides, I do not like it. A poor, struggling doctor should not lift his eyes to a duke's daughter! Bah! 'A man's a man for all that.' I've nothing to be ashamed of in my life. It's not her rank; it's not her wealth; it's her goodness and her beauty that make me feel unworthy of her.

Yet I know she loves me, and means to make me win her. I know it subconsciously. From every worldly standpoint, it is my duty as a man to fight against it. But will not Nature be too strong? *She* does not hesitate. Don't think I'm calling her 'forward'; she is the most modest woman in the world. But she is too simple, too sincere, too *good* (in a word) to pretend to lie to me, or to herself, about the most sacred thing in life.

MARCH 28. What a damnable week! I have suffered intensely. I know – without having been told – why she has gone away. She wanted to look deep in her heart – and to give me time to look in mine – so as to make sure that this our love is no mere impulse.

Such ordeals purify.

And now comes a note: 'I'm back from Brighton. It has been *dreadfully* dull. Won't you call and cheer me up one afternoon?'

MARCH 29. Again the world has conquered Nature. I simply daren't propose on such a short acquaintance. The most beautiful girl in London, and one of its heiresses! And I but a struggling physician, on the brink of bankruptcy. Yet I know inwardly that she wants me as utterly as I want her. Oh God! Oh God! if it be only true.

.... How the devil *does* one propose?

MARCH 30. One doesn't propose; it happens. I daren't trust myself to write, and it is too sacred. (Oh scientific, critical, cynical spirit, where are you flown?) We sat, looking at each other across the tea-table, incapable of speech; a moment later, we were in each other's arms. Don't ask me how!

JUNE 12. Back from Lugano. London promises a most brilliant season. The new house has been admirably decorated. To think I should be in Cavendish Square, a whole house, within three years! And London has suddenly discovered that I am *The Doctor*. I can see myself Physician-in-Waiting to His Majesty within five years! A baronetcy, perhaps! The mountain has come to Mohammed!

AUGUST 10. Anna grows more adorable every day. But I'm overworked with patients, and bored with dinners and dances. We start tonight for the shoot – all day and every day in the heather is what I want!

OCTOBER 3. Back to the old grind! But with Anna life is all pure happiness. I wonder my patients never notice how my thoughts stray. But they're all self-hypnotised; I'm the fashionable doctor, and their health doesn't matter!

This is the last entry. I seem to have forgotten all my old habits – life has been such an even flow of success that I have had nothing to write down! Yet things have not been altogether smooth, to say the truth. The infernal jealousy of my brother (!) physicians has been annoying. It was certainly Hughes who prevented my being called in at his Majesty's fatal illness. I believe I could have saved him – and possibly England. The political crisis has become serious indeed. Anna wants me to stand for Parliament. No, thank you! If they make me a peer, well and good; but to squabble with those low brutes in the Commons – not I! Well, this is indeed digression! None of it throws the smallest light on Anna's state of health. Perhaps I am fanciful; but it is worrying me to death. Possibly, if I were to put down the symptoms in black and white, it would clear my mind. Very likely it is some transitory problem; but I have the gravest fears. No case has ever so bewildered me! I will enter up my daily observations from today, June 18, 1911.

ANNA'S SYMPTOMS

1. I noticed a certain coldness in her manner about Easter: but it passed quickly, only to return, however, at intervals.

2. She has formed the habit of writing almost daily to her aunt, whom she formerly neglected. But this is surely a trifle!

3. She has grown very irritable in small matters, especially before dinner. Yes: I don't like the irritability: her temper has always been angelic. Query – can she be — Oh, impossible!

There! was ever a slighter indictment? Yet, I 'feel it in my bones,' to use the strange old peasant phrase, that there is something seriously wrong. Enough of this for today!

JUNE 19. I must analyse closely the psychology of Anna's behaviour. I went upstairs at 5 o'clock to tea. She came rather effusively to greet me, commented on my appearing fagged out, made me 'cosy,' and showered a dozen little attentions upon me. She even got out my big black pipe, and lit it for me – this struck me as very singular, for as a rule I am not supposed to smoke in the drawing-room. It sounds ideal – well on the way to Darby and Joan! Yet there was something false in it all. I don't mean exactly that she was deceiving me, but that she was acting under some constraint or impatience. So strongly did I feel this suppressed irritability on her part that, were I not a man of such absurdly equable temper, it would surely have communicated itself to me.

JUNE 20. 2 A.M. I am so disturbed that I cannot sleep. So I have come down to the study to write these notes. There is a new incident to record, decidedly strange, yes, I may even call it suspicious. It is a slight thing in itself; but to what may it not point? We had dined with Lord Chillingham, *en famille*, and returned rather late. Anna went to her escritoire, scribbled a note, and gave it to Francis – dear old boy, he has been with her since she was in long clothes – to put in the post. But in his manner of taking the letter and the *very peculiar intonation* of his formal 'Yes, my lady!' I divined a secret understanding. Whatever may be afoot, Francis knows of it!

JULY 1. There has been nothing worth notice in the last week, but I observe a growing uneasiness in Anna – a trace of some anxiety. She keeps on wishing the season were over – and at the same time she is keen to have Aunt Sybil in the house. Which, as Euclid says, is absurd! I'm damned if I'll put up with Aunt Sybil, especially since Anna may be on the verge of a nervous breakdown. There! I wrote it by accident! BUT!! *Can that be it?* There's nothing in the world to cause it. If it were myself, now! That old fool the Grand Duke Fedor walked out of my consulting room this afternoon, just because I told him that he drank too hard – and he does, and worse! After all, I have a secure fortune, and can afford to be honest now and then, even with Grand Dukes!

JULY 3. Anna burst into tears this afternoon, and though I coaxed her with all my skill she would not tell me the cause. She sobbed herself to peace upon my breast, though; whatever may be wrong, I never doubt her love. Thank God for that!

Later. There is certainly some deviltry afoot. The whole evening – Anna went out to the Fitzbras to dinner – the telephone has been ringing. When I go to the instrument, the exchange girl denies that she has called me. I shall write a strong letter to the P.M.G. – or is it that the girl has orders to deny the call on hearing a man's voice at the 'phone? Hum!

Later. Have asked Francis about the 'phone. He answers that he never heard it ring. But I notice such trepidation and change of voice that I am sure he is lying.

Later yet. I have solved the mystery – and it grows deeper. At the next call I sprang to the instrument, and saw with my own eyes that the bell was not being struck. Yet all the while I could hear it! Only one explanation seems possible. An instrument has been installed secretly in some other part of the house. Why? In God's name, why? —

I shall certainly tell *no one* about these things. Whatever may be wrong, no scandal! My wife's good name is dearer to me than the world.

JULY 4. Two infernal annoyances today, though they have nothing to do with Anna.

1. Sir George Bloggs at lunch tells me that the Crédit Lyonnais is involved in some political scandal in France, and may have to close its doors at any moment – something about the Russian loans. Not a soul knows; but I had quietly packed away over two million sterling there! A serious blow indeed should I lose that, for I am more than doubtful as to the safety of the bulk of my fortune.

2. A point-blank refusal, conveyed very politely at teatime by that young fool Radley, to make me a peer. This after the tens of thousands I have poured into their dirty party funds!

Anna is more disturbed and irritable than ever. This may be partly due to sympathy with my own annoyance – I hope so. Yet I thought I had successfully concealed my worries from her.

JULY 6. Aunt Sybil has arrived without a word of warning. Damn! However, I'll pretend to like it; I'm sure, if it does Anna good, all right. I don't mind suffering in a good cause!

Later. Hooray! She's only staying two nights!

JUNE 7. The telephone nuisance recommenced this after-noon – Anna was out. Rather curious that it never plays this game when she's in. *Ergo*, it depends on her to connect and disconnect it. I spoke to Henry about it. Result, amazing. The young ass burst into tears, or nearly, and promised it shouldn't occur again. Then he blamed the exchange! Rather funny logic, eh? There's something damned deep behind all this! Henry must be in it too, anyhow, whatever it is. Really, I am begin-ning to be worried.

JULY 14. The Royal Society have refused to allow me to read my paper on Lesions of the Corpora Quadrigemina in rela-tion to Diabetes. There I trace the influence of that scoundrel Bryant. I shall send it – with just one biting comment – to *The Lancet* for publication; Bryant! who hardly knows the colon from the cranium! I could buy him body and soul ten times over with what I make in a day. And he works against me in the dark!

P.S. Anna is certainly worse today. Her fits of temper are really becoming intolerable. I am convinced it is only illness, or I could find it in me to be angry. Poor girl! I wish to God I knew what's wrong. However serious her trouble may be, I would rather know. I'd call in Sir Simon Pan, but – well, they talk, they talk!

JULY 15. The secret is out – it is disgrace. I feared it. I came upstairs rather quietly, to hear Anna at the telephone saying 'He's downstairs. It's quite safe. Trust me. Nine o'clock, then: my black dress. Yes, I'll tell him.' Tell whom? I opened the door quickly and quietly; Anna was reading on the ottoman, at the other end of the room from the 'phone! I began to believe the Eastern stories of women's cunning! However, I'll make sure. I said to her that I was called away to Edinburgh on an important consultation, and must catch the dining-car train. James packed my bag; Anna drove with me to Easton in the Rolls-Royce. She was intensely affectionate, pretended to be terribly upset at parting from me – she-devil! She made sure I was safely in the train. She forgot it stops at Willesden! I slipped out, taxied back to town, got a detective, and set him to work. I spent the next two nights at the Ritz – and a grand old harking–back to bachelor days it was! I ran into Jimmy Sinclair that very evening at the Empire; and we made the old town think the Germans had carried out their silly threat to bombard us with Zeppelins!

JULY 18. Back from – Edinburgh! The cat was nearly out of the bag last night. It cost me a fiver to prove to a worthy guardian of the peace that I was not 'd. and d.' Anna overjoyed to see me, and I to see Anna. Thank God, thank God! I have wronged her altogether. The detective said there was no shadow of ground for suspecting her actions, though he hinted that if I kept him on the job indefinitely – Thank you, I know that story!

Well, thank God she's true. I must have heard her words wrongly. Yet – moral error I could have forgiven; perhaps that were better than the physical or (worse!) mental trouble which I must now conclude to be the cause of her strange actions.

JULY 31. I am happy again. Anna seems perfectly herself once more. Please God it may last!

AUGUST 24. Scotland – the very word's a tonic. The grouse are plentiful and strong on the wing. I think I'm shooting better than ever. But the ghillies are a surly lot. Old Hamish's temper is quite spoilt. They have an infernal trick of whispering to each other – quite new – puts me off my birds. But I don't believe I'm missing half they say I am. Dogs are not what they used to be; or else some fool's putting up a joke on me.

SEPT. 1. There is certainly something entirely wrong with Anna. She is constantly in tears, and no efforts of mine can drag a word from her. Her irritability, too, is more pronounced than ever. This is particularly curious, for there is something I might almost call abominably self-satisfied in her secret relations with the servants. It seems to me that there is a hidden meaning in every word and glance – but of what nature I am entirely at a loss to divine. It is at least evident that I am the only one left out of the secret.

SEPT. 2. I am sick of the mystery that surrounds me. I shall go straight back to London.

SEPT. 5. Bills! Well, I suppose we have been living extravagantly, but we can afford it, damn it! If these fools knew the vast sums I have laid by in banks and bonds all over the world these last ten years, they'd never ask for payment this century. Now what shall I do? Shall I pay the fools, or shall I keep my secret? The latter, a thousand times!

Later. Anna has given me a cheque. One day soon I will surprise her with the list of my holdings – how happy she will be when she knows that I could fight Westminster or Bedford to a finish, and win out!

SEPT. 6. Anna's behaviour grows more and more extraordinary. I very much distrust Fanchette, who is nowadays constantly in the room, even when I am there, on some trivial pretext. I am convinced that something is going on behind my back, and that all the servants are in the plot.

Later. I took an opportunity to examine Anna's eyes very closely. The pupils are equal. I found the accommodation slow to act, but not very specially abnormal. However, secretiveness and loss of appetite, combined with the really very intense irritability, can only mean one thing. God help me!

SEPT. 8. The more I think it over, the more certain I am that Anna has become – that I should have to say it! – a slave to morphia. Almost I accuse myself. I searched my conduct anxiously – have I done anything to make her unhappy, anything that might drive her to such a dreadful solace? My conscience, humbly yet firmly, answers: No.

SEPT. 12. There is no longer any doubt in my mind. Everything is explained. No doubt the servants are all in league with her. I shall discharge them *en bloc*, shut up the house, and take Anna abroad. There is an excellent specialist in Lausanne.

Later. As I suspected, Anna is furious at my decision. She urges a thousand reasons against it – my practice, and so on. On the surface, she talked very good sense; but I can trace the real feeling beneath the words. In the midst of the storm, she calmed quite suddenly, and yielded gladly – quite her own sweet self. But there again I traced the action of the drug; she evidently feared to arouse suspicion, or thought that she could continue to deceive me.

SEPT. 13. 7 A.M. Last night she made desperate love to me – an obvious trick. About one o'clock this morning, finding that she could not sleep (another symptom, perhaps) she asked me for a hypnotic. (Perhaps this too was a blind.) I laid her out with a big dose of veronal, and while she slept, went over her body with a magnifying glass for marks of the syringe. There were none; she evidently takes it by the mouth, or in some other way.

SEPT. 20. Lausanne. Dr Galmier is an imbecile; tells me he does not believe she has any such tendency. The devilish cunning of the drug fiend! It baffles even the experts. He told me I was looking tired and worried. So I ought to be, with this appalling tragedy to face! He could at least see how thin and pale poor Anna looked. We may very likely winter at St Moritz.

SEPT. 24. Things are going well financially at any rate: I have banked half a million sterling with the Crèdit Génévois, and invested as much more in the French Rente. But what is money, when the only person on earth one loves is attacked by the most terrible of diseases? I am the most miserable man living.

SEPT. 28. (Venice.) By heaven, an idea! I *will* keep her from the drug, and I see now how to do it.

SEPT. 29. All is in order. I have engaged a steam yacht: Anna and I are to go out to Campo Santo in a gondola; the yacht is to spill us with her wash, rescue us, and take us out to sea for a month. In whatever manner she has managed to conceal the morphine, the salt water will spoil it! At least I shall be able to observe the effects of privation. But I shall wait a week, and lull her suspicions first.

OCT. 8. (At sea.) The plan succeeded admirably. I wonder, though, whether the drug was morphine or some other. She shows none of the symptoms of privation, but her nerves are evidently shattered. She seems dominated by some dreadful fear.

OCT. 9. I believe she is getting morphia after all. I caught her just before lunch in earnest conversation with the captain. They changed their manner quite noticeably on perceiving my approach. Anna is magnetic enough, God knows; like that strange Countess Tarnovska, she has the power of forcing everyone to do her will.

Later. Undoubtedly the story has got around the ship. I see the men whispering together; they cast pitying glances at her.

OCT. 10. She knows I know. She is doing all in her power to hide that symptomatic irritability; but it is useless. Daily she grows thin, pale and haggard; the drug is doing its horrible work too well. What have I done, oh my God, to deserve this chastisement? I never took much stock in religion, but I have been a pretty straight sort of chap. Yet I could not be worse punished had I committed the 'Unpardonable Sin' – whatever that may be!

OCT. 11. The captain is certainly an accomplice. Likely enough he is a drug fiend himself; all these Italians have some beastly vice or another.

It is a strange thing; this illness of Anna's has set me to thinking about my 'soul.' (What is a soul?) I am undoubtedly hearing – that is, of course, recollecting – the words 'The soul that sinneth it shall die.' I don't recall them consciously; I can only suppose I heard them as a boy at kirk, or possibly from that old blackguard Rayner of Edinburgh. Yet they literally haunt me; I could almost swear I hear the sailors saying them at me. It shows how Anna's condition has set my own nerves on edge.

OCT. 14. Pretending I was trying a mere experiment, I tested Anna by psychoanalysis. She reacted normally to the words 'drug,' 'needle,' 'morphine,' and some others cognate which I slipped into the list, but violently to 'enemy,' 'black,' 'murder,' 'poison,' 'knife' and 'danger.' Freud would assume that she was in fear of danger of being stabbed or poisoned by some enemy, possibly a coloured man of some kind. If so, this is an insane fear; I hope to God – I must have offended God beyond pardon if it be so – that this is not the case. There is no insanity in her family so far as I know, though I believe her grandfather drank himself to death. But then so did most of those intemperate Early Victorians.

OCT. 15. Experiment continued. She reacts in the most emphatically violent manner to the words 'insanity,' 'delusion' and the like. The worst of all calamities has fallen upon me – it is no more than I deserve, but oh my God, have mercy upon me – a miserable sinner! – my wife is mad. She knows it herself and dreads that I may have discovered it. Poor, poor Anna!

OCT. 16. I have told the captain to go about and put in at Marseilles. Anna must have the best advice that Science can give her. Besides, this is a small vessel, and I feel at the mercy of the storm, with all this bullion aboard. I shall not be happy till it is safely in the vaults of my bank in Paris. Thank God, the danger of a European war is over for a while.

OCT. 20. (Marseilles.) A magnificent dinner *chez* Basso to celebrate our safe arrival! Anna seems much better; it is quite the happy hours of honeymoon again. Yet the shadow of this awful disaster hangs over me all the time – poor Baby! I hope she does *not* know. Let her slide easily into dementia, if it must be, rather than endure the horrors of aggravated and unbalanced consciousness which accompany other forms of madness!

Later. It is difficult to concentrate my thoughts. Some infernal idiot keeps on ringing up the man in the next room, who is evidently out. Damn!

OCT. 21. I went to a priest this morning. Something kept me from telling him the real trouble which weighs upon me like Olympus on the Titans. He, on the other hand, was a shallow, stupid fool. He could do no more than rate me for a 'heretic.' Asses!

Later. The mail has come from England. They have filled my post at the Hospital. It was only to be expected; in my absence there was no way to check the conspiracy of Bryant and Flint and the rest of the accursed gang. I showed Anna the letter, told her she must use her family influence. She merely burst into tears – at dinner, too, before fifty people. Alas! it is only one more evidence of the great calamity.

OCT. 22. Have been out all night seeking distraction – and finding it, in a way – wandering about in the lowest quarters of the town. It has done me good; I can face Fate for the moment.

Later. A most extraordinary thing has occurred. Walking down the Cannebière, a Frenchman (I will swear to it, no make-believe) called in my ear as he passed: 'We'll get you yet! We'll get you yet! We'll get you yet!' and the accent was perfectly English, and the tone that of my own father, dead these twenty years! It sounds a foolish fancy, and I should have dismissed it as such, but that it happens to fit in very curiously with certain *extremely* serious matters that I have been *most particularly* careful not to mention in these notes. But *now* I see – I never did till now – how this whole business is linked up with Anna's terrible illness.

I must think further of this – perhaps I have the key at last.

Later. Good God! Can such things be possible? I have the answer to the whole damned riddle in the one word – Flint!

Very good: to England; I know what to do. With my wealth it will be easy to – well, I won't write what, even here.

NOV. 2. The banquet is for tomorrow night. Oh! I'll unmask the villainy! Flint Anna's lover all these years! Half London in a plot to drive me mad! Anna's own madness simulated, part of their scheme to drive me further into the toils! And why, in God's name, why? Ah – I dare not – oh God, thou knowest I dare not – write the reason. Thou alone knowest my secret guilt! Thou knowest me, that I am of all men the most damned. Thou knowest also that I must admit myself most worthy of damnation. The devil himself must have prompted me to the one means which assures my salvation in this frightful emergency: I am known at nearly every bank in the whole world as their heaviest depositor. Besides, there is nearly a ton of gold in the big Panhard – and Earl is faithful, even if all the rest have betrayed me. He will know how to throw the hounds off the scent. Since I picked him up in Unter den Linden, in fact, I think he is the devil himself! I owe much to his promptings.

Oh God! eternal fire of hell! I do not blame Earl even, or Satan, or whoever he may be. *Mea culpa! mea maxima culpa!*[1] I have committed the Unpardonable Sin!

* * *

CRAZED POISONS WIFE
AND FRIENDS AT FEAST

LONDON, Nov. 3. Fashionable London was thrown into horrified amazement this evening by a series of tragic events. It appears that Dr Simpson, of 308B Cavendish Square, on his return from a trip to the continent, had invited a number of friends, social and professional, to dine with him and his beautiful and fascinating wife, *née* Lady Anna Cleveland. After the dinner was ended, the doctor rose, ostensibly to propose a toast in the English fashion. Instead of doing so, he denounced the entire company as being in a conspiracy to ruin him, his wife and Sir Hugh Flint the eminent surgeon being described as guilty soulmates. He accused them of having founded the confederacy to ruin him. He further announced to the astounded guests – who took the speech as a joke – that they were all poisoned, and rushed from the room, intending to do a clean get-away. The chauffeur, however, Earl Baumann, a level-headed German lad, drove the madman to the nearest police-station where, after a violent struggle, he was overpowered. He announced that he was the richest man in the world, and offered the sergeant in charge millions of pounds sterling to release him. The station doctor pronounced him to be suffering from acute religious mania, with delusions of grandeur and of persecution. At the house the frightened servants hastily summoned aid, but it unfortunately proved too late. The maniac, having understood his work too well, had administered enormous doses of aconitin, the deadliest known alkaloid, in the coffee. Not only Sir Hugh Flint and Lady Anna Simpson, but the entire party are dead. Many of the corpses still await identification.

New York Evening Telegram

---

[1] [Through my fault, through my grievous fault.]

The Bald Man

I

The Bald Man was the key of the position. It was the best observation post for fifty miles in either direction. Besides this, there ran a vital rail five miles hither of its sheltering crest. If the Germans could get up their guns, it was goodbye to certain fortresses which had already taken their toll in seven figures, and, it might easily be, the loss of several armies. For these reasons, the Bald Man had been contested time and again, until his slopes ran red. But for several months the Germans had left him alone. The French had bitten in two salients, one either side of him, so as to pocket any possible spearhead.

Alan Archer smoked his pipe in quiet, week after week, in the Ambulance Hut by the stream in the valley behind the crest. It was only now and again that he had to pick up chance victims of long-distance firing from among the thin lines that held the ridge.

The Bald Man had not always been bald. Before the war he was tufted with joyous forests; but the shells had left his scalp shining naked under the moon. He was of white limestone, and the shells and the rains had made him pasty as chalk. He was pitted, too, like a face scarred with smallpox in the days before vaccination; and every pit was dangerous with rifle and machine-gun. A fringe of trees remained about his base, and added point to the fantastic nickname.

Alan Archer knocked out his pipe and rose slowly to return to the hut at the call to dinner. He was tired with that alternation of fierce work and boredom which marks all campaigns. He stretched and yawned.

'Come on, Two!' shouted Jacques, the cook of the party.

Alan was called Two because he stood two metres in his socks. He disdained to reply; he was by nature silent. 'Lazy as the devil' – but quite like another aspect of the Prince of Darkness when anything occurred to arouse him. He had a great record as an athlete in America; his cool courage was to swear by yet in his old college.

'Where's Dolly Gray?' he asked languidly as he entered the hut. 'Carrying her bundle, I suppose.' 'Dolly Gray' was one of the Corps; her bundle – a wounded man.

'There's been no firing.'

'Someone with trench fever, then,' put in the surgeon.

It was one of the most important duties of the Corps to dispatch a man, usually by himself, every evening, in order to go over the day's routine with the Observation Officer on the Bald Man, and check up what had been done. In case of his finding a slight case of illness or a trifling wound, this man would attend to the matter himself; if stretcher-bearers were needed, he would signal accordingly to the Ambulance Hut. But the Corps was so short of men and stretchers that one man had often to do the work of two.

'There he comes, through the Bald Man's fringe,' cried Jacques, with a tureen of soup in his arms.

'They call it soup,' muttered a man called Paunchy, short for Pauncefote, an English type who had not quite assimilated conditions.

'Allow me to observe,' quoth the surgeon sententiously, 'that Professor Grill of Columbia has shown that when anything inspires us with extreme disgust, it is really that we wish to take it into our mouths!' Everyone laughed, for Paunchy was so called for his greed.

But the mirth cut short with Alan's exclamation. He had gone to the door. They all sprang to their feet. 'Look, boys! Dolly's running like a rabbit!'

'And he's got no bundle!'

'Good Lord! He's dropped on all fours!'

'Hell! What's doing?'

'Something wrong! Let's go get him!' cried Alan, and ran out with the surgeon at his heels.

But 'Dolly Gray' could give no good account of himself. The man he had been assisting had died suddenly; that was all. For the rest, he was in high hysteria, unable to explain himself. He could not eat his soup. The surgeon thrust out his lip, and got out his hypodermic syringe. 'Shut up, everybody!' said he. 'He'll be fit in the morning.'

But Alan Archer did not sleep that night. He went out and smoked, and watched the moonlight on the scalp of the Bald Man. He knew perfectly well what was wrong with 'Dolly Gray.' It was one of those fits of madness which the Ancients knew, a madness born of loneliness and dread and the horror of empty forests. They feigned that the God of the Forests, Pan, had appeared to such an one, and from Him gave it the name of Panic Fear.

Alan Archer had been terribly afraid, once in his life. It was in Ceylon. He had followed a wounded buffalo into thick jungle; and his beaters had deserted him. He had no idea where the brute might be, from what direction he might charge. And he became aware suddenly of the silence. That moment had taught him that while courage is a matter of heart and character, it depends also upon nervous stability. 'Dolly Gray' was a man of desperate courage, proven five score of times; yet – there was just one thing, probably something utterly trivial, that had power to strike him morally to the level of the invertebrate. Alan Archer bit his lip till the blood came; for he did not know what that thing, in his own case, might be. He thought of Tamerlane, ruthless as dauntless, how a cat cowed him; of Lord Roberts, conqueror of Kandahar, who came nigh fainting at the squealing of a pig; of twenty other similar cases. He was an instant afraid for himself. His thoughts came to a head. 'Curse those blasted Boches!' he cried aloud, 'why the deuce can't they get busy on this sector?' He went up to the Bald Man, and passed the night with a group chatting.

It was dawn when he returned to the hut. The surgeon took him aside.

'I'm sending Dolly home on a special mission,' said he; 'he'll never be any good again. I've had a talk with him. Don't say anything to the rest; I only tell you because – you know.'

'Why can't we get into the war?' growled Alan. 'We've been outraged every way the dirty dogs can think of – Europe's beginning to think we've got a yellow streak, damn it!'[1]

'Oho!' whispered the surgeon to his heart. 'So he's afraid of being afraid. That's the worst of these top-notch psychological types; they know too much. They know that anything whatever can happen.' 'Yes, it's bad luck,' he said aloud. 'You certainly ought to be in a fighting unit.'

'Curse it, I'm a first-rate signaller, to say nothing of gunnery and engineering; and they all laugh at me because I've got Yankee stamped on every inch of my confounded Two Metres!'

'If I were a recruiting sergeant I'd put you down Zulu, and pass you in,' laughed the surgeon.

And then that very day the luck turned! A desultory bombardment began, and Alan's little party were alive again, day and night of ceaseless toil, to bring the wounded from the crest. And by them toiled a sadder party still, a party without hope – the Burial Squad.

---

[1] This story dates from 1916.

2

Three weeks passed by, and then the German sniping ceased almost entirely. They had made one or two tentative movements against the salients which protected the Bald Man, but had been easily repulsed. Alan Archer had made a friend of the Observation Officer, and used to spend evenings on the dome of the Bald Man with him. The officer taught him to read the topography of the position, to comprehend the strategy of possible offensives. 'If it wasn't for us here,' he said once, 'given weather bad enough to keep our airplanes at home, they could clean up the whole show with one good stunt. See over there, now, for instance......' and he went into details.

It was late that night when Alan returned to the Hut. On his way, only a few feet below the apex of the Bald Man, he came across a dead boy. He was lying supine, his face to the young moon. His left flank had been blown away completely, and he was ghastly pale in that wan light, even his lips exsanguine.

'Poor chap!' mused Alan, unperturbed, the case being so common, 'I wonder how the Burial Squad missed him.'

But that night he slept ill. The dead face haunted him. He thought of pictured saints, waxen, calm, chaste, bloodless. In particular, he was reminded of a girl martyr, floating dead upon a river. The moon-aura supplied the painter's ghastly fancy of an aureole. Yes, the days of the martyrs were come again. He wished he had the skill to reproduce the mental image; he would have sent it through America like the Fiery Cross, till every man cried out for vengeance, and every woman bade her man arm for war.

But the next night he stopped by the edge of the shell-hole, in surprise. The Burial Squad had still not passed; the boy still lay there. He went close, to renew his impression. But the face had changed; it was distorted, drawn, the jaw dropped, the eyes glazed and dull. He shivered a little. Indeed, the night was chill. A wind blew out of the north-west, and threatened storm. The intense heat of the last week was stricken to the heart thereby. Alan fastened his coat, and went to the Hut at a quick pace.

The third night the storm broke wild and loud. The white face of the corpse was sickly with the beginnings of decomposition; it flared lurid through the gaps of tempest, while the rain lashed the hill like spindrift.

The dead boy had begun to haunt Alan Archer. He felt a certain morbidity in this preoccupation, and determined to check all thoughts concerning him at their first onset. He was a little doubtful as to whether he should avoid that particular route, or whether it would be weak-minded to do so. Again, the Squad might have removed the remains; it would be silly to be keeping out of the way of what was not there. But in the end his reason vigorously insisted on his taking a different road to and from the summit.

The fourth night the storm blew wilder yet. Alan, staggering blind against the rage of heaven, actually stumbled over the carcass. The boy's face seemed to grin, sardonic and sinister, at him. He cursed and went desperately on. All night he lay awake, furious with the Burial Squad for their neglect. But, worse, he blamed himself; he realised that some subconscious power in him had drawn him to the very spot he had determined to avoid.

The fifth night the storm had somewhat abated, but the wind was still fearfully high, and the black clouds scudded over heaven, showing from time to time a sullen, fitful moon, sickly and angry, through the wrack. Such nights are dreadful to men who walk abroad; the savage gleams, sporadic, serve but to accentuate the darkness. A hideous fascination – the Vertigo of the Abyss, wise men have called it – transformed his fear, just as murderers are impelled to revisit the scene of their crime, and, despite his conscious repulsion, drew him to the edge of the shell-hole. He knew what he was doing, that it was madness, and that he could not help himself. The epileptic violence of the gale had shifted the dead boy, and Alan's imagination read in that swollen and discoloured face the threat of some malignantly unnatural resurrection. The slopes of the Bald Man were slippery with slime, and Alan fell once or twice as he descended. He picked himself up with unnecessary haste; noticed the fact, began to wonder. 'Why do I do that?' he muttered. 'What's talking in my subconscious? Hell!' he slipped again, and strained a muscle with the acrid violence of his recovery.

As he reached the fringe of the Bald Man the wind suddenly dropped. Utter silence wrapped him. It fell dark as a wolf's mouth. He groped slowly amid the trees. And then – he heard footsteps following him. Instantly he thought of the dead man. 'They wouldn't bury him,' he screamed; 'he's coming – he's coming home – with me.' His conscious mind reacted to the threat of its hidden master. 'Nonsense,' he cried aloud; 'the dead don't walk. I know it's sheer hallucination!' But that is just the terror of hallucination; it cares nothing for the conscious mind, with its petty canon of reality, based on the limits of so-called 'normal' experience. One cannot convince a madman; his experience is as solid as a sane man's. Alan realised this fact with fury and horror. 'It's like love,' he thought; 'it's all rubbish to third parties, but it's none the less real to those involved in its maelstrom of mania.' With that he yielded utterly to the impulse of panic; bruised and battered from his wild flight through the wood, he leapt over the meadow to the Hut, and flung himself panting and screaming on the floor.

The surgeon was by his side in a second. 'What's wrong?' he cried. But Alan only sobbed and shrieked. The surgeon gave him a full dose of morphia, and presently he slept.

3

The morning broke fair, but the wind seemed to have gained force from that one lull of yester-even, and blew fiercely from the north. Alan woke refreshed, apparently his own man again; but as the day wore on, he became more and more uneasy. The surgeon, wise as the serpent, had said nothing; it was Alan who approached him at the noon meal.

'Doc!' said he quietly, 'I want to transfer to another sector. I can't tell you why; it's just nonsense. But I've fought it out with myself; and the plain fact is, I can't force myself to go up that hill again.'

The surgeon meditated. Suddenly a shell burst on the crest of the Bald Man, another, then a dozen, and the roar of German drumfire came rolling from beyond the crest.

'There's your answer,' cried the surgeon, slapping Alan on the shoulder; 'work to do, my boy! That'll clear away the cobwebs!' But the big man did not answer. 'Think it over, lad!' said the other, kindly, 'you'll be all right by the time we start.' Alan nodded slowly, and turned away to busy himself with the preparations for the expedition.

The German fire increased constantly in vehemence all that afternoon. The scalp of the Bald Man was like a volcano in eruption, so constantly did the shells burst on it. The time came for the party to set out. Then Alan drew himself up.

'I've thought it all out,' said he, in a dull voice; 'I can't explain. I'm willing to be called a coward. But I can't go. I can't go.' He turned and went to the Hut, and squatted by the open door, his face buried in his arms.

The surgeon thought he would try the other tack. 'We'll go without him, boys,' he cried, loud, so that Alan might hear. 'We're better without yellow dogs.' Alan shuddered, but he did not stir.

At that moment a high explosive shell came clear over the Bald Man and struck the ground within a yard of the party. In the wind and fury of the catastrophe Alan was hurled fifty feet away.

He came to himself unhurt. The Hut was matchwood; the others –
'napoo.' He saw by the sun – a rim of fire on the horizon – that he had
been unconscious over an hour.

The German fire had ceased absolutely. Dead silence held his inexorable court about him. His Fear alone possessed him.

The dead boy was with him, chuckling; he could hear him. Why
couldn't he see him? He wanted to look on that carrion – just once. He
understood, with the struggling remnant of his reason, how fatally perverse was the fancy. It was his duty to go, to report what had happened,
true; but he knew also that it was the Demon in him that prompted
that good argument. A little fillip came from the ruin of his conscious
mind; he recalled the surgeon's word that fear and disgust mean that
we want to put into our mouths the thing that causes it. Yes, he must
crawl up through that worn fringe of trees, fire-scarred; he must writhe
up those slopes of bloody paste to the Scalp of the Bald Man; and he
must batten on the flesh of that dead hero. The sick greens and ochres
of that bloated face; the maggots crawling in and out of their meat, till
it heaved like a sweating she-devil in some brothel of hell – it was his
meat, his, ha! He licked his dry lips.

Now there set in complete dissociation of his personality, and he
strove manfully against the obscene impulse. But ever the same side
of him began to acquiesce in the hallucination that the dead boy stood
by him, a hell-creature goading him with chuckling friendliness to the
mad act. He must – he must. So now he became furtive, fearing lest
his comrades should perceive him and hinder him. He was one of the
company of the damned, a soul sold to Satan. He thought of ghouls,
witches, vampires, werewolves, and laughed aloud, and licked his lips
again. He tossed his head as he loped up the slopes of bloody slime;
and as he loped he howled.

It was his comrades whom he feared now; the dead boy no longer
pursued him. No, they were good friends now. He thought the dead
boy sat astride him, cried Tally-Ho on that foul parody of a hunt.
The full moon met him as he reached the crest; he gibbered wild and
weird; a thick slime dribbled from his mouth. Oho! he was the devil's
hound, hot on the slot; and it was moonlight. Ah, the moon! Dead
queen of sorceries and murders, hail! She was his, hurrah! By her light
he would hunt – he would hunt! Kill and eat! Kill and eat! Wasn't it
Samuel Butler who said that love was only perfect when one ate the
other? Dear old Butler; and, by God, he was right about humanity's
duty to destroy all machines, wasn't he?

As he reached the crest of the Bald Man, the full moon met him, ablaze, in her rising. Ha! Hecate: – he gloated horribly, a thick slime dribbling from his mouth. And then he reached his prey. What was this? The corpse was no longer there, and with an animal growl of baulked greed he scrabbled at the earth with his beasts' claws.

And then a new thought came into his mind. They had bombarded the Bald Man; of course, a shell had hit; yes, there was the new hole, right on the edge of the other.

He suddenly realised that he was Alan Archer of the Red Cross. He called aloud to his friend the Observation Officer. The hill was silent as the grave that it was. Alan understood perfectly that every man had been killed in that fearful blast of cannon-wrath that had raged all the afternoon.

He went up to the Dome. Yes, there lay those brave men. My God! what tragedy! There lay his friend, too. And at the sight of him he became lucid, like a disembodied spirit. He seized his dead friend's field-glasses; they were uninjured. He swept the east. The situation realised itself, a veritable Apocalypse. Look! Two thousand yards below him, what were those grey lines? And there, to the South-East, those masses, far as the eye could reach?

He knew the Germans dared not venture on the slopes of the Bald Man until they were ready to smash in one of the protecting salients. And there was the whole plan, bare to him. It was a major offensive – he understood the scheme from A to Z. Then, what were the French doing? Why were they silent, when the very life-line was threatened? He remembered – some days of storm, his officer had told him. By God, the French didn't know! He thrilled cold through every nerve in his body. He knew, and he alone. He must telephone instantly.

A glance showed him the impossibility of doing so. The whole Dome was a torn mass of wreck. God! God! he cried, feeling the weight of the whole world upon his shoulders. Liberty herself, for that one tragic moment, lay in his hands; and he was – paralysed. He threw up his arms in despair, and cried out to the moon, as it might be a Pagan priest of Artemis. And the moon gave sudden answer.

Yes, she was lifted over the Bald Man so that her light struck clear on Staff Headquarters, far behind in the valley. If he stood up against the sky, he might be seen. He could semaphore with his arms. It was certain death, of course; the act of a madman to raise even a hand in that bright light; but – well, he had been mad already, and less nobly. He climbed to the edge of the shell-hole, collected his thoughts into a brief concentrated message, commended his soul to his Maker, reared aloft his giant frame, and began to signal with desperate speed.

The man who happened to see him said afterwards that he thought it was a man struck lunatic by the pain of a wound, and dancing in the agony of the damned. He got lamps and signalled back.

'Not crazy!' gesticulated Alan. 'Listen! Listen! Listen!' and repeated his message from the beginning. The bullets whined past him, like shrikes darting; but God was for France that night, and he had come to his last phrase before he fell. And ere his eyes lost light he heard the bass crescendo of the French barrage as it broke high over his head, and the raucous yell of the Blue Devils as they raced forward to the assault.

Black and Silver

I

I was sitting only two tables away from where the man was stabbed. The restaurant was of course in immediate uproar; it was not easy to arrest the murderess, a big, stalwart Austrian woman with dyed red hair, who went mad with the realisation of what she had done, and lashed out with her bowie knife and her fists and her feet until the waiters thought that it was a wildcat rather than a woman. Presently the police came in with their clubs, and beat down the excitement as well as the resistance. They will clear the place, I thought, and shut it up until the coroner arrives. For the man was as dead as one of his own western steers; a big, bull-necked brute, he was from Chicago, as we all learnt afterwards from the papers.

The idea of going recalled me to the purpose for which I had waited, dallying with liqueurs. Here was my chance to offer my escort to the solitary lady in the corner. She had come in when I was halfway through my meal, and her entry had produced a sensation even in that restaurant, inured to most bizarre events. It was not only that people turned to look at her. The maître d'hôtel found himself in front of her without appearing to get there, in the way that distinguishes the good maître d'hôtel from the bad one. The other waiters seemed to constitute themselves a bodyguard; they convoyed her to a little table in the corner, and almost before she was seated the wine steward had appeared with a marvellous Venetian glass tall and slim, a masterpiece, like a black opal, and a bottle of Hock that looked as if it might have been the loot of the cellar of Jamshid himself. The maître d'hôtel handed her the menu; she appeared to comprehend it at a glance; she marked two dishes with a tiny silver pencil; he bowed yet lower, and dematerialised. She had taken no notice of any of the fuss; she had not spoken a single word.

Now that she was left alone, I was able to get a good impression of her. She was not unusually tall, but her excessive slimness made her appear so. She had the figure of a young boy rather than that of a woman. Her face was small and delicate, pallid as the moon, with a certain veiled vigilance as if she saw all but disdained to notice it – it reminded me a little of a Frenchwoman of the *vieille régime*[1] on a tumbril ... or a throne. The mouth was exceptionally small and straight and thin.

But the astonishing part of her was her arms and hands. She wore a great hat of black radiating straws, supporting a mesh of adorable lace. It was set very far back on her head, showing fully a very high and intellectual forehead. On it, designed by no man-milliner, but by a true artist, was a gigantic silver spider, the hat being its web. Beneath it were locks of the palest ashen gold, neatly braided and looped, to cover the back of the neck. Her dress was of tight-fitting silk of that charcoal grey of which one can hardly say whether it is black or silver. This note was carried throughout her whole adornment. Her fan was of black paradise feathers in a chased silver frame.

Yet in all this nothing was more than a foil for those wonderful arms and hands. They were extravagantly long and fine. She was in evening dress with shoulder-straps only to the bodice, but her black gloves reached almost up to them. They were of the most intoxicating black kid, almost as fine as silk, and a tiny silver monogram at the top set off their perfect blackness. So long and thin was the hand that one felt instinctively that no bracelet could ever have stayed upon her wrist.

Her dinner was as extraordinary as herself. She had ordered caviar, then *truffes à la serviette*, then black coffee. She did not remove her gloves during the repast, and she looked neither to right nor left. I am bound to admit that she aroused my curiosity to the highest point. 'An intrigue, now, with *that* woman...' I did not finish the thought. It struck me, of course, that she might be a *morphineuse*; everything but her extreme neatness pointed to that conclusion. Yet no; her countenance expressed a settled melancholy, but was astonishingly reserved and self-controlled. Never had I seen a woman so perfectly *grande dame* as this one. Every line of her gave the lie to any hint of self-indulgence. The intensity of her suggested for a second that she might be an international spy; but she was clearly no adventuress. Conjecture revolved vainly in its orbit; all came back at last to the obvious truth: she was a lady.

---

[1] [Old guard.]

Once during the fracas I looked across to her. I had hoped to see alarm; I would cross to her and reassure her. By no means; her tiny white teeth bit into her truffles, one by one, as if she were alone in the café; she lifted her glass and drank that noble Hock as steadily and as simply as the Priest consumes the Wine of the Sacrament. I have some experience of life: Eton, Oxford and the Indian Civil Service, until a certain fatal episode which threw me on the world and forced me to begin again from the beginning, on rather different lines. But I had never seen such absolute aplomb; it could only arise from a hereditary conviction that nothing can ever happen.

The police had begun to clear the café; I had prepared my little speech; I looked across – she had disappeared. On her table lay a twenty-dollar bill.

I am a man of resource; I segastuated myself into the neighbourhood of the maître d'hôtel. I prestidigitated ten dollars into his ever-ready hand. He did not need to await my question.

'It is the Countess Mierka Brzeckska,' he said. 'Her maid appeared one day, about a month ago, with that glass and a case of that Hock – Johannisberger Cabinet 1854 – I have never seen its equal – and said that madame would sometimes lunch or dine here. This is her sixth visit. She never comes twice in one day. She never speaks a single word. She always pays with a twenty-dollar bill, though the cheque is rarely over five dollars. Yes, sir, about forty gentlemen have made enquiry. That is all I know.'

'If they all give you ten dollars, you should be doing well.'

'Thank you, sir, things are fair, fair.' His voice sank to a whisper. 'I got on to Bethlehem at 108. (They were 435½ that day.) Do you think I should get out, sir?'

'When in doubt, take a profit,' I answered, 'and – whether in doubt or not – cut a loss. Good day!'

I thought I had got very little for my ten dollars. But the woman intrigued me hugely; as I turned into the Avenue I struck my cane viciously on the sidewalk and swore to God to follow up the adventure. I dropped into the office of a society weekly whose editor was a clubfellow. Luckily he was in.

'No, dear man,' he replied to my question. 'I won't bore you with the scrap I know. We've had a "par" or two, you know, nothing at all. It's as mysterious as the Origin of Evil. You take my tip and go right down to Pfeiffer of *The Mercury*; he's had a man on her these last two months. Know him, don't you?'

'Sure.'

So off I went to Park Place in a taxi at a cost of four dollars and seventy-five cents – I was keen – and caught Pfeiffer just as he was leaving the office. We drifted into Hahn's for a drink.

'It's the curse of the office,' he began, sipping his highball. 'I put Jones on to her, then Jaeger, then Scott, now Fletcher, and, believe me, nothing doing. She has a suite at the Martha Washington, of all places, respectability and curl-papers to the *n* plus oneth degree; she never speaks, she never telephones, she gets no calls, she gets no letters. She lunches and dines out nearly all the time, always in the best places. She has an electric brougham, black and silver like herself, and the only thing the least bit fishy about it all is that it would take a racing car to catch that tiny runabout. I don't know any longer how many times my chaps have been thrown off by the plain speed of it. And often enough she makes long sprints late at night. Oh yes! there's one other thing. She's not dumb; she sings to herself in the hotel to some kind of a guitar; always French songs, very sweet and innocent; "*pauvre Gaspard*"[1] and "*O mon Dieu vous m'avez blessé d'amour*"[2] and that sort of thing; but nearly every day that melancholy Provençal burthen "*Enseveli, tout mon espoir.*"[3] The French Embassy know nothing about her, and the Russian won't talk. Probably she's a French-woman married to some damned Pole. Very likely he got killed in the war, and she's got the weeps over him. Anyhow, it's all as lively as one's own funeral, and I've got her complaint, for the old man, if he gets wind of all this, will think I'm getting too fat for my job.'

And here it ended. For a month I neither saw nor heard any more of 'Black and Silver.'

2

Suddenly the luck turned, as luck will. I was in Sherry's with a party of friends, dining hastily, going on to a new play. She walked into the balcony, in all parts exactly as before. The staff were not as demon-strative as in the fashionable Bohemian café three blocks away, but they were even more devotional. It was the difference between Angli-can and Catholic worship.

Almost before I had time to think, I was called to the telephone. Free for a moment of my friends, I got rid of the man who had rung me up with little ceremony, and walked to the front of the restaurant.

---

[1] ['Poor Gaspard.']
[2] [Oh my God, you have wounded me with love.]
[3] [Buried one, all my hope.]

There was the electric brougham, the chauffeur as funereal as the rest of the equipment, an old man, in a dead black, silver-braided uniform, with white hair and beard, and an expression like an undertaker.

I made up my mind in a second. I telephoned to Mahoney's. 'Send me your fastest racing car to Sherry's within ten minutes,' I said, 'with a man that would hang on to the devil's own tail.' He said that he had a car that would follow a monoplane across the Rocky Mountains, and I could have it before he rang off. (That is how Mahoney built up his business.)

I went back into Sherry's, told them that my call was from a dying uncle worth eighteen millions, and would they excuse me? They would. I went out; my car drove up in about five minutes; I gave the man his cue and settled down to wait.

Presently she came out. The brougham was at the door with matchless coordination; she stepped in without a word; she drove away. Up the Avenue we sped; through Central Park – and here the auto was put to it to keep track of the wonder-car – up Lenox, across by Columbia University, through a curious and deserted quarter to the 'Grand Concourse,' through Van Cortlandt Park, back beneath the Elevated Railway and so on to Riverside Drive and into Broadway.

'Another foozle,' said I, to myself, 'she's going back to the Martha Washington. She's lost her husband, and a fast car helps her to forget, and that's all there's to it.' But the car kept on steadily down Broadway, and at Madison Square turned once more into the Avenue. At Eighth Street it swung sharply to the right, and stopped dead.

She mounted the steps of a house only a few doors from the Avenue. I was actually startled (by this time) to see her do something natural and normal. My car was drawn up on the other side of the street, two doors further on, as I had instructed. What she did was to take a latchkey from her bag, and open the door of the house. A miraculous silhouette she made, for the house was directly in the light of the street lamps, and the door was dead ivory white against the black of her dress. Her white flesh faded out; it was as if she had become invisible, only the dress remaining. Like a snake in long grass, she gave one twist of her lithe body, and disappeared. I had expected it; I would not even curse; I told the chauffeur to go to Jack's; he put the clutch in ....

'Stop!' I said.

There was no doubt about it. The door was still open, and across its blank lay, like a bar, her arm and hand.

My heart almost stopped. I could not think at all. My brain was dizzy by this time with the beating of the wings of my imagination.

But by some primitive instinct I got out of the auto and began – mechanically, automatically – to cross the street.

Then I stopped. Hang it, what could I do? The position was impossible. Luckily no one was passing.

The arm remained motionless.

3

It could not have been a quarter of a minute; it seemed like hours. Ultimately primæval manhood prevailed in me, I had almost said against me. Like a man in a dream I went up to the door; my hand closed upon her wrist. Instantly, yet very gently, the arm began to withdraw itself; the hand turned and caught my wrist delicately and subtly, a caress, yet a command; the door opened so that I could slip through it, and almost before I knew it I heard it close behind me. At the same moment the blackness became absolute, and I felt an arm about my neck. The thin straight mouth was put firmly on mine with extraordinary passion, yet deliberately and in cold blood, as if it were an effect of will, not of desire. There was no yielding in it, either to itself, or to another; it was imperious and formal, like a decree of execution signed by a king who loved mercy.

The long kiss ended; I raised my head – and started. There was no light of any kind, but a skeleton hung self-luminous in the air. She drew me towards it; I heard the bones clink as we brushed by, and felt the swaying of the velvet *portières* through which she led me. I could feel that I was in a large room, perhaps a studio, for there was a sense of bareness, perceptible even without sight. With perfect confidence she drew me steadily onwards; then we sank down upon a large leather-covered armchair.

Somewhere, loudly and solemnly, a clock ticked. Time, yet one more emblem and signpost of mortality! She must have touched a secret switch; the room glimmered out in light. From a hundred cunningly concealed tubes radiating that ghastly glare of mercury vapour which photographers sometimes use in their studios, and which turns all reds to blues. The natural severity of her face added to the effect; she was a corpse, no doubt. I thought of Gautier's 'La morte amoureuse,' and a thousand other stories of the kind. I was tremendously excited, but not alarmed. This woman was evidently a *détraquée*[1] with a peculiar fashion. Let her have her way! I had plenty of experience of such. After

---

[1] [Psychopath.]

my first year in Port Said – following my misfortune – there was not much that I did not know. I fell in willingly with her caprice of silence.

The light showed me a large studio, a sculptor's, doubtlessly, for there were no canvases, and many statues stood about the room, mostly plasters of antiques. The arm-chair in which I sat, and on whose arm she hovered, was the only piece of furniture in the room, with one exception. Directly in front of me, about ten feet away, was a great coffin of black covered with a pall of woven silver. The foot was facing me; at the head stood two silver candlesticks. But instead of candles they held skulls, which now began to glow with the same infernal mercury-lamp light. It was all very harmless; a variation of the Cabaret du Néant in private life. Such things rather amuse me.

I was recalled to myself with yet another start. Somehow, between the door and the chair, she had discarded her cloak; beneath it was but filmy gossamer frou-frou; she was all hat and gloves and modelled whiteness. Her eyes fixed mine with ghastly fire. I could feel her breath hissing between her teeth. Her right arm was about my neck; her left caressed me with ineffable skill and abandon. My imagination became almost a paroxysm; I really knew no longer anything, but that a great geyser-burst of mad, perverse, incomprehensible passion had surged up in me. I became as one delirious. A million impossible fancies raced through my brain.

Suddenly I woke. She had not moved, from the moment that we came to the chair on whose arm she sat; nay, scarce a muscle; yet now she slipped from me and the light went out. It was only for a moment; a rosy glow pervaded the room from lamps hung high; and she stood before me, the hat removed, her figure wrapped in a gorgeous mandarin coat, and the fantastic, the hashish-thrilled, the murderous hands bare. It was a revelation. Even the supposed coffin was seen for what it was – evidently – an unfinished piece of sculpture over which the dainty-fingered artist had thrown a shawl of silver embroidery.

But there was still another surprise in store for me. Just as I thought that she meant to lapse into human and natural behaviour, she merely led me to the door. Still in my maze, I yet was alive enough to passion to ask her when I should see her again. For the first and last time she spoke, rapidly, incisively, with the calm of all finality, and just a touch of *espièglerie*[1] to make it charming: '*Je ne me donne jamais deux fois.*'[2]

---

[1] [Mischief.]

[2] [I never give myself twice.]

I found myself in the street. The brougham had vanished. I looked for my car. My man drove up. He laughed. I forgave him, for there was I, standing stockishly, like a fool – with a pair of long black kid gloves in my hand.

4

The next morning Mahoney called me up.

'Car O.K.?' he asked.

'Sure,' said I.

'None of my business,' said he, 'but you'd better know. You were followed home last night.'

'Likely enough,' I said, 'the cops are on to that joint, by Hank, you bet your sweet life.'

'Righto,' he said, and rang off.

But that was not the end of it that day. I had a hot time of it in Wall Street standing off the bears, but we won out, and a dozen of us decided to celebrate the victory at the St Regis. We got a bit soused, I'm afraid; anyhow, young Van X. (let's call him that! Willie, his name is – the pet of our bunch – about the best family in Manhattan, and the richest) started in with a story – and, by the Great Horn Spoon, it was my own story! Bar the direction of the drive – he had gone over to Long Island – word for word, the same. Except, too, that in dismissing him she had borrowed Voltaire's answer to his English fellow-experimenter: 'Once, a philosopher!'

To my amazement, the story fell perfectly flat. Van X. showed his annoyance. Oscar L. (the banker) put him wise. 'I guess we've all been there, old sport. Don't care much for that sort of thing myself, but it's all right, once in a while. Damn queer stunt; sounds like a bet; anyhow, she's gone clean through this one burg. Some stunt!'

I tried a little *shikar* at odd times, but to no purpose. Once I found her in Delmonico's; she ignored me. I noticed grimly that a certain young oil magnate followed her out very precipitately.

By-and-by the story was forgotten; I heard (I forget how) that she had left the Martha Washington. Pfeiffer printed a long story in the end, hinting all he dared hint, and hinting – jack high! – that he knew much more. The police raided the studio, too; but nothing was found. And so it ended; all the makings of a great romance and a great scandal – and nothing came of it.

But I always cherished the memory of the episode as one of the strangest and most enigmatic treasures of my mind.

Well, gentlemen, here is the story as I wrote it, thinking it might suit some magazine. (I scribble at odd moments.) I am sorry to have to spoil it.

About three months after her disappearance I received a large, flat envelope, registered, from Montreal. It contained a photograph, and a printed circular offering to sell the negative. A printed circular! The photograph was excessively clear, and eminently recognisable. Perhaps there was no particular harm in it; but it would not have been quite encouraging to one's fiancée or one's wife, if one were encumbered with such! Well – I don't know – to be frank, it would hardly have multiplied one's invitations to social gatherings – bar crap games in coloured circles! The price asked – filled in ink on a blank left purposely – was reasonable enough: five hundred dollars. I wonder what Van X. paid, and old Oscar L.! If only I had not had my little misfortune in India! Well, it saved money for once!

As it was, I replied:

> My dear Countess,
>
> I am deeply obliged for your charming offer; but some eight years ago, at Port Said, I posed professionally for many hundred such pictures, even more unconventional, and I am sorry to say that my collection is complete.
>
> My object in pursuing you was to compromise and ultimately to blackmail you.
>
> All square on the home green?
>
> > Yours etc.

I wonder if we shall ever play the nineteenth hole.

The Humour of Pauline Pepper

I

General Graf von Donner u. Blitzen possessed the most mathematical mind on the Austrian Staff. He not only could calculate everything, from the trajectory of a shell to the m.p.h. of a goulash-cannon, to fifteen places of decimals, but he would; and no one had ever been able to stop him. He had a mind like a chemical balance; and he would plot a curve whenever he wanted to curve a plot!

This exemplary officer was seated in the line at Trafoi, on the Austrian side of what is called the Stilfser-joch by Teutons, and the Stelvio by Italians. His solitary lunch had been laid out like an oasis in a desert of logarithms; for Italy was expected to declare war at any moment, and he was charged with the important work of the final inspection of the frontier posts. He had resolved to motor to the summit of the pass after lunch to make a last survey of the hidden defences.

It is a royal ride, from Trafoi to the Stelvio, with the mighty mass of the Ortler towering on the East, its glaciers aglow with the glory of the sun on their fresh-fallen snows. Here, as one rises by the long zig-zags of the road, new peaks, the Königspitze, Monte Zebrù, the Eisseespitze, and many another, come into startling view, until one suddenly becomes aware of that vast snowy plateau which culminates in Monte Cevedale.

But the General's mind was on more detailed beauties, on batteries concealed in crags, on land-mines cunningly distributed to blow up the road at critical points, and on the arrangement of carefully hidden telephone communications with the base at Meran.

Late that afternoon he signalled from the crest of the pass that his calculations were 'complete and satisfactory'; yet one might have gone through all the stacks of figure-covered papers in his automobile without finding a single reference to Josef Kohn, the delicatessen-merchant from Sixth Avenue.

2

Josef Kohn had a mathematical mind, also, though it ran on different lines to the General's. His speciality was the calculation of profits on pretzels. It had not been worth a Government job to him, but it had enabled him to run a Ford, which he drove in Central Park every evening, wet or fine, with a perfect contempt for the limousines of the millionaires. He never gave a thought to his rich uncle in Trieste, or indulged a hope that he would be remembered in the Will. It was a complete surprise, early in 1915, when the old man died, and left him half his fortune. A less pleasant surprise was when he learnt that there would be difficulty in realising the estate; his lawyer advised him that his best chance was to go over and attend to the matter himself. About three-quarters of a million dollars was the amount, and Josef was not the man to hesitate, though he had a very sick feeling about submarines. Once in Trieste, he found no trouble in collecting his fortune, and transferring it to sound American securities. But, being in Europe, he thought he might as well see Europe, war or no war. At least he could have a fairly good time in the neutral countries. And to Josef Kohn a good time meant motoring.

He was not going to be bothered with a chauffeur; anyhow, he might have some difficulty in getting one. In fact, it was not easy to buy a car. It needed a little bribery as well as a long price to get even the car he did get. This was a discarded military despatch car, a racing pattern of tremendous power, calculated to climb like a goat – and with a kick like a mule. Josef was always half afraid to put the clutch in. He spent a good deal of money getting the car patched up – the steering-gear had been badly messed up by a bullet – but his energy and enthusiasm overcame not only this difficulty, but that of shipping his purchase over to Venice. There, however, his troubles ended, and he spent a wonderful spring touring over Lombardy. The only fly in his ointment was the periodical difficulty with the military authorities, who seemed to dislike the name on his passport, fortified though that was by the most imposing official seals and stamps, and letters of recommendation from all sorts of bigwigs.

3

It was in Bormio that some sportive god picked him up between thumb and finger and proceeded to use him as a pawn in a game of international importance. Of course it would be easy to slip from the hold if it were not for that stickiest of all substances with which the gods lime their destined prey – love.

Josef Kohn would never have been a hero if he had not lost his heart to Pauline Pepper, whom he found sketching in the woods around Bormio on the second afternoon of his little visit. She was a startling blonde, with an impudent scarlet mouth, and a broad tip-tilted nose, a mixture of sensuality and fun. She belonged to a French-Swedish family from Boston, and believed that she could paint. It was an error; she had nothing but beauty and – a sense of humour.

Josef Kohn stimulated this devil in her; she thought him and his delicatessen the most comic of earth's joys, set as he was in such jewel-craft as that sub-Alpine scenery. It made her think of things uncanny. When he became amorous, she found his mixture of shyness and affrontery amazing. He treated her partly as if he had just been presented at court, partly as if he had picked her up on Coney Island. But she did not let him get very far. She heaved a terrible sigh; her blue eyes filled with tears; she uttered but one word 'Belovèd' and sank upon his breast. But, before he could clasp her to his manly bosom, she sprang up with a shriek. 'Alas! unhappy me! I had forgot my tragic destiny. No, Josef, happiness is not for us! Fly! Fly! Forget me!'

Pressed to disclose the serpent secret that was gnawing at her breast, she ultimately revealed that She Was Not What She Seemed. At that she left the astounded and delighted Kohn, her face buried in her hands, her gait calculated to make Hecuba look like a third-rate vaudeville artist. All she would do was to vouchsafe a hint that she would tell him more – 'Perhaps To-Mahorrow!'

The morning came, and with it an explanation that she was not worthy of a Real Man's Love. After teasing poor Josef for about two hours, she finally confessed, with her hair down amid floods of tears, that she had been Deeply Wronged.

'Tell me his name!' hissed Josef Kohn, all worked up. 'His life-blood shall pollute my virgin steel' – or words as nearly to that effect as came within his rather limited vocabulary.

Pauline tried to think of someone as inaccessible as possible, but the Crown Prince, she thought, had been rather overworked; so she hit on a name she had seen several times in the papers as on a tour of inspection of the Austrian Tyrol, just across the Stelvio pass from Bormio, General Graf von Donner und Blitzen!

Josef Kohn refused to regard What Had Happened as any bar to wedlock; to him she was Even More Pewer. But he certainly saw that it was his duty to kill the Libertine; the only difficulty was – how to do it. However, he was not fated to be bothered about this, for Pauline, having promised to marry him as soon as his steel was imbrued in the heart's blood of her oppressor, got very fed up with the vulgar little ass, and began to resent his familiarities. So she came to him with a most portentous look, and told him – what was quite true – that Italy might declare war any minute, and that things would be very unpleasant for anybody named Kohn, passport or no passport. She advised him to get across the pass into Austria, and home to America via Switzerland and France. Besides, she added, once in Austria you will be able to avenge me on my Destroyer.

4

Josef Kohn got cold feet. He saw himself stabbed in nine hundred and ninety-nine places by a frenzied mob of Italians. He went out to think it over, and saw a little Austrian shop being stoned by the people, a rumour that war was declared having come up the valley. He scribbled a note for Pauline: 'Await me; I go to avenge you,' jumped into the big car, and got out of Bormio – as it happened, a few hours before the telegraph closed the frontier.

The further he went, the closer fear gripped him. Up and up he went, the long zig-zags of the road irritating him infinitely with their interminability. His car was of enormous power; it carried him towards the pass at an average of thirty miles an hour.

The gods timed his arrival to a second. He just cleared the frontier officials; before he had got away five hundred yards – which only meant about one hundred measured straight down the slope of the hill – the officer in charge was reading a heliograph message that he was to close the frontier. Also that he was to be particularly careful to look out for Austrian spies with forged American passports.

He jumped to his job. 'Get that man back!' he shouted, 'get him dead or alive!' The Austrian outposts were withdrawn some distance down the valley; some of the Italians started to their feet, and ran helter-skelter down the hill; others started to fire at the flying car. Josef Kohn had been in a panic when he started; he needed no explanation of what was happening. He let her out! His terror keyed him up to the stage when men perform miracles. He cleared the first three corners on two wheels, the next two on one, the sixth by a manœuvre that seemed to him rather like looping the loop in an airplane. But he got round. He was leaving his pursuers well behind, and he was hidden from the sharpshooters by the curve of the hillside.

But seven was never his lucky number; the seventh corner, with an angle of about fifteen degrees, was beyond even a miracle for a car going at ninety miles an hour.

It went quietly through the parapet, and found itself on an immense patch of snow frozen extremely hard; down this it rushed like an avalanche. Josef Kohn became more frightened of the Law of Gravitation than he had been of the Italians; he tried to pull up. Aided by various small obstacles, he very nearly succeeded, and came into the next stretch of road below without overturning. But his momentum was just a little too great; the car lurched through the wall and reached the next slope.

This was no easy slope of snow, but steep and broken crags. The car began to bump and jump. Josef Kohn lost hope. He clung to the wheel by instinct, awaiting the crash.

And then the crags became precipitous. The car took the last fifty feet through the air in one tremendous bound. Down it came almost vertically – on the top of the military automobile of General Graf von Donner und Blitzen!

5

It was a very burned and bruised and battered Josef Kohn that opened his eyes in the Austrian base hospital at Meran. But when he did so, they showed him a pompous procession in the square outside – the funeral obsequies of his Hated Rival.

The automobile, he learned, had not only killed the General and three of his staff, but set fire to all those wonderful calculations which were to annihilate Italy, and which had foolishly omitted to take cognisance of Sixth Avenue, New York, and Mr Josef Kohn.

This important gentleman, convalescent, hastened to write to Pauline, announce the success of his mission, and claim her hand.

Alas! his luck was altogether out. She wrote that her Wicked Uncle had insisted on her immediate marriage to a Man Whom She Could Never Love – the Principe Ravioli dei Spaghetti.

Josef Kohn pocketed the loss; he is a hero in Sixth Avenue; few delicatessen-merchants have slain a general officer and three of his staff, and destroyed the war plans of a frontier, in single combat. He never mentioned Pauline Pepper to Rosina Grossman, who was a very wealthy widow indeed, and dearly loved a hero.

But he will never ride again in a motor-car.

A Nativity

It was by no means a bad street for Brixton, and Jim Gibson had always counted himself a respectable man. In five years he had saved nearly a hundred pounds from his thirty-five shillings a week, and he had done wisely to take a wife, and been lucky as well as clever to find so steady and decent a girl as Liz Day. They lived in a cheery and clean little house of four rooms, and Saturday noon always inaugurated a little honeymoon, lasting till it was time for Jim to go to the works at dawn on Monday.

It was only in the second year of the marriage that this routine met with interruption, from Fact Number One in the life of humanity. There was no shadow of dread in the future; Liz was as healthy as a young panther, and there was plenty of money in the savings bank. But Nature is a fantastic mother, and takes her toll of the mind when the body has been fortified against her. The mere disturbance served to disturb; and, with no fear, the nerves of Jim Gibson were insensibly sensitised.

After all, the ordeal was novel; neighbours of good intention told stories, ranging from the latest layman's version of hospital facts to fables which would have lowered the intellectual standard of a Sussex peasant. Now and again Jim would experience that eerie feeling that one sometimes has in church, sometimes when – perhaps in the desert where one has been alone for hours – one suddenly realises that one is alone. Alarm without cause in reason, but in the innate atavistic memory, in the very structure of the nerves which are trained by heredity to remember the countless accidents of childbirth in the past.

But Jim Gibson was a steady and temperate man; he had no fear of ghosts, and hard work and sane living had made him proof against more than temporary uneasiness.

Yet now husband and wife sat alone, and fell to silence, a deeper communion and a truer sympathy perhaps than when they had passed their evenings in merry talk or lovers' play, but, for all that, a state too subtle and high-strung for anyone not so broad-based and grounded in intellectual knowledge as to find in objective thought a refuge from the strain of constant introspection.

Not that in any conscious sense either of them were so foolish or so unfortunate as to partake of the torture-sacrament which is the daily bread and wine of every artist; but the inherent metaphysical tendency, which haunts even the grossest of mankind in weaker moments, let slip a leash of silent sleuth-hounds on them. They had the scent of the quarry. If love grew truer and deeper, may it not have been under the Shadow of the Wings of that Swan whose name is equally Life and Death?

In the last month of the appointed time, Liz sent for her young sister Olive, a scrubby child of sixteen with big black eyes, a body like a snake's, short curls of black and a thin scarlet slit of a mouth. Her manner was at once languid and acrid, her tongue sly and sharp. But she tackled the housework with contemptuous vigour.

Her advent was a new disturbance; she prevented both the open and the silent communion of the married lovers, the former by her presence, the latter by her talk. She rattled on continuously from supper-time to bed-time. It was a sort of separation, a moral barrier, only the more inevitable because it was so natural and so right. But Jim grew to hate her, just as one hates the harmless unnecessary person in a railway-carriage, whether it be the joys of company or those of solitude that he is spoiling.

The occasional visits of the midwife were a solace; the big motherly woman radiated cheerfulness and gin whenever she dropped in to pass the time of day.

And one Tuesday in May Jim returned to find Olive alone in the sitting-room in a state of suppressed excitement. Her hands were clenched, and her eyes sparkling with some neurosis that she – less than any other woman in the world – could define or name. And she had not prepared the supper.

Liz was upstairs in the bedroom, and the midwife was with her. The husband ran anxiously to the door; the old woman would brook no interference, and bade him wait till he was wanted.

He returned to the sitting room, and walked restlessly round like a caged beast. Olive sat deathly still, and flushed and paled by turns.

Twenty minutes later the midwife called to him to run for the doctor. Five minutes later he returned, with a young man in spectacles, swinging a black bag, and wearing the air of a jaded mule. He brusquely told the husband to stay below, and made for the staircase.

Jim flung himself into a chair. Every nerve was on fire. The craving of the morphine slave was like his mood.

Olive faced him, equally helpless, equally excited. From time to time the groans of the wife pressed their weird weight upon the panting silence.

Suddenly the tension became unbearable. The nameless disquietude of the man and the girl took shape, interpreted themselves as passion. It was the extremity of fear. The groans ceased abruptly; a scream, jagged and rasping, cut the air.

It determined the crisis. In a second, blind and raving, Jim flung himself upon Olive, and crushed her as a bear crushes a hunter.

The girl comprehended herself, scratched and bit.

It was the death-struggle against Nature, to which there is only one end. The screams of the two sisters mingled; as one child was born, another was begotten.

Every Precaution

I

The blind pianist sat in the deserted café. His instrument was situated in one corner on a small square dais of wood. The floor of the café was of black stone, liberally sprinkled with sawdust. The general scheme of decoration of the café was green, as if to commemorate its consecration as a temple of the goddess Absinthe.

The only other person in the room was a too-faithful devotee of that extravagant mistress. She was a woman of between thirty and thirty-five years of age, no more; but her whole life had been eaten up in the service of the goddess. Skin, eye, and nerve testified alike to the tyranny of her idol. It was the custom in this café to prepare the absinthe in the adjoining bar; but this woman insisted on being supplied with the materials wholesale. Thus she was able to steep herself without interruption in the consumption of the faery poison which had rapt her from apprehension of human affairs into a world of her own fancy. She had paid the price of the pilgrimage. A greenish pallor, resembling that of the belly of a fish which has begun to decompose, overspread her emaciated features. Nervous tremblings, interrupted by occasional convulsive spasms, shook her limbs. Her lustreless eyes were horrible to look upon; for in them one could see not only the signs of confusion of actual sight, but also that dreadful preoccupation with things form-less and fantastic which seems to lie beyond the bar of sanity.

The door swung open. Hand in hand, laughing merrily, two children tripped into the room. The girl was not a day over eighteen, fair, blue-eyed, and rosy as the fingers of the morn. One could see at a glance that she had never known a day's unhappiness, or sickness, or distress. The newness of the wedding ring on her plump finger was excuse for her exuberance, and so was the boy with her. He was per-haps twenty-five years old, gay, athletic, handsome as a god, yet with a finely intellectual type of face and the strong jaw and firm mouth that go with high moral character.

The proprietor himself, watching the café through the windowed door that led into the bar, came in to greet them, scenting persons of distinction. The young people seated themselves at one of the middle tables. The blind man began to play a tune. The proprietor took the order – two absinthes – and vanished.

'Myra,' said her husband, 'I want you to have one absinthe, and to promise me that you will never take another. I am not one of those birds, who think that a woman should be innocent – by which they mean ignorant.'

The proprietor brought in the absinthe. 'I should like you to listen,' said the young man to him, 'to what I am about to say: for you, as keeper of this house, hold a great responsibility toward your fellow-creatures.' The good man bowed, and stood attentive.

'Dearest,' he continued, 'we must not fly from evil, but resist it. I believe in education and in experience; I want to see you full-armed in the battle of life. For, make no mistake, dear heart, life is a battle; we do not know, dove, how strenuous or how long; but we do know that sooner or later we must fall. Our success is to be gauged by our works done, and victories won, and by the children that we train to follow us in the fight! Now, sweet wife, I have brought you here to tell you of these things, knowing it for a quiet place. The boat leaves for Havana in an hour; and I wanted you to know, before we mix with other people, what plans I have made, what campaign I have designed. We have youth, health, and money in abundance; it is our duty to ourselves and to our race to take every precaution to preserve these advantages to our descendants. After our month or two of honey, we shall go to the house that my ancestors built long since by Lake Pasquaney. There the air is sweet and pure and keen; the people are simple and honest and high-minded. The climate is perfect; every power of nature seems joined in gentle conspiracy to make life what it surely should be. The estate is spacious, the house well-ordered; there we can dwell, and found a new race – a Sun-race! – that shall combine physical health with moral vigour and spiritual well-being. We shall be the Adam and Eve of a new Eden – and forewarned as to the Serpent!'

'Words of gold, sir!' cried the keeper of the Absinthe House, warmly. 'I wish I could have had your advantages. As it is, I wish you all happiness and success! Excuse me, Madame,' he added quickly. 'I am needed in the bar.' He bowed profoundly and went out.

Myra sipped her absinthe with a very wry face at the taste; but her eyes glowed marvellously as she drank in her husband's wise and noble words. She was the only child of distinguished parents, a grand old stock clear of all taint for centuries; a worthy mate indeed for the young man beside her. With all her heart she loved him; with her first love she loved him. She had been carefully guarded all her life; no flirtations had brushed the bloom from her purity; virgin in mind as in body she had given herself to Howard Poindexter – once and for ever. She had only one thought in life: to help him, to make him happy, to bear him healthy children.

She put her hand on his, and gazed into his eyes.

'Ten days more,' she whispered, 'to the anniversary of our first meeting – Christmas Day!'

Howard Poindexter raised his glass. 'To Christmas Day!' he cried aloud.

The woman in the corner awoke from her apathy at the words. She came forward unsteadily, and rested her arms on the table, thrusting her face into Poindexter's. 'Christmas Day ain't no private car,' said she; 'I've a string on Christmas Day myself.' She went back to her table, brought over her bottle of absinthe, and sat it down on the marble with a determined gesture. 'Days ain't nothing in my young life,' she went on; 'when the green goddess has got you, you don't care nothing about days. But Christmas day, oh yes! Come here, Toby!'

Instead of obeying, the man gave a horrible grimace, and set his fingers on the keys. 'Hark! the herald angels sing,' he chanted to his own accompaniment; and he played words and music with a cynicism so repulsive that the new-comers set their teeth in horror. It was a performance icily devilish. The absintheuse laughed with a sort of senseless malice. 'Come here, Toby!' she repeated. The blind pianist began to grope his way towards the party, guided by the sound of her voice. 'It was Christmas Day I met this doggoned blind gink, wasn't it, Toby? Five years ago! And that night I gave him what took his eyes out; he never saw New Year, curse him! Didn't I, Toby?'

The bride shrank back, appalled. She would have fled the café; the foul coarse accents and the revolting smell of the hag disgusted her almost to nausea. But her husband held her with his eye. It was necessary that she should see degradation at its limit that she might avoid its very shadow, yet perchance understand and lend her aid to those in danger of it.

'Do you love me, Toby?' The blind man reached his arms toward her. 'Shucks! quit fooling!' she growled. 'I love him, too, but not to go dippy. I should worry! See here, mister, you and your precautions. Don't you take no precautions but just one, and that's to drink this green muck till you're blind. Then you don't have no more troubles. I'll show you here's to Christmas Day!' She took up the bottle, and put her blanched lips to the neck, drank nearly half of it. 'Here, drink, Toby, you ——' she ended with a foul oath, 'here's dog-goned Christmas Day!' She brought the bottle down upon his skull. It smashed into a hundred pieces. The blood gushed in every direction from the blind man's head. She sank into a chair, and fell into a silly drunken laughter. Suddenly she was convulsed by an epileptoid spasm, and fell writhing on the floor, twisting off the legs of the chairs in her agony, and snapping at the air.

The proprietor rushed in at the noise of the crashing glass, and the blind man's awful scream; two waiters followed him. One raised the bleeding head of the pianist; the other grappled with the cursing mad-woman on the floor.

Poindexter threw a dollar bill upon the table, caught up his bride, and fled with her from the abominable scene.

The proprietor checked him, 'I must have your name, sir,' he said, 'if the man dies the police will have to come in. You were an eye-witness of the attack.' The young husband drew a card from his case.

> Howard Poindexter,
> Concord Towers,
> Bristol, N.H.

He read slowly. Poindexter nodded, and hurried out.

He knew it would not be necessary to exact a promise from his young wife as to the acquisition of the absinthe habit.

2

A year later. No – not quite a year; the first cold wind had not yet touched the delta of the Mississippi. The 'Green Hour' silently announced itself – the yellow of sunset mingling with the blue, so that the gazer might remember to seek the Old Absinthe House, and take his apéritif.

In the café the blind pianist still strummed; save for the scars of the gashes, time and fate had passed over him and left him scatheless. He may have seemed happier than of old; his song was a little more spontaneous and his fingers lighter on the keys. His love increased with every injury done to him by its object; and so, it may be, did hers also.

At the same table as before the woman still sat, apparently unchanged. Her poisoning was one degree more chronic: she was a little nearer to cachexia; but no one could have said whether she was good for one year more or forty, not even the celebrated alienist who was chatting with the proprietor at a table in the opposite corner.

'I had hoped,' he was saying, 'that you could have shown me a really advanced case of absinthism, one in which hallucinations are constant. I have never seen one in America. In fact, not since I left Paris thirty years ago. I want to make some personal observations to complete my book on insanity.'

'That girl's pretty near it at times,' said the proprietor; 'just before last Christmas she made a murderous assault on the pianist there; broke a bottle over his head, quite without provocation, apparently for fun!'

'Insanity's a funny thing; I could tell you of some strange cases. Our lives and reasons hang literally by far less than a hair, by the inexplicable and even indecipherable hieroglyphs of subtle molecular changes in the cells of the brain. Perfectly normal healthy people sometimes act in the maddest fashion, under apparently slight derangement of a function, or even under purely physiological stimulus.

'There's the boy, you know, who got a splinter of wood under his toe-nail, and had violent fits of mania as long as he was standing. Forced on to a bed, he became quite sane, had no memory of what had happened save that he "felt a little odd"; but he went off into mania again directly there was pressure on the toe!

'Even a simple matter like pregnancy in a perfectly healthy woman may have the most astounding consequences. Doctor Henry Maudsley quotes two cases offered by Shencks;[1] in one, the woman wanted to bite the bare arms of a barber, and made her husband offer him money to allow it; in the other she was consumed by a raging passion to devour her husband himself, and actually killed him, and pickled him, and banqueted on him at her leisure for a month! This case, curiously enough, has been precisely parallelled in America quite recently – within a month or so, in fact – a man named Howard Poindexter.'

'He was sitting here with his bride,' interrupted the inn-keeper, 'sitting at this very table when Norah there broke the bottle over Toby's head. He had been explaining how to avoid misfortune by virtue and prudence; he said he had taken every precaution.'

The two men sat in silence. Then they were conscious of the presence of the *absintheuse* at their elbows. 'And the moral is, gentlemen,' she slobbered with an insane giggle, 'that you might just as well join me in another glass to the little green goddess.'

They drank; but it is not recorded what deity the alienist invoked.

---

[1] *The Physiology and Pathology of Mind.* Henry Maudsley M.D. (New York, D. Appleton & Co., 1871), p. 238, note.

God's Journey

I

The house was very big, and very old, and very lonely. In some parts of Europe, it would have been called a castle, for it stood foursquare with walls two yards thick, and there was a strong tower at one corner. But, here, a hundred miles from Kazan, it was just the House of the Barin.

Little Dascha was never very frightened. The loneliness of the land came natural to her. Nobody knew who she was, but people said that there must be Tatar blood in her because her face was very Mongolian, even as a baby, and her hair was fox colour. Probably it would get darker when she got older.

No, she was never frightened, brave little six year old, not even of Pavel Petrovich Goluchinov in his worst fits of melancholic rage; she had an all-powerful protectress in the pale woman who ruled the house, Maria Ivanovna. For the Barin was a bit of an adventurer. There were periods in his past that would not bear investigation. And his wife was the daughter of a general, a prince of the Empire, a man who stood very well indeed with the Tsar.

The Barin beat everybody else, not only in the house, but for twenty miles around. One does not resist a man whose father-in-law is a general. And, besides, God had afflicted him. He was never quite like the other people. He was more human and sane when he was drunk than at other times, thought the peasants.

But, drunk or sober, he never lifted his hand against the thin, pale, fragile woman whom he had married. And he never opposed her.

She had never had any children, and little Dascha had been adopted to fill the empty place. On that one occasion, indeed, the Barin had registered one last, ineffectual protest. He wanted to know why, if she must have a child in the house, she could not take a boy.

However, there was a good deal of boy in the queer little Tatar girl. She was a wild, scapegrace child, always in mischief. But when thwarted or annoyed, she would retire into herself almost like some Chinese monk might do, sitting motionless in a corner, forgetful of everything but the trouble of the moment.

Maria Ivanovna herself thought there was something unnatural in such fits, and tried to break the child of the habit; but, will for will, little Dascha was the stronger of the pair.

It was a long time, indeed, before her foster-mother could find out what was the meaning of her sulkiness. But once, in an outburst of frankness, the girl said:

'Somebody does harm to me. I say nothing. I tell God. You wait. You will see that good does not come of that.'

'Well, baby,' said the Barinya, 'why does it take you so long to tell God?'

'Oh,' said Dascha, 'God lives a long way off. I am sometimes very tired before I get to him. But I never give up.'

It was a very strange and solitary family that lived in the big house, in the lonely land. The Barinya saw no friends at all, except that now and then some of her relations would come from Moscow or St Petersburg to visit her.

Their estate was an enormous one. It was thirty miles to the next house of any landed proprietor.

Pavel Petrovich had no friends at all of his own rank. Strange stories were told of how he had left the army, and stories even more sinister as to how he had managed to marry into so exalted a family.

He was a short, strongly built man, with a bullet head nearly bald, a long pair of fierce moustaches, and a clean shaved chin. His nose was short and blunt; his eyes, small, beady and malevolent. All his notion of human society was drinking bouts in the Pivnaya with the peasants of the village. His mistress was the lowest and dirtiest of all the serfs.

He had managed after long and careful manœuvres to get her into the house as an occasional helper in the scullery.

The poor lady knew nothing of this, and would not have cared. She had resigned herself to her life of utter loneliness. Like so many Russians of the most strictly religious type, she felt acutely the need of self-torture. She accepted her long imprisonment, for one could hardly speak of it as anything else, as the just punishment for real or imaginary errors of her earlier life.

The Barin might have tolerated any other kind of woman. The cold rigidity of his wife was an abhorrence to him. Indeed, Maria Ivanovna had no softer feelings in her life at all. Her religion was as arid as the Steppes. Her only weak spot was little Dascha, whom she cherished with a love that was really more religious than it was human. Indeed, she had reason to release her grip on life, for she was slowly, very slowly, dying of consumption.

It is impossible to imagine a greater contrast than that between the two women.

Nadia, the maid, was a stout, muscular wench, violent, drunken and degraded, but enormously vital. A fanciful man might have thought of her as a demon sprung from the very soil itself. She was fierce and surly. She had probably not five hundred words in her whole vocabulary, and her ideas were gross almost to bestiality. She was entirely destitute of any moral sense. But beyond this mask lay a brain, which, under other conditions, might have fitted a statesman. You would have got no hint of it, save in the smouldering fire of her wolfish eyes. And even in them, you would probably have read nothing but savage and predatory instinct.

You would have supposed that her ambitions were bounded by the satisfaction of the moment. But, in reality, she had, perhaps hardly formulated in consciousness, a lust of power which knew neither bounds nor scruples.

In any other country, a woman with such ideas would have hastened to grasp at the obvious purifications which lead to power. She would have tried to wash, to dress herself attractively, to acquire some education.

In the country of Catherine the Great, such methods are not necessary. You will remember how John the Pannonian, the blacksmith's bastard, destroyed the Infant Protus and grasped the sceptre in his great gnarled fist without any more ado about it.

So, all that Nadia could see of the whole planet was the big, square house, and she wanted that for her own.

All she could see of humanity was the master of the house, whom she had in her grasp, and the mistress of the house, who prevented her from making use of her victory.

Between the thought of murder and the deed, however, lay an abyss. There was the certainty of vengeance; and there was the dread of the supernatural. But here came to her aid the inexorable patience of the Russian peasant. She had a quality which would have saved Napoleon if he had possessed it. She knew how to wait. She did not even take any steps to gain a firmer grasp, to establish her footing in the household more securely. The Barin was her slave. Of what use would it be to do anything whatever when she had that vantage?

As it so often turns out in life, if one is honestly resigned to wait, one does not have to wait so long after all.

Before she had been in the house a year, the Barinya found her sickness leap suddenly forward. A week's tussle with the Grim Old Man, and she was gone.

It was on the day of the funeral itself that a long heralded storm broke out in the house. The Barinya had wished to be buried with her jewelled cross, crude emeralds and amethysts bubbling from rough hammered gold. When the time came to close the coffin, the cross was nowhere to be found.

Everyone in the house was rather drunk, and a great hullabaloo was aroused. A person of any intelligence would have known who had taken it. The village pope was a notorious thief, and it was not the first time that the spiritual amenities of his presence had had to be paid for by material disadvantages.

But the room where the dead woman lay was filled with beings half crazy with emotion, and nothing was to be heard but accusations and recriminations mingled with passionate protestations and appeals to the Deity to bear witness to what was going on.

There was one person who had not the normal activity of the brain, that superficial quality of swift reaction without reflection, whose evidence is talk. This was a brain that apprehended situations in some deep stratum of the soul, and the result of whose subtle, secret operations is to make decisions which really decide things.

When the hubbub chanced for a moment to be lulled, Nadia, who had been watching the scene silently out of the corners of her sombre eyes, came heavily across the floor towards the master of the house. Her very motion might have suggested some inexorable engine of destruction. She lurched clumsily like a tank, slow, stupid, and yet deadly.

She made most humble reverence to Pavel Petrovich and said, 'I saw Dascha with it.'

The words were quite enough. It let everybody out.

The pope immediately said, 'So that was the glittering thing I noticed in her hand a little while ago.'

And soon other witnesses came forward, including one who had actually seen the child take it from the breast of the dead woman.

The next thing was to find Dascha. The child was playing in a little coppice which fringed the sluggish stream that wound around the great tower of the house.

She denied all knowledge of the cross. When she heard the nature of the accusation, she shut her little mouth firmly, and sat down where she was.

The Barin grew very angry. His wife was dead. There was no one to restrain him. His sullen hatred for the child, pent up for years, broke loose. He shook her and slapped her, punctuating his actions with curses.

The child took no more notice of him than if she had been carved of wood. The moment he stopped, there she was once more sitting like an idol, and nothing but the quick beating of her little heart testified to her emotion.

At last the pope, possibly stricken by some touch of remorse, began to protest.

Pavel Petrovich turned on him with a savage oath, took him immediately by the shoulders, spun him around, and dismissed him with a vigorous kick.

But the others also took Dascha's part. She was so sweet, so playful, so natural, so witty in her childish way, that everybody loved her; that is, when he or she happened to think of it.

But the Barin beat them all off like a huntsman driving the hounds from a dead fox, and, having picked her up by the nape of her neck, flung her across his shoulder. Crying out, 'Foundling she is, now let somebody else find her!' he strode to the stable, leapt on his favourite horse, and rode away across the Steppes with her.

It was a day before he returned. No one ever knew what he had done with Dascha, except Nadia, to whom he confessed that he had given a sum of money to some merchants, who were travelling towards Nizhni Novgorod, to take her with them.

2

Pavel Petrovich was not long in discovering that he had exchanged King Log for King Stork. Nadia closed upon him as if it were a mountain that fell upon a man and buried him.

In a week, she was the absolute mistress of the household; but, having achieved her ambitions, she did not enlarge her horizon. She had got all she wanted, or ever could want, for the simple reason that she knew of nothing else; and she proceeded to enjoy it to the utmost. She turned the house into a pigsty. The servants had no duties any more, save to get drunk. Orgies of the most outrageous character were the rule of the house. She would invite wandering bands of Gypsies to camp in the great hall. The furniture was broken up for firewood, and the glassware used for missiles

She was supremely happy. There was not a cloud on the horizon. She was not one of those women who ruin a man, for she did not know what diamonds were. The Barin's income was more than sufficient for all the debauchery and drink that heart could wish.

He, too, was happy in his hoggish way. He became absolutely slovenly in his dress, and only changed his linen when the whim took him. He let his beard grow long.

The household readily settled down into the new routine. Month after month passed by with scarce an incident beyond the putting out of somebody's eye, or something of the sort, always in a perfectly friendly manner, so that the trifle was forgotten and forgiven as soon as the blood stopped flowing.

There was no doctor in the village. The diseases of the people were attended to at intervals by travelling quacks, who competed with the old 'wise women' who prepared medicines of simples. But if a doctor had chanced to pay a visit to the old big house, he might have warned its master that his course of life was not conducive to longevity.

There is a peculiar action of alcohol which is true with regard to certain temperaments and constitutions. A man becomes as it were preserved in spirit. He never seems to be ill. It is almost as if time passed him by. But, now and again, an accident may break down this mummification of the devotee of Bacchus.

One winter's night, twelve years after the death of his wife, Pavel Petrovich made a wager with a travelling salesman. It was a race across the river which bounded the edge of the village. It was filled with broken ice, heaped up in hummocks at the curve. Black pools of water glimmered darkly between them.

The whole crowd, clutching bottles of vodka, staggered out of the great house down to the stream. The race began. But before he had got half way, Pavel Petrovich slipped on a steep hummock and found himself in the river.

Men from the village, drawn by the drunken shouts of the crowd, had gathered to watch the race; while the revellers laughed and cheered, they brought ropes and pulled out the drowning drunkard.

It was a long while before he came back to life. The chill came near to be his bane. But (luckily for his life) there was a woman in the village who had been a nurse in the Crimean War and understood such conditions. She installed herself in the big house and watched the sick man day and night, while Nadia, perpetually drunk, only came in from time to time to curse him for being sick. It was her way of expressing her love. What she wanted, what she really cared for, was a man to join her in her amusements. And while she had no scruples about fidelity, Pavel Petrovich was the lord of the district, and it was her pride that she had him under her thumb.

There were times in that long illness when the nurse almost despaired, and Nadia understood in her dark soul that his death would be the end of her empire. She said to herself that she ought to have married him long before, and that she must do it now. But the vodka with which she had saturated herself for so many years stepped between idea and execution.

It was Pavel Petrovich who broached the subject. His sickness had washed all gross desires from him. He began to live again in the memories of early boyhood. His religious training knocked at the door of his dull conscience. He began to think, in a quite conventional, bourgeois way, of "making reparation to the woman whom he had wronged.'

A severe sickness is very trying to one's sense of humour.

He spoke of the matter to his nurse, and she, good old soul, thought it her clear duty to confirm him in his idea. The upshot was that one day when he seemed sinking, she sent for the pope; and, dragging Nadia from her carousals with some Gypsies who were passing through, had them safely married.

It is possible that the sick man was really affected in his subconsciousness by the superstitious idea of reparation, for from the moment of his marriage he began rapidly to mend. Ten days later he was up and about.

But he was a man essentially changed. His eye caught the dirt and disorder of the house, which had never once been cleaned in twelve years. He began to remember how different it had been while Maria Ivanovna lived. An ineffable weariness and disgust swept through him. And, yet, such is the force of habit, no sooner had he found Nadia lying drunk in the kitchen, than he called for a bottle of spirits.

But drink is a very curious thing. It requires two parties to the transaction. The Pavel Petrovich who was drinking now was not the Pavel Petrovich who had drunk before.

Previously, his nature had been merely gross, and vodka had accentuated that quality in him. Now, he was purified of bestiality by that close call from death, and the obedient alcohol now accentuated that quality just as it had done the former.

He got drunk, all right, but instead of his losing himself in a fantasia whose theme was animal satisfaction, it gave him clarity of vision, like that of a drowning man who can comprehend in an instant the whole vista of life.

He became melancholy, for that was part of his original nature; but it was not the fierce and irritable melancholia which had characterised that type of mood during his first wife's lifetime. It was a pure, a mystic melancholia, and the chorus was, 'What a rotten thing life is. And, anyhow, what a mess you've made of it.'

And when that thought took clear shape in his mind, his eyes fell upon his wife. In twelve years, she had grown old and fat. She was incredibly dirty. Her hair was matted with mud. Her clothes were filthy beyond words, torn and stained. It did not seem as if she put them on. One might have said that they had grown on her, like moss upon a rotten oak stump.

And, then again, came the fierce counterattack of habit. She was the woman who gratified every vile and perverted habit that he had ever had. To use his own language, she was the woman whom he loved.

As if in answer to this thought, she came out of her drunken stupor. There were several other people in the kitchen, but they never stirred. It was certain that they would not stir for many an hour yet.

Nadia came to her husband, staggering over the flags of the kitchen. She caught him fiercely in her fat arms, and smothered him with drunken kisses. The tumult in his soul increased almost to the point of ecstasy. All the sensual side of his nature, developed through years of indulgence, roused an almost incoherent passion in him. The perceptive faculties in him, rendered exquisitely acute by the emaciation of his sickness and rooted deep in the soil of his earliest training, cried bitterly, 'That thing is your wife!'

He thrilled with horror and disgust. Then rose the other wave, insurgent and insistent; and, alternating, these two violences drove him to the edge of insanity.

A moment came when he could no longer distinguish between them, and it was at that moment that his wife reeled, and dragged him to the ground.

As chance would have it, there was a rusty carving knife lying upon the floor within reach of his hand; and, even as he swooned beneath her kisses, he reached out for it and drove it slowly into her throat.

Pavel Petrovich did not know what he had done for a little while. When he came to himself, the other people in the room were still asleep. He, on the other hand, was more awake than he had ever been in his whole life. His brain had never been very active, but at this moment it was supernaturally acute. He understood perfectly well that he had done murder. He understood perfectly well that he was free from any possibility of suspicion. Furious brawls had been too common in that house. More than once a man or a woman had been wounded nigh unto death. No one would suspect a convalescing invalid of the crime. He had no motive that anyone could imagine. Any one of the dozen people in that kitchen might have done it. When they woke up, it would be their business to look after it.

All he had to do was to take a stroll in the village, and chat pleasantly with the people whom he might find there. He was sure he could do it. He did not feel the slightest tremor, either of remorse or fear.

The lovely sun of spring shone beyond the walls of the old big house. He went quietly upstairs, put on his coat and hat, and went out of the house humming a tune.

3

When Pavel Petrovich came to the village, he found a warm welcome from everybody whom he met. The mind of the Russian is admirably simple and well-ordered. He never mistakes accidents for essentials. A Tsar might be a very terrible person. He might be stamped with every crime. He might be guilty of every oppression. But he is the Little Father, Temporal and Spiritual Head of the Empire, which is the civilised world. And as a father he is to be loved and revered, as the representative of God on earth.

Similarly, the landowner might have been rather a wicked oppressor, and the serfs might be ready to burn down the roof over his head and roast him in the embers; but he never ceases to be the Dear Barin, Vice Regent of the Tsar, one ray of that Tsar's sunshine. The peasants must love him with the love not only of a child for a father, but that of a mother for a child. 'He has been near to death, and God has preserved him to us, and this is the happiest day in our lives.'

And then – there is the mood of reaction against such feelings. It is hard for those who do not know Russia to understand such psychology.

The result of it was that, spiritually exalted with the fine weather and the love of his villagers, Pavel Petrovich suddenly found himself in a world of simple, childlike happiness. He experienced the relief of one whose sins have been washed away, and wished such a state to endure for ever.

It was only when he became hungry that he thought of returning to his house. But the thought of that house was another spiritual awakening. It was not a real house at all to him. It was a nightmare from which he awakened. But, again, his physical being aroused in him the impulse to return to that house, and this was a thing which he understood that he could never do.

He visualised the twenty years he had spent there with absolute lucidity. He could never go there again.

But there was nothing to distress him in that fact; the situation was quite simple. He would go to his friend, Stephen Pavlovich, the merchant, and draw on him for funds. He would go to spend the spring in the Crimea. It was perfectly natural that one recovering from pneumonia should take just that step.

People in Russia do not scrutinise closely the behaviour of individuals. Everyone is allowed to do things in his own way.

There was no reason why he should start from his house with a large number of trunks amid the flourish of trumpets.

So he went to his friend's house and borrowed ten thousand rubles. He engaged a carriage, and set out on his travels, a free man.

The fresh air and the swift motion exhilarated him more than ever. He felt that by his act he had cut himself off completely from his past. He knew perfectly well that he stood in no danger whatever.

The evening had fallen when he came to the market town of the district. He put up at the hotel, deliciously languid after his long drive, so that his soul sighed itself softly away into a spiritual siesta. He dined well, and enjoyed his food like a hunter, drinking heartily with no sting of the passion for drink. A small bottle of light champagne was all that he touched. And when his head sank on the pillow, he slept instantly, dreamlessly, like a tired child.

In the morning, he woke early. He could not think where he was. He could not remember any of the events which had led up to his being in this strange place.

One may suppose that there are few people to whom this experience has not happened at one time or another. It is always a little embarrassing to people of weak mentality, perhaps even a little terrifying. To Pavel Petrovich, enfeebled by his long sickness, and no doubt subconsciously affected by the remembrance of what he had passed through, the situation was one of horror. An impalpable idea, senseless and formless, obsessed him.

It presented itself to him at last in a shape which he had never previously envisaged. He said to himself, 'Now I know who I am, and where I am, and how I came to be here. I am a murderer running away.'

That had been the true reason for his flight, though that aspect had never previously presented itself to his consciousness. He was a murderer, running away, though he had not known it till that moment.

But the idea, once presented to him in such form, took complete possession of him. He immediately began to think of the things which would naturally occur to anyone in such a situation. He did not think of the truth, that there was no chance whatever of anyone suspecting him. He simply thought, 'How shall I escape notice?'

Thus, first of all, it occurred to him that he must change his appearance. So he dressed quietly and quickly, went downstairs and ordered his breakfast. He walked down the street until he came to a barber's.

The proprietor had not yet arrived at that early hour in the morning. The only person in the shop was an assistant, a boy, some eighteen years old, with a mass of chestnut hair, a bright, quick smile, and eyes large, lustrous and intense.

Pavel Petrovich took a swift fancy to him. He exchanged greetings far more cordial than his wont, and asked for a clean shave. It would be easy to make some laughing excuse at the hotel for the change in his appearance. A convalescent going to some fashionable resort in the Crimea does not need a big, black beard. He began to try his excuses on the young barber, who acquiesced in a flow of pleasant conversation.

'This is the time to go to the Crimea,' said the boy, 'the spring wind blows cold from Tartary. You see, Gospodin, how my hand trembles, although the sun is up and shining brightly.

'Yes, this is spring weather. I have waited a long while through a dreary winter.

'Your hair is a little thin on the top, sir. Can't I sell you this elixir, which is made by the cleverest chemist from Paris itself?

'No, sir, you need not be afraid if my hand trembles. I have been shaving people for several years, and I have never had an accident.'

'No, my boy, I would trust you with anything,' laughed the man in the chair, 'I have half a mind to ask you to be my valet. What do you say to leaving this dull little town, and sunning yourself among the fine ladies on the Plage?'

'The offer is tempting,' said the boy, 'but I am on a journey, and I am very near its end. It has taken me a long while to get to this town, which is not far from the place that I have always wanted to go to.

'Strange as it may seem to you, I think there is a God who speeds travellers even when they least expect it.'

'I hope He will speed me,' replied Pavel Petrovich.

'I have no doubt of that,' cried the young barber.

'It seems almost a pity for you to lose that beautiful beard. I admired your appearance so much when you came into the shop. You look quite different now. Of course, I do not mean to say that I do not admire you as you are. Though, perhaps, a man never looks his best with a lot of lather on his face.'

Pavel Petrovich laughed cheerfully.

'Talking of accidents,' said the boy, 'it seems so extraordinary to me that suicides have no more sense. They try to cut through the thick muscles of the neck, or to pierce through the bony structure of the larynx; as a surgical fact, it requires the greatest determination as well as considerable muscular strength to reach any vital artery in this direction. But, on the other hand, the jugular vein lies very near the surface, and I sometimes think that beards were intended as a sort of protection to this part from some cutting or piercing instrument.'

The boy's words, innocent as they were, filled Pavel Petrovich with a clammy terror. Was it not in that vein that he had stabbed his wife?

The boy noticed the change in his eyes.

'I hope that you will let me sell you some of our special cream to use after shaving,' he said, as though purposely ignoring the sweat which had broken out on the forehead of his customer.

'Thank you,' said Pavel Petrovich, 'perhaps it will be as well for me to take a pot with me.' But he spoke through his clenched teeth in cold desperation.

The boy wiped his customer's forehead with a napkin.

'I fear you have been ill, sir,' he said, 'and are not quite recovered.'

'Why, yes,' said Pavel Petrovich, 'I told you I had been ill when first I came into the shop.'

'Ah,' said the boy, 'I do not think you know what illness is. I have a sickness of the soul.

'Shall I go over it twice, sir?'

'Yes, I want to be shaved close.'

'I will shave very close,' said the boy, 'but I will be careful not to cut you.'

Is it possible that the boy did not notice the fearful state of agitation in which his customer now was? It appeared like a coma. His eyes were turned up so that the whites showed horribly. Perhaps he did not know very clearly the nature of his fear. Perhaps he had not the power to analyse the complex of emotion which was agonising him. But the boy noticed – no doubt he noticed well – and he sought to console Goluchinov by endeavouring to awake his sympathy.

'However sick you may have been, sir, I can assure you that, young as I am, it is nothing to what I myself have suffered.

'When I was a child, I was accused wrongfully of a theft. I was thrown out of the house where I had been brought up, and handed over like a parcel to some men who were travelling in the country on their affairs.'

Goluchinov's head swam. Extraordinary that this boy's story should recall his own behaviour towards little Dascha, long years ago! It seemed as if every word was playing with the skill of a Chinese torturer upon his nerves.

'Yes, sir, this is my story,' continued the young barber.

'A little to the right, if you please, sir.

'I have never forgotten the injury that was done to me. I took a solemn oath that I would avenge it.

'Still a little more to the right, if you please, sir.

'I am going to surprise you, sir, perhaps. But, after all, the thing is common in Russia. I am really a girl. But, that I might pursue more easily the plan of my vengeance, I have worn boy's clothes, lived a boy's life, learnt a boy's trade. And, little by little, I worked my way until I am now within a day's journey of the place where I mean to take my vengeance.

'I beg your pardon, sir. The head a trifle farther back, if you please.

'I should have said, I had meant to take my vengeance there. But, as I said before, to one who travels earnestly, it sometimes happens that God comes to meet him on the way. This world is full of strange events. Is it not, sir?

'I think you would find your hair better if you had it regularly singed. It is allowing the hair to grow too long and uneven that makes it possible for the germs to live, which cause baldness. Singeing sterilises perfectly the ends of the hair.'

Pavel Petrovich gasped an affirmative. He did not know anything any more, but fear struck to the roots of his soul in a cold delirium of anguish.

'Yes, sir,' the girl went on, 'even if God does not come half way to meet one, he certainly always comes a little way. I thought myself a day's journey from the author of my misery, and curiously enough he is in this chair, Pavel Petrovich Goluchinov!

'A little bay rum, sir?'

The murderer did not answer. The girl's hand, light as it was, weighed on his head as if it had been the monument of his sins, and the razor was still at his throat.

'No bay rum, sir? A little powder, perhaps? We have exactly the shade of powder you require, Barin. Could I not sell you a stick of alum, in case at any time you should cut yourself in shaving, and find it necessary to stop the bleeding? One cannot really be too careful with that jugular vein. Hardly a touch from the point or the heel of this razor, and it would be all over. No surgeon could do anything if you should happen to meet with such an accident, Pavel Petrovich Goluchinov.'

Little Dascha folded her razor, and hastened to powder her customer's chin.

'There, that is better. That certainly looks fine. Twenty kopecks, if you please, and pray do not forget to remember the barber.'

But he did not hear those words: God had come to meet little Dascha on her journey.

The Colour of My Eyes

My Father employed the Great Angel Sandalphon in his work. And Sandalphon wrought upon a shaft of sunlight, bending it this way and that, until he had made a Rainbow in the Heavens as a ring for the finger of my Father.

Moreover he chose a goddess to tend his rainbow; swift was she, and fair to look upon; and her name was Iris.

And Sandalphon was enamoured of her beauty, because she was like unto the Rainbow that he had made; but she was subtle and elusive, so that whenever he was here, she was there; when flying strongly, he came there, she was gone.

At last, weary and disconsolate, he sat down upon a great rock above a waterfall, and folded his wings over his face and wept.

When he opened his eyes, he saw his lovely Iris playing in the spray of the waterfall, mocking him. But he, being made wise by love, and by the sorrow of love, turned away steadily.

There, on a grassy slope dew-bright, he saw a peacock strutting. Then he said: Lo! the Father hath wrought also wonder of beauty upon earth, where one may grasp and hold.

Now, playing with the peacock, and feeding him with gilded grains of wheat, there was a nymph of the daughters of men. And Sandalphon moved secretly towards her, wondering if his art might not blend the colour of the peacock with her form. But when he looked into her eyes, he saw cloudy skies of blue, like unto the heavens before he had wrought his Rainbow.

And the nymph marvelled at his glory, but with disdain and nonchalance, for she was perfect in herself and in her pleasure.

Sandalphon was content, seeing ice in her eyes; for he understood that their form was apt for the incarnation of an Iris, if only my Father would allow him to work into them the Miracle of Colour.

So then Sandalphon flew away to my Father, and spake his heart. And my Father smiled and bade him do as he best could. Oh! this was long ago, long, long ago – Sandalphon made delight in many a myriad of eyes, but he was never satisfied. At last – just a few years since – he went back to my Father, saying humbly that he understood that the task was too great for him, that this was a thing that only my Father himself could bring to Perfection.

So then my Father smiled, and said to Sandalphon that He would show him how to colour eyes. And they came to me together, and found me a small child lying asleep; and my Father said: 'These will be good eyes for this Work.'

So my Father took my eyes, and wrought mightily with His thumb for an hammer, and the Breath of His nostrils for a forge. And first about the iris of my eyes he put a ring of orange, to wake remembrance of the Sun. And He made the groundwork of violet, like a tropical night, with shades of peacock green and peacock blue, because He wished to commemorate the adventure of Sandalphon by the waterfall. Then He set in them, all about the blackness of the pupil, flecks of pale gold for stars, and sparks of scarlet to be the sign manual of His work.

And when he had finished, He showed these jewels to Sandalphon proudly. But the great Angel became agitated and embarrassed, and hid his face from my Father. Then my Father bade him speak, but he would not. At that my Father smiled indeed, for He knew all things, but sternly He commanded Sandalphon.

Then the great Angel threw himself upon the earth, and abased his brow seven times, and cried through the storm of his sobbing: 'Let me be destroyed in Thine anger, for it is not of mine own will that I blaspheme. But – oh my Lord – although these eyes be of beauty and wonder a miracle to gaze on through Eternity, yet – these are not the eyes that I conceived in mine heart!'

And my Father laughed softly, and raised him, and led him away, and whispered in his ear: 'Oh, Sandalphon, be of good cheer; for I am compassionate of thine artist sorrow. But I have done all that Omnipotence itself can do. As thou seest, that is only half the work. Thou must come back in a few years and look upon these eyes, when they are filled with Love.'

Dedit!

I

The Soul

It was grey English weather for the pauper funeral, with draughty wind and drizzle of rain that by their positive attack seemed almost a relief from the drab chill. By no means an event, this ditching carrion, earth to the earth that bred such vermin parasites, ashes of a dull fire that was never flame but smoke as of raked garbage, dust that had never defied the winds of circumstance or lifted itself of its own will from its chance neighbour grains, from them so undistinguishable that to have named it sounds fatuity, and to have bade it vote, an insane scoundrel's blunder.

Not an event? But the whole countryside is up and out; the village cemetery overflows, and the rain's dubious drizzle is put to shame by honest tears as the wind's shifty casuality by men's strong sobbing. The road, too, is clogged with carriages; on the panels of the first of them is a small initial in dull blue, and a ducal coronet above it.

Ah! there's the Duke, that white-haired octogenarian in shabby black, his worn silk hat, a decade behind the fashion, with a broad band of cloth upon it. He stands, head bowed, by the open grave; stands? hardly; he leans heavily on a gold-mounted cane of ebony, and with his other arm clings to a stalwart man of forty in Colonel's uniform, a man so like him that the least critical stranger would at a glance divine the heir. There are so many more mourners – though not true mourners like the crowd-ing country-folk – that we must ask its secret of the coffin.

A plain deal coffin; not so much as a brass plate! Stay, though! the village carpenter has chiseled some inscription. It's crude; it's hard to read – and when we've read it, it says little. There's the word Claudia; there's the brace of dates; last, the one word DEDIT.[1] A woman it is; she lived three and fifty years and a few months; and somebody gave

---

[1] [She gave.]

something, and someone who knew a little Latin wished to say so. That's all, unless we guess. An arrow at random: Claudia sounds like the name of one well-born. Debrett identifies our Duke, whose second daughter Claudia was born on the same day as our dead pauper. It sounds incredible; she must have been intensely loved and honoured, since high attend her obsequies, and low bewail her loss.

Then why the shallow soil for her, and not the porphyry and malachite vault, with its bronze sculptured doors, of her forefathers? Why the cheap crazy hearse, and the half-foundered nag, the common coffin and the cryptic epitaph, more riddle than answer?

Who is the stout man with the red face, his scanty hair, greyed over the ears, the crow's feet beside and the black pouches under his eyes, his short breath, the effort evident in his carriage, concordant witnesses that his five and forty years add, in his ledger of life, to more than middle age? He is the rector, doubtless, by his cloth, by the familiarity which those who are clearly natives of the place show toward him. He is still speaking by the open grave; his words will perhaps cut the knot that the incongruities of the scene have tied and tangled in our rope of thought.

'—— the destiny of Lady Claudia Cusack.' (We were right, then; the Duke's daughter.) 'Is any stranger here – can there be any stranger to her in the world, any who knows not her story? – who wonders at this burial, bare decency, with yet the mightiest and the humblest in the land made level not only by the democracy of Death, but that of Tears? It was her will, expressed with all the emphasis of passion, that she should lie by whom she loved, in whose society lived, the People. Beside me stand His Grace the Archbishop, my Lord the Bishop, and yet more, all lightnings of enthusiasm, thunders of eloquence: our sister knew that they would come; she prayed them not to speak. She willed that I, the humble priest, whose highest pride is that she called me her friend, should do this office, and pronounce this elegy.'

He halts, he stumbles, this my sorry Pegasus, hobbled by bonds of language, hamstrung by knife of this great grief that has brought us here today.

'She prayed "No eloquence, no eulogy!" She has her will in that; my speech is bankrupt – my heart's in my throat! – and she is beyond eulogy as beyond all earth's imperfections. But, for the rest, she asked no flowers. What then are these thronged children that owe health, wit, often life itself, to her? No wreaths? Her death itself was a victory nine years long. No crowns? The End crowns the Work. No music at her grave? Earth's breast hath suckled mighty children; but not Chopin, nor

Handel, has composed *Dead March* or dirge such as this created by her genius, this that I hear today, the sobs of multitudes that mourn her. No monument? Ah, like the noble Roman, if thou seek one, look around thee! Behold the lives that she has saved, the hearts that she has eased, the cottages that she has built, the countryside that she has nourished as a mother her child – I had almost said a thing unlawful – the world she has created with the sustained wisdom, the care, the love of very Providence!

'Eloquence! Eulogy! My brothers and sisters, the trumpet of silver cannot sound, when silent fact is gold. I will not praise the Lady Claudia; I will state facts, known to nigh all of you at first hand, as crudely and as harshly as a geologist describes a mineral.

'I first came to this village, at that time barely one-fifth of its present size, just twenty years ago last Easter, as curate to your invalid rector, my dear friend and teacher, now with God, Dr Danesbury. Five years later, I lamented him at the graveside, and replaced him (alas! but ill!) at the altar. My first friend, after him, was the Lady Claudia Cusack. Few of us knew her rank, although her beauty, her manner, her refinement, sang their anthem aloud, proclaiming her more spirit than clay. She was by far the richest woman in the district: she lived at that time with a girl to share the work of house and garden, and, since that girl's death, with her young nephew, this twelve-year lad from whom we look to see such great things, fruit of his three years' intimacy with her soul. She worked like any farmer's drudge; her delicate hands were knotted and callous from her grip on earth. Yet her mind soared; she read philosophy, poetry, history, even law; she knew Greek and Latin so well that Æschylus and Ovid were as legible to her as English; she made mathematics her recreation; and it was her telescope, the one luxury she allowed herself, that showed her, ten years since, first of the world's astronomers, that satellite of Neptune whose discovery amazed the learned, and so profoundly modified our theories of the origin of the planets.

'It was I whom she trusted with the secret of her name and her fortune: for she had need of me in her most passionate work: I mean her charity.

'Let me say here that she was no devotee, hardly even a Christian, as the blind hearts of men judge Christians. She rarely came to church, she never communicated; she often spoke contemptuously of religion.

'But if Charity be of the essence of Christ's teaching, the heart of His word, she was the first of Christians. Hers was no organised, systematic charity, that spies upon, that cross-examines, that insults, degrades and pauperises its object – I had almost said its victim.

'It was no condescending charity that humiliates the recipient, no indiscriminate charity that makes the giver mockery of fools and prey of rogues.

'Still less was it that prurient prig's charity that tries to bribe unworthiness, to buy virtue, to whiten sepulchres, and so makes cowards, liars, hypocrites and slaves of all that it infects.

'Her Charity was rarely even bestowed to meet emergencies; for she foresaw, and she forestalled, their assurgence. It was born of her heart's passion, intense as love in a boy, confident as love in a man, wilfully blind to merit, yet with eyes keenly critical to economise means, assure result. It was constructive. It calculated cost. The prize was health, prosperity or happiness; and she sought this without a thought of whether her child – she thought of us all as her children – were worthy. She never reproached; she never sought to influence conduct. She treated everyone as free and responsible. We have not shown ourselves unworthy, on the whole. Most villages have been stagnant, many have decayed; few have prospered and increased; for industrialism has been the spider to suck England's blood. Not one has increased fivefold, in these twenty years, save this; and it is she, she alone, who achieved it. I cannot conscientiously applaud every detail of her work; church attendance has fallen off; there is prevalent a certain looseness of conduct which I deplore, with a freedom of manner, an unserious attitude towards life, and a most exaggerated caricature of the great virtue of tolerance. Illegitimacy is enormously on the increase, and appears not to be condemned by public opinion. I feel bound to say that she deliberately encouraged sexual immorality; she even advocated promiscuity. When I reproached her, she said: "Cricket and football are unsuitable for women." But in our horror at such opinions, we must not hide our faces from fact; and it is not to be denied that our community excels all others in our neighbourhood, in such matters as rate of increase, healthiness, happiness, prosperity, independence, enterprise and intelligence. It is not for us to balance the ledger; we make the entries, and trust God to be just judge.

'To this work she gave all. I sum her life in the word

'DEDIT.

'She could foretell her death day; these last nine years she has been dying of cancer. No one has heard her groan, or seen the smile fade from her face. She measured her Life, and she died penniless.

'DEDIT.'

The rector staggered with emotion and exhaustion. He recovered himself, and would have gone on; but the local doctor, at one shrewd glance, divined mischief, sprang to his side, and with a brisk word in the Bishop's ear, and a gesture to beckon the aid of a bystander, took the sick man by the arm. 'You've got to come home, Dick!' he whispered.

The rector tried to resist, then yielded, almost collapsing; and the two men led him through the swift-posted lane of sympathisers to the Duke's carriage.

'That red house with the tower, among those beeches!' said the doctor, pointing, 'and come back for the Duke!'

'Yes, sir!' and the horses, glad to be off, sprang forward at the touch of the whip.

2

The Body

The doctor and the priest are Siamese twins, born of one mother, the Wizard. The separation is recent, indeed hardly complete; more, the Monistic Philosophy of Science, on the one hand, and Mary Baker Eddyism, on the other, seem to be trying to reunite them. Science is thus inspired by the fact that all priests are quacks, and that a sound soul is one symptom of a sound body; Mrs Eddy by the failure of medicine in America, where doctors are mostly just what Europe found priests were, ignorant thieves exploiting the credulity and fear of the yet more ignorant public.

The rector and the doctor of Lady Claudia's village had hardly understood this tendency. Their respective duties seemed to them divided cleanly, marked like a frontier on a map. They never encroached upon each other. They respected each other, though perhaps the doctor had less faith than the rector in the other's importance.

They were old friends and intimate; the doctor set his patient in a low Oxford chair, gave him brandy, passed a tobacco jar with College Arms on it.

'I was coming to see you, anyhow, Hal; I've been a bit nervous; I don't know why, but I keep thinking it's a – a return of my old trouble.'

'Nonsense, Dick! Nothing less likely. What's the "it," anyhow?'

'I can't say. I'm nervous. Silly of me, I know.'

'Any pain?'

'Headaches lately – rather sudden, but they go as they came. Oh yes! I've had twinges, very sharp, two or three times; shooting pains, starting from the sole of the foot, apparently, a warning of gout, I suppose.

Then there's a curious feeling, not unpleasant in a way, as if I were wearing a belt.'

The doctor tapped the arm of his chair, and began to hum a little tune. He swung round suddenly, took a thin package from a file, and glanced through the papers.

'Let's see!' he said, 'You've not had such a bad time. Twenty years since you've been here, didn't you say? A year longer than I have. Fill your pipe! That's a great jar. I never look at it but I go straight back to our first friendship, when I was a young fellow of Clare, as the limerick says, and you were another. What a May Term we wound up with!'

'When you rowed four, and I rowed seven!'

'And we bumped Lady Margaret, Hall, Third and Jesus.'

'We'd have had First and gone Head if we'd had one more day.'

'Jesus nearly caught them the last two days, after they bumped Third at Ditton.'

'Well, it's late to catch 'em now!'

'Wonder if we could pull an oar – I think I'll run over your reflexes, Tootle-tunn-teh, Oh, adorable friend of my youth!'

He took a little padded hammer from a drawer in his desk, and tapped the knee of the rector.

'Subnormal, decidedly subnormal!'

The clergyman had been studying his friend's face; if he couldn't cure souls, he could read minds.

'You don't like it, I can see. What is it?'

'Might be several things. Just stand up. Attention! Hands to the side! Now throw the head back! Now close your eyes!'

The doctor's strong arm caught a shoulder, and lowered a tottering body to a chair.

'Dizzy fit, eh?'

'No; my mind's clear enough; I seemed to lose my balance.'

'That's Romberg's symptom.'

'Symptom of what?'

'It looks as if you had a touch of Tabes.'

'Tabes – er, wasting or something, isn't it?'

'Tabes dorsalis. Call it locomotor ataxia: same thing.'

The patient paled, and gripped his chair. The basket-work creaked. 'My God!'

'Brace up, old man! It's awkward, and it's painful at times; but it's not fatal. George Meredith had it in his thirties, and lived to laugh at eighty. We can help you more than we could in those days, too.'

But the rector's face had grown extraordinarily bitter; suddenly he broke into a savage laugh. The doctor did not understand, at the moment; he judged the water shallower than it was; and he said the obvious thing.

'You can't complain too much. You've had nearly twenty years of health.'

'Barring a throat.'

'Which I cured in a month.'

'And a bad leg.'

'You call that twopenny ha'penny skin lesion a bad leg? It was well in a week. Hang it all, man, you've not had even a day in bed.'

'And now it breaks loose – today! Trust the Devil to make a good joke – I laughed at it myself just now!'

The doctor looked hard, saw sanity, decided not to ask any questions.

'You've got to thank two wits; mine in knowing how to prescribe for you; and yours, in having had the sense to obey my orders.'

'It was tedious; it was revolting, too, a skeleton at every banquet. I think, another time, I'd rather suffer from the body than have my mind gnawing.'

'I saw a spasm of hate in your face a while ago. Do you reproach yourself, or blame another?'

'I suppose I do. I shouldn't, but my mind seems to have – Romberg's symptom, you called it, I think.'

'Yes, Romberg's symptom.'

'What is it?'

'Let me digress! There's an automatic arrangement in our feet that keeps our bodies balanced with no conscious aid. When you need your eyes to tell you how to hold your feet, that arrangement is out of order. If it gets worse, even your eyes won't serve; the muscles mutiny, and you can't walk. There's no loss of power, only of skill to apply it. You can be taught to walk again, as a child is.'

'I see. My mind's got Romberg's symptom, right enough. It staggers unless I watch it and control it; and nowadays my vigilance sometimes tires, my control weakens.'

'You've no reason to reproach yourself. It's a common accident; it may be as innocent as influenza.'

'I wasn't innocent.'

'We are all innocent in one sense, for we are children lost in a forest, the Night of Ignorance on us, with scarce a star! Why, man, if this were punishment for sin, a thing unjust enough, as I see it, is the further wantonness and infamy conceivable, that such a rod should scourge those who have not sinned, nor their parents?'

'All have sinned, and come short of the glory of God.'

'Then why let some – some of the worst, by Jove! – go free?'

'We cannot understand, and we must not presume to criticise, the ways of God.'

'You're begging the question. That's the fallacy in all theology.'

'I know in whom I have believed.'

The doctor tried another tack.

'I tell you,' he said, 'that sin so-called is often as unavoidable as gravitation.'

'The insane are irresponsible.'

'But where's the limit of insanity? We have definitions for legal purposes, but science has none. Like most moderns, I doubt Freewill altogether.'

'I don't.'

'Three thousand years of thought have left men arguing the point. Let's forget it!'

'I'll exercise my own Freewill, and do so!'

(Good, thought the doctor, I'm getting him over the shock.)

'All that apart, then, I can tell you of impulses to sin as urgent as the need to breathe.'

'Disease, you'd call it?'

'Why should I, when it goes with perfect health of body, with perfect soundness of intellect.'

'One point of the law, you know!'

'He's guilty of all? All right; but who made the law?'

'God.'

'Then – which law? Laws conflict. I prefer to seek divers causes when I find divers effects. Where you say God, I would say Custom, Majority, a Tyrant's whim, a Politician's cunning, Fear borne of Ignorance, anything, everything; but never yet did Truth father a litter of Lies, or Simplicity create Confusion.'

'You're more theological than I am! Hang theories! Give me your judgement in a concrete case!'

He laughed at the thought of the story he was going to tell.

'When I was in Kashmir, I heard of a terrible sinner. As you know, the Maharajah is a Hindu, though most of his people are Mohammedans. It's therefore a capital crime to kill a cow – or indeed to catch a *mahseer*, because one swallowed the Maharajah's soul, and you might catch that one! Well, a man in the Indus valley, high up, got cut off from the world by a landslip either side of him. Rather than starve, he killed his cow and ate her.'

'Was the man a Hindu?'

'Lovely of you to dodge the issue! Oh you parsons! What does it matter?'

'To his conscience, everything!'

'Sin subjective, then?'

'For the purpose of this argument only.'

'My point is: was he responsible for his act?'

'I would rather starve than steal.'

'Ever try it out? And then, is suicide less of a sin than theft? You might atone for theft.'

'All this is sheer casuistry.'

'I apologise for the shape of my collar.'

'We Anglicans hate casuistry.' He really believed what he said!

'Well, here's another case.' A curious smile, subtly sinister, twisted the doctor's mouth. 'It's been in my notes a long while, and, unlike yours, it calls for a folio, if we follow its trail. My mind has been refreshed about it constantly; not a month since, by the same token, I had a new memento.

'This was a woman, sound in mind and body, just as you are, no worse, no less, except that she never happened to develop Romberg's symptom.'

The doctor paused, to see whether his patient would wince at the allusion. But he was calm; he had become impersonal by the road of intellectual interest.

'Till she fell fatally stricken – nothing to do with the other affair – she hadn't a day's ill-health. Her mind was clear to the last minute of life. She was fine morally in every way but one, even by your standards. That one? She was a nymphomaniac. She sprayed disease like a machine-gun; and – it's almost unparalleled in medical history – she remained dangerous all her life. Neither middle-age, nor the tortures of the murderous malady that ended her, abated her desire, her success in securing its indulgence, or her power to poison.'

'Yet you say she was sane?'

'As you or I. She suffered horribly from the knowledge of the misery she caused. She knew something of medicine, by the way; I may tell you I met her first in old Remsen's lab when I was taking stinks, and she was at Newnham. She came to me one day in a rage of despair, and told me a terrible story.'

'We are put here to master ourselves, by the good help of God, and the virtue of Our Lord's Atonement. Temptation should be the touch-stone of our gold; the bar of our High Jump, too!'

The doctor laughed.

'St Satan's boat is put on for us to hump, eh?'

'Safer to do it at Grassy, if we can. Accidents may happen between that and the Railway Bridge!'

'Yes, we should cleave unto Righteousness from our youth up – but I have heard that Solomon himself got progged for smoking in cap and gown!'

'*Si jeunesse savait*,[1] the French say.'

'I thought French authors were always so immoral!'

'Only to those who read them in translations.'

'Publishers translate none but the naughty books?'

'They have to please the British Public.'

'This woman's story would have to be put in French and retrans-lated, or nobody in London – outside Chelsea and the Café Royal – would stand it.'

'I claim the priest's privilege. Go on!'

'Three years before she met me, so she said, she became conscious of the craving. She had fierce horror of indulgence, her breeding, her mind, her training, her pride and her prudence all allied against it. But their combined force didn't hold her back for five poor minutes. She lived in London, and was there when the first attack came on; within half an hour she had won ease. Momentary indeed; some four hours later, the attack was renewed. It was nine o'clock; but she found an excuse to go into the street alone. Her radiant beauty, her elegance, her intense magnetism, made her search easy. Very curiously, she hated dalliance; as she said once, it's not that I like the taste; I don't; I merely need the drink. That night she woke at three o'clock: the streets were empty; and she got frightened; so she returned, and went straight to the room of a young footman. So it went on; she made her plans for gratifying her strange need. They were adventurous plans; liaisons did not please her; she rarely gave herself twice to the same man. It was as if she were a blind man seek-ing a pearl dropped among pebbles. She'd pick up each quickly, in-differently; the touch would prove it to be not what she sought, and she would throw it away, and pick up another. She came to Newnham chiefly to glut herself with the three thousand of us; yet she would

---

[1] [If youth but knew.]

sample Barnwell too, and cycle into the country to catch the chance of the roadside, or try her luck with the horsey denizens of Newmarket, or pray some grace among the pious folk of Peterborough. I want you to realise that this life suited her. Love was a meal she couldn't miss, that was all; and she throve on the diet. When I met her, she was the most splendid animal I had ever seen; and she never talked of love, or thought of it except when the brief spasm shook her. She was a clean-minded pal, cleaner than you, old friend! She was high-minded too; habitually thought in abstract terms, was constantly preoccupied with intellectual problems. She favoured me beyond most men; on and off, we remained intimate in the gross sense of the word for six or seven years. But for love! a mere interruption of the conversation, exactly like a man called to the telephone for a trifle, a matter settled and out of mind the moment the receiver falls back on the hook.

'About a month after I met her, she came to me for medical advice – I wasn't qualified then. Of course I warned her of the danger to others if she went on with her career; I sent her to Jonathan Hutchinson. She never came back from London; I lost sight of her for a year or so. I met her again one Boat Race Night, veiled heavily, in the Empire Promenade. She took me to her flat in Jermyn Street; she told me that she couldn't stop ——'

'But that can't be the terrible story she told you later, since you knew all this at that time?'

'I recognise the acute critic who wrote the commentary on Colossians whose echoes still wake our cloisters! I'm merely laying the table-cloth.'

'The hors d'œuvres, please!'

'Sharp to the taste, and spiced! That night I warned her almost angrily. I was just qualified and had swelled head, and wanted everybody forcibly injected with all sorts of serums, and clothes to be made of carbolic lint, and kissing declared felony. I'd dream the sea was a basin of antiseptic and the air chloroform, and I the surgeon to operate on Mother Earth for Gravel.

'I spoke as the specialist couldn't speak, eagerly, passionately. I drew her pictures – and I coloured them – of the ravages she might cause; I showed her lives cut short, lives crippled, lives deformed; I made her see loves withered and blasted, hearts broken, hopes crushed down, wills baffled. I showed her even the indirect disaster within the scope of the swing of her scourge: parents whose age is suddenly smitten by a son's fall, children unborn with doom already upon them from her curse. It seems that I succeeded in my task of rousing her to fight, as you'll hear later.

'I saw her several times in the following two years. She was usually drunk or drugged; she was quite reckless, and refused to talk seriously. Then came the time I told you of at first, when she confessed.'

'Confessed! What else? What didn't you know?'

'Her secret. Her virtue.'

'What?'

'Her virtue. After that night in Jermyn Street she went to Maudsley. (He was one of the three best men on mind-lesions then living; perhaps the first of the three.) He failed. She tried hypnotic cures, a man in Vienna, for one; no good. She tried quacks. Maudsley had advised her, by the way, that her craving was an idiosyncrasy, and her health being perfect, harmless if she took precautions to protect others; and he supposed that need of these would pass in a few months at most. Her ordeal's fire blazed sevenfold when she found herself still dangerous after the last date set by any of her specialists.'

The rector wiped his forehead. 'In such a case,' he said slowly, 'I almost think – well, no, I can't say it.'

'She thought it, she said it, and she tried to do it. I ought to be in quarantine, she cried, or perhaps in a lunatic asylum. I told her she was just as healthy, just as sane, as I was. I'm a pestilence, she almost shouted, only it's not been labelled, analysed and counter-mined. But I could prove even to you that I am legally mad; and you it was that made me so. I've tried, tried hard, to kill myself. That's madness, under the law? It all depends, I dissented judicially. Well, she went on, you know how gentle I am. I could never use violence, even in playing games. My muscles won't obey my will. I couldn't throw myself from a cliff or a bridge, or under a train; I couldn't kick a chair away from under me. I tried; I could no more than I could fight in the prize ring. I tried poisons, alcohol, morphia, cocaine: I drenched myself only to reach a tolerance where brandy affects me no more than toast and water, the drugs no more than so much sugar. I couldn't even get a craving for them. I couldn't force myself to swallow strychnine or belladonna; the thought of the violence of the convulsions they produce was more loathsome than even my life. I tried Cannabis, Chloral, Veronal; my next best to success was a stupor of three days and nights, from which I woke a giantess refreshed, greedy for pleasure.

'Her toxicological misadventures had rather amused me, from a technical point of view; I suggested charcoal. She had tried it twice. Unfortunately, the idea of anything glowing, from a firefly to a cigarette, brings on one of her attacks, and out she has to go!'

'This story nauseates me. Does it go on much longer?'

'Do you still blame her?'

'I'm upset. I must consider. Later.'

'I'm near the end of the journey. That was her confession; she couldn't kill her desire, or even her power to indulge it; she couldn't thwart it, even by suicide. She went on spreading pestilence, as helpless and as innocent as thistledown. The strange thing was that she never caused a scandal. She was no hypocrite, not even careful to conceal her acts; it was as if there was a universal conspiracy of silence. Brilliant, voluptuous, well-groomed, frank in speech almost to cynicism or to brutality, her name never provoked a smile, a sneer, a jest, an innuendo, or another name to run in harness with it.

'In later days she bore such visible marks of a strange fate that a first look at her would rouse the most incurious, and set the dullest wondering; but none suggested a solution implying any stain upon her virtue.'

'Strange, strange indeed! In this world, too! I'm bound to ask: is this tale true?'

'Word and letter, cynic! The care of souls breeds much contempt for men!'

'Swift was a priest!'

'Sterne for my money, to fight him to a finish!'

'But Sterne was a thoroughly bad person!'

'I know you for a good one, then, after that master-sneer. Well, let me end! I saw her constantly after that tragic day.'

'That's what you used to go to London for?'

The doctor looked at his friend curiously. Was he such a fool as he pretended? His disavowal of Sterne on behalf of his cloth's misanthropy hardly argued it.

'She went to Paris, too,' he answered lightly. 'And to Naples, of course, the nymphomaniac's Valhalla. And to their hashish-dream, gigantic, multicoloured, vibrant, but as real as death and as solid as beefsteak, North Africa.'

'She never visited you here?'

'No,' said the doctor. 'She lived her rational life ——.' He hesitated, noting a queer look on his friend's face. 'A life of infinite credit, with its strange twin, a life cut clean away from the conscious part of her, silently active like her liver, alert, efficient, venomous to the last. Only a month ago there came to me, bearing the wound of the first nail in his Calvary, her nephew, twelve years old!'

The rector took the revelation calmly.

'I thought so. My funeral oration, and then yours! When I pulled through my first funk, I laughed. It puzzled you. Now – you laugh too!'

The doctor searched; but the riddle of this speech baffled him. The rector smiled.

'I give it up, Dick! I've no Scotch in me that I know of except the old and vatted; but I'm hanged if I see any joke.'

'The clergy, if they are to joke with immunity, must joke as through a glass darkly. It was she who gave me my ticket for the journey whose last stop before the Terminus is Romberg's symptom.'

'Your praise of her – her repartee, the resurrection of your long, quiet, half-forgotten curse, sardonic laughter from her grave!'

'I had remembered. I had made my private joke. Long as I spoke, I never moved my eyes from her coffin, inscribed with my terse irony. She gave me – that's what I meant by DEDIT.'

'I think I never knew you until now.'

'Possibly, possibly, man of science! You don't know everything yet!'

The doctor started up as if challenged. 'Nor do you,' he flung back sharply.

'Ah, what do you mean by that? I wonder now. I really wonder. Bluff, in the manner of Haeckel, like enough! Arrogance, or fear to have your armour traced to Wardour Street, or maybe just the unmeaning snappiness of the small dog's bark. All signs of weakness, all blank cartridge, my quick-firing friend!'

'My original remark was humble enough not to have provoked your outburst. And now I come to think of it, why were you so quick on the draw? Is the portrait you draw of me really the secret of your own soul, as artists say they must?'

'Does this recrimination lead us anywhere?'

'Oh yes, if you'll answer my original question.'

'I've forgotten what it was.'

'Do you still blame her?'

'Blame – what does blame mean? But my body won't let me forget, or my mind let me forgive: DEDIT.'

'Your epitaph lacks terseness.'

The parson stared in amazement. 'Could I shorten it?'

'No: but I can. DEDI.'[1]

---

[1] [I gave.]

His voice broke suddenly. As with many clever men, his talk was foil-play, thrust and riposte tempered with the convention that no hurt can come of it. He grasped his own meaning, knew that the button had come off his point. His humanity cried out.

'Old man!——' he faltered – 'I'm – damned sorry.' He held out his hand.

The rector, red face bleached to sickliness of greys and ochres, walked straight from the house. On the steps, he stumbled.

Colonel Pacton's Brother

'Colonel Pacton! Colonel Pacton! Colonel Pacton!'

It was a raucous yell; it had no human note in it. The boy was a machine. His cry had no tone, since his speech had no meaning or interest for him.

Hoarse and crude, rasped from a raw larynx, bellowed from savage lungs, the scream was yet unable to assert itself. Only a few men heard it.

For its auditorium, frond-arched serenity of gloom, was no unhaunted glade or tangle of mangrove swamps, no snowy silence, no sand wilderness, no waste of sea. It was not even a Provençal market, a Dublin riot, a Chemin des Dames, or a city Zeppelin-bombed.

It was the entrance hall of an hotel, the newest, and so, of course, the best and biggest in Flivverton. This city had sprung up like Jonah's gourd, but more so, for it affords shelter to many prophets and to yet more profiteers. Scarce fifty years ago it was a market town and fishing port. Then 'Hen' Flivver made it a city. Soon the capricious tide of the Greenback Sea swept up his river; the city, five years later, was a metropolis. Men had no time to brood; its million bipeds – ninety per cent of them – were crowded in the same type of wooden shacks as had sufficed its pioneer thousand. The business section alone boasted of stone or brick, just as, in God's reign, His Cathedrals stood alone among, yet above and aloof from the town's houses – man's abodes, dark, dirty, comfortless and cramped. God claimed men's lives, their love, their all. His servants' hall was packed with men of wealth, of genius; and when He died, intestate, Mammon, his next of kin, proved equally autocratic.

Genius got the sack, and Talent, far more docile and sensible, served in his stead.

But all that slaves can do his slaves had done; the business section of Flivverton was the Eighth Wonder of the World; proclaimed as such it was wherever its editorial drum-majors swung their batons.

2

'Colonel Pacton! Colonel Pacton!'

It woke an elegant Englishman, just registered as Earl of Granchester, from musings not unlike the above; he looked about him.

The Hotel Rathskeller was to Flivverton what the Parthenon was to Athens. The entrance hall was larger and loftier than Saint Peter's. In style and sanitation it yielded nothing to a London County Council Public Lavatory. It had a frieze with gilt inscriptions expressing lofty sentiments in grandiloquent language; they concerned honesty, hospitality and a mysterious virtue called 'service.' It dwarfed its own offices. It had two hundred telephone booths, and an ice-cream soda counter served by twenty men. It had seats for five hundred. These were all filled; and for each one who sat there were four standing, and three walking. Walking? It was hardly that; rather a scuffling run, not unlike a waiter's, a bad waiter in a cheap eating-house.

Nearly all were shouting. The Earl's general impression was of a railway station in a nightmare.

'Colonel Pacton!'

The Earl rose slowly as a room clerk rushed at him. 'Two thousand sixteen.'

(There were not so many rooms; the number only meant Room 16 on Floor 20; but it sounded big.) A boy snatched up the Earl's valise, fought his way to the elevators; they shot up swiftly; the Earl, in comparative peace, even forgot to sympathise with the distress of the unknown fellow man who wanted Colonel Pacton.

He took a bath and a nap; he had two hours to spare before he need dress for dinner. And he wondered what his host, the millionaire publisher Hans Pumpern – senior partner of Pumpern, Ickel, Sauer and Kraut – would turn out to be like.

3

Hans Pumpern got up from the breakfast table, growling. His house, large as it was, was wooden. It stood on a magnificent boulevard, paved like a motorist's dream of heaven which curved gradually round half the city. Grass plots, planted with trees, served to divide it longitudinally into three. Its arc lamps turned its nights into Jubilees.

Hans Pumpern's wife held his fur overcoat for him. The skins were mangy, the cloth stained, worn through, even torn. His office occupied sixteen rooms in the great Chantage Building 'downtown' that was the pride of Flivverton's busiest corner. (Eight million four hundred and twelve people passed it daily, each one reducing the fatal shocks of ambulation by wearing O'Flaherty's Heels.) He borrowed three dollars from his wife for his lunch. He had to buy a block in the city that morning; but he could not meet the owner and the lawyers at his office, lest the landlord swoop for arrears of rent, four months; or at any rate at his bookstores, where he would have to face his staff, unpaid for weeks, some of them starving. They had to hang on, whether or no, for Pumpern was a Freemason of the Thirty-Third Degree; woe to the man that angered him!

Had they but known! He was in deep disgrace with his Consistory; his brother Masons were grimly waiting to slip a knife to his ribs.

But he was still the millionaire, the leading citizen, the social sunflower. That he had not a dollar in his pocket was rather a point to his credit; such a rich man – he must have some scheme on hand, something so good that he had stripped himself – shirt, socks and viyella – to finance it.

He was a mysterious man, they all knew, and that again earns a rich man respect and a poor man distrust. He had made his millions very swiftly, very secretly; none knew his methods, or could give details of the stages of his career.

His cashier was a raw Welshman, and drew his pay, full tale of it, punctual as sunrise, though Pumpern himself should go dinnerless. For little Owen Evans had good assets. Built less for beauty than for use, his nose was like the salient at St Mihiel, his eyes like a skirmish, the one, a troop of lancers wheeling to take the other, a big gun in flank, his mouth a front line trench, his teeth a well-shelled minster. But he could smell a rat, pick out a wrong figure in a column at the first glance, keep his lips from smile or speech, and use his black fangs to worry, snap, or to hang on.

Thus little Owen was the only man that mattered to big Hans. He wrote the publisher's most paying line of fiction, the Accounts. He wrote three versions for three publics: a Book of Acts for Pumpern and his partners; an Ecclesiastes for the Income-Tax people, and their kind; lastly, a Book of Psalms, but more so, for the eye of anybody who might think of buying shares. He was very proud of his art, and quite content to draw his pittance of fifty dollars a week; for he knew, as nobody else knew, that if the Acts ended with a shipwreck, he was sure of a plank;

if luck smiled, and David reached for his harp – well, he was waiting for just that.

In American business, Fortune is sudden and decisive; incalculable as the ball at roulette – unless the wheel is faked. Pumpern might be a clumsy faker; but even at that Luck might smile upon the suitor that her cousin Trickery spurned. And on that day would Mr Owen Evans hand in his resignation to Hans Pumpern, and in exchange pouch currency for every month he had worked – just ten nice little hundreds!

This morning his eyes glittered; his one friend, treasurer of the city's biggest bank, had a double hook fast in his directors, triple gut, a sound line, a smooth reel and a perfect rod; that friend was going to wind in, and the bank was going to back up Pumpern's new scheme to the limit, and Pumpern would sell his control of the publishing house for real money, and start again elsewhere after having paid the little royalty to his tame novelist. And Owen would build a castle on the land his father farmed, find a gay face ablush with red and honest blood, and found a dynasty; why not M.P., P.C., Secretary for – well, what of the Exchequer? Ha! Ha! – at the end, upstairs again, and die Lord Plynlimmon. Plenty of men had done as much, and more.

He ate his breakfast with one hand, the other scribbling figures for the plot of a new ledger-novel, his fancy's flights outsoaring Sinbad's roc, his lyric ecstasy swearing that Flivverton should be a Shelley's Skylark and make Baghdad by that comparison no more than a snail in a book of old sermons.

And he had no idea, as he thought of going to the House of Lords, that the Mountain might come to Mahomet. For a live lord was at that moment sitting on the edge of a board, his head bowing in bodily fear of the ceiling, his arms and legs in unaccustomed strife with his clothes, the whole not two hundred miles away, and closer every minute by two-thirds of a mile.

The Earl of Granchester was nothing to Owen Evans, not even a name; less therefore than the much-invoked and unresponsive Colonel Pacton was to the Earl a few hours later.

Owen was a poet, in figures; an atheist, he supposed himself, but in reality basing his whole life on the theory of causality. He had a dream, a purpose, a technique, all the virtues that could help to make for himself an idol, and in matter, an image of his dream, an incarnation of his god.

And he trusted cause to mother effect, sage counsel to outwit the whims of folly, constructive order's house to stand firm, though freakish gale or impish earthquake do it spite.

He who believes all this, believes in God, though he deny with an oath, though he blaspheme and curse, though he deride and mock, though when the cock crows he turn not, nor weep, though he face death like a man, while reiterating that he is no more than a dog in the last unfaltering brag.

But he believes in some persistent will beyond his, beyond the race-will of mankind; therefore the Will of Something, call it Matter or Spirit, no odds which, that makes Law; that therefore is presumably a Being, though we cannot conceive its nature, read its mind, or guess its goal.

Had Owen Evans known of the Earl, he would have cared no jot. Had one foretold to him that his career depended on the Earl, he would have shrugged his shoulders, and sniffed: 'I'll cross the bridge when I get there.'

He believed in Nature's 'playing fair.' But yet more mystically, this scoffer at faith believed in himself, in the ugly brat that came unwanted to the mean farmhouse and twelve acres stony and steep, to elbow his three brothers and two sisters. The brat had brains; he had tilled them, ploughed, sowed, manured and watered them; in season they gave corn. They had built ships to carry him from the farm's pebbly rill to the school's stream, then to the broad swift river of college, then to the seas of the world; and in all storms they had proved staunch.

He believed also in his rare gift of imagination. When he wrote three values in his three ledger-epics, he chose by instinct as sincere and sound as ever guided poetry through uncharted seas. His falsest ledgers were not false to him. He created a personality for each of them; to him the rosy mouth of the well-dined, well-wined, well-digesting optimist spoke truth no less than the pale trembling lips of the hypochondriac, whose sparse grey straggling locks ill-kempt framed the slate-coloured face with its blear eyes, its rheumy nose, its drooping mouth. That wheezing breath, that faltering pulse, that groggy heart, that jaundiced liver, those hard kidneys, that quite atrophied manhood; all this must be a picture, lively, convincing, not overdrawn, no caricature. That man must live and think; he must be Virgin Truth, his purity prevail against the brigands, them that take taxes in the name of Government.

His ledger poets were no puppets; they lived, they wrote their lies with most assured integrity.

Part, and no little part, of this strange endowment of the cashier, was his power of divining a man's thoughts. He could put himself in another's place, just as he could do with his own creations. Give him some slight acquaintance with a man, then let an argument start; Owen could tell in the first minute what his opponent would say throughout, and how he would act at the end.

Once he had overheard Hans Pumpern talk with a railroad magnate in the street. Mere small talk; but Owen took his cue from the man's mood, raised every cent he had saved, and sold on a narrow margin a certain stock which the magnate was playing. The close of the market found him more than seventeen thousand dollars 'nearer my God to Thee,' his first million.

Nothing but himself and his own mind were real to him; for even his unconscious faith in the Order of Nature was, fully analysed, faith in himself. He willed, acted, attained; that must be Law, then. He could no more think otherwise than we, who think as Euclid thought, can grasp the possibility of the other geometries unless we have been trained.

4

Owen Evans grinned at his horrible face as he rose from breakfast, and tied his cravat. He reached the office half an hour later; his friend telephoned from the bank that Old Man Stringer (President and mainspring) was in bed with a cold; the conference must be postponed; the city block would not figure in Pumpern's assets for another four-and-twenty hours.

Owen Evans did not even frown; he had waited almost as many years. It never occurred to him that with the Lord a thousand days is as one day, and that things can happen in one spin of our funny old pill which ruin the Character of Nature. A thousand years of Good Conduct, Punctuality, Uniformity and so on; we commend her; she's our show pupil. Regularity! Industry! Propriety! Ah! So we benignly close our eyes; the classroom begins to fade; and when we wake – oh sudden! oh impossible!

Nature's no mother at heart; wise Isis, builder of cities, daughter of God, sister and wife to Him, and in the end His mother!

Nay, there's a madcap wench in her, a maid unwon, a might with no morality. Here is no mind as our mind; nor are her ways our ways.

Owen was in the range of her dance that day; and what happened was not contrary to nature, as he would have deemed, though it upset his plans without intention. So once at Potosí a plant, busied with naught but its own growth, slew countless men, builded new towns and kingdoms, when its roots tore from the soil and showed the silver in their miser fingers.

5

The millionaire had not paid for his house or its contents; he proposed to do so by taking boarders. He thus occupied four rooms only. His wife did all the work, with a man hired by the hour to help occasionally.

She was a splendid child, supple and strong. A mop of fiery chestnut hair crowned her. Her face was a warm cream that flushed when her vivacity would. She had immense grey eyes; they had a haunted look. Did she take drugs? No; she had been thus from a child. Their strange light suggested a liability to some form of madness. She talked with them, for her speech was quite unequal to her demands on it; the interjection was her star actor – a blasphemy, a curse, or an obscenity served her best, her tone and not her choice of word determining the emotion she wished to express. But when she was articulate, the phrase was always brief, an epigram. She always spoke sheer truth, her phrase most passionate and intense. Her soul's distilment of pure spirit dripped limpid from her lips, undoctored, undisguised, unwatered and unflavoured.

Her eyes spoke oftener, and their vocabulary was more varied. They could not only love and hate; they could actually prattle. But as all tunes on the bagpipes must reckon with the changeless three bleats of its drones – the character, may one say, of the instrument – so to whatever message she sent through them, her eyes would add three deeper words: Sorrow; Thirst; and Madness. These three were one.

Her body was trim, slender, and yet robust; in it the panther's stealth and strength elastic, the gnat's restlessness and aimlessness, the deer's timidity and alertness, were united with the fox's furtiveness and the snake's conscious deadliness.

She had married Pumpern without serious thought. He chanced to be there; she could not have what she wanted – it didn't exist, even – so anything was as good or as bad as anything else. Her parents were dead long since, and her guardian, Colonel Pacton, had tired of her violence, her innocence, and her contemptuousness; he rarely saw her.

She thought it a little hard on her to be asked to prepare a banquet for an English Earl, and the ex-horse-doctor, now a Spiritualist Lecturer and Medium, who was to meet him. Credit was in hospital with both legs broken, and Cash was to be nailed down that morning in the coffin of the butcher, or they must play at being vegetarian.

Help? Business boomed in Flivverton just then; anything that had arms and legs was snatched at; men gave it ten, fifteen, even twenty dollars a day.

Let her be praised, this Kohinoor of women! She had been 'finished' in England at a Brighton school, and knew the ways of Earls. She cooked a dinner to his taste, delighted him. The preacher thought it lacked profusion, for his ideals were as his brother the hog's; and her husband loathed delicacy, for his palate was as his forebears', loving to yield to force; it craved voluptuous violences, revelled in discords.

6

The Earl of Granchester, his cocktail poised, observed his fellow guest, the Reverend Doctor Ross, with no small interest. 'Ross' was no doubt one of those higher things to which men rise by making stepping stones of their dead selves; perhaps it had, not long since, been adapted from Rosenthal or something similar. For the long pendulous protrusion that dwarfed his face trumpeted Semite, and that beneath his chest seemed like a kettle-drum, booming forth Teuton. His fishy eyes suggested a pawn-broking ancestry. His mouth was an afterthought stuck on in a hurry, very loosely. It was a misfit, too, three sizes too big for his face. Its owner kept on licking it, but it would not dry. The neck was very thick; its creases conquered the pink collar; their weight and moisture taught mere starch a moral lesson, humbled its pride in its stiffness.

Granchester smiled as he thought of the trivial coincidences, the drifting gossamer, which had determined the composition of the party.

It was mere chance that had sent him to Flivverton at all. He had failed to get a cabin at Liverpool on the *Patagonia* that week; the delay had given time for a letter to reach him. In it a friend, a popular author, asked him to investigate the sales of his past book. He had wired Pumpern. The publisher jumped at the opportunity. He knew of the Earl – the whole world did – as a leader of certain sects devoted to the occult; so he must ask his own private Mediator between God and Man, the inspired Ross, to meet him.

Then – this was really rather curious – he had asked about a portrait on his host's wall. It was in oils, and the Earl was amazed to recognise a butterfly faintly fluttering in one corner.

'You have a Whistler?' he cried in crescendo.

'Whistler? Nothing,' answered Pumpern. 'My wife plays the piano; but we've a big Victrola; after dinner we'll have some.'

'No, no,' insisted Granchester; 'this picture! What is it?'

'Oh that! That's my wife's guardian, Colonel Pacton.'

The Earl started. He knew at once how he had come to pick out the strange name from the din of the hotel; it was familiar, even dear to him. He had admired reproductions of the picture often enough; he thought it one of Whistler's best.

Curious! very curious! And he nearly made the reflection that our world is a very small one.

7

Dinner began with talk of the journey from New York, veered to that city's business outlook, rose to severely moral summits as Prohibition claimed its parenthetical toll of austere virtue's commination, switched to the vastness, energy, wealth, efficiency and high-mindedness of Flivverton itself. Pumpern advanced statistical proof that even at half the present rate of increase, the city would be the biggest in the world in eight years and a month. Nobody proved that a baby who gains two pounds on eight in its first month must (even at half that rate) weigh more than a mammoth by the time it goes into short frocks. The praise of Flivverton took its two corybants like a spasm; it was almost epileptic. The Earl couldn't even assent; their frenzies overlapped. Only a madman would have tried to check them; only a desperate suicide to contradict them.

Then they stopped suddenly, collapsed, like an eight's crew, when, twenty minutes above Putney, they have spurted from Barnes Bridge to Mortlake, and shot first past the post.

Granchester caught the ball. 'I never saw this city till today, and a first glance at Vastness tells so little. The mind is shocked, bewildered, overwhelmed. New York I know: did it prepare me? Nowise. It is a torn back number of an old-fashioned magazine. In its long history – far too long, it's senile! – it has never grown at one-tenth the rate of your majestic world-metropolis. I am unutterably staggered by your progress, by your efficiency. I will not call you the last word in civilisation – let me say rather the first word, the creative Fiat, the God-utterance that shall brand the Past as Chaos. You are the first true Cosmo-Civilisation, a word too often profaned for me to profane it! Let us create a word for the ideal of Flivverton, a word beyond civilisation as Flivverton itself is beyond other cities. Gentlemen, I hail you pioneers, o pioneers of – dare I say it? – Millenialisation!'

The men recovered under this hypodermic; but as they had already said over and over all they knew, they simply sat and beamed.

Granchester went on: 'I hardly dare to sleep – if, indeed, such intensity of emotion as today's permits me – yes, dare I sleep, knowing I shall wake in this reality beyond my dreams? Dare I risk sanity by further draughts of the spiritual rye whiskey that my eyes and ears must gulp? Yes! Neither love nor worship ever slew who seek the Good, the Beautiful, the True! Poetry! by your own God-man, Flivver. I crawl no more on the sidewalks of prose; I roll majestically, as Zeus, swiftly as Hermes, borne in that car that he made, that made Flivverton, I rush on Poesy's intoxicating tarmac!'

They plied him with gobbets of fact.

More automobiles pass the City Hall in an hour than any corner in New York in two.

The daily death rate from car accidents is twelve and a half; two years back it was only three, and they had boosted it by including trolley-cars.

'A distinct variety of sport, I assume,' murmured the Earl.

They became inarticulate. 'More,' 'bigger,' 'progress,' 'dollars,' 'taller' were all the words he caught, and then, yet louder and quicker, they changed from their comparatives to the corresponding superlatives.

Again they stopped, talked out. The Earl, too, was as tired as they; to listen had been an ordeal. He thought of his dentist, drilling inexorably, his whirring weapons always too near the nerve, sometimes right on it. But yet – well, he had hidden his soul behind his half-closed eyes, that languidly watched Elsa Pumpern; her beauty soothed them as it stirred the soul that lurked behind them.

8

This time the conversation – or rather, the succession of speeches – died for good.

They had said all they knew on any subject soever outside their personal business or domestic matters.

Dinner was over; the appalling prospect of evening lay before them like the Sahara. The Victrola, the movies, a lecture: such are the three American alternatives to Silence, Scandal and Squabble.

Or else, get drunk. America knows no other devices to enable its inhabitants to endure either their own company or that of their fellow creatures.

The situation was growing intolerable. It was hardly relieved for Granchester when his host followed his wife into the kitchen, and spent ten minutes storming about over the dinner. He struck her, and stamped back. Three minutes later she came in, sobbing: stood and cried out almost the first phrase she had uttered that evening.

'You promised me the ideals of life, and I've had nothing but scrub-work!' Then she fled back.

But rescue was at hand. The Reverend Doctor Ross had not diverted his Powers of Healing from horse's body to man's soul without warrant.

He saw the Earl's impatience; it would not do at all to let him go. He had not been asked for nothing. The Granchester estates were huge, as Pumpern had found out from a loan broker (whose files had over a million names classed by their credit) within an hour of receiving the telegram. Pumpern had called Ross in to hold the sheep for the shearing.

He must not go! The Earl had no thought of going; Elsa had bound him, faster than once Delilah, with all her Philistines to aid, bound Sampson.

He stared at the canvas of Colonel Pacton. The man was clearly a kind-hearted gentleman. Why, in the devil's name, thought he, did you hand over that child to this ogre?

9

Ross was too bent on his own plans to observe his victim. He had to double-cross his accomplice and his dupe, of course. Just so had Pumpern thought: 'I need this spoon; but I'll lick it clean when I'm through.' It is the natural attitude of business partners in America for one to hate, fear, spy upon, distrust, despise, betray and finally to kick out the other. But first you must get the bear in the trap. Though to cheat your pal of his share of the hide be the more civilised pleasure, it depends on the bear, just as the tedious toil of stocking a shop with goods must be endured if you would enjoy the merry moment of arson, and the more solid pleasure of touching the insurance money.

So Ross played his one trick, the same old game: though the thieves disguise it differently for every new 'sucker.' Its name is Priestcraft.

He gave a sudden whinny, twitched all over, flung back his head, screamed, then as suddenly feigned sleep – the lucid sleep of the prophet.

He saw a stately man behind the Earl, was it his father? 'He has a shining crown. His expression is grave and calm. His name seems to be William.'

'My father's name was William,' Granchester admitted.

'I see a stately pile —.' He described it for five minutes, outside and in, with details that the Earl himself hardly knew until reminded of them. His sisters told their names, threw discretion to the winds as they chattered of their clothes, their children, their amusements, their adventures, everything! The Prophet skated back through history. He knew all Granchester's 'spirit' relations, made them talk, described them. It was amazing: the man made no slip except about the type of armour worn at one particular period.

The vision and the voice took forty minutes. Then he woke up, and pretended to know nothing of what he had said.

'You saw his highness' father,' explained Pumpern; 'then all his family, his castle, his ancestors, that is, I fancy they were that. His highness seemed to recognise everything.'

'It's true,' said Granchester. 'Only one slip, a mere trifle of detail, in a mass of accurate facts, many most intimate and private, family secrets, wonderful, wonderful!

'Now let me say yet more; you could not have read from my mind, for some of it I did not know myself. How do I know they're true, then? Because they explain other things. I never saw your key, but it fits my lock.'

'You are convinced?' cried Ross in eager haste.

'There is one point where I must doubt. You saw the Earl of Granchester – you saw my father. Now there is a little mystery there – you may be right – it's a mere detail – but I'll ask my mother – even if she contradicts you, you have a good excuse for error – never mind – I'll say it flat. I – am – convinced.'

They ran to him; they wrung his hands. Pumpern shed tears. It was indeed a victory for the 'Spirits.'

For, as we all know, the Earl, who was an F.R.S. for his physics, had been all his life the worst enemy of the spooks; and was indeed said to have come to New York to expose a famous medium.

10

They had got him. They could make his father speak, his paternal authority fortified by spirit dignity. Yes, he should watch his son. The inexperience of thirty-seven years should profit by the wisdom of Summerland. He should not squander his estate, or gamble it. Surely his father, who had never appeared before him, now came thus hastily to tell him that this was the critical hour for his house, encumbered with lands and dwindling millions. Death duties? Falling Consols? The super-tax?

It is to smile. The sire was on the watch. He had planned this trip to Flivverton; he knew that there lay

Gold –

Double!

Redouble!

Double again!

No end to it!

And all by using – oh, not risking! merely by using wisely, watchfully, a minnow of cash on the books of business cast by the line System (his mind wandered into similes for everything) in the pool Opportunity.

Right here in Flivverton.

Do it now!

The partners had measured the minnow: about eight hundred and fifty thousand pounds sterling, they thought. More might sound greedy: less, as if they were afraid to ask more.

They were to split fifty-fifty; they swore it with frank gaze and hearty handclasp, the one muttering 'over my dead body' and his friend 'when I get back to Canada.' (There the police wanted him.)

11

Of course they would not spread the net in sight of the bird. Ross would go off again tonight, and have a vision of the father looking anxious. Ross must understand nothing, and be upset about it. Tomorrow morning he will have had a dream.

He will report it, but dismiss it cheerily.

Next, a Ouija-scrawl, repeating one unmeaning phrase, the rest mostly pieties *à la medium*. Next, a long sitting: father terribly urgent and most pathetically unintelligible. About a week of this, and then the Ouija Board again to give a long clear message, entreaty and command in one. But it will be impossible to act on it, as it will refer to some quite unknown matter. But, as the Earl strays home, Fate taps his shoulder! A perfect stranger will have a fit at his feet. The Earl will pick him up, and assist him to reach his palatial residence. Those grateful lips will whisper of reward. 'No; you're a gentleman, I see; not money! Accept a share in the One Deal that will rate Morgan "Also Ran."'

And so on.

And now his father's message is made clear enough. Accept a share? Not he! He must control the trust. Come, Nairne! Come Bradbury! Old notes for new!

It was a good enough scheme; the Third Murderer, having no claim but the blackmailer's on his pals, since he merely plays the small part assigned to him, takes a lump sum of fifty thousand. Either will hardly miss it, especially if he succeeds as well as he hopes in nailing his partner to the double-cross.

A splendid scheme! Not a loose nut or worn washer! But will she start? It all depends on that.

Can we convince him?

And now –

He said it.

Said it soberly, slowly, earnestly.

Said it with well-weighed emphasis.

Said this:

'I am convinced.'

12

The rest was merely formal. 'If your snark be a snark, that is right.'

Once you know that your sucker is a sucker, nothing can go wrong.

The sucker's progress!

It varies as the path of the hooked salmon; a light firm hand, with patience and vigilance to rule it, and soon or late the end is sure. The needle varies not, merely vibrates from boiled to broiled.

Just so. But – but – the publisher may have read English in his cradle, the preacher prattled dialectic to his nurse; they could both swear, and millions more confirm, that they read, wrote, spoke English, understood it thoroughly.

But to understand English is one thing; to understand an Englishman who talks is another.

Their wish fathered their thought: 'I am convinced' was gold.

Yet they were both exponents of the Gilded Brick – what innocents knaves are!

They did not test their gold – they did not ask 'Convinced of what?' If they had, Granchester might have explained: 'the accuracy of your knowledge is indeed a pleasure; its wealth a wonder. Were I to bring together the page in the Sunday *New York Herald*, *Whitaker's Almanac*, and the family file in your local newspaper's "graveyard" I could hardly do better.' And if he had been pleased by their gleam of intelligence in doubting him to be the absolute ass they hoped, he might have saved them a whole world of worry with the words:

'My friends! I knew a man who wished to marry. He spent a year and a fortune in preparing for it; he got everything from the engagement ring to a nomination at his club for his heir. Everything but the girl!'

But when at last he left the house, Ross sat a while in silence. Then he rose heavily.

'There's a snag,' he said slowly. 'Can't see it; smell it. I'll tell you, Pump, call me a liar, all right, it's O.K. See here! You think this spirit stuff of mine is bunk. So do I. But no; not clear through, no, sir. I wish it was. It skeers me. I'd hate to think I'd live for ever, if I was I, and remembered all I've been. And I am skeered; skeered to die; skeered not to fall for some hot air: I know too much by a damned sight.

'But something's true; I dunno what.

'But when I doctored horses, I could sit still and bring 'em, bring 'em from miles around, drop 'em outside my door I could, and all by power o' mind.

'And I kin hear a voice inside me, clean against reason, never speaks but one word.'

'When you want to give away money, it says "Don't,"' jeered Pumpern.

The preacher grew more solemn; a deep flush dyed his neck and rose to his brow.

'It only says: Lost,' he droned. 'I sometimes think it means I'm lost, my soul damned to hell. Billy Sunday stuff, ugh! But I think mostly it means my judgement's lost its way: for it speaks only when I'm cocksure of a thing; and the voice is always right. It hissed at me just now, when he said he was convinced, and I said to myself: Got him.

'Trust me; take no chances: we'll get him, but it'll be with the second barrel.'

He lumbered off without another word.

13

Meanwhile the Earl had gone. The night was warmer than he had thought: he paused by the gap in the hedge which served as the side entrance, to take off his scarf. He found the arms of his young hostess hotter and tighter still.

She bruised his mouth with hers.

She cried, 'I'll follow you to the ends of the earth.'

She ran, half leaping, like a hare, to the side door. As she passed through, the light fell full on her; he, watching, saw the strangest sight of his life.

Over her silver sequin dress, cut high, she had thrown a great black shawl. Its folds made him see a hooded hunchback, carrying a great salver on his head – the edge of the dress, of course.

Then in her passion's vehemence, her face might have twisted and blanched to a bodiless devil's.

But in her hands he saw a kris, fantastically shaped as if to whet the appetite of murder; as if men's blood lust after a while needed spice of perversity, exactly as does that passion's paler sister. And it was no strange kris; it was his own, the most cherished spoil of his Malay wanderings.

How had she got it?
No matter: for it had smitten her throat; the red wedge gaped.
'Twas all impossible. He put the whole day from him: he slept sound.

14

The Earl woke early, turned himself, went to sleep again. The one thought in his mind was his annoyance at finding himself in such a town and such a room. The bell-boy's howls for Colonel Pacton haunted his dreams; and when he woke he suddenly remembered that the familiarity of the name was only half explained by Whistler's picture. It woke him thoroughly; he rang for a cup of tea. But the town had been dry for two years; organisation had triumphed. The waiter, before asking for the order, placed a bottle of whiskey on the little table by his bed. He laughingly refused it; but the incident brought him the missing word.

He saw himself with his friend, Coldstream, driving from a recital of Frieda Hempel's in Atlanta, Georgia into the country to a farm ten miles away where Coldstream was playing at agriculture. He remembered how startled he was when the headlights fell upon a shadowy corner of the road, showing a lightless car manned by masked men, and how Coldstream, after much playful pretence at fear, laughed and stopped the car, and bought a gallon of 'Rye.' He then remembered how the car had been coquettish. The lights, the tyres, the gas, almost everything took it by turns to hold them up. They were an hour late on the top of the last slope that curved gently to the farm; and it was then that Coldstream cheerfully said: 'We're sure to get home now unless Colonel Pacton's brother interferes.' He had made enquiries with the view to calculating the probability of so unwarrantable an attack on individual liberty, and discovered that Coldstream had merely invented the phrase as equivalent to 'unless something utterly unforeseen happens.' There might be a dozen Colonel Pactons, each one with half a dozen brothers of the most malicious type, or there might not. Coldstream professed himself ready to submit to search.

The last cloud lifted from his mind; he was aware of only one desire; that was the passion to remove his body some four thousand miles east of its present lodging. He resolved to go straight down to Pumpern's office, show his credentials, settle the matter of the royalties before lunch, and tear himself, cost what it might, from fascinating Flivverton by the nonstop express to England. The publisher had not arrived: he asked for the partners. The girl at the desk, determined to make her employer pay for the privilege of not paying her for a month, blurted out that the partners had never existed.

'Who is in charge of the office?'

'If it's about money,' said the girl, 'and I suppose you want the same as the rest, better see Mr Evans. He's with Mr Peters from the bank here. When he comes out, I'll ask him. What's the name?'

'Granchester.'

'Whatchye say?'

He told her again.

'I can't put that over to Mr Evans.'

He handed her his visiting card. She read it with disgust.

'Play a straight hand,' she said. 'I want your Christian name, the family name. Whatchye want to hide it for; or haven't you got none?'

The Earl of Granchester began to be amused. 'At my baptism,' he explained, 'I was named William Rodney Wellington St John Palmerston De Lacy Orme Belorme.'

'What's the big idea?' she said.

'My parents were very conscientious about remembering rich relations,' explained the Earl, 'and in England you can have as many names as you like without extra charge.'

'And what's the family name?'

'Orme.'

'Orme, is that all? Sounds French. You a Kanuck?'

'No, but it's French. It means an elm. The elm tree is almost like one of the family. We plant it wherever we go; and the motto of our house is a Latin word which means 'unexpectedly,' because elms have a habit of dropping their boughs without the slightest warning, even on perfect strangers, without the formality of an introduction. We have made it a family habit. We always do the unexpected thing. See how I dropped down here – never heard of the place until Wednesday last week.'

'You're a queer sort,' said the girl. 'What is this Earl of Granchester stuff on the card?'

'That's the new title. I'm only the eighth earl.

'You have the right dope, if I may say so. I'm nineteenth Baron Orme, much more to the point. You ask "Why Granchester?" We bought the place; or, as some people think, we stole it. Why did we want it? Girl, you would dote on Granchester. I have a castle, built six centuries back, on the one hill for thirty miles in any direction. Round it the land is ours for about six miles. The castle is ringed with elms, most of them older than itself, and nine avenues of elms radiate from it leading to nine hamlets —'

'Hamlets?' said the girl sharply. 'What's hamlets? Ain't that Shakespeare?'

'Villages, villages,' he explained to the girl. 'The people cultivate our lands. They are our children. They have no fear that they may lose their jobs through their ill-luck or our ill-will. It has been a custom that any man, if he but bear a twig of elm, may speak on the instant to the head of the family; they two, alone, man to man, equal before their God. And we believe that if a man should lie to us on such an occasion, that when he pays the price of audience, which is to pass the next night beneath an elm, there will drop a bough on him and slay him.'

'You do talk funny,' said the girl, wriggling uneasily. The slightest departure from her well-worn round of familiar fully-explained incidents roused her passions. To her, an unknown word could mean no other thing than her unknown nature; not two incomprehensibles, but one incomprehensible.

'It is at least the fact,' the Earl went on, interested to explore her reactions, 'that no man has abused the privilege within the memory of man. And memory is a great thing among our people, let me tell you. We have a thousand secret treasures in our minds. Some cannot read or write, and their minds are stored more usefully than many a professor's.'

At that moment the door of the inner office swung open. A young man came out. It was easy to see that he was annoyed.

'I'll send your name in,' said the girl to Granchester, 'or some of it, but believe me there's dirty weather ahead. When Mr Peters gets the frozen face, our cashier takes it out on the whole gang. I've seen him stand right up to the boss and call him down.'

'I'm glad it's just like that,' replied the caller, 'my business would have made him angry anyhow. You can't get a quart into a pint bottle.'

15

Evans of course knew Granchester by name. His English childhood flamed in him. He met an Earl! What else could matter!

Fate cannot harm me, I have snobbed today.

He forgot Peters before he had finished saying 'Show him in.'

Yet Peters had not come to chatter about markets, and his gloom was due to something more than the weather, liver, or reflections on the increasing prevalence of questionable business methods. He had tried to catch Evans at his house; just missed him; reached the office two minutes before him; greeted him with the words, 'The old man died at eight o'clock this morning.'

'The deal?' screamed Evans.

'Off,' said Peters.

'Hell!' was the cashier's summing-up.

'I couldn't even do anything at the Bank,' said Peters yet more bitterly. 'The time-locks only release at nine. How could I guess that the old beast would croak? A trifling cold, they said. I sat all afternoon in his room – the safe wide open. I could have taken nearly half a million; it lay loose – graft, every cent – not in the books; only we two knew about it; and now, the fool auditor has his seal on the safe – not a thing to be done. Hell! what a lesson. "Grab while the grabbing is good; chance everything else" is what they'll find on my heart when I join mother.'

Evans expressed a sympathy which he did not feel. 'That's your funeral anyhow,' he said; 'Why can't we pull this deal off?'

'When the old man snapped his silver cord,' replied the other, 'my pull on him snapped too. The bunch don't care a hoot for me. I'm old invaluable Peters, that's all.'

'But a deal's a deal,' urged Evans. 'Hadn't the old man O.K.'d it?'

'Sure he had, and expected the next Board Meeting to develop into a gun fight. The bunch aren't crazy. The old man wouldn't have put a cent of his money against all Pumpern's assets. I was the man behind the gun.'

'Didn't he sign something, damn him?'

'He did,' said Peters, 'just a sort of contract letter.'

'What did it say?'

'He pledged the bank to put up the full amount. Pumpern asked for details to be settled in conference.'

'Isn't that good enough?'

'Why, you poor fish, haven't you seen your boss this week? If that letter had reached him, he'd have been buying the town instead of loafing about in an old rag of a coat that you or I would sell for a dollar if we could find a sucker, and cadging his lunch every day.'

'Who has the letter?' asked Evans.

'Somers, of course – sent to him to countersign. He took it home, and sent it round the fiery cross. Believe me, some clan gathering!'

Evans considered. 'Can we do something with Somers?'

'Wouldn't give Pumpern a dime if he was guaranteed a million dollars to do it. Why, the man's like a nightmare to him – wants to put him out of Masonry, one degree after another, with the peculiar swift kick of each applied in the tenderest spot; after that, ride him on a rail to

Chicago, which Somers hates only one degree less than he hates Pumpern; and after that, think up something serious, and start in again.'

'But Somers can't destroy an official letter.' Evans had Welsh persistence in the same perfection that he had Welsh dishonesty.

'I saw the letter, of course,' said Peters, 'and Jessie has her notes. We were both there when he signed it. But on the technicality, it should be countersigned.'

'Is Pumpern going to sue the bank, compel them to produce the letter, ask the Courts to force somebody to make it good? What's the consideration, for another thing?'

Evans gave up. 'You're right,' he said, 'but let's forget it. What's our slice of that poor lemon? I've got a worthwhile hand to play. I'm in on a deal of nearly fifty millions; and nobody knows I'm there. I'm going to hold 'em up. I'm giving myself just ten – unless they squeal too loud; if so, twenty. Either way, me for the soil that grows nothing but leeks, lambs and liars about six months from now; and if I need you, you'll hear.'

16

At this stage, Peters went off to the bank; and Granchester, who expected to find a raging madman, was met with nods and becks and wreathed smiles. He explained in two minutes that he wanted to glance at the books and satisfy his friend, the novelist, that he was getting all his royalties. Evans behaved as if he had been made State Senator. It took him just twelve seconds to abstract the statement from the file. A glance assured him that his memory was in working order; there were no slips to fear. He took out his Number 3 Romance from the safe – the set of books he called *The Pain in the Neck or The Pessimist's Nightmare* by L. I. Livin. The Earl of Granchester, though a competent mathematician, even a brilliant one, when the figures meant something in science, became completely imbecile when they represented financial transactions. He could no more check his hotel bill than a corpse can measure his coffin; but he could look excessively knowing. In extreme cases, he would take out a pair of horn-rimmed spectacles, and, looking over them, draw his conclusions, not from the figures, but from the other man's face. On this occasion, he completely failed. Little Owen read him without an effort. Anyway, there was no difficulty. The books tallied. Even the dollar mark could not blind Granchester to the consistent identities of totals, whether they meant anything or nothing to him. Owen knew well that there was nothing wrong with the books; he knew, and only he, of Pumpern's private printing press, far away south, where a man who could read was a suspicious character. He knew how the 'best sellers' got reprinted on that press; how Pumpern, under another name, sold them as Bookseller's Remnants at bargain prices, and thus how fifty thousand copies of a book could reach the public while only ten or twelve per cent appeared in any of the documents that concerned them.

Granchester's scrutiny led to no more than a moral conviction that, since the books were so right and the cashier so certain of the fact, such alacrity and rectitude must be a screen for something very wrong indeed in another department. He made up his mind to write to his friend to employ a detective who knew the quaint tribal customs of those who sailed the seas and flew the flag of Flint, or on the highways followed God's commandment by the honour that they paid to their sire Barabbas. All this took scarce ten minutes. Granchester turned to go. The Welshman called inwardly on his forefathers, on the wild men who bearded English kings. He struck the Earl on his raw wound.

'It's two years,' he said, 'since I spoke to a human being. I expect to go home this year; but I'll die first unless you come to the rescue. Don't think me over-officious, don't think me a tuft-hunter. I'm not being rude if I say that a crossing-sweeper from the Thames Embankment would be as welcome. I'm being polite. It's not the Earl I want; it's the English voice and the English way that tear from my heartstrings a mad symphony of agony and rapture. Do come to lunch.'

'I understand perfectly,' said the other, laughing. 'You don't have to tell a man's a man for a' that, after a month or two in a land where it's not even the guinea stamp but the greenback; where dirty paper money tells of the hands that have clawed it.'

Owen caught up the tune. 'The long green is the fig leaf,' he said briskly. 'It hides all sin and shame.'

'Right,' said the Earl. 'This is your town and we're the only men in it. I'll lunch with you at noon —'

'At the Pontiac – the front entrance – noon sharp,' completed the cashier.

'Right, but of course when you next come to happier lands, I shall expect you to be my guest at Orme.'

17

Owen was overjoyed. He was just man enough to set his heel on snobbery, but just snob enough to glow all over at the heroism of his act. 'There are few cashiers,' he could not help saying to himself, 'who, born on a stony slope in Wales, of peasants scarcely higher, by any standard except anatomy, than their own sheep, have won their way by sheer merit to the Degree of Arts which Royalty honoured.' He had proceeded by less worthy methods to make his way up the slippery golden stairs and treacherous social slopes, and might never have been suspected but for a fluke that might not happen again in centuries, and which no cunning could have avoided. It was mere chance that he was guilty; had he been never so innocent he must have been suspected in those peculiar circumstances. That was why he was on Pumpern's trail in this half crazy abscess of a town, instead of being perhaps a Master Dice Thrower in Copthall Court, or the financial adviser to a Kimberley King or a blackmailing journal. But, after all, things were well enough. He was not yet twenty-six – he had accounts with six banks. Each of them had some five thousand dollars for him whenever he so willed it. He knew enough about most of the big men in town to assure him either an income for life at the best, or a free pardon and a getaway at the worst. And today was the day; indeed it was a bit of all right, and no mistake, for Mr Owen Evans. He ran breast-high on a trail of forty millions, and he was entertaining an Earl at lunch – not as the firm's cashier, by David, but by his birthright, by worth of his Welsh blood that has mixed with English for he had forgotten how many centuries, whether on battlefield or in bed-chamber. But he was perfectly well aware that the Earl had been by no means bound to recollect just those particular truths. He might have been the haughty kind, though his father had certainly not lent money, or purveyed beauty to royalty. But he might very well have taken a personal dislike to Owen, who never lied to himself, or forgot for a moment that he was as repulsive an animal as walked the streets. He knew he had only one asset: his brain – an engine of quite exceptional power, scope and order.

18

The upshot of these reflections was that Owen Evans, though he would have liked to kill the Earl, preferably in a duel, because he was such a manifest superior, was also ready to risk his body and soul in the Earl's service. The great man had not patronised him; had not stooped; had not once hinted at the gulf between them. He had joked as if he were an old school-fellow, a brother officer, or a duke. Owen could fancy himself in an Eton jacket and silk hat cribbing iambics from his Lordship. The epaulets tossed on his shoulders as foot to foot with the Earl he led his company to the charge. He felt a bullet strike him. He woke to find the Earl wounded no more nor less than he. The purifying mud of Flanders, the conflagrating blood of Britons made them brother priests to Mars. He saw the King himself pin the Victoria Cross on both their breasts. His fancy whirled him on. He felt the strawberry leaves about his brow; the gold was not a weight. He did not feel shame or surprise when at some brilliant gala, men did not call him 'you,' but said 'your Grace.' They flattered him, they courted him, they ate out of his hand. These daydreams made him reel; his soul was dizzy and drunk; he staggered, caught at his desk, sank with white face and sweating brow into his office chair. His throat moved in small spasms; he jammed his lower jaw against its mate. Tears sprang to his eyes that had not wept since he was whipped at school. He pulled himself together; his eye fell on the little mirror which told him what was passing in the office; he looked unflinchingly at his hideousness.

The Earl had not shown, even by the unconscious start that most men give when they first saw him, that he had noticed that detested ugliness. Hyperion had accepted the Satyr with all the indifference of Hamlet's mother. Granchester was himself splendidly handsome in the way Owen most admired. He evidently scorned his toilet; tropical suns had tanned his face; a sportsman's hardships ringed his eyes; fever had wasted his cheeks and thinned his close-cropped curls. All this was beauty's armour. At thirty-seven he looked forty-four. But all these scars conspired to emphasise the majesty of the brow, a mighty dome where dwelt some wise, calm, conscious God. It added to the fearlessness, to the vigilance, to the swift apprehension and to the mastery of the eyes, to the nobility and refinement of the nose, to the firmness and passion of the mouth, to the resolution and probity of the chin. Then a man's carriage was itself 'distinction.' Owen had watched him as he left the office. He had never seen a man in his life who moved with such elastic ease, such mastery of his motion.

And this man did not shrink when he saw Owen. He had forbidden himself to feel what he was bound to know. Owen had never dared to risk a woman's 'No'; he rarely trusted himself even to speak with them except when business forced him. He thought how the Earl must, all his life, have had the women of the world like spaniels. He saw them with admiring eyes, tender and moist, with their throats parched, crouching as they waited for a whistle. Ariel had not let their contrast come into Caliban's mind. And so, just as he had dreamt of Granchester as a friend, now his wandering eye hypnotically fixed on its reflection; his face faded out. He saw himself as the Earl's rival. He lived Don Juan's life in a few minutes. Empresses, dancers – all were his! He seduced nuns at the very altar, eloped with brides in the

first week of their honeymoon. Again he came to himself. He had
lived Heaven for an eternity despite the clock that swore, with little
contradiction, it was not half an hour. All this he owed to the Earl.
And while the rational self, with its teeth in the crab-apple of life,
would have killed him and trampled him whose mouth was glad with
the rich peach of life, the poet in him touched the truth that sense-
experience could not mask. He, the true Self, the nameless reality beneath the foolish label Owen Evans, wanted to pay that debt, the price
of his gorgeous dream. He wanted to see Owen Evans do for the Earl
of Granchester some service, something signal, something sublime,
something to prove himself worthy of what he knew was nothing less
than his redemption.

19

Over the yellow perch the Earl became most monstrous cheerful. But
that peculiarly local delicacy merely made Owen remark that even so
exquisite a joy was but a Jew's price for a man's soul with his intellectual
pleasures and society of his fellow creatures thrown into the scale.

'I can't see it,' said his guest. 'They tell me there are no amusements
in America. I assure you that in some twenty hours, I've had more
fun, more excitement than I ever got in a month the other side. Why,
Hamlet no longer brings the blush of shame to my maiden cheeks; no
longer do I lack the matter for soliloquy. By all the hollow turnips that
hold candles, let me swear it. My father's ghost's abroad! Like Charles
the First, half an hour after his head was cut off, he walks and talks.
Oh, I'm too gross, encased in sense. He cannot reach me but through
a holy man, a crystal soul to reflect truth, the saint whose name is
Ross – nowadays. Through him I and my sire may pass the time of
day. Ross is a German Jew; to my unsanctified eyes, he looks more
hog than man. In such guise must the Gods walk, lest the profane
pollute them. My father came to me last night; and I am only sorry
to say that what he said was garbled by some deaf and dumb spirit.
He did not say one word with any sense in it, despite his obvious
anxiety, and the almost overstrained use of the saint's well-known influence with God. But this morning, after I left your office, there was
a telephone call. It was my friend and benefactor Ross, who had been
warned of God in a dream. My father, with tears streaming down his
eyes, implored me not to leave the city till I had got his message. I
shall accordingly spend the afternoon trying to find a house, if possible, on a ninety-nine years lease.

'Oh yes, my friend, man shall not live by perch alone, but by every word that cometh out of the mouth of Ross. I would not leave this town – not to be the boss of Tammany.'

20

Never was battle played by the Great General Staff of Germany with more precision than the campaign against the Earl. And certainly, German armies never found foe to do exactly what they wanted him as amiably as did Lord Granchester. It was like a Book of Euclid. Of such it may well be said that, however satisfactory the conclusions, the details of the proof are singularly dry. I will not reproduce the Ouija Board's string of letters, varied now and then by an intelligible word or phrase, like an oasis rare and refreshing. I will not trace the steps by which the Reverend Ross acquired the confidence of the ghost. I jump at once to the great message.

The ghost was minatory, affectionate, hortatory, pathetic, expostulatory, paternal, everything by turns. But the gist of it all was that his son should do a kindness to a stranger, and find that he had entertained an angel unawares. He would be the guardian angel of the family; with his wings he would bear him up lest he hurt his foot against a stone. Not an hour had passed before this stranger punctually flopped at the very feet appointed. The Earl acted with appropriate promptness; rescuer and rescued soon found themselves fast friends. The angel waved his wings, the extraordinary coincidence was discovered, the Earl was duly impressed. The contracts were prepared; there was never a hitch.

21

Owen had been at work at high pressure during this time. Pumpern had set him to work out the figures for the scheme. It never occurred to him, absorbed as he was in fancy's flight, doing, so to speak, with the ten numerals as much as Shelley with his six-and-twenty letters, that there was any connection between Granchester, who never repeated his visit to the office, and the man who was to buy his poetry. Nor did the publisher's wife think that the Earl's daily visits to the house had any other purpose than to see her. She guessed her lover sceptical enough, thought that his long sittings had no other object than to throw dust into her husband's eyes. It was pure chance that stamped 'Received with thanks' at the foot of the little account that his soul had run up with his saviour.

His prospectus completed, he made up his overtime mostly in taking walks about the city. It was pure chance that glued his eyes to a shop window, and delayed his return to his dinner. It was pure chance that he fell into a fit of abstraction, and fell into the wrong turning. The luck of the time and place threw him into a stall at the performance of the Comedy of the Apoplectic Millionaire and the Humane Nobleman. The violence dragged him from his meditations – he recognised both parties. But some instinct kept him from interfering. As he walked home he mused; he thought it devilish strange. He knew the millionaire to be one of the least scrupulous of Pumpern's gang. His mind flashed back to the lunch at the Pontiac. 'That dream!' he thought. A third strand twisted itself in the rope. He remembered Pumpern asking him the rate of Sterling exchange. It came to him in a flash that his friend was the man they were after, the man to be noosed in the lasso of his own figures. He left his dinner unfinished, and went to a telephone booth. The Earl was not in his hotel. He tried again in the morning, and got him.

'I beg your pardon,' said Owen, 'but Mr Pumpern asked me to call you up. Have you got the carbon copy of the rough draft of the Prospectus? There is a clerical error on page three.'

'What prospectus?' said the Earl. 'Never saw one – never heard of one. Anything else?'

2 2

Owen apologised. He fought down his conviction; but his anxiety fevered him. He went about like a man in a dream for three or more days. Then, to his amazement, he found on his desk a note from the Earl.

'My dear young friend,' it ran. 'It appears I am settled. Indeed, I'm the oldest inhabitant. My father likes the climate. So you are the tenderfoot. You must come to lunch with me. I want to warn you. You stand in the gravest danger that can threaten cashiers – you make mistakes in figures. There is no clerical error on page three, or on any other page of that Prospectus. Shall we say tomorrow at the same place and time?'

Over the lunch, Owen told all he knew; so did his host. There was no more to be said. A series of flukes had upset all calculations. As they rose from the table, Granchester said to Owen, 'only one word – act as if nothing had happened.'

The cashier agreed; and each took his own way.

23

Granchester took his own advice. The revelations of the lunch did not alter a single detail of his plans. It was agreed to sign the papers at the office of a lawyer on next Monday morning. On Sunday evening, Granchester asked some friends to dinner. It was served in a private room. There was the millionaire, the angel; there were the publisher and the preacher. Last of all there was a funny little man whom everybody recognised as a friendly rival to Ross. He was a 'trumpet medium,' perfectly harmless, capable of no mischief. But what was he doing there?

'I have a confession to make,' said the host. 'There was a moment when I lost my faith. It all seemed too good to be true. I may say frankly that I prayed about it. I resolved to go in secret to another counsellor. He is here tonight. I thought I would have you all to celebrate my great good fortune. My friend here, though he be least conspicuous, has been essential. I tell you plainly that if he had counselled me against my new investment, I had determined to withdraw. But, as he will tell you himself, my father came at the first sitting. He urged me to go on.'

The conspirators began to recover. They had suspected mischief from the most harmless source. The tension was too great. What with the relief and the champagne the dinner was tremendous. Only one devil resisted every exorcism. That was the preacher's 'still small voice.' He still shivered with superstitious fear. When it was over, the Earl asked a favour.

'Will you, my friends with spiritual gifts,' he said, 'invoke a final benediction on my plans? Will you once more bring to our darkness that clear light that shines from beyond the veil? Will you fortify mortal hearts for the courage of those who have faced death, and found it but the gate to a fuller life?'

They naturally said that they would be only too happy to oblige.

The Reverend Ross went through his customary performances. Then a strange thing happened. He could not fake with his usual glibness. His tongue seemed tied. He forced himself to triteness. The sweat poured down his face. At last he stammered out –

'Yes, it's all right, all right. Yes – go on. I see success – your father's pleased. I'm only afraid, I can't help it, there's something I don't know about. Oh, get those papers signed – then the cloud will pass.'

After about half an hour he yielded the pulpit to his brother augur. This little old man had none of Ross' stunts. He went into trance like a child falling asleep. He was perfectly calm, perfectly confident.

'I see your father plainly. I hear him. He is calling you.'

'Can I speak to him?' said the Earl.

'Yes, yes, he wants you to.'

'Tell me once more, my father, only once more. Is success assured?'

'Yes, yes,' cried the old man, 'provided you stick to your plans. Everything must be done as it was first conceived. Yes, first – he seems to dwell on "first" – "from the very first of all," he says.'

'It's all right, then, once we sign the papers?'

'"Oh yes, oh yes." He smiles so beautifully. I do wish you could see him.'

'That's all right then,' cried Granchester with a sigh of relief.

'Ah, ah, he shakes his head; he speaks; I cannot hear it!'

'Nonsense' replied the host, 'he was perfectly clear. Oh, a thought strikes me! Can it be that something might prevent the completion?'

The medium made repeated efforts to report what he described as the nonsensical words of the ghost.

'Nothing can stop the deal,' he repeated a dozen times or more. Then he got one more word. Unfortunately, it was the word 'unless.' The minutes passed, his spirit wrestled manfully. At last he gave it up. 'The words are clear,' he said; 'but they mean nothing unless there's something which you haven't told us.'

'What are they?' cried the Earl impatiently.

'Nothing can stop the deal,' said the old man in his most solemn voice, 'unless Colonel Pacton's Brother interferes.'

'Don't know him,' cheerfully answered Granchester. The other three were equally at a loss.

'Colonel Pacton is my wife's guardian, of course,' said the publisher.

'I think I understand,' stammered the preacher, though his face had gone livid with fear. 'It's just another spirit.'

'Stop the séance, don't give him a chance, let's all go home!'

The party broke up. But Ross bore off his accomplices to his own house.

'I've got to talk to you fellows,' he said, 'I've got to talk damn straight. Sit down.'

24

'As I've told both of you,' began the preacher, 'I fake this business all I can, but there's always just one little bit left over. You've got to trust to that, and act on it. Whatever your mind tells you, God knows better. Don't laugh, I've seen it work. I've had a hunch from the word go that there was something wrong. You never heard of Colonel Pacton's

Brother – no more did I. But I know who he is as well as I know who you are. You know what Pacton did in the War. He organised the government's protection against spies. I never heard of his brother, as I told you; but I know who he is and his job, as well as I know myself. He's on the doorstep – put a fist to those deeds, and he'll come in, and he won't knock, and we'll all have a government job for the rest of our lives.'

The others declared he was crazy. He argued for an hour; they laughed the more. They went to their homes.

The Earl of Granchester arrived at the lawyer's office as the clock struck ten. He waited. No one came. The preacher's frozen feet had proved contagious. The lawyer rang them up. They were both ill in bed. It was agreed to postpone the conference till a week later.

'It's an infernal nuisance' said the lawyer. 'I know how you want to get home.'

His client breathed a sigh of resignation. 'We can but bear it patiently,' said he, 'when Colonel Pacton's Brother interferes.'

25

The next three days, the Earl pressed an exceptionally luxurious automobile into his service, merely changing his necktie for one more eloquent of sympathy with suffering. He sped from house to house; turn by turn his friends were gladdened by his bedside manner. They found it a bit of a strain, for all that. It was the preacher who first broke down.

'I'll tell you the truth,' he said. 'That message about Colonel Pacton's brother, that knocked me flat. I, too, had had that fear, that nameless fear. It haunted me. Had our friend told of some enemy that we could meet in fight, it wouldn't have mattered. The unknown name made my vague fear more imminent. You will think it weak of me, but I collapsed. It's the same story with the others, I don't doubt for a minute. You see, this business has been organised from spirit-land all through. That's the appalling thing.'

'I thought as much,' said the visitor. 'I had myself to fight, as you so justly put it, not with flesh and blood, but with principalities and powers. But I hope you don't mean to back out of the deal?'

The preacher called out protestations.

'Never mind, never mind,' said the Earl. 'I think I know how to put your minds at rest.'

He drove to his hotel; summoned a bell-boy; bade him page Colonel Pacton. On this occasion, that particular idol of society was found almost at once. He came forward with his visitor's card in his hand. He was a tall grey-bearded man, so excessively distinguished that it almost pained one to look at him.

'I am Colonel Pacton,' said he. 'To what am I indebted, may I ask?' The question trailed away into a murmur which stamped him as belonging to one of the original *Mayflower* families as plainly as if he had worn a sailor hat with the name of the ship on it.

'I'm ashamed to intrude,' said Granchester. 'The fact is that I was about to conclude a business deal. I may excuse myself, I trust yet more, if I mention that the sum involved was sufficiently large to make a quite perceptible difference to my somewhat slender purse, though, of course, nothing at all to such men as throng these halls of marble. It barely reached the forty million mark.'

'Yes,' said Colonel Pacton, slightly more frigid.

'My story is a short one. My friends are very superstitious. A medium told them that one thing alone could spoil the deal. "Nothing can do so," he told them in my presence, "unless Colonel Pacton's Brother intervenes." It frightened them clean out of their wits.'

The Colonel got rather red. 'This is absolute nonsense, absolute nonsense, sir,' he said, the soldier in him elbowing the diplomatist.

'So I say myself,' replied the Earl. 'And what am I to do? Couldn't you reassure them?'

'Why this is madness, madness!'

A sudden suspicion seemed to strike the Englishman. 'I suppose that you are the only Colonel Pacton?' he enquired deferentially.

'I surely am,' replied the veteran; 'and you may as well know right now that I haven't got a brother. I never had one. And both my parents being dead long since, you'll have to find a wonderful medium to persuade me that I'll ever have one now.'

'Tut, tut, too bad!' replied the Earl. 'Not even a spirit brother!'

The old man tapped the floor with his foot. 'What next? What can I do? Pray come to the point.'

'If you would give me an hour of your time, if you would call on my friends in your car, if you would tell them what you have just told me, I think I could complete the deal. I throw myself entirely on your good nature.'

'This city,' said the soldier emphatically and deliberately, 'is full of the craziest people I ever struck in my life. You seem to be sane. Out of gratitude for the pleasure of meeting anybody in that class, I'll be glad to come. Shall we start right away?'

With every possible solemnity, the formalities of the ritual were complied with. All three promised to turn up at the hour of the postponed conference. No further obstacle thrust up its head. Everything was signed, sealed and delivered; copies went to the state archives for record. There was no more to do.

26

'I have one more proposal to make, gentlemen, or, shall I say, one more favour to ask. I can never express in words what a wonderful time this has been. It has been indeed a privilege to watch the wondrous ways of Providence; heaven and earth conspiring to redeem my family fortunes! Still, no word more of that. What I have to say is only as your friend, if you will let me wreathe my brows with that untarnished name. I must go to England at once to raise this money. Will you come with me as my guests? Let my poor castle repay, though in no coin but good will, the hospitality which the majestic castles in your fair city have so gladly granted.'

The plan met with ready acceptance. The long strain had left its mark on the nerves of the conspirators. They might just as well keep an eye on the property until they had cashed in on it, and made their getaway. Only a fortnight later, they were occupying the biggest suite on the fastest liner afloat.

27

The three prominent citizens of Flivverton had become acclimatised to Granchester in the first week of their visit. The third week drew to its close. They stood alone upon the castle terrace. They were waiting for the Earl to return from London. The financial arrangements had been completed. He was to be there for dinner with the whole of the cash. Any train might bring him. They were getting a little nervous again. Every crack of a twig was mistaken for something to do with his arrival. At last, an unmistakable footstep.

'Why isn't he in the car?' growled the suspicious preacher. And then they saw it was not the Earl at all. A young man was standing right under the big elm in front of the house. They had been warned how treacherous elms were. They shouted to him to come out into the open. He still hesitated, shifting from one foot to the other, plainly uncertain what to do next. At that moment the publisher recognised the stranger. It was his own cashier! He gasped out a fierce blasphemy. Dragging the others by their sleeves, he set forward at a shambling run.

'He's going to crab the deal,' he croaked at them. 'At the last minute we're dished. Kidnap him! Stick a knife into him – anything! We've got to get him away!'

But the young man, though he greeted them with an independence of manner which surprised them, behaved as if he had nothing on his mind. He explained his presence in a dozen words.

'I resigned, as you well know, sir, last month, and I've come home to live. That I'm here is all pure luck. I stopped off simply because Lord Granchester asked me to dine with him whenever I came to England. But, to tell you the truth, when I got near the place, I began to feel it rather overpowering. You Americans can't understand that, very likely, but I stood there like a booby, not knowing what to do. I didn't even recognise you on the terrace.'

The three conspirators breathed again. Silence fell for a moment. A slow smile spread across their faces as the sound of a distant motor grew more and more distinct. The Earl was coming – they had turned the trick!

28

Another sound! It was a sharp, dry crack. Before they had time even to look for the source, the biggest bough of the great elm crashed down, and crushed the cashier into pulp.

They were too scared to scream – not one of them was hurt, or even so much as scratched. The fallen bough was perfectly green. The leaves had stroked their faces. It seemed as if the world had fallen away from them. The preacher even wondered – had he made a mistake, and was he dead? And then they saw that the car had drawn up opposite, and that the Earl had jumped out of it to examine the corpse.

'Come away from here,' was all he said.

Even those few words told them that his voice and manner were somehow curiously changed. He led the way in silence to the terrace.

'I want to talk to you gentlemen,' he said. 'Let us sit here, with death just over our shoulders.'

They took seats. The Earl lighted a cigarette. 'First of all,' he began, 'let me assure you that the hour of execution is only advanced by thirty minutes. But that joke of Nature,' and he flung his hand over towards the tree, 'has been a little too much for me. I'd like to cross-examine you a bit, Mr Preacher. You, who know God so well, ought to be able to explain the universe – bits of it – bits like this.

'Here is the machinery of the curious drama which we four have been playing, as I see it with my peculiar squint. I see three forces working. The first I'll call the force that compels your faith, the three of you as a whole I mean. You think that effect must always necessarily follow cause. You base your actions on what your minds are bound to believe to be truth, owing to their quaint construction; and on experience, which tells you that observation of an infinitesimal fraction of nature over a period of time, which is an infinitesimal fraction of time, entitles you to formulate an universal law. You assume the continuity and uniformity of everything even though your actual observation, your direct observation, shows nothing but discontinuity and variety. Shall I read a paper at the Royal Society to prove that all boughs must fall on all cashiers? It would be just as sensible as to deduce from the microscopic and instantaneous phenomenon which we call the solar system, that infinity and eternity must be exactly like it.

'Then, there's the second force: pure chance. That's funnier still. To this hour, I haven't the least idea why that poor boy down there suddenly blazed into a dog-like love for me. By no intent of mine, I promise you! By pure chance, he is delayed in a walk, by pure chance misses his way, and thus it happens that he was a witness of my meeting our apoplectic friend here. He gets it into his head that you three gentlemen are in a plot to rob me. We meet at lunch. He gives me all the details. See how this chance has worked on my behalf! Don't worry, gentlemen, it's all right. You've got the papers signed and sealed, haven't you? You mustn't mind when I tell you, as it happens, I knew everything that he had to tell me, bar a few details, before I'd been twenty-four hours in Flivverton. There we see chance at work. She patiently conspired with such intelligence as to baffle human conjecture; and yet her object seems to have been to break into a house with neither walls nor roof! Chance ends with more grim idiocy yet. Just when a difference of one yard in your positions under the elm would have satisfied every canon of poetic justice, you go unscathed; and the man who had gone clean out of the game lies there.

'Then, there's a third force: supernatural intervention. You and I, Doctor Ross, have given some time to study that. You played your hunches, didn't you? How do you score the game? Did Colonel Pacton's Brother interfere?'

'In a sort of way, he did,' returned the preacher. 'I was afraid of something. My Brother Divine merely gave it a name. My belief in Colonel Pacton's Brother created him. Thoughts are things.'

'Hum,' said the Earl, 'it doesn't bother me at all. Let me tell you that I invented Colonel Pacton's Brother myself, and spent three nights rehearsing the old medium and his part.'

The millionaire began to bluster. 'Do I understand, my Lord, that you have been playing the fool with us?'

'Business, business, please keep to business! You have the papers signed and sealed. Isn't that enough for you?'

The other two men forced their accomplice to make a show of patience.

'I want to assure you, gentlemen, that I take this business more seriously than anything else I have yet met in all my life. Here's an inexplicable thing. I can't begin to imagine a cause for it. I haven't seen the slightest trace of any effect. Do you remember the first night I dined at Mr Pumpern's? I seem to remember that your wife had not managed to suit your gastronomic requirements. When I got out of the house, I found her waiting to grab me.'

Pumpern suddenly got up. 'What in hell do you mean?'

'Tut, tut, metaphysics first, let me beg you. Well, having clinched, she broke away. I saw her in a flood of light which shone from your side door. Her figure looked like a black-hooded dwarf with a silver dish on its head. I saw her right hand clearly. I knew it for hers beyond a doubt. In it she had a Malay kris. This I also recognised as my own. I never saw another anything like it. It hung then, as it hangs now, as a trophy on my walls in my room in London. I cabled that night for news of it. Your wife's face was as bloodless as if she were dead. It was twisted into the most extraordinary contortions. Her throat had been cut by the kris – it gaped like a melon with a slice cut out. It is the most extraordinary hallucination – and the only one I ever had. What did it mean?'

The publisher rose and folded his arms. 'If this is true, Lord Granchester,' he growled with a pomposity which came near to deceiving himself, 'it means the vengeance of an outraged husband.'

'Don't distress yourself, Mr Pumpern.'

'Not at all, not at all.'

'The intrigue, despite its melodramatic opening, went on as smoothly as your own plans for me.'

The publisher opened his mouth again.

'You're much too late, my friend,' said Granchester. 'Your wife got a divorce last week. You aren't an outraged husband. She will be here tomorrow, anyhow, unless the boat's late.'

The millionaire found that he couldn't stand it.

'Are we three businessmen, or are we goats?' he said angrily. 'Can't you see that this is all bunk? I beg your pardon, My Lord, I didn't mean to put it in that way. I meant that you are making this all up to amuse us, as you have so often done before.'

'Quite right, quite right – the business view. We have our papers signed; we have our papers sealed; nothing else matters. Now, back to our supernatural! Here is one hunch you had: something inside you said "There's something wrong."'

'It surely did,' was the surly acquiescence of the medium.

'You never played that hunch. You went in for a business deal, the largest of your lives. You put your business brains together. You worked day and night at it. Yet you omitted the first elementary precaution, a precaution you would take instinctively, any one of you, in a transaction involving half a dollar. I bet you your poor forty million that not one of you has ever missed it before in your lives.'

'Well, what is it?' said the banker. 'I wasn't in this from the start, you know. Have these fools let me down?'

'One moment let me beg of your indulgence. I want to finish with the supernatural. Why didn't you play your hunch?' he said to Ross.

'I didn't know what it meant.'

'I did,' said the Earl. 'You have gone wrong from the first owing to this absurd belief of yours in supernatural intervention. The hunch you didn't play was the only one that was right; and it wasn't a hunch at all. When you went off the handle over Colonel Pacton's Brother it was guilty conscience; your moral conscience. But the other hunch was the prick of your intellectual conscience. It was your mind reproaching you that you had left out one link in your chain.'

The preacher was genuinely interested in the conversation; but the publisher got more stolid every moment, and the third man more angrily suspicious.

'Let me draw you a picture. Ah, here we are,' he broke off suddenly, waving his hand to a tall man some ten years older than himself – a man with a gold eyeglass and a short square beard who was coming down from the house to the terrace. 'Never mind the picture. We'll do a dialogue. Imagine yourselves in the Union Club, New York. Here am I and my friend in a window, frightfully bored. One of us opens a letter. "Bother," he says, "I suppose I may as well." He throws the letter to the other who reads it and says, "Not on your life." "Why not?" says the one. "Mug's game," says the other. "The man's a friend of mine," says the first. "Don't do it," says the second. "Here, you let me go instead of you." "Well, I suppose so," acquiesces the man to whom the letter was addressed, going off to a writing table with a laugh, and scribbling a note to his friend. What do you make of that?'

It appeared that nobody made anything of it. 'Doesn't it suggest anything to you, thou man of God?'

'No,' he grunted.

'Doesn't explain why that little word "lost" kept running round your solar plexus?'

'Not a glimmer.'

'Never imagined that sort of scene?'

He shook his head heavily.

The banker interrupted. 'Excuse me,' he said. 'As you yourself remarked, "business." We still have a slight formality to transact.'

'Just what I was coming to,' smiled the young man sweetly. 'I go into the witness box. Observe the correctness of my attitude. I hereby solemnly affirm that I have never in all my life been honoured with the privilege of intimacy with such imbeciles, dolts and fools as the shrewdest knaves in your city. And I further wish to remark that if I am cast for the part of Paris, and have to hand the apple to one of the three, I choose unhesitatingly my Venus from the remarkable specimen of the Blue-faced Baboon, who, after lying to God and to man since he could frame a phrase, now expects God and man to tell the truth to him. I pick him, also, on more practical grounds. Don't be afraid! It's going to be your turn to say what you made me say – do you remember?'

'Do you expect us to remember all you say?' put in the banker in a tone of acid impertinence.

'Oh no,' returned the Earl with gaiety. 'But surely you have not forgotten the three words on which your whole plan had been laid – 'I am convinced!' Be good enough to stand up for a moment, Doctor Ross, if I may venture to ask you to take the trouble. What I want to say is that you are convinced that as a fool you shine above your colleagues, as they exceed in knavery the common run of thieves in Flivverton, and as the thieves in Flivverton outclass the rest of the world. You say that little scene means nothing? Let me recall another. Do you remember how you ransacked Flivverton for information about the details of my family affairs, for pictures, interviews, biographies; no sprat too small for your creel, fisher of men!'

The medium ventured upon the customary professional denials.

'Never occurred to you that while you were at the microscope there might be something you missed at the telescope?'

The baited man began to lose patience, and the Earl himself was tiring of the torture.

'Will you do me the honour of being so kind as to turn round?'

Ross did so, half afraid. He did not know what he might see. His superstitious terrors aggravated his intuition that he was in a trap.

'Do you recognise that man?'

The preacher hunted in the jungle of his memory. At last, every muscle in his face gone suddenly flat, he sobbed, as a man will after a sufficient dose of the knout, and managed to gasp out —

'It's Colonel Pacton's Brother!'

The two Englishmen, utterly taken aback, burst into a frenzy of laughter.

'Come, come,' said the elder, 'this is undignified. It seems to me that all this trouble has sprung from failing to observe the ordinary customs in usage for centuries past in good society in England. Gold tried in the fire, gentlemen, proved in the forges of time!'

'Well?' growled the banker.

'We have never been properly introduced.' The words came through the black beard with a sort of murmurous and regretful courtesy.

'This gentleman,' said he, coming forward, 'who appears to have been engaged in some very delicate and interesting transactions during the last few weeks, is my young friend and fellow investigator, Sir Roger Bloxam. I have the honour to bid you all most hearty welcome to my poor house.'

The ex-Earl attempted to save the situation by hustling his victims through the formality of introductions. But things had gone too far. The three Americans drew apart – and two apart from one.

'You must have seen Lord Granchester's picture a dozen times when you were looking him up,' said the publisher with a lump in his throat.

'We did everything,' said the banker, his business ability making him more accurate in his pronouns. 'We signed for forty million; and we never identified the principal. Good night!'

'You were our business head,' snarled back Hans Pumpern.

'Business nothing!' said the banker. I was to get a lump sum down, was I? I wasn't even your partner; and I'm glad of it. Damn it all, I'm glad. I'm glad he's got your wife. I'm glad because her money was the only money you had. It was your lunch money, it was your car-fare, you cheapskate. When you get back to Flivverton, what are you going to live on?'

'Don't disturb yourself about that, I beg,' remarked Sir Roger. 'My friend the novelist has it all clear by now, I feel quite sure. Poor Evans confessed to me about your secret printing press. They'll never let you starve. You will never be out of a job.'

'Don't be vindictive,' said Lord Granchester. 'Can't you see when a man's had enough?'

'Sometimes I can,' said Sir Roger, 'but not when he can't see that a woman's had enough.'

'I simply cannot allow this to go on any further,' said the Earl. 'You have made me an accomplice in your pranks, you outrageous young scapegrace. Do you understand what is due to your fellow guests?'

There was a long embarrassed silence. Sir Roger paced the ground; his head was bowed, his eye was caught by the elm. He suddenly straightened his back, and walked up to the four men.

'You're only half right, Granchester,' he said. 'I don't know if it's supernatural. But I heard that boy speak then, as you hear me speak now. It flashed into my mind how it was that he, a scoundrel and a tool of scoundrels, suddenly made amends. It was because I, without the slightest conscious intention, spoke to him with absolute simplicity. I did not even see his body or mind. I told him my business as if I had been talking into a dictagraph. I was the first man who had never noticed the ugliness that he was ashamed of. He was a man, and I was a man. You can get to that either by plain good manners, or by such vivisection as we've been having here today. These men are more than my fellow guests – they are my fellow men; they are yours!'

The Earl drew himself up and frowned. 'What do you suggest that we should do?'

'Well,' said Sir Roger very slowly, 'when you came in and spoilt it all, we were discussing the cause of phenomena. And the only thing that seems to have come off properly, with no misfires, is the force of the practical joke.'

Ross looked at him, tears in his eyes, and a glint as of light in their corners.

'Yes,' said Sir Roger, 'we're on dangerous ground. If a practical joke is the cause of events, am I, well, shall I call it presumptuous?'

'Well, well,' said the Earl impatiently.

'Let's call all bets off,' suggested Sir Roger. 'We're strangers; none of us ever saw any of the others before. We give the high sign when we part. Wipe the slate. No bankruptcy, no prosecutions, everything back where we were as nearly as possible.'

'What about poor young Evans?' said the preacher.

'We don't want him back where he was. Pure chance took care of him. His soul's saved; and all his troubles are over. Forget it.'

'And what about my wife?' said Pumpern.

'Same happy ending; saved her soul; ended her troubles. What? aren't you satisfied, my dear outraged husband? I'll tell them to pay you her income. All over – goodbye – don't you know. Did God make you? Back to the woods – Skidoo – 23 – if you've anything else to say, shut up!'

He waved at them like a conjuror banishing phantoms, turned on his heels, and walked quickly into the house.

The Earl followed him slowly. The three Americans looked at each other; the whole thing had been too much for them. Their brains were not working any more.

The banker rallied them. He put his hands upon their shoulders. He only said one thing; but he said a whole lot when he said it. These were his words – and they will probably be in six foot letters of gold on the new police courts in Flivverton: –

'GO WHILE THE GOING'S GOOD!'

At the top of the steps Sir Roger awaited his friend, a queer smile on his face.

'Granny,' said he, 'we forgot to send the wedding cake to one poor fellow.'

'I'm not curious,' said the Earl. 'Oh well, boys will be boys – what is it?'

'Wedding cake' – Sir Roger always took sentences at their grammatical value whenever he could create confusion by doing so.

Sir Roger choked back a sob. He shook his head most mournfully. He drooped.

'Oh kittens, kittens!' cried the Earl impatiently. 'All right. Get on – spit it out. It's wedding cake, and whom did we forget to send it to?'

'COLONEL PACTON'S BROTHER!'

The Vampire of Vespuccia

As the petty sounds of the Earth's vermin are hushed when thunder rolls through the vast dome of heaven, so in the huge auditorium, each man of the packed thousands held his breath while the orator flung forth his peroration.

The gestures of the tiny black-frocked figure of Judge Sterling produced a weird impression from being the sole movements in that abyss of stillness; from the tiers of boxes he had the effect of a marionette. But his voice seemed impersonal, a force of nature; his last phrase fulminated with terrors more awful than Sinai's; it was a brutal and contemptuous defiance of the hostile multitude whom he had come to address.

'God will look after our rights if we look after our righteousness.'

It was the time and the place that vitalised this pious platitude, challenged the tiger of murder in every heart. For Judge Sterling was no longer a judge; he had resigned a week earlier, that he might be free to throw himself into the ranks of the few fanatics who were protesting against the policy of the President of the United States of America, a policy endorsed almost unanimously by Congress, backed by Wall Street, popular throughout the country, patently profitable to all parties – and yet a violation of the principles of Justice. The rights of the little republic of Vespuccia should be no less sacred than those of its big neighbour; and it was the annexation of Vespuccia which the President had proposed – on this policy he relied for reelection.

The action of Judge Sterling was a bolt from the blue. He had always been respected for his learning, acumen, integrity and independence; but he had never been active in politics. His friends said plainly that he must have gone mad. He had published his letter of resignation – a curt scathing scorpion – hired the biggest auditorium in the city where his opponents were strongest, and enabled them to match their many against his one.

Sterling threw himself back in to his chair, exhausted. Sweat streamed upon his broad and noble forehead, down his high-boned and hollow cheeks, past his thin straight firm mouth, over his resolute square jaw. He had spoken: let the mob lynch him if they liked.

But not a murmur moved in the throng. The echoes of that passionate prophet-plea died away in to a shuddering silence. Every man fixed his eyes upon the President – a phantom of pallor motionless in his box. It was for him alone to pick up the gauntlet which his oldest friend and staunchest colleague had thrown down with such tempestuous suddenness. But the keenest sight and spirit in the crowd could make no guess as to what thoughts vibrated behind that bloodless mask, those fixed inscrutable eyes.

A man started suddenly to his feet. In that silence, the slight sound caught every ear. The audience turned angrily towards the interrupter, shocked at his insolent action. They saw a Herculean figure, tangled grey curls rioting on its head, its satyr face convulsed by a savage impulse: and they understood. For the giant was Pitt Campbell the banker, the President's closest confidant, his spokesman on many an occasion when discretion or propriety forbade the Head of the State to speak in his own person.

The banker was a formidable personality; his relentless energy and uncompromising directness had made him one of the most masterful men in the country. He had been the backbone of the campaign on behalf of the policy which Sterling had attacked. The audience allowed his right to speak. But at his first sentence they began to doubt their senses.

'Mr President,' boomed Campbell, his bass bellowing with brutal violence across the hall, 'I know when I'm licked. We can't afford to play a dirty trick. Me for the penitents' bench! Boys, let's play the game. Three cheers for Judge Sterling, and the Square Deal!'

His hearers sat as if they had been turned to stone. Not a voice answered the appeal. What would the President do, now that his most trusted ally had turned against him without a word of warning? His blank white face never twitched; but he rose slowly to his feet, and after appearing to hesitate for a few moments, turned on his heel, and left the box. At the action, there broke out simultaneously in several parts of the hall a volley of cat-calls and derisive yells. Through them cut coldly the hush rasp of Senator Cross: 'Yah, yellow dog! Hurrah for Fair Play and our next President, Ford Sterling!'

The impulse swept the mutable mob into impetuous ardour. They forgot every motive that had brought them together; they were stampeded into surrender. They stormed the platform; they bore Judge Sterling through the streets on their shoulders, shouting as they marched. Campbell, coolly contemptuous of crowd-psychology, collected a few of the most important men, and convened a conference in his office. In an all-night sitting this committee created a new political party, promulgated a new programme, organised a nationwide machine and planned a whirlwind campaign of oratory and pamphleteering. A month later the 'Sterling ticket' crashed like a cloudburst upon the polls, and the 'crazy crank' who had challenged the community single-handed was the ideal and the idol of his fellow-citizens.

2

Vespuccia is a group of islands in the tropics; they are mountainous and inhospitable, sparsely inhabited by settlers, principally of French and Irish blood, aristocratic rebels against Sansculottism in the one case and Dublin Castle in the other. They had used republican forms to express the patriarchal institutions, by which they governed a contented and prosperous community of mulattos. Few ever emigrated from those enchanted islands; few ever visited their coasts. For Vespuccia was economically independent and commercially insignificant. Neither the products of labour, nor those of the land, offered inducements to the energy of exploitation. But at the period of this story, two accidents had conferred sudden importance upon the republic. The opening of the Panama Canal, the revolutions in naval strategy which followed the invention of new types of warships both floating and flying, the experience of the Japanese-American and the Anglo-Russian Wars; these had combined to make the possession of the Vespuccian Islands essential to the command of the sea. Secondly, the McNab-Sullivan motor had made an epoch in mechanics. It depended on utilising the release of atomic energy by the action of the Q-rays of Reuss; and these rays could only be generated by Lord Forsinard's 'photoanalytic battery' in which Hydrofluoric acid acted on alternating plates of Vulcanite and Spinthrium. This rare metal had been discovered and isolated by Moncoco and Mont de Pierre in a specimen of bordellite, where it exists as the silicate in minute quantities; but, recognising its extreme utility, they continued their researches, and found, three years later, that in the collite of Culvit the Spinthrium had been mistaken for the inert Onanium, and really formed (as the sulphate) 69% of the mineral. Now collite, though it is found in Sicily, Iona and elsewhere, occurs in negligibly small deposits; but it forms the most extensive strata of the mountains of Vespuccia.

This new motor was consequently of no more than theoretical importance unless Vespuccia vitalised it by supplying collite. The overtures of several governments to obtain a concession which would have secured the mechanical hegemony of the world to the successful suitor were rejected point-blank by the President of Vespuccia and his Council. They were apprehensive of sharing the fate of the Crust in Baudelaire's prose poem, torn and trampled in the contest of two ragamuffins. Vespuccia stood firm, and invoked the League of Nations to uphold its sovereignty.

England, after vainly applying persistent pressure and exhausting her diplomatic resources, suddenly reversed her helm and swore to stand by the little republic. The other principal competitor was the United States, whose demands became constantly more imperious, especially after the disasters of the Japanese War had made it clear that Vespuccia was an essential link in the chain of naval defence.

The President, originally elected by a minority, and daily losing popularity by his alleged alliance with inhumane and unscrupulous plutocracy, determined to stake everything on a single throw, and to make the annexation of Vespuccia the fulcrum of the lever by which the people might be moved to renew his lease of office. His campaign had met with success unexampled – until the fatal moment when Ford Sterling had smashed the entire structure single-handed, with one stroke of the sword on whose blade was inlaid this motto: 'Straightness is strength.'

Among the hundred odd millions that populated the United States with so many specimens of our species, there were probably no more than a dozen Vespuccians to rejoice in the escape of their native land. Of these, it may be that the majority had forgotten patriotism in the pursuit of prosperity; but the heart, in one breast, beat hard with elation, with ecstatic, extravagant pride, almost insanely intense. One might have supposed that its owner's mind attributed the enormous event to its own machinations. The absurdity of any such idea is apparent when we summon this patriot to the stage of this story; the footlights show the figure not of a political genius, a power in finance or a diplomat of superlative subtlety, but, on the background of a wooden shack in a cotton-patch, that of a yellow-skinned hag with a narrow forehead, a toothless grin wrinkling her dirty cheeks as she fixes her only eye – a black patch covers its fellow – upon the fragments of a newspaper whose columns are lurid with the 'landslide' in favour of Vespuccian independence.

Had anyone cared to ask the name of this outcast, old at thirty-five, she would have confessed to 'Marguerite Parnell'; possibly adding that 'Mad Maggie' is good enough for her neighbours. All (as she had no shame in admitting) shun her, except the lowest class of men, who visit her now and then in the course of a bout of drunkenness.

She might be induced to boast that one man loves and respects her: her son, Paul, a Washington lawyer. He is a marked man at twenty-one, with the reputation of having the most brilliant brain that ever added honour to Harvard, and the most fascinating and dominating personality that ever found the art of leadership as natural as swimming is to salmon. Paul Parnell, for all that, finds only one meaning in life; he knows no motive but devotion to the mother that bore him and bred him, that trained him with concentrated craft and cunning to accomplish her own private purpose in life, the formulation in fact of the phantom created by her insanity, in whose features were mixed the unreasoning patriotism of a serf, the crude ambition of a mega-lomaniac, and the venomous vengeance of an egoist who would like to destroy the universe every time it reminds him that he is not the almighty and absolute arbiter of events. Yet, insane though she might be, ignorant and obscene as she was, Marguerite Parnell had divined one of the secrets of power. She had insisted on living in misery, vile among vile associates, though she possessed a fortune which enabled her to send Paul to the best schools, and to Harvard, equipped with a spending allowance which put him on terms of equality with the sons of magnates.

Marguerite Parnell grinned over her newspaper with the air proper to a murderer perusing an account of his crime in which the facts are so false, the deductions so misleading, that no misgiving mars his confident chuckle at having outwitted society. Yet in her glance there shot a nobler shaft than mere triumph; one might rather compare its message with the thought of some successful statesman who has achieved his aim so subtly that no man suspects its authorship, or even understands what has happened, much less how. She glowed with the sense of secret power, of superiority such as creative genius has over its puppets, and of that superb self-satisfaction which is peculiar to the feeling that one has ful-filled one's purpose in life, that it has been worth while to embrace the adventure, with all its shame and agony, its daily despair, and its fore-doomed defeat by Death.

The wrinkled woman set a soiled slipper on the disdained newspaper as a lively whistle reached her ears. She threw a scarf over her skinny shoulders, smoothed back her straggling hair, readjusted her patch on æsthetic principles, plastered the ochre cheeks with powder, smeared the thick purplish lips with carmine, and went to the door to meet her son. She had not seen him for two months – nearly three. The boy walked heavily and unsteadily up the mud by-path; but his spirit was bubbling with gladness. His mother took him in her arms with passionate pride and joy, as if the animal instinct for the son were intensified by some spiritual impulse such as a statesman might experience on the return of the soldier whose victories had vindicated his policy. She led him to her bed, laid him down, and covered him up like a child; then mixed him a posset of hot milk and corn whisky, with the yolks of two raw eggs stirred into it – a pinch of heroin and three drops of Tabasco sauce completed this hell-broth, which she called 'Easter Egg-nogg' on account of its potency in resuscitating the human male. She drank with her son to the toast 'Vengeance and Vespuccia.' The young man's physical exhaustion soon disappeared; he insisted on sitting up. He began to tell his adventures, leaning eagerly forward with flame in his velvet-black eyes, while his mother crouched on a rug at his feet and drank his words, with her nostrils twitching with excitement and her fingers plucking feverishly at the fringe of her shawl.

3

Paul Parnell spoke with few interruptions. But when he rolled out Sterling's final phrase, whose fame now rang in every house – 'God will look after our rights if we look after our righteousness' – the painted lips of his mother parted, and she laughed, a loud, lewd, horrible laugh. 'God's truth!' she cackled, 'good for that damned old liar! And a pity he didn't think of it ten years ago!'

Pitt Campbell's intervention brought a sneer to her lips. 'The cowardly crook!' she cried. Her son laughed lightly back: 'The man whose moral courage and integrity are graven in American history!'

His eyes flashed strangely as he described the Presidential surrender, the chalk-white pallor and nervous collapse of the man; in their triumph were mingled horror and grim fear, as well as some perverse form of amused disgust. But Marguerite had closed her eyes; she shook with a spasm of Satanically evil ecstasy.

Paul proceeded to describe the details of the campaign, the strategy of the 'Party of Righteousness,' and the triumphs of their Totem, the Bison. But his hearer seemed to have lost her interest; she rocked herself slowly to and fro with half-shut eyes, musing and muttering.

She sat up suddenly, and snapped: 'What about Sing Sing?'

'He came out last week, pretty sick; I took him to Saratoga Springs to feed up; I guess he'll be right along in a week or so.'

'Ah!' was the only comment.

'Someone coming!' cried Paul, whose quick ear had heard a step on the path. He went to the door.

'Talk of the Devil!' he laughed. For it was the man of whom they had been talking, feeble beyond the right of his fifty years, that came into the hut a minute later, and mingled his tears and embraces with those of Paul and his mother.

The newcomer accepted a cigar from the young lawyer, and the two men discussed trivial things while Marguerite prepared a meal. Not until they had eaten did the conversation become serious; then, bolting the door, the yellow woman bade the two men settle themselves while she told the story of the past ten years.

'I shall begin,' she said quietly to the ex-convict, 'with the day I came to Washington – two years before your trial for murder and arson.'

4

'There have been two Devils at my elbow all my life; the Beauty which made me a Queen at twelve, a siren at thirteen, a strumpet a year later, and a mother within six months of that. The other was my Brain, incredibly cunning and insanely intense. My brain drove me to desert Vespuccia for a world worthy of its ambition; and my beauty allured the first victim that counted for more than comfort and cash; you both know whom I mean – the creature whose cheeks and liver are whiter than the House from whose doors I have just kicked him!

'Through that cur, though, I met Ford Sterling; and met love. I loved, soul and sense, for the first and last time. That love became flesh – Ford Sterling is your father, Paul!'

She took two slips of paper from the packet and threw them on the table. The men read them, stupefied. One witnessed the marriage of Marguerite Parnell to Ford Sterling; the other the birth of Paul Sterling eleven months later.

'But my brain rebelled against Love; all my pride and happiness were nothing to me, to the gnawings of my insane craving to make mischief in the world. I had instinctively insisted on keeping my marriage a secret from everybody; when I came to live in Washington I pretended to be a rich Creole; I hired a high-class chaperone, and saw Ford only by stealth. Paul was brought openly to me, with a story that my widowed sister had died and left her son in my charge. Ford Sterling forged documents to prove it; there they are!'

She threw a docket on the table.

'The moment I realised that my husband was in my power, my love dropped dead like a shot dove. I smelt a new mouse, and set my claws in that hulking fool, Pitt Campbell. The verminous creature was yellow all through, a sneak and a thief. In my hands he was soft clay; his gross animal instincts made him my dog. He gave himself into my power, body and soul; there are the proofs that would put him in gaol for the rest of his rotten life!'

With a gesture of repulsion, the thin fingers of Marguerite Sterling flung a thick envelope before her hearers.

'I worked wildly and craftily, like the madwoman I am. I never wasted a week. I made myself mistress of men's fate; the woman they took to be a sensual sorceress was insensible to aught but the pleasures of power. I have trampled down my temperament; no saint ever conquered himself to serve God as I did to serve the Devil within me. It was rarely that I allowed myself to indulge even in the raptures of hate. But when that yellow dog thought he would kennel in the White House, I remembered that he had been too clever for me. I had no power over him. It was an insult. I set traps for him. His midnight visits to me? The sly cur had arranged for an alibi, and for men to swear that some other man had been guilty. I could only ruin myself – and he would save me the pains unless I obeyed him. It was then that I thought of the old witch that nursed me, her Voodoo: I gathered the herbs that she had told me, sure, faithful, silent friends to hatred; I made the ointment, harmless to woman, fatal to man; and the next time that he celebrated his victory over me, its price was the poison that has left his face bloodless and taught his nerves to betray him in his need.'

The ex-convict gasped like a fish thrown in a boat; he stared wildly at the impassive face of the woman before him.

'He won through the acute stage after six weeks of desperate struggle; and his first care was to revenge himself on me. But too many men were in my power; he soon found out that overt action would not avail him. But having become the Governor of his State, he had the police under his thumb; he set their thugs to beat me up in broad daylight on the high road; they left me after breaking two ribs and an arm, smashing my teeth and gouging my eye. The Devil of my Beauty quit me; but he left the Devil of my Brain far stronger now that he possessed me wholly and solely. I sold my house in Washington and came to live in this nigger shack. The only one of my friends that followed me was you, my friend, Jack Mason!'

Tears filled the old man's eyes.

'You did not know my nature or my story; you loved me purely and unselfishly; or, rather, you loved the image of your ideal that your senses fooled you into seeing in me. I played on that devotion with all the devilish art that my despair could command. I tricked your truth into the service of my revenge; you thought yourself the chosen weapon of Eternal Justice, the champion of Innocence, when you swore to bring that reptile to a reckoning! Once more his vigilance outwitted me; he feared me more than ever; his spies never lost your trail. They invented a motive for you to set fire to Phillbrock's farm; they arranged for you to be present on the appointed night; and they blackjacked the boy whose corpse was found in the burned barn.'

The sombre hatred of her eyes was tinged with a faint gleam of human pity; she quenched it with an angry gesture of scorn at what her insane mind considered weakness.

'I concentrated all my efforts upon making Paul the minister of my revenge. He has never caused me a moment of fear lest he might fail me. I cared not a jot for you, Jack Mason; your sentence meant to me only one more defeat, one more humiliation, at the hands of the man I hated.

'In these lonely years I suppose that my mind began to lose its grip. I lived in the memory of my childhood; Vespuccia became to me like a heaven from which I had been exiled. When Paul told me last year of the proposal to annex it, I was inflamed, like some ancient prophetess; wrath gave me genius; I passed a wild-eyed wakeful night; in the morning I had planned every detail of my campaign of patriotism, which would at the same moment glut my private vengeance and my lust for secret power.

'My first step was to make the position of the President politically untenable. I sent Paul to interview the British Ambassador, armed with the evidence – here, in this letter with the red seals! – that he had sold diplomatic secrets to the Stein group of bankers. He gave it to me as a pledge of confidence – my price for the mechanical mummeries he called love. Paul learnt that England had withdrawn from her designs on Vespuccia because Sir William Waghorn had found Spinthruim in enormous quantities in the mineral assolite whose deposits are so extensive throughout Warwickshire. The McNab-Sullivan motor had been secret adapted by the Government to the uses of war; England was assured of a walk-over in the next conflict. I instructed Paul to return to the Embassy the next morning, to convince my one-time lover that it was idiotic to allow America the opportunity of equalising matters by annexing Vespuccia. A week later we learnt that the British Government was as purblind as usual, and refused to interfere. I put my foot down, and forced the Ambassador to present a forged ulti- matum at the White House, saying that the annexation of Vespuccia would be regarded as an unfriendly act by the Court of St James!

'There was no course open to the President but to climb down. I employed Paul to interview my various victims and explain the situation. I selected my husband to succeed that mongrel in the White House; I had long since forgiven him for preferring his "rights" to his "righteousness" by claiming from me the same conjugal duties which had ceased to interest me. I put up Pitt Campbell to be the bellwether of the political flock; and planted the most leather-hinged of my late lovers at points of strategic importance in the auditorium to start the stampede. The President, knowing from the start that he was beaten, even apart from the action of his fellow-citizens, was forced to accept the humiliating role that I assigned to him. For myself, I have maintained my position of never using my power for personal profit; but I am glad to think that on this one occasion, I demanded the instant release of my loyal, my much-injured friend – Jack Mason! You are free to finish the task by doing justice upon the scoundrel who sent you up the Hudson!'

Jack Mason rose. 'Never! Two wrongs don't make a right. I pity him. I forgive him.'

The woman uttered an appalling shriek. 'Then I am baffled after all in the very hour of victory. The Devil deserts me. My life is blasted at the root! Earth is no longer tolerable; I will back where I belong – in Hell!' She caught up the carving-knife from the cracked dish, set its point to her throat, and collapsed, a crumpled mass, into her chair.

5

The lady rose and stretched herself. 'Ten minutes of nine!' she exclaimed in a totally altered tone. 'We ought to get back to Atlanta.'

Jack Mason and Paul rose from their seats respectfully; one held open the door, while the other took a furred mantle from a closet, and adjusted it to the shoulders of 'Mad Maggie' as she removed the facial sections of her make-up.

'By the way, get me a youngish actress for next week,' the eminent novelist said, stepping into her automobile; 'she has to have eloped with you, Paul; you are the chauffeur of the Duke of Durham – that's you, Jack – taking the family jewels. I dare say you saw the affair in the papers this morning.'

The men bowed in understanding silence.

As You Were!

A TALE OF THE NINETIES

DEDICATED TO JOSEPH CONRAD

Mine host of the 'Angler's Rest' caught the warning in the eye of his visitor. Being a sensible man, he knew that an elderly aristocrat with a hawk nose and a square jaw was not to be trifled with, especially when, as in the present case, accoutred in the full panoply of an Archdeacon.

'Please do not forget for a moment,' ordered the Senior severely, 'that I am the vicar of the adjoining parish.'

The words caught the ear of a loudly-dressed youth, redolent of horse and dog, who entered the taproom at that moment with a lounging swagger, flung himself on to the settee in the bow window, and called for old ale.

'Certainly not, Dr Bompas,' replied the inn-keeper respectfully, as he hastened to serve the newcomer with a tankard of the foaming amber.

'It is an act of ordinary courtesy,' pursued the Archdeacon, as if no interruption had occurred, 'that has dictated my visit. It appeared to me not improbable that a member of my own cloth might welcome an introduction to the clerical society of the vicinity; and hearing, in the course of my matutinal ramble, that one of your guests was in Holy Orders, I determined to extend my peregrinations to this hostelry.'

The rubicund landlord passed his visitors' book across the bar.

'I can't read the gentleman's writing,' he explained; 'I never had any call to ask his name.'

The calligraphy of the person in question presented no difficulty to the archidiaconal eye. He read the entry aloud with a throaty relish. 'Rev. Newman Justin Daly, Seamen's Home, The Causeway, Wapping.'

He wiped his spectacles, and remarked amiably that in his spare moments it amused him to play with the fancy that he might have made an excellent detective.

'It affords much relaxation to my brain,' he observed, 'to pass an occasional hour in solving the puzzles and rebuses, or even the Chess and Draughts problems, which occupy the appropriate columns in some of our higher-class periodicals. I have frequently thought that much may be learnt of a man by so simple a method as considering the import of his name. In the present instance, Mr Ladd,' he continued, 'it is clear that your guest is of Irish family. We may further deduce an hereditary interest in sacred matters, since not the individual but his parents are responsible for his baptismal appellations. From the name Justin it is clear that his family was not ignorant of hagiology. It might even be plausible to hazard the suggestion that the name affords a clue to the day of his nativity. Still more remarkable indications occur to the mind in connection with the name Newman. It is at least probable that the great controversies which agitated the Anglican church in Victorian times are responsible for the choice of the sublime, if mistaken, protagonist of the revival of Romanism in England as the first name of my colleague. So much,' concluded the Archdeacon, with an amiably childlike smile, 'the ingenious mind may discover from so apparently insignificant a datum as an entry in the register of a Riparian Inn.'

The Herculean occupant of the settee lowered the sporting paper behind which he had entrenched himself, and interrupted in a booming bass which might have been magnificent if it had not been for its hoarse and surly intonation.

'Ah, Sir Garnet,' he growled; 'but maybe that isn't his name, and then where are you?'

The Archdeacon turned almost fiercely, hesitating for a moment whether to ignore the insolence of his critic or to crush him. He decided on the latter course.

'Do you presume to suggest,' he rasped out with acerbity, 'that a consecrated priest would condescend to an alias?'

The young man emptied his tankard and rapped on the table for more before replying.

'Perhaps he isn't a priest,' came the slow malignant words.

The Archdeacon was undaunted. He countered with satirical lightness.

'Do you consider it decent, sir, to put forward the hypothesis that, in this age of education and progress, so blasphemous a masquerade would be adopted by anyone calling himself a man?'

This retort, stinging as it was, merely drove his antagonist to a third line of defence.

'Perhaps he isn't a man,' grunted the cantankerous youth; 'great blue eyes like plates and a mop of curly hair and no more beard than a baby, and he talks as if he were afraid someone might hear him. Do you call that a man?'

The old clergyman sprang instantly to the defence of his colleague. There was biting acid in the tone with which he replied.

'You will excuse me if I point out that there are different standards and ideals of manhood.'

It was part of the business of the worthy landlord of the Angler's Rest, especially on Saturday evenings, to play the part of peacemaker. There were moments when alcohol inflamed local antipathies to the point of expression, or the jealousies of rival Waltonians caused them to forget the obligations of Piscatorial Freemasonry. He hastened to intervene.

'The young man is certainly a rum 'un. I can't say myself as how I exactly cotton to him. If a man isn't a sportsman, bless me if I know how to take him. And what could have put it into the head of this here Rev. Daly to stay down here is more'n I know. He don't fish – As for that, Mr Powell, no more do you. He don't go out of the house, not scarce once in a week. His lamp's going all night pretty well, to judge by the oil he burns.'

'The midnight oil, the midnight oil,' purred the Archdeacon in a mellow murmur.

'All he does,' continued mine host, 'is reading. His room's full of books, Latin and Greek, I dare say; I looked at 'em, couldn't make head or tail of the business. It's a queer sort of game, the way I see it.'

'French novels, more likely,' muttered Powell, half under his breath.

The Archdeacon indulged in a smile gently patronising. 'How old would you say he is?'

Mine host scratched his head. 'A bit of a boy,' was his verdict. 'Two and twenty mostlike.'

'Very good, very good,' remarked Dr Bompas. 'The case is perfectly clear and presents no feature in the slightest degree unusual. It is obvious that Mr Daly has come down here for a period of quiet study and repose. He is probably engaged in preparing himself for some examination, or in composing a thesis.'

The figure on the settee refused to be mollified. He discarded his newspaper entirely, called for a further supply of old ale, and took up the cudgels once more.

'Likely enough,' he argued, 'on what you know. It's what you don't know that upsets favourites. My room is next to your studious curate's, and what he does after dark – well, I'm not going to guess; but whatever it is, I know I lose my sleep.'

'He has possibly formed the habit of reading aloud to himself,' suggested the Archdeacon. 'Such was my own case when absorbed in my studies.'

During this conversation Doctor Bompas had been attentively observing his opponent, whose appearance puzzled him not a little. For his age, enough of the hobbledyhoy remained to make it certain that he was not yet twenty-one. His dress and manners denoted the stable; and yet there was something in his carriage which the observer instinctively recognised as not being that of a servant; perhaps he might be the son of a rich bookmaker, employed by his father to tout for the latest news in haunts frequented by trainers and jockeys.

Yet what could a boy of this type be doing down here? He had noticed his name in the register – Hopgood Powell, 1, Wellcome Crescent, Upper Holloway – and he had apparently arrived at about the same time as that very different specimen of mankind, the mild young curate. At the Angler's Rest, there was literally nothing to do but to fish. There were no hounds for many miles, practically no society, nothing to shoot, scenery of the tamest – it was the most forgotten corner of England; with only one merit, the excellence of the fishing. As to the quality of the young man's mind, the Archdeacon could only diagnose dull obstinacy, mottled with patches of surly irritability. And yet he could not help being impressed by the ingenuity with which Powell had found positions, however untenable, to rebut his own common-sense speculations. He decided to draw the badger.

'Well, Mr Powell,' he said, with a pleasant smile, 'I'm sorry indeed that you suffer from insomnia even in so ideal a haunt of repose as this inn. I imagine, if you will pardon the curiosity and presumption of an old man, that you came here yourself with the very object of finding peace and forgetfulness. Terrible, terrible: insomnia! I have been at times myself a sufferer!'

Powell heaved a Gargantuan sigh.

'Indeed,' he said heavily, 'mine is a hideous story. You are not far from the truth. Yet that truth is worse than the most gloomy forebodings could imagine. You see me, young, robust beyond the average; my worldy circumstances are easy, my heart is unscarred by love, my mind unburdened by thought of any description; I may boast humbly that my conscience is as clear as cherry brandy, and being, like yourself, an Anglican, my soul feels as safe as the most famous masterpiece of Griffiths. What then can ail me? I rely frankly on the intellectual powers of which you have recently given so signal an example, to divine what doom has driven me to so desperate a deed as taking up my residence in this infernal inn.'

It appeared as if the Archdeacon hardly caught the sense of these remarks, he was so overcome with amazement at the sudden change in the character of Powell's delivery. But before he could reply, the situation was altered by the appearance of a newcomer who roared a hearty greeting from the doorway. The three men saw a burly bronzed athlete who might have been within two years of forty either way. He was dressed in riding breeches and top boots, a cheque coat, a scarlet waistcoat and a hunting smock. He swung a heavy crop as he strode. Dr Bompas went quickly to meet him.

'Why, this is indeed a pleasure,' he chirped. 'I need not ask how is my dear old friend, Squire Randall?' He put out his hand with peculiar vigour; his keen eyes darted a look of penetrating power as if to warn their object against some action which might disconcert certain designs which the two men had in common. Indeed, there seemed to be a momentary hesitation, covered by the exaggeration of the grasp; but it passed like the flurry of a startled pheasant.

'Good gad!' thundered the Squire, 'you're looking in good shape yourself. Well, Mr Ladd, can you spare a drop of the old ale for a thirsty man?'

An acute observer might have remarked a shade of embarrassed surprise in the manner of the landlord, as he grasped the Squire's extended hand before proceeding to serve him.

'Just rode over from the Hall,' cried Randall; 'couldn't pass the old place without taking a drop for the good of the house. Eh, could I now?'

The Archdeacon acquiesced, and remarked slyly that he thought he might break his rule for once, that some of the same would do him no harm.

It seemed that Powell was annoyed by this interruption to his conversation. He joined the others at the bar.

'Three I have had,' he groaned; 'I feel no better. However, I'll try what a fourth can do.'

Bompas thought it better to introduce Powell to the Squire, and did so.

'We were talking,' he went on, after the men had shaken hands and glared at each other the armed neutrality peculiar to new acquaintances in England. 'I really came here to look up a young colleague of mine, and Mr Powell and I were discussing the question as to what he was like. I fear our young friend is a sad sceptic. He threw doubts on all my theories.' He gave a little laugh as he added, 'He even suggested that Newman Daly, so far from being a priest, was not even a man.'

'Daly!' cried Randall, slapping his thigh; 'that settles the business. Rum; very rum, Mr Powell. I'm sure you'll forgive me for saying that even the youngest of us may sometimes drop bricks. By all that's wonderful, Newman Daly! – rum, very rum! Damn queer – beg pardon, Bompas – how things happen. I was dining with Blackett and his wife last night – Blackett's our local Galen – we played bridge till all hours. I sculled back by moonlight and, bless my soul, what should I see on Wareham Reach but a punt with two men! The face of one shone bright in the moonlight. I knew it – and yet I didn't! You know what I mean? But the minute you said Daly, why of course! He doesn't know me, but I know him. He rowed six for Oxford two years ago; no, three years. So you see he's a man, Mr Powell!'

Refutation of an idle theory could hardly account for the look of consternation with which Powell received this remark, and there seemed no explanation whatever for the almost savage glance of reproof which the Archdeacon darted at the speaker. He hastened to turn the conversation. But before he could speak, the young man burst out:

'I don't understand. Some mistake. Daly doesn't know a soul here. Him row six for Oxford? – rats! That kid? He isn't eight stone four! And what would he be doing in a punt in the middle of the night?'

Bompas gave a deprecatory cough. 'Mr Powell,' he said, very suavely, 'was telling his troubles when you came in. He asked me to formulate a theory as to their nature, but in view of the data he supplied, I frankly confess myself at a loss.'

Powell accepted the challenge. 'It may seem comic rather than tragic to men like you, who have faced life and conquered,' he began with a certain dignity. 'You have no doubt often thought how dull and imbecile are the sorrows of the Werthers, Hamlets and other young men who take themselves and their woes seriously.'

The landlord stared, uncomprehending; the two other men nodded and sighed, as if to say that they too had had their share of sentimental suffering.

'The world,' continued the youth, 'is like a backwater full of drainage, covered with slime, choked with sedge; no fish, hardly so much as a water-rat.'

Dr Bompas murmured something about Schopenhauer, and Randall observed that he always felt that way after backing a loser, but that Blackett insisted on putting part of the blame on the liver.

'May I ask,' interrupted Bompas in the sympathetic tone which he usually reserved for widows or mothers of unmanageable offspring, 'the particular application of this affliction?'

'I could bear up against personal griefs,' replied Powell in a melancholy monotone; 'I almost wish I had one – a bullet to bite on, as you might say. But worse luck! The whole world seems such a rotten show! Here, look at this! This is the sort of thing!'

He lumbered over to the settee and returned with the newspaper. His thick forefinger found a column headed 'Cried in the Cri,' from a contributor known as Tom Thumb. The second paragraph ran thus: he read it in a voice of toneless despair, though it was obviously intended to sparkle with the sprightliest persiflage.

> The younger bloods are musing over a problem in theology which might have made Thomas Aquinas wriggle on his chair. If God helps those who help themselves, will he or won't he help the Duke of Durham? We all love Dolly, and we miss him quite a lot. We also mourn for him; and when we are through mourning, we wonder where he is, and why? And did he fall or was he pushed? He certainly helped himself in one sense, and yet we fear that someone helped to help him. Alas, poor Dolly! Take him for all in all, we shall not look upon his like again!
>
> By the way, as the sub-editorial hangman snarls over my shoulder, this column may be read by somebody in Tasmania who will fail to catch the drift of these remarks, and forget to renew his subscription. I beg to inform him, with apologies, that Dolly Durham is our most darling duke; that he is a ward in Chancery, a legal infant who is liable to be sent to penal servitude for life if he should wink without the consent of the Lord Chancellor. Judge then of our anxiety at his elopement with the fairest and most fascinating flapper of frivolous France, Claire St Lo, who danced her way into diamond dog-collar circles last year, and has broken her engagement at the Alcazar as if it were a mere man's heart, in order to commit matrimony with the aforesaid scion of strawberry leaves. The sleuths of Scotland Yard are baying on the trail, which has already led them to Algiers; the Sahara Desert has been divided into sections which are being systematically patrolled by æroplanes. It can only be a matter of days before Dolly is brought back in chains and sent to build breakwaters for his contempt of Court; while his companion will, no doubt, be turned over to French justice to expiate her kidnapping in the climate of Cayenne.

'The Duke is a dear friend of yours, no doubt,' said the Archdeacon sympathetically.

'Never met him in my life, and don't expect to!'

Squire Randall gave a chuckle. 'Aha, you had your eye on the lady, eh?'

'No,' said Powell, 'I can't say that I know the lady. I wish the Duke joy of her.'

The Archdeacon saw light. 'There is a sympathy of youth for youth,' he suggested pompously; 'you feel their sorrows as if they were your own. A very noble trait.'

'There's something in what you say,' returned Powell; 'and yet there isn't everything in what you say. What gets me is the rottenness of the whole business. Why can't chaps leave a chap alone? Here's everyone, from the Lord Chancellor and the police to this damned penny-a-liner and his Tasmanian toad-in-the-hole, chivying this silly Duke, instead of frying their own fish – to say nothing of Claire Whatever-her-name-is getting her claws in his fur. But he's the luckiest of the lot. I've heard enough about Dolly Durham to risk a bob that he can take care of himself. He rowed four three years for Oxford, and there isn't a better heavy, bar pugs, in England. He could dodge the devil himself, as any Oxford man will tell you. He'll clear the hurdles. And he's got the finest girl that walks – clever and pretty and straight as a die. He's in luck, all right. My sympathy goes to her for being tied up to such a walloping fish, having to waste herself on stupid society and all that. Oh, it's rotten, rotten! It's a rank, rotten show! Let's forget it. Another of the same, Mr Ladd!'

The Squire and the parson exchanged bewildered glances. Powell's explanation of his anxieties made them less intelligible than ever, but it was calculated to excite their curiosity to the highest point. The Squire insisted.

'Excuse me, sir; I must seem very stupid to you, but I really can't see where the shoe pinches. This Dolly, now —'

Powell cut him short with an angry gesture. 'I said, let's forget it!' he cried; 'it's not to the point. I only took it by chance – one case in millions and billions, and all simply rotten. It's a rotten world,' he went on, raising his voice, 'a rank, rotten, ridiculous world!'

He stopped abruptly, and stuck his face into that of the outraged Archdeacon. 'Mine,' he said with grim intensity, 'is a hideous story.'

His hearers began to wonder whether Powell was not one of those lunatics whose mild melancholia, finding no focus, expresses itself in vague unreasoning pessimism without even being able to formulate a fanciful grievance.

But the current of their thoughts was diverted. The door opened stealthily; with a gliding motion, without audible footfall, they were joined by the slight clerical figure of the mysterious curate. He addressed the Archdeacon with a charming modesty, free from embarrassment or timidity on the one hand, and from self-assertion on the other.

As he advanced, Powell withdrew to the window, abruptly yet adroitly; the two elder men, facing the newcomer, could not perceive the extravagant vehemence of the gesture which accompanied the retreat. The young clergyman could not have failed to notice this strange conduct; but whether he interpreted it as a threat, or a defiance, he did not allow himself to be betrayed into showing the slightest surprise.

'Permit me to introduce myself,' said he in low clear tones whose musical modulation had no touch of affectation or artificiality. 'I am Mr Daly, of the Seamen's Home at Wapping. I happened to see you pass my window, and resolved to make myself known to you as soon as I had completed my hour of Patristic study.'

With the same impenetrable cunning of manner that had marked his retirement, the horsey youth swooped back to the bar, and stood at the curate's elbow. A sinister sneer smouldered in his sidelong eyes.

'I am indeed glad to meet you,' returned the other graciously. 'I am Archdeacon Bompas, the Vicar of the adjoining parish. The cause of my visit was indeed that I heard of your presence among us. I may say that you have been the subject of our conversation.'

Before Daly could reply, Powell turned upon him with a sort of malignant intensity.

'I may as well tell you,' he said with a snarl, 'I have told these gentlemen that I think you are an imposter.'

The curate coloured and shrank back. He tried to speak; words seemed to fail him; Bompas instantly came to the rescue.

'You mustn't mind what Mr Powell says,' he cried in tones of incisive authority. 'The conversation has made it clear to us that Mr Powell has some very peculiar and original ideas. Very interesting, very interesting, indeed, I freely admit; though I will not pretend that I am perfectly clear in my mind as to their exact purport in all cases.'

'I twig,' said Powell. 'I'm not as dippy as all that. I saw you thought I was a bit balmy long ago, and so I may be – so may every blooming one of us. What's more, I believe we all are! That's my grouse, with six to the Ace-King-Queen. But I know a hawk from a hand-saw. Look here! Just for the fun of the thing, and no hard feelings – here's my quid, Squire Randall —'

He clapped a sovereign on the bar. 'Put yours to that. Let the Archdeacon here ask Mr Daly a few straight questions, and if he's not clean bowled in the first over, you take the pot.'

After a moment's hesitation on the part of the elder men, the curate decided them to humour their eccentric acquaintance.

'I beg of you,' he said firmly, 'to feel no false delicacy about hurting my feelings. I demand as a right to vindicate myself after so open a challenge.'

Randall gave a queer laugh, as if amused by something incomprehensible to the others. He slapped his stake on the bar and shook Powell's hand, with the words: 'It's a bet!'

Dr Bompas seemed far from comfortable. He eased his neck from his collar with a fidgety forefinger, but seemed unable to commence his cross-examination, except by repeatedly clearing his throat.

'Well, sir?' smiled Daly, who had completely recovered his self-possession.

Bompas collected his faculties, and asked where and when Daly had received Orders.

The answers came as glibly as the questions were laboured. Dr Bompas professed himself satisfied. But Powell protested at the perfunctory character of the inquiry. He pointed out that any imposter could invent names and dates in the absence of books of reference.

'Try him on points of doctrine,' he insisted. 'He probably doesn't know the Thirty-nine Articles from the butt-end of a broomstick.'

'Very good, very good,' acquiesced the Archdeacon. 'The suggestion is timely – very much to the point. Perhaps, Mr Daly, you will give us your views on this matter of the Thirty-nine Articles?'

'With humble deference,' said Daly, 'I believe them to be essential; very essential.'

Dr Bompas evinced the liveliest satisfaction at these words, but Powell made the sour comment that they scarcely bore witness to any profundity of knowledge of the subjects involved.

'It's up to you,' he added, with insolent emphasis, 'to give me a run for my money, when I'm betting against your friend.'

The old clergyman could not resent the remark, rude as it was, and Randall himself banged his fist on the bar.

'Fair enough!' he shouted. 'Plough the beggar, if you can!'

The Archdeacon seemed to be racking his brains. There was a moment of silence.

'I must ask you,' he said at last, in severe accents, 'to quote your authorities for maintaining the attitude, the wholly admirable attitude, which you have expressed.'

The curate raised his hands, and spread his slim white elegant fingers to tick off his points as he phrased them.

'In this company and place,' he began, 'I prefer to take for granted names so sacred as those of St Peter, St Paul and St John?'

'Yes, yes; by all means,' concurred Bompas.

'In that case, I will begin with Slawkenbergius.' He watched the face of his questioner with the keen alertness of a skilled fencer. What he read in it seemed to satisfy him.

'Next, and perhaps greater,' he continued, 'we may mention Dean Schwenck Gilbert. I refer to the famous passage in his letter to Canon Lehár in which he refutes Rabbi Cohen.'

Bompas nodded appreciatively.

'Third, Archbishop Cranmer. After him, Ridley and Latimer's tract, *The Candle*; Luther's *Lustige Witwe*; Pascal's incomparable *Viens, Poupoule*. Need I enumerate the lesser lights?'

The young man's display of learning appeared to overwhelm the Archdeacon, who grew more purple and more ill at ease every moment. He replied by an apoplectic nod.

'In my turn,' pursued Daly, as if roused to the point of inviting a controversy, 'may I ask you to throw the light of your ecclesiastical experience on a question which has recently perplexed me?'

The burly Squire concealed his uncontrollable delight at the turn affairs were taking in the huge pewter tankard which Ladd had just replenished. Dr Bompas seemed to have been struck speechless.

'What precise meaning,' went on the inexorable Daly, 'do you attach to that remarkable phrase of the twenty-sixth Article, "The validity of canonical exegesis is neither independent of, incompatible with, nor insusceptible at, the coherent consubstantiality of ecclesiastical custom"?'

The Archdeacon smiled a pitying smile. 'Ah me, my dear young friend,' he answered unctuously; 'there speaks the voice of youth. How well I recognise my own early enthusiasms! Surely you know that this sublime passage which troubles you has been the source of equal perplexity to the very greatest minds in the Anglican Church? How can you expect me to elucidate a difficulty which has daunted men as superior to myself as Sir Isaac Newton to a Chinese coolie?'

At this answer the curate turned, with a glance of mild triumph, upon his accuser.

Powell pushed grudgingly the two sovereigns over to Randall.

'Oh, well; you seem to be the real thing,' he muttered. 'But for all that, there's lots of things about you that look to me just a bit off. What does a pillar of learning, and the church, like you want in a punt when everybody's in bed except the prowling poacher and the busy burglar?'

'I take it,' answered the curate with mild reproof, 'that you have not been privileged to move, to any great extent, in what I may term University circles? You may not be aware that night and solitude, amid scenes breathing the peace of Nature, are favourable conditions for the pious exercises of meditation.'

'Now I've got you,' retorted Powell; 'whatever else you are, you're a liar. You talk about solitude – how does the other man in the punt fit in with that?'

At this fierce onslaught, Daly seemed to shrink into himself. It was as if a pit had opened unawares beneath him.

But while the two younger men had been confronting each other, the Archdeacon had taken Randall quietly by the sleeve, and whispered earnestly in his ear. The Squire saved Daly by walking up to Powell with the demeanour of a provoked pugilist. He made hardly any pretence of politeness, saying point-blank:

'It's all very well for you, Mr Powell, to pick holes in the conduct of inoffensive strangers, but I want you to know, without any beating about the bush, that you need to be explained yourself.'

'Oh, do I?' growled the young man. 'All right, what is it? Cough it up!'

Dr Bompas intervened. 'We don't wish to create any ill feelings,' he began in conciliatory tones, 'but, as you have yourself admitted, you are rather a curious character, with your somewhat aimless suspicions (if you will pardon my saying so), and your incomprehensible dissatisfaction with the Universe, to say nothing of the incongruity of these psychological points with your physical appearance. But, beside all that, your presence in this district is undeniably mysterious. In default of an intelligible motive, I am bound to say that to the censorious it may seem calculated to arouse suspicion.'

The young man gave a dreary laugh. 'Aren't we all in the same boat?' he growled. 'What are we any of us doing here, or anywhere? Aren't we all incongruous? Isn't all life mysterious and meaningless? Tell me the motive of anything in creation. You know the church can't do it, philosophy can't do it, science can't; why bother with one penny puzzle when everything's a rotten riddle?'

'You exhibit remarkable ingenuity in evading our enquiries,' returned Bompas. 'Excuse me if I press them.'

'Anything to please,' replied the other. 'I am a human being, male, born twenty years, eleven months and nineteen days ago. My father was a sort of farmer with a taste for racing. Part of his life he took some interest in soldiers and all that. My mother never did much more than keep house and gossip. He was the eldest son, two brothers, one went soldiering, one went to sea. Three sisters, two of 'em married, one to some kind of preaching chap, t'other to a fellow in Canada, or one of those places; the youngest still to let. As for myself, I got the usual sort of schooling. I'm fond of anything in the open air. I drifted somehow up to London, and got married, like a young ass, to a fairish sort of kid – nothing to talk about, I dare say. She suits me well enough, and that's the main thing.'

Daly had listened to this speech with keen attention, as if to see whether he could spy an opening for revenge. The last item, apparently, suited him.

'Forgive me if I ask how it comes, in that case, that you are here without your wife?'

Almost in the same breath, the Squire burst out: 'You haven't told us how you earn your living!'

'My father left me a bit,' explained Powell, 'and I make a bit at cards and on the ponies. I rub along somehow. About my wife – that's what I'd like to know myself. If she isn't here, why isn't she here? Ah, you're right there – it would be a wise man that could tell me what she's doing now!'

'You don't seem to take it much to heart,' said Dr Bompas.

'You don't seem to be looking for her very hard,' Randall chimed in.

'You don't seem to have a proper sense of your responsibilities as a husband,' cried the curate sharply.

'Oh, she's all right,' drawled Powell, lifelessly. 'I don't worry one bit about her. I can find her when I want to. About my duty – that's all poppycock. When she complains, it's time enough for me to fuss!'

The Archdeacon pursed his lips with displeasure. 'You still avoid any direct answer as to the reason of your presence here.'

Powell gave a snort of impatience. 'Oh well, oh well,' he grumbled; 'if you must know, I'm here because I like the place. I know this part of England pretty well. One moment, now! Where do you live yourself, Squire?'

There was a momentary pause. Bompas flashed a commanding glance at his friend.

'Greenleigh Hall,' answered Randall, with obvious unwillingness.

'Arising out of that answer,' cried Powell quickly, 'what has happened to Sir Archibald Barker?'

The most superficial observer could hardly have failed to see how inconvenient a question had been put. The Squire darted a savage glance at his friend, who returned it with a subtle smile. The diplomatic landlord swept two glasses to the floor, and began an incoherent lamentation.

Randall took advantage of the confusion to go to the window, and exclaim that his horse had got loose. On this pretext he ran out of the room, leaving his friend to bear the brunt of this unexpected counterattack. For a full minute, his eyes met Powell's in a silent contest of will. Then the young man said in a low voice:

'May I have the pleasure of a few words in private?'

The other man assented with a certain suppressed eagerness, and followed Powell through the winding passages of the inn to the large bedsitting-room, overlooking a deep pool, where the young man was quartered. Its owner threw himself on a couch and motioned his visitor to the huge basket-chair. Neither of the men seemed willing to speak. The silence became oppressive. The soft noise of the eddying water began to get on their nerves.

'I'll see you,' said Powell, at last. 'It may be a busted flush, after all. I have to know – put down your cards.'

To this strange speech the Archdeacon seemed at a loss to find the proper reply. He attempted to gain time.

'I don't understand,' he said, half angrily.

The other yawned as if to imply that assumed obtuseness was a diplomatic mistake.

'I'm not the kind,' he said with a sort of haughty weariness, 'to give away something for nothing, and, as it happens, it's rather hard to avoid committing myself, even if I tell you what you very well know that I know about you.'

'Perfectly true,' flashed back Bompas, 'but you've done it, you see, in saying that. You may as well put it plain.'

'I'll risk it – it doesn't matter so much after all. I think I can guess the length of your foot within a very few inches. I don't mind saying this much then. Of all the archdeacons I know, you are not the most archidiaconal.'

The other man looked honestly puzzled.

'I did expect a man in your line,' pursued Powell, 'to jib at Dean Gilbert and Canon Lehár, even if you didn't include Slawkenbergius in your repertory. You should, though; it's pitiful that parsons don't model themselves upon Sterne.'

Dr Bompas permitted himself something between a blush and a wince.

'I know my limitations,' he apologised; 'but I could hardly have foreseen that I should have been called upon for quite such technicalities. That swine let me in,' he growled.

'I observed that your colleague had his own sense of humour,' smiled Powell appreciatively. 'However, to put it plainly, *cucullus non facit monachum*.'[1]

---

[1] [A cowl does not make a monk.]

'Another blind spot,' confessed Bompas, with the air of a convicted bluffer.

'Yes, a few Latin tags would help out, as Thane Cedric discovered in his visit to Front-de-Bœuf's castle. In English, the collar doesn't make the clergyman. You're no more a priest than I am a poet. My little book of verses merely proves it.'

'All right,' said the other, beginning to show irritation at the air of contemptuous superiority with which he was being treated. 'But if I'm not an Archdeacon, what am I?'

'That I don't know,' said Powell, 'and I certainly don't mean to guess. But I do want to know, and what's more I jolly well mean to know, what you're doing down here in this comic costume, and what you want with my reverend neighbour, the curate?'

'I've nothing to hide,' came the answer in very decided accents, after a pause, as if he had made up his mind with an effort; 'I'm doing my duty. I'm an officer of justice – I have the Lord Chancellor's warrant in my pocket. On information received, I came here with my colleague. We have been on a false trail. The people I'm after were pretty spry with their red herring. It came to our ears that two very curious cards were staying here. We thought it worth looking into.'

'Very interesting, I'm sure,' returned Powell nonchalantly, stretching himself and yawning. 'Would it be impertinent to enquire whether I may offer you my congratulations?'

The other man scratched his head. 'I can't say, I'm sure,' he admitted. 'You do look a bit like the party I want, and that fellow Daly might be the other. But what beats me is the way you talked. If you're my man, we know you're as clever as they make 'em. Then why did you start that hare about Daly being funny?'

'That might be explained on the principle of "The Purloined Letter"; but like so many other explanations, it would be totally wrong.'

'Why don't you put your own cards down?' asked the other; 'whoever you are, there's a lot about you that looks pretty rum.'

'There is,' admitted the youth. 'We thrashed out all that in the bar. But let's get to business. If I were what you think, what about it?'

'I should have to do my duty and ask Your Grace to accompany me to London.'

The young man jumped up from the bed as if he had had the surprise of his life. 'What!' he cried; 'you think I'm Durham! By Jove, that's really too rich. That's something to tell my grandchildren! You don't really think anything so absurd,' he continued more soberly; 'do tell me how ever you got the idea.'

The man in black seemed staggered. He bit his lip.

'Spit it out, Sherlock!' cried Powell.

'Well, you see,' said the other, 'we know His Grace likes his joke. When you were pulling my leg in the bar, you said some queer things. You told us a pack of lies; and yet, if you are His Grace, they were perfectly true. The late Duke *was* a kind of farmer – 80,000 acres was about his mark. He *did* have a fancy for horses – won the Derby twice; and he *was* interested in soldiers – First Life Guards, Colonel; and Secretary for War after that. The Duke's brothers, same game; and his sisters, one married a Bishop and the other a Colonial Lord-Lieutenant.'

'Dear me, that's exceedingly clever! But after all, it may be only coincidence; far stranger things have happened. You should read up the *Transactions* of the s.p.r. It must be one of the dangers of really brilliant detectives to rely too implicitly on their fascinating faculties.'

'You can't put me off like that,' came the obstinate answer. 'If you're not the Duke of Durham, who are you?'

'That's hardly your business, is it? I'm not the Duke; why prolong the agony?'

Before the elder man could reply, his opponent stopped him with an imperious gesture.

'But about your duty? Is that such a pillbox? I don't want to insult you, but couldn't you put the glass to your blind eye if the other eye saw something pretty? This duke of yours seems pretty clever – why not clever enough to make your employers believe that he fooled you? Professional pride is all very well in its way – but is it as good as, shall we say, a thousand in cash?'

The tempter's prospective victim paced the room in perplexity.

'That's plain talk. You've as good as admitted you're caught.'

'Not the least in the world. I'm only putting a case.'

'I don't see why it matters so much,' answered the old man. 'Another two weeks, you come of age. The worst that can happen to you is to get a rap on the knuckles for contempt of court.'

'Put with your customary acumen,' said the young giant. 'With me it's merely a matter of personal pride. I object to being caught as much as the oldest trout in the pool here. Besides, I'm on my honeymoon. It would bore me extremely to break my routine of daily dalliance and romantic rambles after dark. The one thing I loathe is lawyers.'

'Well,' said the other, shortly, 'if I did say "yes," what price Randall?'

'The same price,' drawled his antagonist coolly. 'Tell you what, I'll go and get him.'

The other man shook his head. 'That cock won't fight. I know him – he's a fanatic about duty. What's more, I wouldn't do it myself. It's not so much the principle of the thing, but if it ever came out – my career is worth more than a thousand pounds to me.'

'No harm in talking it over,' replied Durham. 'I'll go and get him. Give me ten minutes; if I can't convince you by then, all right, go ahead and arrest me.'

'It's a deal. I'll help you to find him.'

The young man smiled to himself at the simple-mindedness of this human bloodhound, who knew so little of the ways of the quarry he spent his life in stalking as to suppose that the Duke of Durham would condescend to the ignominious expedient of escape.

They found Randall chatting calmly with the demure young person with the big blue eyes, and the quartette returned to the pleasant riverside apartment. The Archdeacon broached the subject with almost indecent directness. The indignation of Randall was unbounded. When at last it found words, they gushed forth in a stuttering storm. The blonde figure in the curate's costume positively quailed at the vehemence of Randall's outraged integrity. The stipulated ten minutes were fully occupied by his unbridled eloquence. It came to an end only because of the limits of physical endurance. The horsey youth's face fell like a barometer before a hurricane, and his accomplice's blue eyes were dimmed despite all the efforts of resolution to repress emotion.

'Well, it can't be helped,' said the baffled tempter, rising to put an end to the scene. 'It's a fair cop, I believe is the correct expression. I'll come quiet. I suppose you don't want to clap the Darbies on me?'

Both men protested that they had not dared to dream of inflicting such an indignity.

'Will it be all right,' asked their victim, 'if we go up to town in my car?'

His captors consulted in whispers.

'Quite the proper thing,' said Bompas. 'We don't want any fuss; we want it to look quite natural and friendly.'

The little party adjourned to the bar, where the principal defendant insisted on a final round of drinks.

'I have persuaded my friends here,' he said to the landlord, 'to join me in a little spin. Expect us when you see us.'

The worthy host of the Angler's Rest effusively wished them a pleasant excursion. Five minutes later, they were on the road to London, laughing and joking as if, by common consent, they had forgotten the serious object of the journey. The Squire rallied his colleague with boyish ebullience as they approached the 'adjoining parish.'

'So these are our pastures,' said Randall, mockingly. 'What a pretty old church we have! Have you prepared your next Sunday's sermon, my dear Doctor?'

'Oh yes,' laughed back the other; 'my text is "The wicked flee when no man pursueth."'

'I didn't flee,' the victim of this gibe retorted from the wheel, 'and I could have got away clean if I had wanted to. I spotted you almost from the first. I don't want to be rude – I only say this to encourage you; but your disguises are awfully thin. You can't get the style – no amount of perfection in detail will make a man look what he isn't.'

'I confess the failure,' replied Bompas; 'but, after all, it served its turn. The proof is that we've got you. Besides, such acute observers of life as Your Grace are the rarest of mortals. Our disguises are quite good enough to deceive ninety-nine men out of every hundred.'

The hundredth man gave an incredulous gesture.

'Very good; I will prove it,' replied the other with a shade of irritation in his tone. 'Stop when we come to the vicarage.'

A delightful old house, in an admirably kept garden, stood just beyond the church. The owner of the car obediently came to a standstill opposite the porch. A moment later, a dignified manservant came down the pathway to the kerb.

'Lunch for five, James; and tell Parker to put this gentleman's car in the garage.'

The man addressed as James, whatever he may have felt, manifested no mark of surprise. He bowed and opened the door. In bewildered amusement, the two young people, arm in arm, followed their seniors towards the house. At the door stood smiling an elderly lady, who received the party as if its leader were in fact the Archdeacon, which he was.

'I know you can keep a secret, Ellen,' he said pleasantly, 'and this is a Privy Council one. Let me present Their Graces the Duke and Duchess of Durham.'

Mrs Bompas received her romantic guests with unaffected delight, and asked Sir Archibald Barker after the health of his family.

'Lunch will be ready in twenty minutes,' promised the purring hostess, after the first few commonplace compliments, and directed the butler to put the best spare room at the disposal of the now cheerful culprits.

The heavy-footed youth closed the door with exaggerated care. His eyes met those of his companion, and the room shook with innumerable laughter. The blue eyes were the first to clear away their mist. 'We must keep it up,' said their owner, setting his delicate jaw with extreme firmness. 'It would break their hearts – they're enjoying the time of their lives.'

'Keep it up? You bet! A lark like this will go straight to the pater's heart; I can run up to town tomorrow.'

'Yes, it's all right for you, Powell, the Stewards won't warn you off for a bit of harmless spoof; but it were better for this man that a millstone should be hanged about his neck and he were cast into the depths of the sea than that this escapade should come to the ears of my bishop.'

'Nothing for it but to trust your luck,' was Powell's gloomy consolation. 'By the way, Daly, did you think they were 'tecs any of the time?'

'I saw them in this very garden on my morning "grind" two days after I got here. Besides, I saw Augustus John's portrait of the Archdeacon in last year's Academy, and Barker actually gave me my Greek Verse prize, my last term at Malvern! What about you?'

The other laughed aloud. 'Old Bompas preached the 'Varsity sermon the term I was sent down, and Sir Archibald has one of the best stables in England. I've seen him fifty times at various meetings.'

Meanwhile, the elder men were washing their hands in a small room leading out of the archidiaconal library.

'The amusing part of it – the nailbrush after you! – is that I coached young Durham last "Long."A In fact, it was at Lady Conderton's Charity Sale that he met Claire St Lo – he was fatally struck at first sight. She didn't mind his club foot!'

'I knew her well,' returned Barker, 'a big, husky woman with venomous black slits for eyes. I'm sorry for young Durham – I met him at the Old Boys' dinner last year – he pulled a first-rate oar.'

Only a Dog

It was not even his own dog. He said it barked, and had the mange. Most dogs bark; and if it had a tenth of the diseases he had, it would have been kindness to kill it. But what business was it of his? It was her brother's dog; it was her mother's pet.

Anna had come up to my room in the hotel. I had explained the truth (God's truth, not man's) to the clerk, so there was no difficulty. Besides, you can get away with anything in America, if you have an English accent. She had her mother's letter in her hand when she came in. I had never heard of Jock before – Jock was the dog's name – I only knew there had been some trouble about a dog. Now the whole story came out. He – that's her husband, only he was never that, more than twice her age, and a permanent invalid – hates everything and everybody and himself into the bargain. A little like Count Genesi, without the nobility of the passion. A little like Guido Franceschini – and to tell you the truth, that's what I'm afraid of. Well, his hatred concentrated on this dog. He's a liar and a coward; he kept off enquiries for weeks, saying he had sent it away to be looked after, or given it away, or – oh! any lie that sounded plausible. And now the truth was out; he had confessed to Anna: he had had it murdered. So she had come straight round to me. Poor little Jock! If it did bark, what affair was that of his? A few days, and he would be going away, West perhaps – probably – I pray God – never to return.

Of course he is mad. I have suspected softening of the brain for some time. His brother's death last year shook him heavily. He hears his brother's voice calling him – that's insanity without doubt. And he bursts into violent rages or violent tears on no provocation.

He is an utterly vile old man. He has even tried to make Anna's sisters his mistresses. (And he threatens me with the Blue Laws!) However, this is the main point: he is mad. The neighbours are all ready to testify; if he makes one more step against us, we shall assume the offensive and send him to Matteawan or wherever it is. Then Anna will have no further scruple in divorcing him. Only her sense of duty has stood in the way so far. Her heart's so beautiful! She will suffer anything herself rather than give pain to her worst enemy. So there she is, tied to this monster, and I honour her so for her pure heart that I won't urge her to do otherwise. But I'm not bound in any such way myself: I'll free her somehow. (Oh God! God! I pray God for her freedom!) Yet I would not hurt him. I would only put an end to his unhappiness. For he is utterly wretched, as are all who hate. And when she met me, and loved me (that very first minute), and went back to his house, he saw it in her face that she was happy, and for that he hated her the more. What I am so afraid of is that his madness may break out into violence, that he may murder her as he murdered the poor little dog.

I don't know which of us began it. I was sitting in the big armchair; Anna was standing against the wall with her hands behind her, resting against them, and swaying on their lovely elasticity. She told me all the story so simply and so sadly. Yes, I think I began it, because she came over when she saw me fighting with the tears, and knelt beside me, and took me in her arms, and petted me, and hushed me – but it was no good. We broke down, both of us; we cried for quite ten minutes in each other's arms. I was so ashamed of myself; it was so silly to cry over a dog I didn't even know. But it was so cruel and so senseless that it seemed a very parable of the universe itself. There was *Weltschmerz*[1] in those tears, be sure.

Then it was time for me to play the man, to console her – as God gave me grace and power to do. *Amor vincit omnia.*[2] But I am still moved by the crime; months later, as it is, I cannot think of it without something pulling at my heart. If there be a soul of good in all things evil, it may here be this, that Anna knew then without possibility of doubt how utterly tender I am of heart, and childlike. I am not really ashamed that I cried; I would be ashamed if I had not. For another thing, the incident may help to steel her when the crisis comes.

For he is coming East in a week or so, and her sister and I have agreed to strike home, if there's half a chance of it. Even Jock, who was only a dog, and barked, and had the mange, may find avengers.

But what strange creatures women are! Anna's mother had written a letter full of tears, so simple, so pathetic: 'Where is my little dog? I want my little dog.' All the while it was lying dead. Anna wrote back and told what the monster had at last confessed – and the next time

---

[1] [World-sadness.]
[2] [Love conquers all.]

her mother wrote, it was to minimise the tragedy; after all, Jock was 'only a dog.'

My own heart's of different stuff; I'll not forget Jock – whom I never knew – so long as I live; and if God put not forth a hand to avenge him, I will. Only a dog!

The Virgin

'And this,' said the Curator, 'is the ordinary reversible bomb. Shake it, or strike it, or even burn it – it is perfectly harmless; but turn it bottom up long enough for the acid in this tube to soak through, and in a few moments there will be a devastating explosion.'

He paused, to watch the effect of words so startling.

The worn-out harridan who was chaperoning the girls hardly heard him. She was in mental torture; lovers were scarce; and in physical torture, for the breast – the breast that a thousand men had kissed beneath the Rossetti mane that she loved to throw over it – was swollen with some foul disease. She was fighting against the pain, and the fear that it might be cancer.

The eldest of the three girls was as uninterested. Hot from a stolen hour of passion with her aunt's chauffeur, she sniffed the air like a horse neighing before battle. A hint of petrol would have excited her as patchouli excites some debauchees.

The second girl too; her natural British stolidity dulled all life for her. She looked at the bomb with less interest than a cow would have done. A cow would at least have tested if the strange object was edible.

The youngest of the three, indeed, acted much like this. She attended to the curator's words with avidity; but, deciding that they did not affect her, turned away with open boredom, even irritation.

She was a tightly-knitted child: a touch of blood-colour in her black tresses, heavy and curled. Her bust and hips were firm, though too large for perfect beauty; and on her face sat purity. Purity alarmed and vigilant, like the mind of a man who, exploring some new coast, should find the traces of something possibly terrible because utterly unknown.

Viola Walker was just turned twenty-four. She had been thrown among actresses, was indeed fresh from a short but brilliantly successful season on the concert boards, she had read the works of Elinor Glyn and Mrs Humphrey Ward and Victoria Cross. But her knowledge was wholly intellectual; she had a don's attitude to life; there was not one drop of dew on the dry dust of her mind. But the difference between her and a don was that she understood her limitation, and hated it. Only the knowledge of certain ruin held her back from the one course which seemed to offer her a Key to the Closed Palace of the King.

The Curator would have been huffed by this feminine inattention if his fifth listener had not happened to be the ideal. Gregory Philpotts could and did talk by the hour on every subject under the sun; and the sole source of his information was the sixpenny reprint of the Rationalistic Press. His mind was active and logical, but totally uneducated and incapable of concentration. Sensible of his own inferiority, he was vain and a braggart. The most pompous fool in Europe – and possibly its most well-meaning man.

So he explained to the Curator how the Law of Evolution explained bombs, and how the system of education in this country was hopelessly unscientific, and how the death of Queen Victoria was the knell of art, and —

The harridan struck in, and swept the party away. She was nearly fainting with the gnawing agony of her breast, the blood and ooze from which she could feel trickling to her knees. She fancied that a third lump was forming. By some trick of conscience she thought of her three husbands, the first who had divorced her, the second whom she had killed in the first three months of marriage, and the third who had blown out his brains when he awoke from his delirium and found what manner of woman he had wedded.

She had read, too, much about cancer and its 'secondary deposits.' What internal horrors – thought she – would fulfil the symbol of all the girls that I have ruined and infected? She had this great gift, necessary to the perfect hypocrite, that to herself she never lied.

So, ashen under her ill-smeared rouge and powder, she staggered out of the Museum.

Gregory Philpotts at the tail of the party 'went bellowing on to the last.'

2

If it was the mission of Gregers Werle to be the thirteenth at table, it was assuredly that of Gregory Philpotts to be the third in bed.

It was hardly to be expected that he would prove the most congenial of companions to Edward Innes, whose mission was unquestionably to be first. But the brazen-faced fellow, with his tin-pan voice, had thrust himself on the latter's hospitality. When Innes had to go to Oxford for a week to lecture, he left Gregory the key of his flat.

'I hope you don't mind, dear old chap,' said Gregory, 'but I want to bring a lady for a day or two.'

'Don't let her steal my ivories,' was Innes' contemptuous retort.

He was, consequently, not surprised when, running up to London for an afternoon, he found a charming girl seated on the arm of his ancestral chair, bending over the smiling Gregory. Whether she was kissing him or no is a question not here to be determined. He thought so himself; but a week later was prepared to believe it an illustration of the fact that one is liable to see what one expects to see – so startlingly used in fiction by Mr Zangwill in *The Big Bow Mystery*.

He was introduced, found her a delightful companion, witty and gay, and was altogether ravished with her singing. A week later, he found that he could not forget her, and asked her to come and sing to him one afternoon.

She replied from Berlin, where she was (according to Gregory's statement) staying with him; her card promised a call for the next week.

She called, and Innes, though thinking her a mere drab, kissed her carelessly and asked her to dinner.

Gregory's contempt of her had been so open that Innes never troubled to ask his permission, and was casual enough about asking hers. He would ask her to dinner, he thought, forget himself for an hour, and be done with the girl. He did not care for her; but politeness demanded the male tribute to her charms.

So it came to pass that Underham's cosy cupboard of a restaurant grew sparkling and pink to them with oysters and Burgundy. A curious Burgundy it is; Innes called it 'Petard' – never dreaming that he (poor engineer!) would one day be hoist with it!

They went back to his flat, laughing rather wildly, with just enough protest from the girl to save her face. Alas! it was not her face that was in danger!

Innes had fitted up a large conservatory as an Oriental Divan. He threw her unceremoniously among the rugs and cushions and began to strip her. This time she did protest, vigorously enough; but he, perfectly confident in his knowledge of her real character – judged by her face, flushed and eager, and by Gregory's detailed story – went on with the quiet determination of a doctor performing some necessary service for a lunatic.

The protests continued, and he enjoyed the joke immensely; but when, an hour after, just as he wearied of the sport, they changed to lamentations, he lost his temper and told the truth. He hinted, in fact, that, historically and anatomically considered, her story was a little thin. But she had such plausible explanations for everything that he began not only to admire her cleverness, but to suspect a conspiracy.

But nothing would have shaken his disbelief, founded as it was on both *à priori* and *à posteriori* data, unless, seeking in his mind 'What is the real, the unmistakable test of virginity?' he remembered the Dictum of Dorothy.

Dorothy wears with distinction – practically unchallenged – the Lady Leg-Puller's Association World's Championship Garter. And this had been her deliberate definition: 'A virgin always does the wrong thing at the right time.' Now this applied to Viola, who was tearfully disturbing his chastened sadness – and asking him the silliest questions.

If she were lying, he was bound to admit, she was lying so wonderfully well that – there was a baffling hypothesis. Was she simply there to make a fool of him? He decided that it was so, and treated her as a brilliant swordsman might treat a well-matched foe, with a subcurrent of annoyance. For he was an overworked man, not in the mood for fencing. He had wanted a quiet, animal evening: and here was tragedy or melodrama so well imitated that the comedy was acute.

Ultimately, he got rid of her rudely enough and went to bed in a temper.

3

The days passed by, and their friendship did not pass, though they never renewed intimacy.

She communicated her kindness to him; she even extorted his respect.

There could only be one end to such an imbroglio: Innes was obliged to explain his own abominable conduct by quoting his authority. Luckily he had a letter to show.

'Dear Innes' (it ran) 'Thank you for not hinting to Miss Walker that she had stayed with me at Sonnenschein's – she would have been so distressed if she thought I had told you' – and so on.

Miss Walker was naturally furious, and answered Philpotts – who besought interviews – in the most threatening terms. These letters – with comments – were sent on by Gregory to the hapless Innes, accusing him of treachery.

As a final blow, he rang up Innes on the telephone, and confessed that his whole story was a lie, the folly of an empty braggart mixed with the spite of a foiled seducer. And if there was another reason for it, it was the desire to pull his host's leg by tempting him to try his skill on a fortress that he knew to be impregnable!

Was all this a Pelion leg-pull on the Ossa leg-pull of the lady? As Olympus, at the bottom of the pile, he felt asphyxia approaching. Poor fool! Had he guessed how improbability would ally itself to improbability, things monstrous, things incredible, things certain, he would have swallowed Jonah's whale and the notion, and gone into a monastery as the only chance to save his reason.

Viola's anatomical explanations had dealt in part with chills and gastritis and false diagnosis. The pains continuing, he sent her to a doctor, a friend of his own. The doctor said 'Specialist'; and the Specialist said: we shall know the sex of it in another semester.

Thirty-seven days after the first date possible to the theory of the Anti-Leg Pull League! And Innes' divorced wife, since dead of alcoholism and specific disease, had been a doubtful case three months before the birth of her child!

He began to wonder whether he had been wise in allowing his medical friend to practise urethral dilatation on his vile body. The medical friend had predicted remarkable results – but nothing like this!

Innes didn't like it; quite frankly, he didn't like it. He decided to run over to Paris where people are sane about sex, and consult Dorothy the Pythoness infallible.

Every fact fitted two hypotheses; one, the truth and purity of Viola Walker; two, the deliberate villainy of the harlot and her ponce Gregory. Was the scheme blackmail – or what? It seemed aimless. One does not invoke Jupiter when Ganymede will serve, unless –

Oh, could it be that they wished to wrest the Laurels of the Amateur World's Championship under the auspices of the Cosmopolitan Leg Puller's Association from him?

His forehead felt already bare.

He was keen on the girl, too. She might develop genius from talent. A second experiment might show him the truth of the matter. When she telephoned him next, he said: 'I don't want to hear anything. Stick a nighty in a bag, and we'll make a night of it in Folkestone: meet me at two o'clock sharp at Charing Cross.'

But at 2.15 she was not there, and he ran distractedly up the platform, out of the barrier.

Then he saw her.

Thinking it safer, he turned without greeting her.

'Good afternoon, Innes,' said Gregory Philpotts, walking rapidly, but in the tone of one who expected to meet him there.

He sat stunned in the Pullman – and had to pretend that – Good God! what hadn't he to pretend?

And if anybody can finish this story for me I shall be exceedingly obliged.

4

My name is William Armstrong. I am the junior partner in the firm of Nevis, Masterson and Armstrong, solicitors, 227 Chancery Lane, London. I have known Edward Innes for twelve years, and my firm has acted for his family for four generations.

I am asked to complete the unfinished MS. of my friend on account of the light which my narrative throws upon the sequel.

It is clear that Innes began to write this story as fiction. Part 1 is imaginary – the opening sentences appear inspired. The artistic presentation of the facts seems to have been too difficult a task for him; Parts 2 and 3 are little better than a journalistic jotting.

For myself, I shall endeavour to make my story as simple a record of things heard and seen as possible, for to adequately, even – how much more then to artistically and in fine language – narrate the incidents which came under my notice would demand a more skilful writer than I can pretend to, at all events *coram populo*,[1] be.

I arrived at Folkestone late on the evening of the 12th of June last. The people in the next room to mine had retired apparently to bed, but not apparently to rest, and they created a great deal of disturbance, so that, tired as I was, sleep refused to visit my couch. There were audible cries and kisses, and sharp ejaculations as of pain, with oaths and imprecations.

My tentative knockings upon the partition only produced short bursts of smothered laughter.

How long this continued I cannot say, but the clock struck three before I sank into a troubled slumber.

I woke early, for I had forgotten to draw down the blind, and the sun was streaming full in at the window.

There was still a noise in the next room; apparently of someone washing, for I heard the jug's clatter, and splashing and rubbing. Then I heard the looking-glass (as I suppose) creak, and a girl's voice, charming, although thick, unsteady and hysterical, said 'I'm ready, dear.' Then her

---

[1] [In front of the people.]

laugh cooed and trilled, very pleasantly. Then 'Wake up, silly!' Then laughter again, but this time harsh and uncanny. Suddenly a shriek broke in, a terrible treble, rising in pitch and intensity until the voice broke in a tuneless scream.

I was thoroughly alarmed; and, throwing on my ulster, went into the corridor. At the same moment the door of the next room opened, and there stood the girl, her hair dishevelled, naked, shriek after shriek of laughter pealing from her.

'I've won! I've won!' she cried, and dragged me into the room.

My eyes fell upon the dead face of Edward Innes.

'Good God!' I cried, bending over him.

At the same moment she sprang on my back like a tigress, and buried her teeth in the lobe of my right ear; I have the mark to this day, and shall carry it to my grave.

Fortunately the hotel servants were alarmed; medical aid was summoned; I was released from my painful and undignified position.

The girl was removed, a hopeless, raving maniac, to an asylum for the insane.

The facts were suppressed at the inquest; heart failure was given as the cause of death. It is in response to the posthumous request of poor Innes that I gave this narrative to the public.

WILLIAM ARMSTRONG

(I am satisfied of the exact truth of Mr Armstrong's story, and of the facts detailed in the MS. left by Mr Innes. Their value as a contribution to pathological psychology has induced me to include the document in this volume. It has been thought desirable to alter names, dates and places, etc.)

A Masque

Pan, night, a cloud, Arcadia, and the moon.

Browning

I

There was not enough glimmer prescient of moonlight even to show the cloudbank on the horizon. It might only be divined by the absence of stars; for a little higher, in the hot haze that hung upon the sea like a veil, one might perceive dim clusters. Indeed, there was a watcher. In a house that stood outpost to either the jungle or the sea, as you will, was a light from an open window, and framed in the window was a Madonna of Fra Angelico. Had one looked in, one's eyes would not have rested on the snows of the low couch, or upon the ebony and ivory of the great crucifix upon the eastern wall, or even upon the sanctuary lamp that hung from silver chains before a picture of Our Lady, though these were the only objects in that most austere and sumptuous room. For it was wholly dominated by the personality of its tenant, who stood with clasped hands looking eagerly out of one of the two windows that opened seaward.

She stood entranced, her hands clasped in the energy of prayer, her eyes hungry with the intensity of her aspiration. Her lips were thin and pale, her nostrils fine and quivering, her forehead pure and thoughtful, with the straight blue-black hair brushed well away from it, and twisted into a thick plait that hung almost to her feet. Some acuter observer might have guessed sinister obscurities in this night-like mane: it uttered contradictions of the face, with its small nose, its delicate sweetness, its gentle and refined purity.

The girl was dressed for sleep in lace that seemed like the patterns which frost makes on glass. But the night held no frost. It was a dreadful menace that ended a day of furious sunlight. The stillness was insufferable. There was no breeze to stir a leaf; and all the voices

of nature were unnaturally hushed. The sea seemed to have forgotten
the call of the children of Latona, and the waves had ceased to lap the
sand; or, if they moved, it was but as in silent prayer, as in imitation
of the lips of that young girl that looked out to the black sky beyond
them, and besought God for moonlight – the moonlight of the soul.

The only answer was that threat of storm that lay far down upon the
sky line. The heat was overwhelming; one might have wondered how
she stood, so slender as she was. Clearly it was the soul that stayed her.

She had remained there, motionless and chastely ardent, for perhaps an hour when a sudden glint shone like a sword upon the water.
The rim of the full moon thrust up its arch of glory. The base of the
storm cloud, jagged as the mouth of the swordfish, caught the silver,
and stood, a silhouette of horror, motionless as a wild beast in am-
bush. The sea flashed the thin ray along its unrippled inkiness.

Margarita started as if she had been struck. The light leapt at her as
if an arrow were shot against her by some god. And at the same time
she put her hands convulsively upon her sides, and a sharp cry escaped
her whitening lips.

As if in sympathy, the cloudbank lit with a livid jag of lightning, and a
low horrible growl of thunder answered it. Then all was silent as before;
the moon rose stealthily; the girl resumed her pose of eager beatitude,
her body quivering with pleasure or excitement whose nature it would
have been impossible to guess but for the chaste and devout sparkle of
her eyes, so pale a grey that they were barely warmer than mother-of-
pearl, the jet circles of her pupils being thus the only true relief to a
marble face.

And suddenly they danced with fear. The moon had risen, and the
storm cloud, approaching the shore, had left a space for her orb. It
was on this that there intended a black point, like the onset of an
eclipse. But, growing, it did not grow as a curve, the shadow of the
innocent Earth; it grew as a face, and that face the shadow of the very
soul of hell.

2

The face protruded itself upon the moon, then vanished. It might
have been the hallucination of a damned soul created by the fury of
his fear that hell, after so many ages, might hold a terror still untried.

It reappeared, this time in the full glow cast from the window. Scars
and weals added but little to the deformity of a face warped utterly
from God's likeness by the malicious master-craft of some cynical
fiend. It was rugous and rugged, the skin tanned brick by the sun.

The nose was immense, almost too fearful to be credible: it was as disproportionate as an elephant's trunk. The right eye had a cast which lent a sinister meaning to what might have been mere ugliness. The brow was abnormally lofty, and sloped back like an idiot's; the lower jaw, heavy and square, was thrust forward like a gorilla's. The mouth was vast, and lipped vilely with mere bolsters of red flesh; between them yellow and black fangs, as fantastic as dolomite peaks, were like hell fallen in ruins.

The Madonna face at the window showed no surprise at the apparition; instead, she drew back slightly and to one side. A knotted hand was laid upon the window-ledge; the hunchback swung himself, lightly as an ape and silently as the shadow of death, into the room. The girl disappeared in blackness; her hand had extinguished the sanctuary lamp before the image of the Virgin.

An half hour passed before the moon rose sufficiently to cast her light upon the couch. There, like a turkey's breast, was the hideous cone heaving strenuously as if impatient of the ivory restraint of the clasped hands, fragile, transparent, and tremulous, that gripped its hog's back summit.

The moonlight lingered, curiously enamoured, for a few moments. Then the jealousy of the storm struck furiously to blot out that vision of nameless wonder. Just as the great hunch, quivering, arched itself more catlike – it might have reminded one of the rage of a porcupine – just as the hands slackened and fell apart, the calm glamour of Diana was replaced by the fiery lance of Jove, one fearful felony of lightning ripping the cloud, and answered by the crash of a thousand thunders. In a second the sea was lashed into life by the million whips of the rain, great drops like bullets. And in the blackness, above the yell of the wind and the roar of the thunder, shrilled one cry, the cry of a young girl in agony. Only one word: 'Tonight.'

But the squeal of glee that answered it was like the curtain of some devil-comedy in hell. It was the hunchback's word: 'My child!'

The world itself acquiesced in the sardonic episode. The thunder rolled not the rage but the deep-throated mockery of the gods; the wind screamed no more with pain but with laughter; the sea itself bubbled as with suppressed mirth. All that had been horrible, terrifying, exciting, suddenly threw off the mask. The tragedy was pantomime. So now in inky blackness nature wrestled with her incubus of electrical surcharge, and the woman with her burden of shameful love. It seemed as if night herself could not endure the violence of her agony, and as if the girl, racked and torn by the forces of life, were the very incarnation of that tempest. For four intolerable hours the powers of hell had sway; then with a last supreme cry the child-mother achieved her purpose as the last flame of lightning tore the last rag of storm, and sent its shattered cohorts down the wind.

The moon shone bright into the room, and fell upon the face of the hunchback, agog with ecstasy expectant. One last wisp of cloud flew down the wrack, and its shadow passed from the mother. Her virginal face was lit with an unearthly rapture; her fingers, fainter and fairer, were fastened on the tiny limbs of a man-child. And those limbs were fashioned of obsidian; the moonlight, falling full upon them, seemed to pale at the infamy it disclosed.

The face of the dwarf changed; the sight blasted his joy; the hideous smile gnashed into a blaze of fury. Out shot the hairy and distorted hand; he seized the child, wrung its neck like a chicken's, and flung it against the wall. The crucifix crashed to the ground and broke into a thousand fragments.

The hunchback whipped out a great knife and plunged it into the belly of his mistress; he turned and vaulted lightly from the window.

The moonlight fell upon the dead girl's smile.

The Escape

The hall of the hotel at Wasdale in Cumberland, where men go to climb the crags of Scafell and Great Gable, is too full of wet boots and stockings and ropes to be a satisfactory place to sit in after dinner, so that on returning to the hotel, after physiological satisfaction and meteorological speculation, it is usual to turn to the left and open the first door on the left hand side of the passage. It is a small room, but has been big enough to hold nearly every man whose name is famous in the annals of mountain-craft in England.

On Easter Saturday a few years ago the two chairs next the fireplace were occupied, one by a man of nearly fifty years of age, with a well-established black beard – the other by a man some twenty years his junior, with a beard of about three days' growth. The stockinged feet of both formed an attractive overmantel. Both were dressed untidily even for Wasdale. Both were of great stature, with features expressing unusual sternness and resolution.

The elder seemed an incarnation of strength, the younger of agility. The older was occupying himself with a notebook and pencil in an endeavour to express the number 113 by the figure 4 used four times with the assistance of conventional mathematical signs. It would have been impossible to guess what the younger man was doing; the phrase 'doing nothing' expresses a species of activity which would have amounted to libel upon his idleness. The rest of the room was occupied by a number of petulant youths, whose conversation was excessively afflicting to the three or four elder men who were compelled to listen to it.

Two or three of the least distinguished of the company were breathlessly recounting those of their exploits which appeared to them the most heroic. They did not seem at all embarrassed by the fact that three of the men present were university professors of European reputation, and that the two men by the fireplace shared between them practically all the world's mountaineering records, and had climbed more new peaks than the youngsters knew the names of.

'Well, when I got out under the chock-stone,' said the egregious Phelps, 'I found that the left wall of the gully was absolutely perpendicular, and not a ledge one could get one's little finger on, and I was too far out in the gully to be held if I came off. So I got the second man up under the stone, so that he could hold my foot on the wall while I tried to get an arm over the jammed stone, and after about half an hour, I wriggled up, somehow. It was a devil of a climb. I hope some of you chaps will go out tomorrow and try it – quite a jolly little piece of work.' He really meant that he thought no one else could get up.

The rain beat incessantly on the window, and the conversation in the room continued with neither variableness nor shadow of turning, though towards ten o'clock it had loosened slightly from mountaineering shop to the discussion of less specialised dangers, such as drowning and burglars.

The two men by the fireplace had all this time posed as statues of silence, when suddenly the younger man, without shifting his attitude or altering as much as the expression of his eyes, came into the conversation like a mammoth into a marketplace. He was interrupting at least three people, and he spoke with the certainty of an archbishop.

'The tightest place I was ever in,' he began, removing an enormous briar pipe from his mouth, 'was in Chihuahua.

'There were four of us, Gibson, Andrews, Mackenzie and myself. My own name is Dillon.'

On this announcement he replaced the pipe, relighted it, and puffed solemnly, but no one ventured to interrupt.

'We were riding,' he pursued, 'from San Juan de Cordilla to Zacatlán. The distance is a hundred and fifty miles, and for a hundred and twenty of these miles the track lies through a plain of alkali. There is no water, except at forty miles from Zacatlán where a stream runs down from the Sierra de los Cojones, and loses itself in the desert. The journey in itself is therefore severe, and a trifling accident might render it dangerous, but we had good horses, and were well provided.

'Before leaving San Juan, however, we heard that a number of bad Indians were out. It was far from likely that we should run across them, and did we do so we were well armed. Every one of us was a crack shot, and we felt that we could hold our own against ten times our number.

'It was at dawn on the tenth of April 1901 that we left San Juan, and we had every expectation of camping by the stream to which I have previously referred. Misfortune, however, dogged us almost from the start. Before we had ridden forty miles, Mackenzie's bronco went lame, and it was two hours before we were able to resume the trail. There were two further accidents of a minor nature, which delayed us still further, and only just as night fell did we see on the horizon the peak of the Sierra.

'We decided to camp, as we had plenty of water, and resume the journey when the moon rose, which would be some time after midnight. We hobbled the horses, made the fire, ate our bacon, and lay down to rest.

'Andrews, who was keeping watch, woke me at about ten o'clock to call my attention to the uneasiness of the horses. We listened long and keenly, but could make out no cause, but almost as we had decided to lie down again, I thought I heard a cry in the distance. It was sufficient for us to wake the others, and the fire was hastily extinguished by one of us, while the others saddled the horses. Andrews, with his wonderful sight, watched the horizon in the direction of the fancied sound. He swore that a star had been momentarily occluded.

'Silently we got to horse. As ill-luck would have it, the supposed Indians, although not between us and the mountain, were sufficiently near to that line to make it advisable for us to diverge considerably from it. Moonrise therefore found us no nearer to the Sierra than before. Worse, by its light Andrews was able to make sure that the Indians had really divined our presence and were following. He thought, however, that it was only a small party.

'By four o'clock it was light enough to see that there were only six of them, and that they were about two miles away. Gibson and I wanted to turn and fight, but we decided first to draw such a circuit that we were between them and Zacatlán in case we wanted to make a running fight. We therefore continued our route at top speed.

'About half an hour later, Andrews, standing in his saddle, uttered a low curse. Directly in our path was a large and well-mounted body of savages.

'There was only one thing to be done; and that was to strike straight for the Sierra, though to do this would bring us easily within shot of the first party. Even as we turned, the larger body perceived us and gave chase. Riding hard we passed within five hundred yards of the first body, who had swerved to cut us off, firing as we went. We dropped two of them, and the others hesitated, and lost sufficient ground to give us a closer passage towards Zacatlán. The larger body, in full pursuit, were about three miles away.

'At six o'clock we had gained ground on the pursuers, and almost counted ourselves saved when, mounting a rise in the ground, the last fagged-out end of a spur of the Sierra, we saw ourselves confronted at a distance of barely a thousand yards by over a hundred mounted men in full war paint.

'On seeing us, they shouted, brandished their rifles and their toma-hawks, and galloped to meet us. Only one course was open to us: to mount the Sierra and endeavour to find amongst its rocks some spe-cies of natural fortress, which we might hold until the *rurales* came out to round up the brigands.

'Here fortune for a moment favoured us: a small valley ran into the mountain, and an excellent winding track was visible. The Indians would not dare to follow armed men at full speed along it, and in any case they would be obliged to adopt single file. We gained this path in safety, and were soon in the mountain, temporarily protected by its precipices. Gibson turned at the first corner and emptied his magazine at the pursuers, in order, if possible, to delay them for a few moments.

'The sun had now risen, and was becoming very hot, but we had gained over a thousand feet in height, and were on the borders of the forest which fringed the mountain. It now seemed to us practi-cable to strike over the shoulder of the mountain, and so on to Za-catlán, but hardly had this hope been formulated in our minds when, turning a corner, we found the path completely blocked by a giant Sequoia which had fallen across it. There was nothing for it but to leave our horses, and climb over the trunk. So enormous, however, was its girth, that this was only to be accomplished by making a living pyramid of four men. The leader got hold of a branch; No. 2 clung to his ankles, and No. 3 to the ankles of No. 2, while No. 4 clambered up the human ladder into safety.

'A descent on the other side proved easier. But we had been forced to abandon, not only our horses, but also our rifles and provisions. We had nothing left but our revolvers. The Indians, however, were likely to be delayed even longer than ourselves, and we had every hope of finding a cave or some other easily defensible place where we might hold out a little longer.

'We toiled on for over two hours under the burning sun, the valley becoming ever narrower and steeper and the track rougher. We had passed out of the region of trees, and the precipices above and below were so steep that no diversion from the track would have been prac-ticable. The Indians were now about a mile away and once or twice the leaders, catching sight of us, risked shots. They had left their horses, of course, but had managed to bring over their rifles.

'Suddenly, turning the corner of great escarpment of precipitous rock, we found that the track consisted only of a rough bridge so steeply sloping downwards as to be almost like a ladder. Nothing would be easier than for us to cross it and destroy it behind us. It might take the pursuers many hours to find a way round.

'This we did without difficulty, and plunged on with lighter hearts. About half an hour later, the final misfortune occurred. The track ended suddenly, and a sheer wall as smooth as glass cut us off from advance. We spent ten minutes in endeavouring to find a way out – there was none. At the end of this time we heard renewed shots. The Indians had either improvised a ladder to cross the gap, or had managed to jump it. As the land lay, the last hundred yards of the path was on an inward curve. We could see the Indians crouching opposite, uttering loud whoops of triumph as they came into view.

'There was a moment's pause; then simultaneously we opened fire.'

Dillon, for the first time, shifted his position, knocked the ashes out of his pipe, refilled it very deliberately, and lighted it again.

'The Indians were astonishingly bad marksmen; but at the end of an hour Mackenzie had a flesh wound in the shoulder, Andrews had the bone of his arm broken, and Gibson had an artery cut. He was only keeping alive by an improvised tourniquet. I alone was unwounded. On our part, we had killed fourteen of them outright. But we had no more ammunition for our revolvers – we had not even kept the final shots, by which so many preferred to save themselves from death by torture.'

Dillon's pipe was burning very badly, and he relighted it with great attention.

'At the last moment, we had only to roll over the edge of the precipice,' continued Dillon, as though wearily.

'Well, gentlemen, that was our situation. Four men disarmed, all but one wounded too seriously to resist attack, on an exposed ledge, from which there was no escape, and within two hundred yards of them, some six score well-armed savages, thirsting for their blood.'

The pipe again went out – tobacco claims too much attention to coexist with memories so poignant. But the pause was so long that Phelps breathlessly enquired:

'Well, what happened?'

Dillon grew even more sombre; with slow emphasis he replied:

'They killed us every one.'

'Suppose,' said the man at the corner of the fire, putting away his notebook, 'that we have a last pipe in the open, before turning in?'

NOTES AND SOURCES

Abbreviations

HRC/UTA. Harry Ransom Center, University of Texas at Austin.
OTO/CG. Ordo Templi Orientis Archives, Cody Grundy Accession.
OTO/KA. Ordo Templi Orientis Archives, Kenneth Anger Accession.
YC/WI. Yorke Collection, Warburg Institute, School of Advanced Studies, University of London.

Sources: Serials

The English Review. London. Edited by Austin Harrison.
The Equinox. London. Edited by Aleister Crowley. J. F. C. Fuller, Mary Desti and Victor B. Neuburg, subeditors.
The Idler: An Illustrated Monthly Magazine. London. Edited by Robert Barr.
The International: A Review of Two Worlds. New York. Edited by George Sylvester Viereck. Aleister Crowley, contributing editor (1917–18).
Pearson's Magazine. New York. Edited by Frank Harris.
The Smart Set: A Magazine of Cleverness. New York. Edited by George Jean Nathan and H. L. Mencken.
What's On? Where, When and How to See. London. Edited by Robert Haslam.

Sources: Books by Aleister Crowley

The Collected Works of Aleister Crowley. 3 vols. Foyers: Society for the Propagation of Religious Truth, 1905–07. Facsimile reprint Des Plaines, Ill.: Yogi Publication Society, n.d. [ca. 1970].
Konx Om Pax: Essays in Light. Foyers, Inverness-shire: Society for the Propagation of Religious Truth; London and New York: Walter Scott Publishing Co., 1907. Reprinted Des Plaines, Ill.: Yogi Publication Society, n.d. (ca. 1970). Facsimile reprint with introduction by Martin P. Starr, Chicago: Teitan Press, 1990. Holograph MSS. and page proofs are at HRC/UTA. Two first edition copies at HRC/UTA have holograph annotations: Copy A, Crowley's personal copy (no. 1), catalogued in MSS. with the page proofs, and Copy B, another annotated copy catalogued with the rare books. Another first edition at at YC/WI has transcriptions of annotations by Gerald J. Yorke.

The Spirit of Solitude: An Autobiography, subsequently re-Antichristened the Confessions of Aleister Crowley. 2 vols. of a projected 6 or 7. London: Mandrake Press, 1929. Abridged unauthorised 1-vol. edition, *The Confessions of Aleister Crowley*, ed. John Symonds and Kenneth Grant, London: Jonathan Cape, 1969. Authorised unabridged edition, New York: O.T.O. (in preparation, 2015).

The Stratagem and Other Stories. London: Mandrake Press, 1929. 2d rev. ed., *The Stratagem and Other Stories*, ed. Keith Rhys [pseud. William Breeze]. Brighton: Temple Press, 1990.

The Sword of Song, called by Christians the Book of the Beast. Benares [London]: Society for the Propagation of Religious Truth, 1904. Holograph MSS. and page proofs are at HRC/UTA.

THE THREE CHARACTERISTICS

Written in 1902. First published in *The Sword of Song* (1904), appendix I, p. 93. Republished with copious annotations in *The Collected Works of Aleister Crowley*, vol. II (1906), p. 225.

PAGE 9. '*spretæ injuria formæ*'   [Virgil, *Æneid* 1:26–7, paraphrase, referring to Juno's anger at being passed over in the 'Judgment of Paris.']

PAGE 11. **'the hathis pilin' teak / In the sludgy, squdgy creek'**   [Adapted from Rudyard Kipling, 'Mandalay.']

PAGE 13. ***The Nineteenth Mahākalpa***   [The journal *The Nineteenth Century*.]

PAGE 13. **Huxlānanda Swāmi**   [The British biologist Thomas Henry Huxley (1825–1895).]

PAGE 14. *pansil*   [See 'Pansil,' *The Collected Works of Aleister Crowley*, vol. II (1906), p. 192.]

AMBROSII MAGI HORTUS ROSARUM

Written in 1902. First published in *The Sword of Song* (1904), appendix II, p. 107. Republished with extensive annotations in *The Collected Works of Aleister Crowley*, vol. II (1906), p. 212. Crowley's marginalia to the first edition that provided the basis for the annotations added in *Collected Works* are extant, in Crowley's copy of *The Sword of Song* at HRC. Crowley had incorporated only a small percentage of these marginal notes, probably due to reasons of space. The additional marginalia are included in this edition wherever possible.

PAGE 16. **I, Ambrose, called I.A.O.**   [Crowley used the amusing pseudonym Isadore Ambrose O'Rourke during his residence in Mexico in 1900–01, calling himself 'the Chevalier O'Rourke.' For his use of the full name see 'Today's Arrivals,' *The Mexican Herald*, July 12, 1900, p. 2, as well as later news reports including an interview; see Crowley, *The Early Diaries*, ed. William Breeze (in press), passim.]

PAGE 17. **S.S.D.D.** [Florence Farr Emery (1860–1917). Soror Sapientia Sapienti Dona Date in the Hermetic Order of the Golden Dawn.

PAGE 18. **H. *et* S.V.A.** [This probably means 'H[oros] and S.V.A.' The American psychic and con artist Ann O'delia Salomon (1849–?) was known as Mme. Laura Horos and Soror S.V.A. when she infiltrated the Golden Dawn group led by S.L. MacGregor Mathers in Paris. She had many names, some through marriage but several invented: Mrs. Joseph H. Diss Debar *née* Editha Loleta Landsfeldt Montez; Anna O'Delia Salomon Messant; Swami Vive Ananda; Marie Louise de la Commune. Her last husband was an accomplice, Frank Dutton Jackson (1866–1948), known as Theodore Horos or Frater M.S.R. in G.D. circles. A 1901 sex scandal in England led to their arrest, trial and imprisonment until 1906, as well as much negative publicity for the G.D. See John Mulholland, *Beware Familiar Spirits* (New York; London: Scribner's, 1938).]

PAGE 18. **Deo Duce Comite Ferro** [One of the mottos of the co-founder and genius behind the Golden Dawn, whose preferred full name was Samuel Sidney Liddell MacGregor Mathers (1854–1918).]

PAGE 19. **Vestigia Nulla Retrorsum** [The Golden Dawn motto of Moina MacGregor Mathers *née* Bergson (1865–1928).]

PAGE 29. **'Qabalistic Dogma'** [First published in Crowley, *Collected Works*, vol. 1 (1905), p. 265; republished in *The Equinox* 1(5) (1911), p. 83.]

PAGE 30. **Abracadabra** [This is the earliest instance of this formula, which Crowley related to the letter *cheth* (ח) and 418. Why Crowley used this spelling and not Abrahadabra, as he spells it in a later annotation (given as a footnote for this edition) and almost always used in his later writings, is not clear. It appears to be related to the Father's remark on p. 35. that 'The chariot (Ch.) is not, and the chariot (H.) is at hand.' *The Book of the Law*, discussed below, is a work that heralded numerous changes of esoteric initiatic formulæ; it features the word 'Abrahadabra' prominently.]

PAGE 30. **Ain Elohim** [In adding quotation marks for dialog in this edition the repetition of 'Ain Elohim' raised the question of whether the Fool or the Father spoke the phrase. Crowley, in 'An Essay upon Number,' *The Equinox* 1(5) (1911), p. 110, has this passage: '*Dixit Stultus in corde suo:* "Ain Elohim"' ('Said the Fool in his heart: "There is no God"'). This tends to confirm that it is part of a monologue by the Fool. The editorial note to the text gives '= Negative Unity' (cf. "Liber Had")' as it was thought misleading to translate the phrase literally as 'Not God' without some qualification.]

PAGE 36. **V.N.** [George Cecil Jones (1873–1960) was Frater Volo Noscere in the Golden Dawn.]

PAGE 37. **the Book of the Law** [Crowley's use of this title in a story which he dated to 1902 might, at first sight, suggest a prophetic early reference to the all-important text he received in 1904 E.V., *Liber AL vel Legis, The Book of the Law*, the cornerstone of his religious philosophy of Thelema. Alternatively, to those unwilling to accept his 1904 reception story for the book, it might be evidence that he had planned it years earlier. It is however far more likely that Crowley revised this paper when adding it to the appendices to *The Sword of Song*, which appeared in October 1904. No MS. or TS. survives.]

THE WAKE WORLD

Written 1906–07. First published in *Konx Om Pax* (1907), p. xiii, as 'The Wake World: A Tale for Babes and Sucklings.' This work is 'Liber XLV,' a 'suggestive' work in Class C, in the curriculum of Crowley's teaching order the A∴A∴. Three pages of untranslated foreign language quotations appear on pp. xiv–2 in the first edition and are omitted. Crowley's marginalia to this story in the annotated *Konx Om Pax* HRC/UTA copy B were limited to terse source citations for these quotations and copy A has none. The annotated copy at YC/WI has three notes; two are given in the text, and one is given below.

PAGE 38. **Lola Daydream** Vera Snepp, of *Clouds without Water*.

[Vera Snepp (1888–1953) was one of the inspirations of Crowley's suite of love poems, *Clouds without Water* (1909); see *Confessions*. She became Mrs Henry Algernon Claude Graves, and acted as Vera Neville.]

T'IEN TAO

Written ca. 1907. First published in *Konx Om Pax* (1907), p. 53, as 'Thien Tao: A Political Essay,' with Chinese titles giving 'T'ien | Tao | Kwaw| Li | Ya'; the inner titling has 'T'ien Tao, or the Synagogue of Satan.' It is 'Liber LXI,' a 'suggestive' work in Class C, in the curriculum of the A∴A∴. Chinese translations of subheads have been omitted. Crowley's extensive marginalia from the annotated *Konx Om Pax* HRC/UTA copy B are given as footnotes.

PAGE 57. **'My object [...] fit the crime'** [W.S. Gilbert and Arthur Sullivan, 'Song – Mikado,' from *The Mikado: or, The Town of Titipu* (New York: William A. Pond, 1885), p. 33; quotation conformed.

PAGE 57. **the demonstration of St Thomas Aquinas** [The HRC/UTA copy B *Konx Om Pax* has the marginal note 'Quote' but Aquinas did not say this; he qualified this optimism (derived from Plato as restated by Peter Abelard) in *Summa Theologiæ* i, q. xix, a. ix; q. xxv. aa. 5–6. Leibniz, *Theodicée* (1714), §10, has 'everything is for the best in the best of all possible worlds,' and it appears in Voltaire, *Philosophical Dictionary*

(English trans. 1843), vol. 2, art. 'Optimism,' and most famously in
Candide (1759).]

THE STONE OF THE PHILOSOPHERS

Written ca. 1907. First published in *Konx Om Pax* (1907), p. 69, as 'The
Stone of the Philosophers which is Hidden in Abiegnus, the Rosicrucian
Mountain of Initiation.' It is 'Liber LIII' in the curriculum of Crowley's
teaching order the A∴A∴ preserved in a transitional TS. of *Liber ABA
(Book 4, Part 3, Magick in Theory and Practice)* at University of British
Columbia Special Collections. Crowley made two corrections in HRC/
UTA A (one of which was repeated in YC/WI); these were incorporated
silently. Other topical footnotes to the pages are from HRC/UTA A, one of
which also appears in YC/WI. The other marginal notes give biographical
details of interest to specialists and are provided here as endnotes. A few
notes from HRC/UTA A are in Fuller's hand, as noted, but these appear to
be by Crowley.

PAGE 69. **Holbein House**   [YC/WI:] Fuller was living here in 1907 (I
suppose) after his marriage. I must have met him autumn 1906 but
saw little of him at first. [HRC/UTA A, in Fuller's hand:] Near Sloane
Square. 118. Fuller's rooms.

[J. F. C. Fuller (1878–1966), a founding officer of the A∴A∴, was then
a British Army Captain; he later rose to Major-General and became a
prominent and prolific author and military theorist.]

PAGE 69. **once a man lay dead in his room for seven weeks**   [HRC/UTA
A, in Fuller's hand:] A man found dead in it. *Vide* daily papers Nov. or
Dec. 1906. [From *The Derby Daily Telegraph*, 18 Jan. 1907, p. 3:]

STARTLING DISCOVERY IN A FLAT

Colonel's Mummified Body Found

On Thursday, at Chelsea, a coroner's inquiry was held into the
strange discovery of the mummified body of Louis Whewell, 74, a
retired Colonel of Volunteers, in his flat at Holbein House. He was
eccentric and reticent, preferring to live the life of a hermit. During his 13 years' occupancy of the flat he had never allowed anyone
inside, and had never spoken to the other tenants. He was last seen
alive at the beginning of December, and when the body was found
a number of letters dating from December 11 were found. [...]
death was due to pneumonia, and had occurred at least five weeks
previously.

[HRC/UTA A, in Fuller's hand:] And again the body of woman at the
end of 108 at beg[inn]ing of '09. [HRC/UTA A, p. 69, has an unsourced
clipping pasted in that is undated, but ca. March 19-20, 1909:]

FROZEN IN A FLAT

Lady Found Dead in Her Bedroom at Sloane Square

Frozen hard by the bitterly cold weather, the body of an old lady, Miss Isabella Greig, aged seventy, has been lying, unknown to anyone, in her flat at Holbein-House, Sloane Square.

The superintendent of the mansions fancied she had gone on a holiday, but suspicion arose, and on forcing an entrance she was found dead on the bedroom floor.

Clad only in a dressing-gown, the body was froze [*sic*] through, and the skin was quite hard.

The fact that no letters had been opened since February 19 shows it was about the time when the old lady died.

Death from natural causes was the jury's verdict to-day.

PAGE 69. **the blank wall opposite**   [HRC/UTA A, in Fuller's hand:] As at 118.

PAGE 70. '**هو الله الذى لا اله الا هو** or the Devil's Conversion'   [Qu'ran 59:22, 23, 'He is Allah, other than whom there is no deity'; corrupted in the first ed. where the fifth word *ilaha* was given as Allāh, and corrected here.]

PAGE 71. See [*Liber*] 777   [Crowley issued this qabalistic reference work anonymously as 777 *vel Prolegomena Symbolica ad Systemam Sceptico-Mysticae Viae Explicandae Fundamentum Hieroglyphicum Sanctissimorum Scientiae Summae* (London: Walter Scott Publishing Co., 1909.) For Gabriel, see tables LIX, p. 18; XCIX, p. 22.]

PAGE 71. G∴D∴ **lecture on telesmatic images**   [See S. L. MacGregor-Mathers, 'Telesmatic Images and Adonai' (G.D. Flying Roll XII); excerpted in Israel Regardie, *The Golden Dawn*, vol. IV (Chicago: Aries Press, 1940), pp. 61–3; rev. ed. *The Golden Dawn: A Complete Course in Practical Ceremonial Magick* (St. Paul: Llewellyn, 1989), pp. 488–9.]

PAGE 73. **The Crown is Kether – the Highest – and I like anything that symbolises that Crown**   [This marginal MS. note is given as a footnote to p. 73. The MS. can be read two ways. One is given in the text (as quoted above); another has 'I like anything that symbolises that Crown' – very amusing in the context and the sort of joke Crowley loved. However, the unity theme supports the reading given in text.]

PAGE 75. **'Ovariotomy'**   [YC/WI:] Kathleen Bruce, who had her ovaries removed.

[The British sculptor Kathleen Bruce (1878–1947) was one of Crowley's lovers in Paris (1902) and London (1907). In 1908 she married the polar explorer Capt. Robert Falcon Scott (1868–1912). In 1922 she remarried, to Edward Hilton Young; he became the 1st Baron Kennet in 1935 after which she was styled Baroness Kennet.]

PAGE 85. **Inspiration**   [YC/WI:] With Tankerville.

[George Montagu Bennet, 7th Earl of Tankerville (1852–1931) was in a sense the first student in the nascent A∴A∴. Crowley first became involved with him and his wife in 1907 when they sought his assistance with psychic attacks they believed they were experiencing.]

PAGE 86. **'The Gilt Mask'** [YC/WI:] Kathleen Bruce, now Lady Kennet.

PAGE 89. **'The Mosque Bewitched'** [YC/WI:] Tangier.

PAGE 91. **'The Suspicious Earl'** [YC/WI, HRC/UTA A:] Tankerville.

PAGE 93. **I swear by all the stars that stream [...] Granada** [YC/WI:] With Tank [Lord Tankerville].

PAGE 94. **Titan Eve** [YC/WI:] Evelyn Hall.

[Evelyn Beatrice Hall (1868–1956), also known as E. Beatrice Hall, was the daughter of the Anglican rector of St Clements Eastcheap, and one of Crowley's mistresses in 1899–1900, appearing in his 1900 'Abramelin' diary. Under the pseudonym Stephen G. (or S. G.) Tallentyre, she published studies of Voltaire, Mirabeau and the women of the French salons, as well as fiction. Crowley's description of her in the poem 'The Symbolists' as 'thewed and sinewed' appears to be borne out by her 1896 portrait by Alfred-Pierre Agache, *The Sword (L'Épee)*, at the Art Gallery of Ontario. The poem's emphasis on theology and the reference to her 'father's fancy hats' tend to confirm the identification.]

PAGE 95. **'La Gitana'** [YC/WI:] With Tank.

THE MURDER IN X. STREET

This was probably written in late 1907 or early 1908. Crowley's diary for March 7, 1907 records his meeting with Robert Heywood Haslam (1878–1954), editor of the weekly *What's On: Where, When and How to See*. This piece was his first contribution, and ran under the heading 'Our New Competition' from February 8 through March 7, 1908. It is not a true short story, but has interest as showing Crowley's early prose development. Its minimal plot and characterisation serve to set up puzzles which readers are invited to solve. The last installment of the story on March 7 stated that 'the various answers to the many problems set will be published in our number dated March 21st, for the week ending March 28th.' However, 'Our Competition,' March 21, p. 13, advised that 'The solutions of the various problems are unavoidably held over this week, owing to a lack of space.' The solutions may have appeared in the April 18, 1908 issue, a number missing in the British Library, which holds the only extant run of this journal. It seems more likely that Crowley played an elaborate practical joke on Haslam, his editor; the solutions probably required as much space as the story. A few easy answers are given below.

PAGE 99. **'Who is she?'** [The solution is ERG ('A measure of work'), DYE ('A device to conceal age and shabbiness') and SUN ('The all-beholder'), which gives 1 - G, 2 - R, 3 - U, 4 - N, 5 - D, 6 - Y, or 'Grundy.' Mrs. Grundy was a recurring figure in English literature epitomizing a conservative prig with outraged morals; the name first appeared in a play by Thomas Morton, *Speed the Plough* (1798).]

PAGE 100. **Where, I wonder?**   [His third yard = 2^2 = 4 inches, his fourth = 2^3 = 8 inches, so his 200th = 2^{199} inches, a vastly larger distance.]

PAGE 102. ***Read the cipher and signify the letters***   [The cipher text is 'WHEAT is often cornered, always beaten. SEA is always wet. TOE is WHAT WE usually have ten of. NEST has a bird in it. WEST has a star in it. Better THAW your NOSE. Rub it with SNOW.' The key is 1 - W, 2 - H, 3 - A, 4 - T, 5 - S, 6 - O, 7 - N, i.e., *What's On*, the name of the weekly.]

PAGE 103. **rules for clerks, of whom there were six**   [Crowley took this problem from exercise 407 in John Neville Keynes, *Studies and Exercises in Formal Logic* (3d ed. 1894), pp. 440–43; this had been his college logic textbook at Cambridge. Its solution takes over a page.]

THE DRUG

Written ca. 1908. First published in *The Idler Magazine* XXXIV(76) (Jan. 1909), p. 403. The *Banyan Tree* version in OTO/CG is an 8 pp. fragment with about half the story, and the annotation '64a West 9th Street N.Y. City'; it also has the note '*The Idler*.' It has errors not present in the *Idler* version, which was the copy text. It was republished as *The Drug* (Cambridge: privately printed [Nicholas Bishop-Culpeper], 1996); another edition was *The Drug* (Austin: 100th Monkey Press, 2014).

PAGE 107. **my quiet friend**   [The brief description suggests Allan Bennett (1872–1923), who worked in analytical chemistry and introduced Crowley to various drugs. The character may however be based on Dr Samuel Perry (1869–1952), an early member of one of Crowley's orders, the A∴A∴, and a second-generation physician and pharmacologist in Spalding, Lincolnshire, which resembles the setting of the story. Perry was one of Crowley's most advanced students, attaining the 5°=6□; he became the A∴A∴ Chancellor by 1911.]

PAGE 108. **Kelly [...] "partaker of the mysteries of the creation"**   [Sir Edward Kelly (or Kelley, 1555–1595), who developed the Enochian system with Dr. John Dee. The quote translates the Enochian '*Odo kikale Qaa*'; see the Call or Key of the Thirty Æthyrs, 'Liber Chanokh,' II, *The Equinox* I(8), p. 127.]

CANCER? A STUDY IN NERVES

Written in Venice in the spring of 1908; first published as a three-part serial in *What's On?* VIII(93–95) (2, 9, 16 Jan. 1909), pp. 12, 14 in each number. Republished in *The Equinox* I(9) (Mar. 1913), p. 81, credited to Crowley; the table of contents has the note 'Reprinted from *What's On?* by kind permission of Robert Haslam.' A TS. titled 'The Cancer: A Study in Nerves' was part of the J. F. C. Fuller collection and is now HRC/UTA 10/8.

PAGE 114. **Bertie Bernard** [The *What's On?* version had Bertie Brenner, a name combining those of two sculptors Crowley knew from Paris, Bertie Longworth and Michael Brenner. The character itself is based on the French Symbolist painter Eugène Carrière (1849–1906). Crowley recalled their meeting in 1902 in his *Confessions*: 'He had just recovered from an operation for cancer of the throat, and I remember principally his remark, calm to the point of casual indifference, "if it comes back, I shall kill myself."' The story quotes this episode.]

PAGE 117. **Dr Maigrelette** [Based on Crowley's own doctor in Paris, the American physician Edmund Louis Gros (1869–1942), founder of the American Hospital in Neuilly-sur-Seine. He would treat Crowley's drug addiction in the early 1920s.]

AT THE FORK OF THE ROADS

Written ca. 1908. First published anonymously in *The Equinox* 1(1) (Mar. 1909), p. 101. Republished in *The Fourth Mayflower Book of Black Magic Stories*, ed. Michel Parry (St Alban, Herts.: Mayflower, 1976). In his marginalia to *The Equinox*, Crowley noted: 'This story is true in every detail. Date of occurrence 1899 E.V. May or June.'

PAGE 126. **Hypatia Gay** Althea Gyles.

[Althea Gyles (1868–1949) was an Irish artist and illustrator whose work was championed by W. B. Yeats; several of his early editions feature cover illustrations by Gyles.]

PAGE 126. **Count Swanoff** Aleister Crowley.

[Crowley leased his first London flat at 67–69 Chancery Lane, the setting of the story, under the pseudonym Count Vladimir Svareff.]

PAGE 126. **Will Bute** W. B. Yeats.

PAGE 126. **why do you threaten me** [A gloss of 'why do you threat me.']

PAGE 127. **The master** Allan Bennett.

PAGE 127. **signs and letters upon the vellum** A talisman from *Greater Key of Solomon*, I think. It is preserved in an old book of talismans among my papers.

PAGE 128. **publisher in Bond Street** Leonard Smithers.

[The Decadent publisher Leonard Smithers (1861–1907).]

PAGE 128. **drawings** These were for *The Harlot's House* by Oscar Wilde.

[Oscar Wilde, *The Harlot's House* (London: 'imprinted for subscribers at the Mathurin Press,' 1904); it was illustrated by Althea Gyles.]

PAGE 128. **a certain drug** Valerianate of Zinc.

PAGE 129. **secretly distributing the drug about the house** There was a huge row about this from the landlady; but a Russian nobleman could do no wrong! Gyles gave the powder to a chemist to analyse, and he reported that it was bone-dust!!!

PAGE 130. 'You have ruined me – Curse you!' This is the only touch of exaggeration in the story.

THE DREAM CIRCEAN

Written in Paris in 1908, probably in the spring. First published in *The Equinox* I(2) (Sept. 1909), p. 105, under the pseudonym Martial Nay. Republished in *The Black Magic Omnibus*, ed. Peter Haining (New York: Taplinger, 1976; U.K. ed. London: Futura, 1977). Crowley made three textual changes in marginalia to a copy of *The Equinox*, incorporated silently. He also noted: 'Written (I think in Paris) after my first visit to the Lapin Agile. I fancy Nina Olivier, Hener Skene and Victor Neuburg were of the party. I was then loving a girl Marcelle in a brothel in the Rue des Quatre Vents – see reference in "John St John"' (a reference to his fall 1908 diary in *The Equinox* I(1) (1909), supplement). The Lapin Agile was a cabaret on Rue des Saules in Montmartre associated with Picasso, Modigliani and Apollinaire. For Nina Olivier, see the note to 'The Ordeal of Ida Pendragon.' Hener Skene (1877–1916) was a cousin of Kathleen Bruce (ibid.), later Kathleen Scott; he became the dancer Isadora Duncan's piano accompanist. The poet Victor B. Neuburg (1883–1940) was one of Crowley's more advanced magical students and a subeditor of *The Equinox*, as well as his lover.

PAGE 131. **Grand old Frédéric** [Partly based on the expatriate Irish painter Roderic O'Conor (1860–1940), who played the cello.]

PAGE 132. **At Lourcine** […] **At Clamart** *Les pourris de Lourcine et les morts de Clamart.* Ed[mond] Haraucourt.

['The rotten of Lourcine and the dead of Clamart.' Misquoted from La Sire de Chamblay (Edmond H…) [Edmond Haraucourt], *La légende des sexes: poëmes hystériques et profanes* (Brussels, privately printed, 1893). The original is '*Cons pourris de Lourcine, et cons morts de Clamart,* | *Je vous ai vus, baignés d'un jus multicolore,* | *Nager, flasques, dans une odeur de vieux homard.*' ('Rotten cunts of Lourcine, and dead cunts of Clamart, | I saw you bathed in multicoloured juice, | Swimming, flabbily, with the smell of old lobster.') L'Hôpital Lourcine was famed for treating syphilis, and the Paris suburb of Clamart had a pathology centre that dissected unclaimed corpses.]

PAGE 132. **The Scotch Count** [Samuel Liddell MacGregor] Mathers.

PAGE 133. '**Where are the snows of yesteryear?**' [François Villon, 'Ballade des dames du temps jadis' ('Ballad of the Ladies of Times Past'), trans. Rossetti.]

PAGE 135. '**Circumstance bows […] miss a chance.**' [Crowley,] *Clouds without Water* [1909].

PAGE 143. 'Look not upon the Visible Image [...] Fatality' [A combination of two of *The Chaldæan Oracles*, §148, 'Invoke not the visible Image of the Soul of Nature,' and §149, 'Look not upon Nature, for her name is fatal.']

PAGE 143. Éliphas Lévi Zahed [The French magician and author Alphonse Louis Constant (1810–1875).]

ILLUSION D'AMOUREUX

First published in *The Equinox* I(2) (Sept. 1909), p. 187, under the pseudonym Francis Bendick. In marginalia to *The Equinox*, Crowley noted:

PAGE 146. the gilded lily with geranium lips Ada Leverson.

[The writer and novelist Ada Leverson (1862–1933) was briefly Crowley's lover in 1907.]

THE SOUL-HUNTER

Written in Paris in spring 1908. First published anonymously in *The Equinox* I(3) (Mar. 1910), p. 119. In marginalia to *The Equinox*, Crowley made one correction, taken silently in this edition, and noted: 'Written in Paris, about the same time as the "Three Poems for Jane Chéron."' Republished as a pamphlet by the 100th Monkey Press, Austin, 2014.

THE DAUGHTER OF THE HORSELEECH

First published in *The Equinox* I(4) (Sept. 1910), p. 201, under the pseudonym Ethel Ramsay. In marginalia to *The Equinox*, Crowley noted:

PAGE 156. G.O. Varr Jehovah.

PAGE 156. L.O. Heem Elohim.

PAGES 156–157. [On the descriptions of the spiritual entities, Crowley noted: 'These descriptions are all according to [*Liber*] 777 analysis of the names throughout.']

THE VIOLINIST

Written in spring 1910. First published in *The Equinox* I(4) (Sept. 1910), p. 277, under the pseudonym Francis Bendick. Republished in *The Second Mayflower Book of Black Magic Stories*, ed. Michel Parry (St Alban, Herts.: Mayflower, 1974).

PAGE 160. The girl was tall and finely built [Leila Waddell (1880–1932), an Australian violinist and Crowley's lover beginning in spring 1910.]

THE VIXEN

First published in *The Equinox* I(5) (Mar. 1911), p. 125, under the pseudonym Francis Bendick. Republished in *The First Mayflower Book of Black Magic Stories*, ed. Michel Parry (St Alban, Herts.: Mayflower, 1974), and in *New Witchcraft* I(1) (1975).

PAGE 163. **To and from N.I.L.B.W.** [In this dedication to Leila Waddell, Crowley jumbles the initials of her names Leila Ida Nerissa Bathurst Waddell.]

Patricia Fleming [The title character, based on Leila Waddell.]

THE ELECTRIC SILENCE

First published anonymously in *The Equinox* I(6) (London, Sept. 1911), p. 53. Its introductory note states 'This parable is a synopsis of *The Temple of Solomon the King*, with which it may be collated,' referring to the serialised account of Crowley's magical career in volume I of *The Equinox*, the first four installments of which were primarily written by J.F.C. Fuller. Crowley annotated 'The Electric Silence' in his copy of *The Equinox* to explain various allusions, and to provide autobiographical keys to real persons and events; these have been taken from a Yorke TS. of the notes (from HRC/UTA) and a TS. in the O.T.O. Archives, Jack B. Hogg, Jr. Accession. These notes are given as footnotes to the text in this edition. While this work is not fiction, but rather a highly stylised prose autobiography, it could be read as such by readers unfamiliar with Crowley's life and career, and is included in this collection as it has a particular type of experimental prose. Crowley described the circumstances of its writing in a note to his copy of *The Equinox*: 'Written at Eastbourne immediately on my return from second journey to Sahara. I had expected a wire from Leila Waddell, and was upset at not getting it.'

THE ORDEAL OF IDA PENDRAGON

Written in Paris in 1911, probably in the spring, and first published in *The Equinox* I(6) (Sept. 1911), p. 113, under the pseudonym Martial Nay. Crowley noted in his copy of *The Equinox*: 'Written at the Panthéon Tavern. I think in Paris on my way back from second Sahara journey.'

PAGE 176. **To I, J, and K** Ida (i.e., Leila Waddell), Jane Chéron, Kathleen Bruce. Ida Pendragon is a combination of these three.

[For Leila Waddell, see notes to 'The Violinist' and 'The Vixen'; one of her middle names was Ida. Jane Chéron (also known as June and Jaja) was a well-known artists' figure model in Paris; she later married the *New York Times* Moscow correspondent Walter Duranty (1884–1957). For Kathleen Bruce, see endnote for 'The Stone of the Philosophers.']

PAGE 176. *Porcus e grege Epicuri* [Horace, *Epistles* I.4, paraphrase: '*Epicuri de grege porcum.*']

PAGE 178. **Absolute Grand Patriarch of the Rite of Mizraim** [The Rite of Mizram is a masonic rite of French and Italian origin that was reorganised and worked by John Yarker (1833–1914), who wrote that 'it has been reduced to 33 degrees, and designated the "Reformed Rite of Mizraim." In a quiet way it is still conferred in this country under its own Supreme Council.' Yarker, *The Arcane Schools* (Belfast: Tait,

1909), p. 489. Yarker had folded the Rite of Mizraim into the Antient and Primitive Rite to form 'a Sovereign Sanctuary for Great Britain and Ireland in 1872 [which] introduced the Rite into Germany in 1905 [*sic*], where it has numerous Craft Lodges'; ibid., p. 490. In 1902 Yarker chartered Theodor Reuss (1855–1923) and others to lead a German section, which Reuss organised from London. Crowley joined this, becoming a Patriarch Prince Administrator after Yarker's death. The Antient and Primitive Rite was further reduced when it was adapted as the masonic basis for the modern Ordo Templi Orientis (O.T.O.).]

PAGE 189. **Ninon** [Nina Olivier (1882–1949) was known as 'Nina of Montparnasse' when she was one of Crowley's Paris lovers in 1902; her maiden name was Eugénia Victoria Auzias. During 1908–09 she began a complex relationship with the American art critic and collector Leo Stein (1872–1947) that led to their marriage in 1921. Gertrude Stein became her sister-in-law.]

PAGE 185. **'Ar – ar – it – a.'** [ARARITA is a Qabalistic acronym from a 13th century text attributed to Rabbi Hammai, *Sefer ha-ʿIyyun*, *The Book of Contemplation*.]

PAGE 185. **'One is His beginning […] his permutation one.'** [A paraphrase of 'Liber DCCCXIII vel Ararita sub figura DLXX' 1:0, *The Holy Books of Thelema* (1983), p. 217.]

APOLLO BESTOWS THE VIOLIN

First published in *The Equinox* I(7) (Mar. 1912), p. 244, credited to Crowley. It was inspired by Leila Waddell; see endnotes to 'The Violinist' and 'The Vixen.'

ACROSS THE GULF

Written in the summer of 1911, probably in Paris or Fontainebleau; first published in *The Equinox* I(7) (Mar. 1912), p. 293, credited to Crowley. This story is 'Liber LIX,' a 'suggestive' work in Class C in the curriculum of the A∴A∴. The holograph MS. was part of the J.F.C. Fuller collection and is now HRC/UTA I/I. A TS. is in YC/WI OS LI2, 60 pp.

PAGE 202. **I discovered my stèla at Bulaq** [Crowley first encountered the funerary stela of the Theban priest Ankhefenkhons i in the weeks leading up to his reception of *Liber AL vel Legis*, *The Book of the Law* over April 8–10, 1904. He referred to it as the Stéla of Revealing. For accounts of the Stèla of Ankhefenkhons i and the lead-up to the writing of *Liber Legis*, with its aftermath, see the editorial introduction and Part IV (*The Equinox of the Gods*) in Crowley, *Magick (Liber ABA, Parts I–IV)*, rev. 2d ed., ed. Hymenaeus Beta (York Beach: Weiser, 1997); see also the editor's preface and the Egyptological Appendix A to Crowley, *The Holy Books of Thelema* (*The Equinox* III(9)), ed. Hymenaeus Alpha and Hymenaeus Beta (New York: Weiser, 1983). A new edition of *The Holy Books of Thelema* (New

York: O.T.O. Publishing, in press 2015–16) has an expanded Egyptological appendix that examines Ankhefenkhons i in some depth, and provided material for the notes to this story.]

PAGE 202. **obtained certain initiations**   [A gloss of 'obtained certain initiation' as it also appears in the TS.; the MS. was not consulted.]

PAGE 202. **Twenty-Sixth Dynasty**   [At the time Crowley was writing, Egyptologists had placed Ankhefenkhons i and his contemporaries too late, in the 26th Dynasty. He is now placed in the 25th.]

PAGE 202. **child of Ta-nech [...] and of Bes-na-Maut, priestess**   [This shows Crowley's curious naivete with Egyptology, even when dealing with names and concepts that had direct bearing on his personal magical work, as here with these names from the Stèla of Revealing. Ta-nech (Taneshet) was Ankhefenkhons i's mother, while Bes-na-Maut (Besenmut) was his father. While Crowley managed to reverse their names, he was on solid theological ground in emphasising the importance of the parents of Ankhefenkhons i as his high offices were hereditary, from both sides of his family.]

PAGE 202. **At my birth**   [Crowley is here describing his natal astrological chart. He had the first decan (Aphruimis) of the sign Leo rising, with Uranus (Herschel) in the First House. His Sun was conjunct Venus (not Jupiter, the usual planet attributed to Amun) in the second decan (Atrechinis) of Libra, at the Nadir or bottom of the chart (which he terms the Abyss). He mistakely has his Moon in Aries in the Ninth House; it was actually in Pisces.]

PAGE 203. **On the roof of the palace [...] astrologers of Pharaoh**   [Ankhefenkhons i was a 'god's father beloved of god' (*it-ntr-mri-ntr*) in the temple of Amun-Ra at Karnak (Thebes). He was also a stolist (*sm₃* or *sm₃ty*) or robing priest, who dressed the god's statue each day. To enter the inner shrine of Atum and touch the god – and especially to face him – were rights and duties reserved in principle to the Pharaoh as head of the Egyptian priesthood, but except on the great annual processions or other occasions of state importance when the Pharaoh officiated, priests of high rank served as the king's proxy. Ankhefenkhons i also served as 'opener of the doors of the sky in Karnak' (*wn ꜥꜣwy nw(t) pt m ipt-swt*), opening the symbolic 'doors of heaven' in the daily temple ritual. Günther Vittmann suggests that these doors led to the inner shrine of Amun (see Vittmann, art. 'Türoffner von Himmels,' *Lexikon der Ägyptologie* VI, pp. 795–6; see also Gerard Broekmann, 'Theban Priestly and Governmental Offices and Titles in the Libyan Period,' *Zeitschrift für ägyptische Sprache und Altertumskunde* 138 (2011), p. 94). However, 'opener of the doors of the sky in Karnak' may relate to another office held by Ankhefenkhons i, 'phylarch of the second phyle of the temple of Ra on the roof of the Amun temple.' The Festival Hall of Thutmose III (Akhmenu) held the principal shrine of the god Amun, who was conveyed from his inner sanctuary to a solar temple on the roof of the Festival Hall to be exposed to the rays of the sun-god Ra. The 'doors of the sky' probably led to this upstairs temple, where Amun would have been placed on an alabaster altar in a ritual process central to the fusion of the distinct deities Amun and Ra as Amun-Ra. The solar temple itself was dedicated to Ra-Harakhty (Ra-Hoor-Khuit), Amun-Ra and *pꜣwty tꜣwy* (primordial god of the two lands). Texts also link Khepri Horus, identified with Horus Behedite (Horbehutet or Hadit), and as it was open-air, it was undoubtedly also sacred to Nut (Nuit), the sky-goddess through whom Khepri passes each night to be reborn at dawn, though this is not explicit. See Pierre Barguet, *Le temple d'Amon-Rê à Karnak: essai d'exégèse* (Cairo: IFAO, 1962), pp. 287–90, and the studies by J.-Fr. Carlotti and J.-Fr. Pécoil *et al.* in the series *L'Akh-menou de Thoutmosis III à Karnak*, online at http://www.cfeetk.cnrs.fr/. See also http://dlib.etc.ucla.edu/projects/Karnak/feature/Akhmenu. There were no sources for this when Crowley wrote; his instinctive grasp of Egyptian religious practice far exceeded what could have been gleaned from the Egyptological literature of his day. He did derive the related concepts of the four stations of the Sun – Ra, Hathor, Atum and Khepri – from the text of the Stèla of Ankhefenkhons i. He made their ritual observance a daily practice in the neo-Egyptian religion he founded, Thelema, in 'Liber Resh vel Helios sub figura CC'; they also occur in *Liber AL vel Legis (The Book of the Law)*.]

PAGE 203. **as Tum drew to His setting [...] threatening moment in the night** [This again alludes to the daily service of the rooftop Ra temple. Similarly, the Zelator ritual of Crowley's initiatory order A∴A∴ begins with the setting of Atum (Tum, Tmu or Temu). Like the sun, the candidate dies and passes through the underworld of Duat (Tuat) – the 'threatening moment in the night' – before emerging in the morning as Ra-Horakhty (Ra as Horus of the Two Horizons), able to declare the affirmation of the Stèla of Ankhefenkhons i: 'I have made a secret door / Into the House of Ra and Tum, / Of Khephra and of Ahathoor.']

PAGE 204. **Horus – or Mentu, as we called Him in Thebai** [Crowley learned his early Egyptology from the Hermetic Order of the Golden Dawn, which taught that Montu had another form, compounded with Horus, called Horus-Mentu. The G.D. probably intended the common Theban hybrid deity Montu-Ra. Crowley here goes further and seems to suggest their equivalence in Thebes, which would not be correct.]

PAGE 217. **Priest of Asar in Thebai!** [The Stèla of Ankhefenkhons i was the only artifact for this priest with which Crowley was familiar, and it describes him only as a priest of Montu and as 'the one who opens the doors of the sky in Karnak.' Crowley was unaware that other artifacts from his funerary equipment were also found, and that these gave his additional religious offices. Asar is an obsolete spelling of Osiris, and one of Ankhefenkhons i's more interesting titles was '*ḥm-nṯr* priest of Osiris supervising the Mansion of Gold' (*ḥm-nṯr n wsir ḥnty ḥwt-nbw*), where the images of the gods themselves were crafted and animated through the Opening of the Mouth ceremony. Crowley also correctly intuited, in this story, that the cult of Osiris began a tremendous rise to prominence in Thebes during this period.]

HIS SECRET SIN

Written in the summer of 1911, probably in Paris or Fontainebleau; first published in *The Equinox* I(8) (Sept. 1912), p. 49, credited to Crowley. An O.T.O. Archives TS. with variants was not followed. It was collected in *The Stratagem and Other Stories* (London: Mandrake Press, 1929). Crowley dedicated this collection 'To the Memories of Three Dead Friends'; these included Eugène John Wieland (1880–1915), for a time the publisher of *The Equinox*, 'who bowled me out over the third' (i.e., the third story in the book, 'His Secret Sin').

PAGE 238. **Inscribed admiringly to Alexander Coote**   [William Alexander Coote (1842–1919), the secretary of the National Vigilance Association for the Suppression of the White Slave Traffic (N.V.A.) in London, a group of moral vigilantes who fought 'vice' by 'going underground' to become informants and privately prosecuting brothel-keepers; see his absurdly titled account of the N.V.A.'s work, *The Romance of Philanthropy* (1916).]

PAGE 241. **The Stolen Bacillus**   [H.G. Wells, *The Stolen Bacillus and Other Incidents* (London: Methuen, 1895).]

PAGE 241. **Mrs Grahame**   [Crowley's lover Lilian Horniblow (ca. 1874–1958). Crowley refers to Mrs Horniblow by her *nom de amour* 'Laura Grahame' in his heavily coded 1900 diary.]

PAGE 241. **Colonel Grahame**   [Brig. Gen. Frank Herbert Horniblow (1860–1931), Lilian Horniblow's husband, who was a colonel when the story was written.]

THE WOODCUTTER

Written in the summer of 1911 in Paris or Fontainebleau; first published in *The Equinox* I(8) (Sept. 1912), p. 79, credited to Crowley.

PROFESSOR ZIRCON

First published in *The Equinox* I(8) (Sept. 1912), p. 91, credited to Crowley.

THE VITRIOL-THROWER

First published anonymously in *The Equinox* I(9) (Mar. 1913), p. 103.

PAGE 254. **To Kathleen Scott**   [Kathleen Bruce – see note to 'The Stone of the Philosophers.']

PAGE 257. **'The world [...] proud of her whoredom'** [Crowley, *Summa Spes* (London: privately printed, 1903); in *The Collected Works of Aleister Crowley*, vol. II (1906), p. 200.]

THE TESTAMENT OF MAGDALEN BLAIR

First published in *The Equinox* I(9) (Mar. 1913), p. 135, anonymously but signed at end V. English, M.D., and dedicated to Crowley's mother, Emily Bertha Crowley (1848–1917). Crowley had given the holograph MS., titled 'The King of Terrors' and dated Nov. 11, 1912, to the American collector John Quinn (1870–1924), inscribing it 'To John Quinn the MS. of my best story (so far). Christmas 1914, a tiny tribute from Aleister Crowley.' See *Complete Catalogue of the Library of John Quinn: Sold by Auction in Five Parts (with Printed Prices)*, vol. I (New York: Anderson Galleries, 1924), p. 230. It is now HRC/UTA 12/2. It was collected in *The Stratagem and Other Stories* (London: Mandrake Press, 1929). This story was anthologised in *The Nightmare Reader: Volume 2*, ed. Peter Haining (London: Victor Gollancz, 1973; rpt. London: Pan, 1976), *Isaac Asimov Presents Tales of the Occult*, ed. Isaac Asimov and Charles Waugh (Buffalo: Prometheus, 1989), and *Don't Open This Book!*, ed. Marvin Kaye (Garden City: Doubleday Direct, 1998).

PAGE 262. *Athanasia contra mundum* [A feminised variant of '*Athanasius contra mundum*' ('Athanasius against the world'), referring to the theological battles of Athanasius, the 4th c. Bishop of Alexandria.]

PAGE 268. **Dr Barbézieux** [Clearly based on Dr Georges Barbézieux (1860–?), a French physician Crowley met in Yunnan, China in 1906.]

PAGE 268. **stertorous and strangling breath [...] convulsion** [Crowley dedicated the 1929 collection *The Stratagem and Other Stories* 'To the Memories of Three Dead Friends'; they included Allan Bennett, Bhikkhu Ananda Metteyya (1872–1923), who 'suggested the second' (i.e., the second story in the book, 'The Testament of Magdalen Blair'). The story may reflect Bennett's own experience as a child. In 1884 his mother died at home of tuberculosis of the throat (psthisis), whose victims slowly suffocate. Her obituary noted that she suffered a "v[ery] lingering death"; it was of sufficient medical interest that an autopsy was conducted.]

PAGE 284. **V. English, M.D.** [In spring–summer 1899 Crowley was somehow involved with – or at least aware of – a Legitimist plot to run guns to the Spanish Carlists, via France, using the *Firefly*, a British steam yacht that belonged to Bertram Ashburnham, the 5th Earl of Ashburnham (1840–1913), the most prominent Jacobite and Carlist organiser in England. The nature and extent of Crowley's involvement is not known; he did not feel himself at liberty to describe it in his *Confessions*. He had become a commissioned Carlist officer – even awarded a knighthood – but he was not on board the *Firefly*, as is sometimes claimed. Lord Ashburnham had taken the precaution of employing a temporary captain for the *Firefly*'s mission, Lieut. Vincent English, R.N. (ret.) – clearly Crowley's inspiration for the name of the story's narrator, V. English, M.D. The *Firefly*'s regular captain was Milnes Patmore (1848–1906), the son of the poet and British Museum librarian Coventry Patmore (1823–96). Capt. Patmore's wife was the author and historian Katharine Alexandra (*née* Stewart) Patmore (1865–1942), and Bennett's first cousin. It is thus likely that Crowley was introduced to the Carlists by Bennett, and his use of the name V. English in a story inspired by Bennett was a coded acknowledgment of the connection.]

ERCILDOUNE

First published in *The Equinox* I(9) (Mar. 1913), p. 175, credited to Crowley. The holograph MS. with author's revisions is HRC/UTA 11/7.

PAGE 285. **Roland Rex**   [Loosely based on Crowley, who attempted the Himalayan peak K2 in the Karakoram range via Askole and Skardu in 1902.]

PAGE 287. **his headman, Salama**   [Salama Tantra, Crowley's headman on his expeditions in the Himalayas and China.]

PAGE 290. **True Thomas**   [Thomas the Rhymer, or Thomas Learmonth, the 13th c. Scottish laird and prophetic poet, whose seat was Ercildoune (modern Earlston).]

PAGE 303. **all the hearts of the great house**   [Glossed; the *Equinox* had 'all the hearts of great house.' The MS. was not consulted.]

THE STRATAGEM

First published in *The English Review* 67 (Jun. 1914), p. 339; republished in *The Smart Set* L(I) (Sept. 1916), p. 229. The *Smart Set* version has a redrawn variant of the illustration. It was collected in *The Stratagem and Other Stories* (London: Mandrake Press, 1929). Crowley dedicated this collection 'To the Memories of Three Dead Friends'; they included Joseph Conrad (1857–1924), who 'applauded the first story' (i.e., the first story in the book, 'The Stratagem').

PAGE 339. **Bevan**   [In a case of life imitating art, Crowley was detained by French police in 1922 on suspicion of being the fugitive financier Gerald Lee Bevan, chairman and managing director of the City Equitable Fire Insurance Co Ltd; see *Confessions*.]

PAGE 342. **my grandmother was […] a Higginbotham**   [Anne Heginbottam (or Heginbotham) (1840–1921) of Coventry, Warwickshire, was employed by Crowley's uncle Jonathan Sparrow Crowley (1826–1888) as a governess; she became his second wife. Crowley called her Aunt Annie, and she was the relative with whom he was closest. She was not however a blood relation.]

LIEUTENANT FINN'S PROMOTION

First published in *The International* IX(8) (Aug. 1915), p. 243. The holograph MS. is Warburg YC OS C3 (c). The 'Key' does not appear in MS.

THE CHUTE

First published in *The International* IX(11) (Nov. 1915), p. 347. The holograph MS. is YC/WI OS C3 (f).

A DEATH BED REPENTANCE

First published in *The International* XI(7) (Jul. 1917), p. 201. Dedicated to the writer Samuel Butler (1835–1902). The holograph MS. is YC/WI OS 2 (g).

PAGE 368. **John Nelson Darby** [The preacher-theologian John Nelson Darby (1800–82) was a prominent early leader in the Plymouth Brethren and founded the splinter Exclusive Brethren.]

PAGE 369. ***Father and Son*** [Edmund Gosse, *Father and Son: A Study of Two Temperaments* (London: William Heinemann, 1907).]

PAGE 369. **another writer sprung of the loins of the Brethren, the poet of *The World's Tragedy*** [Crowley, *The World's Tragedy* (1910).]

PAGE 370. **close friend of [...] Crowley** [Crowley's father, the Plymouth Brethren preacher Edward Crowley (1829–87).]

FILO DE SE

First published in *The International* XI(8) (Aug. 1917), p. 241. The copy text is Crowley's set of *The International* (O.T.O. Archives), which has a few corrections to quotations; a holograph marginal note is given as a footnote.

PAGE 379. **'take death [...] reaching it'** [Algernon Charles Swinburne, 'Phædra.']

PAGE 379. **'I alit [...] aside to die.'** [Percy Bysshe Shelley, *Prometheus Unbound* i, 719–22.]

PAGE 380. **'I am idle [...] no more money.'** [A paraphrase of Florizel in Robert Louis Stevenson, 'The Suicide Club.']

PAGE 381. **'This little life [...] after death.'** [James Thomson, *The City of Dreadful Night* (1874).]

PAGE 383. **'For dried is the blood [...] the vein'.** [Algernon Charles Swinburne, 'Dolores.']

PAGE 383. **'*Novem continuas fututiones!*'** [Catullus, *Catulli Veronensis Liber* 32.]

PAGE 384. **Cecil Chesterton** [Cecil Chesterton (1879–1918) was the younger brother of G.K. Chesterton and a close associate of Hilaire Belloc. A Catholic convert and prominent theorist of Distributism, he edited and published the weekly *The New Witness* 1912–16.]

THE ARGUMENT THAT TOOK THE WRONG TURNING

First published in *The International* XI(10) (Oct. 1917), p. 309.

PAGE 386. **quiet man** [Crowley.]

PAGE 386. **young and beautiful woman** [Rose Edith Crowley, *née* Kelly (1874–1932), later Mrs Joseph Andrew Gormley.]

PAGE 386. **My wife's father** [The Rev. Frederic Festus Kelly (1838–1918), Vicar of Camberwell.]

PAGE 386. **His wife** [Blanche Kelly *née* Bradford (ca. 1845–1935).]

THE PROFESSOR AND THE PLUTOCRAT

First published in *The International* XI(11) (Nov. 1917), p. 348, under the pseudonym S.J. Mills. Crowley indicated his authorship in a table of contents in his annotated set of *The International*, O.T.O. Archives. Slight edits have been made for publication here.

PAGE 388. **Professor Bugsby** [Based on Lindley B. Keasby (1867–1946), professor of institutional history at the University of Texas at Austin. His pro-German politics during WWI blocked his widely expected appointment as university president, and eventually cost him his tenure. He bought *The International* in 1918 and it promptly folded.]

PAGE 389. **my *Distanzliebe* is as *lebendig* as your *Pattvereiningdungingen* is *starr*!!!** [A possible translation has been provided in a footnote to the story: 'My love-at-a-distance is as vital as your stalemated organisation is fossilised!!!' However, the German neologism *Pattvereiningdungingen* cannot be fully translated, and thus seems corrupted; it seems likely to have included *vereinigung* ('union') with the causative suffix *-igen*, i.e., *Pattvereinigungigen*. The word *Distanzliebe*, for love at a distance, was then current in psychoanalytic circles.]

ROBBING MISS HORNIMAN

First published in *The International* XII(4) (Apr. 1918), p. 103. The MS. is YC/WI OS 40 (a). A Yorke transcription TS. is in HRC/UTA 10.6, 9 pp. The copy text is Crowley's set of *The International*, O.T.O. Archives, which has holograph edits. Except for Annie Horniman, the women mentioned were all part of the bohemian artistic scene centred on the Café Royal and the Cabaret Club (the Cave of the Golden Calf) during 1910–13.

PAGE 391. **Hilda Howard** [A Hilda Howard appears in one of Crowley's lists of lovers, and was probably a part of the early bohemian scene in Paris or London. The poem 'The Priestess of Panormita' in *The Winged Beetle* (1910) was dedicated to her.]

PAGE 391. **Izeh** [Izé (or Izeh) Kranil (1888–1958) was a dancer in Paris in 1912, and on the pre-war London café scene. In 1918 Crowley described her as 'Algerian by birth, half French, half Arab, and is one of the best-known figures in literary and artistic circles in Europe,' an exaggeration. Her entry in one of his lovers lists has a question mark. He published his translation of her 'Aux Pieds de Notre Dame de l'Obscurité' as 'At the Feet of Our Lady of Darkness' in *The International* (Feb. 1918), and she was the basis for Fatma Hallaj in *The Diary of a Drug Fiend* (1922). She settled in England, changing her name to Dolora Vaghya in 1935; she had previously used the name Iris Vaghya as an 'Egyptian authoress.' The UK National Portrait Gallery has several photographs, miscatalogued under Tzet Kranil.]

PAGE 391. **John** [The British painter Augustus John (1878–1961).]

PAGE 391. **Euphemia** [The artists' model Euphemia Lamb (1887–1957), *née* Annie Euphemia Forrest. She married the British painter Henry Lamb (1883–1960) in 1906, but was famed for her affairs. She later became Anne (or Annie) Euphemia Grove.]

PAGE 391. **Shelley** [Lilian Shelley (*née* Milsom, 1892–?) is best remembered as a model for Augustus John and Jacob Epstein. She got her start singing in the Cave of the Golden Calf and other London clubs, which led to a successful 1914 English tour as 'Crazy Lilian Shelly, the Merry, Mad, Magnetic Comedienne.' In 1914 she married a friend of Augustus John, the Irish painter John Flanagan (1889–1976). Flanagan is best remembered for his later relationship with the singer Gracie Fields (1898–1979); see David Buckman, *Artists in Britain since 1945* (Bristol: Art Dictionaries Ltd., 2006), and *Sing as We Go: The Autobiography of Gracie Fields* (New York: Doubleday, 1961).]

PAGE 391. **Little Billee** [An obscure singer-dancer in the London clubs of the period who took her name from a character in George du Maurier's novel about Bohemian Paris, *Trilby* (1894).]

PAGE 391. **Harry Austin** [Austin Harrison (1873–1928), editor of *The English Review* 1910–23.]

PAGE 391. **Spalding** [A small town in Lincolnshire, probably known to Crowley through a visit to Dr Samuel Perry; see notes to 'The Drug.']

PAGE 392. **Miss Anne Horniman** [Annie Horniman (1860–1947), a British heiress and theatre patron who financed W.B. Yeats' Abbey Theatre, Dublin, as well as theatre organisations in England, and for many years the patron of Hermetic Order of the Golden Dawn cofounder S.L. MacGregor Mathers and his wife Moina. The story misspells her first name as Anne, perhaps on the assumption that Annie was a diminutive, but the latter was her birth-name.]

THE IDEAL IDOL

First published in *The International* XII(4) (Apr. 1918), p. 110, under the pseudonym Cyril Custance. Crowley noted his authorship in a table of contents in his annotated set of *The International* (O.T.O. Archives). Crowley's copy also has revisions, incorporated here.

FACE

First published in *Pearson's Magazine* XXXI(9) (Sept. 1920). The holograph MS. is YC/WI OS 8 (b). The primary TS. with holograph revisions is in *The Banyan Tree*, OTO/CG, with the holograph note 'Published in *Pearson's* N.Y. Spring 1921' [*sic*]. Another TS. is HRC/UTA 10.6, 18 pp., which has the Germer-era O.T.O. Archives catalogue number 7607.

WHICH THINGS ARE AN ALLEGORY

First published posthumously in *The Stratagem and Other Stories*, ed. Keith Rhys (Brighton: Temple Press, 1990). The holograph MS. is YC/WI OS CI (c). A note to the MS. by Gerald Yorke dates it to 1905 or earlier. Several TSS. in OTO/KA were prepared by Leslie Huggins.

THE CRIME OF THE IMPASSE DE L'ENFANT JÉSUS

Unpublished; probably 1910 or earlier, as it was part of the J. F. C. Fuller collection; the holograph MS. is now HRC/UTA 11.3, 29 pp.

ATLANTIS

Written in Moscow in the summer of 1913. This story is 'Liber LI,' a 'suggestive' work in Class C in the curriculum of the A∴A∴; it is also in the curriculum of the O.T.O. Based on a TS. in the Jane Wolfe Papers, O.T.O. Archives, 52 pp., prepared by Karl Germer, who proofed it carefully against his source. Germer made annotations addressed to Phyllis Seckler, who was preparing distribution TSS. Another TS. in the O.T.O. Archives, Helen Parsons Smith Accession, with a brief foreword by Wilfred T. Smith (not integral to the story and omitted here), was the basis for the Yorke transcription TS. in YC/WI OS LI2 (a); in his transcription Yorke describes the Smith TS. as corrupt. The Germer TS. is the copy text; it has better readings, and preserves a long paragraph in chap. 4 as well as sentence fragments. This 'novel' was first published posthumously by Kenneth Anger and David Jove from the Yorke transcription TS. as *Atlantis* (Malton, Ont.: Dove Press [1970]); this edition omitted the Smith foreword but included a one sentence foreword by Anger: 'The time to fathom this sex-magical treasure by Aleister Crowley is NOW!' An undated TS. with holograph revisions, auctioned at Sotheby's London in December 1996, is in a private collection and has not been consulted; it has a credit line 'by Brother Astralogus the Greek' not present in other TSS. As the Sothebys TS. was unavailable, it is not known whether it represents an earlier or later version than the Germer TS.

PAGE 424. **was cut off from its fellows**   [A gloss of a bad reading in TS., 'was cut from its fellows.']

PAGE 454. '*Si monumentum quæris, circumspice.*' [A variant of the epitaph of Sir Christopher Wren at St Paul's Cathedral, which he had designed: '*Lector, si monumentum requiris, circumspice*' ('Reader, if you seek his monument, look around').]

PAGE 455. **it was obliged to adopt** [A gloss of a bad reading in TS., 'was obliged to adopt.']

THE MYSTERIOUS MALADY

Written in New York in late fall of 1915. A holograph MS. titled 'The Mysterious Malady' (apparently a second draft) is YC/WI OS 1(a); a note to the MS. by Gerald Yorke gives the date of its writing and the original title, 'Lady Anna's Illness.' A TS. with holograph revisions is in *The Banyan Tree*, OTO/CG, 23 pp.; it has a note with the address '9 West 47th.' Another TS. is HRC/UTA 12.6, 20 pp., which has the Germer-era O.T.O. Archives catalogue number 7602; it lacks the MS. revisions in *The Banyan Tree* TS. but is better punctuated. A Yorke transcription TS. in in OTO/KA, 8 pp.

THE BALD MAN

Written in 1916, according to Crowley's footnote to the story. Unpublished; taken from a TS. with holograph revisions in *The Banyan Tree*, OTO/CG, 15 pp.

PAGE 477. **But the Corps was so short of men** [A gloss of a bad reading in TS., 'But the was so short of men.']

BLACK AND SILVER

Written near Bristol, New Hampshire in summer 1916. Unpublished; taken from the TS. with holograph revisions in *The Banyan Tree*, OTO/CG, 15 pp. The TS. has the holograph note 'Buggered up by *Vanity Fair* N.Y.' It was perhaps submitted, badly edited and left unpublished, as it does not appear with Crowley's *Vanity Fair* contributions from his New York period.

PAGE 485. **the man was as dead** A gloss of a bad reading in TS., 'the man was dead.'

PAGE 488. *pauvre Gaspard* ['poor Gaspard'; see Léon Devbel, *Léliancolies: La chanson du pauvre Gaspard: Poèms* (Paris: Revue Verlainienne, 1912).]

PAGE 488. '*O mon Dieu vous m'avez blessé d'amour.*' ['Oh my God, you have wounded me with love.' Paul Verlaine, *Sagesse* (1880).]

PAGE 490. **Gautier's 'La morte amoureuse'** [Theophile Gautier, 'La morte amoureuse' (1836); see *Récits fantastiques* (Paris: Bookking International, 1993). English trans.: *The Dead Leman and Other Tales from the French*, ed. and trans. Andrew Lang and Paul Sylvester (New York: Scribner and Welford, 1889); *Spirite / The Vampire / Aeria Marcella*, ed. and trans. F.C. de Sumicrast (*The Romances of Theophile Gauthier*, vol. 5) (Boston: Little, Brown and Co., 1912).]

THE HUMOUR OF PAULINE PEPPER

Unpublished; taken from the holograph MS., YC/WI OS 7, and a TS. with a few holograph revisions but many corruptions in *The Banyan Tree*, OTO/CG, 7 pp. This TS. has the note 'Aleister Crowley 64a West 9th Street, New York City' – which dates the note, though not necessarily the TS., to 1918; the address is scored through and 'c/o King Features Syndicate, Mr Seabrook' is added. Another TS. is HRC/UTA 10/6, 8 pp. which has the Germer-era O.T.O. Archives catalogue number 7555. Another TS. is in OTO/KA, 5 pp.

A NATIVITY

Unpublished; taken from the TS. with holograph revisions in *The Banyan Tree*, OTO/CG, 4 pp. It has the scored out address '225 West 42nd Street N.Y. City' and the address '64a West 9th Street N.Y. City,' which dates the TS., though not the story, to 1918.

EVERY PRECAUTION

Unpublished; taken from a TS. with holograph revisions in *The Banyan Tree*, OTO/CG, 9 pp. The holograph MS. is YC/WI OS 8 (a). It probably dates from Crowley's stay in New Orleans, December 1916–January 1917. A note at the end shows that Crowley considered omitting the last two paragraphs.

GOD'S JOURNEY

Probably written in spring 1918. Unpublished; taken from a TS. with holograph revisions in *The Banyan Tree*, OTO/CG, 28 pp. Lavroff's name was typed in but crossed out, and the revisions are in Crowley's hand, making his authorship certain. This TS. incorporates holograph edits from an earlier TS., YC/WI OS F2 (1), 38 pp. A Yorke transcription TS. is in OTO/KA, 13 pp. The pseudonym Marie Lavroff or Lavrova suggests the possible collaboration of Maria Rolling (1891–1969, *née* Eliasberg or Elsberg). She was briefly Crowley's lover in spring 1918, and used the name Marie or Maria Lavroff as a lecturer, changing her married name Roehling to Rolling around the time she became a Jungian analyst. The Warburg TS. gives St Petersburg, whereas the later *Banyan Tree* TS. has the post-1924 usage Petrograd. As the story's setting seems to be pre-revolutionary, the St Petersburg reading is taken. Russian proper names have been modernised.

THE COLOUR OF MY EYES

Probably written in spring 1918. Unpublished; taken from a TS., YC/WI OS F2 (5), 4 pp. Another TS. is a Yorke transcript, OTO/KA, 2 pp. Credited to Marie Lavroff; see note to 'God's Journey.'

DEDIT!

Written on June 20, 1920. Unpublished; a TS. with holograph amendations is in *The Banyan Tree*, OTO/CG, 20 pp.

COLONEL PACTON'S BROTHER

Written over a 24-hour period August 25–26, 1920, and revised in early January 1922. Unpublished; taken from a TS., YC/WI OS F2(12), 71 pp., with holograph corrections, most of which are in a Yorke transcription TS., OTO/KA, 38 pp.

PAGE 538. **Flivverton** [Detroit.]

PAGE 539. **Earl of Granchester** [Based on the Hon. Everard Fielding (1867–1936), son of the Earl of Denbigh and secretary of the Society for Psychical Research. Granchester may be based on the family seat at Newnham Paddox, Warwickshire.]

PAGE 539. **Hotel Rathskeller** [Possibly the Detroit Athletic Club.]

PAGE 539. **Hans Pumpern** [He is closely modelled on the Detroit businessman, bookseller and publisher Albert Winslow Ryerson (1872–1931). He owned the Ryerson Building, and brought Crowley to Detroit in 1919 in an abortive attempt to organise the O.T.O. with a group of 33° Scottish Rite freemasons.]

PAGE 544. **His wife [...] a splendid child** [This character is based on Albert Ryerson's second wife, Bertha (or Bonita) Almira Bruce (1888–?). Her 1919 marriage to Ryerson was either one of convenience, or of such serious inconvenience that it ended very quickly; it was never legally registered. As Soror Almeira, she was Crowley's fifth Scarlet Woman. Crowley's portrait of Bruce in the story is especially valuable as she is the least well known of his Scarlet Women; no photograph survives, and nothing is known of her life after 1941.]

PAGE 553. **Coldstream** [Based on the American journalist, author and adventurer William B. Seabrook (1884–1945), who apparently used a similar pseudonym, Eugene Coldbrook, for the magazine article "Aleister Crowley – Man or Demon?,' *True Mystic Science* (March 1939).]

PAGE 561. **Ross** [A composite of the psychic Bert Reese (1841–1926) and the Danish-born New York psychic and lecturer Christian P. Christensen (ca. 1871–?).]

PAGE 571. **as a trophy on my walls** [A gloss of 'in a trophy on my walls.']

PAGE 574. **Sir Roger Bloxam** [A Crowley pseudonym; see his autobiographical experimental novel *Not the Life and Adventures of Sir Roger Bloxam*.]

THE VAMPIRE OF VESPUCCIA

Written on October 4, 1921. Unpublished; the MS. is in YC/WI OS L2.

PAGE 579. **Q-rays of Reuss** [Theodor Reuss (1855–1923), Crowley's predecessor as Frater Superior (O.H.O.) of Ordo Templi Orientis. 'Q-rays' suggests *Heb.* ק, *qoph* = Tarot trump XVIII, 'The Moon,' probably intended to imply a lunar quality.]

As You Were!

Written in fall 1921. Unpublished. A TS. with holograph revisions is in *The Banyan Tree*, OTO/CG, 38 pp. Another TS. is in YC/WI OS F2. In the Warburg TS. the dedication to Joseph Conrad was crossed out; relying on *The Banyan Tree* TS., it has been retained for this edition.

PAGE 596. **Slawkenbergius** [Hafen Slawkenbergius is a character in Laurence Sterne, *The Life and Opinions of Tristram Shandy, Gentleman* (1759-69).]

PAGE 597. **Dean Schwenck Gilbert** [The English dramatist, librettist, poet and illustrator Sir William Schwenck Gilbert (1836–1911), author of *The Bab Ballads*, and (with Sir Arthur Sullivan) comic operas.]

PAGE 597. **Canon Lehár** [An operetta by the composer Fritz Lehár (1870-1948) was titled *Die Lustige Witwe* (1905, English adaptation *The Merry Widow*, 1907). Crowley here attributes a work of that title to Martin Luther.]

PAGE 597. **Archbishop Cranmer** [...] **Ridley and Latimer's tract, *The Candle*** [The English Reformation martyrs Thomas Cranmer (1489–1556), Archbishop of Canterbury, and the bishops Nicholas Ridley (ca. 1500–55) and Hugh Latimer (1487–1555). When the last two were burnt together, Latimer reportedly said 'Be of good comfort, Master Ridley, and play the man; we shall this day light such a candle, by God's grace, in England, as I trust shall never be put out.']

PAGE 597. **Pascal's incomparable *Viens, Pou-poule*** [*Viens poupoule*, one of the most popular songs of Belle Époque France, written and sung by Félix Mayol (1872–1941); see Jean-Pierre Moulin, *Une Histoire de la chanson française* (2007), p. 36. With his hyphen, Crowley turns 'come to me baby' into 'come to me, prostitute louse.' *Poule*, 'chicken' or 'hen,' here has the sense of 'baby' as a term of affection, and is also slang for prostitute.]

Only a Dog

First published as *Only a Dog* (Cambridge: privately printed [Nicholas Bishop-Culpeper], 1987), which used Crowley's first draft TS. with holograph edits. Bishop-Culpeper's copy of this TS. is now in O.T.O. Archives, and was the source for YC/WI OS F2 (7), 4 pp., and a Yorke TS. in OTO/KA, 2 pp. The story as published here is the final revised version from a TS. in *The Banyan Tree*, OTO/CG, which has Crowley's final holograph edits.

PAGE 606. **Matteawan** [Matteawan State Hospital in Beacon, New York was a hospital for the 'furiously mad.']

The Virgin

Unpublished; taken from the only known version, a TS. with holograph revisions in *The Banyan Tree*, OTO/CG, 13 pp.

PAGE 610. **Gregers Werle** [A character in Henrik Ibsen, *The Wild Duck* (1884).]

PAGE 613. **swallowed Jonah's whale and the notion** [The word 'notion' is an editorial best guess and gloss. The TS. had 'precaution' struck out, changed to a word ending in 'tion' that is partially cut off in OTO/CG.]

A MASQUE

Unpublished; taken from a TS. with holograph revisions in *The Banyan Tree*, OTO/CG, 6 pp.

THE ESCAPE

Unpublished; taken from a TS. with holograph revisions in *The Banyan Tree*, OTO/CG, 8 pp. It has a holograph MS. note 'October' but was never published, so far as is known.

PAGE 620. **Wasdale** [Also spelt Wastdale; the region in Cumberland where Crowley learned rock climbing as a young man.]

PAGE 620. **a man of nearly fifty years of age** [Oscar Eckenstein (1859–1921), an analytical chemist and rail transport engineer, was Crowley's preceptor in mountaineering and yoga as well as his lover.]

PAGE 620. **a man some twenty years his junior** [Crowley.]

PAGE 621. **Dillon** [Crowley.]

PAGE 621. **tenth of April 1901** [Crowley and Eckenstein were climbing in Mexico on this date, at Calimaya, near Toluca, in Mexico State. They did not explore in Chihuahua, which is in the far north.]